A lifetime of sailing boats in untamed weather had honed his reflexes and made him indifferent to danger. Catching those flapping reins was just like laying hold of a loose halyard in high winds; battling the beast to a standstill not much harder than wrestling with a net-load of fish reluctant to die.

And besides, it seemed a shame for a fine animal like that to break a slender leg just 'cause some royal folderol couldn't keep his arse in the saddle.

"It'd be fine, I reckon," he said, determined that this elegantly clad prince was a man, like him, who pissed and farted same as all men did, and had nothing more special to recommend him than an expensive tailor. "Don't seem like the beast's taken any harm, barrin' a fright."

The prince glanced up at him. A flicker of recognition lit his eyes and he nodded. Standing straight, he looped the reins over one arm and then dusted his hands on his breeches. "So it would appear, Barl be praised." He kissed the solid gold holyring on his left forefinger. "He was a gift from His Majesty."

"A grand gift," said Asher. "Glad I could save 'im for you. I be fine too, by the way. You know. 'Case you were wonderin'."

Books by Karen Miller

Kingmaker, Kingbreaker
The Innocent Mage
The Awakened Mage

Fisherman's Children
The Prodigal Mage
The Reluctant Mage

A Blight of Mages

The Godspeaker Trilogy
Empress
The Riven Kingdom
Hammer of God

Writing as K. E. Mills

Rogue Agent
The Accidental Sorcerer
Witches Incorporated
Wizard Squared
Wizard Undercover

KAREN MILLER

THE INNOCENT MAGE

KINGMAKER
KINGBREAKER
BOOK ONE

www.orbitbooks.net

New York   London

Copyright © 2005 by Karen Miller
Excerpt from *The Awakened Mage* copyright © 2006 by Karen Miller
All rights reserved. Except as permitted under the U.S. Copyright Act of 1976, no part of this publication may be reproduced, distributed, or transmitted in any form or by any means, or stored in a database or retrieval system, without the prior written permission of the publisher.

Orbit
Hachette Book Group USA
237 Park Avenue
New York, NY 10017
Visit our Web site at www.orbitbooks.net

Orbit is an imprint of Hachette Book Group USA, Inc.
The Orbit name and logo is a trademark of Little, Brown Book Group Ltd.

Printed in the United States of America

Originally published by Voyager, Australia: 2005
First Orbit edition: September 2007

16   15   14

To my parents, for their blind, unbending and oftentimes bemused faith. Couldn't have done it without you, guys.

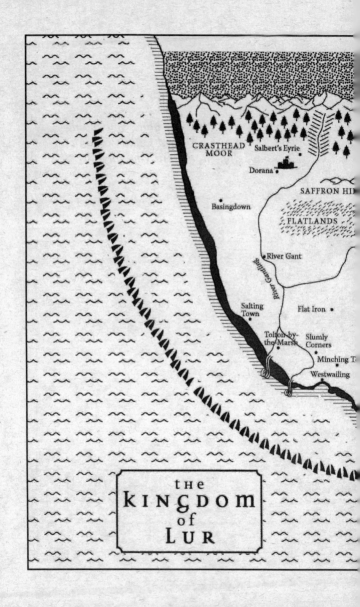

CRASTHEAD
MOOR

Salbert's Eyrie

Dorana

SAFFRON HI

Basingdown

FLATLANDS

River Gant

Salting
Town

Flat Iron

Tolton-by-
the-Marsh

Slumly
Corners

Minching T

Westwailing

the
KINGDOM
of
LUR

BEYOND THE WALL

BARL'S WALL

BARL'S MOUNTAINS

THE BLACK WOODS

• Sapslo

• Jerring

Colford
•

THE
DINGLES

Struan Caves

Dinfingle

• Schoomer

Rillingcoombe

Bibford •

charven•

• Dolphin Head

vrock•

r's•

DRAGON TEETH REEF

THE
INNOCENT
MAGE

PROLOGUE

Nine hundred and ninety-seven . . . nine hundred and ninety-eight . . . nine hundred and ninety-nine . . . one thousand!

Asher opened his eyes. At *last*.

Time to go.

Holding his breath, he slid out of his old, creaking bed and put his bare feet on the floor as lightly as the rising sun kissed the mouth of Restharven Harbor.

In the other bed his brother Bede, mired in sleep, stirred and grunted beneath his blankets. Asher waited, suspended between heartbeats. Bede grunted again, then started snoring, and Asher sighed his silent relief. Thank Barl they didn't still share this room with Niko. Bloody Niko woke cursing if a fly farted. There'd be no chance of creeping safely out of the house if Niko still slept here.

But after Wishus finally got hisself married to that shrew Pippa and moved out of his solitary chamber to his own stone cottage along Fishhook Lane, Niko had taken belligerent possession of the empty room. Claimed it as his own by right of being the oldest brother still living at home—and with his fists if nobody liked that reason.

As the youngest, Asher didn't rate a room of his own. As the youngest he didn't rate a lot of things. Even though he was twenty years old, and a man, and could be married his own damn self if he'd wanted to be. If there was a woman in Restharven or anywhere else on the coast who could make his heart beat fast for longer than a kiss and a fumble on the cliffs overlooking the ocean.

Pausing to scoop up his boots, left conveniently at the end of the bed, Asher tiptoed into the corridor and past Niko's closed door. At Da's room he hesitated. Looked in.

Da wasn't there. Shafting moonlight revealed the sagging double bed, empty. The blankets undisturbed. The single pillow undented. The room smelled musty. Abandoned, even though somebody still lived there. If he closed his eyes, he could almost catch the sweet suggestion of Ma's perfume.

But only almost, and only if he imagined it. Ma was long since dead and buried, and all that remained of her perfume was a single cracked and used-up bottle Da kept on the dusty windowsill.

Asher moved on, a ghost in his own house.

He found his father in the living room, sprawled snoring in his armchair. An empty ale jug sat on the table by his right hand; his tankard was tumbled on the carpet at his slippered feet. Asher wrinkled his nose at the sourness of spilled beer and soaked wool.

The living room curtains were still open. Moonlight painted the floor, the armchair. Da. Asher stared down at him and felt a pang of conscience. He looked so *tired*. But then he had a right to. Sailing towards sixty, Da was.

When you saw him on the ocean, bellowing orders and hauling nets over the side of whichever family smack he'd chosen to captain that day, or watched him gutting fish and bargaining the prices afterwards, it was hard to believe he had seven sons grown and was a grandpa eleven times over. There wasn't a man in all the Kingdom of Lur, Olken or Doranen, who could beat back the waves like Da. Who could catch a leaping sawfish with just a hook and a rod, or snatch a bright-scaled volly from right over the side of the boat and kill it with his bare hands alone.

Looking at him now, though, all black and silver in the moonlight, his uncapped head sparse with graying hair, his weathered face sagging in sorrowed sleep, belief was all too easy.

Da was old. Old and wearing out fast, from work and worry.

Still holding his boots, Asher crouched beside the armchair. Gazed into his father's slumbering features and felt a great wave of love crash over him. He was going to miss this face, with its crooked nose, broke in a drunken brawl over Ma when they were courting, and its scarred chin, split by slipping on a storm-heaved deck five seasons gone.

"Past time somebody did the worryin' for you, Da," he whispered. "Past time y'had things soft, 'stead of hard. I said I'd do this for you, one day, and I reckon that day's come."

Trouble was, it was easier said than done. To make good on his promise he needed more than dreams, though he had plenty of those. He needed money. Lots and lots of money. But he wasn't going to find it in Restharven.

Not just because it was Restharven, but because of his brothers. In a family business, money made was money shared . . . and the youngest got the smallest slice of the pie.

Well, sink that for a load of mackerel.

He was off to find his own pie, and he wasn't going to share it with anybody. Not till the pie was big enough to buy him a boat of his own, so he and Da could leave Zeth and the rest of them to their own devices, sink or swim, who cared? He and Da wouldn't. He and Da would have their own damn boat, and with all the money they'd make fishing it, just the two of them, they'd live as grand as the king hisself.

For two years now, he'd been scrimping and saving and going without, just so he'd have enough to get by. Enough to get him all the way to the grand City of Dorana. He had it all worked out.

"It's just for a year, Da," he whispered. "I'll only be gone a year. It ain't that long a time, really. And I'll be back afore y'know it. You'll see."

The clock on the wall struck half past ten, loud chiming in the silence. The Rusty Anchor would be closing soon, and Jed was waiting with his knapsack and purse. He had to go. Asher leaned over the armchair, pressed a kiss to his father's weathered cheek and slipped out of the small stone cottage he and all his brothers had lived in from birth.

When he was sure it was safe to make a noise he stamped into his boots then hurried from shadow to shadow until he reached the Rusty Anchor. The pub was full, as usual. Asher pressed his nose to the bobbled windowpane, trying not to be seen, and searched for Jed.

Spying his friend at last amongst the crush of carousing fishermen, he tapped and waved and hoped Jed would notice him. Just as he was despairing, Jed leapt away from an enthusiastically swung arm, stumbled, turned, and saw him.

"I were about to give up on you!" his friend grumbled as he came outside, a fresh tankard of ale in his hand. "You said ten o'clock, or soon after. It be nigh on closin' time now!"

"Don't look like y'missed me over much." Asher swiped the tankard from Jed's clutches and took a deep swallow of cold, bitter ale. "Did y'bring 'em?"

Jed snatched the tankard back. "'Course I brung 'em," he said, rolling his eyes. "I'm your friend, ain't I?"

"A friend would let me drink that tankard dry," said Asher, grinning. "It's a long ways between me and the next pub, and from the looks of you, one tankard more'll be one tankard too many."

"Ain't no such thing," said Jed. Then he relented. "Here." He shoved the tankard at him. "Bloody bully. Now come on. I've stashed your things round the corner. If you stop fritterin' my time and get along I'll manage a last mouthful meself afore the Anchor closes."

Asher took the tankard. Good ole Jed. There wasn't another soul he'd have trusted his precious purseful of trins and cuicks to, or his goatskin of water and knapsack stuffed with cheese and apples and bread and clothes. Nor his dreams, neither. They'd been friends their whole lives, him and Jed. He'd even offered to take Jed to the City with him, but there'd been no need. Jed wasn't plagued with a school of brothers. He was all set to inherit his da's fishing boat in a few more years.

Lucky bastard.

"You take care now," Jed said sternly as Asher guzzled the rest of his ale. "Dorana City's a long ways from here, and it be a powerful dry place. Not to mention swarmin' with Doranen. So just you watch your step, Meister Asher. You ain't the most respectful man I ever had the pleasure of knowin'. Fact is, I ain't sure those magic folk up yonder be ready for the likes of you."

Asher laughed and tossed him the empty tankard. "Reckon those magic folk up yonder can take care of 'emselves, Jed. Just like me. Now you won't forget to see my da first thing tomorrow and let him know I be fine and I'll be back a year from today, will you?"

"'Course I won't. But I still reckon you ought to let me tell him where you'll be. He's bound to ask, y'know."

"Aye, I know, but it ain't to be helped," said Asher. "You got to keep that flappin' tongue of yours behind your teeth, Jed, 'cause two seconds after you tell him he'll tell Zeth and the rest of 'em and that'll be the end of that. They'll find me and drag me back here and I won't ever get enough money saved to set Da and me up all grand and comfy. Just 'cause we're related and I be the youngest they think they own me. But they don't. So it'll be safest all round if you just act like you ain't got the foggiest notion where I am."

"Lie, you mean?"

Asher pulled a face. "For 'is own good, Jed. And mine."

"All right," said Jed, belching. "If you say so."

Asher tied the water-filled goatskin to his belt and hitched his knapsack over his shoulders. "I say so."

Jed sighed mournfully. "You'll miss the festival."

"This year. We can drink twice as much next year to make up for it. My shout. Now get yourself into the Anchor, would you, afore somebody wonders where you've got to and comes lookin'."

"Aye, sir," said Jed, and bruised Asher's ribs with a clumsy hug. "Have a grand time, eh? Bring yourself home safe and sound."

"I aim to." Asher stepped back. "Safe and mighty plump in the pocket to boot. And mayhap I'll bring a tidy armful of City Olken lass home with me and my money!"

Jed snorted. "Mayhap you will at that. Provided she's half blind and all foolish. Now for the love of Barl, it be ten minutes till closing time. If you don't get out of here now you'll be leavin' with an audience."

Which was the last thing he needed. With a smile and a wave Asher turned and hurried up the street, away from his friend and the pub and the only life he'd ever known. If he walked all night, fast, he'd reach the village of Schoomer in time to hitch a ride on one of the potato wagons heading for Colford. From Colford he could hitch to Jerring, from Jerring to Sapslo, and in Sapslo he could buy a seat on one of the wagons traveling to Dorana.

No way would his sinkin' brothers ever work out *that* plan.

As he strode up the hill towards the Coast Road he looked out to the left, where Restharven Harbor shone like a newly minted trin beneath the full-bellied moon. The warm night was full of salt and sound. A rising breeze blew spray in his face and his ears echoed with the pounding boom of waves crashing against the cliffs on either side of the keyhole harbor.

He felt his heart knock against his ribs. A year in dry

Dorana. A year without the ocean. No screaming gulls, no skin-scouring surf. No pitching deck beneath his feet, no snapping sails above his head. No racing the tide and his brothers back to port, or diving off Dolphin Head into surging blue water, or scoffing grease and vinegar fresh-fried fish for dinner with Jed and the other lads.

Could he stand it?

Ha. "Could" didn't come into it. He had to. There were dreams to fulfil and a promise to keep, and he couldn't do either without leaving his heart and soul behind him. Without leaving home.

Head up, whistling and unafraid, Asher hurried towards his future.

PART ONE

CHAPTER ONE

*H*e's here."

Caught unawares, Matt straightened sharply and stared at the woman framed in the stable doorway. Her thin fingers clung tight to the top of the bolted half-door and her angular face was taut with suppressed excitement. The startled horse he was saddling tossed its head and snorted.

"Easy, Ballodair, you fool," he said, one hand on the dancing brown hindquarters. "Sneak up on a body why don't you, Dathne?"

"Sorry." As usual, she didn't sound particularly repentant. "Did you hear what I said?"

Matt ducked under the stallion's neck and checked the girth buckles on the other side. "Not really."

Dathne glanced over her shoulder, unbolted the stable door and slipped inside. From the yard behind her, the sounds of voices raised in bantering laughter and the clip-clopping scrunch of iron-shod hooves on raked gravel as two of the stable lads led horses to pasture. "I *said*," she repeated, lowering her voice, "he's here."

The gold buckles on the horse's bridle weren't quite even. Tugging them straight, frowning, Matt glanced at her. "Who? His Highness?" He clicked his tongue. "Early again, drat him. Nine o'clock he asks me to have Ballodair ready, some meetin' or other somewhere, but it ain't even—"

Dathne made an impatient hissing sound. "Not Prince Gar, you clot-head! *Him*."

At first he couldn't make head or tail of what she meant. Then he looked, really looked, into her face, her eyes. His heart leapt, and he had to steady himself against Ballodair's warm, muscled neck.

"Are you sure? How do you know?" His voice sounded strange: cracked and dry and frightened. He was frightened. If Dathne was right . . . if the one so long awaited was here at last . . . then this life, which he loved despite its dangerous secrets, was ended. And this day, so bright and blue and warmly scented with jasmine and roses and fine-boned horseflesh, marked the beginning of the end of all things known and cherished.

The end of everything, should he and Dathne fail.

Dathne was staring at him, surprise and annoyance in her narrow, uncompromising face. "How do I know? You of all people ask me that?" she, demanded. "I *know*. He woke me out of sleep with his coming, late last night. My skin crawls with him." Then she shrugged, an impatient twitch of her bony shoulders. "And anyway, I've seen him."

"Seen him?" said Matt, startled. "In the flesh, you mean? Not vision? When? Where?"

Pulling her light shawl tight about her, she took a straw-rustling step closer and dropped her voice to a near whisper. "Earlier. I followed my nose till I found him coming out of Verry's Hostelry." She sniffed. "Can't say I think much of his taste."

"Dathne, that was foolish." He wiped his sweaty palms down his breeches. "What if he'd seen you?"

Another shrug. "What if he had? He doesn't know me or what I'm about. Besides, he didn't. The City's thronging with folk for market day. I blended with the crowd well enough."

"You don't reckon . . ." Matt hesitated. "D'you think he *knows*?"

Dathne scowled and scuffed her toe in the yellow straw, thinking. "He might," she said at last. "I suppose." Then she shook her head. "But I think not. If he did, why would there be need of us? We've a part to play in all this that hasn't begun yet." Her dark eyes took on a daunting, familiar glow. "I wonder where it will lead us. Don't you?"

Matt shivered. That was the kind of question he'd rather wasn't asked, or answered. "So long as it's not to an early grave, I don't much care. Have you told Veira?"

"Not yet," Dathne replied after a heartbeat's hesitation. "She's got Circle business, trouble in Basingdown, and beyond him being here I've nothing to tell. Not yet."

"You sound so calm. So sure!" He knew he sounded accusing. Couldn't help it. There she stood, strong and certain and self-contained as always, while his guts were writhing into knots and fresh sweat damped his shirt. Sensing his distress, Ballodair blew a warning through blood-red nostrils and pinned back his sharply curved ears. Matt took a strangled breath and stroked the horse's glossy cheek, seeking comfort. "How is it you're so sure?" His voice was a plaintive whisper.

Dathne smiled. "Because I dreamed him and he came."

And that was that. Stupid of him to expect more. To expect comfort.

Dathne was Dathne: acerbic, cryptic, unflustered and alone. After six years of knowing her, arguing with her, deferring to her, a drab and fluttering moth to her flame, he knew it was pointless to protest. She would be as she was and there was an end to it. As well to complain that a horse had four legs and a tail.

A grin, fleeting and impish, lit her plain face. She could read him as easily as any of the books she sold in her shop, drat her. "I should go. The prince will be here for his horse any moment, and I have things to do."

Something in her gleaming eyes unsettled his innards all over again. "What things?"

"Meet me in the Goose tonight for a pint," she invited, fingers lightly resting on the stable door. "Could be I'll have a tale to tell."

"Dathne—!"

But she was out of the stable, bolting the door, *snick*, behind her, and the sun was bright on the raven-black hair bound in a knot close to her long straight neck. "No later than seven, mind!" she called over her shoulder, stepping neatly aside from young Bellybone with his buckets of water dangling left and right. "I need my beauty sleep . . . for all the good it's done me so far!"

Then she was gone, slipping like a shadow through the stable yard's arched main entrance, and coming through the door in the wall leading to the prince's Tower residence was the prince himself, ready for riding and for business, bright yellow hair like molten gold and the easy smile on his face that hid so much, so much.

With a sigh and a last frowning stare after the woman he was soul-sworn bound to serve and to follow, Matt thrust aside his worries and went forth to greet his sovereign's son.

In the great Central Square of Dorana, capital city of the Kingdom of Lur, market day was in full, uproarious swing. First Barl's Day of every month it was held, regular as rainfall, and even though the sun had barely cleared the tallest turret on the distant royal palace the square was crammed full of buyers and sellers and sightseers, flapping and jostling like fish in a net.

Asher stood in the midst of the madness and stared like a lackwit, his senses reeling. A rabble of noise dinned his ears and his nose was overwhelmed by so many different smells, sweat and smoke and cow dung and incense, flowers and sweetmeats and roasting fowl and fresh-baked bread and more, that his empty stomach churned.

Most of the stallholders were his own people, Olken, dark-haired and industrious, selling their wares with cheerful ferocity. Fresh fruit, vegetables, butchered meat, live chickens, cured fish, candles, books, jewelry, saddlery, furniture, paintings, haircuts, bread, clocks, sweetmeats, pastries, wool, work clothes, fancy clothes . . . it seemed there was nothing a man couldn't buy if he had a yearning, and the money.

"Ribbons! Buy yer pretty ribbons here, six cuicks a dozen!"

"Teshoes! Ripe teshoes!"

"Oy! Mind how ye go there, lad! Mind how ye go!"

Asher spun on his heel and stumbled clear just as a bull handler, chocolate-brown beast in tow, ambled past on his way to the Livestock Quarter. The bull's polished nose ring flashed in the sunshine, and its splayed hooves clacked on the cobblestones.

"'Ere, you great lump, git out of me way!" grumbled the fruit seller, a fat Olken woman with her dark hair straggled back in a bun, her bright green dress swathed in a juice-stained apron and a brace of plump pink teshoes in one capable hand. "You be trippin' up me customers!"

Because he'd sworn a private promise to ask whoever he could, he said to her, "Would you be needin' a body to hire?"

The fruit seller winked at the crowd gathered about her barrows and cackled. "Thanks, sonny, but I already got me a man wot'd make two of you, I reckon, so just be on yer way if you ain't buyin' none of me wares!" A roll of her meaty shoulders heaved her abundant bosom, and her lips pursed in a mockery of invitation.

Around him, laughter. Hot-faced, Asher waited till the ole besom's back was turned, nicked a teshoe from the pile at the front of the stall and jumped into the swift-flowing stream of passers-by.

He finished the fruit in three gulps and licked the tart juice off his stubbly chin. It was all the breakfast he'd get. Lunch, too, and maybe even dinner if he didn't find work today. The purse tucked into his belt was ominously flat; it had taken nearly all his meager savings just to get here, and then last night's board had gobbled up most of the rest. He had enough for one more night's lodging, a bowl of soup and a heel of bread. After that, he was looking at a spot of bother. But even as doubt set its gnawing rat teeth in his guts, he felt a wild grin escape him.

He was in Dorana. *Dorana*. The great walled City itself. If only Da could see him now. If his *brothers* could see . . . they'd puke their miserable guts out, right enough.

Ha.

Long before devising the plan that had brought him here, he'd dreamed of seeing this place. Had grown up feeding that dream on the stories Ole Hemp used to tell the eager crowd of boys who gathered round his feet of an afternoon, once the boats were in and the catch was cleaned and gutted and the gulls were squabbling their fill on the pier.

Ole Hemp was the only man in Restharven who'd ever seen the City. Sprawled on his favorite bench down by the harbor, puffing on his gnarly pipe, he used to tell tales that set all their hearts to thumping and nigh started their eyes right out of their heads.

"Dorana City," Ole Hemp would say, "be so big you could fit Restharven in it twenty times over, at least. Its houses and hostelries be tall, like inland trees, and painted every color under the sky. And its ale houses, well, they never run dry, do they. And the smells! Enough to spill the juices from yer mouth in a river, for in their kitchens they roast pigs and lambs and fat juicy bullocks over fire pits so big and deep they'd hold a whole Restharven fambly, near enough."

And the listening boys would sigh, imagining, and rub their fish-full bellies.

But there was more, Hemp would say, so hushed and

awestruck his voice sounded like the foam on the shingle once all the waves had run back to the sea. In Dorana you could see Barl's Wall itself, that towering golden barrier of magic bedded deep into the sawtooth mountain range above and behind the City.

"See it?" the boys would gasp, unbelieving, no matter how many times they'd heard the story.

"Oh aye," Old Hemp assured them. "Barl's Wall ain't invisible, like the spells sunk deep in the horizon-wide reef that stops all boats entering or leaving the calmer waters between coral and coast. No, no, Barl's Wall be a great flaming thing, visible at noon on a cloudless blue day. Keeping us safe. Protecting every last Olken man, woman and child from the dangers of the long-abandoned world beyond."

That was when somebody would always ask. "And what about the Doranen, Hemp? Does it protect them too?" And Hemp would always answer: "'Course it do. Reckon they're like to build a wall as won't save their own selves first and foremost?"

But he always said that quietly, as though they could hear him, even though the nearest Doranen lived over thirty miles away. For Doranen ears were magic ears, and they weren't the sort of folk who took kindly to criticism.

Unsettled and suddenly homesick, Asher shook himself free of memories then looked up and over the marketplace into the distance beyond the City, where Barl's Wall shimmered in the morning sun. Ole Hemp had been right about that much, any road: there the Wall was, and there it would stand, most like until the end of time itself.

A laughing group of Doranen sauntered by. Asher couldn't help himself: he stared.

They were a tall race, the Doranen. Hair the colors of silver and gold and ripe wheat and sunshine, looped and curled and braided with carelessly expensive jewels. Eyes clear and fine, glass hues of green and blue and gray, and their skin white, like fresh milk. Their bones were long and elegant, lightly fleshed and sheathed in silk, brocade, velvet, linen, leather. They carried themselves like creatures apart, untouched, untouchable, and wherever they walked the dust of the marketplace puffed away from them in deference.

That was magic . . . and they wore it like an invisible cloak. Wrapped it around their slender shoulders and kept it from slipping with the haughty tilt of their chins and the way they placed their fine-shod feet upon the ground, as though flowers should spring blooming and perfumed in their wake.

Down Restharven way, you'd hardly see a Doranen from one end of the year to the next. The king, at Sea Harvest Festival. The tax collector. The census taker. One of their fancy Pothers, if a good old-fashioned Olken healer couldn't fix your gripes or your broken bones for you. Other than that, they kept themselves to themselves on large country estates or in the kingdom's bigger towns and here, of course, in the capital. What they did to amuse themselves, Asher had no idea. Farmed and fished rivers and grew grapes and bred horses, he supposed, just like his own people. Except, of course, they used magic.

Asher felt his lip curl. Living your life with magic . . . it wasn't *natural*. These fancy yeller-headed folk with their precious powers to do near on everything for them, to make the world bend to their wishes and whims, who'd never raised the smallest blister in all their lives, let alone an honest sweat . . . what did they under-stand about the world? About the way a man should be connected to it, should live steeped in its tides and rhythms, obedient to its subtle voices?

Nowt. For all their mysterious, magical powers, the Doranen understood nowt.

With an impatient, huffing sigh, he moved on. Stand-ing about like a shag on a rock wasn't going to get him any closer to finding a job.

With his elbows tucked in and one hand hovering pro-tectively over his purse, he navigated the crowded spaces between the market stalls, asking each stallholder for work. The little girls back home, picking winkles at low tide, put fewer shells in their gunny-sacks than the rejec-tions he collected now.

His heart was banging uncomfortably. This wasn't the way his dreams had gone at all. He'd reckoned finding a job'd be a damn sight easier than *this* . . .

Scowling, he stopped before one of the few Doranen stalls in the marketplace. The pretty young woman tend-ing it smiled at him and snapped her fingers. The cun-ningly carved and painted toy dog prancing among the other toys immediately barked and turned a somersault. With another Doranen finger-snap a jolly fat clown dressed in spangled red began juggling three yellow balls. The little dog yapped and tried to snatch one out of the air.

The stall's other onlookers laughed. Just in time, Asher caught and swallowed a smile. Snorting, he turned his back on the dog and the clown and the pretty young woman and stumped away through the streaming crowd. Bloody Doranen. Couldn't even flummery toys to amuse spratlings without reaching for a spell.

At the heart of the marketplace stood a fountain, spewing water like a whale. Its centerpiece was a carved greenstone statue of Barl, with arms outstretched and a thunderbolt grasped in one fist. Beneath the bubbling surface, trins and cuicks winked and flashed in the sunshine. Asher fished a single precious copper cuick from his purse and tossed it in.

"It's a job I be needin'," he said to the silent face above him. "Nowt fancy, and all in a good cause. Reckon y'could see your way clear to helpin'?"

The statue stayed silent. Moisture slicked its carved green cheeks like tears . . . though what Barl had to cry about, he surely didn't know. Turning his back, Asher slumped onto the lip of the fountain's retaining wall. Not that he'd expected the statue to actually *speak*. But he'd half hoped for some kind of answer. An inspiration. A bloody good idea. For sure he wasn't the most *regular* of chapel-goers, but like everybody else in the kingdom, he did *believe*. And he obeyed the Laws. All of them. That had to be good for something.

He refused to accept his dream was dead before ever it drew breath. *Somewhere* in this noisy walled City there had to be an Olken in need of an honest young man with a strong back and a willingness to put in a long day's toil for a hot meal, a soft bed and fair pay at the end of it. Some kind of working man, or woman. No point botherin' with any of the fancy Olken. They were almost as bad as the Doranen. Fancy City Olken with fancy City houses and soft City hands and more money than sense, they'd be wanting workers—no, *staff*—with references and posh accents and clothes worth a year's catch of mackerel. He had no use for that malarkey, and the folks that did would have as little use for him.

No. He was a Restharven fisherman born and bred and he knew his worth. Somewhere in this City he'd find someone else who did too. Statue or no statue, he was going to get hisself that job.

He had to. He had a fortune to make and promises to keep.

Cutting through the babble of noise in the square, the indignant bellow of a cow. Asher snapped out of his slump. Of *course*. The Livestock Quarter. *Fool*. He should've tried there first, 'stead of traipsing from stall to stall getting nowt but a fistful of "no" for his trouble. In the Livestock Quarter he'd find farmers, cattlemen. His kind of folk. For certain sure there'd be somebody there wantin' the kind of service Asher of Restharven could provide.

He jumped up, hope rekindled. On the other side of the square, sound and movement distracted him. Shouting. Whistles. Applause. Glimpsed between the market stalls and crowding bodies, a flash of dark heads and blue and crimson livery: the City Guard, marching down the sloping road from the palace, which gleamed like a settled seagull up on the hill above the City.

Asher went to look. The Livestock Quarter wasn't going anywhere, and he was curious. Five minutes here or there weren't like to make a difference.

"Way now!" a stern voice shouted, carrying over the bubble and froth of the marketplace. "Make way for His Highness Prince Gar!"

Asher felt himself jostled and bumped forward with the rest of the crowd as it surged and seethed around him. He didn't understand the commotion. Why get so excited just because the prince was coming? The prince lived here in the City, didn't he, along with the rest of the royal family? Didn't City folk get to see him most every day of the week? Aye, they did. So why break a body's toes to lay eyes on him now?

But even as he muttered and cursed and shoved back, he had to admit to a breath of excitement. Not even Ole Hemp had laid eyes on a member of the royal family. This would put him one up, and no mistake. Da would be tickled pink.

With the roadway cleared of shoppers and stallholders, the prince was free to ride his bay blood horse with only one hand on the reins. It was a beautiful animal, mincing and dappled and harnessed in jewels. Asher felt his throat close in envy. That's what being a prince got you: a wondrous beast like that one, and a hundred more at home just like it, most prob'ly.

For the first time in his life, he was fleetingly sorry to be himself.

The approaching prince looked as well bred as his horse. His corn-silk hair, as long as a girl's, was caught in a tail at the nape of his neck. His green silk shirt and tan leather breeches were immaculate. The gloss on his black leather boots was blinding. On his head gleamed a beaten silver circlet of rank, studded with rubies. His thin face was lively with appreciation as he waved and smiled at the well-wishers to his left and right.

Thrust to the edge of the road by the heaving crowd, Asher eyed him up and down. So. This was His Royal Highness Prince Gar. Even down in distant Restharven they knew about *him*. Gar the Magicless. Gar the Cripple. Even, some whispered into their ale pots, Gar the Disgrace. Too blond to be an Olken, too magickless to be Doranen. That's what folks said about His Royal Highness Prince Gar . . . at least down Restharven way.

But from all the hooting and hollering of the City Olken around him it seemed they didn't mind the prince couldn't do magic. That he'd not be the one to take over the WeatherWorking once his father the king wore out. No, the City Olken seemed to think he was something to screech and dance for. Why? What use was a magician who couldn't do magic? About as much as a ship without sails, to his mind.

And it seemed he wasn't the only one to think so.

Barely a handful of Doranen had stopped to cheer their king's son as he rode off to spend a strenuous day in the countryside sniffing flowers, or whatever it was he did to amuse himself. A few had paused to smile and nod. A lot more, though, paid him no mind at all, or watched him pass with bland faces and judgement in their eyes. Did the prince see it? Did he care? It was hard to tell. For sure his dazzling smile didn't falter and his hand stayed steady on the reins . . . but mayhap there was a flicker in the green eyes. A momentary coldness, or stifled hurt.

Asher snorted. Catch him wasting time feeling sorry for a prince.

The king's son was drawing level now. In a moment would be close enough to reach out and touch if he'd had a mind to. Determined to remain unaffected, Asher stared into the smooth, careless face of royalty . . . and royalty stared back.

A frown. A jolt: of interest, or rejection, or something in between. Then an Olken lass tossed a rose. It struck royalty's prancing horse on the neck. The horse shied, objecting, and the prince had his hands full.

Disconcerted, Asher stepped back from the edge of the road, heedless of the trampled toes and curses behind him. Despite himself, and despising himself for it, he was impressed. There *was* something about the prince. The king's son possessed an aura of authority. Of grace, even. Something inborn, of blood and bone and breeding, not circumstance. Something that made him . . . different.

Codswallop. The prince was rich, magic or no magic he was Doranen, and he was royalty; probably it was that and nothing more.

Asher shook himself, breaking the unlikely, unwelcome spell. All this standing about gawping at royalty. Da would've clipped him over the earhole long afore now. Time he took care of his own business.

He turned away. From six feet further along the road came a loud bang. A scream. Asher turned back to see a whirling, whizzing rush of light as the rockets in a fireworks stall erupted into blazing glory, shooting skywards in a shower of green and yellow sparks. The crowd shrieked.

Already unnerved, the prince's blood horse whinnied in fright and reared. His Royal Highness fell off backwards to land his royal arse hard and hurting on the dirty ground. Panic-stricken, preparing to bolt, the animal bunched its hindquarters and spun about, eyes wild. Foam flew from its gaping mouth.

"*Ballodair!*" the prince cried as the horse launched itself over his head in a great leaping bound.

"Catch him!" cried another voice, sharp and commanding, buried somewhere close by in the crowd.

Without thinking, Asher jumped into the path of the frightened horse. A lifetime of sailing boats in untamed weather had honed his reflexes and made him indifferent to danger. Catching those flapping reins was just like laying hold of a loose halyard in high winds; battling the beast to a standstill not much harder than wrestling with a net-load of fish reluctant to die.

And besides, it seemed a shame for a fine animal like that to break a slender leg just 'cause some royal folderol couldn't keep his arse in the saddle.

Shod hooves striking sparks, the horse plunged and spun. The screaming crowd scattered. Swearing as the horse's head collided with his own, seeing stars and shouting as an iron-clad foot ground his booted toes into the cobblestones, Asher struggled to keep the animal in one place. Blood from his split eyebrow blurred his vision. His sweaty hands slid on the leather reins as the horse grunted and thrashed and struggled for freedom.

In the end, Asher won. Defeated at last, the horse stood with all four feet on the ground, trembling. Its nostrils were red and wide open as ale pots as it huffed hot, hay-scented breath. Its eyes stared but no longer rolled, white-rimmed. Asher bent over, gasping.

Without warning the reins were plucked from his grasp and a shaking voice said, "Ballodair! It was just some fireworks! Are you all right, you fool of an animal?"

Head pounding, blood warm and sticky on his face, Asher straightened.

The prince, running an anxious hand down the animal's legs, was searching for damage. Paid no heed to the man who'd saved his wretched horse's hide. Offended, Asher cleared his throat. "It be fine, I reckon," he said, determined that this elegantly clad prince was a man, like him, who pissed and farted same as all men did, and had nothing more special to recommend him than an expensive tailor. "Don't seem like the beast's taken any harm, barrin' a fright."

The prince glanced up at him. A flicker of recognition lit his eyes and he nodded. Standing straight, he looped the reins over one arm then dusted his hands on his breeches. "So it would appear, Barl be praised." He kissed the solid gold holyring on his left forefinger. "He was a gift from His Majesty."

"A grand gift," said Asher. "Glad I could save 'im for you. I be fine too, by the way. You know. 'Case you were wonderin'."

The returning crowd gasped and muttered. A City Guard, his cheeks still pale from what might have been, frowned and stepped closer. The prince held up one hand, halting him, and considered Asher in unsmiling silence. Heart pounding, Asher lifted his chin and considered the prince right back. After a moment, the prince relaxed. Very nearly smiled. "Not so fine, I think. Your head is split open and your wits are addled from the blow. Have you taken any other hurt?"

The crowd buzzed its surprise, pressing to get a closer look at the ramshackle newcomer in such close conversation with royalty. Asher touched cautious fingertips to his eyebrow and shrugged as they came away red. "This ain't nowt. Reckon I've had worse shavin'." Then he scowled. "And my wits ain't addled, neither."

Horrified, the City Guard prodded Asher in the back. "Lout! Address the prince as 'Your Highness' and show some respect or you'll find yourself in one of Captain Orrick's cells!"

Again the prince lifted a hand. "It's all right, Grimwold. I suspect our reluctant hero isn't from around these parts." Smiling, he pulled a handkerchief from his shirt pocket, then unclipped a leather flask from his saddle and doused the fabric with its pale green contents. "Wine," he explained, offering it to Asher. "It'll sting, I'm afraid, but that's better than horse sweat in an open wound. Where are you from, by the way?"

With a grunt—and if the prince wanted to consider himself thanked, then fine—Asher took the handkerchief and dabbed his face with it. The alcohol burned like fire against his raw flesh; he couldn't swallow the pained hiss fast enough. "Restharven," he muttered. "Your Highness." Face clean of blood and dust, he glared at the soiled handkerchief. "Y'want this back?"

The prince's lips curved in faint amusement. "No. Thank you."

Was the king's son laughing at him? Bastard. "Got hundreds, have you?"

Now the smile was in full bloom. "Not quite. But enough that I can lose one and not repine. I've never been to Restharven."

"I know," said Asher. Then, prompted by the guard's glower added, sickly sweet, "Your Highness."

"How is it," asked the prince, after a thoughtful pause, "that you come to dislike me so thoroughly? And after I've given you a pure silk handkerchief, moreover."

Asher felt his face heat. Hadn't Ma always said to him, *Asher, that unruly tongue of yours will land you in such trouble one day* . . . "Never said I dislike you," he muttered. "Don't even know you, do I?"

The prince nodded. "That's very true. And easily remedied, what's more. Grimwold?" The silently scandalized guard snapped off a salute. "I believe we've provided enough entertainment for now. Move the people about their business. I'd like a private word with this gentleman." He turned to Asher. "That is unless you've pressing business to conduct elsewhere?"

Asher bit his tongue. Stared into a fine-bred face vivid with amusement, and a challenge. He cleared his throat. "No. Your Highness."

"Excellent!" declared the prince, and clapped him on the shoulder. "Then I shall steal a few minutes of your time with a clear conscience! Grimwold?"

With an obedient nod Grimwold did as he was told. The crowd dispersed in dribs and drabs, murmuring . . . and Asher was left alone with the Crown Prince of Lur.

CHAPTER TWO

Asher spared the grudgingly moving townsfolk a scathing glance. "Load of ole mollygrubbers. You fell off your horse, I caught it for you. Ain't no need for fuss. Ain't none of their business, I reckon."

Arms folded, head on one side, the prince regarded him with fascination. "Do you know, not even my enemies are as rude as you. At least not to my face."

Asher stared. Enemies? Since when did a prince have enemies? Then he scowled. "Rude? I ain't rude. I'm just me."

"Is that so?" said the prince, and laughed. "And who would 'me' be, exactly?"

It took Asher a moment to realize the prince was asking his name. Smart-arse. "Asher."

"Well, Asher—from Restharven—it's certainly refreshing to make your acquaintance. What brings you all the way from the coast to the City?"

Asher stared. Questions, questions and more bloody questions. Next time he'd let the horse bolt and break all its legs, he surely would. "A private matter," he said. Then added politely, because say what you like, Ma never raised her sons to be *rude*, "Your Highness."

"I see," said the prince, nodding. "Anything I can help with?"

Asher shrugged. "Prob'ly not. I be lookin' for work."

"Work?" The prince raised his pale eyebrows. "Hmm. So tell me, Asher. Since you come from Restharven, am I right in thinking you're a fisherman?"

"Aye."

The prince pushed aside his horse's questing nose. "Ah. Well, I can't say I've noticed a lot of fish in Dorana, unless you count the ornamental ones in the palace garden fishponds, and I don't think my mother would approve of you netting those." Another smile, reminiscent this time. "Besides, I ate one when I was four and it tasted disgusting."

"I can do other things aside from fishin'," said Asher, goaded.

"Really?" The prince considered him. "Such as?"

Such as : . . . such as . . . sailing. Except there weren't no boats in Dorana, neither. Damn the man. "Lots of things. I can . . . I can . . ." Punch you in the nose for askin' damn fool questions. Which most likely would earn him a night in a cell. Oh well. It'd save him the cost of a room at Verry's if he had no luck in the Livestock Quarter. "I can—"

A voice, polite but with a brisk air of confidence, said, "Your Highness?"

Asher turned. A woman. Middle height. Maybe a year or three older than himself. Thin. Sharp-faced, sharp-eyed, with an intensity about her that could never be restful. No feminine frippery about her, makeup or jewelry or suchlike. Slung over one bony shoulder a string bag half filled with packages. She glanced at him, an air of disinterest behind the good manners, then returned her attention to the prince.

He was smiling again. "Dathne."

She offered him a scarecrowish curtsy, all knees and elbows. "Forgive me for intruding, sir, but I saw what happened. I trust Your Highness is unharmed?"

"Aside from the odd bruise to my posterior—and my pride," said the prince, rubbing one hip. "I should know better than to go tumbling off like that."

She shrugged. "Accidents happen. Sir, if I may be so impertinent . . . Matt was saying only last night that what with young Tolliver going back to his family's farm, he could do with another pair of hands about the stables."

"Was he indeed?" The prince turned to Asher. "Well?"

Asher stared. "Well, what? Sir?"

"My stable meister is a good man. Strict, but fair. All the lads like him." When Asher didn't reply, the prince added, impatiently, "I'm offering you a job."

"I were goin' to ask around in the Livestock Quarter."

"Well then," said the prince, grinning, "I've saved you some shoe leather, haven't I? So. Are you interested?"

Careful, careful. Only a fool dives headfirst into strange waters. "What if I am?"

The prince shrugged. "Then you're hired." He nodded at the woman, pleased. "A lucky coincidence, Dathne."

Her lips curved in a faint smile. "Yes, Your Highness. Would you like me to see him safe to Matt? You're on your way somewhere, I think."

"On my way and horribly late," said the prince. "So yes. You could take him up to the Tower. Thank you,

Dathne." Gathering his reins, he slipped one booted toe into the stirrup and swung himself into the saddle with a lithe grace. "Tell Matt to get Asher settled in, and have him send for Nix to see to that cut. You can start your duties proper in the morning, Asher. All right?"

Taken aback by all the brusque efficiency, Asher nodded. "Aye. Sir."

"Certainly, Your Highness," said the bony woman.

"And after you leave the Tower, Dathne, you could stop by the palace and see if the queen is free to speak with you. I believe there's a book she's looking for."

Another curtsy. "It would be my pleasure, Your Highness."

"Excellent," said the prince, and nudged his horse forward.

Asher stared after him, mouth agape. "Wait a minute! You can't just give me a job and then ride off without so much as a—"

"I can, you know," the prince said over his shoulder. "It's one of the few advantages of being royal."

"*Wait* a minute!" Asher shouted, and hustled after him, ignoring a handful of staring bystanders and the distantly hovering Grimwold. "You ain't said how much you'll pay me!"

The prince swung his horse 'round. "Twenty trins a week, plus suitable work clothes, bed and meals."

Asher choked. Twenty trins? *Twenty trins*? Da had only ever paid him seven, and nearly not that, what with all of brother Zeth's complaining about him being the youngest with no family of his own to feed. He took a deep breath. "Thirty!"

The prince laughed. "*Thirty*?"

"I saved your precious Ballodair, didn't I? Sir?"

Another laugh. "And I can see your act of derring-do is going to cost me dearly. Twenty-five, and not a cuick more. Tell Matt. Anything else? Say no."

"No," said Dathne, who'd joined them. "Good-day, Your Highness."

Asher watched the prince ride out of sight, dumb-founded, then turned to stare at the skinny, interfering woman who'd just got him a job in the Prince of Lur's stables for the unheard-of sum of twenty-five trins a week, plus clothes and bed and board.

She grinned. "Well, well. It looks like I'm stuck with introducing you to Matt, so let's get it done, shall we? I'm a very busy bookseller and I don't have all day." She snapped her fingers under his nose and turned on her heel. "Follow me."

The wine-soaked, bloodstained silk handkerchief was dry now. Asher shoved it into his pocket and followed.

For all that she was a good head shorter than he, Asher found himself scuttling to keep up with the woman's impatient haste along the rising High Street that led, apparently, to the palace. The roadway was lined with shops; he would've liked to stop for a minute, have a stickybeak through their sparkling windows, but the sinkin' woman just kept forging ahead as though a shark had plans to swallow her for supper.

"So what's this Matt like then, eh?" he asked, hitching his knapsack back onto his shoulder for the fourth time.

"You heard His Highness," she replied. "He's an excellent fellow. You'll like him." She spared him a side-long glance. "The question is, will he like you?"

That stung. "Ain't no call for him not to be likin' me!

Reckon I be as good a man any day as some fancy prince's stable meister."

Her eyebrows lifted. "Well, that remains to be seen, doesn't it?" Taking him by the sleeve she tugged him off the main thoroughfare and down a quieter side street lined with balconied private dwellings. Just as Hemp had claimed, they were toweringly tall and painted all different colors. "This way."

Asher stopped staring at one high, narrow house painted yellow—*yellow*—and stared at the skinny woman instead, suddenly distrustful. He pulled his sleeve free and slowed, almost halting. "Where are we goin'? I thought we were headin' for the palace."

"We are, more or less," she replied. "His Highness hasn't lived in the palace itself since his majority. He has his own separate establishment in the palace grounds now. Going this way saves time." She favored him with a sly grin. "Mind you, if I weren't in a rush I *would* take you the long way round. Make sure you were in a suitably humbled frame of mind before meeting Meister Matt."

Asher scowled. "What did the prince say your name were again? Mistress Clever Clogs?"

Surprisingly, that made her laugh. "It's Dathne," she said, and bustled on.

"Ha." With a leap he blocked her pell-mell progress along the quiet street. "And why would you be interested in doin' a favor for me, eh, Mistress Dathne? You don't know me from a hole in the ground."

Eyebrows raised again, she looked him up and down. "Who said the favor was for you? I thought to help Matt out—but if you're going to be this disagreeable, could be I'll think again."

"Y'can't!" said Asher, alarmed, feeling those precious twenty-five weekly trins trickling through his fingers. "The prince said—"

"Whatever he said can as easily be unsaid. He doesn't interfere with Matt's running of the stables, so long as he's happy with how the horses are looking. And trust me, His Highness is very happy. If Matt says he won't have you then you'll be out on your ear, Meister Fisherman, and all for the sake of a little civility. Is that what you want?"

After a struggling moment, Asher shook his head. "Never said that. I just like to know where I stand, Dathne. That's all. Don't like owin' folk. Especially strangers."

She favored him with an enigmatic smile. "But we're not strangers, Asher. And as for owing me . . . well." Pushing him to one side, she started walking again. "I'm sure if I put my mind to it, I'll be able to come up with some way for you to pay me back."

Asher stared after her, mouth open. Did she mean . . . ? He hoped not. Skinny lemon-tongued shrews weren't his catch of mackerel, not by a netful they weren't. And then he pushed the thought aside, because she was turning another corner and in a moment he'd have lost her, and what kind of an impression would that make, eh, with his twenty-five trins still hanging in the balance?

Hoisting his knapsack to safety yet again, he hurried to catch up.

The palace grounds were enormous. Stretching the entire width of the walled City, they were girded by an impressive pale cream sandstone wall with a number of entrances each guarded by a pair of liveried Olken resplendent in crimson and gold. The two sentries decorating the gates that Dathne led him towards straightened at their approach, smiling.

"Morning to you, Mistress Dathne," they murmured, waving her under the stone archway with a single, disciplined glance for the unkempt stranger tagging at her heels.

"And to you, Pamfret, Brogan," Dathne replied. Taking Asher's elbow again, she hustled him along a raked blue gravel pathway that wound through lavish garden beds.

After the hubbub of the market square and their breathless rush up the sloping High Street, the garden's tranquility was like a cool draft of ale. Asher reclaimed his elbow and slowed, sucking in the perfumed air. Took a moment to consider his surroundings. To his far right rose the pure white walls of the palace, and to his left, just visible behind a belt of massive oak trees, a single column of midnight blue stone pointed fingerlike to the sky.

Dathne caught him staring at it. "The Prince's Tower."

"You mean he lives up there?"

"And works. Why? What's wrong with that?"

Skin crawling, Asher stared at the stone spire. "Houses ain't s'posed to be *tall*," he muttered, remembering Restharven's cozy stone cottages. "It ain't *natural*. What if it fell down?"

Dathne laughed. "It's nearly three hundred years old, Asher. If it was going to tumble it would have done so long before now. Besides, the Doranen don't build anything without stitching it up tight with magic. Trust me, it's perfectly safe."

"You've been in there?"

"Of course I have." She started walking again, fingers plucking at his sleeve to keep him with her. "Dozens of times. I often have books the prince finds interesting. He's probably the finest scholar in the kingdom, you know. Reads the original Doranen texts as fluently as if they'd been written yesterday."

"Oh aye?" said Asher, profoundly uninterested. "Good for him."

She looked at him sidelong, one eyebrow raised, a gleam of mischief in her eyes. "Do you like books?"

He'd never owned a book in his life. He could read, after a fashion; Ma had insisted on enough schooling for that, at least, before the wasting sickness whittled her to bones and eyes and put her in the ground. Once she was dead and gone, though, the sea had swallowed him whole and school had become a haphazard affair, his days there as scattered as flotsam on Bottlenose Beach. He shrugged. "Books? Don't think on 'em much one way or the other."

"Of course," she said. "Too busy fishing, I expect."

Was she laughing at him? He glared. "Fishin's a grand life. I ain't found one grander."

"Did I say it wasn't?" She raised her hands in mock surrender. "You're too easily prickled, Asher of Restharven. I don't know anything of where you come from. Could be you're the most important man in the village, and if that's so then I'm pleased for you. But a word to the wise now. Here you're the new boy and Matt won't stand for brangling. It upsets the horses, and in his eyes there's no greater sin. Is your skin so tender you can't take a little teasing?"

Asher felt himself burn. With six brothers unloving

and Da pickled and stewed and blinded with grief, he'd learned early to meet aggravation with greater aggravation or pay a heavy price. He scowled. "Any brangling won't be 'cause I started it. A body's got a right to earn a livin' without havin' to sleep with one eye open 'cause some iggerant shit-shoveler can't leave well enough alone. And if your precious Matt ain't a man to see that, then I'll turn round right now and find m'self a different job."

She stopped and swung about then, bony fingers closing hard on his wrist. In her face, a riot of uncertainty. Her eyes, plain brown and piercing, searched his face over and over as though looking for answers to a question she didn't care—or dare—to speak aloud. Her brows were knitted and her teeth pinched her lower lip bloodless. There was a blazing ferocity in her he didn't understand . . . but the heat of it backed him up a pace.

And then she smiled, the heat snuffing out of her like a wind-blown candle. Stepping back again, she let go of his wrist. "I expect you're right," she said lightly. "It never hurts to let people know you won't be trifled with. Now come on. I really don't have all day."

At length the graveled path led them to another wall, this one of rough-hewn bloodrock speckled with some kind of crystal that winked and flashed in the sunshine. An elaborate cast-iron gate stood wide open in welcome; passing through it, Asher saw the blue tower much closer now, yet still partly obscured by the oaks standing tall around its base. Straight ahead, though, was a grand curving archway of cream and ochre sandstone connecting two long, low ochre brick buildings. There were windows ranged at intervals along their walls, the open shutters painted a rich dark green. Through several of them horses poked long faces of brown and chestnut and gray, nostrils quivering, ears pricked, dark eyes wide and curious. Ringing into the surrounding quiet, a hammer struck echoes from an anvil.

"And here we are," said Dathne. "Matt's little kingdom." When Asher looked at her askance she added, "You think I'm jesting? Trust me, I'm not. The horses are his heart, and he protects them as keenly as any king does his subjects. Keep that fact pinned to your mast in plain sight, Meister Fisherman, and you'll not go far wrong."

"Ha," said Asher.

They passed beneath the sandstone archway and into the rich-smelling world of horses. The stables were arranged in a large square, each box opening onto an expanse of herringboned brick and dark red gravel. The yard was immaculate, swept and raked and clean as a cook's kitchen. At its center gloried a lavish, bee-buzzed flowerbed.

The sound of hammering was louder in here, but had changed. Off to the left in a covered, open-fronted alcove a massive gray horse stood snorting with displeasure. A young Olken lad gripped its plaited leather lead hard in both hands. A giant of a man, Olken and mountainously muscled, crouched over one of the horse's raised hind legs, cradling the fetlock and hoof between his bent knees. His black hair was clipped neat as a hedge. One large hand held a hammer and pounded nails into the horse's hoof with such precise power that Asher, staring, had to wonder what it might feel like to be felled by a punch from him.

Be best, prob'ly, if he never found out.

Beside him, Dathne made a pleased sound. "There he is." She raised her voice. "Matt!"

Matt took a moment to tap the nail-head home with one final metallic blow, then shuffled carefully back to front, hand supporting the horse's hoof, so he could finish off securing the shoe. Settling into his new position, hitching the hoof high onto his thigh, he glanced up. Saw Dathne, saw the stranger with her, and froze. His brown eyes widened, and his lips parted, sucking in an astonished rush of air. Then his expression smoothed, became completely noncommittal.

"Dathne." His voice was deep and instinctively soothing. "Be with you directly." He glanced at the lad clutching the horse's lead rope. "Make sure you've got a good grip there, Boonie, he's tensing up." He made a hissing sound and jiggled the horse's leg gently. "Settle down, old son, it's nearly over."

Quickly, with an economy of effort and a minimum of fuss, the stable meister resumed his task. Asher, watching closely, was impressed. You could trust a man who knew his job and did it well, without boastful flourishes.

Finished at last, Matt guided the horse's hoof back to the ground and nodded at the lad. "Put him in his paddock now, Boonie, and mind he doesn't kick you when you turn him loose."

The lad bobbed his head. "Aye, Meister Matt," he said, eyes aglow with respectful worship, and led the gray horse away. Matt watched them for a moment, eyes warm, then stuck his hammer through his belt and crossed the yard to Dathne and Asher.

As he opened his mouth to speak, Dathne said

brightly, "Matt, this is Asher of Restharven. His Highness has hired him to replace Tolliver."

Matt looked at her. "Oh he has, has he?"

"There was an incident in town, you see. Ballodair—"

"Ballodair!" Matt exclaimed. "Dathne, if you—"

She clapped her hands under his nose. "The horse is fine, Matt! Stop fussing!" She rolled her eyes at Asher. "Now do you believe me?"

Matt took a deep, steadying breath. "Just tell me what happened," he said with gritty patience.

Asher decided he'd had enough of other people speaking for him and deciding his fate. "Some fireworks went off, the horse took fright, tipped the prince onto his arse and tried to bolt. I caught it, and the prince offered me a job."

Matt was staring at Dathne, the warmth in his eyes chilled now. "Fireworks?" His voice was ominously quiet.

"One or two rockets," she told him, equally ominous. "No harm done."

"This time."

Asher scowled. From the looks of them, these two were set to start brangling like cats any tick of the clock. Something was going on here, some kind of lovers' spat, most like, and he wanted no part of it. Let 'em tussle on their own time. "Who do I see about recording my wages? Twenty-five trins a week I'm to get."

"Twenty-five?" Startled, Matt turned. "That's—"

"What the prince said he'd pay me," said Asher, truculent.

"He did," agreed Dathne.

"That's as may be," said Matt, still glowering, "but is he worth twenty-five trins a week?"

"Why should you care?" Dathne replied. "It's not your money, is it?"

"No," said Matt, "but it's my yard and my headache if the other lads hear—"

Her hand lifted, silencing him midsentence. Turning to Asher she said, "Are you going to blab to the other lads how much you're being paid?"

Asher snorted. "'Course not. What kind of a fool d'you take me for?"

She turned back to Matt. "There. You see? He's the soul of discretion."

Matt gaped at her for a moment, then closed his mouth with a snap of teeth and glared at Asher. "What do you know of horsekeeping, any road? You've not the look of a horseman, that much I can tell."

Asher glared right back. "Reckon I know enough. His Highness went and hired me, didn't he? Don't reckon I need to give you more of a recommendation than that. Why don't y'wait and see what kind of a fist I make on the job afore you count me no good, eh? Mayhap you'll get yourself a pleasant surprise."

Matt shook his head. "Oh, I'm already surprised, Asher of Restharven." His scowling gaze snapped sideways to Dathne, and the air fairly sizzled between them. "Whether or not it's pleasant remains to be seen."

Definitely, something was going on there. Asher took a small step to one side, putting distance between himself and the bookseller. "Y'won't regret hirin' me on," he said. "I ain't a wastrel, nor a shimshammery tyke neither. If I take a man's money, I give 'im proper weight for it."

Matt looked at him then, really looked at him. In his piercing regard there was a strange echo of the way Dathne had stared at him earlier. After a long moment, the stable meister nodded. "So you say. But words are cheap. I'll judge you on deeds, if I judge you at all."

"And I'm sure nobody could ask for better than that," said Dathne briskly. "Now, Matt, once Asher's settled in His Highness wants Nix to have a look at that cut on his head. Your precious Ballodair did that, so probably you owe Asher an apology. I must be off, I've to go see the queen, and then it's back to my little shop before I lose any more business today!" She waggled her fingers at them and turned on her heel.

Matt took a thunderous step after her. "*Dathne!*"

Striding away, she called back to him, "Tonight in the Goose, Matt, remember? No later than seven or you'll be paying!"

Matt stared after her, face stormy. Then he raised his fisted hands, stamped one booted foot to the gravel and exclaimed in heartfelt tones, "Barl save me! That *bloody* woman!"

"Aye," said Asher, and shook his head. "She be a slum-skumbledy wench and no mistake."

Matt blinked and lowered his fists. "*Slumskumbledy?*"

"Brangling," explained Asher. "Contrariwise." He shrugged. "A pain in the arse, if y'must know."

Matt shoved his hands in his pockets and stared at Asher. Asher stared back. Abruptly, spontaneously, they exploded into a duet of baffled, rueful laughter.

"A pain in the arse?" Matt echoed, eyes bright. "Asher of Restharven, I doubt I could've said it better myself!"

And just like that, though Meister Matt was the boss,

and a handful of years older than his new stable lad, they were friends.

At five after seven that evening Matt shouldered his way into the Green Goose Inn, favored watering hole and gossip mill of many royal staff, whether they served in the palace or the Prince's Tower. The Goose was a popular meeting place for several reasons: it was only a short walk from the palace grounds, useful for when a body's legs were all unsteady from an excess of cheer; the ale was cool and tasty, the food hot and plentiful, and their host, Aleman Derrig, could be sure to keep out any nuisances hoping to importune favors of a royal nature.

Though his name was called a dozen times as he ducked his head under the lintel, Matt just raised an acknowledging hand and did not stop to dally. All his attention was on Dathne, wedged comfortably in a corner booth with an ale-foamed tankard and a steaming bowl of soup keeping her company.

Sliding onto the bench opposite, he planted his elbows on the scarred, smoke-soaked table between them, leaned forward into the fragrant waftings from the broth bowl and said, his voice shaking with outrage, "That's him, isn't it? What in Jervale's name d'you think you're *doing*?"

"Keep your voice down. There's no need to tell the world and all his cousins what we're about."

Matt looked around the crowded inn. Humperdy's Band was racketing away in the far corner, fiddle and pipe and tambourine and drum filling the spaces between floor and rafters with raucous music. Many of the evening's rowdies were singing along, in tune and out of it. Heels banged away under benches and tables, more or less in time with the ditty, tankards thumped in counterpoint, and above that was the cheerful bellowing of friends gathered in good-natured banter. He doubted anyone standing even two feet away had overheard him.

He glared. "Stop trying to change the subject."

Dathne sighed and shook her head. "I did what was needful, Matt. No more, no less. I'm sorry to fret you. It wasn't my intention. But I must act when the push comes upon me, you know it, so don't sit there like a frog on a log pulling faces. We have him under our noses now, which is exactly where he should be. What's the rest of it compared to that?"

Matt bullied his face straight and stared at his freshly bruised knuckles, where one of the yearlings had tried its teeth that afternoon. "The rest of it?" He lifted his gaze to look at her. "Fireworks and bolting horses and all those people watching? Dathne—"

She waved an impatient hand. "Nothing happened that shouldn't have. And if you've a mind to bleat about your precious damned Ballodair again, I swear I'll throw this tankard of ale in your face then get the price of it off you straight after!"

That made him scowl again. "It's my job to worrit on the horses, Dathne."

She leaned close, eyes slitted with temper. "Your job is to do what I tell you and see that all runs as it should. What we're about here is worth a hundred Ballodairs, and our lives besides, and hating me for saying so doesn't change it. So you'd best make up that flitterbug mind of yours once and for all whether you can stomach the task or not. I can't do my part without a second pair of hands

I can trust. If they're not to be yours then I need to tell Veira so she can find me another."

Stricken silent, Matt looked down. Around him the room heaved with laughter and eating and generous drinking. His friends, for the most part, folk he'd known half his life and longer. Simple, hardworking Olken, blissfully ignorant of the secrets he'd kept for nearly ten years. Good people who were set to suffer and die if he and Dathne and the others of the Circle failed. His stomach rolled over, thinking on it, and the room disappeared in a blur of anguish.

Cool strong fingers on his wrist brought him back.

"Jervale's Prophecy is fulfilled, my friend," said Dathne. The sharp edges were gone from her voice: she sounded sad and tired and not like herself. "The Innocent Mage is come, and we stand at the beginning of the end of everything. I know you hoped the Final Days would pass you by, that the folk called after us would be the ones to face the fire, but that hope's dead and buried now. Digging it up and crying fresh tears on it won't change the truth. Like it or not, Matt, you and I are the ones born to the days Jervale foretold."

"How long have you known?"

"Long enough."

"And you're sure?" he whispered. "There's no doubt? No chance you might be mistaken?"

She shook her head. "Visions don't lie."

"They might."

"That's fear talking. Strangle it before it leads us all to disaster."

Matt winced as his guts cramped. "You may be Jervale's

Heir, Dathne, but that doesn't make you perfect. You could be wrong!"

"I could be, but I'm not. I was three days short of my tenth birthday the first time I dreamed Asher's face. The next afternoon I was told some cousin I'd never met had died overnight and it was my duty to take his place as Jervale's Heir. And then I was told what that meant. I haven't had an easy night's sleep since."

There was pain in her, fiercely denied. Matt wanted to reach out, to touch her, comfort her, but he didn't dare. Something deep and dark and implacably cold inside her stopped him. He felt his heart break. "Dathne . . ."

Her chin came up, and in her eyes glittered a scornful self-derision. She mocked her own pain, even as she mocked his pain for her. "Since that first time I've dreamed Asher . . . oh, more times than I dare think of. Him, and other things."

"What things?"

"Things," she said, and shivered. "They're not important now."

"I say they are. I want to know."

Hollow-eyed and direly foreboding, she stared at him. "No, Matt. You truly don't."

He had to persuade her. She shouldn't have to bear this burden alone. "Tell me. Please. I've got broad shoulders, Dathne. I can help. Even the best of us make mistakes when we're tired. Sad. Besieged."

"Not me. I'm never wrong, Matt. Not about this. Call my dreams visions, call them warnings, call them echoes of Prophecy. It's all just words, whipped to nothingness on the wind. I am Jervale's Heir and I *know*. Asher is the Innocent Mage. The Final Days are coming. And I am the

last living of Jervale's descendants, born to guide our ignorant fisherman to victory . . . or fail, and doom our
world to death and despair."

His chest was so tight he could hardly breathe. "And
me? What am I?"

She looked away, frowning. "My compass. My anchor.
My candle in the dark."

Warmed and angered at once, he lowered his voice.
"Then if I'm all those things, why did you never tell me
any of this when we met? Barl save us all, Dathne, I
could've done more, I could've—"

"No. You couldn't," she said gently. "Besides, I didn't
know you then."

"You know me now! You've known me for years! You
should've told me!"

Her smile cut him like a razor. "Matt, Matt. Why
would I weigh you down with such cruel knowledge a
heartbeat before you needed to know it?"

He could've wept. "I still say you might be wrong. We
should talk about this properly, we should—"

"There's nothing to talk about." The iron was back in
her voice, her eyes. "I am the Heir. You swore an oath to
follow wherever I might lead. So I ask you here and now,
Matt, and on my oath to the Circle I will never ask you
again: are you with me?"

Helplessly he stared at her. Was he with her? He'd
been with her from the moment they'd met, when he was
new to the king's stables and she was setting up her bookshop, and word had come from Veira that he'd been chosen to stand by Jervale's Heir and do his duty however
she saw fit.

Was he with her? He was with her even as he despaired

of her, when she rode roughshod over his cares and concerns, acted out of impulse or instinct or sheer bloody-mindedness, when she danced down pathways that he, unsighted, could never glimpse.

Was he with her?

He was with her till the bitter end, whatever that might be.

He brought his other hand to rest lightly on the fingers that still held his wrist with a desperation she'd die before admitting, and nodded. "Aye, Dathne. With you, for you, behind you. Always."

For a moment he thought he might see her shed a tear, for the first time ever. Her lips softened, and her gaze, and the fingers on his wrist tightened hard enough to tingle. And then she laughed and let go of him, the mocking light returned to her eyes. "Good. Now put a smile on old Derrig's face and fetch yourself an ale, Meister Matt. Fetch me another one while you're at it, too, for I think I've a mind to get drunk."

Almost he opened his mouth and asked if she thought that was wise. Just in time, though, he caught the words behind his teeth. Swallowed them. Said instead, "As my lady commands."

There was, after all, more than one way of crying.

CHAPTER THREE

Asher's days trotted briskly by, filled sunup to sundown with the exacting business of horses. Aside from Barlsday mornings in the palace chapel, and those times when the prince came into the stable yard to discuss stud business with Matt or fetch Ballodair to go riding, he scarcely saw his employer.

Which suited him just fine. What did a fisherman and a prince have to talk about anyways, eh? Nowt, save for the weather. And once you got past "That were a nice drop of rain your da organized for last night, eh?" "Oh yes, wasn't it?" there wasn't much left to say. So let the prince keep hisself to hisself up in his fancy Tower. Asher of Restharven was happy to perform his horsekeeping duties untroubled by princes, count twenty of his twenty-five hard-earned trins into his own personal and private chest at the Royal Treasury at the end of each week . . . and gloat on the thought of returning home to Restharven the same time next year a rich, rich man.

At first his nights were tossed and turned by dreams of the life he'd left behind. The sweet salt air, and the slap and suck of the tide against the hulls of the fishing fleet in the harbor. Jed's mad giggling. The wheeling, whirling gulls and the music of the village's menfolk come singing home from sea. Da's cracked baritone, butchering another ditty and making them all laugh.

Barl save him, there were mornings he'd wake with the memories so fresh it would be several pounding heartbeats before he knew where he was, and why the world smelled of horses. Before he remembered the names of the lads roused grumbling from their dormitory beds by Matt's merciless cowbell, and why they weren't his brothers.

Then he'd have to wait, hands fisted in his blankets, treacherous face hidden in the pillow, until he could greet the sunrise uncaring.

Those mornings were hard.

But the choice had been his. There was no point complaining about it, and no-one to complain to any road. This was his life now. Best get on with living it.

In spare hours Matt taught him to ride properly on the prince's retired brown hunter Dauntless, because—the stable meister said, comically despairing—he couldn't stand to see a man so woeful ignorant of decent basic horsemanship.

It was a far cry from his bareback slipping and sliding on Dotte, the family's decrepit half-blind nag who pulled the fish cart to and from Restharven Harbor. At first he wasn't sure about the notion of learning fancy riding. Especially when Dathne shut up her bookshop and came to watch, and laugh.

Turned out, though, he was an apt pupil with a knack for staying put in the saddle. Pretty soon Dathne wasn't laughing much at all, nor the lads neither, Boonie and Bellybone and Rinnie and the rest. Pretty soon he could walk, trot and canter ole Dauntless in figure-eights with his eyes closed, his arms folded across his chest *and* no stirrups. Ha!

So Matt promoted him onto Folly, with a wicked glint in his eye that said *"Right then, Meister Fisherman. Think you're a horseman now, do you? Well let's just see about that . . ."*

Folly had a pigroot in her that could turn a body inside out and back again faster than a frog catches flies. But Asher wasn't going to be beaten. Not by her, and not by smirking Stable Meister Matt. The tricky chestnut mare's antics had him eating dirt four times on the first day, twice on the second and never again after that. So, with an admiring grin and a proud slap on the back, the stable meister pronounced him fit to be seen in public.

That meant he joined Matt and his string of lads riding out every morning on the prancing apples of His Highness's eye: blood horses bred and cosseted for the purpose of fetching a tidy sum of trins at auction, or commanding high stud fees from hopeful folk with promising mares, or winning the races run every week for the entertainment of Olken and Doranen alike.

Within weeks, the sea dreams dwindled and life settled into a comfortable, comforting routine. In the evenings after work he tramped down to the Green Goose with Matt and the other lads. There they hobnobbed with other royal staff, supped ale, threw darts and swapped tales taller than the tallest house in the City. Often he'd argue amiably over a game of knuckles with Matt, then work up an appetite dancing with a comely Olken lass. Or Dathne.

In the softening light of the inn's lamps, when she let her hair loose onto her shoulders and a tankard or two of ale had smoothed the knife edges from her face, the bookseller was . . . well, not ugly. And she wasn't such bad company, either, once she'd blunted her sharp tongue on the hide of whoever was handy.

He learned soon enough to make sure it wasn't him.

Same as the other lads, he was only required to work five days out of six. So he spent his day off each week exploring the City on foot, or its surrounding countryside on borrowed horseback. Swam bare-arsed in River Gant. Fished for silver spotties off Dragonshead Bridge with a homemade rod and line, sometimes alone, more often with one or more of his new-made friends: the stable lads, a few of the junior City Guards, a handful of palace staff. Sometimes he even rode with Dathne in her wagon when she trundled off to investigate reports of old books for sale in other towns and villages.

Not that he was interested in old books. Or her. It was just nice to enjoy a change of scenery once in a while. To see how other Olken lived. To talk about things nowt to do with colic and fetlocks and worming elixirs. And if he came back from those occasional outings with a smile on his face, so what? Weren't no law against smiling, was there?

Riding. Swimming. Playing darts and sinking a few pints here and there. Dancing with pretty barmaids and aye, right, flirting with 'em too. All that on top of making fists of money without breaking too much of a sweat over stable yard chores.

If there was a better way to occupy a year of self-imposed exile from the ocean, Asher was hard put to imagine it.

So he didn't even try.

He was on his own in the yard one sleepy afternoon, pottering with bits and bobbery while Matt was out on errands and the other lads minded their own business mending harness, polishing carriages and collecting manure from the pastures, when a tingle between his shoulderblades told him he was no longer alone. He stopped sweeping the brickwork outside the currently empty sick box, and turned.

Prince Gar. Leaned against a convenient hitching post watching his fisherman stable hand earn those twenty-five weekly trins. Wearing his official ruby and silver circlet, what's more, which meant he was off to somewhere important. His clothing was officially flash, too: a crimson silk shirt under a gold and black brocade weskit and indigo fine wool britches, with his boots like polished black glass. Asher pulled a face. Fancy that for a job, eh? Primping a prince's boots till you could see your face in 'em. Poor bastard stuck with that chore must be near out of his skull with boredom by now.

"A touch of indigestion, Asher?" inquired the prince kindly.

Asher straightened his expression. "No, sir. Afternoon, sir. Somethin' I can help you with?"

Still leaning, still considering, the prince let his gaze stray around the immaculate stable yard. "Perhaps. How's the job working out?"

"Fine, sir," Asher said cautiously. "Thanks for askin'."

"No problems adjusting to your new life?"

"I been here nigh on two months, sir. Reckon if there were goin' to be problems I'd have stumbled across 'em by now."

The prince's lips twitched. "Yes, I reckon you would have." He sobered. Nodded. "That looks nasty. What happened?"

Asher looked down at his bare left forearm, revealed by the rolling up of his sleeve, where a thick white scar like old rope wound from elbow to wrist. "Cut m'self."

The prince blinked. "No. Really? How?"

Taking Jed up on a damn fool drunken bet was how. He'd pinched Young Mick's solo sailer and skimmed the waves all the way out to Dragonteeth Reef, intending to snap off a bit of coral and bring it back as proof, and a trophy.

Dragonteeth Reef had pretty near snapped off his arm instead.

Which wasn't the kind of thing he felt like telling this pretty prince, so he shrugged. "Just an accident. Fishin's a chancy life. Accidents happen all the time."

"Do they?" murmured Prince Gar. "Remind me not to take it up as a hobby in that case."

He kept a straight face, just. "Aye, Your Highness."

If he knew he was being laughed at, the prince didn't show it. Instead he smiled. "Matt says you've settled in well. It seems the horses like you as much as you like them."

Unsettled, Asher started sweeping again. Matt and the prince had been discussing him? He didn't much care for the sound of that. "Aye. Sir."

"Do you have a favorite?"

"S'pose," said Asher, with a one-shouldered shrug

he'd picked up from Dathne. "I like Cygnet. He's a good horse."

The prince grinned. "Good? He's the best I've ever bred. You've a keen eye, Asher."

Asher shrugged again. "I'm learnin'."

"It's an admirable trait."

Still sweeping, Asher frowned. Something wasn't right here. Princes didn't make a habit of wandering about stable yards paying compliments to minions with brooms, did they? Not bloody likely. So. Time to land this fish and see what he'd caught. "Your Highness—"

The prince didn't let him finish. "Listen. I've seen for myself that you're quick in a crisis, and brave. Matt says you're a competent if reluctant reader, and your handwriting is legible, although a trifle undisciplined. He also says the rest of the lads look up to you, you're a cheerful drunk, you ride like a man born in the saddle even though everyone knows you weren't, you know when and how to hold your tongue, you never have to be told anything twice and you don't suffer fools gladly." A small smile. "Well. At all."

"He does, does he?" His fingers were clutched so tight around the broom handle he was getting splinters. Bloody Matt and his great big mouth. There'd be words down at the Goose that evening, oh aye, and none of them complimentary.

"Yes," said the prince. "He does. Is he right?"

Sweeping could wait. Asher leaned the broom against the nearest wall and scowled. For all his negligent post-leaning, the prince was . . . edgy. Like a colt with one ear cocked for the sound of wind and an excuse to helter-skelter madly with its heels kicking the air.

"Right enough," he admitted. "And what if he is? What's all that malarkey got to do with how well I shovel shit? Sir?"

The prince shook his head and smiled again. "Nothing. How old are you?"

"Four month older'n you." He'd surrendered to curiosity about the prince's age after a week and asked Dathne. "Why?"

The prince didn't answer, just stared into the distance instead, lost in thought. Waiting, Asher reached for the broom again and tipped it upside down to pick out two dirty bent stalks of straw from between the bristles. Matt surely went spare if his precious brooms weren't put away prissy like unmarried maidens. To hear him go on, you'd think the bloody Wall itself would tumble down otherwise.

"Do you have something to wear that's a little less . . . industrious?" the prince said abruptly.

Asher looked down at his green cotton shirt, brown cotton trews and sturdy brown leather boots. "No use blamin' me for how I look. Some ole biddy up at the Tower gave me this clobber."

"Mistress Hemshaw. My housekeeper. I know. But do you have anything else? Anything—I don't know . . . smarter?"

Asher scowled. Over his bitter protests Dathne had made him squander half his precious first week's pay on outfits that were neither fishermen's homespun nor Tower-provided working clothes. Not silk, ha, or leather, or superfine wool either. Lawn for the shirt and second-card wool for the trousers. Expensive enough. He'd only worn them twice. Didn't want to wear them out completely before he got home again to show them off.

"Smarter? Aye," he said reluctantly. "Sir. Why?"

"Good." The prince pushed away from the wall to stand with his hands on his hips. "Go and get changed then. Quickly. The carriage will be here any moment."

Asher gaped. "Carriage?"

"Yes. I always travel to Justice Hall in His Majesty's carriage. As the Lawgiver I speak with his voice. Arriving in his carriage sets the proper tone for the proceedings."

"Justice Hall?" Asher stepped back. The broom in his hands lifted, a flimsy barrier between himself and the might of royalty. "*Court*, y'mean? You be takin' me to court? Why? I ain't never broke the law and whoever said I did be a drowned liar!"

The prince raised a calming hand. "Peace, Asher. You're not in trouble. I want you to witness today's hearing, that's all."

"Why? Sir?"

"We can discuss that afterwards. Now go and change, quickly." The prince grinned. "We don't want Justice Hall smelling like a stable, do we?"

"And what about Matt?" said Asher, retreating slowly. "If he comes back and I ain't done with—"

"Matt knows you'll be absent this afternoon."

Oh, did he? Bloody Matt. No wonder he'd been so insistent that the stable yard be swept and raked again, even though Bellybone had done it well enough that morning. Wanted to make sure the prince'd have no trouble finding poor ole mushroom Asher.

And now he was off to Justice Hall? With the prince?

In the king's carriage? *Why*? What in Barl's name was going on?

"*Asher*!" said the prince, all patience fled. "*Now*!"

Asher took the hint. Dropped the broom and ran for the dormitory, swearing under his breath with every pounding step.

Bloody Matt! Bloody Matt! Bloody bloody bloody Matt!

They were nearly halfway to the main palace gates, the king's magnificent enclosed carriage riding smooth as melted butter, when they heard a pounding tattoo of hooves approaching from behind. Scant moments later one of the smartly trotting carriage horses whickered and a young, feminine voice cried: "Hold up there, Matcher! I want a word with His Highness!"

As the coachman shouted a reply, Asher looked at the prince. Gar's face was pinched with displeasure and his manicured fingernails were drumming on his knee. "Barl save me," he muttered. "What does she want now?"

The carriage slowed. Stopped. The prince pulled down the sliding window beside him. "I'm in a hurry, Fane! Whatever it is will have to wait!"

Fane. Her Royal Highness the Princess Fane. Prince Gar's younger, only sister. A prodigious magical talent, so the gossips down at the Goose said, and the king's undisputed heir. Beautiful, too. Asher had never met her, or seen her even. He wriggled a little on his seat to get a glimpse.

"It can't wait!" retorted Princess Fane. Mounted on a panting sweaty brown pony, dust marring her rose silk tunic and crimson leather leggings, her annoyed face was almost level with her brother's. "Do you think I'd have galloped all this way like a madwoman on some servant's inferior plug if it was something that could wait?"

"You gallop everywhere like a madwoman, Fane," the prince replied, sighing. "On anything with four legs. Why should this time be any different?"

They looked eerily alike, the princess and her brother. Slender. Fair, even for Doranen. The same elegant eyebrows, the same straight nose, molded lips, firm chin. Her eyes were blue, though, her lashes extravagantly long and darkened with something. She was exquisite, just like the gossips had said. But that beauty was marred now with temper; her grip on the reins was so tight the pony's lips had curled back and its eyes were rolling in protest.

"Just be quiet and listen!" she snapped. "I absolutely must have that copy of *Trevoyle's Legacy* you borrowed from Durm. I'm being examined on the Schism the day after tomorrow and—"

"I told you this morning, Fane, I returned it to the Master Magician last week."

"He says he doesn't have it."

"Then I don't know what to tell you."

The pony grunted as Her Highness bounced in the saddle. "*Gar*! You were the last one to see it. There isn't another complete copy of that text in all the kingdom and I *need* it! Do you *want* me to fail my examination?"

"What I want, Fane, is for you to go away. I'm due at Justice Hall and I can't be late. Have you tried a seeking spell?"

The princess's cheeks flushed. "Yes, I tried a seeking spell."

"Oh." Her brother bit back an unwise smile. "Well. Even I know they're unreliable. Why not ask Mama? She's the best in the kingdom when it comes to finding lost objects."

"Mama is locked up all day with a bunch of stupid women talking about stupid things like flower fetes!"

"Can't Durm do a seeking spell for you? Or Father?"

The princess's blush deepened. "Durm won't, and he's told Father not to either. I'm supposed to find it for myself."

"Well," said the prince, one hand on the windowpane ready to push it closed again, "let me know how you get on. I certainly wish you luck. And now I'm leaving. Goodbye."

Ignoring her outraged shriek he shoved the window shut, then tugged on a short blue bell-rope overhead. There came a musical jangling, the sound of a whip cracking, then the carriage rocked gently and rolled forward as the harnessed horses sprang into their knee-snapping trot.

"My sister," said the prince as they continued on their way. "Princess Fane."

Asher nodded. "I figured as much."

Arms folded over his chest, the prince considered him broodingly. "Do you have a sister?"

"No. Brothers."

"How many?"

"Six."

"*Six*?" the prince said, startled. Then he relaxed. "Of course. The restrictions don't apply to the fishing community." He shook his head. "Six brothers. I can't imagine it. Do you miss them?"

Asher was hard-put not to laugh out loud. "Not at all. Sir."

The prince looked surprised. "No?"

"We don't get along."

"Really? Why not?"

Asher scowled. Nearly said, *Prob'ly the same reason you can't stand your sister*, but thought better of it. Prob'ly that'd be a good way to get tossed out of the carriage on his arse.

"Lots of reasons," he said instead, shrugging. "They reckoned six brothers in the family was enough. Split a business six ways and you ain't lookin' at much on your plate. Split it seven and it be that much less. And I were a bit sickly as a spratling. Made Ma soft on me. Da, too."

"You don't look sickly now."

"I ain't," said Asher. "I be strong as an ox now. Just I had fevers and the trembles when I were little. My brothers never had a day sick between 'em. Thought I was makin' it up. I weren't . . . but they'd never believe it. And they didn't much care for the cossetin' I got, when they never did."

The prince nodded. "That seems unfair. I'm sorry."

Another shrug. "Don't matter. That's them and here's me and there's an end to it."

"Indeed," the prince said briskly. "Now tell me, Asher, how familiar are you with our kingdom's laws?" He grinned. "You must know something of them, since you were so certain before that you'd not broken any."

"Well," said Asher cautiously, "I s'pose that depends on what you mean by 'familiar'."

The prince waved an impatient, dismissive hand. "Oh, never mind. Just pin your ears back and listen while I explain what you should know before we reach Justice Hall. You'll find the whole experience much more interesting if you have a vague idea of what's going on."

Asher swallowed a sigh. Justice Hall interesting? Not bloody likely. But he'd better not say so; like it or not this folderol princeling was the source of his twenty-five weekly trins. Only a fool would risk the loss of such bounty.

And Da's little boy Asher might be a lot of things, but a fool weren't one of them.

Justice Hall sat cheek by jowl between Dorana City's public Barl's Chapel and the City Guardhouse. Together, the three impressive buildings made up one entire side of the central market square. A typically tall Doranen building, with walls of pale cream sandstone and roof tiles of blue clay, Justice Hall's narrow window frames housed panels of stained glass in every color magic could imagine. Each panel depicted a momentous event in the kingdom's history: the coming of the Doranen, the holy covenant between the Olken and Doranen peoples, Barl's great sacrifice, the horrors of Trevoyle's Schism, the Healing Treaty's signing on the place where now bubbled Supplicant's Fountain.

The Hall's enormous oak front doors were bound and studded in polished brass and flanked either side with a sculptured relief. On the left stood blessed Barl, smiling benevolently down on those who entered seeking justice. On the right hung an unsheathed sword, reminding justice seekers that the truth cut two ways . . . and that the penalty for wrongdoing was both swift and merciless.

Asher had barely noticed the building on his first day

in the City. He'd been too busy looking for work and then, amazingly, finding it. On one of his early days off he'd stood on Justice Hall's sandstone steps and marveled at the place, listening to Dathne explain what each carving and stained-glass panel meant, but he'd felt no need to go inside.

Yet now here he was, riding in a fancy royal carriage on his way to doing just that. And he *still* didn't know why.

The prince said, "Asher! Are you listening?"

Asher jerked his wandering attention back to the present. "Aye. Sir. Of course."

"Good. Now, you're perfectly clear on the differences between Olken and Doranen legal jurisdictions, are you? You wouldn't like me to run through them again? Only once we're in the Hall I'll have to leave you to your own devices."

"No, sir. Reckon I got it straight," said Asher. It took an effort to keep his teeth ungritted. Did the prince think he was a knucklehead? "All criminal and civil matters Olken to Olken, up to and including malice *and* grievous damage inflicted with intent, stay in the Olken district courts. Any charge higher than that, like murder—not that we wander about killin' each other much—goes to the Olken central court." He pointed out of the carriage window. "That's over yonder, three streets behind the Grand Theater, on the other side of the square. Next door to the City Library."

"Indeed it is," agreed the prince. "Visit the library often, do you?"

"No. Leastways not for me. Picked up a book for Dathne once or twice." He sniffed. "Don't see what she's wantin' borrowed books for. Got enough for sale in that shop of hers, ain't she?"

"Some knowledge is priceless," said the prince. "And must be made available to anyone who desires it, regardless of their personal wealth. Or its lack. Go on. That's the Golden Cockerel Hotel we've just passed. We're nearly there."

Asher strangled a groan. When was he ever going to need to know about the law? This was such a load of bollocks . . .

"All civil and criminal matters Doranen to Doranen get judged at Justice Hall, before the Master Magician," he recited dutifully, "along with any branglin' between Olken and Doranen, no matter where they live. Any civil or criminal matters Olken to Olken what can't be sorted between ourselves go to Justice Hall, and you decide."

"Which is why we're going there today," said the prince. "Exactly. And cardinal crimes?"

Asher shuddered. There'd been no cardinal crime committed in Lur for years. You had to go back to when his long-dead great-grandpa was a spratling for the last one.

But that wasn't so odd. No fool in his right mind, Olken or Doranen, went about committing cardinal crimes. Not if he wanted to keep on breathing, any road.

"All cardinal crimes are tried before the king," he said as the carriage slowed and turned into a side street off the main market road. "Or queen. Whichever it is. And their Privy Council. Whether the trial be made public or not depends on circumstances."

The prince was staring at him. "Remarkable."

"What?" said Asher. "That I got a good memory? No

it ain't. Your Highness. My ma, Barl save her, she had herself a memory twice as nimble as mine."

The carriage drew to a halt. As waiting attendants hurried to stand by the horses' heads and open the doors, the prince said, frowning, "Your mother is dead? I'm sorry."

Asher shrugged. "Happened a long time ago. Reckon I'm past grievin' now." Then, because that felt disloyal, he added, "Not that I don't miss her, like. Just . . . you get used to it, I s'pose. Sir. I mean, what other choice is there?"

The prince nodded. "So, you're a practical man, Asher of Restharven."

"Practical be my middle name." Asher gestured at the open carriage door. "After you, sir."

The rear of Justice Hall was, in its own way, as imposing as the front. There was a stable block to house the horses and carriages of those involved in the proceedings, complete with liveried Olken staff to take care of them. There were three separate entrances to the Hall, each with its own set of steps, each barricaded by its own pair of uniformed Olken City Guards. There were neat gardens, trimmed trees, and an ominously well-trodden path leading into the grounds of the guardhouse next door. Another path led in the opposite direction, towards the public chapel. Despite its location in the heart of the City, the atmosphere was hushed. Reverent, almost. As though the weighty matters decided inside the Hall discouraged unmannerly noise outside.

After greeting the various staff by name, and receiving smiles and greetings in return, the prince headed towards the Hall's middle entrance. Asher trailed in his wake, feeling like a barnacle in a bed of roses. The surprised, curious stares of the stable hands and guards burned his back. He knew that as soon as he was out of sight they'd be whispering.

Well, let 'em whisper.

The chosen entrance's decorative wooden surround was painted in crimson and gold. Above the lintel sat a carved relief of the WeatherWorker's crown, embossed with gold and silver leaf and set with chips of ruby and diamond. As the prince approached, the door's guards rapped their ceremonial pikes smartly on the ground and stood aside. The prince nodded and smiled and Asher followed him, into the cool splendor of Justice Hall.

As they passed from sunlight to illuminated shadow his first impression was one of space. The floor, empty of furniture, was tiled in green and gold, with an enormous mosaic of an unsheathed sword in the middle. Gold-framed paintings covered the sandstone walls; past trials, Asher guessed, seeing as how there was a crowned and robed king or queen in each, and somebody smiling, and somebody else in chains, surrounded by guards and looking like their best boat had just sunk. There were two wooden staircases against the back wall, leading up to crimson velvet curtains, each one door-shaped. Between them, set into the rear wall, was a single wooden door. There were two more in each of the side walls. As the prince crossed over the mosaic sword, one of the right-hand doors opened and a Doranen woman emerged. She was middle-aged, smothered in somber blue silk and brocade.

"Your Highness," she said in a soft, calm voice, and offered a small bow. "Both parties, complete with speakers and witnesses, have arrived and await your adjudication."

"Excellent." The prince turned to Asher who was hovering in the background. "Marnagh, this is Asher. He'll be observing the proceedings today. Could you find him an inconspicuous chair in the Royal Gallery?"

Marnagh swept Asher up and down with a single shrewd look. Whatever she thought of him stayed locked tight behind her pale gray eyes. "Of course, Your Highness."

"Asher."

Asher stepped forward, hands clasped tight behind his back. "Your Highness?"

"This is Lady Marnagh. She keeps order in Justice Hall. Without her we'd all be hopelessly lost and I wouldn't look half as wise as I do, or know a quarter as much about the law."

Marnagh laughed. "Your Highness is too kind."

"Better that than too green, which is what I was scant months ago. And don't bother trying to deny it."

Asher managed an awkward bow. "Lady Marnagh."

She acknowledged him with a nod that made him feel six years old again. He scowled. She smiled.

The prince started for the staircase on the right. "I must prepare for today's session, so I'll leave you in the Lady Marnagh's capable hands, Asher. If there's anything you need to know, she'll tell you."

"Aye, sir," said Asher, and watched him run up the staircase and disappear behind the crimson curtain. "I don't bloody believe it," he muttered. "He's gone and done it *again*."

"Done what?" asked Lady Marnagh mildly.

"Dropped me in it, then left me in the clutches of some woman I don't know!" said Asher, unthinking.

"Indeed?" said Lady Marnagh. "Well, if that's the worst thing royalty ever does to you, young man, I'd be eternally grateful!"

Abruptly aware of his audience, Asher flushed. "Sorry. Never meant no disrespect."

Her severe lips softened. "Yes. Well. If you'll come with me?"

He followed her up the left-hand staircase. Behind the shrouding red velvet was a screened gallery complete with comfortable chairs and an excellent view of the Hall.

"You can observe from here," said Lady Marnagh. "Please remain absolutely silent while the hearing is in session. It would be best if you stayed seated once His Highness has commenced the proceedings. To all intents and purposes anyone in the gallery is invisible to the Hall, but movement can be distracting." She frowned. "In fact, choose a seat now and don't leave it again until His Highness gives you permission."

Disconcerted, Asher stared. "And how long'll that be? I mean, what time's all this malarkey s'posed to end?"

"That depends entirely upon the matter at hand," said Lady Marnagh, her plucked eyebrows raised.

"Well, but, what if I need to . . . you know . . ."

The eyebrows rose higher. "Then I suggest you cross your legs—Asher, is it?" She smiled; he'd seen friendlier sharks. "Now I must attend to my duties. I trust you will find this afternoon's . . ." She paused and looked down her nose at him. "*Malarkey*, educational. Certainly I hope you know how privileged you are, being invited to watch the hearing from the Royal Gallery, as His Highness's personal guest."

Oh aye, he was privileged all right. Stuck in a box halfway up a wall with no way down again till the prince had finished his business, being told to cross his legs— ha!—if nature called, all for reasons that nobody saw fit to tell him! Privileged? Put upon, she should've said. Used and abused and taken advantage of, and what Matt was going to say when he came back to find none of the mangers scrubbed clean, like he'd ordered, and the yard only half swept and raked, and the lads doing evening stables without him . . .

Lady Marnagh was waiting for an answer. Her eyebrows had climbed so high they'd nearly disappeared into her pale yellow hairline, and her lips were thin with disapproval.

Asher sighed. "Aye, Lady Marnagh. Reckon there ain't been a body so privileged as me in all the history of Lur."

Lady Marnagh left the gallery. The way she twitched the velvet curtain closed behind her suggested that she wasn't amused. Oh well. Too bad. The prince wasn't paying him near enough to cover extra duties like keeping snooty shark-impersonating Doranen women smiling. He heaved another sigh and leaned his arms along the screened gallery's railing so he could get a decent look at what was happening down below.

Justice Hall was split down the middle by a wide aisle, and from side to side two-thirds along with a solid wooden barrier, maybe waist high on a man. Behind the barrier there was nothing but rows and rows of benches. For the public, Asher guessed, seeing the smattering of folks, mostly Olken, dotted about the Hall. The few

Doranen all looked young. Students, most likely, from the university. They had an older Doranen with them, wearing a chivvying face. Asher grinned. Poor bugger. Be a good bet he'd happily change jobs with the prince's boot polisher, any day. Everyone, Olken and Doranen, was dressed up in their holyday best. Most of them wore hats, plain and flat for the men, tall and nodding with flowers and feathers for the women.

In front of the barrier there were chairs, and a wide wooden table on each side of the aisle. There were Olken sitting there, too, and seeing how serious they looked, he supposed they were the—what had Lady Marnagh called them?—the parties, their speakers and witnesses. So. The folks doing the brangling.

At the top end of the Hall, set into the wall, was a door. On the other side of it, he suspected, was the chamber where he and the prince had come in. Set some six paces in from the wall was a crimson dais. On it stood a high-backed wooden chair, padded and covered in crimson and gold velvet. Beside it, a slender wooden stand bearing a golden bell and hammer. On the wall behind the dais hung an enormous tapestry of an unsheathed sword. Just in case folks forgot what they were doing here, most likely.

Aye, right. As if *that* was like to happen.

Off to the right side of the dais was a small desk and a plain unpadded chair. The desk had a pile of paper on it, but no inkpot or pen. Asher couldn't see the point of that. He shrugged; the mystery would surely be explained sooner or later. And if it wasn't he could always ask the prince later.

Although whether the prince would *answer* him was

another matter entirely. Too bloody secretive by half, was His Royal Highness Prince Gar.

The sound of hushed conversation rose from the floor of the Hall like the rolling of waves onto a distant sandy shore. Filtering through the stained-glass windows, sunlight from the world outside splashed a palette of colors over every face and turned the attending City Guards' uniforms into patchwork quilts. Asher counted twelve pike-wielding, po-faced officials: one on each side of the main doors, four along each wall, and the last two flanking the raised platform beneath the hanging sword. None of his friends was among them. Pity, that. He could've amused himself pulling faces at 'em.

The Royal Gallery he occupied in such solitary splendor ran almost the full length of the Hall. There was a similar gallery directly opposite, but it was completely filled in. A private place for the prince or the king or the Master Magician to gather his or her thoughts before hearing folks go on about their troubles, he guessed.

The door in the Hall's rear wall opened, then closed behind Lady Marnagh. Her silk and brocade tunic had been smothered with a plain robe of dark green. She crossed to the small table and stood behind it. The guards on either side of the dais rapped their pikes onto the tiled floor hard and sharp, three times. At the Hall's entrance, the guards flanking the open doors swung them closed with a muffled thud. Silence fell like an axe.

Then everyone seated in the Hall stood, eyes turned towards the end of the private gallery. A moment later a section of the gallery floor detached and descended with slow majesty. Asher felt his jaw drop. No ropes or mechanical devices guided the platform's progress: it moved by magic.

Of course.

Inch by inch, the unsmiling form of the prince was revealed. He was draped neck to knee to ankle in a gold and crimson brocade robe. His silver circlet had been replaced by a heavy, plain gold crown. His expression was grave. Thoughtful. He looked . . . older.

The platform stopped a mere whisper above the floor. The prince stepped down and took his seat on the dais. Then he lifted the hammer from its hook and struck the bell three times. The air inside the Hall chimed. Shimmered. Asher felt something cool and invisible dance across his skin.

"We are gathered today, by His Majesty's authority and in his name, for the purposes of justice." The prince's voice carried effortlessly to every corner and listening ear. "Barl give us grace and wisdom and honor in its seeking." Bowing his head, he kissed his holyring.

"As you ask," murmured the crowd, "Barl mote it be." All round the Hall, lips were pressed to forefingers, ringed or not.

The prince replaced the hammer, then rested his hands on the arms of his chair. "Be seated. And let us hear the vexatious matter that brings us hence today."

With a sigh and a rustle and a scraping of the petitioners' chair legs on the tiles, everyone sat.

Intrigued despite himself, Asher waited to see what would happen.

CHAPTER FOUR

Who seeks my judgement in this matter?" asked the prince.

A young woman seated at the right-hand table stood. She was short and plump, her dress an unflattering shade of custard yellow. "I do, Your Highness."

The prince nodded. At the small desk Lady Marnagh closed her eyes and twice passed her left hand across the stack of paper before her. Orange sparks ignited, flared and faded. She returned her hand to her lap and glanced at the prince.

"State your name and place of residence for the records," he said.

"Mistress Raite of Deephollow Vale, Your Highness."

Asher pressed his face to the gallery's screen. Just barely, he saw orange fire dance across the top sheet of paper. A single line of words glowed for a moment then winked out.

So. Who needed pen and ink when magic could be had at the snap of the fingers?

"Thank you. Be seated," said the prince. "Who contests your claim?"

At the other table a middle-aged Olken man leapt to his feet. "Me, Your Highness! *I* contest my cousin's ridiculous, ungrateful complaint!"

He was tall and broomstick thin. His satin suit, frothed with lace at neck and wrists, was a bilious pea-green. Asher pulled a face; looked like color blindness ran in the family.

The prince frowned. "I requested your name and place of residence, not your legal opinion."

Even from halfway up the wall and behind a screen, Asher could see the man's face turn tomato red. He grinned. So the king's son had a bite in him, eh? That was interesting. He'd been thinking all that silk and velvet might've softened the prince's sinews.

Useful to know that wasn't the case.

And what kind of a sinkin' fool was the pea-green man, to set up the prince's hackles against him in the first few minutes?

"Meister Brenin, Your Highness," the cousin said. He sounded perilously close to sulky. "From Tolton-by-the-Marsh."

As the man sat down again, whispering to one of his cronies at the table, the prince turned his attention to the young Olken woman. "Very well. Mistress Raite, for the record, state your complaint."

Flustered but resolute the woman stood again. The man seated beside her—husband? brother? too young to be her da, any road—reached for her hand, squeezed it tight, then let go. Asher leaned back in his chair, propped

his heels on the railing inside the gallery's screen and prepared to be entertained.

The trouble had started when word was sent to Mistress Raite of her Uncle Vorlye's mortal illness. He was
dying, and there wasn't a herb or potion in the kingdom
to save him. Would she be able to nurse the poor soul in
his fading days? Cousin Brenin was a busy man, with no
wife at hand to shoulder the burden. Of course it meant
three hours a day of travel, but they were family, weren't
they? A good woman mindful of Barl's Laws would
surely ignore a little inconvenience for the sake of a dying
man.

What of the hospice in Salting Town, a mere half-hour
from Tolton-by-the-Marsh? the prince wanted to know. It
was a fine facility; he had attended its dedication by Her
Majesty and Royal Barlsman Holze just last summer. The
Barl's Brethren there were devoted to nursing the sick
and dying. Uncle Vorlye would have been well cared for,
and Mistress Raite not put to so much hardship. Meister
Brenin?

Blustering, Meister Brenin pointed out that the
Barl's Brethren, doubtless holy folk to the youngest
novice, couldn't be held the same as a man's family,
Your Highness.

Not to mention family wouldn't ask for a donation of
fifteen trins a week towards the costs of ministering to a
dying man, was the prince's dry observation. Asher snick-
ered approvingly; he liked a man with a sense of humor.

Next, Mistress Raite became a trifle agitated. It
seemed that dear Uncle Vorlye, who remained well in
his right mind up to the very end, was so touched by her

tender care that he saw fit to leave her a little something in his will.

"A *little* something?" her cousin snarled. "The bloody woman addled his wits, Your Highness! Tricked him into leaving her half his fortune! A scurrilous villainy of wickedness it was, sir, and the District Magister agreed! He overturned that poxy will in a matter of moments and fined the wretched woman accordingly. Only by a miracle did she escape a harsher penalty!"

"Peace, Meister Brenin," the prince said coolly. "Your turn will come." He turned to Mistress Raite. "You have good reason for refusing to accept Barl's Justice in this matter?"

Mistress Raite's chin lifted. "Yes, Your Highness. I'm innocent. The legacy was two hundred trins, not half his fortune, and I never asked for a cuick of it."

"Yet the District Magister upheld your cousin's claim."

"Yes, he did, Your Highness," she agreed. "And that would have nowt to do with how the District Magister and my cousin hunt regular together every week through winter, or play catch-ball in the lighter months, or race each other to the bottom of a wine barrel three nights out of six, now would it?"

Asher dropped his feet to the floor and leaned forward, impressed. Convicted and custard yellow she might be, but Mistress Raite was a persuasive speaker. He couldn't see a skerrick of guile in her. Just honest distress.

Staring down at the prince's shuttered face he tried to figure what the king's son was thinking. Was he convinced by Mistress Raite's tale of woe, or not? There was no way of telling; all thought and feeling were locked tight behind his Lawgiver's mask.

The prince was silent for long moments, considering. Then he looked at Meister Brenin. "Mistress Raite speaks the truth? You and this District Magister are friends?"

Meister Brenin looked down his nose. "We are, Your Highness." His lips curved into a thin, self-satisfied smile. "I have many friends, sir. I am a man of influence and standing in Tolton-by-the-Marsh."

The prince's answering smile glittered like a naked sword. "We are not in Tolton-by-the-Marsh, Meister Brenin."

Asher swallowed a hoot of amusement as Meister Brenin flinched. "I was unaware that such a friendship was frowned upon, Your Highness," the man said stiffly.

"Friendship is never frowned upon, Meister Brenin." The prince's faint emphasis on the word "friendship" wasn't lost on his audience; Meister Brenin wilted. The prince let his cold gaze linger a moment longer on the man's downcast face, then looked at Mistress Raite. "You have speakers present who will attest to the truth of your claims?"

"I do, sir."

The prince nodded. "Then let them be heard."

One by one, Mistress Raite's speakers rose and confirmed her version of events. When they were done, excited whispering from the audience drowned the silence and had to be quelled by the guards.

Called upon to answer the accusations, Meister Brenin lost his temper and swore at Mistress Raite. The prince cautioned him. On second thoughts, Meister Brenin's speakers declined to exercise their tongues on his behalf.

Meister Brenin swore at them, and was given a final warning. Meister Brenin subsided, cowed at last.

"This hearing will pause while I withdraw and consider the charges and evidence laid before me," announced the prince. "Due to the sensitive matters raised this afternoon, the City Guards will prevent the withdrawal of any person here attending, until my judgement is rendered." Taking the hammer, he struck it against the golden bell three times.

On cue, the guards on either side of the Hall's double doors took two steps towards each other and extended their arms. There was a thunk of iron against iron as their pikes met in a cross between them. The exit was barred.

Asher grimaced. The way things were going, there'd be a whole lot of folks sitting with their legs crossed before this day was done.

Lady Marnagh, released from monitoring the magically recorded proceedings, pushed her chair back and stood. In response, everyone followed suit. Once the last man had found his feet the prince stepped down from his dais. As the platform lifted him to seclusion, Asher whooshed his lungs empty of air and sagged in his seat.

Well, sink him bloody sideways. If anyone had told him an afternoon in Justice Hall could be *exciting*, he'd have laughed.

Abruptly tired of sitting, he leapt up and marched the length of the gallery, arms swinging. Below, the hearing's captive attendees buzzed like bees in a stick-poked hive. A wise decision, to keep them penned until a judgement was reached. They'd be off and prattling on this in a heartbeat, given half a chance, embroidering and embelishing the plain facts like a pack of ole biddies in a sewing circle.

"Well?" said the prince's cool voice behind him. "What do you think so far?"

Asher turned. "What are you doin' here, sir? Ain't you s'posed to be cogitatin' your decision?"

The prince considered him, the faintest of smiles warming his eyes. He was still draped in the gold and crimson robe, but the heavy crown had been set aside.

"You're not in the least bit in awe of me, are you? Even now."

Fidgeting, suspicious, Asher said, "Is that another way of sayin' I'm rude? Sir?"

"Not . . . exactly. Perhaps forthright would be a better word. Or independent."

"I don't know about that. I was just surprised to see you, is all."

The prince nodded. "I'm here because I'm interested in your opinion of how I should rule in this matter."

Heedless of protocol, Asher dropped into the nearest chair. It was that or fall down completely. "*My* opinion?"

"Yes." If the prince cared that Asher sat while he was standing, he didn't say so. "Why should I believe Mistress Raite over her cousin Meister Brenin?"

"Aside from the fact he's a fartin' fool, y'mean?" said Asher, grinning. "And not a one of his fine friends'll stand up for him?" When the prince's grave expression didn't alter he sobered, and tried to think of a sensible answer. "Well . . . he's rich, and he reckons that makes him better than folk who ain't. He used drinkin' and sportin' with the Magister to do down a woman who nigh on killed herself, I reckon, lookin' after his da, when his da should've been his concern, *and* he disrespected his da's wishes when he did it." He snorted. "Just to snatch back two hundred trins, which from the sound of it would mean nowt to him, and all to her."

"I see," said the prince, nodding. "So even if he were in the right, and she were in the wrong, it wouldn't matter because he's rich and he'll never miss two hundred trins?"

"I never said that," Asher protested. "Don't you go puttin' words in my mouth. Sir. Point I'm tryin' to make here is he's mean, as well as twisty."

"Twisty?"

"He turned the law into a pair of hobnailed boots, and then he kicked her with 'em," said Asher slowly, scowling with concentration. "That ain't what it's for. The law's for helpin' folks do the right thing by each other, so's we can all live side by side without bangin' each other in the shins over piddlin' trifles. Or takin' what ain't ours just 'cause we want it. And if it can be bought for the price of a wine barrel, it ain't worth nowt at all."

"Then if not the price of a wine barrel, Asher, what? What monetary value can we assign to the law?"

"Well . . . y'can't," said Asher. "The law's priceless. That be the whole point of it. I thought. Sir."

The prince took a moment to adjust the folds of his robe. Then, as he turned to leave, he said, "This business shouldn't take much longer. You'll be home in time for supper."

"Oh," said Asher, bemused. "Aye. Right. That's good, sir. Sir? What—"

But the prince was gone.

"Sink the bloody man," muttered Asher, and jumped up to resume his pacing.

He'd marched there and back along the gallery five more times when the prince, once again wearing the crown, returned to the Hall and the hearing continued. After thanking the audience for their forbearance, the prince declared himself ready to render judgement. Mistress Raite and her cousin Meister Brenin stood and waited. The Hall was so silent Asher could hear a trapped fly battering at a nearby window, and voices in the street outside.

Judgement, said the prince sternly, fell in favor of Mistress Raite of Deephollow Vale. She was free to leave the City with her good name intact; all findings previously rendered against her were expunged, and fines made void. The bequest of two hundred trins accepted in good faith would be restored to her forthwith.

As for Meister Brenin, he was to remain in Dorana, in the custody of the guardhouse, while further investigations into matters arising from this hearing were undertaken. He could expect charges to be laid against him in due course. A summons for his friend the District Magister was even now on its way to Tolton-by-the-Marsh; they would be sharing a cell by sunset tomorrow.

The golden bell rang out three times. And that was that.

The prince withdrew to his private gallery. His departure released every trapped tongue in the Hall. As a score of excited conversations dinned the air, two guards took possession of a shocked and silent Meister Brenin. Mistress Raite took a step towards him, hands outstretched, face creased with concern. Her cousin's soundless snarl scurried her to the shelter of her companion's arm—

husband for sure, Asher thought—and the congratulations of her witnesses and friends. Meister Brenin was escorted from the Hall through the door in the wall behind the dais.

Lady Marnagh approached Mistress Raite and her husband. After a brief conversation they followed her through the same door. A moment later a young Olken man entered, retrieved the official record from the small table, and left again. With the Hall's double doors once more unbarred and open, the still excited, still voluble crowd of onlookers dribbled out. The doors were closed behind them, and the remaining City Guards left through the door that had swallowed their fellows.

Asher was alone.

He waited. When nobody came to collect him from the gallery, he made his own way back behind the red velvet curtain and down the wooden stairs to the rear of the Hall. There he found the prince in deep and solemn conversation with Lady Marnagh. Both had removed their ceremonial robes. The prince glanced at him, held up a finger, and continued talking. Asher couldn't make out what he was saying.

Eventually he finished. Lady Marnagh nodded, bowed and without so much as a glance in Asher's direction returned to the room she'd been in when he and the prince arrived. The door thumped shut behind her.

"Home," said the prince. He looked tired.

The carriage was waiting for them. Sunk in thought, scowling out of the window as it carried them back to the Tower, Asher was only reminded of the prince's presence when his employer cleared his throat and said, "Well?"

He sounded amused. Startled, Asher pulled his gaze away from the passing faces and buildings. "Sir?"

"Do you agree with my decision or not?"

Feeling suddenly cautious, Asher examined his knees. "Don't reckon it be for me to agree or disagree."

"Asher!" The prince appeared shocked. "Please, *don't* go getting shy on me now."

"Shy? I ain't shy. I just reckon there's one of us in this carriage as shovels shit for a livin' and there's another what wears a crown in Justice Hall, and last time I looked I didn't see no crown in my boot-box."

"That doesn't mean you're not possessed of an opinion," the prince replied. "I'd like to hear it."

Perplexed, exasperated, Asher sat back and stared. "And I'd like to know what's got you so interested in the opinions of a fisherman stable hand. Sir."

The prince grinned. "That's more like it. I'll tell you what. You answer my question and I'll answer yours. Fair?"

"Fair," Asher said grudgingly. "Right then. My opinion, for what it be worth, is it were right to find in Mistress Raite's favor."

"But?"

"But I don't know why you said she were to get the two hundred trins and nowt more. That miserable bloody cousin of hers be a rich bastard, and where he's goin' he won't be needin' a pile of money. Not to mention he caused her a right load of heartache, one way and another. Reckon he should be punished for that."

"And he will be," the prince said quietly. "Meister Brenin and his friend the Magister conspired to pervert the course of Barl's Justice. I promise you, Asher, when this is over they'll be sorry they ever met."

"So where's the harm in makin' him give her more than the two hundred trins? That sort needs punchin' in the purse, if you reckon to drive the message right home. I know. We got one just like him back in Restharven."

The prince sighed. "Remember what you said about the law being priceless? It's the same with justice. The uncle wanted his niece to receive two hundred trins. The cousin took that money away, and I restored it to her. I also restored her good name in the eyes of the kingdom. That is justice. But to give her more than that would be to flout her uncle's expressed desire. Worse. It would be to say there is money to be made in defending Barl's Laws. I can't condone or encourage that. The Laws must be honored and upheld because it's right to do so, not profitable."

"Huh," said Asher. "Good point, that."

"I'm glad you agree." The prince sounded sincere.

Pleased, and determined not to show it, Asher shrugged. "Still reckon it be a right shame you didn't get to kick 'im in the purse strings, though."

"Yes, I imagine it would've been fun," the prince said gravely.

Asher glared. Was that a joke at his expense? The prince's expression was politely patient, so . . . prob'ly not. He grunted. "All right. I answered your question. Now you can answer mine. Sir."

"Why do I care so much about your opinions?"

"Aye."

The prince looked out of the carriage window. They'd turned into the palace grounds. The Tower wasn't far away. Reaching up, he tugged on a red cord dangling above his head beside the blue bell-rope. A hinged flap fell open.

"Matcher?" the prince called through it.

From above them, the coachman's startled voice said, "Your Highness? Is owt wrong, sir?"

"No, nothing. But you can stop the carriage here and let us out. We'll walk to the Tower."

"Right you are, sir," said the invisible Matcher.

"Walk?" said Asher, scandalized. "Why? It'll take forever, and I got chores—"

The prince closed the ceiling flap. "No, you haven't. I told you, Matt knows you're with me. Are you suggesting he'll presume to tell me I can't borrow one of my own employees?"

"No, but—"

"Then that's all right, isn't it?"

The carriage slowed to a halt. The prince opened the door and stepped down, Asher at his heels, then closed it and thumped on the side with his fist. "Off you go, Matcher!" As the carriage pulled away, he turned to Asher and grinned. "That's better. We'll have time to finish our conversation now."

He started walking. Asher stared after him, dumbfounded. He was beginning to think he had no idea who this man really was. In the market square, the day they met, he'd been . . . almost an equal. In Justice Hall, dressed in all that legal finery, weighed down by the solid gold crown and duty, the prince had been remote and unreachable. Stern. Frightening, almost. Had seemed years and years older. Now, whistling his way into the distance, he seemed as young and foolhardy as Jed.

Regular folk picked 'emselves a person to be and stuck with that. Trust royalty to be different.

Huffing in annoyance he undid a couple more shirt buttons and rolled up his sleeves. Then he jogged after the prince, caught him up, and fell into step beside him along the crushed and pounded blue gravel road that led straight to the palace. The wide thoroughfare was lined both sides with statuesque djelba trees. Their branches met overhead in a dappling canopy. Waxy pink blossoms the size of dinner plates soaked the cooling dusk air in sweetness.

"I'll start," said the prince, as though they'd never stopped talking, "by answering your question with a question of my own. How would you like to work for me, Asher?"

Asher glanced at him sideways. "I am workin' for you."

"Indirectly, yes. Directly, you work for Matt. I want to know if you'd be willing to work for *me*. With me. As my assistant."

"Assistant to what?"

"The announcement has yet to be made public, and I expect you to hold your tongue until it is, but His Majesty has appointed me the kingdom's first Olken Administrator. In many ways, it's just a formality. Practically speaking, I've been fulfilling the position's duties for nearly a year. Ever since my majority. Until now they've been tasks traditionally performed by the reigning monarch, so I've been performing them in His Majesty's name. In a nutshell, it means I attend to matters of concern that touch both our peoples, wherever they arise throughout the kingdom. It's like being a living bridge between Doranen and Olken. The title "Olken Administrator" may be new, but the work itself began the day Barl and my ancestors came over the mountains and into this land."

"Oh," said Asher cautiously. "Sounds like a bloody big job, sir. Why don't the king want it?"

" 'Want' has nothing to do with it," the prince snapped. "It's a question of how best can His Majesty's resources be used for the good of the kingdom. He is consumed by the WeatherWorking. My sister studies night and day to become his worthy successor. Her Majesty and the Master Magician also have their duties, with no time to spare for extra burdens, whereas I—"

Asher watched the prince's lips whiten with pressure. He didn't need to hear the sentence finished. Gar the Magickless needed something to do with himself, and his da the king had found it for him.

For the distance of two and a half trees, they walked in silence. Then the prince finished the sentence anyway. "Whereas I," he said carefully, "am in a unique position to be of use, not only to His Majesty but to all the people of Lur, Doranen and Olken alike. I consider it a privilege . . . but I can't do it alone."

"Alone? You got y'self a whole Tower full of folks, ain't you, all fallin' over 'emselves to do what you want?"

"I have a staff, yes, and they are invaluable," agreed the prince. "But I've learned a great deal since I started this work, mostly about how much I don't know about your people. I find myself needing something more than secretaries and clerks. Some*one* more. I need an Olken to work hand in glove with me, Asher. Someone who can help me be that bridge between our peoples. Someone who is unimpressed with the trappings of royalty, the seduction of court life, the social advantages of an elevated position. Someone with an instinctive sense of justice, who I can trust to be my right hand, my eyes, my voice, who won't be swayed by the flattery of those seeking favor and who I know will always tell me the truth, whether I want to hear it or not. In short, Asher, I need you."

Asher couldn't help it: he laughed. "You need your head read, more like."

"Really? Are you going to tell me I'm wrong about you? That you do care for all the pomp and circumstance and fawning flattery that royalty so often inspires?"

"No, sir! I couldn't care less for all that codswallop!"

"Well, then?" said the prince. The way he said it was a challenge.

Asher shook his head. "Well then, I don't want to do it."

"Why not?"

"Why d'you reckon? You'll be wantin' me to wear fancy clothes, won't you? Shirts with lace on 'em and little bits of ribbon and embroidery and suchlike. You'll expect me to stop soundin' like m'self and talk like a posh City Olken instead, won't you? Aye, you will! And I'll have to hobnob with folk who can't eat a meal less they use seven different forks, and think an honest workin' Olken man like me be good for nowt but opening doors for 'em!"

The prince was nodding. "I see. You're afraid."

"I ain't no such thing!"

"No?" The prince's expression darkened. Became grim. "Well, I am."

"What of?" said Asher, surprised. "Seems to me y'be doing a bang-up job. The way the folks cheer you in the streets. How you sat in Justice Hall today, as grand as the king hisself, you—"

"Don't." The prince stopped walking. "Don't ever compare me to the king. It's not . . . proper."

Asher swung round to face him and shrugged. "All right. But still. Y' can't be bollocksin' things up too bad or he wouldn't be making all this official, would he?"

They'd reached the turn-off that led away from the palace to the Tower. The prince started walking again, along the narrower road, and beckoned Asher to keep up. "I'm muddling through, Asher. I'm treading water, and so far I've managed not to drown myself, or anybody else. But I can trust to luck no longer. I've known for months now I needed Olken help to do this job properly. I was beginning to despair of ever finding the right person to be that help."

"And you reckon the right person is *me*?" said Asher. "You must be runnin' a fever, I reckon. Or else that crown you had on today's gone and bent your brain."

The prince frowned. "I love my father, Asher, as doubtless you love yours. I cannot fail in this. If I do, the king will be forced to resume those responsibilities I've assumed. At all costs, I must prevent that."

"Why? You said all this bein' a bridge malarkey usually got done by the . . . the reigning monarch. Why can't the king do it?" He watched the prince's face go very still, and his heart boomed hard against his ribs. "All right, sir. I reckon it's time you and me started rowin' this boat in the same direction. What ain't you tellin' me, eh? What's so sinkin' important about *you* doin' this Administrator stuff, and not the king?"

For the first time since Asher had laid eyes on the man, the prince looked uncertain. "Can I trust you?"

Asher sighed. "What kind of a daft bloody question is that? One minute you're askin' me to be your right-hand man 'cause I be so upright and incorruptible, and the next you want to know if I can be trusted? Reckon you need to make up your mind. Sir."

Temper flashed lightning-fast across the prince's face. "I'll thank you to keep a civil tongue in your head, Asher. The fact that I'll permit you a certain amount of leeway is hardly the same as allowing you to—"

"I see," said Asher. "So when you said you wanted someone who'd tell you the truth whether you wanted to hear it or not, *sir*, what you *really* meant was—"

"*All right!*"

Silence as the prince collected his thoughts and feelings. Asher pushed his hands into his pockets and amused himself by humming one of Da's favorite ditties under his breath. When he was done, and the prince still showed no sign of moving, he said, "If we stand around here much longer, some bird's goin' to think we're statues and shit on us."

The prince stirred. Looked at him, all uncertainty banished. "What do you know of WeatherWorking?"

Asher shrugged. "Nowt beyond what any spratling knows. The WeatherWorking and the Wall march hand in hand. Without Weather Magic we'd go back to the old days, when the weather was unchancy. We'd be at the mercy of storms and floods and droughts and famine. WeatherWorking feeds the Wall, keeps it strong. If it fails, the Wall fails, and there'd be nowt to keep us safe from all the evil that lies beyond the mountains. It's our duty to live our lives according to Barl's Law, so that never happens."

Lurking humor resurfaced, briefly. "A neat summary. Which means you can't have slept through *every* Barlsday sermon you ever heard."

Asher winced. Damn. How could the prince have noticed that? The royal family sat up the front of the palace chapel, while he always made sure to find the most shadowy corner right down the back. "Sir?"

"Relax. I won't tell. Holze is a good man, but even I have to admit his sermons are a trifle longwinded. The trick is to doze with your eyes open."

"Oh," said Asher. "Right." He'd be sure to try it, very next Barlsday.

"Anyway. About WeatherWorking. The thing is, it's very difficult and requires enormous amounts of energy. His Majesty gets tired." The prince frowned. "Exhausted. And before I assumed these extra duties, he would deplete his reserves of strength attending to them. At first he resisted the idea of relinquishing the obligation, but in the end Her Majesty, the Master Magician and I prevailed."

So. Not so much a case of "find the poor magickless prince something to do", mayhap, as a matter of necessity. Or both. Two fish caught with the same hook. Asher thought of his own da. The arguments they'd had about slowing down. Taking care.

"Reckon fathers don't take too kindly to their sons reminding 'em they ain't as young as once they were."

The prince sighed. "No. Mind you," he added sharply, "this in *no* way suggests that the king is unfit. Let me make that abundantly clear. He is as capable today as he was at his coronation. The kingdom could rest in no stronger hands."

"I never said otherwise. You just want to do the right thing by your da. Help him, like a good son should. Reckon I can see that. Reckon I admire you for it."

"So you do see, then, how important it is that I not fail as Olken Administrator? Failure would mean he'd resume those duties. Tax his strength, when all his strength must be given to WeatherWorking. And failure, *my* failure, would be used against him to—"

Another silence. The sun was sinking fast now. Long shadows crept across the manicured grounds on either side of them, through the trees, across the road. Asher swallowed.

"What d'you mean, used against him? Who'd want to use you to hurt the king?"

CHAPTER FIVE

N obody," said the prince eventually, not looking at him. "It's complicated. Just tell me you'll change your mind, Asher. Tell me you'll take the job."

Feeling cornered, pressured, Asher stamped his heels into the roadway. A flock of nightbirds flew overhead, their harsh cries scraping the sky.

"This be politics, eh?" he said accusingly. "You be askin' me to mucky myself with politics. That ain't my job. My job's fishin' and sailin' and shit shovelin'. *Honest* dirty work. I leave politics to the likes of . . . of . . ."

"Me?" said the prince, smiling faintly.

"You're different," muttered Asher. "You got born to it without a say-so. You want me to *choose* it. On *purpose*." He released a hard-held breath. "Look. There's got to be a hundred Olken out there who'd lick the road clean from the City gates to your front door to get a job like this."

"That's true," said the prince. "Which is just one of the many reasons why you're perfect for the position. As my right hand, you'd be advising me on a wide range of Olken matters. Customs. Ways of thinking and experiencing the world that I, as a Doranen, might never understand. No matter my good intentions or willingness to learn. It means that in some cases I'd be letting you make the decisions altogether if I thought you were the better qualified to do so. Most people would eventually be overcome by that much power. They'd abuse it. But you're not most people, Asher. In all honesty, you're not like anybody I've ever met before. Olken or Doranen."

"And that's what today were all about, eh? Checkin' to see if I thought about things the right way?"

The prince hesitated. "Partly. Partly it was to see if you thought about things at all. Not everybody does."

Asher felt his lip curl. "And especially not fishermen turned stable hands?"

"Don't be ludicrous," snapped the prince. "Some of the biggest fools I've ever met in my life can boast a university education and blood lines that trace back to the Founding Families. If I thought like that, Asher, we wouldn't be standing here in the middle of the road discussing this, would we? You'd be in the stable yard shoveling shit and I'd be . . . somewhere else."

Fair point. "So why are we standin' here in the middle of the road discussin' this? Sir?"

"Because I started thinking about appointing an assistant a week after His Majesty agreed to let me take over from him, and nearly a year later you're the only man I've met who I can imagine trusting to do the job!'

Asher stared. "You're stark staring bonkers. You don't hardly know me from a hole in the ground."

"I know enough!"

It was impossible not to feel flattered. Hating himself

for it, Asher scowled. "And what about all the other palaver? Clothes and—"

"Naturally," the prince said carefully, "you'd need to dress a little more formally than you do now. But there's no law that says you have to wear lace. As for your accent . . ." He smiled. "I confess it could do with a little citifying. Not because there's anything wrong with it, as such," he added, holding up a hasty hand, "but because, like it or not, first impressions count and you'll want people to be impressed with your abilities, not distracted by the way you speak."

"Huh." Asher sniffed. That didn't sound *too* bad. "All right. Say I agree. How much'll you pay me? 'Cause I don't reckon to be gettin' myself all hot and bothered over politics for a miserly twenty-five trins a week."

The prince's expression was a mingling of relief, hope and amusement. "What about fifty trins a week, plus all meals and a suite in the Tower, plus a wardrobe more fitting to your new station. And a horse. Say . . . Cygnet? Is that recompense unmiserly enough?"

Asher nearly swallowed his tongue. Cygnet? For his own? And fifty trins, every week? Forget about buying a lone modest, second-hand smack. He'd be able to buy a whole *fleet* of fishing boats, every one of 'em brand new, when he went back home to Restharven with that kind of money.

The dizzying thought stirred his conscience to life. He sighed, and shook his head. "Reckon it's more than enough, sir. But I can't do it. Sorry. Thanks for askin', though. I be right flattered."

Taken aback, the prince stared. "Why can't you? Don't

try to tell me you're not interested. You're not that good a liar."

Asher scowled, hating to turn his back on all that money. Hating the prince for offering it to him. "'Cause I weren't plannin' on stayin' in Dorana longer than a year, all right? And this job you want me to do, that's the kind of job as goes for longer than that. For life, maybe. I mean, if your da's tired now he ain't goin' to be less tired this time next year, is he? You're goin' to be Olken Administrating till your hair's gone gray and your teeth've all dropped out. And you'll be needin' yourself an assistant as can go gray alongside you. That won't be me. I got other fish to fry."

"It's true I'll be Olken Administrator for as long as His Majesty reigns," said the prince. "And I pray Barl grants him many more years to pursue his sacred calling." His lips pressed hard against his holyring. "But no man lives forever. Our Doranen magic can do many things, Asher, but it can't make us immortal. What my sister will want of me once she becomes WeatherWorker is anyone's guess. It might well be that both I and my assistant will find ourselves without a purpose the day after she ascends the throne."

"All right, so mayhap you won't be Olken Administrating without your teeth. But the thing is, I made a promise to *my* da, see? I promised him I'd be away one year and not a day longer. I ain't about to go back on my word, not even for fifty trins a week and a horse like Cygnet. You can't expect me to. And if y'do . . . well . . ." He glared, defiant. "Then I reckon you ain't the man I thought you were."

The prince ignored that. Stared at the ground instead,

thinking. "Of course you must keep your promise," he said at last. "But that doesn't mean you can't accept this offer. You can still make a valuable contribution, Asher. And when the times comes, I won't stop you from leaving. You have my word."

Oh. So that was one objection down, a score more to go. Politics. The claptrap that went with royalty. The ruckus of change. He had hisself a good life in the stables. The work wasn't demanding, it wasn't beyond him, and he had friends there. Even more important, he had no enemies.

None of that, he suspected, could be said of being the prince's Assistant Olken Administrator.

"And what happens if I say I'll do it, and after a week of workin' hand in glove we be hatin' each other's guts?"

"Then you can go back to the stables for as long as you like, and I'll find somebody else to assist me."

Or he could just find somebody else now and be done with it. Let them worry about the politics and the polite conversation and the sorting out of a hundred people's problems day in day out . . .

Except it were *fifty trins* a week. And *Cygnet*.

"Look," said the prince. "It's a lot to consider, I know. And I've sprung it upon you without warning. Why not take the night to think it over? You can give me your answer in the morning. I'll be exercising Ballodair first thing, you can tell me then. All right?"

"All right," said Asher, relieved.

The prince nodded. "Good. Now we'd best be getting along before somebody panics and sends out a search party."

In silent accord they continued along the road. At the entrance to the Tower forecourt they parted, the prince disappearing into the tall blue building, Asher breaking into a jog to reach the stables before Matt lost all patience and had his guts for garters. It was almost dark by then, and clouding over. The warm air pressed damp and heavy against his skin.

Though the inside of his skull was battered with conflicting thoughts and feelings, within the chaos he felt a fleeting moment of curiosity about the king. Borne the WeatherWorker, decreed by Barl to carry the weight of the Wall and their world upon his flesh-and-bone shoulders. Even now, while the rest of Lur busied itself with heedless living, in the secret place where all such wild magics were conjured the prince's father prepared to offer himself in the service of his people, Olken and Doranen alike.

Prepared to call the night's rain.

Exhausted, the prince had called him.

Asher shivered, and jogged along a little faster.

The stable yard was a puddle of light in the gathering gloom. Unheeded, he stood in the shadow of the sandstone archway and watched the other lads as they bustled back and forth across the lamplit gravel, carrying feed and hay and rugs, scoffing and laughing and tossing jokes to each other in passing. He watched the horses, too, his other new friends. Stared hungrily at Cygnet, gleaming like a pearl.

"In case you hadn't noticed," an exasperated voice said behind him, "we've already got ourselves a scarecrow. And the last time I looked we didn't need a guard dog. So what d'you think you're doing standing there with your thumb up your arse while all the lads are running their feet off for evening stables? Which are late as it is, seeing how we were short-handed all afternoon. Where've you been, anyway?"

Matt.

Asher turned. "Justice Hall."

"Justice Hall?"

"Aye, and it be all your fault. What did you want to go witterin' on to the prince about me for, eh? All that guff about me bein' so reliable and hardworkin' and clever? I never asked you to praise me to royalty, did I? Never said I were lookin' for work other than what I got here? If y'had to say somethin', why not that I'm no better or worse than I should be? Eh? It's the truth."

Matt walked past him and into the yard proper. "Prince Gar offered you another position?" His voice was calm, conversational, but there was tension in the set of his shoulders and the way his fingers held tight to his belt.

"Aye." Asher took a step forward himself so he could see Matt's face. "Some blather about bein' his right-hand man up in the Tower. He's bein' announced as the Olken Administrator, see. Says he wants, me as his official assistant." Too late, he remembered. "Oh. Damn." He pulled a face. Lowered his voice. "Weren't s'posed to mention that. Don't tell anyone, eh?"

"I won't," said Matt. "I'm good with secrets."

"Aye, well, so'm I s'posed to be, if I do this job. And there's me blurtin' out the first one he trusts me with!"

Matt half smiled. "I wouldn't worry over-much. It gets easier as you go along." The smile faded, and his gaze shifted until he was staring far into the distance at the mellow golden glow of Barl's Wall rising out of the mountains. For a moment some strong and secret emotion bleached the color from his tanned face so that all of a sudden he looked old and weary. Then the moment passed and he was himself again, wry and purposeful and full of spirit. "What he's offering you . . . it's a big compliment. And a big step. Did you accept?"

"I said I'd think on it," said Asher, shrugging. "And I will. But I don't know, Matt. Aye, the money's bloody good and the work sounds interestin', I s'pose, but . . . I'm happy here. I ain't one of them fancy folderol Olken as works up in the Tower, like Darran or that pissant Willer. Reckon I'll stick out there like an eel in a bowl of goldfish. I mean, I don't want to go makin' a bloody great fool of m'self, do I?"

"I reckon it's only natural to feel a little fear when a prince makes you an offer like this. There's a lot at stake."

"This ain't got nowt to do with fear!" said Asher, offended. "I be weighin' the fors and againsts, is all, like any sensible man should." He kicked at the raked gravel. "Like I said, this be all your fault. Reckon he never would've thought of me if you hadn't flapped your lips at him."

Matt took a deep, considering breath and let it out with care. "If His Highness is as good a judge of a man as he is of horseflesh, Asher, and I suspect he is, then he knows the right one for a job when he sees him. I doubt I had much to do with this at all. Some things are just . . . meant to be."

The mosquitoes were starting to whine; Asher slapped one to death against his bare forearm and scowled at the smear of blood it left behind. "So y'reckon I should say yes, eh?"

"I reckon," said Matt, unsmiling, "you should talk it over with someone else. Could be I'm not the best person to ask."

"Who?"

"Who else do you trust?"

Asher tugged at his bottom lip, thinking. "Reckon I trust Dathne," he said reluctantly. "She drives me near to distraction with her pokin' and proddin' and expectin' me to widen my horizons, read all those books she keeps on givin' me and then answer bloody questions after, but I trust her. She may be slumskumbledy but she's got a good head on her shoulders, I'll give her that."

Matt looked away. "Yes. You could talk to Dathne. I'm sure she'll tell you . . ."

"What?"

"What she thinks," said Matt, and looked back again. "She'll be down at the Goose in an hour or so. And you'll be finished around here by then."

"Huh," said Asher. Confide in Dathne, eh? Dathne was so sharp it was a wonder she didn't cut herself twice a day. Sharp, and never short of an opinion. She'd surely have an idea or three of what he should do. What all this could mean. And over the weeks she'd become an unlikely friend. "Mayhap I will ask her at that."

Matt clapped him on the shoulder. "Good. Now help the lads finish off evening stables, will you? It'll be raining any minute, and I've got the red mare to physic, a loose buckle to sew back on a rug and an order for feed to write up. I don't have time to stand around gossiping, and neither do you. Even if this does look to be your last night getting your hands dirty with the rest of us." He smiled, then, just a little, to take the sting out of his words . . . but Asher could sense a chill beneath it. Where it came from he didn't know.

And he wasn't sure he wanted to find out, either.

* * *

Two hours later he was sitting in a booth opposite Dathne, spooning the Goose's fragrant mutton stew onto slabs of fresh brown bread and telling her all about the prince's remarkable offer, this time without a mention of what the job was actually called.

Like Matt, Dathne was impressed. Unlike Matt, she was admiring too.

He liked that.

"And you didn't say yes on the spot? Asher!" Reaching across the benchtop, she pressed the back of her hand to his forehead. "You must be fevered."

Despite the stomach-growling goodness of the stew, he scowled. "Reckon I be the kind of fool what jumps into new water without testin' the depth first, do you?"

Dathne shrugged. "No. But are you the kind of a fool who turns down fifty trins a week just because he thinks he's a better man than a prince in pretty clothes?"

He tossed his spoon into the stew pot and banged his fist beside it. "I never said I thought I were better. Reckon he's all right, for a Doranen."

"If he's willing to pay you fifty trins a week, would it matter if he wasn't?"

Asher pulled the pot close again and shoveled in the last few mouthfuls. Buying some time. "It might."

"So you do *want* the job?"

"Don't reckon as I've decided one way or another yet." He brooded into the empty pot. "It does matter, him bein' a good man. And he is. Y'could see Justice Hall were important to him. Getting it right. Being fair. He cared about that. Y'could see he takes it serious."

"Well, that's good, isn't it?" she said encouragingly.

"Aye!" he retorted. "But that ain't really the point, eh?

I only just got m'self settled good and proper in the stables. All this choppin' and changin' be enough to make a body seasick, I swear!"

Dathne took a deep draft of ale from her tankard, smacked her lips together and considered him with her head tipped to one side. "So do you really want to know what I think, or am I just here to be shouted and banged at?"

Asher felt his cheeks heat. "I ain't shoutin'. Might've banged once or twice. Whole thing's took me by surprise, all right?"

"I'll take that as a yes," said Dathne, rolling her eyes. "If it's living in the Tower that's got you worried, don't be. For a prince, His Highness maintains a remarkably informal household. I'm sure you'll fit right in. Of course Darran won't like you, but who cares? He won't be paying you."

Asher's jaw tightened aggressively. "Who said I be worried? And I don't care if that ole Darran likes me or not."

She smiled. "Good for you. So . . . is it you're afraid you'll fail?"

"No, I ain't afraid I'll fail! I ain't failed at a single thing I ever put my mind to, startin' with lacin' my own boots when I were a spratling of three. Why's everybody thinkin' I be afraid?"

"Well, it's only natural, isn't it?" Dathne eyed him over the top of her tankard. "A rustic young fellow like you thrown in the deep end with Doranen royalty. Put in charge of all kinds of important, secret things. Surely it'd be odd if you *weren't* afraid."

A hot bubble of outrage swelled in his chest, then burst into angry words. "Rustic? You reckon I be *rustic*?"

Dathne's eyebrows lifted. "Me? Of course not. But then I know you, don't I?"

He banged the benchtop again and leaned close. A few heads turned at nearby booths, curious. He ignored them.

"You know bloody nowt if y'reckon I be afraid to do this job just 'cause I were born in a small fishing village days and days from this here fancy big city!" he said hotly. "Let me tell you a thing or two about *fishin'*, missy."

"By all means," said Dathne, and put down her tankard. "I'm all ears."

Her gentle sarcasm was lost on him. Eyes burning, fists braced on the benchtop, he leaned even closer. "The coast of this kingdom be the only place left what sees weather the way it used to be. The way it were afore the Doranen came. Uncalled. Untamed. *Wild*. The spells Barl put in Dragonteeth Reef keep us invisible, and that be all. They don't stop nature. We get storms along the coast, blowin' in from the open ocean, blowin' over the coral and teeth-first into our faces. Water twisters what can suck up a whole boat and all her crew to the last man or boy and spit 'em out again in pieces. Hailstones big as your head. Giant waves just itchin' to slap you down like a hand of iron. Winds that'll blow you right clean out of your boots, and sleet to slice y'to the bone."

"It sounds terrifying," murmured Dathne.

"Aye, it bloody well is! But it don't stop us. We respect it, but we ain't afraid." He jabbed a pointed finger at her. "And *that* be why the WeatherWorker comes to us every year for Sea Harvest Festival. 'Cause the WeatherWorkers know we be different from other Olken. Aye, and from all the Doranen too. The WeatherWorkers know us fishin' folk face the weather their precious magic can't tame, *and* we survive it."

She stared at him, her intensity so fierce it fairly crackled in her hair. "You're proud of that, aren't you? Proud that your people are the closest to what we all were before the Doranen came."

"'Course I am," he retorted. "Who wouldn't be? The storms what blow inland run smack bang into the Weather Magic no more'n half a mile from the water, and it kills 'em stone dead. They never reach the next nearest town or village. So aside from us fishin' folk, there ain't a man, woman or child in this whole kingdom knows what wild weather be like. What Lur used to be. Those folk livin' close enough to the coast to find out, Olken *and* Doranen, they hear thunder on our horizon and hide 'emselves under their beds till it's gone."

"You're scornful . . . but can you blame them?" said Dathne. "Is it their fault they weren't born fishermen? Thanks to Barl and the WeatherWorkers, the people of this kingdom have lived for more than six hundred years in peaceful prosperity, looking upon the weather as a friend. A gift. As a tool to be used, like any hammer or nail or needle. Not as something unsafe, or lethal. Even if you could, would you change that? Give the kingdom back its wild weather? Break the chains of magic and abandon us all to chaos? To hurricane and earthquake? Famine, flood and drought?"

Scornful. Frowning, all pent-up indignation released, Asher sat back and rubbed the tip of one forefinger across the grain of the wooden benchtop. "Don't be daft. Why'd I want to do a thing like that?" He looked up. "And I don't blame no-one for nowt. I'm just sayin' it ain't right to go around disrespectin' folk 'cause they ain't all City-born and sophisticated, like."

"I never said I disrespected you. And it's good to know you don't disrespect yourself either. Asher . . ." Dathne hesitated, her dark eyes somber. "The day we met, I said you were too easily prickled. And you were. Has that changed? Because there'll be people who say, to your face and to your back, that they could do this job better. That the prince should've asked them. That you're an upstart rustic who should've stayed in the stables or, better yet, on your da's leaky little boat far away from here. And instead of shouting, or thumping tables or even, Barl forbid, thumping *them*, you'll need to smile and walk away. Can you do that?"

He glowered at her. "My da's boat don't leak. And I don't care two tubs of fish guts what other folks say. I be good enough for the prince, and that's all I care about. I can do whatever he asks."

Considering him thoughtfully she said, "Does that mean you'll say yes?"

He shook his head. Shrugged. "I d'know . . ."

Reaching across the table, she patted his arm. Her touch through his thick cotton sleeve was warm and familiar. It shivered him, somewhere deep inside. "Oh, come on," she coaxed. "At least give the job a *try*. All bluster aside, you know you want to. If only to prove to all those folk you don't care about that they're wrong. And he said you could go back to the stables if it didn't work out, didn't he?"

He sniffed. "Talk's cheap."

"I'll agree that nothing is certain save sunshine and rain," she said carefully, "but for what it's worth, Asher, I believe Prince Gar is a man of his word. And I think you do, too."

He couldn't deny it. "I s'pose."

She sat back again, eyebrows raised. "Look at it this way. If you *don't* give this new job a chance you'll spend the rest of your life wondering what might have been. *And* you'll be a lot poorer while you're wondering it. Fifty trins a week? That's not a sum to be sneezed at."

"Huh," said Asher. "Easy enough for you to say. You ain't the one lookin' at lace on his collar and seven forks to eat a bowl of soup." He scratched his chin, then shoved his emptied stew pot to one side. "Reckon I'm done here."

She smiled. She had a nice smile, when it wasn't pretending to be an unsheathed dagger. "You're welcome."

With a nod, he slid out from behind the benchtop and shouldered his way across the Goose's crowded dance floor.

Dathne watched him go. "*Missy?*" she said to herself, remembering, and laughed.

Asher opened the door and was lost to the mizzling night. He didn't see Matt lurking nearby in the shadows, waiting for him to leave.

Dathne looked up as the stable meister approached her habitual corner. Her eyes were triumphant.

"*So.*"

"Just tell me," said Matt, easing onto the seat Asher had abandoned, "that you had nothing to do with it."

Her straight black eyebrows shot up indignantly. "Of course I didn't! But at least now you have to admit that what I *did* do turned out to be the right thing. He's about to enter the House of the Usurper. Prophecy continues."

Matt sighed. "He said he'd take the job, then?"

"No. But he will. I told him he should, and he wants to. All that lovely money." She laughed softly, and swallowed some more ale. "And though I suspect he'd die before admitting it, he's proud as punch the prince has asked him. In fact, my friend, I'd say nine-tenths of that young man's backbone is nothing *but* pride." She paused, her expression thoughtful. "Which isn't such a bad thing, provided it's put to good use."

Matt rubbed his eyes. "There'll be folks none too pleased to see a stable lad elevated so far above the rest of us. He's bound to lose some friends over this. Or worse, make enemies."

Dathne shrugged. "He's not here to be popular. He's here to fulfil Prophecy."

"It doesn't bother you?"

"What? That I told him what would serve my purposes before his?" Another shrug. "I'm not here to be popular either, Matt."

He couldn't meet her eyes. "I feel like muck." His voice was so low he could barely hear it himself. "He's my friend, and we're using him. Without his knowledge, or his consent. It's wrong."

Her hand snapped out to close about his wrist, ink-stained fingernails biting deep between tendon and sinew. "*Look at me.*"

Reluctantly, he lifted his gaze.

"Saving kingdoms is a mucky business. We can soil our hands a little now, you and I, or we can see them soaked in blood later. Either way, we get mucky."

"And what if I don"t like getting mucky?"

Dathne bared her teeth in a fierce smile. "Then I'd say

sorry, bucko, but it's a bit late now." The smile disappeared and all that remained was ferocity. "You listen. He's not your friend, Matt. He's a pawn, just like you and me. Prophecy's tool. You don't make friends with a tool. You use it, and you keep on using it until the job it's designed for is done."

"That's cold," Matt whispered.

Her teeth bared again. "You mean *I'm* cold."

"I mean there might be another way. A better way."

She shook her head. "There isn't."

"But—"

"*There isn't.*" With a visible effort, she controled herself. "There's a reason Prophecy calls him the Innocent Mage. He doesn't get told a thing, Matt. Not one *thing*. Not until he has to be told. Not until there's no turning back. Understood?"

A fraction more pressure from the fingernails on his flesh and she'd draw blood. He sat motionless, heart pounding, and endured her flame-filled eyes. Then he nodded, feeling scorched to his bones' marrow. "Aye. Understood."

She nodded sharply and released him. "Good. Now go fetch yourself a mug of ale and wash away that mopey look before somebody thinks you asked me to marry you and I said no."

"Ha!" said Matt, and shoved away from the bench. He didn't want a mug of ale. If he drank so much as a mouthful, his quivering guts would heave themselves onto the floor at his feet. "Ask you to marry me? That'll be the day!"

He saw his words strike home. Saw them hurt her.

To his shame, he wasn't sorry.

CHAPTER SIX

Darran, Private Secretary to His Royal Highness Prince Gar and self-appointed Guardian of the Tower, reached for his cup and took a genteel sip of his morning tea.

Gulping was for peasants.

"Darran?"

Darran replaced the cup in its saucer with a faint chink of porcelain. "Yes, Willer?"

His assistant and protégé was staring vexedly at a sheet of official parchment topping a pile of official parchments teetering untidily before him. "I think we have a problem."

With a sigh, Darran drummed his manicured fingernails on his pristine desktop. "Willer, *how* many times must I say it? In this office we do *not* have problems. We have interesting developments. We have challenges. If we absolutely *must* we may, on occasion, have a slight difficulty. But under *no* circumstances whatso*ever* do we have *problems*. Now. What is it?"

As befitted his subordinate position, Willer's desk was

small and situated between the door and the bookcase, which was neatly filled with publications detailing the genealogies of all the kingdom's Doranen families, plus sundry other reference works such as *Dorana City By-Laws*, Fabrit and Delbard's *A Short History of Lur* and, of course, the indispensable Polger's *Etiquette, Precedent and Protocol*.

Squirming round in his chair—really, the boy ate *far* too many pastries, Darran thought—Willer held up the offending document, his expression trepidatious. "It's His Highness's diary for next month."

"Yes? What of it? How many times must I remind you, Willer? Above all else, a good private secretary is *lucid*."

With a grunt Willer shoved his chair back, got up and marched across the circular office's plush carpet waving the parchment in question. "Well, Darran, he's *lucidly* gone and declined all of next month's invitations except the one to the Brewers' Guild banquet."

"Don't be ridiculous." Darran held out an impatient hand for the diary. "He can't have. Declined Lady Scobey's soirée? Refused to attend Lord Dorv's hunting party? *Again?* Turned down the chance to go boating on the Gant with the Council? Tut! You've misread his—oh. Oh dear." Staring at the list of social engagements to which His Highness had been invited, noting with despair the decisive pen strokes through every invitation bar the least prestigious, he felt a sudden stab of pain between his eyes. "Barl preserve us!" he cursed, and thrust the parchment back into Willer's waiting hand. "What is he *thinking*?"

Wisely, Willer didn't reply.

"Lady Scobey is going to be furious! I've had her

wretched cook in and out of here a dozen times this week, wanting to know His Highness's favorite dishes. He *can't* say no to her, I'll never hear the end of it!" Scalded with outrage, Darran snatched the diary back again and stared at it with loathing. "The *Brewers'* Guild? Is he out of his mind? That motley assortment of inebriated reprobates? There's not a man among them who knows how to tie a cravat properly! In fact, I doubt there's even one who knows what a cravat *is*! Barl *preserve* us!" He tossed the diary onto his desk and went so far as to stand and pace towards the window and back again. "Well. Clearly this is unacceptable. Willer, present my compliments to His Highness and request the indulgence of a short—"

There was a smart *rap-rap* on the closed office door.

"*What*?" cried Darran.

The door swung open to reveal His Royal Highness, and behind him a disreputable-looking Olken wearing deplorably scruffed shirt and trews and boots clotted with mud, or something worse. He looked vaguely familiar, was some kind of manual laborer about the place, possibly, but what he was doing here, in the ordered beauty of the Tower, with the prince . . .

His Highness smiled, that sweet, mischievous smile the hardest of hearts could not withstand. "Don't tell me, Darran. Let me guess. Willer's just shown you my acceptance list for next month's social engagements."

"Your Highness!" gasped Darran. "Oh sir, *forgive* me."

His Highness, sauntering into the office, waved a dismissive hand. After a slight hesitation the disreputable Olken followed him over the threshold. "It's all right. I didn't expect you to be happy about it."

Mortified at being discovered raising his voice in disarray, Darran took a deep, calming breath and reached for the diary. "As it happens, Your Highness, I did wish to consult with you on the matter of next month's engagements. I'm sure it's just an oversight, but—"

"Sorry," said His Highness. "No oversight."

Darran felt his heart plummet. "Your Highness, forgive me, but is this . . ." He hesitated. ". . . *wise*? To say no to all of these important Doranen personages, your peers, and then accept an invitation from the . . . the . . . Olken Brewers' Guild?"

His Highness shrugged. "I like the Olken Brewers' Guild."

"You do?" said Darran faintly.

"Well, I like the members. Their meister is best sipped in half-pints only. But yes." The prince sighed. "And clearly you think that's inappropriate."

"I do not presume to have an opinion," said Darran, avoiding Willer's gaze. "But I would be doing you a grave disservice did I not remind you that as the king's son you have social obligations and a duty to—"

"Be bored out of my mind in the name of politics?" said His Highness dryly.

"Well . . ." Darran ventured the very slightest of smiles; a little judicious sympathy went a long way in greasing the wheels of appropriate princely conduct. "Please don't mistake me, Your Highness. I do understand that sometimes it's difficult."

"Difficult?" murmured His Highness. "I think the word you're looking for is impossible."

"Yes, sir. I imagine it is. But, sir, if you could please bring yourself to reconsider . . . find a way to accept *one* other invitation . . . just one . . . it would be the politic thing to do."

His Highness sighed. Held out his hand. "Show me then."

Darran gave him the diary, stepped back again and cleared his throat. "If I might make a suggestion, sir?"

His Highness glanced up. "Short of gagging you, is there any way I can prevent it?"

"Oh, sir!" Darran protested with a deprecating laugh. "So amusing."

"I'm glad one of us thinks this is funny. Your point, Darran."

Darran nodded. "Of course, sir. My point is this: I happen to know that Lady Scobey has gone to great lengths to design her soirée in such a way as can only be highly pleasing to your palate."

"Lady Scobey," said His Highness, frowning, "is hoping against hope that I'll succumb to the dubious charms of her youngest daughter and offer myself as a husband. Lady Scobey, shrewd mama that she is, seems to have reached the flattering conclusion that my lack of magical ability is outweighed, just, by the fact that my father is the king and my sister heir to the crown. I suppose I should be grateful . . ."

There was an embarrassed silence. After a moment Darran cleared his throat. "Well, if the idea of Lady Scobey's soirée displeases you, sir, then perhaps—"

The prince's face twisted with a repressed and violent revulsion. "*Displeases* me? Why would it displease me? Lady Scobey's eldest daughter has just announced her engagement to Conroyd Jarralt's firstborn son. Now the good mama thinks to get her feet under both our tables and who can blame her? She's only thinking of her family. No, no, what *displeases* me, Darran, is—" And then he stopped. Shook his head and managed a rueful smile. "I'm sorry. You can't possibly be interested in Doranen romantic gossip. And of course you're right. I can't attend only the Brewers' banquet. Privilege has its price, after all. Give me a pen."

Darran nodded sharply at Willer, who inked a quill and handed it to the prince. His Highness scrawled a circle around the notation for Lady Scobey's party, crossed out his original rejection and wrote in the neat hand that Darran admired so much: *Invitation accepted—under protest.* Then he handed both diary and pen to Willer.

"Thank you, Your Highness," said Darran, scrupulously neutral. "Lady Scobey will be delighted, I'm sure."

That made the prince laugh; a mirthless sound. "Only until I make it quite clear that I've no intention of marrying her daughter."

The pain in him, imperfectly masked, was painful to see. To endure, without offering comfort. But Darran knew that while His Highness might, on very rare occasions, refer to his ... imperfection ... such references were never *ever* to be ratified by comment, or even acknowledgement.

"Is there anything else Your Highness requires?"

His Highness's expression cleared. "As a matter of fact, Darran, there is." He beckoned to the swarthy Olken, still silently loitering just inside the doorway. The ruffian hesitated then stepped into the office proper. "Asher, this is my private secretary, Darran. I believe you've heard of him. Darran keeps my life in order whether I want him to or not. And the young gentleman there in the startling pink weskit is his assistant, Willer."

The Olken nodded. Darran waited for him to speak, waited a little longer . . . then realized with an unpleasant jolt that an abrupt jerk of the chin was the only recognition he was going to receive.

How . . . offensive.

He looked this Asher up and down. A rough, unprepossessing fellow. Capable enough, most likely, in a purely brutish fashion. His face was scarred: a faded white line ran irregularly along his right cheekbone. It gave him a threatening, brawling air which was echoed in the muscled breadth of his shoulders and the blunt, square power of his hands, hanging relaxed by his sides. How old was he? Hard to say . . . Contemporary to His Highness, it was safe to assume, but with a wealth of dubious experience in his dark, calculating eyes. His complexion was weathered, suggesting a lifetime's exposure to a climate harsher than most in the kingdom. The chin was firm. Stubborn, even. And in him raged a crackling vitality, a brooding force of personality that hummed the air around him like an invisible dynamo.

Darran, who prided himself on being a swift and accurate judge of character, felt his spine stiffen.

Here was trouble.

His Highness placed a hand on the ruffian's shoulder. "Darran, this is Asher of Restharven. He's the man who caught Ballodair for me after I fell off in the market square, you recall? I offered him a job as thanks, and he accepted."

Slowly, Darran nodded. "Yes, sir. I do recall the incident." He shifted his gaze a fraction, let it rest on the ruffian's calm face. Was that dumb insolence he could see lurking behind the mask? He thought it was. The hairs rose up on the back of his neck.

Oh yes indeed. Here was trouble all right, and everything that trouble implied.

The prince slid a sidelong glance at the fellow. "Well, I've decided he was being wasted in the stable yard, so I've invited him to work with me here, in the Tower."

Willer made an incautious, strangled sound in his throat. Darran burned him with a look. "Really, sir?" he said, fighting the impulse to clench his hands into fists. "How interesting. If I may ask, sir, in what capacity will this—will Asher be working here?"

Again the fleeting, mischievous smile. "*Well*," said His Highness, "once upon a time he'd have been known as the Prince's Champion."

That startled a reaction out of the ruffian. "Eh? Champion? You never said nowt about me bein' a champion. Sir. Champion of what anyways? Folderol and footlin' about?"

Darran shuddered. Barl save them all, that *accent*! Thick enough to cut with a knife! And the disrespect. *Appalling*. He felt his stomach roll queasily. His world was unravelling right before his eyes and he had the most awful suspicion he was powerless to stop it.

The prince laughed. "Don't you like it? I do. *Champion*. I think it sounds quaint."

"Quaint," the brute echoed, voice dripping with disgust. "Ain't no call for quaint, I reckon."

"No? Well . . . perhaps not," His Highness said regretfully.

"Champion," the dreadful man said again. Then he

smiled, a scornful twist of his lips. "Got that from one of them books Dathne's always fetchin' you, eh?"

His Highness appeared completely unperturbed. "As a matter of fact, I did. We had champions prancing all over the countryside a few hundred years ago, particularly during that bad patch after King Trevoyle died without an heir. But once the dust settled and all the bodies were buried it was decided we'd do without them for a while, and that was that. So, in deference to the past, we won't actually call you my champion. Not in public, anyway. I reserve the right to use the title in private, though, if ever I'm in a mood to irritate you. Instead, we'll call you my . . ." He fell silent, thinking.

Mistake! Darran wanted to shout. Call him your mistake, come to your senses and toss him back on the dung heap where he belongs! It''s not too late!

The prince stirred. "Do you know, I believe I've a mind not to worry about the past and its refined sensibilities after all. Trevoyle's Schism was a long time ago. A champion's job was to stand at his lord's right hand, defending him from all harm. He spoke with his lord's voice in matters of local dispute and calumny and was relied upon to provide his lord with intelligence, information and advice whenever it was required." Again, the mischievous grin. "He was also expected to die on his lord's behalf . . . but probably we won't need to worry about that."

The jumped-up stable hand was staring. "Oh, aye? Reckon that's a relief. Sir. But if you got to call me something, Assistant Olken Administrator'll do. Reckon the lads are goin' to give me a hard enough time about this as it is, without you taggin' me as a champion."

Darran swallowed an anguished cry. Assistant Olken Administrator? His Highness had decided to appoint himself an assistant—without consultation? Without guidance? Had appointed this man, this *awful* man, to the post? What was he *thinking*?

The prince frowned for a moment, then nodded. "Yes. I hadn't considered that. Very well. Darran . . ."

Feeling ill, Darran said, "Sir?"

"As of today, Asher is the kingdom's Assistant Olken Administrator."

He flinched. Hearing it said like that, baldly, with no suggestion of doubt or equivocation, not even a hint of needing a wiser opinion, a moment to think . . . the effort of controling himself would likely give him a hernia. Driven to desperation he said, delicately, unwisely, "Sir, does His Majesty . . . ?"

The prince's answering look was dangerously bland. "Does His Majesty what, Darran?"

Know? Approve? Permit? Darran cleared his throat. If he wasn't extremely careful, the next sound he heard would be that of thin ice cracking. He took a prudent step back to safer ground. "Well, sir, it's just your official appointment has yet to be announced."

"The news will be made public on Barlsday," said the prince. "Along with the announcement that I have chosen an Olken to work with me in this important undertaking." He smiled, but his eyes remained chilly. "As one who pays such close attention to politics, Darran, I thought you of all people would appreciate the gesture."

"Yes! Yes, sir, naturally I do!" And would appreciate it even more had the chosen one been anybody but this smirking lout. If the prince had thought to ask his vastly

experienced private secretary who best would fill such
important, such political shoes . . . But the boy could be
so *impulsive*. As surely as Barl came over the mountains,
this would end in tears and tantrums, he could feel it in
his bones.

"I'm pleased that you agree," said the prince. "And
now, if there's nothing else that can't wait, I'll give my
new assistant a guided tour of the Tower."

Darran throttled a gasp. "You, sir? Surely that is something more properly done by—" The protest withered and
died in the face of His Highness's cool gaze. "Yes, sir.
Certainly, sir. I have no further pressing business for you
at this moment, sir."

"Good. I, however, do have some for you," said His
Highness. "Reschedule the remainder of today's appoint-
ments and then inform my tailor and my bootmaker that
I shall want to see them here as soon as possible, for
Asher's fittings. Oh yes, and advise the palace provi-
sioner that Asher and I will come and see her at some
point this afternoon about furnishing the Tower's Green
Floor to his tastes."

Darran nearly moaned aloud. His Highness was lodging the brute *here*? In the *Tower*? But *nobody* lived in
here, saving His Highness. Staff lodged elsewhere,
mainly the palace, and walked to work.

Lodging the ruffian here was an unprecedented mark
of regard.

His Highness was staring. "Darran?"

"Yes, sir. Of course, sir."

"Naturally, you won't refer to Asher by his new title.
Yet."

After a quick glance to make sure Willer was taking notes, Darran nodded. "Certainly, sir."

The prince frowned. "You'll need to inform the kitchen, too, so we all have enough to eat. And something else—oh yes." He stopped his headlong rush towards disaster and looked at the lout. "You've not changed your mind about Cygnet, have you? You'd not prefer another horse?"

Darran choked. A *horse*? On top of everything, His Highness was giving this peasant a *horse*? Worth an absolute *fortune*? Oh dear Barl preserve them.

"No, sir," the lout said. "Cygnet'll do me just fine."

"All right then," the prince said, nodding. "Darran, let Matt know he's just lost himself a stable hand, and that Cygnet henceforth belongs to Asher. Now, is that everything? Yes, I think it is."

"Wages," said the lout, scowling.

"Ah, yes. How could I forget that?" Taking the pen back from Willer, His Highness found a scrap of paper, scribbled on it, folded it in half and held it out. "Here is Asher's revised wage, Darran. It's a confidential matter, you understand?"

Darran took the proffered note with numb fingers. "Of course, Your Highness," he said woodenly. "Your Highness, a question, if I may be so bold."

The prince frowned. "Of course. Since when do you need my permission to ask a question?"

Since you foisted this uneducated braggard upon me and called him your champion! Somehow, Darran managed a deferential smile. "I'm sorry, sir. It's just that I find myself a trifle confused as to the correct etiquette involved. To be blunt, sir, does this—your—does Asher report to me? Or do I report to him?"

"Neither," replied the prince. "You both report to me. On occasion, Asher will have cause and leave to speak with my voice. You will know when he does so. Otherwise I expect you to work together as equals with separate duties. Is that clear?"

Darran inclined his head. "Quite clear, sir. Thank you. And just one final point, a very small point I know, but it's best to be clear on these things from the beginning, don't you agree?"

The prince sighed. "What?"

"Where, precisely, does Willer fit into these . . . new arrangements?"

"Willer?" His Highness said blankly. "He doesn't. Willer's your assistant. Asher's mine. But if he should require any help, of course Willer will give it to him happily. Won't you, Willer?"

Willer flushed. "Yes, Your Highness. Of course, Your Highness."

The prince nodded. "Excellent. Well, we'll leave you now to get those messengers organized. Thank you for your time, Darran."

Darran bowed low, despite the scarlet ache in his middle. "Not at all, sir. My time is yours to command, as always."

The office door closed with a thud behind the prince and his boorish companion.

Willer, choking, spewed forth a laugh laced with horror and spite and collapsed into his chair. "Darran, I can't believe it. Can you believe it? His Highness has gone *mad*! Should I send for Pother Nix?"

Because the situation was so dire Darran decided not to flay Willer for his undisciplined outburst. In truth, it was something of a relief to know that his feelings were so perfectly shared. Heart pounding, mouth dry, he opened the slip of paper the prince had handed him and looked at the amount of money His Highness was prepared to throw away every week on the loutish ruffian he had, so incredibly, so inexplicably, taken into his employ.

Fifty trins.

Only twenty-five trins less than he earned himself after a lifetime of loyal service and immense personal sacrifice.

Hot thick hatred stirred. Who was he, this ruffian, this lout, this *stranger*, to march into all their lives and turn them topsy-turvy in such a fashion? Prince's Champion? Champion troublemaker, more like. Champion disturber of the peace. Champion error of judgement, and if he could say so he would, save that he knew his prince well enough to recognize the signs of an unwise idea firmly rooted. Knew, to his everlasting despair and from bitter personal experience, that no amount of wisdom or sage and loving advice would breach the determined certainty of royalty bent upon indulging an intemperate whim.

"Darran?" said Willer.

He refolded the scrap of paper into a tiny lump with swift, furious precision. "What?"

"Pother Nix. Shall I send for him?"

"Of course not! His Highness isn't ill, he is merely . . . enthusiastic. That ill-bred lout won't last a week."

Willer chewed his lip. "But what if he does? What if he lasts, I don't know, forever?"

Darran felt his stomach lurch. "Nonsense. I can assure you, my dear Willer, that he won't last anywhere near that long. You and I will see to that."

"We will?" said Willer, a delighted smile lighting his pasty face. "Excellent!" Then the smile collapsed. "Um . . . how?"

With a contemptuous flick of his fingers, Darran disposed of the little paper wad into the rubbish basket. "I don't know, precisely. Not yet. But I'll tell you this, my friend: if we give Asher of Restharven enough rope you can be sure that sooner or later he'll hang himself."

As he climbed the spiraling Tower staircase behind the prince, Asher chuckled. "Dathne were right. Reckon that Darran don't care for me at all."

The prince sighed and glanced over his shoulder. "Don't take it personally. Darran doesn't care for anybody overmuch; he was born under a disapproving star. But he's served my family all his life and he really is very good at his job, so I bear with his foibles. You'll just have to bear with them too." A sudden chuckle. "Do you know, I think this is going to be *fun*."

Asher snorted. "Well, I reckon it's goin' to be *somethin'*. Don't reckon I'd swim a long way to call it *fun*.' He frowned with sudden thought. "Eh. What am I s'posed to call you, anyways?"

The prince swung about, walking backwards. "Well, in public you continue to call me 'sir' or 'Your Highness'. Around here, and whenever it's just us, you'll call me Gar, of course. Why? What did you think you'd be calling me?"

"Mad," said Asher cheerfully. "As a gaffed fish."

By the time the late-setting summer sun had sunk into shadow, a bewildering array of things had happened. Asher had an entire floor of the Tower to himself, acres of space, with a bedchamber and his very own privy closet and a sitting room and library—a right waste of space, that—and an office even, since Gar seemed to think he'd be up to his eyebrows in work soon enough.

More than that, each room was now filled with furniture chosen from a vast array of beds and tables and sofas and desks and cupboards and whatnots stored in an entire wing of the palace. Even as the last stick of it huffed and puffed its way upstairs on the stout backs of various servants, there were maids with dusters and polishing cloths and sheets and pillows and towels and who knew what else rushing in to make his new accommodation fit for a prince.

Or, in his case, a prince's champion.

He grinned at the thought. Though he'd drown himself before admitting it aloud, he quite liked the sound of the title. For certain sure it'd make Da smile when he found out.

After the cheerful, crowded disorder of the stable lads' dormitory the solitary splendor of the Green Floor was nearly too much to take in.

And that wasn't all.

Much to his dismay the summoned tailor had arrived as bidden, breathless with excitement and rushing, with a whole school of underlings in his wake. Before Asher could open his mouth to protest they had him stripped down to his drawers and were crawling all over him with tape measures and fabric samples, cotton and lawn and brocade and wool and linen and velvet and silk and leather, most of them in colors he wasn't exactly sure a man should wear. When he started to say this the tailor, a small man with busy fingers and a voice like the crack of a bullwhip, rapped him on the knuckles with his shears and told him to hold his tongue, what did a brawny muscle-bound bubblehead know about the finer points of fashion, pray?

Knuckles stinging, temper seething, he'd held his tongue.

Gar, drat him, had nearly fallen over with laughing before being diverted by a disapproving Darran to deal with a newborn crisis somewhere in the City.

By the time the tailor and his scurrying minions were done there were plans for some twelve different changes of clothes, plus extra shirts, weskits and trews and two sets of riding leathers. Even as he stood there being poked and prodded and stuck with careless pins, three of the sweating underlings had set up two treadle sewing machines and a portable cutting table, rolled out bolts of brown and black and blue and green and dull bronze fabrics and, following some quick sketches by their employer, somehow produced three shirts and two pairs of britches for him to be going on with.

When they were done, Asher dressed himself in blue and black and gazed at his unfamiliar reflection in the mirror, shocked to silence. Such fine clothes! He looked practically posh. If his brothers could see him now, they'd *puke*. He grinned. Well, see him they would in a year's time. He'd make sure to wear the fanciest weskit he still had left, just for the pleasure of their slumguzzled faces.

While the tailor and his underlings were making their last-minute adjustments the bootmaker arrived. More measuring. A servant was sent to his shop with instructions to bring back some on-hand boots and shoes that would do, at a pinch, until the made-to-measure items were ready. Asher, slipping his feet into butter-soft dark blue leather, couldn't imagine any boot could be finer. But the grimacing bootmaker said that while such journeyman items might be fine for an Olken off the street, for a personage as grand as—as—the prince's assistant, well, they were barely up to snuff.

Asher stared. It was his first inkling that perhaps his life was going to change in a lot more ways than he'd bargained for.

Eventually the last bowing and scraping body left and he was alone in his grand new apartments. A message was delivered from the prince: family matters would keep him at the palace that evening; he should feel free to dine whenever he felt hungry.

"Ha," said Asher, staring at the hastily scrawled note. Now what was he supposed to do with himself? In reply his stomach grumbled demandingly, so he went down to the kitchen for his dinner. There, the scandalized cook sent him away with a scolding lecture about the dire consequences of important personages running their own errands.

Suitably chastened and thoroughly educated on the uses of Tower lackeys, he went back upstairs and amused himself by rearranging furniture until his supper arrived.

After his meal, a delectable chicken casserole with baked leeks, and a raspberry fool for dessert, he sat back in his solitary sitting room and sipped the last of the crisp white wine that had accompanied his dinner. Some bright spark had left a pile of books on his bedside table—Gar, most like, being funny—but he couldn't begin to care about *Olken Law as it Pertains to Equal Weights and Measures in Commerce* tonight . . . or, possibly, *ever*.

Adrift, chartless and lost in unsailed waters, he headed for a familiar port.

As he'd hoped, he found Matt doing the rounds of his stable yard, quietly checking each horse, making sure no rugs had slipped, no bellies were colicking, no legs had filled with heat and swelling unnoticed. Hearing the crunch of boots on gravel, Matt turned. The flickering lamplight from outside each stable shadowed the look on his broad face into a mystery.

"Cygnet's a fine animal," he said. "He'll take good care of you."

"Aye," said Asher, and headed for his new mount's stable. The horse, a shimmering silver gray with eyes like blue glass, shifted in the straw and poked a cautious nose over the stable door. Rippled velvet-soft nostrils and nickered, a flirty little sound inviting apples.

Matt reached into his pocket. "Here," he said, and tossed Asher half a Golden Dewdrop. Catching it one-handed, Asher let Cygnet lip it from his fingers. Inhaled the rich scent of horse and crushed apple, and for the first time thought that perhaps he hadn't made such a blundering great mistake after all.

"I keep thinkin' I'm dreamin'," he said, tickling his horse under the chin. Cygnet's lower lip drooped, wobbling, and his eyelids half closed in simple pleasure. "One minute I'm muckin' out stables and the next . . ." Baffled, almost afraid, he shook his head. "And I still don't see how I'm s'posed to make a success of it."

There was an upturned bucket outside Ballodair's stable. Matt eased his way over to it and sat down, elbows braced on his knees, fingers laced to cradle his chin. The prince's stallion came to investigate. Blew in Matt's close-cropped hair, lost interest, and returned to eating hay.

"I think," Matt said, slowly, "by being the prince's friend."

"His *friend*?" Asher stared. "Me? Why? He's got hisself scores of friends, ain't he?"

"I don't think so." Matt's expression was sober, his voice melancholy. "He has . . . hangers-on. Toadies. Opportunists who see in him their own advancement and royal favor. But friends? No."

"Why not?"

Matt looked at him. "You know why not."

"Asher tugged gently on Cygnet's forelock, frowning. Yes, he knew. "How'd he get hisself born without magic anyways?"

In the flickering lamplight Matt's expression echoed the sorrow in his voice. "Nobody's sure. It just happens. Not often, though, and never before in the royal family."

"Still, it ain't his fault. And he ain't contagious."

"No. But he reminds the other Doranen that they and their magic are not invulnerable, or invincible. And they hate him for it."

"*Hate*?" said Asher, startled. "But he's the king's son."

Matt lifted one shoulder. "Which is why their enmity is subtle, Asher. A handshake released too quickly. A smile that doesn't quite reach the eyes. Nothing a body could point to and say, see? But it's there, and he knows it. He's no fool, Prince Gar. He knows it." He shook his head. "You watch your step, my friend. Like it or not you're in their world now . . . and there's more than one kind of shark swimming in the sea."

Asher snorted. "I grew up with sharks, Matt, and six

brangling brothers besides. Reckon I can take care of m'self."

"Yes," said Matt, and once again his face was shadowed. "Yes, you probably can. Now I'd best say goodnight, for I've more stables to check and other work besides."

"I'll help,' said Asher promptly. "I may be *important* now, Barl save me, with folk bowin' and scrapin' and fallin' over 'emselves to put a smile on m'face, but I ain't too pretty or proud to lend a hand."

"No, there's no need, you shouldn't—" Matt began. Then he stopped. Looked to be making a decision. "All right then," he said, and smiled. "Can't say I won't appreciate the company. Thanks."

Asher grinned. "That be thanks, *sir*, I reckon," he said. And laughed as Matt threw an apple at him.

CHAPTER SEVEN

"So," said Dana, Queen of Lur, as her gathered family shared the evening meal, "was I imagining things, Gar, or did I hear one of the maids say that you'd hired a young Olken man to replace Darran?"

Her husband's fork stopped halfway to his mouth. "What? You've pensioned off Darran?" King Borne demanded. "Barl's nightcap. He'll be heartbroken!"

"I do wish you wouldn't swear," Dana complained gently. "At least not at the dinner table. And not in front of Fane."

"Oh, Mama," Fane protested. "Honestly. That's not swearing. *Swearing* is—"

"Inappropriate for the heir presumptive," said Durm. "Exercise a little self-control, madam." The Master Magician's fleshy face, carved with deep lines of experience and the trials of containing strong magics, reflected his displeasure. Beneath sparse gray eyebrows his eyes snapped and sparked, seething power never far from the surface of his skin.

But Fane was not afraid of power. "Well, if it's

inappropriate for me, why is it all right for Papa? *Papa* swears all the time, and he's the king!"

A lively debate erupted. Gar sighed, sat back in his chair with his goblet of red wine and waited for the storm to pass. Once, just once, it would be nice to dine with his family without some trivial matter starting a battle royal. No pun intended. But Fane had been born under a quarrelsome star and it seemed a day could not go by without her living up to that birthright with a vengeance. Pity the poor fool who ended up marrying her.

After some five minutes of his sister's vigorous opinionatedness it was their mother, as usual, who held sway.

"Well, I don't care if Barl herself rushed about the countryside shrieking *rot my toenails*, I won't have that kind of language at the dinner table!" she declared. "Do I make myself clear?"

Borne took her hand in his and raised it to his lips. "As crystal, my love." His expression rearranged itself into somber contrition. "We are duly chastized."

"Ha!" said Dana, and tugged his beard. "If only I thought you were!"

Gar hid his grin in his goblet. Fane groaned. "Oh, must you? *Flirting* at the dinner table is—"

"The prerogative of your parents," said Borne, affectionately severe. "Stop being tiresome, brat." As Fane subsided, pouting, he considered Gar and added, "Well? Have you?"

"Have I what?" said Gar. "Pensioned off Darran? No, of course not. Much as I'd like to." He shrugged. "But I have hired myself an assistant."

Fane speared a minted baby potato and nibbled it from her fork. "An assistant?" She was looking especially pretty this evening, with her silver-gilt hair loose and gently curling round her face, and her soft skin glowing in the glimfire light. Her tunic was the particular shade of blue that brought out to perfection the diamond clarity of her eyes. "What for? You don't do anything."

Gar watched his father's gaze sharpen and shook his head, fractionally. There was no point. Fane was Fane, and he'd long grown used to her viperish tongue. Voice determinedly light he said, "And now I'll be able to do even less. Aren't I lucky?"

Borne frowned into his wine. "What kind of assistance are you expecting this person to provide?"

"The Olken Administrating kind." Borne looked up. Gar met his eyes steadily, and added, "I thought you might have it mentioned on Barlsday. Two announcements for the price of one, so to speak."

Dana, spreading butter on a fresh piece of bread, smiled at him. "You always were an economical child. So who is this person? Do we know him? Her?"

"Him," said Gar. "No. You've not met. His name is Asher, of Restharven."

Borne's frown deepened. "The fisherman you hired on as a stable hand?" Fane choked back laughter, and he raised a swift hand, silencing her. "Gar, is this wise? Surely Darran—"

"Darran has more than enough to do already," said Gar. "Besides, he's not suitable for my purpose."

Borne's eyebrows lifted. "And a stable hand is?"

"A man is not merely his employment, sir. Were you to start mucking out stables tomorrow, still you'd be who and what you are."

"Yes, dear, that's true, but even so . . ." Dana hesitated.

"You must admit, it's rather a leap. There'll be a bees' hive of gossip once the appointment is made public. It's unusual to say the least, to elevate a stable hand so high. You can't think there won't be some . . . consternation."

Gar shrugged. "People will talk no matter who I choose. Since it's impossible to please everyone I decided to please myself and let the rest of the beehive buzz itself to strangulation."

Fane turned to the Master Magician. "What do you think, Durm? Gar's mad to hire some smelly ruffian he barely knows anything about to be his personal assistant, isn't he?"

"My opinion is irrelevant," said Durm, politely smiling, "given that this matter is unrelated to magic."

"Huh," said Fane with a toss of her head. "Well, I think he's utterly deranged. I mean, what could a fisherman stablehand possibly know about anything besides horse manure and fish guts? Gar's going to be a laughing stock. Which means *I'll* be a laughing stock too, because it's my stupid brother who hired this—this—"

"Darling . . ." said Dana, shaking her head.

Ignoring Fane, Gar stared at his father. "I assure you, sir, my decision wasn't made upon a whim. I've given this matter a great deal of thought. I chose Asher carefully, and for good reason."

The king sat back in his chair, one finger tracing the etched base of his wine goblet. "Indeed. And while you were ruminating on your choice did you happen to consider the reaction of a man like Conroyd Jarralt, once the news got out?"

"There you go being rude about Conroyd Jarralt again," said Fane, pulling a face. "I wish you'd explain why you don't like him. *I* like him. I think he's very charming and terribly good-looking. Even if he is old enough to be my father."

Gar turned on her. "Charm and good looks being in your tiny little book the most important attributes for leadership!"

She flushed and her eyes glittered dangerously. Lips curved in a poison-sweet smile she said, "At least he's not a cr—"

"*Fane!*" said Borne. His fist crashed on the tabletop so that all their goblets and the silverware jumped. Wine splashed, scarlet, on the white damask tablecloth. Fane retreated into sulky silence.

"It's all right," Gar said, his voice low. "It doesn't matter. Father, I'm truly sorry if I've displeased you. That wasn't my intention."

Borne's expression thawed. "Then why did you proceed without first asking my advice? You've not even been officially declared, Gar. If you must have such an unlikely-sounding assistant, and I'm still not convinced you should, why not at least delay announcing him until—"

"Because it wouldn't make any difference, sir," said Gar. "A few days, a week, a month, even: in the end it would be the same. Regardless of how long I wait to announce Asher's appointment, Jarralt will still carp and cavil at the idea of an Olken elevated to such a high position. So I choose to announce it now. And in proceeding as I have, without your involvement, his censure will fall solely upon me."

"You think so?" said Borne with a smile that did not quite reach his troubled eyes. "You give him too much credit. He'll say your poor judgement and want of conduct reflect a shabby discipline and a sad lack of upbringing."

"He may indeed say that," said Durm, stirring in his chair. "But not with impunity."

Gar watched his father and his father's best friend exchange swift grins. Opposite him, his mother sniffed.

"At any rate," she said, "I'm sure I don't see what concern it is of Conroyd Jarralt's if Gar decides to appoint an assistant. If Con does complain, Borne, tell him to mind his own business and be done with it." Another sniff. "Besides, his real problem is that he's never forgiven you the fact your great-great-great-grandfather bested his in the Crown Trials after Trevoyle died."

"I think you'll find," Borne replied, "that his pique springs from a more . . . domestic source. If he is unforgiving, my dear, it's because I won the prize he so desperately desired for himself."

"I neither confirm nor deny your theory," she said, dimpling. "Instead I would point out that poor Conroyd carries a grudge like a dog with a very old, very smelly bone. Somebody needs to smack him on the nose and tell him to drop it, once and for all."

"By all means," said Borne, his face alight with love and laughter. "Provided it's not me expected to do the smacking."

Dana smiled back at him. "Oh no. I'll do it. Barl knows I smacked him often enough when he was courting me."

Borne pressed a kiss to her palm. "It delights me beyond words to hear it."

"By the Wall," moaned Fane, spirits revived, and

dropped her napkin over her face like a veil. "I'm going to be indelicately ill."

Laughter banished the last of the lingering tensions. The remains of the main course were cleared away, a careless word from Durm removed the wine stain from the tablecloth, and dessert was served. Pushing aside his berry compôte and cream scarcely touched, Borne tapped his fingernails on the table.

"If I may briefly and, I promise, sweetly, return to this matter of your new assistant, Gar . . ."

Gar nodded, masking his wariness with a smile. "Certainly, sir."

"I simply wonder why you'd choose an unsophisticated laborer to aid you in your duties when there must be dozens of polished, trustworthy Olken eager to serve you, and their people, in the position."

Gar hesitated. How to explain a feeling? A tickle in the brain that said, illogically, irrationally, that in Asher he'd found a man who could be trusted with any secret, any sorrow, any task no matter how trivial or tremendous.

He couldn't. At least not here, in front of Durm and Fane.

He said, obliquely, "Matt speaks very highly of him. He's courageous, hardworking and forthright, with a refreshing lack of obsequiousness." Leaning over the table towards his father, Gar willed him to understanding. "Sophistication, sir, is an overcoat that any man may put on, but it can't hide the flaws beneath. I'll take honest unrefinement over sophisticated flattery any day."

Dana laughed. "Gracious, Gar. This young man sounds a positive paragon!"

"Darran doesn't think so," said Gar, grinning. "Darran

is more appalled by him than Conroyd Jarralt could ever be, I promise you. Nor do I think he's a paragon, either. But I do believe Asher of Restharven will be invaluable to me as I seek to deepen my understanding of his people, so that I may serve them, and His Majesty, more diligently."

Fane sighed and rolled her eyes. "They're Olken, Gar. What more is there to understand?"

"That is an ignorant observation, madam," said Durm, his expression heavy with disapproval.

Fane turned to him, flushed and resentful. "That's not fair! You've no opinion of them either, you know you don't! 'A race with little to recommend them save their muscle and a degree of business acumen.' That's what you think, you said so not a week ago!"

Gar stared into the cooling remains of his berries and cream, unwanted now, for fear Durm should see the look on his face. It shamed and embarrassed him to hear his people disparage the Olken like that. How much worse did it sound, then, such sentiments coming from the kingdom's Master Magician? It set a bad example. He wished he could say as much to Durm, point out to him the unfortunate impression he was making . . . but of course, that was impossible.

Once, long ago, he and Durm had been master and pupil, and friends of a sort as well. But then had come the dawning realization that the king's precious heir was, incredibly, devoid of magic, scarcely better than an Olken, and their circumstantial friendship hadn't survived the ensuing frustrations and disappointments, the battles to wring from him even the smallest hint of magical ability. Bitter days.

Then the unthinkable happened. The WeatherWorker sired a second child. And with Fane barely walking and already showing promise of a talent unimaginable, he'd been discarded entirely. Left to the devices of mere scholars and bookmen. The pain of that abandonment had been shot through with a sobbing relief.

Now he and the Master Magician were courteous strangers whose paths crossed in Council, during official functions and at family dinners like this one. Because Durm was the king's best friend and closest confidant after the queen, they maintained a superficial cordiality . . . but it was a sham, and they both knew it. He could not forgive Durm's lack of understanding and compassion, and the Master Magician would not forgive his former pupil's failure.

Durm said now, his full face glowering, "It is true that I described the Olken thus in private, because it is my private opinion and I make no apology for it. But I have never said the like in public. Nor have I ever said, madam, publicly *or* privately, that the Olken were not to be understood. One day, Barl grant it be long hence, you will be this kingdom's WeatherWorker, charged with the sacred duty of keeping it safe. Therefore it is imperative that you comprehend the Olken's place in Barl's great design. Granted it is insignificant, but that is not the point. As WeatherWorker, every life in the kingdom will depend on you. *Every* life, Olken as well as Doranen."

Eyes brilliant with tears Fane said hotly, "I know all that! You tell me almost every day! All I meant was—"

Durm raised his plump hand, silencing her midsentence. "Your meaning was lamentably clear. You are not interested in the Olken, and therefore you dismiss them as unimportant. But if they were unimportant, Barl would have deemed them so and she did not. You and I may fail to understand her reasoning, but we must never question it. That is blasphemous ignorance, and an ignorant monarch is to be abhorred. You know as well as I that your father relies upon your brother's counsel and commitment in matters concerning the Olken. In due course, if you are wise, you will find yourself relying upon them too. Especially if you persist in this scandalous refusal to recognize what is important and what is not."

Choking back sobs, Fane shoved her chair away from the table and stumbled out of the dining room. As the door banged shut behind her Dana favored the Master Magician with a furious glare.

"Why not send for a stick to beat her with while you're about it, Durm? For certain she can't be properly chastized until she's bleeding on the outside as well as within!"

It was Durm's turn to flush. "Majesty—"

"Oh, never mind," she snapped. "I'd tell you to remember that for all her talent she's still a child, but I'd be wasting my breath."

Borne reached his hand out to her. "My love—"

She shook him free. "Yes, yes, you defend him, Borne, just as you always do. Are you as blind as he, then? Barl save us all! Why can't you see her as she is, here and now, instead of what she'll become one day? I'm not saying she was right. She was wrong, we all know that. *She* knows that. But there was no need to tear her down in such a fashion, not in public. Not in front of you."

Borne sighed. "Dana, my heart, you must accept the truth. Fane is fifteen years old and the days of her childhood are dwindling. There is little time left for indulgence and excuses."

Now the queen's eyes were bright with unshed tears. "But I don't accept it," she whispered harshly. "I shall never accept it. *Never*."

Borne's face twisted with a sudden grief and he reached for her again. His hand trembled. "Dearest—"

"No," she said. "I'm sorry. I must go to her." Pulling away from him a second time she followed her daughter from the room, waving the doors open and then closed behind her with an impatient hand.

"It is I who should apologize," Durm said into the stricken silence. "Perhaps I was too harsh. But Fane is so talented, so rare. When she says such ill-considered things I—"

"It's all right," said Borne wearily. "Fane has never been one to take a rebuke lightly, you know that. As for the queen, well . . ."

"Indeed," said Durm.

"You are dear to her, old friend, never doubt it," Borne insisted. "But she worries, and it makes her short of temper." With a barely stiffled grunt, he got to his feet. "So I think, if you'll excuse me . . ."

Durm shook his head and stood. "No, Borne. You and your son doubtless have more to discuss on this matter of his assistant, and any soothing of ruffled feathers is best done by the one who ruffled them."

Slowly, Borne sat down again. "If you're sure . . ."

Durm smiled. "I am always sure." He pressed a hand to his heart and bowed, favored Gar with a noncommittal nod and withdrew, closing the dining room door quietly after him.

"Well," said the king with a short laugh. "So much for our jolly family dinner."

"Mama has a point." Gar reached for the wine carafe so he could refill his goblet. "Fane is still young."

"There have been kings and queens of Lur younger than she." Borne massaged his temples, and between his closed eyes the skin was pinched with pain. "Weather Workers all. She needs to grow up."

"And so she will, in time," said Gar. "But youth isn't the only pebble in her shoe."

Borne's mouth set in a thin, mulish line. "You're wrong."

"Of all the reasons there are to admire you, sir, your loyalty is the greatest. But loyalty needn't be blind. Indeed it mustn't be, for blind loyalty is no kindness at all. It's a curse."

"I don't wish to hear this from you," said Borne. "Fane is your sister. She loves you."

Gar sighed. Fortified himself with a long swallow of wine. "My sister knows precisely why she was born, and what will be forever denied her, and given her, because of it. There are few things more wearing, Father, than an unwelcome obligation. Were Fane's feelings for me contained in a coin, and were you to flip that coin, there's no saying which side would land face up: love, or hate."

Borne's head jerked at that, and his eyes blazed. "That is a monstrous thing to say!"

Gar nodded. "I know. But it's true."

"You are *wrong*."

"Father—"

"She is young. Too young for the burdens placed upon

her shoulders, too young for the knowledge Durm burns into her morning, noon and night."

"But not so young she doesn't understand conversations overheard in corners, the scurrilous speculations repeated by those who should know better than to speak in the presence of a child." Gar tipped the rest of his wine down his throat.

"You babble like a brook," said Borne, his face turned away, his fingers knotted on the table. "You make no sense."

"You think I've not heard the rumors too? The stories? The gossip?" said Gar, knowing he failed to banish all bitterness and hating himself for it. "They say her talent is unnatural. They say she received the magic that should have come to me, as well as her own share. They say—"

" 'They' are fools, Gar! And Fane doesn't believe the ignorant ramblings of—"

"Yes, she does, Father," Gar said quietly. "You know she does. Even though she understands the tales are rumor, half-truths, distortions of fact. Deep inside she thinks she's a thief. The sight of me is a knife in her heart, pricking."

"*You are wrong.*"

Gar shook his head. "No. You simply wish I was."

Borne stood, his back turned, his head bowed. "It must stop, Gar. The bickering, the blame. It must *stop*."

"How? Will you tell her she can't feel? She was born to correct a mistake and for no other reason. Every waking moment of her life is dedicated to that end. If you forbid Fane her feelings, Father, what does she have left that belongs to her and her alone?"

Slowly Borne turned. "And if you were not as you are? If you had your birthright? Would you feel as she does?

Trapped and prisoned and born for a purpose not of your own choosing, but mine?"

Gar shrugged. "How can I know? I'm not the WeatherWorker-in-Waiting."

Borne seized the back of his chair, gripping it with a white-knuckled ferocity. "Do you wish you were?"

Gar flinched. Reluctantly he met his father's burning gaze. All his life a conspiracy of silence had shrouded this, his family's festering wound. The wound he had caused by being born incomplete. That had only partially been healed by Fane's birth and the discovery that she was a prodigy whose powers might one day rival those of Blessed Barl herself.

He said, very carefully, "You've never asked me that before."

His father nodded. "I'm asking you now. Do you wish you were my heir?"

Gar stared at the tablecloth. Did he wish it? Did he envy Fane the birthright that should have been his? Covet the power that danced at her fingertips and lit her eyes like lanterns? Did he want to one day be the kingdom's WeatherWorker, even though he knew better than almost anyone breathing what that meant? The sacrifices and the savagery?

Oh yes. A thousand times yes. He wanted it so badly the desire ate his belly like an acid, churned in him and welled unbidden from his eyes in the hollow privacy of the night.

He looked up and smiled at his father, seeing in the tired face a maelstrom of dread and hope. He shook his head. "No, sir, I don't. I'm content with the life Barl has seen fit to give me."

And because he'd had a lifetime of practice in conceal-
ment, or because the need to believe was so desperate, or
both, his father believed him.

Fractionally, Borne's whitened knuckles eased their
grip on the back of the chair, and some of the strain eased.
"I'm glad," he said, and sat down again. A small sigh escaped his pale lips. "And not because I fear the king you
would have made, Gar. In truth, I think you'd be a king
without peer, for reasons having nothing to do with
magic. Reasons that Fane must learn if she's to be the
queen this realm deserves and requires."

Another thing that had never before been said. It was
long moments before Gar could trust his voice again.
"Thank you, sir. I value your opinion above all others."

"You must help her see," his father said. "Durm can
teach her everything there is to know about magic and the
uses of power. Your mother can advise her on protocol
and the womanly arts. I can explain from sunup to sundown the intricacies and hidden traps of government . . .
but only you can help her see the richest crop in all our
kingdom. The Olken, Lur's original children. You possess
in abundance the one thing Fane lacks. The common
touch. The Olken love you."

"And you!" Gar said swiftly.

Borne smiled and shook his head. "After a fashion,
perhaps. Though I think it's more reverence than love.
The functions I perform on their behalf, rather than myself. But you? You they hold in genuine and heartfelt affection and I thank Barl for it. I wish Fane were held in
half as much respect."

"Give her time," said Gar. "Her life is circumscribed

by study. She has yet to come to know them as I have these past months."

"Perhaps," Borne agreed. "I hope it is that and nothing more. She'll be queen soon enough and then it will be too late . . ."

Gar felt his heart constrict. "Again you raise the spectre of a diminishing hourglass, sir." His voice sounded harsh, almost accusing. "What haven't I been told? I wish you'd confide in me. I'm no longer a child. Are you unwell?"

Startled, Borne lifted his head to look at him, then smiled. "Unwell? Why, no. No more than usual. Did I frighten you? I'm sorry. I didn't mean to."

"You look tired," said Gar, his voice low.

"I am, a little," Borne admitted. "It's summer, and nearly time for harvest. The magic is strong now. Difficult to contain. Less a matter of subtlety, and more of brute strength. Today's WeatherWorking has given me a headache, that's all. It's nothing. There's no need to fret on my behalf."

But Gar, staring at him, thought there was. He looked weary. Worn down. "I wish I could help you," he said, his throat tight and hurting.

"You help me every day," his father said firmly. "You do as much as any member of either Council. More. Sometimes I think you do too much. When was the last time you went out riding with friends, hmm? Frolicked on a picnic? Asked a pretty girl to dance?"

Discomfited, Gar shrugged. "I've been busy."

"Yes, I know!" Borne retorted. "It seems of late that every time I see you your nose is in a book or you're rushing off to yet another meeting somewhere. You're a young man, Gar, with a lifetime of meetings and books ahead of you. There's more to living than work, my son. You must make time for entertainment, for amusement." He smiled, an anxious upturn of lips. "For romance."

"Father . . ."

Borne slapped the table with the flat of his hand. "If you tell me once more you're determined to deny yourself a wife and children, I promise I'll become angry. Gar, you can't—"

"*Please*, Father!" Gar flung himself away to stand with his back turned, so he didn't have to see the look in his father's eyes. "I beg you, not again. The choice is mine and it's made. Please respect my right to make it, even if you don't agree with the decision."

"How can I agree with it?" Borne cried. "It's the wrong one!"

Gar turned around, made himself stare steadily into his father's face. "For you. Not for me."

Borne's imploring hands reached out across the dinner table towards him. "But Nix says—"

"That he can give no guarantees. A child of my body might well be fully functional . . . or it might not. I can't take the chance. I won't. Besides, there's still Fane. She'll give you grandchildren. She'll continue House Torvig's line."

Borne surged to his feet then, on a roar of anger. "Unfair! *Monstrous* unfair! Do you think I care only for the line?"

"If you didn't care," said Gar, distantly, "you never would've fought with the Privy Council for the right to conceive her. You and Durm would've chosen the next WeatherWorker from amongst the foremost Doranen in the kingdom. It's all right. I understand. It's why I've chosen this path." He held his father's gaze and added, gently, "You know I'm right, Father."

The king's eyes were bright with anguish. "I do not!"

Gar smiled. "Yes, you do. As things stand, I'm just . . . an unfortunate aberration. Inconvenient, but not threatening. Could you say the same if I were to have a child, and that child were . . . like me? That would no longer be considered an aberration. It'd be seen as a pattern and a shadow would fall over Fane. Before we knew it men like Conroyd Jarralt would be arguing that our line is tainted, that it's grown weak, that the crown would be safer on a different head. *His* head. Even though some would argue his line has a taint all its own. And so it would begin again: the nightmare of dynastic warfare, the struggle for the throne, and who knows where it would end? The last such war brought us to the brink of disaster and the Wall nearly to ruin. You didn't raise a son so selfish that he'd drag a whole kingdom to the edge of that abyss just to spare himself a little loneliness."

Silence, then, as Borne struggled . . . failed . . . to find an argument he could stand against his son's austere logic. "You've never told me any of this before. Never explained why . . ."

Gar bit his lip. "Talking about it doesn't change anything, it only—"

"Makes things harder," Borne whispered. "I'm sorry." He turned away then, pressing his sleeve to his face.

"Don't be," said Gar, his voice a hair's-breadth from breaking. "It's not your fault. It's not anybody's fault. It's just the way things are."

"Is there something I can do? Tell me what I can do."

"You can accept my decision. And promise me you'll never question it again."

Silence. Gar waited, holding his breath.

At last his father nodded, his back still turned, his shoulders bowed.

Gar released the air from his aching lungs. "Thank you."

His father straightened and turned around. In his face nothing but determined good humor, all lingering traces of pain vanished. Banished. As though their last exchange had happened months ago. Or not at all. He sat.

"So. You're set on having this fisherman fellow as your assistant, are you?"

Weak with relief, Gar eased himself back into his own chair. "I took him with me to Justice Hall yesterday. For—an unsophisticated laborer, was it?—he demonstrated a remarkably keen grasp of legal niceties and a fine sense of right and wrong. Not to mention he saw through my motives for taking him there as though they were glass. Asher will grow into the task, Father, and not let me down. I'm sure of it. What's more, I think you'll like him too. Though he's rough around the edges, still there's a quality to him I know you'll recognize, and approve."

His father was frowning. "Justice Hall," he murmured. "A bad business, that. We were lucky to catch the rot before it spread any further. You did good work yesterday, my son. I'm proud."

"Thank you," said Gar, and let his warm pleasure show.

Pleased by that, smiling again, his father summoned the carafe closer with a snap of his fingers and refilled their goblets. "So. When do I get to meet this roughly likeable Asher, that I may judge his virtues for myself?"

Gar grinned. It only felt a little forced. "Actually I thought I'd bring him to the next Privy Council meeting."

His father snorted. "*After* he's been publicly announced as your assistant, you mean? In other words, you're putting off dealing with Jarralt's inevitable tantrum for as long as possible."

"You don't approve of the tactic?"

"On the contrary," Borne replied. "If you hadn't suggested it, I would've." He took another mouthful of wine and rolled it savoringly over his tongue before swallowing. "You do realize you're throwing your assistant into the deep end?"

"Well," said Gar, shrugging, "he is a fisherman, Father. I'm sure he knows how to swim."

"Is that so?" Borne lifted his goblet in salute, and warning. "Let us hope you're right, my son . . . for his sake, and the sake of us all."

CHAPTER EIGHT

With a sigh of satisfied weariness Dathne closed her accounts book and put down her pen. Record-keeping was a tiresome chore but it had to be done. And there were times, especially after a brisk day's trading, when she almost found it pleasant. Although the bookshop was little more than an excuse for her presence in the City, she did enjoy running it, was relieved she had a knack for business. Closure of the bookshop would lead to awkward disruptions and, worse, would interfere with her breezy access to both Tower and palace—access that was vital now that Asher had arrived to usher in the Final Days.

The Final Days. It was at once a terrible and irritating phrase, raising questions without answers, fears without remedy. For one thing, how many of them were there? A month's worth? A summer's? A whole year? Was Lur living them now or were they not due to arrive until this time next year, perhaps? Could it be that Asher's arrival in Dorana was merely . . . Prophecy clearing its throat?

She had absolutely no idea. Prophecy didn't say.

In the Final Days shall come the Innocent Mage,
born to save the world from blood and death.
He shall enter the House of the Usurper
He shall learn their ways
He shall earn their love
He shall lay down his life
And Jervale's Heir shall know him, and guide him,
and enlighten him not.

That was it. That was all she had to help her, enlighten her, those few lines she'd been gifted with on her first day as Jervale's Heir.

Obscure didn't begin to describe it. What a shame her revered ancestor hadn't left a calendar complete with helpful hints and important dates marked in red to go with his damned foretelling.

Every night since Asher had at long last tumbled out of her dreams and into her life she'd gone to bed with the same prayer on her lips, in her heart: Jervale, send me another sign. Guide my steps. Show me what to do next.

But Jervale remained stubbornly silent.

A whisper from the shadows of her mind said: What if your prayers go unanswered because Jervale is as blind as you? What if he knows nothing beyond the verse he scribbled down all those centuries ago, when the Olken and the Doranen made their fateful pact? Or . . . what if he can't even hear you?

Shuddering, Dathne shoved her accounts book into the till and slammed shut the drawer. *No.* She wouldn't believe that. *Couldn't* believe that. Couldn't even let herself wonder. The kingdom of Lur depended on her remaining cool and controled and confident.

There was no place in her life for doubt.

With the last of the day's shopkeeping duties seen to, habit sent her back to the front door, to double-check the locks. Not that theft was likely. The penalties were severe and the City Guard vigilant, but when young men drank an ale or three too many, as they were sadly wont to do, what might seem inadvisable in the sober light of day often became a rattling good idea in the tipsy rollick of the night.

Approaching the front window display of Vev Gertsik's latest romance she felt the tingle of magic, a breath of invisible power, breeze over her exposed skin. She frowned, shivering. It was the only drawback to her chosen, necessary profession: the constant whispering hum of Doranen books.

The Doranen disdained the use of ink and roller, the painstaking assemblage of type by industrious, unmagical fingers. Not for them the sweat of laborious effort, the rattling, banging cheer of the typesetting workshop where Olken men and women used nimble skill to transform manuscripts into books that wore the badge of their imperfect creation proudly, like a flag.

No. Doranen books were sleek and polished and perfect. No misaligned letters, no smudging, no bleeding of color on cover or frontispiece. Doranen books were birthed by spells and charms woven in a seamless song to call forth smooth pages and immaculate bindings. They attained a symmetry that the Olken Bookmakers' Guild could admire but never match.

As she checked the locked front door Dathne eyed askance the Gertsik book's cover with its languishing blonde heroine and stalwart blond hero locked in an unlikely embrace. The author's romances flew off the shelves almost as fast as they were unpacked. Gertsik was the darling of the Doranen, and a good many Olken readers as well. But Dathne couldn't bring herself to read them or approve of those Olken who did. Even though it wasn't their fault they were ignorant of all the other stories that could be, should be, told. Their own stories. Olken stories.

Vev Gertsik wrote soppy tales of Doranen love set in their Old Days, centuries dead and gone now and thus ripe for romanticizing. The Old Days, when Doranen magic was limitless, when Barl and her lover Morgan had kissed, not killed, and war was as unthinkable as exile.

The Old Days, before civil strife and the desperate pitting of mage against mage had riven the long-lost land of Dorana with bloody lightning and given birth to a monster for whom no repression was too harsh, no punishment too cruel, no dark magic unimaginable. The Old Days, which had seen Barl and the other survivors of that terrible conflict stumble from their ruined cities in search of peace and freedom and a land where the monster Morg could not find them.

Before the coming of the Doranen the Olken had called Lur their own. They'd lived in thriving rural communities bound together by a dedication to the rhythms of life in all its tempestuous beauty and stark danger. The Olken of those long-dead days had lived small lives, true, but that didn't mean they were without value. On the contrary, those Olken lives had been priceless because they were theirs and wholly theirs. Untouched by foreign hands. Uncorrupted by an alien magic.

But there were no books written about the Old Days of the Olken. There couldn't be. Almost no one alive in these modern times knew that once, before the coming of the fair-haired Doranen with their brash and brutal magic, the Olken had possessed power of their own. A soft and singing earth magic that bound them to the land and to each other without the need for mastery or control.

The only Olken who still recalled that magic, the way things used to be, belonged to the Circle. Sworn to secrecy and the scant words of a prophecy they didn't understand but were willing to die for, they remembered. In silence and sad dreams they kept the buried truth alive.

The loss of her people's heritage wrung Dathne's heart, though it had happened centuries ago. She would *never* accept that what they'd lost—no, what they'd given away, surrendered, sold—was worthless, no matter how glittering the gift in exchange. How safe and secure the life that had replaced it. And she'd sworn a fierce vow that one day every last Olken man, woman and child would learn their true heritage, reclaim their power, and that the bookshops of Lur would abound with stories of *their* Old Days.

If, after the Final Days were ended, there were still bookshops. If there was still a Lur.

Impatient, Dathne turned away from the locked front door and the book display, tugging at her haphazardly braided hair. That was enough maudlin sentimentality for one day. She had dinner to prepare yet, and after that orders to wrap ready for the morning's mail coach. With a swish of her skirts she headed out to the back of the shop and the staircase that led up to her small apartment.

The vision smote her halfway to the apartment door. Tripped her and sprawled her face down against the wooden stairs. She tried to rise. Failed, limbs leaden. She felt a tightness in her chest, heard a moan die in her throat.

Her head moved restlessly against the scuffed timber, scraping her cheek. Her clutching fingers found splinters.

With her eyes shut tight and her mind a soundless scream of protest, she saw the future she'd been born to kill.

Hailstones of fire raining down from a sky the color of clotted blood. Strong proud trees split asunder by spears of lightning. The River Gant rising, rising. Funnels of green cloud reaching thin, cruel fingers to pluck whole houses from the earth and fling them stone by stone by human bone into the howling winds. The Wall, pulsing, writhing, great holes like some gross leprous disease turning it to tatters. Broken bleeding bodies flung heedless into piles, into holes. Discarded. Disdained. And pressing down upon her an enormous smothering weight, crushing the air from her lungs and strangling the pulse in her veins. Within it a baleful intelligence: malevolent, insatiable and infinitely patient, squatting like a toad. Watching. Waiting.

Gasping for air, Dathne wrenched herself free. The effort sent her sliding backwards down the stairs till she came to a bruised and spread-eagled stop on the floor of the bookshop's workroom. Head and heart pounding, she stared at the worn blue carpet inches from her eyes and struggled to breathe, to forget, to remember. She felt befouled, her skin and soul smeared with the unspeakable detritus of evil.

When at last her heartbeat and breathing slowed she sat up, pushing sweaty strands of hair out of her eyes.

"Well," she said aloud, needing to hear her voice, any voice. Even a thin and frightened one. "They do say be careful what you wish for . . ." Breathy laughter shook her. Threatened to collapse into sobs. She pressed the back of her hand against her mouth, hard.

She'd always known the end would be terrible. For years she'd glimpsed snatches of it. Received scanty images bad enough to wake her sweating in the middle of the night. The knowledge of their possible future, the ultimate culmination of the Final Days, had dogged her like a shadow, visible only from the corner of her eye. But now she knew precisely the taste and sound and smell of what she and the others fought to prevent. Knew exactly *how* terrible, to the last drop of blood and the final, fading cry, Lur's death would be. The fear of that fate was merciless: a serpent coiled in her belly, waiting to strike.

Cold, Matt called her.

He didn't understand, and she could never explain it to him. There was only one way to defeat the serpent. Sheathe herself in ice. Freeze the tears that threatened when she thought of what would happen if she failed in her duty as Jervale's Heir.

Freeze her heart.

Panting, she closed her eyes. A mistake. Images of death and destruction flared. Her stomach churned. Sour saliva flooded her mouth. Lurching to her feet she scrambled upstairs to her tiny privy and emptied her spasming belly of the stewed rabbit and poached greens she'd eaten for lunch. Bile burned her throat, searing tears from her eyes. When at last she was empty she pressed her face into a damp towel. Swilled water round her mouth and spat it out.

Veira must know of this. She must be told that what they faced, what they and Asher must fight, was an intelligence. A person . . . or something pretending to be a person. It was unclear, and too terrible to dwell upon, at least so soon after enduring its fetid touch. Nevertheless, Veira must know.

Somewhere beyond the fragile safety of Barl's great Wall something . . . some*one* . . . was waiting. Not that Veira could do anything about it, of course, but it would be better if somebody else knew.

Less lonely.

Because she still felt unnerved and desolate she drank two full glasses of strong green wine, one straight after the other. Then, with warm lamplight dancing shadows on the walls of her small living room, she knelt by the fireplace and rummaged in the blanket box her mother had given her as a leaving-home gift. Buried at the bottom, beneath papers and letters and shawls with holes in she'd get around to mending one of these days, and frayed cushions she didn't want to throw out, was her precious Circle Stone. Gently withdrawing the blanket-shrouded treasure she unwrapped it, put it on the low wooden table by the window and sank cross-legged to the floor.

To anyone unknowing it was just a lump of rough quartz crystal, cracked and crazed and more dull than shiny, but to her it was priceless, her link to Veira and, through her, the rest of their Circle: a conduit to comfort and sanity when the weight of being Jervale's Heir grew too great for bearing. Her crystal and Veira's were twins, halves of a whole, forever joined no matter how vast the distances between them.

Using the Stone was at once simple and challenging. She was Olken. Her secret magic was a subtle thing, a matter of insinuation and gentle cajolery, soft as a whisper amidst the drowning shouts of brash and bossy Doranen incantation. Finding a quiet place in the chatter and noise of their magic was never easy: down the centuries its raucous echoes had soaked the City right down to the cobblestones. If she went deaf tomorrow she'd still feel its thrum against her skin and hear the racket of a thousand thousand charms ringing inside her skull.

The only good thing about the Doranen's loud magic was that it made detecting her a virtual impossibility. Somebody would have to be looking, and even then it was unlikely they'd hear her hushed voice in all the din.

Despite the evening's warmth, she shivered. "Don't be a fool, Dathne," she said aloud. "How can anybody be looking? No Doranen alive or dead knows you exist."

Which was just as well, given the consequences of discovery.

Closing her eyes, letting the lingering tension drain out of her neck and shoulders like rain sieving through sand, Dathne conjured Veira's face before her inner eye. Round and wrinkled like an aging apple. Framed in a tangle of salt-streaked hair. Long bony nose. Dimpled chin. Eyes the color of moss, which shimmered and shifted with her mercurial moods, now snapping with temper, now softened with sympathy.

Her fingers caressed the crystal, seeking the subtle vibrations that would lead her to the inner road, the pathway her thoughts would travel across the unknown miles that lay between her and Veira. The old woman's whereabouts were a secret . . . just in case.

Perfect peace. Perfect harmony. Breathe in. Breathe out. Thoughts like thistledown, floating on a breeze. *Veira* . . .

And Veira was with her. In the crystal, in her heart and mind, a warm, quizzical presence that never failed to calm and encourage. Or scold, if it seemed that scolding was called for.

It's been three days, child. I was beginning to worry.

Dathne felt her lips move, framing each word as it winged its way along the invisible connection joining her crystal to Veira's. "I'm sorry. I didn't mean to concern you, I—" She stopped. Was shamed by a sudden rush of emotion at the sound and touch of the old woman's voice.

Child, is aught amiss? There's an echo of something wicked and wild in you tonight. What's happened?

Haltingly, Dathne told her. Reliving the vision broke sweat upon her brow and clenched her fingers around the crystal. "I've never been given images like that before, Veira. I've been praying to Jervale, asking him for guidance, but I never thought . . ."

You have no doubts? It was the Final Days you were given?

"What else could it be?" She shivered. "Veira . . . it was terrifying. How can I hope to prevail against such evil?"

Prevailing isn't what you're here for. That's the Innocent Mage's destiny, child. Yours is to see him safe to the moment when the battle is joined.

"And how will *he* prevail? The mind I sensed, Veira, it was terrible! An evil beyond speaking! Asher's untried, untested, completely unprepared!"

Then we must prepare him, child, to the best of our abilities. Stop fretting, it does no good. The cup is pressed to our lips now. All we can do is sip and swallow.

"And if that's poison in the cup? What then?"

Then, child, we die.

"Veira!"

Hush. I can hear your bones rattling from here. If there was no hope of victory we would not know what we know, or have been given the tasks that bend our backs and break our hearts. You are Jervale's Heir, child. It is your duty to resist despair. Tell me of Asher. What news?

Reprimanded and comforted both at once, Dathne wrenched her mind away from the vision and thought instead of Asher. "It was announced in chapel yesterday. His Highness is officially named Olken Administrator and Asher is appointed his assistant. Although apparently it pleases the prince to tease him with the title of Champion."

And does it please Asher as well?

Dathne felt herself smile. "From the look on his face when he told me, no, I don't think it does. A gaggle of royal heralds rode out this morning to spread word of the appointments to the rest of the kingdom. Asher's about to become the most famous Olken in Lur . . . and I don't think that much pleases him either."

The link hummed with Veira's fat satisfaction. *But it does please me. So. He is taken into the Usurper's House. Prophecy continues.*

"Veira . . . I don't know what to do next. How to proceed."

You must do nothing.

She felt impatient anxiety ripple through her. "I can't do nothing."

Then wait. Waiting is not nothing. Waiting is what the Circle has done for six hundred years. Waiting has brought us safely to the here and now. It will serve.

"But I'm not the only one waiting! And I can't see what

comes next. There must be a way forward from here, I just can't see what it is, or how I should arrange matters."

What makes you think you are the one to arrange matters?

"Of course I am! The vision—"

An irritated snort. *The vision is but part of the mosaic, child. It is important, I grant you. But so is Asher important, and the prince, and any number of puzzle pieces yet to be revealed. You must not let yourself be intimidated by dreams. They are sent to guide and inform you, not render you helpless with fear. Forewarned is forearmed goes the saying, and so, now we are forearmed. We know now something of the taste and texture of that which will oppose us, and this is all to the good. Be content with that, child. Doom rushes towards us fast enough without we raise the dust in hurrying to greet it halfway.*

Dathne felt her ribs expand and contract in a sigh. "I know."

Now tell me, what of our good friend Matthias?

The thought of Matt made her frown. "He holds. Just."

You sound uncertain.

She shook her head, even though Veira couldn't see the gesture. "No. Not of him. Not exactly."

Then what, exactly?

"He refuses to abandon this unwise friendship with Asher. I've told him it's madness but he won't listen. He's going to be hurt, I know it, but nothing I say will sway him. I tell you, Veira, I'm sorely tempted to take his hammer and hit him over the head with it until he sees sense!"

Are friends like pebbles on the road, child, so numerous they can be kicked aside uncaring?

Dathne let her own tone sharpen to match Veira's.

"The butcher who befriends the lamb is a fool, and worse than a fool, for might not a family starve if for love he can't use his knife at the appointed hour?"

True. But consider this . . . what if we talk not of butchers, but shepherds?

"The shepherd delivers his lambs to market, knowing it's the butcher's money he'll put in his purse when they're sold. In the end, it's the same."

Veira sighed like a ghost, frost in the invisible air. *Be not harsh with good Matthias, child. Can you say for certain he is wrong in this? I know I cannot. You are not the gatekeeper of wisdom nor the sole one among us with a purpose. Until the song is sung and the musicians have all gone home, not even you can tell which notes made the melody.*

Rebuked again. Not harshly, but even so. Stinging, Dathne felt her head bow. "You are wise, Veira."

A whispering chuckle. *I am old. Sometimes it amounts to the same thing. Will you tell Matthias of this new vision?*

Dathne hesitated. She'd seen Matt weep for a dead baby sparrow dropped out of its nest. His heart was too soft: try as he might, he couldn't freeze it.

"No. There's no need. It's enough that I've told you. And besides, he won't have any more idea than I do right now how we're supposed to stop it from happening." Fear chilled her all over again. "Veira—"

Child, do not fret. We have trusted Prophecy so far, and so far it has not led us astray. I think we can—Wait, the Basingdown crystal calls me. Do you stay indoors tonight?

Dathne felt her heart leap; in Veira's thoughts, a

discordant chiming of alarm. "Basingdown? You said that problem was behind us . . ."

Perhaps I spoke too soon. Stay within reach of your Stone, child. I will call you when I can.

Before she could reply, the connection was broken. The severance was so abrupt, the echo of Veira's alarm so jangling, that behind her eyes pain bloomed like blood in water.

Dizzied, adrift, she bumped from wall to wall like a bird encaged, unable to settle, nerves thrumming. She didn't know the exact nature of the Basingdown trouble any more than she knew the name of the Circle members who lived there. Only Veira knew each individual of the group. It was safer that way.

But something terrible had happened, she knew that much: every instinct she possessed was shrieking and her stomach clenched and unclenched like a fist.

Just when she thought she must go mad with waiting her crystal flared, and from its heart pulsed a soft white light. Deep in her mind, the insistent tug of Veira's thoughts to her own. Dathne flung herself to the living room carpet and feverishly sought the connection. Three heartbeats and she had it, hot and humming with alarm.

"What is it? What's happened?"

Calamity and woe, child. One of our number is revealed.

If she hadn't already been on the floor she would have fallen. Struggling for air she pressed her palm against her chest. "Revealed? How? Veira, what *happened*?"

The link between them vibrated wildly with the old woman's distress. *Four months ago Edv—*

Shocked, Dathne interrupted. "No *names*, Veira!"

Peace, child. It matters little now.

Dathne smothered her rising fear. Never in all their long years of friendship had she heard Veira sound so defeated. So heartsick, or afraid. "Sorry. Go on."

Edvord of Basingdown judged the time was ripe to bring his son Timon into the Circle. Edvord has a canker. He is dying. He was afraid to leave it any longer lest his failing wits desert him before what is needful could be completed. Timon is talented, but proud and impatient. Edvord told him he must wait, be guided, and so did I, but wise words fell on deaf ears. An hour ago Edvord's son was taken by the Town Magisters for the illegal practicings of magic.

Dathne knuckled a moan back behind her teeth. "He was seen?"

Yes.

"In Jervale's name, what was he *thinking*? Veira, we're undone!"

Veira rallied; through the link, Dathne could feel what it cost her. *Perhaps not. He was caught attempting Doranen magic.*

"*Doranen* magic? *Why*? Wasn't he told—"

Of course he was told, child! Did I not say Timon is proud and impatient? He refused to believe it is a song we cannot sing. He thought to prove his father wrong and be a hero.

Dathne swallowed a fresh rush of bile. Shut her eyes tight and willed her hands to stop shaking. "At least there's something to be thankful for. If he'd been caught casting Olken spells it would mean the end of everything."

Yes.

She smashed a fist against the floor. "Barl's *tits*!"

Edvord swears his son will die silent.

"Edvord is hardly unbiased." Another rush of bile. "This Timon must be dealt with, Veira. If he should attempt to save himself by betraying us . . ."

He hasn't yet. Besides, he is beyond our reach now. The magisters are taking him to the City as we speak. They'll be there by sundown tomorrow. A rider has gone on ahead, to alert the king.

"And the prince. As Olken Administrator he'll be up to his pretty green eyes in all of this. Which means that Asher will be too."

Through the link, Veira's mind echoed with sorrow and dread. *Once news of this disaster spreads, the people of Lur will bay for Timon's blood like hounds in the hunting field. He has broken cardinal law. It will mean an execution. How will that affect Asher, child? He is destined for magic.*

Dathne chewed her lip. "I . . . don't know."

You must find out, then. And you must repair any damage caused by Timon of Basingdown. Should the Innocent Mage refuse his destiny we are all of us doomed.

Dathne felt suffocated. *Hailstones of fire . . .* "What if I can't repair it? What if Asher himself leads the baying pack?"

You are Jervale's Heir. You must.

Just like that. The old woman made it sound as easy as sewing a new button on a shirt. It wasn't . . . but she had no choice. "I will. But Veira, there's a more immediate danger to consider. You know what will happen now."

Yes, child. I know.

The last breaking of cardinal law had been over a century before. Trial and execution a matter of one day's ex-

amination and five minutes with the royal headsman . . .
but the seeds of suspicion and mistrust sown that day had
taken root to flower and poison the air with an ill-
smelling perfume equal parts fear, anger and blame. The
aftertaste had lingered for months, years, the lifetimes of
those who had seen the head fall.

A repeat of those unfortunate days was the very last
thing they needed. Doranen eyes, woken from trusting
sleep, would be newly sharpened by this violation of cardinal law, would look twice and more than twice at every
harmless Olken gesture, every blameless Olken gathering, every thoughtless Olken laugh. Even on a good day
the Doranen were apt to be jealous of their magics . . .
and the days ahead promised to be anything but good.

Worse still, the Olken of Lur would be twice as vigilant, twice as suspicious as the Doranen. Eager to prove
their devotion to Barl, to the Law, to their own preservation, they'd report the smallest doubt to show the world
they could be trusted.

And in their midst the secret Circle . . . and Asher, the
Innocent Mage.

Damn this wretched Timon of Basingdown and damn
his dying father, too, for putting them all in danger, for
risking the Circle and everyone in it and all that it meant
for the future of Lur. What fools they were, like father
like son, and did this now mean the end of all the Circle's
hopes and plans and painstaking sacrifices?

The end of Lur?

Reading her mind, perhaps, Veira spoke. *There is yet
hope. Hopeless though things appear. This is not the first
storm the Circle has weathered. And I have known*

Edvord longer than you've been alive, child. If he says his son will hold true to his oath I believe him.

"Well, you know him, Veira. And you know I trust your judgement," Dathne replied. "But if this fool does look like talking out of turn then I'm well placed to hear so. Asher is in the habit now of confiding most things to me. I swear I'll pluck Timon's wagging tongue from between his teeth before he can do us damage."

Vengeance will not serve us, child.

Dathne took a deep, rib-creaking breath. Let it hiss out again between her clenched teeth. "Our survival, Lur's survival, rests on the nerve of an idiot whose arrogant recklessness has brought us to the brink of disaster. We hang by a thread, Veira. At all costs, the damage must be contained. Vengeance has nothing to do with it."

Perhaps not. But anger does. Do not let it lead you astray.

"Are you saying I have no right to be angry?"

Of course not. Nor should you think yourself alone in your fury.

Which was true. Through the link, beneath the muffling pain for an old friend's agony, she could feel Veira's rage. Though frightening it also gave her a strange measure of comfort. Allowed her to step away from her own feelings and focus on what was most important.

"We can't allow this to distract us from our purpose, Veira. No matter the public outcry, the increased scrutiny, the fear and doubt this will rouse in the rest of the Circle . . . we must hold firm. Tonight's vision was sent to me for a reason. It's a warning, a harbinger of the evil yet to come. We ignore it at our peril and the ruin of every man, woman and child in this kingdom. *Nothing* can be allowed to sway us from the path upon which we toil, or failure and death are certain."

You speak wisely, as befits the Heir of Jervale.

Dathne didn't know if that made her feel better or worse. All she knew for certain was she could easily fold flat to the floor, crushed by the increased weight of her responsibilities. "As soon as I know anything, Veira, I'll contact you so you can keep the Circle calm and focused. That must be our priority if we're to survive the coming days."

Indeed, child. I shall await your sending.

The connection between them broke. Exhausted, Dathne wrapped her Circle Stone once more and replaced it at the bottom of the blanket box. Though her empty belly was growling she had no heart for food. All she wanted now was sleep. Her mind and body cried out for it. Even Matt would have to wait; she'd tell him about Timon and his mad foolishness in the morning. There was nothing he could do about it tonight. Nothing he could do at all, so why worry him?

Stripping herself naked in her tiny bedroom, letting her skirt and blouse and stockings and underthings fall where they liked, she crawled between cool cotton sheets and closed her eyes. Her last conscious thought was a prayer:

Please, Jervale. Let me not dream.

CHAPTER NINE

Asher stood in his underclothes and stockinged feet in front of his open wardrobe door, filled to the gills with the fine breakfast he'd shared with Gar in the Tower solar. Washed and shaved and smelling faintly of spice, he stared at the clothes dangling from their hangers. What to wear, what to wear? Not the blue shirt or the black britches, since he'd worn them yesterday. The green was good, a sea color, reminding him of home. But on the other hand the bronze was a fine strong shade for a man. And it would go well with the chocolate-brown britches, snug and soft and cut to fit him like a second skin.

He'd never given much thought to clothes before, except as useful coverings for bare skin. Never considered himself much above average-looking. But now, buttoned up in his whispery silk shirt and his lined wool britches, stamping into shiny black boots that came right up to his knees, he thought he looked mighty fine. In fact, once he'd finished tugging his forelock to all the fancy lords in the Privy Council Chamber he just might wander down to town and see if there was some kind of book or other he could bring hisself to buy from Madam Hoity Toity the bookseller. Not that he wanted to spend any of his precious trins on books . . . but what other reason was there to go into Dathne's bookshop?

A pity none of the weskits was ready yet. A fine brocade weskit would finish him off just perfect.

Downstairs, waiting for Gar in the Tower's ground floor foyer, Asher winked at a scurrying chambermaid, what was her name again? Cluny? A blush tinted her cheeks, and he grinned. Oh yes indeed. *Mighty* fine.

"And what do you think you're doing, loitering about the place like a reprobate?' a snippy voice demanded.

He turned. Darran, all sour lemons and spite, coming down the Tower's spiral staircase. Experimenting, Asher discarded his first, instinctive response and smiled instead. "Mornin'," he said expansively. "As it happens, I be waitin' for Gar. We're off to see the Privy Council any tick."

Darran crossed the foyer's gleaming tiled floor silently, like a cat who's lost its collar and bell. "You are attending a Privy Council meeting?"

"Seems so," said Asher with exaggerated cheer. In truth he felt as incredulous as Darran sounded, but he'd not be admitting that any time soon. Off to the Privy Council to hobnob with the king . . . could his strange life get any stranger?

Darran sniffed. "I see." From the way his Adam's apple bobbed furiously in his scrawny throat it looked like Gar's secretary wanted to say a lot more than that, and none of it complimentary. After a short, silent struggle the ole crow nodded. "Well. I'm sure you'll find the experience educational. Have you ordered the carriage?"

"Carriage?" echoed Asher. "To go from here to the palace? Why would we be wantin' a carriage? Our legs ain't broke. We'll walk."

Darran's lips curved in a thin smile. "Oh dear. You do have a lot to learn, don't you? His Highness does not *walk* to official duties. He travels in a manner commensurate with his position." Crossing to a marble-topped display table he picked up a small shiny hand-bell and tinkled it sharply. "If you can't arrange even this small matter without supervision, I don't imagine you'll be remaining as His Highness's assistant anything for long. Observe."

Seething, Asher watched as a young boy dressed in black and green livery darted out of an adjacent room, skidded to a halt before Darran and bowed. "Sir?" he piped.

"His Highness shall be leaving the premises shortly. Kindly repair to the stables and—"

"No, don't bother," Gar called out as he descended the staircase. "Off you go, Remy. I won't be needing a carriage this morning."

The lad Remy bowed again and scuttled back into his messenger-boy bolthole. Scandalized, Darran turned to the prince, offered a punctiliously correct bow of his own and protested. "No carriage? But, Your Highness—"

Gar had changed from his casual breakfast attire of shirt, loose trousers and bare feet into a gold-beaded tunic of stiffened dark green brocade, dull black silk britches and black leather half-boots. His hair was caught back from his face in some kind of gold and green enamel clasp, and a gold and emerald circlet bound his brow. To

Asher's eyes he had the air of a man preparing to ride into battle. That wasn't a good sign . . .

Smiling, the prince touched one hand lightly to Darran's shoulder. "It's a fine morning for a walk. Besides, after the copious amount of bacon Asher ate for breakfast he needs the exercise."

Ha. Very funny. But then so was the look on ole Darran's face.

"I see, sir," Darran said limply. "You know your own mind, of course. Shall I send a carriage to fetch you then, once your business at the palace is concluded?"

"Let's see, shall we? If I want one I'll let you know."

Darran bowed. "Certainly, sir. You can send Asher with a message."

Asher held his tongue, just. Gar sent him a sidelong glance, brimful of repressed hilarity. "I might just do that, Darran. Now don't let me keep you from your business."

In other words, buzz off, busy little bee. Busybody. Still experimenting, Asher sent the secretary on his way with a wide, wide smile, and was rewarded with a venomous flash of temper, swiftly smothered.

"Y'know, he really don't like me at all," he said happily. "But I don't mind. I don't like him neither. Starin' down his snooty nose at me just 'cause I ain't all flash and folderol."

Gar sighed. "Don't be difficult. I've told you, he does me valuable service."

"Ha," said Asher.

Now Gar was looking him up and down. "You seem presentable at any rate. Now come on. We can't afford to be late."

Instead of taking the road to the sprawling splendor of

the palace, Gar chose a grassy pathway winding through carelessly scattered gardens and past older, abandoned apartments and residences that once had been home to other kings and queens of Lur. Long dead now, they were all laid to rest in tombs on the far side of the palace grounds.

Asher stared at the forlornly empty buildings and shook his head. "Seems like a bloody great waste to me. Perfectly good rooms and whatnots, ain't they? Why don't folk live in 'em any more?"

"I don't know," said Gar, shrugging. "Too many ghosts, perhaps. All those memories, pressing down. Sometimes people just want a fresh start . . . and who can blame them?"

Aye. Maybe. And speaking of which . . . "Thanks for not havin' me mentioned in the dispatches to the coast," he said as they left the old palace behind. "Reckon I'm grateful for that."

Gar's sideways glance was curious. "That's all right. I still think you're mad, but . . ."

"You wouldn't if y'had my brothers," Asher said flatly. "This news'll keep just fine till I'm home again."

"Yes. Well. As I said before, it's your decision." Gar waved a dismissive hand. "Now, about this Privy Council meeting . . . there's no need to be nervous." Another sideways look. "*Are* you nervous?"

Asher flicked a fly away from his ear. "Well . . ."

"Don't be. They won't bite. At least not while I'm there." Gar pulled a face. "Or not very hard anyway."

"And that's s'posed to make me not nervous, is it?"

Gar grinned. "Of course."

"Ha!"

"Besides, this is really just a formality. As my assistant you'll have more to do with the General Council, which takes care of the day-to-day business of running the kingdom. Guild issues, common legal matters, that sort of thing. Privy Council meetings are more . . . rarefied. You won't often be required to attend."

Asher hid his relief. Last thing he wanted to do was front up to the king and his personal advisers on a regular basis. "Suits me."

"I know the privy councilors are the most powerful men in the kingdom, but they're still men. Not ogres. That being said, however . . ."

"Oh aye?" sighed Asher. "Here we go. What?"

Gar was frowning. "His Majesty has many virtues but they don't include a wink and a shrug at inappropriate informality. No matter what happens this morning, remember that you are addressing the king or one of his chosen confidants. You may not . . ." He hesitated, searching for the right words. "Our interactions, Asher, are characterised by a degree of familiarity that would never be tolerated by His Majesty. Whatever you do, don't make the mistake of confusing us."

Like there were much chance of *that* happening. Asher rolled his eyes. "Don't worry, I won't." Then, as they took a short cut through yet another arrangement of perfumed flowerbeds, he added, "You sorry you hired me now, are you?"

"Don't be ridiculous," Gar said, flushing. "I just want your introduction to the Privy Council to proceed smoothly. You must realize that whatever I do reflects upon the king. And whatever you do reflects upon me."

That was fair enough. But . . . "If that's true, then how

come you don't care if I speak my mind around the Tower and everywhere else? Folks ain't deaf, Gar. They'll hear what I think, and they'll hear I ain't one for mincing my words. And they'll flap their lips about it too."

"That's entirely different. All my people know I encourage—insist upon, in fact—open, honest and vigorous debate. But the Privy Council is different. Privy Council meetings are . . . political. Even when they're not. Every word, every gesture, can be interpreted in a variety of ways, and some people will always interpret things in the harshest light possible."

Asher considered that. "You sayin' it ain't just you that's got enemies?"

This time Gar's glance was chilly with warning. "No. His Majesty is beloved by all his subjects."

"Come on, Gar," said Asher, gently derisive. "Y'reckon the Doranen are the only folk with a taste for playin' politics? My da used to represent Restharven in the Coastal Alliance. I'd lay odds on the Westwailing Fishermen's Board agin your precious Privy Council any day of the week. So, who's the rotten fish in the barrel?"

That made Gar smile, if only briefly. He hesitated, then said, "Keep your eye on Conroyd Jarralt. In Privy Council and out of it. If he can do you a bad turn, he will."

"Why?"

"Because he's Conroyd Jarralt."

"And?"

"And that's all you need to know. For now. Asher—" Gar slowed, and stopped. Asher stopped beside him. "Think of Privy Council meetings as an elaborate game.

One in which waving the flag of your indifference to almighty Doranen prestige will *lose* you points. Not win them, as it does with me. I'm asking that you watch your step. That's all. If you don't, well, chances are we'll both be sorry that I hired you."

So. The prince was nervous about the Privy Council meeting too. Mayhap even more than just nervous. Resisting the urge to clap Gar on the shoulder, Asher started walking backwards, arms outstretched. "Don't worry," he said. "I ain't about to let you down." He pressed a hand to his heart. "My solemn word." Which he'd keep, sink or swim. No way was he about to lose those fifty trins a week.

"Good," said Gar with a brief smile. "I knew I could count on you."

They hurried on, and five minutes later reached the newest section of the palace where Gar's family lived and worked. The pure white sandstone gleamed in the sun like freshly fallen snow. Some twelve stories high, it was topped with blue and crimson roof tiles and sparkled at regular intervals with elaborate stained-glass windows. A grand sweeping courtyard, scattered thickly with blue and white gravel, stretched from the base of the centrally placed white sandstone steps and ground-level balcony, down to the mouth of the winding tree-lined driveway that led towards the City.

Side by side Asher and Gar ran up the steps, past the ceremonial guards and into the royal residence.

The palace's interior shocked Asher to a standstill. All height and breadth and radiant stained glass, it made Justice Hall look . . . *plain*. Cut flowers in ceramic vases splashed color over every flat surface and sweetened the cool air. Exquisitely carved crystal birds wrought in shades of rose, sapphire, ruby, amethyst and emerald, tipped in gold, adorned indigo-marble display stands.

Two wide and winding polished timber staircases reached like arms to left and right of the grand entrance, embracing visitors, inviting exploration. The floor beneath Asher's feet was a riot of tiny blue, white, crimson and gold tiles in patterns his eyes could barely take in. The walls were papered in dull gold and bronze stripes. Breathtaking oil paintings, portraits so lifelike he'd swear their subjects were breathing, glowed at eye level, demanding admiration.

He had to guess they were members of the royal family, because there was Gar, years younger, with his arms round the neck of a fat black pony. A man and a woman—the king and queen? Had to be, 'cause there was Princess Fane. Maybe just six or seven years of age, but still beautiful. Bronze lamps jutted between the precisely placed frames, blazing with the same strange light he'd noticed in Justice Hall. Not candles. Not oil.

"Glimfire," said Gar. "It's magic, which is why you won't find it in the Tower."

Asher scarcely heard him. "Sink me bloody sideways!" he breathed. Recalling his own family's stone cottage back home, all shabby shadows and crowded coziness, he shook his head in wonder. He'd easily fit his bedroom in here three times over. "You used to *live* here?"

Mellow laughter spun him to his right. Descending the staircase was a tall Doranen man, lean and proud, with lines of experience—or pain—carved deep into his face. His ceremonial likeness hung on the wall scant feet away.

In the flesh, though, he was simply clad in a dark blue silk tunic and trousers. His eyes were green, like Gar's, but older. Seasoned by years and sights unseen by other men. An immaculately trimmed beard framed his strong jaw. A crown of twisted gold announced his rank. The royal house's emblem, a lightning bolt crossed with an unsheathed sword, was stitched in gold thread onto his collar points.

Asher swallowed. He'd seen the king before, down in Westwailing at festival time, but only from the arse-end of a huge crowd. Gar's da had been little more than a blond stick-figure then, waving indiscriminately at the thousands of fisherfolk gathered to celebrate Sea Harvest. Up close, he was magic made flesh. The aura of raw power surrounding him dimmed everything beyond it to tawdry tarnishment.

Gar bowed. "Your Majesty. Good morning."

Somehow, Asher managed his own inadequate bow without falling over. "Y'Majesty," he muttered.

King Borne approached and stretched out one ringed hand. "You must be Asher of Restharven. My son has spoken most highly of you, and of his hopes that you'll prove invaluable to him in his work. Welcome to Dorana City."

Asher stared at the king's hand. Now what? Was he supposed to kiss it? Shake it? What?

Gar chuckled. "Barl save me. I believe my new assistant is lost for words."

"No, I ain't," said Asher, rallying. He took the king's hand and shook it. To his surprise it felt cold and thin, with something close to a tremble deep between the slender bones. All that power, and in the end Lur's monarch was still only human. Somehow he hadn't expected that. "Thank you, Y'Majesty. Reckon I be about the luckiest Olken in Lur. I won't do wrong by His Highness. Or you. I promise."

The king withdrew his hand. "I'm sure of it, Asher." A glance passed between himself and his son and his pale lips softened into a smile. "Now, shall we make our way to the Privy Council chamber? We have a full morning's work ahead of us."

Gar extended his arm towards the left-hand staircase. "By all means, sir. Lead the way. Asher and I are ready."

That earned him another swift look from the king. "You think so? Well. By all means let us see, shall we?"

Conroyd Jarralt was an outrageously handsome man even when flushed with anger and shouting. A Doranen in his glorious, powerful prime, dressed in purple silk brocade and seed pearls, with his falcon house-emblem emblazoned on his chest in silver and jet. His aristocratic face was as perfect as a carving in marble, his athletic vigor overwhelming. In contrast, despite his magical power, the king looked pallid and drained of all vitality. Like a moon dimmed by the sun.

Jarralt banged his fist on the chamber table. "This is *insupportable*, Prince Gar! An *Olken*? With unfettered access to this Privy Council, its members, its decisions? I think not, Your Highness. Barl's mercy, what possessed you to do such a thing without gaining our permission? To have this reckless appointment announced in chapel without first doing us the courtesy of discussion? And then to refuse an accounting of yourself until now? Insupportable, sir! Insufferable!"

Exquisitely polite, Gar said, "I discussed the matter with His Majesty, my lord. As for declining your invitation to discuss it further . . . as I said, I felt it to be a topic best reserved for the privacy of this chamber."

"Indeed." Jarralt's burning gaze turned on the king. "So. He discussed the matter with you. And you said *yes* to this insanity?"

"I did," said the king. "Obviously."

Jarralt clenched his jaw. "I see. Well. One is forced to wonder what will come next. Olkens marrying into the Founding Families, perhaps?"

"Now, now, Conroyd . . ."

Asher, seated beside Gar on the other side of the table from the raging Doranen lord, slid his gaze to Barlsman Holze, on Jarralt's left. The elderly cleric's expression was pained, his lips pursed in disapproval. Steepled forefingers tapped against the tip of his bony nose. Voice mellow, reproving, he continued: "I think we must—"

Jarralt silenced him with a white-hot glare.

At the end of the rectangular table, sitting directly opposite the king, Master Magician Durm contemplated the plain white ceiling with a vast, unnerving indifference.

And the king? Well, the king was smiling. Not nicely, but in a guarded way that hinted at possible unpleasantness should Jarralt travel any further down his current path. Asher winced.

"Intermarriage between our peoples is strictly forbidden, Conroyd," His Majesty said, deceptively mild. "Gar knows that as well as you do. Surely you're not suggesting he advocates the breaking of Barl's Second Law?"

"Of course he isn't, Your Majesty," said Holze, one thin hand resting on Jarralt's rigid forearm. His once blond hair was mostly silver now, and thinning. Cut unfashionably short for a Doranen. A single braid, tightly wound with Barlsflowers to denote his devotion, dangled to his frail left shoulder. "Conroyd was merely expressing an understandable concern for this—forgive me, Your Highness—potentially rash decision."

"Rash?" Conroyd Jarralt snatched his arm free. His dark gold hair was unbound and fashionably long, with just the hint of a curl. Beautiful hair. Girl's hair, thought Asher, then quickly discarded the thought in case it showed on his face. "Rash is too kind a word, Holze," the lord continued. "I'll thank you to answer for your own utterances, sir, not mine."

He had the most amazing voice, like magic given a tongue. It was a voice to drink deep of, as a thirsty man swallows water. Instinctively Asher stiffened his spine against it. He didn't trust a man who could say something wrong yet make his listeners swear black and blue it was right because the way he said it sounded nice.

Holze, defeated, dipped his head. "As you say, Conroyd. You must speak for yourself."

"And I do!" said Jarralt. "I want to know what the king was thinking, to approve this ridiculous appointment. To foist this Olken upstart upon his Privy Council without so much as a by-our-leave!"

The king did not answer immediately. Hands clasped loosely before him on the tabletop, he considered the demand for a moment, then said, "Are you saying you doubt me, Conroyd?" His manner was surprisingly calm, but there was a dangerous glint in his eyes. Jarralt saw it, and colored faintly.

So. The king could bring Conroyd Jarralt to heel when

he wanted. That was good to know. Beside him, Asher felt Gar twitch. The prince's gaze switched abruptly to the other end of the table, where Durm continued to inspect the ceiling for spiderwebs or inspiration or whatever it was he hoped to find there. Feeling eyes upon him he slowly lowered his own regard. Considered Gar in speculative silence for a moment, then returned his attention to matters seemingly above the heads of everybody else in the room.

"All I doubt," said Jarralt, "is the wisdom of the decision. Ordinary, uneducated Olken have never concerned themselves with the running of this kingdom and I see no reason for that to change. They should tend to their farming and their shopkeeping and leave important matters of government to those who can best address them."

Patronizing bastard. Asher cleared his throat. Lowly Olken or not it was time he let certain folk know he wasn't some kind of deaf mute simpleton. Or a horse to be sized up and debated on, complimented on the strength of his back or criticized for the knockiness of his knees.

"Y'Majesty?"

The king looked at him. "You have something to add, Asher?"

Heart thudding, Asher nodded. Under the table, Gar kicked him. He ignored the warning. "Yes, Y'Majesty. I just wanted to say it be an honor and a pleasure to sit at table with you and these other fine lords. And, beggin" your pardon, Lord Jarralt, I reckon you be gettin' y'self all knotted up over nowt. I ain't come here to fret and fust you. His Highness be after an extra pair of hands on the halyards, is all, and I reckon if there be somethin' I can do to help him and His Majesty, here, then sink me if I won't."

Silence. Then: "I'm sorry," said Conroyd Jarralt, staring around the table and sounding not the least bit sorry at all. "*What* did he say?"

Another kick under the table, harder this time. "Asher merely assured you, sir," Gar said quickly, "that he has no intention of causing any problems for this Council."

"Did he?" retorted Jarralt. "How can you be sure? The man is scarcely comprehensible! But if that *is* what he said then I'm bound to point out to you, Your Highness, that the assurance comes too late! His very *existence* is a problem!"

"I disagree," argued Gar. "Anyone who can help me do my job as Olken Administrator more efficiently can only benefit His Majesty *and* this Privy Council."

"You expect this . . . this . . . *Olken* to improve your efficiency?" said Jarralt. "How? You'll be spending all of your time translating for him!"

"Asher has recently arrived here from the coast." From the look of him, Gar was only just keeping hold of his temper. "Olken fisherfolk are wont to speak in a colorful vernacular, it's true, but I have every confidence he'll soon adjust to the more measured speech of the City."

Shifting in his chair a little, moving his still-smarting ankle out of Gar's reach, Asher frowned. Speaking slowly, trying to mask the effort of mimicking the likes of Darran, he said, "Prince Gar has employed me to be his assistant, Lord Jarralt. As an honest man I'll do my best not to disappoint him, the king or this Privy Council. I may be just a magickless Olken, but that don't—

doesn't—mean I ain't trustworthy." Well pleased with himself, he sat back in his chair and smiled.

Jarralt leapt to his feet. "*What*? You have the gall to *mock* me?"

"Mock you?" said Asher, bewildered. "I weren't mockin' you, I were just tryin' to explain how—"

Now Jarralt was leaning across the table, pointed finger stabbing. "I am the head of a Founding Family! My house is second only to that of the royal family! I will *not* be mocked by an ignorant Olken fisherman! Your Majesty, surely you can see this appointment is folly! Madness! This Privy Council is a solemn gathering of learned men whose sacred duty is the protection and governance of this kingdom. How in Barl's holy name can we be expected to uphold our oaths if we must constantly consider what we say before this . . . this interloper! He cannot be granted membership of this Privy Council! It is an affront to everything we stand for!"

"Asher, for the love of Barl *hold your tongue*!" hissed Gar, then turned to Jarralt. "My lord, it appears we are at cross-purposes. It was never my intention that Asher should join the Privy Council. I apologize if that's the impression I've given. As my assistant he'll be helping me—helping us all—continue this august body's ongoing dedication to the betterment and prosperity of Lur. Naturally he will not be concerned with the making of policy or interpretation of law or any other Privy Council duty. I merely wished you to meet him. That's all."

Unappeased, Jarralt bared his teeth. "In other words, you are incapable of carrying out your duties as Olken Administrator without help from an uneducated laborer.

If that's the case, perhaps the matter of your appointment to the position should be revisited?"

The king looked at him through narrowed eyes. "Have a care, Conroyd. And take your seat."

As Jarralt obeyed, lips thinned, Gar raised a hand and turned to his father. "It's a fair question, sir, if ungraciously framed." He turned back to Jarralt. "My lord, I've learned many things since assuming the responsibilities of Olken Administrator, but the most important is this: that nothing but good can come from a deeper Doranen understanding of Olken society. History shows us a score of examples where unpleasantness and discord might well have been avoided if only we truly knew each other better. Can you at least agree with that?"

Asher smothered a grin as he watched Jarralt's expression congeal. "Agree?" the lord echoed suspiciously. "Possibly. But that doesn't—"

"Good," said Gar. "And surely we can also agree that nobody is in a better position to occasionally advise this Privy Council upon matters important to the Olken than one of His Majesty's Olken subjects?"

Jarralt glowered. "Yes. I suppose. In *theory*. However—"

"So if," Gar continued ruthlessly, "by appointing Asher as my assistant I can facilitate future harmonious Doranen and Olken relations, then it must logically follow that this Privy Council—as the decision-making instrument of our kingdom—can only benefit. And if *that's* true, I'd say I've proven my fitness for the position of Olken Administrator, not undermined it. Wouldn't you?" Spreading his hands wide, he appealed to the table at large.

Holze's smile was gentle and approving. "Well said, Your Highness. Above all, Barl desires Doranen and Olken to live peacefully side by side in the paradise she created. If this is indeed your objective, I see no reason to thwart this young Olken's appointment as your assistant. Can you, Lord Jarralt?"

Jarralt snorted. "Oh, to be sure, it *sounds* well and good. But what of practicalities? How often can we of the Privy Council expect this incomprehensible addition to grace us with his dubious presence? How much credence are we to lend to his profoundly experienced observations of good government? Tell us, Prince Gar, is it your intention that we allow your fisherman to lecture us? Instruct us? If it is, then I'm afraid I must decline the honor. The day some upstart Olken can march in here and presume to tell me my business—"

Durm cleared his throat. Jarralt swallowed the rest of his objection. Eyes narrowed, the Master Magician lowered his piercing gaze and considered the now silent lord. "You are raising a storm in a teacup, Conroyd. And that, I believe, is solely His Majesty's prerogative."

Jarralt stared. "Does that mean you *approve* of this . . ."

Durm shrugged. "It means, Conroyd, I have been given no cause to *dis*approve of him." His cold glance flickered. "Yet."

Seared by that swift look Asher stared at the table. Suddenly he knew how a mouse must feel when the shadow of the hawk passes over it.

"So," said Jarralt. For the first time, he sounded subdued. "Your mind is made up . . . Your Majesty?"

"Yes, Conroyd," said the king, his voice and face

implacable. "And not to be unmade. I have complete faith in my son's choice of assistant."

"As have I," added Holze. "His Highness has proven himself a most capable Administrator. Isn't that so, Conroyd?"

Conroyd Jarralt laced his fingers and frowned at them. "Most capable."

Gar said carefully, "Your Majesty, my lords, I thank you. It was never my intention to take up so much time with this trifling business. I merely wished you to know that should there be anything of an Olken nature you wish to discuss or have clarified, Asher shall henceforth be at your disposal."

"And on behalf of this Privy Council," said the king, "I welcome his knowledge and assistance, wherever and whenever it may be extended to us."

There was an expectant pause. Asher, feeling the weight of all those Doranen stares, coughed. "Like I said," he muttered. "Reckon it be an honor to serve the Privy Council."

"Indeed," said the king. "Then I declare this subject closed."

"Well done," Gar murmured in Asher's ear as Jarralt and Holze exchanged whispered comments and looked at their paperwork to discover the next problem for discussion. "Now I think it's best if you go back to the Tower. Ask Darran for a copy of next week's scheduled appointments and be ready with your thoughts when I return. Don't forget to ask His Majesty's permission to withdraw."

Half out of his chair, Asher straightened and offered the king an awkward bow. "Y'Majesty. His Highness has work for me back at the Tower. Can I get on with it?"

Was that a smile, strictly denied? Maybe. And if so, what did it mean? That he had the king's support, or that he was little more than a joke? He couldn't tell and he didn't much care. He just wanted out of the small, crowded chamber. He could feel Conroyd Jarralt's eyes on him, staring.

The king nodded. "By all means, Asher. Return to your duties. Doubtless I shall see you again in the fullness of time."

"Y'Majesty."

Straightening from his farewell bow, Asher looked square into the frozen fury of Conroyd Jarralt's gaze. The force of it made him step back. Thudded his heart and stole his breath. That was *hatred* in the Doranen lord's eyes . . .

"Well go on, then," said Gar, nudging him. "Don't stand there with your mouth open, catching flies. I'll see you later."

Deeply disconcerted, Asher headed for the door. But as his hand reached for the handle it opened all by itself. An agitated young Olken in City Guard livery shoved him aside and barged into the chamber. He rushed to the king, dropped to one knee and held out a rolled parchment.

"Forgive the interruption, Your Majesty," he gasped. "An urgent message from Captain Orrick."

Frowning, the king accepted it. Untied the scroll's binding scarlet ribbon. Unrolled the message, read it, read it again, and blinked. Asher, looking closely at his face, thought he was in sudden pain.

"Very good," the king said quietly. "Return to the captain. Tell him to make the appropriate preparations and await further instructions. And tell him also—discretion is paramount."

The young City Guard nodded. "Yes, Your Majesty."

As the chamber door banged shut behind the guard, the Master Magician spoke.

"What is it, Borne? What has happened?"

CHAPTER TEN

Something bad, Asher judged, if the king's face was anything to go by. It had lost all its washed-out color, leaving him as gray as the paper in his hand. He looked a score of years older, just as Da had looked a heartbeat after Ma exhaled her last rattling breath.

Gar was on his feet, one hand reaching out. "Sir, what is it? Mama? Fane? Are they—"

The king shook his head. "No. It's not family. It's worse." Lifting his gaze from the message he stared the length of the Council table and locked eyes with Durm. "Barl's First Law has been broken. The man is in custody and being brought to the City as we speak. He will be here by this evening."

Asher bit his tongue. What? Some bloody fool Olken had been caught pissin' around with magic? *Why?* Olken couldn't do magic, everybody knew that. And everybody knew that to try, to muck about mouthing words of Doranen power overheard in passing even, was as bright as jumping off Rillingcoombe Cliffs when the tide was out.

As bright . . . and as fatal.

It was Holze who shattered the shocked silence. "Your Majesty, there must be some mistake. Perhaps a misunderstanding . . ."

"No," said the king, still looking at the message. "No misunderstanding."

Holze shook his head, his blue-veined hands tight-clasped and trembling. "I find this quite incredible. There must be an explanation."

Lord Jarralt laughed, crudely amused. "Of course there is. They're jealous of us, any fool knows that. It's not enough that we provide them with a perfect world to live in. Predictable weather that is never too hot or too cold, too dry or too wet. Heat, light, plumbing . . . a veritable cornucopia of domestic comforts. They want more. They want to subvert the proper order of things. Usurp power that does not belong to them."

Well, that was just a lie, pure and simple. Asher opened his mouth to put Jarralt straight, caught Gar's glare and swallowed his angry denial. A curt nod directed him away from the door and against the wall, where he could observe unnoticed. Gar sat down again, his expression unreadable.

"No, no," protested Holze. His voice shook with distress. "Barl's Laws are taught throughout the kingdom. I cannot believe any Olken would willingly break the first and greatest of them!"

"Advancing age has withered your brain, Holze," Jarralt sneered. "This isn't the first attack on our most sacred law and unless we show no mercy to this blasphemous criminal it won't be the last!" He turned to the king. "You must make an example of this vile traitor. Every Olken man, woman and child must be shown, once and for all, what happens when Barl's sacred edicts are transgressed."

Holze reached out an imploring hand. "Conroyd, please! Curb your wrath! As our precious kingdom's most senior caretakers we must remain calm. We must seek Barl's guidance."

"Holze, you amaze me." Jarralt's tone was one of utter contempt. "As Barl's holiest representative among us you should be leading the outcry!"

Holze drew himself upright and stared at Jarralt with wounded dignity. "My lord, nobody knows better than I what duties are owed by me to our blessed, beloved Barl. Shame on you for implying otherwise!"

Jarralt flushed. "I imply nothing. I merely suggest—"

"Your suggestion offends me, Conroyd. And it hurts me too. I thought you knew me—respected me—better. I do not say this man should go unpunished. But you make it sound as though every week sees a new Olken transgression of the laws! You mustn't be so intemperate or unfair. It is a hundred years at least since this crime was last committed!"

"One hundred and thirty-eight," said Durm. "During the reign of Ancel the Red. The criminal was a woman named Maura Shay. She was beheaded, as will this man be."

The king sighed. "Yes. He will." His fingers convulsed around the message, crushing it. "The fool."

"So *now* will you reconsider your son's impetuous elevation of this Olken fisherman?" Jarralt demanded. "Clearly this is not the time for any Olken to be seen wielding power, no matter how meager."

"You're wrong, Lord Jarralt," said Gar. "When news of this unfortunate business spreads, and it will no matter how discreetly Captain Orrick handles the matter, tensions in the Olken community will escalate. They'll feel vulnerable. Examined. Guilty by reason of association. This man's short-sighted—"

"Short-sighted?" said Conroyd Jarralt. "You consider this blasphemous, criminal act to be nothing more than a lapse in judgement, do you?"

Asher watched Gar's lips pinch tight. "Of course I don't. I'll thank you not to put words in my mouth, sir. What this man has done is unforgivable. His actions will have dire repercussions for all of us, Doranen and Olken alike."

Jarralt snorted. "They'll have dire repercussions for him, I know that much. In fact, I say a private beheading is too good for him. He needs to be broken. Literally and publicly, to drive the message home once and for all: Olken disobedience and blasphemy will meet with no mercy."

Gar leaned across the table. "You can't possibly be such a fool. The test here isn't how we deal with this stupid Olken, it's how we conduct *ourselves*. Even you must see that!"

The king raised his hand. "Gar, please . . ."

"But, Your Majesty!" Gar pleaded, ignoring Jarralt's salt-white fury. "Lord Jarralt is wrong. If we wreak vengeance instead of justice, what message will we be sending then? That the purpose of this Privy Council is to mete out heavy-handed retribution. That the Doranen hold all Olken accountable for the actions of one. If that's the message we send, sir, we'll undermine all trust between—"

"Trust?" said Jarralt. "What trust, when an Olken has

been caught breaking Barl's First Law? Attempting magic. This short-sighted act has risked all of our lives, Your Highness. It has threatened the peace of your father's kingdom, sir, and jeopardized Barl's Wall."

Gar banged the table with his fists. "Hardly that, Lord Jarralt. Barl's Wall has stood unwavering for centuries. It took Trevoyle's Schism to weaken it, and that went on for eight months. One thoughtless, reckless act by a single Olken can't possibly have done any real harm."

If he could have Asher would've slapped his hand over Gar's mouth then, because Jarralt's eyes were shining like a shark's scenting blood in the water and all his teeth were on show. "So. You're questioning Barl's Laws now, are you? Your Highness?"

Too late, Gar realized where his passion had led him. Asher closed his eyes briefly, wincing, as the prince snapped back in his chair. "No."

Now Jarralt was all mock sorrow and solicitude. "Forgive the contradiction, sir, but I think you were. Barlsman Holze?"

The old man's sallow face was troubled. "I'm sure His Highness has nothing but the deepest respect for the laws. He knows, as do we all, that they form the foundation of this kingdom. They are the warp and weft of our existence, and have been for over six hundred years. Barl said: *Let no Olken raise his voice in magic, for it is not their way or their right or their purpose in this land. And let the Olken who does so pay with his life, as all would pay if my Wall were to be disturbed by such a lawless act.* To this first law must we all hold true, or pay a terrible price in blood and tears. Is that not so, Your Highness?"

"Yes, sir, it is," said Gar. His clasped hands rested on

the table before him, white-knuckled with pressure. "With all my heart I believe it, and I challenge anyone here to dispute my faith. But one can be a man of faith and still question. There's more to the warp and weft of this kingdom than Barl's Laws, important though they are. *People* are the true fabric of Lur, gentlemen. Olken and Doranen. And if we don't handle this matter with tact we'll tear the fabric of this kingdom apart." He turned to his father, naked appeal in his temper-flushed face. "Am I not right, Your Majesty?"

Asher looked at the king. His expression was remote, chilled; stare as he might, Asher could see no softness there. No mercy. No sorrow even, for the death that would soon come to one unthinking Olken. For all the similarity of bone structure, the arch of an eyebrow, the curve of a lip, he and his son looked no more alike than did ice and a flowing river.

"If you're in any way suggesting that this act can be excused," said the king, "then—"

"Excused? No, sir, not excused," said Gar. "I know that's impossible."

At the other end of the table the Master Magician stirred from his silence. "What, then? What would you have us do?"

Gar turned to him. "Lord Jarralt is . . . mistaken. Yes, this man must be punished, but not publicly."

"Why not?" Durm's eyes were hooded, his expression smooth as glass. "His crime was public."

Gar took a deep breath and let it out slowly. "Because, sir, it can't seem that we take any pleasure in his death. If we turn his execution into a spectacle, as though it were . . . were street theater . . ." His voice was shaking.

"For the same reason, his punishment can't be cruel. If he's truly guilty of this crime then he should die as precedent dictates. But that death must be swift, sure and with all the mercy we possess. And Asher *must* remain as my assistant. What better way is there for this Privy Council—for His Majesty—to show all the kingdom that the Olken people will never be held responsible for the actions of one misguided man?"

Jarralt's lip curled. "You seem inordinately concerned on this point, Your Highness."

"*Inordinately* concerned, sir?" Gar echoed. "You wouldn't say that if you'd bother to study your history. One hundred and thirty-eight years ago, when Maura Shay was found guilty of the same crime, innocent Olken were dragged from their beds, locked up and terrified, and for no other reason than fear. That was a crime too. We may be Doranen, sir, we may have magic . . ."

Asher winced as Gar hesitated. As Jarralt raised an eyebrow at him, imperfectly hiding his scornful smile. Pale now, Gar continued.

"But having magic doesn't make the Doranen impervious to flaws, my lord. Speaking plainly, as Olken Administrator it's my duty to ensure this business doesn't interfere with the good name or wellbeing of the Olken community."

Air hissed between Jarralt's white teeth. "So. Now we come to it. You would place their welfare above ours, Your Highness. Isn't that so? You would side with *them* against your own people."

"Why must you talk of sides?" demanded Gar. "There are no sides here, Jarralt. As His Majesty's subject and a child of Barl I want the law upheld. As Olken Administrator I want it upheld justly. Why would you criticize that?" He turned to the king. "Your Majesty?"

Asher, barely breathing, stared at the king. Was he going to let this argument rage unchecked forever? Who did he side with, his son or his enemy? After a long silence Borne stirred and lifted his heavy gaze. Considered Durm.

"I think I would know what my Master Magician has to say."

All eyes turned to Durm. A large man, generously fleshed, he seemed to Asher not the least bit put out by the hot and anxious stares. His vast robed shoulders lifted in a shrug. "And I, Your Majesty, would know the opinion of our newly appointed Assistant Olken Administrator."

The king's pale eyebrows lifted. "Would you, indeed?" He turned. "Well, Asher? This business concerns you as much as any of us. Satisfy the Master Magician's curiosity. And mine."

Asher bit his lip. Now everyone was staring at him. He didn't like it, not one little bit. His grand new trousers fit too tightly for him to shove his hands in his pockets, which was what he wanted to do. Instead, he crossed his arms over his chest and scowled.

"What do I reckon?" He glanced at the Master Magician then looked back at the king, because it was easier. "I reckon I ain't to blame for what this sinkin' fool's gone and done, Y'Majesty. And I reckon y'should chop the stupid bastard's head off five minutes after he gets here. That'll teach him to go muckin' about with things as don't concern him, eh?"

Barlsman Holze leaned forward. "You are harsh, young man."

"Am I?" said Asher, chin lifting. "Look. Sir. I ain't the most religious man you'll ever see in your chapel, but I reckon I know right from wrong. Olken don't do magic. And if they try, and they get caught, then too bad. They can't snivel they didn't know it were wrong, or what would happen. Everybody knows."

The king said slowly, "The idea of an Olken dying such a horrible death doesn't distress you?"

Asher shrugged. "No. It's only what he deserves."

"So," said Conroyd Jarralt. "You have no loyalty to your own people."

Asher sneered, just a little. "Sure I do. But my first loyalty be with the king. And the law. Ain't yours?"

"Leave him be, Conroyd," advised the Master Magician as Jarralt's face clenched with fury. "You provoked that. Your Majesty . . ."

The king smiled, the very faintest softening of his cold face. "Durm?"

"His Highness is right. There can be no repeat of what occurred the last time we had a conviction of this kind. I see no detriment in this Asher remaining as your son's assistant. Let him be seen freely by His Highness's side as we prosecute this law-breaker. Let the Olken of Dorana City know by word and deed that we cherish them as we have ever cherished them and grieve as they grieve at this gross betrayal of Blessed Barl by one of their own."

The king nodded. "As ever, old friend, we are thought and echo. It shall be handled as you suggest," He turned his attention to Asher. "Leave us. Attend to your duties as my son has requested and hold your tongue on this unfortunate business until he gives you leave to speak publicly."

Swallowing relief Asher bowed, to the king and then

the rest of the Council. "Aye, Y'Majesty," and escaped the chamber before something else could go wrong.

On returning to the Tower he collected his copy of the next week's appointments from a prune-faced Willer, ordered himself an early lunch from the kitchen and settled down in his office to eat and work until Gar returned.

The prince walked in three hours later, looking tired and on edge. He threw himself into the nearest armchair and propped his dusty boots on the edge of the desk. "What are you doing?"

Asher shoved his pen back in its ink pot. "What you asked."

"Oh," said Gar. His fingers drummed on the arm of the chair. "Are you finished?"

"Just about."

Still drumming, Gar nodded. "Good."

"I had a question, though, on—"

Gar lifted his hand. "Tell me. Did you mean what you said?"

Asher considered him warily. "About what?"

"Chopping off this man's head. Did you mean it?"

Oh. That. With a sigh, Asher shoved aside his laboriously scrawled notes, leaned back in his chair and kicked his own heels onto the desktop. If it were good enough for a prince . . .

"'Course I meant it," he said. "Did you think I didn't?"

Gar frowned. "No. At least . . . I thought . . . I wondered—Jarralt was being so difficult . . ."

"Aye. He's a right bastard that one, eh?" Remembering, Asher scowled. "You said he might do me a bad turn.

You *never* said he'd hate my guts. If he had his way, Gar, I'd be a slimy red—"

"Don't worry," Gar said flatly. "It's nothing but bluster. Ignore him. Politely." He brushed a smudge of dust from his knee, still frowning. "Asher . . . I hope you know we're not all so arrogant. About your people. Doranen like Jarralt, like . . ." He hesitated. "It's just that some Doranen hark back to the days when our magic was less . . . restrained. They're fools, of course. That kind of magic destroyed us. Brought us here and changed a lot of things forever. Besides, most if not all of the incantations are centuries lost. But even if they weren't, Barl's Laws are clear. It's prohibited, with penalties as severe as any the Olken face."

Asher snorted. "Oh aye? So if one of your lot were caught pissin' about with magic as didn't concern 'em, would you turn y'self inside out worryin' for 'em?"

"No, I suppose not," said Gar, sighing.

"Then why fret me on not carin' what happens to this Olken fool in custody now, whoever he is?"

"His name is Timon Spake," said Gar. "He hails from Basingdown."

"Never heard of him. But even if I had—"

"Yes?" Gar stared at him. "If you had? If you knew him? If it was Matt, say, who'd been caught breaking the law and not this stranger? Would you still be so eager to see his head struck from his shoulders?"

"Well, for a start I ain't eager to see *anybody's* head struck off their shoulders," Asher pointed out. "I just want to know it got done. And Matt would never break Barl's First Law. He ain't a fool like this Spake man."

"You know what I mean."

Asher sighed. Yes, he did know. "Gar, it's the law. What are you tryin' to say? That the rules should be different for your lot and mine? Or we should forget about 'em if we happen to know the law-breaker?"

Gar thumped his boot heels to the floor. "No! No, I just—I wish—"

"'Cause y'know that'd never bloody work. The only reason your lot and mine rub along as well as we do is 'cause everybody's livin' under the same rules and nobody plays favorites. You start muckin' about with that and the next thing y'know we're all in the water and some of us is drownin'."

With his elbows on his knees, Gar pressed his face into his hands. "I know that," he said, muffled.

"Well, then," Asher said bracingly. "Now we got that settled, how's about we get started on all these appointments you got lined up, eh? I been thinkin' on 'em, just like you asked. Even got some ideas. I'll tell 'em to you, so long as you promise not to laugh."

It took a moment, but Gar finally looked up. "I promise I'll try," he said, with a faint smile. "But that's as far as I go."

Their discussion of the next week's calendar took the rest of the day. Gar had meetings scheduled with the Sheep-growers' Association, the Miners' Guild, the Bakers' Guild, the Vintners and more. Asher's head whirled. He didn't have hardly a clue what any of them did or what they thought their problems were. So Gar had to give him a quick history of each guild, who their meisters or mistresses were, what they wanted, who they were feuding with and how each one impacted on all the others. By the end of it he wasn't sure whether he was horrified at all the things he was going to have to learn or impressed by the fact that Gar knew them so well already. Most of the ideas he'd already come up with had to be thrown overboard, which meant he'd have to come up with some new ones, quick smart.

He started to think that at fifty trins a week, he'd be *under*paid.

Dusk was fast approaching by the time they finished. Groaning, Asher slumped against his chair-back and rubbed his eyes. "Don't reckon I can see how you been managin' on your own. Did the king have all this claptrap to go on with as well as his WeatherWorkin'?"

Just as slumped. Gar nodded. "A lot of it, which is why I stepped in. Of course since I made myself available for consultation and assistance the workload has gradually become heavier and heavier. Hence you."

Asher grinned. "No good deed goes unpunished, eh?"

"Something like that." Gar fought a yawn, and lost. "I hope you're not too alarmed. Most problems can be solved by sitting down and talking them through. A lot of the time people just like to know they've been listened to. Once you're familiar with who's who we can—" A knock at the door interrupted him. It was young Remy, carrying a note. "Yes?"

Remy bowed. "'Scuse me, Your Highness, but this just come from the palace."

Gar took the note and dismissed the lad with a nod. He read it and sighed. "Timon Spake has been delivered to the guardhouse. There's to be a preliminary enquiry before the Privy Council in the morning."

Asher sat up. "What does that mean?"

"It means he'll be asked formally, under oath, if he's guilty of the crime. If he says no we proceed to a full and public trial."

"And if he says yes?"

Gar's expression was bleak. His fingers worried at the note and his gaze was distant. "Then he'll not see another sunrise."

"That fast?" said Asher, surprised.

"There's nothing to be gained by prolonging the agony. Asher, I want you to do something for me. Go down to the guardhouse and make sure this Timon Spake is well situated. He must be decently housed and fed and not subjected to unnecessary restraint. At this moment he's only accused, not convicted, but the crime is so heinous I fear for his safety."

Asher stared. "In the guardhouse?"

"Captain Orrick is an honorable man and an excellent officer," Gar said carefully. "But feelings will be running high. I want it made clear to him and his subordinates that regardless of personal outrage and the severity of the accused's crime, we mustn't run ahead of the verdict."

Slumping again, Asher swallowed a groan. "You want me to go right now?"

"Yes." Gar reached across the desk and pulled paper and pen towards him. As he scrawled a quick note he said, "I can't go myself, for obvious reasons. As my assistant, however, you'll be speaking with my full authority." Finished with his writing, he folded the note and held it out. "Give this to Orrick. It'll ensure his complete cooperation."

Asher took the note and studied it. "Only if he believes it's come from you. What if he accuses me of makin' it up or somethin'? Decides I'm in cahoots with this Timon Spake? He might, seein' as how he's so diligent and he don't know me from a hole in the ground. I mean, he knows someone called Asher's your new assistant, but he don't know for sure that's me."

Gar frowned, took the note back again and headed for the door. Asher scrambled after him and they hurried downstairs to Darran's office.

"Your Highness?" the ole crow squawked as they marched in. "Is something wrong?"

As Gar sealed the note with crimson wax and pressed his house ring into it he said to Darran, "You'll need to send messengers out at once canceling all my appointments for tomorrow."

"Yes, Your Highness," Darran said faintly. "May I ask, Your Highness, what reason I should—"

"No," said Gar. Ignoring Darran's offended shock and Willer's fish-faced goggling, he handed the sealed note to Asher. "Be thorough but don't linger. Report to me the minute you return to the Tower."

"Aye, sir," said Asher, and tucked the note into his pocket. "What d'you want me to do if I find—"

"Whatever you deem appropriate," said Gar. "Bearing in mind I shall have to answer for it to the Privy Council."

"Aye, sir," said Asher, glumly, and withdrew. Not even the look on ole Darran's face had the power to cheer him up. Damn. If this was what bein' Assistant Olken Administrator were all about, then he was *definitely* underpaid.

The last person Dathne expected to see come riding down the High Street from the direction of the palace was Asher. But there he was, scowling and unimpressed on top of his precious silver Cygnet, making his way through the crowd in the City's central square. When he saw the milling, muttering Olken as they bumped and gathered around Supplicant's Fountain and stared across the square at the guardhouse entrance, his scowl melted into dismay, then returned more ferociously than ever. She saw his lips move and imagined the cursing.

She didn't blame him; she felt like cursing, too.

Pushing her way through the bodies she called his name and waved. "Asher! Asher!"

Startled, he drew rein and stared down at her as she reached him. "Dathne? What are you doin' out here?"

"I could ask you the same thing," she said.

He nudged his horse sideways until they were pressed flank and knee against the Golden Cockerel Hotel's front wall. "Official business. Now what's all this rabble-rousin' about?" He leaned over Cygnet's wither as she crowded close and lowered his voice. "You got any idea what's amiss?"

She nodded, one hand steady against the gray colt's warm, sleek shoulder. "I know exactly what's amiss. And so does everybody else here. With or without an official announcement from the palace, by this time tomorrow I expect every man, woman and child in the City will know."

"That some fool's got caught messin' about with—" Stiff-faced with angry surprise, Asher glanced at the mob and reconsidered. "How did you find out? The king only got word this mornin'."

"And Timon Spake was taken yesterday afternoon," she replied, shrugging. "Enough people here have family in Basingdown, Asher. The dressmaker two doors down from my shop has a sister there. Are you forgetting messenger pigeons? It only takes one or two, and after that it's running feet and gabbling tongues. Did you really think you'd keep something like this a secret?"

Asher frowned. "The king did."

"The king was wrong then, wasn't he?" She glanced over her shoulder. Moment by moment the crowd was growing, and as it grew the muttering swelled to an ominous rumble. "I don't like the look of this."

"You and me both," said Asher with another worried look at the gathered Olken. "What are they all doin' here? What do they want?"

She shrugged. "Reassurance. Revenge. The last time this happened a lot of innocent people were hurt. That's not been forgotten. I think the Olken of Doranen want to make it perfectly clear from the outset where their loyalties lie." She shivered. "I'd say if Spake walked out here now they'd tear him limb from limb." Another shiver. "This is going to get ugly."

Even as she spoke, a stream of guards flowed out of the guardhouse, each one armed with a long pike and a short truncheon. They took up positions along the front of the guardhouse railings and planted the butts of their pikes beside them. Their faces were grim. All around the square and along the City streets glimfire flickered into life inside the public lanterns that sat atop light-poles, dangled from gates and shopfronts and hung suspended from wires over street corners. The light threw long shadows, painting the world with danger.

Asher was staring at the thickening crowd. "Wonder if the king knows about this?"

"If he doesn't, he soon will," she said. "What are you doing here anyway?"

"Gar sent me. He be worried about this man Spake. Wants to make sure he ain't gettin' treated unfairly in there." He nodded at the guardhouse. "Reckon he wants to be more worried about this mob out here. Dath, I got to get goin'. You should go too, back home. Might not be safe out here much longer if these folk take it into their heads to get rambunctious."

Dathne nodded, her mind racing. Asher was going into the guardhouse? To see Spake? *Perfect.* Here was a gift unlooked for. A way to salvage this sorry situation. To save her life's work and a kingdom besides from the folly of one heedless idiot. She put her hand on his knee. "Asher, let me go with you."

Dragging his frowning gaze away from the crowd, he laughed. "Don't be daft."

"I mean it. I need to get in there. I must see this Timon Spake."

"Why?"

Because I have to stop his mouth before he talks or there won't be enough empty cells in all of Dorana to hold the victims of his arrogance. "Because he's by way of being family," she said with all the wide-eyed sincerity she could summon. "Only indirectly, a cousin of a cousin of a cousin. You know how it goes. I've never actually met him, but no matter how distant the connection he's still family. If I could just see him, make sure he's—"

"No, I said!" snapped Asher. "I'll tell you how he is, and you can tell whoever asks. But you ain't comin' into the guardhouse with me. If Gar—"

"I'm sure the prince wouldn't mind. He knows me.

And I won't be a nuisance. I won't even speak, I promise. I'll be as quiet as a mouse." She tried a winning, winsome smile. "Please, Asher? You wouldn't even have this job if it wasn't for me. A favor for a favor."

"Dathne!"

Clearly her winning, winsome smile needed some work. "Look, you say you're here to make sure this Spake is all right? Well, I can promise you he's not. He's in that guardhouse, locked in a cell, probably terrified. Probably being fed on pig slops because he'll have no friends in there. After what he's done he's got no friends anywhere. I could run back to my place, it won't take long. I've sweet cakelets I baked just this morning. He's welcome to them. And a book to take his mind off things. I'm sure the prince would approve of that, showing mercy to a condemned man. It's why he's sent you, isn't it? I'd just be helping. Who could object?"

Asher let out an angry huff of air. Chewed at his lip and banged his fist on his thigh, thinking. "Run fast then," he said at last, grudgingly. "Ten minutes I'll wait, and after that I'll be goin' in there without you."

She bolted. The cakelets were on the kitchen windowsill; after setting three onto the benchtop she rummaged in the back of a cupboard. Found the small glass vial she was after and the thin hollow straw she needed. The sickly-sweet smell of tinctured draconis root made her blink. With the straw she cautiously sucked the poison out of the bottle, then dripped it with immense care into the heart of each cakelet.

It wasn't murder. He was going to die anyway, so you couldn't call it murder. And his silence, ensured, would save the lives of hundreds. Maybe thousands. Maybe everyone alive in the kingdom. Veira would be angry, but so long as the old woman was angry after the fact that didn't matter. As Jervale's Heir she had a duty to ensure the smooth passage of Prophecy . . . and she would do whatever she had to, no matter the cost.

She felt a brief, burning hatred for the man who was making her do this. Forcing her hand to take his life. Who had sworn the same oath she had, to silence, to the Circle, to death before betrayal . . .

The bastard should have killed himself.

When it was done she wrapped the cakelets in a clean tea towel, put them and a book into her string bag and bolted all the way back to Asher.

"Just in bloody time," he muttered, eyeing the packed square uneasily. "Stick close now. I reckon this mob's goin' to start a riot any second."

Fingers wrapped tight around his stirrup leather, holding hard against Cygnet's trembling side, she pushed with him through the surging crowd. The air was thick with ugliness, with fear and fury. Looking around her she couldn't see a single fair head anywhere, only dark ones. Only Olken. The press of bodies parted reluctantly, complaining, and they continued forward until a guard standing at the entrance to the guardhouse lowered his pike point-first and challenged them.

"Let me pass," said Asher curtly. "I'm Asher, the Assistant Olken Administrator. I've come on the prince's business."

Dathne watched the guard's tense gaze flicker over the expensive horse, its rider's expensive clothes and lastly his face. The pike's point dropped, fractionally. "The woman?"

"Is with me. Now stand aside." Asher touched his spurs to Cygnet's flanks. The horse snorted, ears pinned back, and danced a little.

"Pass," said the guard, and stepped sideways.

Asher eased his hand on the reins and Cygnet jumped forward. "Easy, you ole fool." He glanced down. "You be all right there, Dathne?"

She took a deep breath. Her heart was booming and her mouth was dry. She could still smell the draconis. "I'm fine. Let's just get this over with, shall we?"

"Aye. Let's," said Asher, and together they walked through the gates of the Dorana City guardhouse.

CHAPTER ELEVEN

Captain Orrick of the City Guard was a lean, hatchet-faced man of middle years who wore his plain crimson uniform like a second skin. His dark, silver-threaded hair was clipped even closer than Matt's and his gray eyes were cool and calculating. He stood in front of the guardhouse lobby desk and twice read the note Asher handed him. Then he looked up.

"I'd heard someone was appointed His Highness's Assistant Administrator."

"Aye, well, that someone'd be me," said Asher.

"So you say." Orrick considered him. "But we've not been formally introduced."

Asher shrugged. "It only just happened. Reckon His Highness'll get around to officially tellin' you it's me in his own good time. Mayhap he's been too busy trimmin' his toenails to think of it."

Orrick's thin lips tightened. If they hadn't been surrounded by the captain's nervous subordinates, all looking out of the windows and muttering about the gathered crowd outside, Dathne would have trodden on Asher's toes, hard. Pellen Orrick was the last man in Dorana to be amused by an eccentric sense of humor.

"His Majesty has charged me straight to keep the prisoner isolated," Orrick said. "Do I understand you expect me to disobey a lawful order from the king?"

"Look," said Asher, sighing. "I don't know nowt about that. All I know is Prince Gar sent me hotfootin' it down here to have a quick gander at this Spake from Basingdown. You be holdin' his note of authority in your hand. If you want to get in a brangle between the prince and his da, that be your business. Mine's doin' as I'm told by the man payin' me a fat sum of trins every week not to stand around arguin' about every little thing. Right?"

Orrick's chill gaze shifted. "You're not mentioned in His Highness's letter of authority, Mistress Dathne."

"No, but I am," said Asher. "And she's with me. Brought a mite of comfort for the prisoner. You sayin' you ain't goin' to let a condemned man have a mite of comfort in his last days? That's hard, that is."

Unprompted, Dathne held out the string bag. Orrick took it from her and inspected the contents. "It's not much," she said. "But a little is better than nothing."

"You know what crime it is this man stands accused of?" said Orrick, handing back the bag.

"Yes, Captain. Word's got about, it seems."

Orrick's face tightened. "And knowing it, still you'd bring him comfort? This blasphemous traitor?"

"As you say, Captain, he is but accused," she said, keeping her gaze discreetly lowered. "And Barl believed in mercy as well as swift retribution. If guilt is proven he'll be punished soon enough."

Orrick made a disgusted, impatient sound. "Very well.

You have five minutes to satisfy your prince's concerns, Meister Asher." Turning to one of his guards he snapped his fingers. "Bunder. Take the prince's assistant and Mistress Dathne here along to see the prisoner Spake. Stay with them while they count his fingers and toes and bring them back smartly thereafter."

Bunder saluted, then took the brass ring of keys Orrick handed him. "Yes, Captain!"

Dathne favored Orrick with her best smile. "Thank you so much, Captain. I'm sure His Highness will be well pleased, won't he, Asher?" When Asher scowled she did tread on his toes.

"Oy!" he said, annoyed, then took the hint. "Aye, he'll be tickled pink." He glanced out of the nearest window, then looked back at Orrick. His expression softened. "Reckon you got a bit on your plate tonight as it is, Captain. We'll be out of your hair directly."

Orrick's eyes lost a little of their chill. "I would appreciate it. Bunder?"

There was a stout wooden door to one side of the main desk. The guardsman opened it for them, let them pass, then closed it and led them along a corridor towards the rear of the building. The cells on either side of the passageway were empty. Dathne wasn't surprised; the guardhouse tended to fill up only at the end of the working week, when an excess of cheer and ale and lost bets on the horses caused trouble. As she followed Bunder's stiff spine and squared shoulders, the string bag bouncing on her shoulder, Dathne felt her heartbeat booming louder, faster.

It was a terrible thing she planned to do, terrible and dangerous. Draconis was not an obvious poison. It acted slowly, weakening the blood vessels in the brain. Some hours after consumption it induced violent seizures, mimicking the natural effects of a stroke. After suffering a series of convulsions, the victim lapsed into a stupor from which he could not be roused, then faded away over two or three days. Twice to her knowledge it had been used in other, equally dire circumstances and in neither case had the Olken healers or Doranen pothers summoned for aid detected its presence. Like so many other things, the knowledge of draconis root had slipped into darkness.

Still, she was taking a dreadful risk. Captain Orrick was a diligent man, jealous of his authority and jurisdiction. There was a chance he might on principle suspect foul play, even though she knew it most likely the brainstorm would be blamed on an Olken's tampering with magic. If the stakes hadn't been so high she never would have contemplated such a dangerous act. But if this fool Spake's nerve failed and he attempted to save himself by implicating others . . .

She felt vilely sick, with nerves and revulsion for what she was about to do. As poisons went draconis was relatively painless, but even so . . . *Jervale forgive me, I have no choice. Either I soil my hands a little now, or see them soaked in blood later.*

At the end of the corridor there was another door. Bunder selected a key from the ring he carried and unlocked it. Swinging the door open, he ushered them through.

The room beyond was small and windowless. Most of it was a cell, partitioned from the small front section by floor-to-ceiling metal bars in which a narrow door had been set. It was heavy with padlocks. The cell contained a bench, a bucket and a man. Its floor was strewn with fresh straw. Two small barred vents high up on the rear wall allowed fresh air to flow into the restricted space, but it wasn't enough to mask the stench of recent vomiting.

Hearing the door open, the prisoner looked up from his hunched squat over the bucket. The first thing Dathne thought on seeing him was: *Veira! Why didn't you tell me he was so young?*

Young, slight of body and plain with it. His face was unremarkable, his chin a trifle weak, his eyes mud brown and his black hair cut unbecomingly above his ears, which stuck out ever so slightly. There were freckles on his nose. It was hard to imagine him shaving. Harder still to imagine him whispering the words of forbidden magics.

She glanced at Asher, solid and silent by her side. His expression was smooth, unflustered; she was beginning to learn that it meant some deep consternation. Behind them Bunder closed the door and stood before it, feet wide and arms crossed over his chest. Fingers tight around the neck of the string bag, Dathne took a deep breath to calm her roiling stomach and waited.

"Is Hervy coming? Hervy Wynton?" Timon Spake asked uncertainly. He had a pleasant voice, deep for a young man, and it shook only a little. "He's a family friend. He said he was coming."

"I ain't the one to tell you that," said Asher. "I'm from the prince, to make sure they're treatin' you fair."

Spake's shoulders slumped. "Oh. I see." With a grunt and a grimace he got to his feet, one hand pressed to his middle.

'Well?" said Asher. "Got any complaints, do you?"

"No," said Spake.

Asher glanced over his shoulder. "Sure you ain't just sayin' that cause he's listenin'?" He jerked a thumb at Bunder.

"No," Spake said again. He was very pale, and there was a twitch beside his right eye. "I'm all right."

"Hungry?"

Spake shuddered and glanced at the bucket. "No. They gave me something a while ago but it's just made me sick."

Dathne felt a wave of despicable relief. Surely that would help muddle the cause of death, hint at something wrong before ever she got there . . . unless the cakelets made him ill, too, before the draconis could do its work. She tried not to frown. It couldn't be helped, she'd just have to hope for the best. *The best*, as she stood here face to face with the man—the boy—she was plotting to kill. She could easily have been sick herself. Not for the first time she wished she'd been born anything, anyone, other than Jervale's bloody Heir.

Asher said, "Well, there's some cakelets here for you, and a book anyways. It's bound to be a long night, you might as well have somethin' to take your mind off things. And Dathne's cookin's got to be better than prison slops. But then you'd know that, eh, what with her bein' family."

Spake stared, clearly puzzled. "Family? I'm sorry, I don't think I—"

Damn. "Distant family," she said quickly. "Cousins of cousins, several times removed. You've probably never heard of me except in passing mention." She took a hard breath then, and let it out again softly, instinct warring with caution. "Although . . . I think we both know Aunty Vee . . ."

The young idiot didn't make the connection. With a kind of hopeless courtesy, Spake raised a hand. "No, no. Thank you, but—" He blinked. "Did you say *Aunty Vee*?"

"Aye, y'fool. Be you deaf as well as gormless?" Asher said roughly. "Go on, take 'em, whether you know her or you don't. She needn't have brought anythin' for you, Spake. And you might be glad of somethin' in your belly afore the sun comes up."

She wouldn't, she couldn't, raise her voice to cajole the boy further. She'd done enough, invoking innocent Veira's name. But she held up the string bag, of a size to slide between the prison bars, and took a step forward. Just then somebody hammered on the door behind them and burst through it, shouting. Unprepared, bellowing, Bunder rocketed forward and sideways. Crashed straight into Asher, who yelled and crashed into her. She went down hard beneath his weight. Landed on the string bag and the cakelets and the book, crushing them all together in a sticky mess.

The guard whose fault it was stood panting and red-faced in the doorway. "Captain Orrick says you're to come at once! There's folks barged into the guardhouse and he says he wants the prince's man to send them away again or he'll fill the cells to bursting and a pox on all their guildmeister heads!"

Winded, groaning, her ribs bent almost double and her thoughts in shrieking disarray, Dathne lay on the cell floor as Asher and Bunder found their feet and cursed the stupid guard who'd skittled them.

"Bloody idiot, Torville!" Bunder raged. "You might've broken all our bones!"

Asher reached down a hand and pulled Dathne to her feet. "You all right?"

"I'm better than the cakelets," she said, and didn't know whether to laugh or cry. This had been her one and only hope of saving the Circle from Edvord Spake's arrogant son. Now all their lives were in his foolish, trembling hands . . . and she didn't know how she felt about it. She kicked the string bag with the toe of her shoe. "They're fit for nothing but rubbish now."

He patted her on the shoulder. "Never mind, Dath. It were a kindly thought, and that's what counts."

Picking up the string bag she took out the book, which had escaped the worst of the mess thanks to the tea towel she'd wrapped around the cakelets. After swiping her sleeve over it she thrust it through the prison bars. "Here."

"Thank you," said Timon Spake, taking the book. He looked at its cover and read the title. "*Heroes of the Old Days.* I've never read this one."

"It's very good," she said, and fixed her grim unblinking gaze upon him. "It's about brave men facing dire consequences with courage. Men who keep to their oaths despite all danger and temptation."

"Oh," said Timon Spake. Nothing showed in his face, but in his sad, troubled eyes questions were dawning. "It sounds . . . inspirational."

"It is," said Dathne, still holding his gaze. "It surely is." She lowered her voice. "You could do worse than follow their example."

"You must come now!" Torville insisted in the doorway, sounding shrill. "Captain Orrick insists!"

So they left the prisoner to his book and his thoughts and hurried back to the guardhouse lobby, where pandemonium ruled. Somehow a great gaggle of well-dressed City Olken had forced their way past the guards in the street outside and were now all shouting and stamping their feet and banging their fists upon the desk. Captain Orrick was standing behind it on a chair, trying to make himself heard above the din.

"Here!" he shouted as Torville practically shoved them through the door. "Here is Asher, His Royal Highness Prince Gar's Assistant Administrator! If you damn fools refuse to listen to me, then listen to him! For if you don't I swear I'll see you all locked up for a month of Barlsdays!"

Dathne dug her elbow into Asher's ribs. "Go on then, introduce yourself. After all, they had to meet you sometime, didn't they?"

"Ha. Don't reckon Gar had this in mind when he mentioned me gettin' to know a few people."

The largest well-dressed Olken pushed to the front of the crush around the desk. "*Who* do you say he is? I have never seen this man before!"

Cornered, Asher shot Orrick a dagger-drawn look then lithely leapt on top of the desk. "You heard 'im! I be Asher, Prince Gar's Assistant Administrator, as was newly appointed and announced last Barlsday. Who are you?"

The large man swelled inside his velvet and furs. "I? I, sir, am Norwich Porter, Meister of the Brewers' Guild!"

"Ah," said Asher. "Got yourself the prince's acceptance to the banquet, have you?"

Norwich Porter goggled at him. "What? Well . . . yes . . . as a matter of fact it arrived—"

"Well, you can set an extra place for me. I'll be there,

and so will His Highness—provided you quit all this caterwauling and get on home where you belong!"

Norwich Porter's face flushed dark red. "How dare you, sir! We are going nowhere, *nowhere*, do you hear, until we get satisfaction! We represent the will and the wishes of all the Olken guilds and we demand—"

"You ain't in the right place to be demandin' nowt!" said Asher. "Who do you think you are, eh, come bargin' into the City guardhouse, blusterin' and bossin' Captain Orrick, here, who's doin' the job your taxes pay him for. The job His Majesty King Borne told him to do just this mornin'. In Privy Council. Where I heard him with my own ears."

Dathne, smothering a smile, thought Norwich Porter was going to fall to the floor in a foaming, spluttering heap. All around him his fellow guild meisters and mistresses gasped and protested and waved their fists. Asher, bless him, was supremely unimpressed.

Norwich Porter said, incredulous, "You dare—you dare—by what right do you stand there and insult—"

"What insult? I'm just tellin' you what's what."

"No, sir," Porter retorted. "I shall tell *you* what's what. It is rumored that Captain Orrick has in custody a vile, treacherous, *evil* law-breaker. We will have him brought to justice! We will see him for ourselves! We—"

"Will end up in the cell next door if you don't quit flappin' your lips and listen!" shouted Asher. "Aye, there be a man here. He's accused—only accused, mind you— of a terrible crime. First thing tomorrow he'll stand afore king and Privy Council and then we'll know the truth of it. Until then he ain't standin' afore anybody, least of all a rabble what comes in here over lawful restraint tryin' to usurp the king's privilege!"

A shocked silence fell. After a moment, Norwich Porter cleared his throat. "I can assure you, sir," he said stiffly, "that nobody here intends to usurp the king's privilege."

"No?" said Asher, one eyebrow raised. "You could've fooled me."

Norwich Porter deflated a little further. Glanced uneasily at the guild officials on either side of him and took a small step back from the desk. "You say this man is to stand before His Majesty and the Privy Council?"

Asher smiled, fiercely. "Aye. Unless you got an objection, which I'd be more than happy to pass along to the king."

Behind Norwich Porter, the other guild meisters and mistresses exchanged furtive looks and began unobtrusively inching towards the front doors. Facing defeat, Norwich Porter rallied himself for one last blow. "And you, sir. Asher, you call yourself? Precisely how are we to know you are who you say you are?"

"Aside from bein' introduced by Captain Orrick here?" Asher smiled again, and Norwich Porter winced. "Come and say hello at your banquet next month. I'll be the one sittin' next to His Highness. Chances are I might remember you."

Dathne had to turn away, the urge to laugh was so strong. She doubted Guild Meister Porter had ever received so public a set-down in all his life.

Giving ground, Norwich Porter tried to gather the shreds of his dignity. "You are rude, sir. I shall be sure to mention that to His Highness the next time we speak."

"Well, you can if you want to," said Asher. "Only I figure he's noticed already. Ain't stoppin' him from payin' me, mind."

As the guild meister, by this time almost completely deserted by his peers, gasped and gobbled a string of incoherent threats and imprecations Orrick got down from his chair and came round to the front of the desk. "Guild Meister Porter, these are fractious times. I appreciate your concerns but the City Guard has everything under control. Do your duty, sir, you and your fellow meisters and mistresses, and tell your members outside to go home. There is nothing to be done here this night."

With a final glare at Asher, Norwich Porter and the handful of remaining guild officials with him departed.

With a pleased smile Asher leapt down from the desk. "So," he said cheerfully. "That be what they call public speakin', eh?"

Orrick favored him with a considering look. "Public bullying, more like."

Asher shrugged. "Silly ole farts, the lot of 'em. Ain't they the ones s'posed to be settin' an example for the rest of us?"

Orrick's lips twitched. "That's the idea."

"Well, a fine bloody example that was."

"Yes," said Orrick. His gray eyes were warm with amusement. "It certainly was." To Dathne's surprise, he held out his hand. "Well done, Meister Asher of Restharven. Welcome to Dorana. I'm sure you'll do very well here."

Despite her protests, Asher insisted on walking Dathne home, Cygnet clip-clopping at his side, even though the gathered crowd had mostly dispersed by the time they left the guardhouse. She bade him goodbye at her bookshop door and for a few moments watched him climb onto Cygnet and trot away up the street, back to the Tower.

Once inside her small apartment she put the string bag and the ruined cakelets in the hearth and burned them. Then she made herself a solitary supper and after that went straight to bed. She wasn't going to tell Veira what she'd almost done that night. It was one secret she'd take to her grave. Because she didn't wish to hurt her friend and mentor. Because she didn't want to argue the merits of an action that in the end was not taken. And because if she never spoke of it, ever, she might one day be able to forget what she'd found herself capable of doing.

Asher found a note pinned to his bedroom door when he finally got back to the Tower. *See me.* Cursing under his breath, he climbed the spiral staircase up to Gar's suite. Bloody worry-wart of a man. Spake wasn't going anywhere, was he? Couldn't this have waited till after he filled his empty belly?

"Spake's fine," he said, wandering into the prince's library. "Scared spitless, but fine. So—"

Gar's raised hand stopped him. "*Deverani, deverani,*" he murmured, staring at an unrolled parchment on the desk before him. He glanced up. "Contextually speaking, which is the closest modern Doranen word, do you think: *undone* or *released*?"

Asher blinked. "You're askin' *me*?"

"Well . . . yes," said Gar, and shook his head. "Though I don't for the life of me know why. Did you want something?"

"Aye," replied Asher, and thunked his shoulder against

the nearest handy bookcase. "Dinner. But there's this note on my door, see, and—"

Gar's expression clouded. "Oh. Yes. Sorry. I was deep in the Fourth Century."

"Huh," said Asher. From the look on the prince's face he wished he was still back there. "Spake's fine. I saw him, spoke to him. He ain't complainin'."

"Did he say anything at all?"

"Not really."

"He didn't . . . I don't know, confess? Explain *why* he'd want to—" Breaking off, Gar pinched the bridge of his nose.

"No," said Asher. "But then I didn't ask him, did I? Don't see what difference it makes any road. Who cares why? *Why* ain't goin' to change things, is it?"

Gar sighed. "No. I suppose not."

"All that matters now is Orrick's doin' his job fair and proper. You got nowt to fret on where that's concerned."

"Good," said Gar, again staring at the parchment. "That's . . . good."

Asher sniffed. "Mind you, things got a mite interestin' for a moment, seein' as every guild meister and his best friend was crammed into the guardhouse tryin' to drag the fool outside and hang 'im from the nearest lamppost . . ."

Gar's head snapped up. "*What*?"

"It's all right," Asher said quickly. "Me and Orrick sorted 'em out."

"Which means, I suppose, that by lunchtime tomorrow I'll be up to my armpits in outraged Olken guild meisters?" Gar stifled a groan. "How in Barl's name did they find out?"

Deciding not to take offence, Asher shrugged. "You weren't never goin' to keep it a secret."

"Not a secret, no, but I'm sure His Majesty would've liked at least one day's grace!" Gar pressed ink-stained fingers to his temples. "I know I would." He sighed. "Oh well. What's done can't be undone. And you're *sure* Spake is comfortably situated?"

Briefly, Asher debated telling him about the small cell and the prisoner's sickness and his terror, barely leashed. About how young he was and how unlikely, how pathetic, a criminal. But what was the point? Gar couldn't change any of it. And he'd see for himself soon enough, when the boy was brought before the Privy Council for examination.

"I told you," he said, pushing away from the bookcase, "he's fine. Now, if there ain't anythin' else, I'll see about my dinner. Reckon I be halfway to starved and—"

"Wait," said Gar. "There is something."

Caught in the doorway, Asher swallowed an impatient groan and swung around. "Aye?"

"I want you there tomorrow. At Timon Spake's hearing."

"Me? Why me?" Asher demanded, incredulous. "I don't need to be there. That's Privy Council business, it's got nowt to do with me. Besides, that Lord Jarralt—one look at me and he'll shout the guardhouse down."

Gar's eyes were cold, his expression unyielding. "He can shout till his head falls off for all I care. By this time tomorrow there's a very good chance Timon Spake will be dead. Executed by command of the Privy Council. I want an Olken witness. Justice must not only be done, it must be seen done. I want someone there who can tell whoever may ask that this man's life wasn't taken from him lightly. I want you, Asher. And I won't take no for an answer."

Silence. Staring at Gar, Asher knew he stood at a crossroad. If he refused this order it was all over. He might as well hitch a ride on the next wagon back to Restharven because nobody would hire on a man who walked away from His Royal Highness Prince Gar. And if he accepted it . . .

If he accepted it, there'd be no turning back. Whatever else he became in the future, however rich he was when he finally returned home or how many boats he bought and sailed and sold, he'd always be the man who once had served the son of a king . . . no matter what was asked of him. A man whose dreams of independence were paid for, in part, by the blood of a guilty fool.

Question was, could he live with that?

Well, Timon Spake was doomed, whether Asher of Restharven was there to see him die or not. And Gar was right about one thing, sink him. They did need an Olken witness to Spake's trial, someone who could stand on top of the tallest building in the kingdom and shout for every Olken man, woman and child to hear: *See? See what muckin' about with magic gets you?*

That was important. It might mean the end, once and for all, of such mad foolishness. Could be that by being there, by seeing first-hand how fair the Privy Council dealt with such a blasphemous criminal and then telling what he saw, he'd *save* lives. That was a good thing, right?

Besides, if he did walk away, who would profit? Who'd be saved then? Timon Spake would be just as condemned. Asher of Restharven would be forced home poor, back to the bruising domination of his brothers. And Da would go to his grave never knowing the comforts he deserved.

With a sigh deep enough to make his ribs creak, he nodded. "Right, then. Seein' as how you're so set on it, reckon I'll see you in the mornin'. What time?"

If Gar was relieved or sorry he didn't show it. "Be downstairs by nine. Make sure you're dressed . . . soberly."

Asher nodded. "Soberly. Right."

Their eyes met. There was such angry despair in Gar's face Asher had to look away.

"You can go now," the prince said. "I won't need you again this evening. Close the door behind you."

Dismissed, and glad of it, Asher left him to his rage and his reading and headed back downstairs to his own rooms.

All of a sudden, he wasn't hungry any more.

CHAPTER TWELVE

"Barl have mercy," King Borne exclaimed, shocked. "This Timon Spake is practically a *child*! Why did no one inform me?"

As Captain Orrick rummaged through the paperwork piled on the table before him, Asher avoided Gar's accusing gaze. The prince'd thank him for not saying anything. Eventually. From the looks of him Gar had barely slept a wink the night before. If he'd known just how beardless a youth it was they had in custody he'd have fretted himself to a standstill, with nothing to show for it by sunrise save a face fit to curdle cream.

Weighed down with chains, his face half hidden as he stared at the flagstoned floor of the guardhouse examination room, Timon Spake of Basingdown knelt in silent disgrace. A City Guard stood on either side of him, strong hands pressing hard on each shoulder as though at any moment he might sprout wings and fly away from the fate that awaited him.

Orrick looked up from his parchments. "The prisoner

is sixteen, Your Majesty. Under the law he is a man, and as a man must stand trial for his crime."

The king nodded. "Very well. In that case let the examination commence. Barlsman Holze?"

Holze lowered his head until his single silver-yellow braid dangled, and pressed his hand to his heart. "Let all here now entreat Blessed Barl's guidance, that we may know the truth and speak it unreserved to the glory of she who made the Wall and the comfort of all her children. O Blessed Barl, we stand before you in this place and at this time to hear the grave charges laid against your son, Timon Spake of Basingdown . . ."

Asher swallowed a sigh. If he'd known there'd be Holze sermonizing he'd have found himself something to sit on. Now he had to stand and wriggle his toes so his legs didn't fall asleep while the ole cleric prosed on and on and on . . .

After surviving a single scorching glare from Jarralt as they arrived at the guardhouse he'd wedged himself into one unobtrusive corner of the examination chamber while the hearing's preparations were concluded. From there he could witness the proceedings as commanded without actually getting involved.

The more he thought about it the more *not getting involved* seemed like a very good idea. This grim stone room was a far cry from the beauty and splendor of airy, stained-glass Justice Hall. In Justice Hall, though important matters were daily decided, there was still a kind of brightness. An unstated recognition that even though the hearings were serious there yet remained light and laughter in the world.

Not so in here. Light and laughter had no place in this

plain, crowded place. In here, without beauty or splendor, the lives of men were stripped bare and judged, and if found wanting . . . ended.

The examination chamber was full of people: the king and his Privy Council, a wall of disapproval and dire consequence implacably ranged against the grubby miscreant cowering at their feet. Lady Marnagh from Justice Hall, seated at the table beside Orrick and once more acting as justice's official record-keeper. Two more faces Asher couldn't put a name to. Speakers for the accused? Or against him. He couldn't tell. There were three other guards as well, one on each side of the prisoner's entrance to the chamber and one at the examiner's entrance.

In keeping with his royal authority Borne was seated on a tall gold and crimson chair set upon a raised platform that ran the length of the bleak examination room. Austere in black velvet, his crown flashed green and crimson fire in the glimlight. At his left hand stood Master Magician Durm, somber in a black brocade robe. Gar stood at his right hand, equally grave in midnight blue silk. Droning Holze, wrapped in white as befitted the Royal Barlsman, stood next to Gar with Conroyd Jarralt, magnificent in peacock blue, beside Durm.

Asher stiffled a curse. So many bodies: surely they'd soon breathe up all the air in the stuffy, windowless room. Already he was sweating, trickles down his spine, behind his ears, stinging his eyes and soaking his armpits. At this rate his suitably sober green shirt and brown weskit, sent along from the tailor yesterday afternoon with all his other clobber, would both be ruined with stink and salt.

Holze's prayer still showed no sign of ending. Asher stared at the king. Could be it was his imagination but he thought Gar's da looked even more stripped clean of flesh than he had the previous morning. As though some terrible fever had rushed rampaging through him overnight, stealing meat and muscle from his bones unopposed. His clear green eyes, Gar's eyes, had sunk deep into his skull, and the unguarded moment of surprise at first beholding the prisoner, which had flushed his hollow cheeks, was vanished without a trace. Now Borne's face looked like a winter snowfield, cold and clean, with all emotion frozen.

Gar's face was a bonfire in comparison; leaping behind his eyes the flames of passionate revolt, their shadows flickering, their heat washing his cheeks red with reflected warmth. Though he stood motionless at his father's side, it seemed to Asher that the prince was shaking, so extreme was the tension in every line of his body.

As for Durm and Jarralt . . . they more closely resembled the king. Their expressions were chilled, their gazes laden with ice. Even Holze, praying, appeared unsympathetic. Timon Spake of Basingdown had but one friend on that platform, and Gar would never prevail in such company, even if he wanted to.

Barring intervention from Blessed Barl herself, Timon Spake of Basingdown was doomed.

Sixteen years of age, and never to see seventeen. Never to kiss another girl or fondle a woman's breast or dandle a milk-sucking son upon his knee. No more springtimes. One last sunset.

What a waste.

At long last Holze's prayer ended. The king said gravely, "Read the charge, Captain Orrick."

Orrick bowed and unrolled crackling parchment. "On this day, the sixth day in the second month of summer in the year 644 After Barl, it is alleged that the prisoner, one Timon Spake of Basingdown, did upon the fourth day in the second month of summer in the year 644 After Barl wilfully and absent coercion break Barl's First Law: to wit, that before witnesses he exhorted magic in the full knowledge that he is Olken and thus forbidden to do so on pain of death." He looked up then and stared stonily at every face in the chamber. "Whosoever does dispute this charge speak now or be hereafter silent."

When nobody spoke, Borne nodded. "Thus is the charge heard and ratified and entered into record. Who speaks against the accused?"

One of the men Asher didn't know stepped forward. Serious in dark brown velvet, draped in chains of office with a feather nodding in his cap, he bowed to the king then again to the rest of the Council.

"Your Majesty, I am Bryne Fletcher, Mayor of Basingdown. It was my daughters who did come upon this man in the woods and so espy his blasphemous and criminal conduct."

Borne's hands rested quietly on his knees. His keen, cold gaze considered the Basingdown mayor in silence. When he spoke his tone was level, his manner dispassionate. "And where are your daughters now, Mayor Fletcher?"

"At home with their mother, Your Majesty. They are but maids, eleven and thirteen years of age. I have given the guard captain their sworn and witnessed statements, as prescribed by law."

"It is so, Your Majesty," said Orrick. "I have the statements here."

A shadow of disquiet crossed Borne's brutally sculptured

face. "And are your daughters sure beyond doubt of what they saw, Mayor Fletcher? In capital matters tender years are no defense against a false accusation. Children have fanciful imaginations, sir. I know, I have two of my own. Before we proceed in this matter I ask you most strictly: do you stand by the witnessed statements of your offspring? Knowing that should this charge be challenged and a full, public hearing be demanded by the accused, as is his right, you and your wife will be held equally accountable for their claims should they be proven false?"

The mayor's florid face lost its color, but his forthright gaze held steady. "I stand by my girls, Your Majesty. Their mother and I have raised them to honor Barl, to obey the law, to daily do right by their neighbour and without exception turn away from wrongdoing. Your Majesty, they have nothing to gain from this and much to lose. They know Timon and are fond of him." The mayor hesitated. Glanced once at the prisoner and cleared his throat. "We are all fond of him. But my daughters know their duty and have done it. My wife and I are proud of them, sir."

"I see." Borne held out his hand. "The statements, Captain." Orrick presented them to the king. Borne read each one, pale brows drawn low. When he was done he gave them to his Master Magician, who read them also, and from him they passed in turn to the other Council members to be read and considered.

Gar was the last to see the witness statements. When he was done he passed the papers back to the king. Borne read them a second time then gave them back to Orrick, who returned to his seat beside Lady Marnagh.

"The statements are in order," Borne said. "And therefore stand in evidence against the accused. Thank you, Mayor Fletcher. Your duty is done. You may commend your daughters on our behalf."

"Yes, Your Majesty," said Fletcher, breathless. "Thank you, Your Majesty." Dismissed, he stepped back again, visibly relieved.

The king said, "Who now speaks for the accused?"

The second man unfamiliar to Asher presented himself. After an unsteady bow he clasped his hands to his drab woollen chest. "Your Majesty." His voice was scarce above a whisper; a gently aging man, he seemed overcome. "My name is Hervy Wynton. I am friend to the Spake family. Edvord Spake, father of the accused, was too ill to make the journey from Basingdown. He has a canker and is dying. He asked me to speak for him in this matter."

Borne nodded. "And what would the accused's father have you say on his behalf?"

Hervy Wynton licked his dry lips. His troubled gaze rested briefly on his friend's son, chained and kneeling, then returned to the stern figure of the king. "Your Majesty, Timon is a good boy. A loving son. He is all that my friend Edvord has left to him in the world. Whatever Timon has done it was never with malicious intent. He is no blasphemer, Your Majesty. Just a rash youth who thought to amuse himself with something he did not understand. Edvord knows his time is short, Your Majesty. He implores your mercy, that his last days be not spent in bitter grief and ceaseless tears."

If the king was moved by the old man's plea there was nothing to show it. "And do you or the accused's father challenge the charge as it stands? Can you show evidence of false accusation? Of wilful slander? Of any dark design intended to bring harm to Timon Spake of Basingdown and thereby benefit the accuser?"

"No, Your Majesty," whispered Hervy Wynton. "We accept . . . that the girls saw what they saw."

Borne nodded. "Very well. You may tell your friend Edvord Spake that his words were heard by king and Privy Council."

Hervy Wynton bowed again and shuffled back to stand beside the mayor. Now all eyes turned to the accused. Borne's thin fingers tightened once upon the arms of his tall chair, then relaxed. "Timon Spake of Basingdown, you have heard the charge leveled against you. What now have you to say for yourself? Are you guilty or falsely accused? Say you guilty and sentencing shall follow. Say you falsely accused and a public trial shall be held, with no shadowed corner left unlit until this matter is illuminated to the full."

For the first time since he'd been brought into the chamber, forced to his knees and held in silence as his life was pulled to pieces around him, Timon Spake of Basingdown looked up.

Asher saw Gar's face contract, saw him flinch as though someone had struck him a painful blow. He scowled. So the blaspheming law-breaker looked no more dangerous than a half-grown hound. So what? He'd still shown his teeth, hadn't he? He'd still put a kingdom—a people—at risk. His own people, if this whole disaster had got out of hand. He looked pitiful now, aye, but that didn't change what he'd done. On purpose. With not a man there to twist his arm and make him cry if he didn't.

Da always said, *Talk is cheap and so be a sorry smile*.

"Answer the question, Timon Spake," the king said coldly. "Your life depends upon it. Are you guilty or falsely accused?"

The chains that bound him looked heavy. They must be hurting him, Spake's thin muscles must surely be shrieking beneath their weight by now. And his knees, pressed unpadded into the unforgiving stone floor, had to be hurting too. Grudgingly, Asher had to admit he admired the fool's nerve not to show it.

Mayor Fletcher's head bowed low, awaiting the answer. Beside him, Hervy Wynton cried out.

"Dispute the charge, Timon! Give yourself a chance! Think of your father, boy! Must I go home without you and break his dying heart?"

"Be silent, man," the king commanded. "We have heard from your own lips your belief that this is a true and lawful charge untainted by deceit or ulterior motive. Do not encourage the prisoner in dishonesty lest justice turn its eyes upon you."

Reprimanded, Hervy Wynton shrank back against the wall and turned his face away. Solitary and splendid in his tall chair King Borne leaned forward, hands braced on his knees, and bent a piercing gaze upon his prisoner. "I ask you a third time, Timon Spake of Basingdown, and give you fair warning: I will not ask again. Are you guilty or falsely accused?"

Timon Spake of Basingdown's weak chin lifted and his chained shoulders braced themselves. When he spoke his voice was calm. Resigned. "Your Majesty, I am guilty."

Borne turned his head to left and right, raking his winter gaze along the faces of his privy councilors. "Gentlemen, you have heard the accusation and the prisoner's reply. Out of his own mouth is he convicted and therefore public trial is rendered moot. Before sentence is pronounced, is there any one of you who would raise his voice in mitigation? If so, raise it now."

One by one Asher looked at the men of the king's Privy Council. He could read nothing in Durm's fat face; it was as smooth as a bladder of lard. Barlsman Holze looked unsurprised and gently sorrowful. Conroyd Jarralt was smiling, a small fierce flashing of teeth. And Gar . . .

All the flames behind Gar's eyes had died, the passionate hope crumbled into ash. He looked ill and tired and unspeakably sad.

Not one of them answered the king's call.

Borne sat back in his chair. On his head his jeweled crown danced color across the gray stone walls. "Timon Spake of Basingdown, you have been heard by king and Privy Council in strict accordance with law. By your own admission and the unchallenged statements of honest witnesses you are found guilty of the charge laid against you. The penalty is death. Therefore I, King Borne, by Barl's grace named WeatherWorker of Lur, do declare your life forfeit and claim it in recompense for the crime committed. Captain Orrick?"

As Timon Spake stared blankly at the floor and Hervy Wynton's harsh sobs punctured the silence, Orrick stood up from his chair and bowed. "Your Majesty?"

"Have you a headsman at hand?"

Orrick nodded. "Yes, Your Majesty."

"Is his axe sharp?"

"Sharp and waiting, Your Majesty."

"Can you think of any impediment to the immediate culmination of this proceeding?"

Now Orrick was frowning, the merest hint of concern. "No, Your Majesty. Everything is ready."

Borne's fingers laced themselves tightly in his lap. His eyes were hooded, his face untouched by any human feeling. "Then let it be done, and done swiftly."

Orrick hesitated. "You mean now, Your Majesty? In here?"

The king considered him. "The kingdom is not served by a public spectacle, Captain. Or unwarranted delay."

"Of course not, Your Majesty." Orrick bowed again. "If Your Majesty and the Privy Council would care to withdraw to my office, then—"

"Withdraw?" said Borne. "For what reason? Justice must not only be done, Captain. It must be seen done or it is not justice at all."

"Your Majesty, I will be here. The guards will be here. Justice—"

"Demands that those who pass judgement shall witness judgement," said Borne. "And if not justice then surely conscience. No more discussion. Captain. Proceed."

Orrick nodded. "Yes, Your Majesty. There will be a short delay. Certain items that—"

"See to them. Quickly."

Orrick turned and flicked a commanding finger at the guard standing alert by the prisoner's entrance to the chamber. The man nodded, opened the door and went about his business. The mayor covered his face with his hands and turned away from Timon, who knelt unmoving, as though in a trance. Heedless of any personal danger Hervy Wynton cried out again and flung himself forward to land on his hands and knees at the king's feet.

"Have mercy, Your Majesty!" he begged, his voice rough with tears. "Give me an hour alone with the boy, give him one more night, at least let him see another sunrise, oh please, *please*, Your Majesty—"

For the first time, Durm spoke. "To what end, Wynton?" He stepped down from the platform and pulled the man to his feet, away from the king. "What can Timon Spake do between now and another sunrise that will make the least bit of difference?"

Wynton's face was ravaged with grief. "But . . . but . . ."

"It's all right, Hervy," said Timon. "Don't fret. This is my doing, not yours. Take my father a message, would you?"

As Durm stepped back onto the platform Wynton stumbled two steps towards his friend's son, then halted as the guards raised warning hands. "What message?" he asked brokenly. "I swear I'll deliver it."

Now there were tears on Timon Spake's white cheeks, and his lips were trembling. "Tell Papa he was right. Tell him I'm sorry. Tell him I did the right thing at the end, when it mattered."

"I'll tell him," Wynton whispered. "Dear boy, I'll tell him."

"Hervy Wynton," said Borne, and beckoned the man to him with a single raised finger. "It is not necessary that you stay and see this matter concluded. If you would care to wait outside . . ."

Wynton shook his head. "No. No, Your Majesty. I'll stay. I owe his father that much, having failed him."

For a moment Asher thought the king might touch

Hervy Wynton. Lay a hand upon him. Pat his shoulder, or hold his thin wrist briefly. The impulse was in Borne's cold face, he could see it, the swift desire, the fleeting need. Then it passed. "You did not fail him, Wynton. Timon Spake has failed himself. Failed all of us who labor night and day for the greater good of Lur."

Slowly, the old man nodded. Dipped his head in a bow. "As you say, Your Majesty," he replied, and stepped back.

The king looked at the Mayor of Basingdown. "And you, sir?"

Fletcher's face was the color of skimmed milk. "I— my wife—my girls—"

"You may go," said Borne.

Then came a flurry of activity as Orrick's paperwork was removed along with the table and chairs. Lady Marnagh took her records and departed. Mayor Fletcher went with her. More guards entered the chamber, carrying armfuls of straw and a roughly shaped wooden block and a basket. The king turned his head. "Holze."

"Certainly, Your Majesty," murmured Holze, and went to the prisoner.

Asher, disregarded and disbelieving, watched as the Barlsman knelt beside Timon Spake. Rested a gentle hand against his cheek and began to speak softly in his ear. Whatever he was saying seemed to give the boy a measure of comfort. He began to nod. To cry more freely. Holze sang a hymn and the boy joined in, haltingly, his forehead lowered to Holze's white silk shoulder.

Asher looked at Gar. Wasn't it about time he spoke up? Said something along the lines of, "Well done, Asher, you can go"? His da had just pronounced sentence of death on that stupid, beardless youth. Any minute now they were going to chop off his stupid head, right in front them, in front of *him*, and when he said he'd witness the hearing that didn't include the head-chopping bit afterwards.

As though reading his mind Gar looked at him. Shook his head, the very slightest of motions. Spoke not a word, but instead let his face do the speaking for him.

You wanted him dead. You can watch him die.

Stunned, furious, Asher felt his sweaty hands clench into fists. This wasn't *his* fault. Timon Spake was the criminal here, not him, so why was he getting punished? Why did he have to see poor bloody Timon Spake get his head hacked off? That wasn't fair. Well, one thing was bloody certain. Fifty trins a week didn't cover *this* kind of aggravation.

No amount of money covered this kind of aggravation.

The prisoner's entrance door opened again and a tall man in black, wearing a black mask and carrying a wicked-looking axe, stepped into the chamber. Asher felt his stomach heave, all his partly digested breakfast rising hot and acid into his throat. He was sweating in earnest now, rivers of horror pouring down his back, his chest. He could hardly breathe, and there were little red spots dancing before his eyes.

The straw had been spread on the flagstone floor to the far right side of the chamber. Well beyond spraying distance of king and Council, Asher realized. The wooden block squatted in the middle of that yellow, absorbent sea and the basket waited on one side. Now Holze was kissing Timon Spake on the forehead. Was helping him to his feet so he could take the faltering steps that would place him within reach of that block, that basket. Now Spake was kneeling again, Holze's tender hands helping him down, down, to the thick and golden straw. The headsman was taking his position. The boy, bound in chains, convicted out of his own mouth, bent over. Lowered his head. Stretched across the wooden block. It was rough. He must be getting splinters in his throat. Holze withdrew. The room was hushed, no speaking, no sobbing. Time stood still.

The headsman looked at the king. The king nodded.

The axe came down, a single strong and steady stroke. The blade bit through flesh and bone and deep into the rough-hewn timber of the block. Timon Spake of Basingdown died. The golden straw around him turned red, the airless chamber filling with the rank iron smell of fresh blood. Hervy Wynton vomited.

Asher didn't, but only just.

The king rose from his tall chair. His hands were steady, his face untouched by tears or anything else. He went to Hervy Wynton, who was wiping his mouth with a handkerchief. "You may take Timon home now, Meister Wynton," he said softly. "Lay him to rest with kindness. He wasn't a bad lad. He lacked judgement. But Barl's Law must hold for all of us, the wise and the foolish alike. My sorrow to his father."

"Yes, Your Majesty," whispered Hervy Wynton. "Thank you, Your Majesty."

Borne turned away from him. "Captain Orrick?"

Orrick, seemingly unmoved, bowed. "Yes, Your Majesty?"

"Assist Meister Wynton. Then see that word is spread throughout the City. Justice is served. Barl's Law is upheld. This business is done, and done. The king's mercy on Lur's people and Barl's blessings as well."

"Yes, Your Majesty."

Borne and his Privy Council left the chamber. Asher, his legs unsteady, followed them out of the guardhouse and into the fancy courtyard out the back, where all their carriages were waiting. The air was clean and fresh. Unbloodied. The sun was shining. There were people in the streets beyond, perhaps the same people who last night had gathered and muttered and called for vengeance. They were bustling now, preoccupied, going about their daily business. As though nothing had changed. As though no one had just died. When they found out, would they be sorry? Or would they dance with delight?

Gar turned to him. His expression was cold. Distant. "I'm returning to the palace with His Majesty. You can take the carriage back to the Tower if you like. I won't need you again today."

Dumbly Asher stared at him. Took a deep breath and rediscovered his voice. Even to his own ears it sounded strange. Thin, and unfamiliar. "I don't want the carriage. I'm goin' to walk for a bit."

"Suit yourself," said Gar, shrugging. "I'll send it back to the stables then."

As Gar turned away, Asher reached out his hand. Brushed his fingertips against the prince's elbow so that he looked back. "Did you know that were goin' to happen?" he demanded harshly. "Did you know Spake were goin' to be killed right then and there?"

Gar's glance flickered towards the king, who was climbing into his carriage. Durm, dismissing the groom, held the door open for him. Holze and Jarralt were already tucked neat and tidy into their own carriages, waiting for Borne to take his leave so they could retreat as well. The prince shook his head.

"No. Of course I didn't. But Durm was right. Today. Tomorrow. What difference did it make? He was always going to die."

Asher watched him wave their carriage away, climb into the king's carriage and pull the door shut. Watched the dark brown horses respond to Matcher's whip, and trot away.

He turned on his heel and started walking.

As the bookshop door closed behind another customer Dathne let her head drop to her hands and groaned aloud. It was tempting, so damned tempting, to hang her "closed" sign in the window and shoot home all the bolts, even though it was barely an hour past lunchtime. And she'd do it, she really would, if one more person rushed in to her today and gasped, "Have you heard? There's going to be a trial. They say he planned to bring down the Wall! Barl have mercy, what is the world coming to? I hope they hang him from the top of the guardhouse. I hope they beat him first. I hope they make him pay. To bring such shame on innocent Olken. To make the Dora-nen question our loyalties. Our gratitude. What a wicked man. What an evil deed."

Her head was pounding with their fear, their indignation, their fervent desire for swift punishment and an even swifter return to normality. A pretence that none of this had ever happened. Her mouth was sour with it, her insides knotted. As if she didn't have her own fears. As if she weren't on tenterhooks, waiting. Wondering. Dreading.

Every time the shop door opened she looked up expecting to see a City Guard with her own death in his face.

When it did swing wide again and the little warning bell jiggled and rang, the noise scraped her raw nerves like fingernails down a plaster wall. Swallowing a scream she pinned a smile to her lips and looked up.

Asher. Smart as new paint in a fancy weskit and brand-new shirt and breeches, although, looking more closely, they seemed a little the worse for wear. Something dreadful lurked in his eyes. She slid out from behind the shop counter, one hand reaching for him. "What is it? What's happened?"

He looked at her and her heart twisted. "It's over," he said. There was an undercurrent of savagery in his voice. "He's dead."

It was like a fist to the stomach, violent and unexpected. "Spake?"

Ignoring her outstretched fingers he began to pace, hands shoved deep into his breeches' pockets, stretching them all out of shape. "He confessed. The king had his head cut off on the spot."

She had to sit down. Groping her way back behind the counter again she bumped herself onto the shop stool and tried to steady herself. "Oh."

Adrift, staring at the bookshelves but seeing something else entirely, Asher shook his head. "There was so much blood. Didn't expect that. Spent most of m'life beheading fish, y'know, and pullin' their guts out for good measure, but they hardly bleed at all. Don't know why." He shuddered. "Spake bled. He bled everywhere. All over the floor. Up the wall, even. Made a right bloody mess. Ha." Frowning, he shook his head. "Weren't like he was a big bloke, either. Scrawny little runt really. Hardly fair to call 'im a man, even though he was sixteen, and legal."

She remembered to breathe. Timon Spake was dead, and the Circle lived. "I know."

Asher's dark expression melted into something softer. Sorrier. "Stupid bastard. Why'd he want to go fartin' about with magic anyways? Stupid, stupid bastard."

A little color was seeping back into his face. Going to him, she took his hand. It was like ice. "Tell me what happened," she coaxed, tugging him towards the little sofa by the window where customers liked to sit and browse and chat. "Tell me *everything*."

After he'd finished she poured a glass of brandy down his unresisting throat. Then she poured one down her own. He said, vaguely, "I never asked you what you thought."

"About what?"

He waved his hand. "Spake."

"It doesn't matter what I think," she said, cramming the cork back into the brandy bottle. "He's dead. It's over. Life goes on."

Brooding, Asher stared into his empty glass. "Bloody Gar. I didn't need to see that. Bastard. Reckon I've got a good mind to—"

Dathne went cold. "You can't," she said, snatching the glass from him. "You have to stay. We Olken need you here working with the prince, now more than ever. You can't quit, Asher."

He glanced at her and his lips twisted in a lopsided smile. "I know. I need the money, don't I?" He stood. "Thanks for listenin', Dath. I needed it."

"You're going?"

He shrugged. "Got some more walkin' to do, I reckon. Got to see if I can't leave what happened a bit further behind me."

He bent to kiss her cheek, and she let him. "If you need to talk more, you know where I am."

"Aye," he said. "Reckon I do."

She locked the door behind him then dashed upstairs and contacted Veira.

You have news, child?

She took a deep breath to calm her racing heart. "It's done, Veira. Timon Spake is dead, and we are safe."

Dead? Already? How?

Quickly she explained. "I'm as surprised as you. I never dreamed it would be dealt with so swiftly."

Poor Edvord. This will finish him. He was only hanging on for the boy. For us.

"It seems he knew best in the end. His son kept the faith. Prophecy will continue."

Edvord can take comfort from that, at least. But what of Asher?

"What of him? He's shaken, but he'll be all right."

The link between them fell to humming silence as Veira considered. *Tread softly, Dathne*, she said at last. *This may go deeper than you know. He's seen first-hand the consequences of what we do. When the time comes for him to join us . . .*

"He'll join us," she said. "Prophecy says so."

Another silence. *Is that Seeing, child, or hoping?*

"Seeing," she said, with far more confidence than she felt, remembering Asher's revulsion and his milk-white face.

Jervale grant it be so. Thanks, child, for the news. I'd best be with Edvord now.

"Veira!"

Yes, child?

"We are going to be all right now, aren't we? With Timon dead, the Circle will be safe?"

There was another, longer silence. Shocked, through the link Dathne thought she could feel Veira weeping.

"I'm sorry," she whispered. "I forget sometimes. You knew him. You know us all. This must be so hard for you . . ."

It is hard for all of us, child. Prophecy is a cruel master. As to your question . . . yes, I think we are safe. Our secret is unspoken, our existence still unknown. But I'll warn the others to have a special care. You tread lightly, too, and Matt.

"We will, Veira. I promise."

With the link severed, Dathne went back downstairs, reopened the shop and let business and the swiftly spreading news of the blasphemer's just desserts crowd out all her other clamoring concerns.

They were safe. Prophecy continued. Now all she had to do was wait.

CHAPTER THIRTEEN

When Asher finally wandered into the Tower stable yard, his feet blistered from walking so far in new boots and his guts still burning from the brandy Dathne had bullied him into drinking, Matt came to greet him. All around them the lads scurried about their afternoon chores as the horses hung their heads over their stable doors, whickering hopefully for food. Butterflies danced above the flowerbeds.

Seeing him, the lads laughed and waved. Bellybone catcalled, grinning, and wagged a rude finger. Asher wagged back but couldn't quite manage a return grin. Suddenly, sharply, he missed the rough simplicity and uncomplicated companionship of the stables.

"Where've you been?" said Matt, looking him up and down with appraising eyes. "The carriage got back from town ages ago."

Asher scraped a line in the gravel with his heel. "Walkin'."

"For three hours?"

"So? Ain't no law against it last time I looked."

Sighing, Matt hooked his thumbs into his scarred leather belt. "You've been avoiding me lately. Why?"

Asher shrugged. "Didn't want to talk about Spake."

"Who says I did?"

"You sayin' you didn't?"

Matt pulled a face, admitting defeat. "Word is Spake's dead. Executed."

"I know. I was there."

Matt's expression changed. "You all right?"

Asher smiled, tiredly. Was he all right? No. Not really. "Y'know, you be the first one to ask." He sighed. "I'm fine. Just . . . when I got up this mornin' I surely didn't count on . . ." He shrugged again and shoved his hands deep into his pockets. "*That*."

"Who would?" said Matt, one eye on the lads. "Bellybone!" he called sharply. "You're dropping hay all over the countryside!"

Bellybone stopped. Looked. "Sorry, Matt!" he shouted, grinning. His skinny arms clutched a hastily stuffed sack of dried grass like it was his last hope of true love. "I'll pick it up directly!"

Despite the cold lump of miserable anger in his gut, Asher smiled. Bellybone was contagious. Always grinning, no matter what, infecting everybody around him with smiles. Even Matt was fighting to keep his face stern.

"Mind you do!" the stable meister retorted. "Or you'll find it on your dinner plate tonight and that's a promise!" As the other lads hooted and whistled he turned back to Asher. "Timon Spake was a fool."

The brief amusement died. "Well, he be a dead fool now," said Asher grimly.

Matt's hand came to rest on his shoulder. "It had to be done."

"I ain't sayin' it didn't. Just . . ."

"Saying it and seeing it are two different things?"

"Aye."

Letting his hand drop, Matt stared over the treetops and into the cooling blue sky. Toward the mountains and the indirect cause of Timon Spake's lonely death.

"The Wall's all there is, Asher, keeping us safe. You can't let misplaced mercy put a whole kingdom at risk. Not after six hundred years. It's sad a man died, but if his meddling had brought down the Wall, how many more deaths would there be? It's one life against tens and tens of thousands, my friend. And anyway, Timon Spake knew the price of law-breaking, just like the rest of us do. Now he's paid it."

Asher nodded. "That's pretty much what Dathne said."

"Did she? Well, then. You should listen to her. She's right. And so am I."

He was really very tired. "I know, I know. You're right, she's right, the king's right. Everybody's right. And that poor bastard's dead. And Gar . . ."

Matt picked up an errant stick of straw and began shredding it with his strong, blunt fingers. "What about him?"

"He's . . . sorry."

The stick of straw disintegrated. Matt tucked the tattered remains in his shirt pocket and considered him. "And you're angry."

Bloody oath he was angry. Despite hours of walking and silent swearing, still angry. He turned away, simmering resentment hunching one shoulder. "I agreed to witness the hearing. Nowt more. Weren't me passing judgement on Spake, eh? Weren't me had the power to speak up for him and didn't. That was Gar. He should've let me leave with the others. *Bastard*."

Matt frowned. "Do I have it wrong? Was Spake's guilt not certain after all?"

"No. It was as certain as I be standin' here. He admitted it. And there were sworn witnesses. Two little girls . . . but sworn, all the same. Their father's a mayor. He vouched for 'em."

"So. Spake was guilty. And you agree the law's got to be upheld?"

Now what was Matt getting at? "'Course I bloody do! What's your point?"

"Then you judged him, didn't you?" Matt said gently, using the voice he saved for especially fractious colts. "And if you judged him you owed him witness of his death. That's only fair."

Because it was Matt, whose opinion he'd come to value, he didn't swear and stamp off back to the Tower. "I s'pose," he muttered grudgingly.

"Tell me something. You say Gar wouldn't let you leave? Fair enough. You were stuck there. But he couldn't force you to watch, could he? When the moment came you could've closed your eyes. Or looked away. Why didn't you?"

"How d'you know I didn't?"

Matt's smile was melancholy. "It's written all over your face, Asher."

He glared at the ground. "I couldn't. The stupid little bastard had guts, didn't he? Never begged. Just owned up. He . . . he put his head on that bloody chunk of wood like he was in bed and that were his feather pillow!" It was an image he knew would haunt him for nights to come. Maybe forever. "Sixteen, he was. Not a man, I don't care what the law says. And he knew he was goin' to die. But he sang a bloody hymn with Holze and he knelt in all that damn straw and he let 'em cut his head off with an axe . . . and he never once said they shouldn't or begged 'em not to."

"He was brave then."

"As brave as he was stupid! And Barl knows he was as stupid as they come. If y'want the truth, Matt, I don't know if I could've been so calm. So I s'pose I—I felt like I owed it to 'im not to look away."

"Despite everything then, Spake was a good lad." Matt's voice was thick with feeling. Shocked, Asher saw tears in his eyes. Matt turned away, embarrassed. Plucked a faded bloom from a nearby rosebush and crushed the wilted petals in his fist. "His death's a stupid, shameful waste. If he'd lived, he might've been . . ." Unheeded, the ruined rose petals drifted to the ground. His voice fell to a whisper. "He might've been anything."

"Aye, well," said Asher once the silence had stretched a good ways beyond comfortable, "it's all over now any road, and a damn good job too. Reckon I've had enough blood and death to last me a lifetime."

Matt stared at him, frowning. "Well . . . it's not *quite* over," he said, and nodded at the other side of the stable yard. "Cygnet's saddled and waiting for you."

Following the nod Asher saw his horse's bridled head poke over its stable door, ears pricked. "Why?"

Matt met his challenging stare with a challenge of his own. "His Highness rode out of here nearly an hour ago and I didn't much care for the look of him. I think he was—" He reconsidered. "He'd been drinking. Said he was going out to Salbert's Eyrie. You know where that is?"

"Aye. Bellybone and Mikel took me to see it my second week here." Asher thought about that. "The Eyrie? And he's drunk, you say? Sink me bloody sideways! Matt, you don't reckon he'd do somethin' daft like—"

"Would I be standing here if I did? What I think is you should go after him. Forget you're angry. Forget what you saw. Just . . . go after him. Now."

Asher went. Even though it meant leaving dinner behind, Cygnet was glad of the gallop; his enormous strides ate up the eight miles between the Tower and the popular picnic park and lookout over Lur's deepest, wildest valley gorge.

Nobody was picnicking there now. The Eyrie was deserted save for Gar's horse Ballodair, tied to a safely distant sapling and dancing at Cygnet's arrival . . . and Gar himself. The fool had blithely, stupidly ignored the safety railings and the warning signs and perched himself on a rock several feet distant from the official viewing platform. Sighing, Asher tied Cygnet next to Ballodair and joined the prince in his folly.

"If you be thinkin' of jumpin' don't expect me to follow you down," he remarked. "I ain't got no head for heights."

Gar glanced at him sideways then returned to his contemplation of the bone-breaking drop below them. The valley floor was hidden. All that could be seen was a sharply sloping terrace of boulders, bare dirt, scrubby saplings and tangled undergrowth, then nothing but tree after tree after tree, spreading for miles like a green and leafy ocean.

"What are you doing here?" asked the prince. His expression was remote. Uncaring. If he was in his cups the excess alcohol hadn't spilled out of him yet.

Asher hunkered to his heels cautiously. Peered over the edge of the precipice and pulled a face. "Buggered if I know." He shrugged. "Came to talk, I s'pose."

"How . . . convivial . . . of you."

Moving at a snail's pace, mindful of the merciless drop mere inches away, Asher sat down. "But not prince to fisherman, mind. I'll tell you straight, I ain't in the mood for that kind of conversation just now."

That earned him a dark look. "Are you ever?"

So. His Royal Highness was a surly drunk, was he? Well sink that for a load of mackerel. "Look. If you don't want company, Gar, just say so. I ain't—"

"Stay," Gar said. "Please. And we'll talk like fr—like two men in plain clothes with not a crown in sight."

Asher stretched out his legs again. "Fine."

"Good." Reaching inside his black tunic Gar pulled out a silver flask inlaid with mother-of-pearl, unscrewed the lid and trickled something smelling of old peaches into his open mouth.

After a moment, Asher said, "My ma always said it were polite to share."

Gar tipped the flask upside down. It was empty.

Asher snorted. "Ha. That'd be bloody right."

Contemplating the wild and unforgiving valley, the flask discarded beside him, Gar said, "It'll be night soon."

Asher looked at the fading sky, the swiftly sinking sun. "I noticed. Reckon we should think on headin' home in a bit, eh? That ole Darran's like to be piddlin' his panties, worryin' on where you've got to."

Frowning now, Gar picked up a handful of pebbles from the rock beside him. Juggled them in his palm. "I've been wondering. Would it've hurt, do you think, to have given Timon Spake one more sunrise?"

Asher shrugged. "I don't know. Would it?"

The pebbles trickled slowly through Gar's spreading fingers. "I think I'd want another one."

"And another one, and another one . . ." Asher picked up a fist-sized chunk of loose rock and threw it over the edge of the Eyrie. Listened for a moment as it bounced from boulder to boulder below them, rousing echoes. "It had to be done, Gar."

Gar looked at him. Beneath an icy surface his eyes reflected all manner of uneasy things. "You can still say that? Even now? Even after seeing . . . what you saw?"

"Even after. Though I reckon I'd say the same even if you hadn't made me stay and watch."

The prince stared at his booted toes. "You're angry about that."

Asher sighed. "I was. I ain't so much now."

"Why not?"

"Matt and me had some words. He made sense."

"Don't you want to know why I made you stay?"

"I know why."

Gar looked at him. "Oh?"

"Aye."

"Well then, don't stop there. Tell me. Explain. Elucidate. Show me," said Gar, savagely, "to myself."

"All right. Only I ain't best pleased with you just now so don't say I didn't warn you."

"I won't.'

Asher took a deep breath and hissed it out between his teeth. "Well then. Why is because misery loves company. Because law or no law you didn't want Spake to die and I did. Because that made you angry. Because even though you're a prince and the very important Olken Administrator and you were up on that platform alongside all the most powerful men in this whole bloody kingdom, you were as chained-up and powerless as stupid Timon Spake. And you didn't like how that felt one little bit. So you turned around and you chained *me* too. To prove you do have power. To prove you ain't helpless after all. *That's* why."

Very slowly, Gar turned to look at him. "You *bastard*."

"Aye." Asher raised an eyebrow. "But that don't mean I'm wrong."

Gar's eyes glittered. "You are if I say you are."

"Oh, here we go." Asher pulled an obsequious face. "Deary me, Your Highness, *that's* a pretty crown. A present from your da, was it?"

With a wordless cry of rage Gar snatched up a nearby shard of rock and flung it into the valley. Sudden fury lent him strength, so that the rock tore through the tops of distant trees and sent birds shrieking into the fading light. "It's Barl who's wrong! It's a *stupid* law!" he shouted. "Olken can no more do magic than I can! They—*you*—can't possibly damage the fabric of the kingdom or Barl's Wall! It's a stupid, senseless law! And today a man *died* because of it!"

Behind them the horses' bits jangled as they threw up their heads, protesting the noise. Asher glanced over his shoulder to make sure they were still secure, because it was a long walk back to the Tower and he had enough blisters to be going on with. Then he looked at Gar. Risked a kindly mocking smile.

"Prob'ly you shouldn't go round sayin' things like that where folks can hear you."

Breathing heavily, Gar stared. Accepted the mockery and managed a twisted smile. "Yes. Well. You're folks."

"Aye, but I'm different."

"You certainly are." He glanced longingly at his empty brandy flask, then dragged a hand over his face. "He was so brave."

"I know," said Asher. "So what?"

"So what? So we'll never know now, will we, what he might have given this kingdom? All his unfulfilled promise has gone to feed the worms!"

"I know what he gave this kingdom," Asher said roughly. "Fear and uncertainty and mobs in the street. He was a traitor. He betrayed you, your da *and* his own people. Your folk and mine might be chalk and cheese, Gar, but we got one thing in common. Lur. Keepin' it safe. Keepin' that Wall standin' strong and shinin'. Where all that's concerned there ain't no you and me, there's just us. Timon Spake? He were the enemy. And you don't cry for enemies. You kill 'em."

Gar stared down into the valley. "Yes. We do." His face spasmed. "*I* do. Well. It's nice to know there's one Doranen thing I'm good at anyway. Seems I'm not a complete cripple after all. Although it's fortunate we used an axe. I couldn't have killed him if magic was part of the proceedings." He laughed. "Now why didn't I think of that before? *Damn*! I could've gone to the king and said, you know, sir, since we Doranen presume to have the right of life and death over our lesser Olken brethren, why not go the whole hog and show them how superior we *really* are? Why don't we kill Timon Spake with *magic*? That'd make those pesky inferior magickless natives sit up and take notice, wouldn't it? Conroyd would *love* that. He'd be your new best friend. Oh, and since I'm nothing but a useless cripple, what you might call a walking talking birth defect, I'll leave the whole trial and execution with magic details to you. All right?"

Appalled, Asher stared. Walking talking *birth defect*? Where was this coming from? Was it the brandy putting wild words in his mouth or did he really *believe* . . . "Gar, you're ravin'! You can't—"

"Blessed Barl save me!" Gar lurched dangerously to his feet. "I'm the Olken Administrator! I'm supposed to *help* your people, Asher, not *kill* them!"

This was getting out of hand. If Gar wasn't careful he really would go over the edge of the precipice. Asher stood, slowly, and took the prince by the arm. "You do help, Gar," he said, and inched him backwards towards safety. "You be a fool to think otherwise. That woman in Justice Hall, remember her? She'd be in prison today or ruined or both if it wasn't for you. Stop frettin' on stupid Timon Spake! You didn't kill him. He bloody well killed himself, near enough!"

"I know!" Gar shouted. "I know, I know. But I had a chance to speak for him and I didn't. I'm the Olken Administrator, it's my job to take care of your people. I could've said *something* in his defense and I didn't."

"*What*? What could you have said? In front of your da and his precious Privy Council? Pellen Orrick, and all those other Olken? Knowin' that every word in that chamber was bein' recorded by Lady Marnagh? What could you have said to help Timon Spake when he was doomed by his own words?"

Suddenly boneless, Gar folded at the knees and slumped to the ground. "I don't know . . ." he whispered. "Something."

"Oh, aye? Something like, 'Barl was wrong, it's a stupid law'? And what would've happened then d'you think, you mad fool! Don't you know Conroyd Jarralt's just *waitin'* for you to make that kind of a mistake? Grow up, Gar! You may not have magic but you're still Doranen. *Royal* Doranen. And this is what bein' royal is all about. Protectin' the kingdom. Keepin' it safe and sound . . . even from the people who live in it. Even when it hurts like murder."

Gar's voice was stark with pain. "That's what I mean, Asher. What happened today. What I did in that chamber. It may have been lawful. It may have been necessary. But it still feels like murder."

To Asher's dismay Gar's voice broke on the last word. "Don't," he said, horrified. "Don't do that. What's the use of cryin', eh? What's the bloody use, Gar? Ain't goin' to bring that Timon Spake back, is it? Ain't goin' to help his poor bloody father?"

Gar was beyond hearing him. So he stood, staring over the shadowed gorge, and waited until the harsh, gasping sobs faded into silence. Stars came out overhead and the first sharp cries of hunting owls pierced the gloom in the valley.

Face hidden behind one muffling hand, Gar said, "I received two letters about you this morning, before we—" He cleared his throat.

"Two letters afore the sun's properly up?" said Asher, determinedly bracing. "Ha. You'd think folks'd have better things to do with their time, now wouldn't you?"

"The first one was from Guild Meister Norwich Porter, castigating you for, among other things, your rude, high-handed and disrespectful tone towards him during a trifling misunderstanding at the guardhouse last night."

Asher snorted. "The only misunderstandin' that puffed-up ole geezer had were in thinkin' I could be knocked arse over eyeballs by a fancy title and some bits of dead animal hair nailed to his weskit. Who were the other letter from, then?"

Gar raised his head. "Captain Orrick. He wished to compliment me on my recent choice of an assistant. He found you efficient, decisive and of great help in breaking up a nasty confrontation at the guardhouse last night."

"Ha," said Asher, pleased. "He's a good man, that Pellen Orrick."

"Yes," agreed Gar. "He is. While Norwich Porter is a puffed-up ole geezer with a fancy title and—and—"

"Some bits of dead animal hair nailed to his weskit," Asher said helpfully.

"Yes. Thank you. The rest of the guild is all right though. I'm sure we'll have a wonderful time at the banquet next month."

"Aye, sir. If you say so."

Silence. The last thin line of light on the horizon died. Gar said reflectively, "Asher? I think I'm drunk."

Asher sighed. "Aye, well, I think you are too. Reckon you can ride or do I send back a carriage for you?"

"I can ride." A pause as Gar tried and failed to stand.

"It appears I can't get up, but I'm sure I can ride. Assuming of course I can find where I left my legs."

Leaning down, Asher took him by the forearm and hauled him to his feet. "Don't worry, we'll go nice and slow and that ole Darran can just find himself a dry pair of panties to put on, eh?"

Gar started haphazardly brushing dirt from his fine clothes. "I have the nasty creeping feeling that tomorrow, when I wake up with a terrible headache, I'm going to remember I made a fool of myself here this evening."

Holding his breath, trying to forget the sheer drop somewhere ahead, Asher retrieved Gar's silver flask and gave it back to him. "No, you won't. Nowt happened here today but two friends havin' a bit of a chinwag. Where be the foolishness in that?"

Gar tucked the flask back inside his tunic. Stared at Asher, unsmiling. "Is that what we are? Friends?"

Asher blinked. Were they? Did he want them to be? He thought maybe . . . yes. Why not? Gar wasn't Jed, or Matt even, but he wasn't bad company. For a Doranen. And if he'd ever met a man who needed a friend it was Gar, just like Matt had said. Sink him. Trouble was, the decision weren't up to him. "You tell me. Your Highness."

"I thought you said this wasn't a prince to fisherman kind of conversation," said Gar, eyebrows lifting.

"It ain't."

Gar grinned. "So there's your answer. Come on . . . friend. It's time we went home."

Side by side in the silent star-pricked darkness, letting the horses follow their noses, they rode back to the Tower stables where Matt was patiently waiting and all the lamps were lit.

PART TWO

PART TWO

CHAPTER FOURTEEN

Honestly," said Princess Fane in an undertone to her mother, "I don't see why we have to suffer through all this nonsense just because Papa is another year older. It's all right for Gar, it's not as if he's got anything better to do with his time, but Durm and I are right in the middle of a very difficult sequence of incantations. It's *stupid* for me to be stuck here in this stuffy pavilion with people I can't stand watching silly men prancing about on their ponies and attacking defenseless bits of wood. Not when I could be getting important work done!"

Her mother sighed. "I know you don't believe me, dear, but your father's birthday celebrations are work too, equally as important as your arcane studies. You'd do well to be guided by Gar in this. Your brother understands the importance of such occasions."

"Well, being decorative is the only thing he's good at," Fane said impatiently. "And since he does it so well, why do you need me?" She knew she was being petulant. She didn't care. A private family dinner to celebrate her father's birthday would have been a much better idea. She hated all the froth and bubble of public occasions. Despised the feeling of being on show, paraded like one of Gar's wretched horses in the sale ring. All those looks and whispers everybody thought she was too young to notice or understand.

Too young. Fools. She was sixteen, not stupid.

Her mother's expression was a blend of exasperation and affection. "Oh, Fane. Gar's royal duties involve a great deal more than being decorative and you know it. Besides, do you think Durm would be here if participation in this event weren't as vital to the well-being of Lur as the most perfect calling of rain?"

Fane pulled a face and snatched a pastry from a passing silver platter. Around a mouthful of crabmeat and mayonnaise she replied, "Durm is Papa's best friend. He doesn't want to hurt his feelings."

Dana sighed again and reached out a slim finger to coax a wisp of Fane's silver-gilt hair back into place. "Whereas you, being merely his daughter, are above such trifling considerations?"

Fane blushed. "That's not what I meant."

"Then be more careful when you speak," her mother said with an edge to her mellow voice. "It's one day, Fane, out of an entire year. Tell me I haven't raised a daughter so selfish that she can't spare her father one single day from so many."

"That's not fair! All I want to do is get back to work!"

"I know." Her mother looked suddenly sad. "But the work will always be there, darling."

As Fane opened her mouth to argue, a roar went up from the enormous crowd of spectators crammed shoulder to knee in the tourney field beyond the royal pavilion.

King Borne turned aside from watching his Birthday Games, and with laughter smoothing the lines grooved deep in his face called, "Come along, you two! Have done with your gossiping and join us! Asher has just gone one up over Conroyd and looks in fine enough fettle to win the competition!"

"Please, Fane . . ."

Fane met her mother's cool blue gaze and felt some of her heated impatience cool in return. With a pang she realized that Dana was looking tired, worn. Older now than even a few short months ago. Heart-wrung, she pulled her mother close and kissed her on one smooth, violet-scented cheek.

"I'm sorry," she whispered. "I don't mean to be awful. I'm just a little—I'm feeling—" She swallowed. "Durm told me last night I'm ready for my first Weather-Working."

Her mother's eyes went wide. "Oh," she said. "I see."

"I promise I won't spoil Papa's day."

"I know you won't, Fane." After a moment, her mother smiled. "And besides, you've still got your surprise present to give him. I can't wait to see what it is, you've been so mysterious."

Fane grinned. "Yes. I have." She laughed, then whirled in a kaleidoscope of silk and brocade and joined her father on the pavilion's flower-strewn balcony. "What did you say? *Asher* win the King's Cup? Darling Papa, exactly how many birthday toasts have you drunk today? He'll never wrest it from a horseman like Conroyd Jarralt!"

Seated with her father were her brother, Durm and sundry obscure lords and ladies who for whatever reason had been deemed worthy of the honor. As the sundries laughed politely, Borne raised amused eyebrows at her, Durm smiled and Gar looked down his brotherly nose.

"Don't be so certain. Asher's been practicing his javelin skills for weeks."

"Really? Then for his sake I hope you found somebody halfway decent to help him. Your aim is so bad you couldn't hit the side of a stable with a shovel of wheat! How many strikes did you manage to score in the first round? One? I could've beaten that blindfolded."

And would have, if they'd let her compete. But no. That was too dangerous a pastime for the WeatherWorker-in-Waiting. She might take a tumble and break her pretty neck, and then where would they be?

Gar was smiling. "I don't doubt that." In his eyes, understanding. Pity. She felt rage scald her. She'd have no pity from a cripple. For a moment she wanted to claw her fingers into talons and scratch out those green eyes of his that saw so much. Too much.

And then she remembered her birthday surprise and her fingers relaxed. She smiled. Talons could come in many different shapes, after all.

Still watching the competition, her father said, "Young Asher has proven himself an object lesson to all of us, I think, not just Conroyd, in how dangerous it is to judge a man on looks and bearing alone."

Gar glanced at him sidelong, smiling smugly. "If these weren't your birthday celebrations, sir, I'd be tempted to say 'I told you so'."

"I think you just did," Borne pointed out, and laughed. Patting his son's arm he added, "But that's all right. I'm more than happy to be proven wrong on this occasion. I like him very much, you know. He's a man of uncommon good sense, hard-working, honest and refreshingly forthright. And he's a good friend to you, I think."

"An excellent friend," said Gar. "I doubt I'd have achieved anywhere near as much this past year without his shrewd counsel on Olken matters."

Borne let his considering gaze roam the faces of the lords and ladies, and Durm, before resting it again on his son. He lifted his voice slightly, making sure everyone could hear him. "Yes. The Olken are lucky to have him working so hard on their behalf." Another pat on the arm. "They're lucky to have both of you, Gar. And so am I. This precious kingdom would be poorer without you."

Gar flushed. "Thank you, sir. It's good of you to say so."

"Nonsense," the king said briskly. "It's nothing but the plain, unvarnished truth. Isn't that so, Durm?"

"Indeed," Durm agreed. "As ever, Your Majesty has the right of it."

Pretending to stare over the tourney field where Conroyd was so majestically defending Doranen honor, Fane rolled her eyes. Of course Durm would agree in public. In private, though, they felt the same way about useless crippled Gar, and Asher and the rest of his lumpen, magickless brethren. Not even her tutor's vast affection for her father could change that.

Another throat-ripping roar went up from the crowd. Rising above the excited clamoring, the competition adjudicator's amplified voice: "And Lord Jarralt makes a perfect run to score three targets out of three! We have a tied match! Fresh targets, if you please!"

Fane laughed. "There you are. Your precious Asher

hasn't won anything yet, Gar. My money is still on Conroyd."

"Or it would be if you were allowed to bet, which of course you're not. Goodness, it is exciting though, isn't it?" Dana said brightly, scooping Fane into the guardianship of one encircling arm and easing her away from Gar to a spare seat on the other side of Durm. "I can't remember the last time the competition ran so close. Now tell me, Borne my dear, who do you honestly think has the best chance of winning your beautiful Birthday Cup?"

As befitted his social stature Darran watched the king's birthday celebrations from the royal household enclosure, where palace and Tower staff enjoyed some of the best seats available and were liberally plied with sweetmeats and chilled ale by the servants roaming among the spectators. Beside him sat Willer, as was only right and proper. Why should he suffer alone, after all?

He released a lugubrious sigh. This was the last place in Lur he wanted to be. Not because he resented spending his time helping to celebrate His Majesty's latest birthday. Not at all. No, what he resented was being made to celebrate it by watching that wretched Asher make a spectacle of himself in public.

Willer shifted irritably in his seat. The boy looked like a pudgy peacock in his shiny blue and gold satin. He was dusted with sugar powder, soaked in scent and querulous with pique. "For the love of Barl, can't we please go? Five minutes more of this rubbish and I'll fall down dead of a brainstorm, I swear."

Darran permitted himself another discreet sigh and rearranged his long legs. "We leave when His Majesty leaves and not before. Now stop fidgeting or I shall have your pay docked for impertinence."

Willer scowled. Fixed his glowering gaze on the crudely muscular figure of their employer's indispensable assistant and said viciously, "Who does Asher think he is anyway? Competing for the King's Cup. Presuming to ride against the Doranen nobility. He's just an Olken like us, no better than you or me. In fact he's a damned sight worse."

Darran glanced around the enclosure, full of Asher's friends, and rapped his knuckles on Willer's soft knee. "Keep your voice down. You and I may know the truth of him but we are lone voices crying in the wilderness."

Willer snorted. "We certainly are, Darran, and I for one am getting a damned sore throat! How much longer must we suffer his presence? It's been over a year now! Give him rope, you said, and he'll hang himself. Well, we've given him so much rope he could knit a blanket big enough to cover the kingdom and he's *still* here. Basking in His Highness's affection, wallowing in the ignorant adoration of the masses, making our every waking hour a misery!"

Darran's meager lips stretched in a thin smile. "Patience, Willer. Even a long road must eventually come to an end."

"I know, Darran, but when? I've been patient! I've been patient till I'm practically choking! I don't think I can go on being patient for very much longer!"

"You must," Darran replied, and summoned one of the roaming servants with an imperious finger. It was hot and he was thirsty, and he feared that only more ale would sustain him to the end of this lamentably tedious affair. "Have faith, Willer. Patience is always rewarded, sooner or later."

*   *   *

Down on the tourney field, Asher ran a reassuring hand along Cygnet's sweating neck and turned to smile at Dathne. She was sitting on the grass by the roped-off tourney field, Matt at her side.

She nodded back, all cloudy dark hair, brown skin and gleaming cat-slanted eyes, and waggled congratulatory fingers in her typically offhanded way. He felt his heart race at the sight of her, and cursed. *Never you mind about that now, fool! You got a cup to win!*

Matt raised his clenched fists high over his head and hollered cheerfully. Seated on the grass with them, Mikel and Bellybone and some of the other lads shouted and whistled too, oblivious to the Doranen looks their loud support attracted.

A short distance away Olken lackeys scurried back and forth across the turf, pounding in fresh rows of wooden pegs ready for the final bout between himself and Conroyd Jarralt. A silly sort of game it was they were playing. Sticking the pointy ends of long javelins into tiny wooden targets. What his sensible da would have to say on it when he told the tale, Asher didn't like to think. But there was a pleasure in aiming true and holding fast, and if it meant knocking Jarralt off his lofty perch, well, where was the harm?

Swallowing impatience, he waited. The enormous mixed crowd of Olken and Doranen spectators buzzed and hummed like a tame swarm of bees and the royal band played loud and hard enough to break their strings and bend their brass. Perched in his official seat, the tourney adjudicator blew foam off a fresh mug of ale and Conroyd Jarralt shouted at his Olken servants as they

struggled to saddle a fresh and fretful horse for the ride-
off. Asher felt his lip curl and turned away before his
lordship noticed the disrespect. The bastard always made
sure to pay back any slights, real or imagined, and he had
a vicious, inventive tongue.

Fresh horse . . . Asher snorted, and gave Cygnet's
damp silver neck another pat. Even if he owned another
horse—and he could if he wanted to now, aye, more
horses than a body would need in a lifetime—he'd not insult Cygnet in such a fashion.

With the last wooden peg secured the lackeys scurried
off to stand on the sidelines. The adjudicator swallowed
the dregs of his ale and strutted to the middle of the field.
Beneath the pomp and ceremony of his adjudicator's
scarlet regalia he was Ruben Cramp, Meister of the
Butchers' Guild. Asher knew him well now, and liked the
unpretentious ole fart.

"Attention, please . . . might I have your attention, my
lords, ladies and gentlefolk!"

Heaving a weighty sigh, Asher eased his leather-clad
buttocks in the saddle. Talk, talk, talk. Couldn't they just
get on with it?

The buzzing crowd hushed. Into the sudden silence the
stamp and jingle of impatient horse as Jarralt's fresh
mount objected to restraint. Jarralt jerked his hand and
the chestnut threw up its head, eyes rolling in protest
against the sharp bite of the bit.

Asher scowled, and Ruben Cramp continued his address. "And so, Your Majesties, Your Highnesses, Master
Durm, my lords, ladies and gentlefolk, the bout be tied,
with Lord Jarralt and Meister Asher on six strikes each!"

The tourney ground exploded into applause. Asher

bowed towards the royal pavilion, punched the air with a clenched fist then blew Dathne a kiss. She pretended not to see it. Always playing hard to get was Dathne. Drat her.

As the cheering subsided, Ruben concluded: "Therefore the winner of the King's Cup will be decided by a tie-breaker, the best out of three runs. Gentlemen, be you ready?"

Asher raised his lance in reply, and was echoed by Jarralt. Their eyes met, and Asher smiled at the fury and hatred burning in the Doranen lord's gaze. Fool of a man. As if it mattered. It was a game, just a game, with some poxy ole tin pot the prize. How could it possibly matter?

The band blew a flourish of mellow notes into the high blue sky. Ruben reached into the folds of his fancy overcoat and pulled out a bright scarlet pennant. "Gentlemen, make ready!"

Asher closed his calves on Cygnet's silver sides and the horse pranced to the starting mark. In a flourish of spurs and flying foam Jarralt galloped to the far end of the target run and took his mark.

Ruben raised the pennant high overhead. "On three, sirs, and may the best man win! One . . . two . . . three!" He opened his fingers and the scarlet cloth fluttered to the ground like a wounded bird. A roar went up from the crowd. Sudden thunder rolled around the tourney field as iron-shod hooves hammered the green grass.

Asher forgot everything: Jarralt, Dathne, the stupidity and futility of the game he played. He forgot the watching king and queen and prince, unlikely friends; the princess, the Master Magician and other enemies. Forgot that this life would soon be left behind, and that the difficult leaving of it still lay ahead. All that existed in that moment was the pounding horse beneath him, the outstretched lance before him and the driving need to pierce a tiny wooden target through the heart and win himself a golden cup.

"First pass, and it be a peg to Meister Asher, a miss to Lord Jarralt!"

As the crowd greeted Ruben's announcement with excited shouting Asher lowered his lance for the lackeys to remove the speared and splintered wooden target and kept his fierce eyes far away from Jarralt. His lordship was cursing his horse, which was only to be expected. Didn't Da always say: *It's a bad workman as blames his tools, boys, and let that be a lesson for you.* Privy councilor or no, there was far too much of the bad workman in Jarralt. It was an ongoing wonder to Asher that the king kept the man on the Council or listened to him when he spoke.

Within moments it was time for the second pass. Time to win the cup and get down to some serious celebrating with Dathne and his friends down at the Green Goose.

Except that when he reined Cygnet in at the end of their second thundering run, it was Jarralt who waved a wooden-tipped lance in the air and he who was left looking a fool, his target abandoned on the turf.

Damn.

He kicked Cygnet into place and waited, breathing quietly, for Ruben to drop the pennant a third and final time.

". . . three!" the butcher bellowed. "*Three*!" the crowd bellowed with him as the scarlet scrap of cloth drifted on an errant breeze and Jarralt buried golden spurs in his horse's bloodied sides and Cygnet pinned his ears back, no need to be told what to do.

Out with the lance, Asher, down with the tip, aim for the heart, strike, pierce, hold, lift, lift, stay there, you beauty, you bastard, stay there, you're dead, you're mine, where's Jarralt, he's dropped it, he's dropped it, I win, I win, Da, ain't this somethin', I win—

Buoyant on the crest of the band's joyous music and the crowd's shrieking admiration, Asher rode his victory lap with head and lance held high. Pink-cheeked Olken lasses threw him their flowers and giggled behind their hands. Mikel and Bellybone and the lads pulled faces and pretended they weren't impressed. Matt hopped and hollered, and Dathne speared his heart with a smile as Cygnet cantered dulcetly by.

Those he worked with in the Prince's Tower were dancing on their chairs in the royal household enclosure. He stood in his stirrups as he pounded by them, waving one fist in the air. Laughed when he spied Darran and Willer, looking as though they'd swallowed curdled milk. A pox on the pair of them, the moldy ole crow and his jackdaw lackey.

In passing the royal pavilion he eased to a slow trot and brandished the lance in a salute to the king, who stood on his balcony and applauded, laughing. On Borne's left stood the Master Magician; Durm spared him a spurious smile, gray-green eyes warm as glass. On Borne's right and grinning like a split melon, Gar. They pulled a face at each other. He nodded and smiled at the queen, and her Most Royal High Snootiness Princess Fane, and then the royal pavilion was behind him and it was time to collect his prize. He passed Cygnet over to young Jim'l for a rub-down and a cool drink, then waited for the king to join him, Ruben and a glowering Conroyd Jarralt in the center of the tourney field.

Borne took his hand and shook it as though they were

equals, or old friends. "An impressive display, Asher. Congratulations."

He bowed. "Thanks, Your Majesty. It's an honor."

Borne grinned. "It's a cup, actually," he said and gave it to him, a glittering golden affair studded with a few careless gemstones and not much good for anything except maybe a daffodil or two. As the prize changed hands the band struck up a lively jig, the crowd cheered and Jarralt accepted the king's commiserations and made his escape. Onto the tourney field danced a troupe of gymnasts, acrobats and clowns, and under cover of diversion Borne leaned close and said, "Come. My son wishes to congratulate you in person. A short delay, and then you'll be free to celebrate with your friends."

Matt and Dathne would be waiting for him under the Cobbler's Tree, as arranged last night in the Goose. But work always came first. "Aye, sir. Of course."

Together they walked towards the royal pavilion. One jeweled royal hand found a place on his shoulder; surprised, Asher slowed a little to match the king's easier pace. Without warning, Borne stumbled. For two strides and a heartbeat Asher carried the king's full weight. Then Borne regained his balance and held up his other hand to silence concern. His face was marble white and sheened with sudden sweat.

"I'm fine, Asher," he said curtly. "Perhaps a touch too much wine at luncheon. All those birthday toasts. Our little secret, yes?"

Asher opened his mouth to argue. The king looked abruptly unwell. His clear green eyes were fogged with discomfort, his tightly gripping hand palsied with strain. "Your Majesty—"

The king frowned and removed his hand. "*Asher*. I am fine."

He lowered his eyes. Nodded. Clasped his hands behind his back lest anyone presume to think they hovered in case the king should misstep himself a second time. "Aye, sir," he murmured dutifully. He'd mention it to Gar, once they were safe inside the pavilion. Gar wouldn't get tossed into one of Pellen Orrick's prison cells for arguing with his own father.

He scowled as his entrance into the royal pavilion was met with a hailstorm of applause. Lords and ladies, who'd be hard put to give him the time of day anywhere else, crowded forward to congratulate him, to proclaim his prowess, exclaim his skill, to reassure themselves and any royal personage who happened to be watching that they had nothing but respect and admiration for the low-born Olken who rode so high in the royal estimation.

Well used to it by now, he accepted their compliments as though they meant something. Caught sight of Gar's amused face, imperfectly hidden behind a glass of wine, and rolled his eyes.

Elegant in azure and silver brocade, fine gold hair swirled and savaged with gemstones, the queen came forward to greet him. She passed the King's Cup to a servant to mind, took his hands in her own and pressed a sweet-smelling cheek to his sweat-grimed and stubbly one.

"Dear Asher," she said, ocean eyes sparkling. "And to think that a year ago you didn't even know one end of a lance from the other."

Borne laughed. "Or a horse, for that matter." He still looked pale. Surely somebody would notice?

Not Gar, too busy scoring points. "I confess he's been an adequate pupil."

Despite his concern for the king, Asher grinned. "And Stable Meister Matt's been a damn fine teacher!"

Amidst the dutiful laughter Dana protested, "Really, Gar! The least you can do is say 'Well done, Asher'."

Gar offered him a mocking bow. Hidden beneath it was genuine admiration. "Well done, Asher."

He bowed back. "Thank you, sir. You owe me a hundred trins."

Gar groaned. "I know. That'll teach me."

"Aye, sir. It will."

"Well," said Dana, still holding his hands, "I think it was a thrilling competition. We're all so pleased you won, Asher." Around the silk-walled pavilion, blond Doranen heads nodded their vigorous agreement.

"Thank you, Your Majesty," he said, and raised her fingers to his lips: the queen was a fine liar and he loved her for it. Kissing her thus was a daring gesture, almost improper, but she was smiling and so was the king, so what did it matter if Durm looked thunderous? Then Lord Jarralt entered the pavilion and politics demanded that the queen greet him in a scented cloud of sympathy. As the noble lords and ladies gathered around their fallen comrade Asher stepped aside and lost himself amongst the fernery along the far wall.

A razor voice dipped in honey said sweetly, "Well, well, well. Who's a clever little Assistant Olken Administrator, then?"

Fane.

Concealed in a high-backed chair drawn out of the mainstream, she sat straight-spined and elegant in gold silk, her slender white fingers juggling three balls of glowing glimfire. Her blue eyes watched him sideways and carefully over and around the spinning magical spheres. She was so beautiful, the way splintered ice and a new harpoon and sea storms were beautiful, and just as dangerous. What she'd be like once grown out of adolescence and crowned WeatherWorker, Asher didn't like to think.

He raised his eyebrows. "Jealous, Your Highness?"

Anger danced beneath the surface of her face, but her voice was placid and bored as she replied, "Desperately. It is my life's ambition, Asher, to stick sharp metal spikes into eensy teensy bits of wood."

He was impressed with the juggling, even though he didn't want to be. Glimfire was unchancy stuff. Useful if your candle snuffed out, to be sure, and you were Doranen and able to conjure it, but in the last year he'd seen more than one nasty burn when some humor in the air ignited a flare-up.

She was her mother's daughter in some things, Fane, and could read in his face what he was feeling. "Now who's jealous?"

"Of parlor tricks?" he retorted, and thought *ha* as her eyes sparked fire. She hid the lapse quickly, smoothed over the annoyance with a spurious, friendly smile and leaned a little closer to him, confidingly.

"Come now," she encouraged him. "You can confess to me, Asher. I won't tell. Have you never been tempted, even the tiniest bit?"

"To try my hand at magic?" Deep-sunk memory surfaced, flashing like the belly of a breaching fish. *Timon.* He felt his expression freeze. "No."

She leaned closer again and lowered her voice. "I'll bet you have."

Slapping her would be a mistake even if she did deserve it, so he swallowed the impulse and shook his head. "Sorry. I like my head where it is, Your Highness."

She pretended surprise at that; the glimfire balls danced a little, echoing. "Asher! You don't think my brother would let someone cut off his best friend's head, do you? Even for breaking Barl's First Law?" She laughed, a tinkly little sound with shards of ice in it. "I don't think even the *king* would let it happen!"

Now what was the little minx playing at? There was a glitter in her he mistrusted to his marrow. "With respect, that's a foolish thing to say. His Majesty holds no man above the law."

She pursed her pretty pink lips. "I'm not so sure. You should've heard him singing your praises before, Asher. Do you know, if he could I think he'd embrace you as a second son. Barl knows you've more in common with Gar than I could ever have."

Bitch. With an effort he kept his expression bland and offered her a bow. "A man could do a lot worse than have qualities in common with your brother. Now, it's been delightful chatting with you, Highness, but I got some friends outside tappin' their toes, so if you'll excuse—"

In other, maybe more important ways she was her father's daughter. Discarding one line of attack, she chose another. It was in the shining of her eyes and the set of her chin. "Oh no, Asher, you musn't leave!" She blew on the balls of glimfire with her mint-scented breath; they turned into little dancing butterflies and fluttered away. "Gar and I have a special gift for the king." Leaning around the edge of her chair, she searched the room for her brother, found him, and raised her voice: "Gar!"

In the midst of conversation, Gar lifted a hand in apology to his audience and turned a little in her direction. "Yes, Fane?"

"I need you!"

Gar excused himself and threaded his way through the talking, laughing, eating throng to stand a cautious pace from her side. "What do you want?"

Fane's eyes glowed with anticipation. She leaned closer to her brother. "Did you find one?"

"Yes," said Gar, "but—"

"Excellent," she replied. "Fetch it."

"This is ridiculous," muttered Gar, but he went to his official chair, dropped to one knee and groped beneath it. A servant paused and offered help; Gar waved her away and came back a moment later clutching a dead brown stick.

"Show me," said Fane. Took the stick, inspected it, and handed it back with a glowing smile of approval. "Perfect."

"For what, exactly?" Gar said, exasperated. "I wish you'd stop being so mysterious and just tell me—"

"If I told you," said his sister severely, "it would ruin the surprise." She unfolded gracefully from her chair, wrapped her skilful fingers around his wrist and tugged him after her. "Come on."

As brother and sister cleared a path to their father, Asher stepped further into the fernery and chewed his lip. Whatever she had planned, he wanted no part of it. Bad enough he'd have to cope with Gar afterwards. The prince always came off second best in Fane's little schemes. Why Gar allowed himself to believe she'd ever mean him anything but hurt, he never knew. He'd long since given up arguing about it.

With one overhead sweep of her arm Fane ignited a starburst and effectively silenced the room. Every eye fixed itself upon her, and she smiled. "Your Majesties. Master Magician Durm. My lords and ladies. On this day of celebration my brother and I would honor the king with a special gift. Gar?"

Bemused, Gar stared at her. Asher watched the assembled nobility, searching for the expressions that were too still, for lips that twitched or eyes that shone with sudden, undimmed hilarity. Noted faces, and names, and held his breath as his friend trembled on the brink of a new disaster.

Gently, Fane prompted her brother. "Our gift, Gar. You're holding it."

Gar stared at her. At the stick. No escape. "Happy birthday, Your Majesty."

Borne took the offered stick. "Thank you, my son. I don't quite know what to say."

"Please," said Gar, cheekbones sharp beneath the skin, "don't say anything."

Fane broke the anguished silence. "That stick, Your Majesty, represents our lives without you. Dead. Dry. Lifeless. Gar chose it himself. Now, if I may?" She took the stick from her father. Held it between her hands, closed her eyes and concentrated.

At first nothing happened. Then the stick shivered. Rippled once along its dry, brown length. Rippled again. A flush of green rolled along it, as though someone had upended an invisible beaker of paint and poured it from end to end.

"Ah," breathed her spellbound audience, and crowded a little closer.

Gar curved his thinned lips in the semblance of a smile and kept his unclenched fists forcibly relaxed by his sides. Asher groaned under his breath and closed his eyes briefly.

The dead brown stick, now green and supple, swelled with buds. The buds blossomed. Delicate leaves unfurled. One end of the stick swelled, larger and larger, until it exploded into petal and drenched the room with a glorious perfume. Silver and gold and shimmering, it glowed with vibrant life and bloomed in perfect symmetry.

As Fane's audience erupted into wild applause she held out the living miracle to her father and curtsied. "And this sweet rose, Majesty, represents all that we have with you as our king."

Borne took the vibrantly alive flower, his green eyes dark with emotion. "Well. Now I truly am speechless. Thank you, daughter. And you, too, Gar. Thank you both."

"It was nothing, sir," said Gar. And stepped back as Fane entered their father's embrace, trembling with triumph.

"I was so afraid it wouldn't work!" she exclaimed, watching as the rose was passed from hand to eager hand and the gathered nobility chorused its admiration. "Durm and I have been practicing for weeks, haven't we, Durm?"

The Master Magician was smiling, his habitually stern expression softened into something more approachable. "I never doubted your skills as a student, Highness."

Borne punched him lightly on one elaborately robed shoulder. "Or your own as a teacher, you old rogue! Thank you! It is the most beautiful gift."

Under cover of exclamation, Fane turned a little in the proud circle of her father's arm and smiled at her brother. Then she caught sight of Asher's face. He couldn't have said exactly what she saw there but it killed her smile stone dead. For a moment an unfamiliar blush of shame stained her cheeks. Then her chin lifted, her eyes cooled and she turned her back on them both. The voluble crowd closed in around her, around the king and Durm, and mercifully hid them from sight.

Asher made a move towards Gar then, his own breath painful in his lungs. The prince held up a hand, sharp as a blow.

"Don't," he said. His voice could have shattered ice.

After more than a year, Asher was impervious. "Smile, or she wins," he said, barely above a whisper.

"She's won already," Gar replied distantly. He was very pale. "As always."

"Only if you let her. Only if you show that it matters."

Gar shrugged. "It does matter. Pretending otherwise only makes me look more foolish."

"And not pretendin' makes her happy!" Asher retorted.

Gar looked him up and down. "A churlish brother I would be, to begrudge a sister's happiness."

"*Gar*—"

"Enough," said Gar. "You don't understand. I doubt you ever will."

Scowling, Asher looked elsewhere for help. Captured the queen's stricken gaze with his own. She understood. Dana took a step towards her son, her eyes stormy—and was halted by a cry.

"Help here! The king! The king!"

It was Durm's voice, almost unrecognisable in its

dismay. The clustered nobles staggered backwards, aghast, to reveal Borne, ashen-faced and swaying on his feet. Clutching at his chest. With the stunned room watching he collapsed at Durm's feet.

"*Majesty!*"

As Gar leapt to his father's side and Durm fell to his knees to take Borne in sheltering arms, Dana turned to Asher.

"I'll find the pothecary," he said.

Her eyes were enormous, and brilliant with fear. Her voice was faint. "Quickly."

He looked back once from the door of the royal pavilion. Borne was unconscious, gray and slimed with sweat. Durm held him in a close embrace, furious with fear. Fane wept on her father's still chest. Gar supported his mother, or she supported him. They were too closely entwined to tell. The servants clustered together against one wall, wide-eyed and horrified. Their expressions were mirrored in the faces of the noble guests.

Well. Most of them anyway.

And abandoned on the floor, crushed and trampled and broken, the beautiful birthday rose.

Asher let the heavy curtain drop down behind him and ran.

CHAPTER FIFTEEN

The palace runner caught Willer as he was going out to lunch.

"A message for His Highness," piped the child. "From the Master Magician."

Willer snatched the rolled letter from the boy's hand and waved him away. Curse it, now he'd be late, and if you didn't get a luncheon table at Fingle's within the first ten minutes you might as well not bother getting one at all.

He cast an unenthusiastic glance up the Tower staircase. Even worse, he'd have to go and disturb His Highness with this missive, which doubtless meant he'd have his head bitten off for daring to put his nose across the library threshold. There'd been shouting and banged doors already this morning, and Darran disappearing into their office in a secretarial huff. For a whole week now, ever since the poor dear king's collapse, His Highness had been a positive *bear* to live with.

Not that one could complain, or would. His Highness was beside himself with worry for the king, which he supposed was only to be expected. But the gloom and despair were infectious. Even the Tower maids kept dashing into linen closets to cry. And if he tripped over one more snuffling boot-boy he really was going to scream. Or take off his belt and give someone a thrashing. Or both. Really, it was so unnecessary. Hadn't Pother Nix announced officially that the king would make a full recovery? Yes, he had. So what was the point of all this temperament? There wasn't any, but it had Darran in as fractious a mood as the prince. Really, between the pair of them life was hardly worth living.

Willer heaved a put-upon sigh. He did hope the king would make his full recovery *soon*, so that life could get back to normal.

Behind him the Tower's heavy oak front doors banged open. Swallowing a startled shriek he whirled, the message clutched protectively to his velvet-swathed chest.

Asher grinned as he sauntered into the lobby, stripping off his sweat-stained gloves as he came. "What's that then, Willer? Not another love letter? Does Darran know?"

Hot with dislike and humiliation, Willer uncrumpled the rolled parchment. "*You*," he said with awful disdain. "And where have you been?" As if he didn't know. Carousing. Gallivanting. Prancing about on personal business when his duty lay at the feet of their prince. *Reprobate*.

Asher tucked his gloves into the waistband of his disgusting leather britches and looked down his crooked nose. "Out."

Willer sniffed. It was beneath him to rise to such obvious provocation. Instead he held out the Master Magician's message. "This has just come from the palace for His Highness. Take it up to him."

Insolence informing every grubby line of his face, Asher snorted. "Take it yourself, Willer. I ain't your servant."

A gentleman never resorted to violence, no matter how justified it might be. With rage thick in his throat Willer retorted, "No, you're *his*, and more's the pity for it too! I swear you'd know the meaning of good manners if you were answerable to *me*. If that were so you'd no more dream of entering His Highness's official residence dressed like—like a *highway rider* than you would of flying over the Wall! Barl save us! Couldn't you at least have *bathed* before coming in from the stables? You reek of sweat and horses!"

Asher smirked. Oh, how Willer longed to wipe that look from the upstart's face! "Better than reekin' of lavender water," was the insufferable reply. "Or rosewater or old tea leaves or whatever it is you douse yourself in every mornin'. No wonder you're gettin' love letters, eh? Or is it just your smelly recipes they're after?"

With a restraint that nearly caused his veins to burst, Willer swallowed his instinctive reply. Darran had made himself abundantly clear on many, many occasions: the prince would brook no disrespect to the kingdom's Assistant Olken Administrator. So instead he clung to his precious talisman, Darran's promise: *give him enough rope* . . .

Such dreams he had, such pleasant dreams, of a stretched brown neck, and feet vainly kicking the indifferent air!

"I am very busy with work for Darran," he said through stiff lips. "Be so good as to take this message to His Highness immediately. It's from the Master Magician."

A little of the arrogance seeped from Asher's face. Even his monumental pride faltered before the mention of the kingdom's second most powerful magician. "Fine," he muttered and held out his hand. "Give it here then."

With silent contempt Willer handed the message over, waited till Asher was round the first bend of the Tower staircase, then hurried out of the side door. If he walked *very* fast, he might just reach Fingle's in time after all.

Asher took the winding staircase two treads at a time, scowling. He'd happily live with the honest stink of sweat and horse in his nostrils, but leave him for five minutes in that prissy sea slug Willer's company and he was itching for hot water and soap.

Gar was working at his library desk, surrounded by towers of ancient books, piles of yellowed and crumble-edged parchment and pages of notes. Ink-stained and harassed, he muttered under his breath and streaked his blond hair blue with dragging fingers. Asher paused in the doorway and frowned. This was getting beyond a joke.

Without looking up from his jottings Gar snarled, "Darran! For the love of Barl, man, I said I didn't want to be—"

"Mind now," Asher interrupted mildly, entering the room. "You'll hurt my feelings, and we wouldn't want that." As Gar sat up, blinking, he threw himself into the nearest comfortable armchair and slung a leg over one side.

Gar pulled a face. "Sorry. He's been pestering me all morning."

"Try tellin' him to turn into a bug and beetle off then."

"I did in the end," Gar admitted. "Although not quite

in those words. Look, amuse yourself for a moment, would you? I just need to finish this . . ."

Asher sighed. Books, books and more books. Ever since the king's collapse Gar had buried himself in parchment and ink pots. Fool that he was. At this rate he'd work himself into a bed right next to his ailing da, and then three guesses who'd get the blame for it? By his reckoning, Gar hadn't set foot outside in six days. Ballodair was so short of work he'd bucked Matt off that very morning; the bruised and limping stable meister wasn't amused.

And Gar was looking short of work too, or at least fresh air. His thin face had grown thinner and there were lines of temper and worry engraved around his eyes and mouth. All this time and he'd still not seen his father. The strain was wearing him down, winding him tight as a lute string ready to snap.

This whole bloody mess was a pain in the arse and no mistake. Just as he'd *finally* been set to tell Gar it was time and past time he packed his bags and went home to Restharven . . .

He'd been meaning to do it for nigh on a month now, but unforeseen circumstances kept getting in the way. First off, right on the anniversary of his arrival in Dorana, a tricky dispute had arisen between the Brewers and the Vintners and it had taken a week's worth of persuasion from both him and Gar to avert an alcoholic disaster. Hard on the heels of that excitement there'd been the Barlscoming Anointments; it would've been cruelty to dumb animals if he'd left Gar to cope with all that religious fervor on his own. And after *that*, the king's birthday celebrations.

Which he *easily* could've missed, and should have, except he'd made the mistake of drinking one glass of wine too many and accepting Gar's bet that he couldn't make the final four of the King's Cup competition. After all, there was nowt to it. He'd seen Conroyd Jarralt win the cup the last King's Birthday holiday, and if Conroyd Jarralt could do it, *well* . . .

Naturally, he'd had to stay on and defend his honor. Da would understand that. Course he would. It had meant spending every spare waking hour on horseback learning the hard way how not to skewer himself or his mount with a stupid steel-tipped javelin as he tried to stab stupid bits of wood at a passing amble.

He'd done all right in the end, though.

Thinking of the gold cup, now sitting in his bathroom holding his razor and shaving brush, he smothered a grin. Actually, he'd done more than all right. Conroyd Jarralt still wasn't speaking to him: two prizes for the price of one.

But he'd promised himself that would be the end of it. The birthday celebrations would be his private going-away party. Once all the bunting was put away for another year he'd bid his farewells to Dorana City and go back to where he truly belonged. The coast. Restharven. Home.

And then what had to happen? The king had to go falling over sick with a fever, didn't he? Now Barl alone knew how long it would be till His Majesty was hale and hearty again and he could in good conscience quit the City for home. At this rate he'd have to send a reassuring message ahead of himself, damn it, and ruin the surprise.

Scratch scratch scratch went Gar's inky pen over the paper as he translated yet another of his precious bloody parchments . . .

Although, if he were being dead honest with himself, turning his back on Dorana wasn't looking to be as easy as once he'd expected. In his first weeks here, with home-sickness a blight, the year of self-imposed exile from Restharven had seemed a length of time without mercy. Now, though, *now* . . . He swallowed a sigh. Truth be told, he'd almost welcomed all those very good reasons for delaying his departure. Without ever meaning to he'd made a lot of friends in the City. Amongst the guilds. The guards. In the royal household and the Tower, especially. Well, not Darran. Or Willer. But Matt. Definitely Matt, and the rest of the lads down at the stables. The house-maids and cooks, like a bloody great gaggle of sisters and aunties and well-meaning grannies.

Gar.

Asher rubbed at a mud spot on his knee, frowning. If anyone had told him a year ago that one day he'd look on a Doranen prince like a brother he'd have laughed him-self sick. Yet a year later here he was. As fond of Gar as he'd never been of Zeth or Wishus or any of the others.

Damn it. That hadn't been part of his plan . . .

Bloody Gar, with his mercurial moods, his devotion to family, his courage in the face of magic and its lack in him-self. His besottedness with horses and books and history. His sly sense of humor, and his imperfectly hidden pain.

In the aftermath of Timon Spake's execution, feelings in Lur had run high and wild. Fear, both Olken and Dora-nen, tainted the sweet air of City and countryside alike. During those dangerous, difficult days he'd watched the prince work himself near to a standstill, mending fences, building bridges, soothing the turbulent kingdom and preventing any echoes of long-past unrest sounding in the streets of her towns and villages. Watched him lay flowers on the grave of Edvord Spake, who'd followed his son into death three days after receiving his boy's body home from the king's justice.

And the hard work hadn't stopped there. Long after the stormy waters of Timon Spake's death had calmed, Gar labored on behalf of his father's magickless subjects. Laughed with them when their babies were born, wept when their mothers died, danced at their weddings and calmed their quarrels in guild meetings all over the kingdom. Listened to them in Justice Hall and agonized afterwards in case he'd not heard their hearts correctly.

Thanks to Gar, Asher of Restharven had been a part of all that. He'd helped solve those disputes. He'd danced at those weddings. Held meetings with the most important Olken in the kingdom and stood before the king in Privy Council to speak his heart and mind on things that had come to matter. *And* he'd been listened to. Plus he was a rich man now, a different, cannier, wiser man, and that was also thanks to Gar.

Some folk would say leaving was a sinkin' poor way to repay such a debt. He might even say it himself. Might not go at all, at least not just yet, not this year, if it weren't for Da.

But he'd made his father a promise, so that was that.

And then . . . there was Dathne.

How did a body know if they'd fallen in love if they'd never been in love before? And of all the women he'd ever met, at home and here in Dorana, that he could've fallen in love with . . . why *Dathne*?

In body and mind she was an angular woman, all sharp corners and flat, hard planes. Not even when drunk could he ever call her beautiful. And yet she stirred him, deeply. Her secretive eyes. The curve of her lips. The long smooth column of her throat. The way her hands shaped the air when she talked. She provoked him beyond bearing. Teased him. Challenged him. Made him laugh. Made him think. He'd learned as much in a year of knowing her as he had working with Gar. And that was saying something, because sometimes he thought his head would burst like an overripe melon with everything he'd learned working with Gar.

But how could he be certain sure it was love, not . . . something else? Was it because whenever he was with her he felt strangely whole? Because he looked forward to seeing her the way he'd used to look forward to sailing? Or did he know because the thought of leaving her behind when he went home raced his heart and dried his mouth? Made him feel ill and panicked and all of a jitter?

That could be it. A lifetime without Dathne in it? He might as well say he'd settle for a lifetime without the sea.

He didn't think he could do either.

So. He'd just have to say something, wouldn't he? Not that she'd ever given him a sign, as such, nor what most men would call encouragement even when they were both tipsy in their cups. But she liked him. He was sure of that much. They saw each other three or four times a week without fail, and she was always asking how he was, what was happening in his life. Inviting him on jaunts about the countryside. Giving him books to read and asking him what he thought of them afterwards. Showing an interest.

Listening, with her eyes as well as her ears. A woman didn't do that if there wasn't *something* going on.

Still: He'd be happier if she'd said something . . . dropped even the smallest of hints . . .

Of course it could be she was shy, like him. Uncertain. Unwilling to risk a rebuff. To be fair, he'd not exactly shown his hand either. But then he'd seen Dathne rebuff other would-be suitors: it wasn't a pretty sight. So he'd sort of . . . let it slide. Told himself he had plenty of time. That some women weren't for rushing. Had put off declaring his feelings again and again and again, waiting for the perfect moment to declare his love.

Well, he was fast running out of moments, wasn't he? Perfect or otherwise. He'd have to risk speaking soon or he might never see her again.

He imagined telling her, at long last. Imagined the feel of her hands tight in his. Her gasp of sweet surprise. The blush on her cheeks and the warm glow of pleasure in her eyes. He imagined kissing her . . .

"What are you smiling at?' said Gar.

Startled, Asher blinked. "What? Nowt. Nothing, I mean. I was just thinking."

Gar returned his pen to the ink pot and leaned back in his chair, groaning at the tug of stiff muscles. "Careful. You might sprain something." His lips curved briefly, the closest he was coming these days to a smile. He took in Asher's disheveled appearance and lifted his eyebrows inquiringly. "You've been out?"

"Aye," said Asher, and grinned. "Takin' care of the Guigan brothers."

Gar considered him. "And?"

"And I reckon they've seen the error of their ways."

Asher flexed reminiscent fingers. "Once they realized we were onto 'em they changed their tune right enough."

"Excellent. The carters have enough to contend with at this time of year without being short-weighted on their fodder. Penalties?"

Asher shrugged. "Thirty percent discount to all their regular customers until the end of Fall. I got a good long list of deservin' names that'll need checking, double-checking and, like as not, checking again. Be nice and say I can give it to Darran, eh?"

Frowning, Gar said, "Thirty percent's a little harsh, isn't it? If I recall correctly we discussed twenty."

"And twenty it would've been, right enough, except they got themselves a little mouthy. Couldn't let 'em get away with that now, could I?"

"I suppose not. Although I imagine they're not very happy."

Asher grinned. "Not very happy at all, no. But as I said to 'em, they could do things my way and be unhappy in the comfort of their own shop, or their way and be unhappier still standin' afore you in Justice Hall explaining what they'd been up to and why. Funnily enough, they decided to do things my way."

"Ah," said Gar. "Thus showing that greed and stupidity don't necessarily go hand in hand. Good job." Then he noticed the rolled letter balanced in Asher's lap. "What's that?"

Asher tossed the scroll at him. "A message from Durm."

Gar's expression changed. "Idiot," he said curtly. "You think the Guigan brothers are more important than this?" Ripping off the neatly tied ribbon, he yanked the letter open and devoured its contents with eyes gone suddenly opaque.

"Well?" said Asher, fingertips drumming on the arm of his chair. "What's the ole spell-crow want now?"

Gar opened his fingers and let the paper rustle to his crowded desktop. "The king wishes to see us," he said distantly. Shifting in his chair, he stared out of the library's stained-glass window into the gardens below. His lips, unsteady, pressed tight together.

"So he's feeling better," said Asher. "That's grand." Then he paused, and listened again to Gar's pronouncement. "Wait a minute. He wants to see *us*? As in you and me? Why?"

Gar pushed free of his chair and headed for the door. "I must make myself presentable. You'd best do the same. Bathe and change, for Barl's sake. You reek of sweat and horses. I'll meet you downstairs in ten minutes."

"All right, all right," Asher grumbled, following him out of the library. "But make it fifteen. And you ain't answered my question, neither. What's the king need to see me for?"

No reply. Swearing lustily under his breath, Asher hurried to his apartments.

Now what?

Master Magician Durm was waiting for them in the anteroom to Their Majesties' private chambers. A light, bright, airy room it was, but dragged down to dirt level by Durm's heavy frown and the way his plump lips tucked in tight at the corners, forbidding smiles. His glossy brown robe hung on him with less grace than it would on a coathanger, its heavy folds mimicking the bloated lines of his body. Following in Gar's hurried footsteps Asher hung back a little and let the prince be the first to feel the embrace of Durm's warm welcome.

"You took your time," the Master Magician announced, sharp white teeth snapping the tail from his greeting. Cold gray eyes, tinged green like wet slate touched with lichen, slid briefly sideways to notice but not acknowledge Asher. "His Majesty is waiting for you. Be brief. Pother Nix and I are satisfied with his progress but he is still swiftly wearied."

For Gar, a lifetime of the man had blunted his impact. Indifferent to censure, thrumming with anticipation, he said, "Has Nix decided yet what caused the fever?"

"As I suspected," Durm replied, soft hands folded across his comfortable girth, "it was a matter of exhaustion and overwork. The king's crown weighs heavy, Your Highness. Even the strongest of men will stumble from time to time."

Gar gnawed his bottom lip. "There must be something I can do."

"We have discussed this. His recovery is in hand, Your Highness."

"You should have let me see him before now." Gar's voice was bladed, his eyes no longer opaque.

Durm unfolded his hands, spread them wide. "To what purpose? Nix, Her Majesty and I are doing all that can be done. He finds other visitors fretsome."

Gar glared. "You're saying he'd find me fretsome? I am his *son*, Durm."

Now the hands reached out, patted Gar's shoulders in a gesture doubtless meant to reassure. Asher, watching from a safe distance, mistrusted the paternal smile that accompanied the gesture. "And as a good son you've held his best interests highest. Now shall we be about our business? It will soon be time for His Majesty to sleep."

Gar nodded, turned his head far enough to meet Asher's neutral gaze and flickered an eyelid. Stride for stride, they made their way towards the closed chamber door.

Durm stepped forward and reached out, catching Asher's passing elbow between finger and thumb. "Where do you think you're going?"

He pulled his elbow free. Not roughly, never roughly, but with a polite, restrained violence. "The message said His Majesty asked for me too. Sir."

Durm shrugged. "He asks for many things, as unwell men are wont to do. He may not be strong enough to see you. Wait here until—"

"Asher!"

Gar, calling impatiently from his mother and father's private room.

A dangerous grin. An apologetic shrug. Don't see the venomous look in the spell-crow's eye. "If you'll excuse me, then," he said with awful courtesy, and slipped out of harm's way into the king's inner sanctum.

Borne sat up in his bed, swaddled in blankets and buttressed with pillows. The ravaging fingerprints of fever were plain upon him. Thin, pale, his eyes sunken to depths Asher hadn't seen since the day of Timon Spake's trial, he was decently robed to the throat in finest linen. His silver-blond head looked naked without a crown, yet somehow he still managed to look like a king.

An open fireplace roaring in the chamber's far corner billowed heat into the shuttered, curtained room. Something scented had been cast into the flames; the stifling air hung heavy with perfume. Glimfire cast fuzzy pools of light from sconces on the walls. Seated on a chair by his side, the queen demurely embroidered some folderol stretched tight in a sewing hoop. She looked up as Asher entered and bowed, and gifted him with a smile. Then she put aside her amusement and her stitching, kissed her husband and stood.

"There, now. I'll leave you fine gentlemen to your plottings. Don't tire yourself, my dear. Remember what Pother Nix said."

Borne pulled a face at her. "How could I forget, beloved, when his words are engraved upon my liver?"

They exchanged a private smile, then Dana turned to her son. "Come see me in my parlor when you've finished, Gar. It seems an age since we've talked."

Two paces from her side, Gar stood and stared at his father as though at a stranger. Asher could see the shocked dismay locked safe and tight behind his eyes and the small half-smile that curved his lips. Stirring, the prince turned away from the altered man in the bed and reached for his mother's hand to kiss it. "Of course, Mama. I'll be with you shortly."

In return she kissed his cheek. Smiled again at her husband, gathered her silk skirts about her and left. As the door was closed behind her, Gar moved nearer to the bed. Asher drifted sideways, to conceal himself in shadows.

"You sent for me, sir," said Gar.

"I certainly did. Sit, sit." Borne patted the arm of the chair by the bed, then glanced into the shadows at the foot of the bed. "And how are you, Asher?"

Asher cleared his throat and stepped forward into

flickering light. "Very well, thank you, Your Majesty. It's a great relief to see you looking better."

"Rubbish," said Borne. "I don't look better, I look like the walking dead. Or I would, if Nix would let me walk. But your kind dishonesty is appreciated nevertheless. I'll talk with you in a moment. First I must speak with Gar."

"Yes, Your Majesty."

He returned to the shadows as Gar slid into his mother's chair and laid the back of his hand briefly against his da's forehead. "How are you feeling, sir?"

"I'm fine. Really. This is naught but a storm in a teacup."

"That's not what Durm says."

Borne pulled another face, deepening the newly mined hollows in his cheeks. "Durm's as bad as Nix. I am fine. Or I would be, if it weren't for the pills and potions I'm made to swallow."

Gar hesitated, frowning. "Durm says there's nothing I can do to help you while you're convalescent, but I don't believe that. There must be something. I wish you'd tell me."

"It's funny you should ask," said Borne after a small pause. "There is one important thing I can't do. It would ease my mind considerably were you to do it for me."

"Name it," Gar said promptly. "I'll do anything."

"You can take a trip to the coast."

Asher twitched. The coast? Why the coast? And why now? Then he saw it. Damn. Of course. Borne was going to send Gar south to Westwailing for the annual Sea Harvest Festival. Well, well, this was going to make things tricky. He'd thought to go home via the festival himself. All those thousands of people. They could hide him from his brothers. Let him find Da and smooth things over without trouble from Zeth and the rest of them.

Well, *damn*.

Gar was frowning. "The coast, sir?" Then his expression cleared. "Oh. I see. It's coming up to Sea Harvest Festival time, isn't it? But surely you'll be—"

Borne shook his head. "I am forbidden to put so much as a toe out of bed for another week. And it's to be a full three weeks of naught but gentle strolling after that. Someone needs to go to Westwailing in my place, Gar. I thought you might enjoy the experience. Besides, it's past time the Olken of Lur's south met you."

Asher bit his tongue. *Gar*? Sing the *festival*? Was the king mad? Gar couldn't sing an uncracked note to save his life. Fever must have addled Borne's brains.

To be fair, Gar was looking just as surprised. "I don't know, sir. I'm not sure I'm the right person for this. Surely Fane is the obvious choice. Especially since—"

Borne's lips thinned in displeasure. "Magic has nothing to do with this, Gar. Sea Harvest isn't a ceremony of power. It's a symbolic event honoring the ancient pact between the Olken and ourselves. Celebrating the ocean's bounty, Barl's reward for the dutiful observance of that pact. A royal presence is what matters, not whether your voice is good enough for public display. Or whether you have magic. You couldn't possibly—"

"Spoil things?" Gar finished for him, his expression twisted. "Of course not. You wouldn't be asking me to do this if there were any danger of that. Would you?"

The king's face flooded with hectic color. "*Gar!*"

"Forgive me," Gar said distantly. "But we both know it's true."

"What's *true*," the king snapped, "is that I thought to have you take my place in Westwailing. You are the Olken Administrator, Gar. Important in your own right. You should be seen by—"

"And Fane is Lur's next WeatherWorker."

"Your sister is full occupied with her studies," said Borne, plucking at his blankets with impatient fingers. "And even if she weren't I'd still want you to do this. I don't understand your attitude. What makes you so prickly? Has something happened I should know about?"

Asher sighed quietly. Had something happened? Only his father seemingly at death's door, his sister poised to be made WeatherWorker and Durm barring the king's only son all access to his grievously ill parent.

Hardly anything really.

Gar shoved out of the chair and moved to stand with his back half turned to the bed. "I'm sorry if I appear ungrateful. It isn't my intention. You must know, sir, this has been a trying week."

In the king's face was all the anguish that his son, prideful to the marrow, would never willingly show. "And I'm sorry, too, for worrying you with this foolish fever. Truly, it looks much worse than it is. I'll be up and about in no time, I promise. Please, Gar. Sit. Let us discuss this matter like men of good sense."

Put that way, by a man who looked to have his left foot planted firmly in the grave, refusal was impossible. Gar resumed the chair by the bed and managed to unknit his brow. "Of course, sir."

"I would not force you to do anything you mislike," Borne said, his hand reaching out to rest on Gar's knee.

"If the idea of representing me in Westwailing displeases you so greatly, just say so and—"

"It doesn't." Gar's voice was unsteady. "It shames me to think I've given you that impression. When do I leave?"

"You're sure?"

Gar nodded. "Sure. As well as humbled, and honored."

"Good. I'm glad." Borne's tired eyes sparkled with vicarious excitement. "You'll leave next week. I suggest you meet with Darran on this, and be guided by him. He knows to the last detail what's involved in the festival. In fact I think it would be best if you took him to Westwailing with you."

Gar grimaced. "Must I?"

"Oh, come," Borne said. "He's not so bad as all that."

"Of course he's not," agreed Gar, faintly smiling. "After all, you loved him so well that on the morning of my majority you gave him to me as a gift."

"He knows his business, my boy, and was exactly what you needed in setting up your own affairs. Admit it. Your office runs like clockwork, doesn't it? You never miss an appointment or find yourself unprepared for a meeting or at a loss when important men come to call?"

Gar sighed. "I know. I know. But he fusses. And he hovers. And he refuses to wear anything that isn't black."

"And he'll tell you all you need to know about the Sea Harvest Festival," Borne added, "and the part you'll be playing in it. Including all the words to the Sea Harvest Hymn."

"Can't Asher do that? He used to be a fisherman, after all. Who better to teach me what I need to know than him?"

Borne's gaze flickered to the shadows, then back again.

"I have no doubt Asher will be of invaluable service to you during your journey and time in Westwailing. Indeed I'm counting on him to be your strong right arm, as usual. But Darran knows the protocols and procedures from our perspective, Gar. Trust me, you will need him."

Gar sighed. "Oh, all right. I'll take him with me." And added, uncertain, "Tell me. You are sure about this? If I should give you cause to regret your offer, sir, I—"

Borne lifted his hand. "*Never,*" he said, voice thickened with emotion. "You could never make me regret, Gar. You're my son, and I love you."

Gar nodded. Took his father's hand and tightened his fingers. "I won't let you down, sir. I swear it."

"I know." The king cleared his throat and adopted a bright smile. "Now run away and visit your mother while I have words with your assistant here. She misses you."

"Yes, sir," said Gar, and withdrew from the chamber, giving Asher a hard glance in passing. *Don't tire him. Be polite.*

Asher rolled his eyes and stepped out of the shadows to meet with the king.

CHAPTER SIXTEEN

Borne indicated the chair by the bed, inviting Asher to sit. "The queen tells me you were a great help to her the day I fell ill. I wanted to thank you."

Perching on the edge of the comfortable armchair, Asher shrugged. Politely. "I didn't do much, Your Majesty."

"I think the queen would disagree. She says you—" Borne broke off, squinting with pain.

Asher leaned forward, alarmed. There was a sudden sweat on the king's brow and his pale face had turned a sickly yellowish green. "Majesty!"

Weakly, Borne indicated the crystal jug of water on his bedside table. Asher poured him a glass. Slipped his arm around the king's shoulders and held him off his pillows to drink.

"Thank you," Borne whispered after three sips. Asher laid him gently back against the pillows and put the glass aside. "If you could stir up the fire for me, Asher? This cursed fever—I'm afraid I feel the cold."

Asher's shirt was sticking to him in the heat, but he

lumbered another huge log into the fireplace and stirred the flames to bolder life, choking a little at the cloying wave of scent that wafted around the room.

That done, with fresh rivulets of sweat pouring down his spine, he sat down again and waited for Borne to say whatever else it was he wanted to say. A year in the service of this family had taught him one important thing: there was regular time, and there was royal time, and it did a body no good at all to get the two confused.

Eventually Borne stirred, and sighed. "I love my son, Asher. Not a day passes that I don't regret . . ." He stopped. Folded his thin fingers in his lap. "I love my daughter, too, misunderstand me not. If there has been any good arising from Gar's affliction it is that I have her to love as well. Fane will make a strong WeatherWorker when I am gone. The Wall will hold fast, never fear, once it comes within her care."

"Aye, sir," said Asher. And added, riskily, "But Gar has the love of the common folk."

"Fane is young, yet," Borne replied, smiling gently. "Just sixteen. She will learn. Gar has had six more years than she to polish his manners."

Asher kept his expression unremarkable. Six years, six decades, six centuries even. He doubted it would make any difference. Fane might be a magical prodigy but there was more warmth in an icicle than the whole of her regal little body. And there were no point at all in telling that to Borne. Fathers could be strangely blind to the faults of their children. Hadn't he grown up seeing it first-hand for himself?

"Aye, sir. As you say."

"I will confess, Asher," said the king, lightly frowning,

his thin fingers smoothing the blankets, "it caused his family no little surprise to learn that Gar had hired himself a champion."

Asher blinked. He'd been summoned to the king's bedside to chat about things a year and more old? "Aye, sir. Reckon it might have done, at that. But you know, I ain't really his champion. He only calls me that to rile me up."

The frown became a smile. "And does it 'rile you up'?"

Another polite shrug. "Not really. Not any more. But I let him think it does. Gives him a laugh."

That made Borne laugh, but his amusement ended in more coughing and another sip of water. When he could speak again: "Making no bones about it, Asher, I wasn't sure Gar hadn't made a mistake, in the beginning. But I've been watching you, perhaps more closely than you know, and he was right. You've done an admirable job as his assistant. And, moreover, you've been good for him."

"Oh, aye?" said Asher cautiously. Something was coming, he could smell it like rain in the wind. "That's good to hear, Your Majesty."

Borne nodded. "My son is less solitary now than once he was. Less inclined to live inside duty and books. He smiles more. I think you've shown him that a life lacking magic can still be a life filled with joy. In your company he forgets he is a cripple."

"Barl bloody save me!" snapped Asher, unthinking. "He ain't a bloody *cripple*!"

Melted with fever, wan and reduced, Borne stared at him in silence.

Appalled, Asher stared back. "Your Majesty," he

added, wincing. Then thought, *sink it*. He was leaving, wasn't he? When would he get another chance to put Gar's father straight on a few things? "He ain't a cripple, Your Majesty," he said again, this time remembering his manners. Keeping his tone moderate. Suitably deferential. "I know there's folk think he is. *He* thinks he is. But he ain't. He's a good man who works hard for you and everybody else in Lur. He'd kill himself for this kingdom, I reckon, if he thought it'd do any good."

"I know that," the king said quietly. "He is my son. Do you think I don't know that?"

Asher gestured helplessly. "Well, then . . . ?"

"Well then, Asher, you may say he's not a cripple. And so, in the privacy of my bedchamber, may I. But the truth remains that he is without magic. And a Doranen without magic is no true Doranen, just as a bird without wings is not truly a bird. *If* you accept that the base property of birds is the ability to fly. Do you?"

Asher stared at the carpet. "Aye," he muttered. "But I still reckon it ain't fair."

"You say it's not fair? *You* say? He sprang from *my* seed, Asher! He is the fruit of *my* loins. And yet you sit there and say *you* think it's not fair?"

"Codswallop to that!" retorted Asher. "It ain't no more your fault than Gar's, Your Majesty. It ain't anybody's fault. It just happened. And sayin' otherwise, thinkin' it even, well that just adds more grist to the mills of folks like Conroyd Jarralt. And what bloody fool would want to do that, eh?"

With a grunt of effort, Borne sat himself more upright against his raft of pillows. His lips twitched. "Well. Not this bloody fool, certainly."

Asher put his head in his hands. "Sorry, Your Majesty. I'm sorry. I'm so used to Gar, we shout and we brangle and we call each other names and I *forget*—"

The king's hand brushed against his knee in a brief benediction. "Gar told me once that above all else he treasured your honesty. He said he could trust you, as he trusted nobody else, to always tell him the truth. Whether he particularly wanted to hear it or not."

Slowly, Asher lifted his head. The king's eyes were kindly and his lips were curved in a smile. "Don't see the point of tellin' him anythin' else, sir."

The smile faded. "Can I trust you'll always do the same for me?"

"Of course, Your Majesty."

Borne slumped a little. Let his head fall back against the pillows. "He also told me you'd said you wouldn't be staying in the City above a year. That you had plans beyond that."

Mouth dry, Asher nodded. "Aye. I said that."

"But it's been more than a year now, and you're still here. Have your plans altered?"

It was hard, but he made himself meet the king's gaze squarely. "No, Your Majesty. In fact I were thinkin' on it just this mornin'. How I'd have to be makin' arrangements in the next few days for gettin' back home to Restharven."

Borne stared at his lackluster hands. "What can I say, what can I do, to make you change your mind? There must be something you want . . ."

"I want nowt, Your Majesty. Except my home."

With his tired gaze still averted the king said, "I could command you to stay."

Asher felt his heart leap. Ignored it. "Aye, sir. You could."

"I don't understand." Borne looked up again. "Are you unhappy here? Have you been mistreated? Are your duties as Assistant Olken Administrator no longer to your liking?"

"No, Your Majesty. I like 'em just fine. I like everythin' about bein' here. And that's the truth."

"Then why leave? You must know it will make Gar unhappy! If you are truly his friend you would avoid doing that at all costs. He depends upon you daily to help him with his work. In truth, *I* depend upon you in that regard. As do your fellow Olken, in the City and beyond it. You aren't a fool, Asher. You must know you've become a man of influence. What does a small life in a small fishing village have to offer that your current life here in the capital does not?"

Helplessly, Asher stared at him. "My da lives in that small fishing village, Your Majesty. And he's waitin' for me to come home."

Borne stared. Sighed. "I see."

"I made him a promise," said Asher, leaning forward. "And I aim to keep it. I know it'll hurt Gar but I ain't got a choice. This is family. D'you think I'd hurt him for anything less?"

"No," said Borne. "And if your father needs you then of course you must go."

He should have felt relieved. He should have felt like turning cartwheels. Instead he felt like some kind of traitor. "I'll never forget what the prince has done for me, Your Majesty. I'm a wealthy man, thanks to him. I got a wardrobe full of fancy clothes. Books to read. A fine horse.

I know things now I never knew I didn't know, if that makes any sense. And I've made a lot of good friends. Never would've had any of that without Gar."

"When do you plan on telling him?"

"Soon. I thought—"

"Wait," said the king. "Wait till you're in Westwailing and the festival is done. I want you to guide him through it safely, Asher. He's never seen the festival. Never even seen the ocean. As a child he used to beg me to take him with me to Westwailing but the queen and I . . ."

Didn't want to parade their magickless son in front of a gawking crowd. Asher nodded. "Aye."

"Wait," Borne pressed. "Don't give him anything else to fret about. After everything you say he's given you, it's not so much to ask, is it?"

Asher chewed at his lip. He didn't want to wait. With his mind made up to go didn't want to keep the decision secret. It'd been hard enough these past few months, knowing his time was running out, making plans with Gar for various projects, discussing ideas. He'd felt like a liar and a cheat because all the time he'd known he wouldn't be there to see them through.

"Asher?" said the king. "Please. As a favor to me, and to his mother."

A king was begging a favor of him. Of all the strange things that had happened to him since setting foot in Dorana City this had to be the strangest. Asher frowned. "But he'll guess, sir. He'll know somethin's in the wind when I start packin' all my—"

"Then don't pack. At least no more than you'd take if you were going down to Westwailing and coming back again. I'll make arrangements for all your possessions and your money to follow you safely down there a day or so after you leave. You'll not be short-changed by so much as a single cuick."

Asher sighed. So he'd spend a few days feelin' uncomfortable. He'd survive. He'd felt the same way in the weeks leading up to his departure from Restharven, hadn't he, and that hadn't killed him. "All right, Your Majesty. I'll wait till the festival's over and done."

Relief washed some color into the king's white face. "Thank you. And speaking of the festival . . ."

"I'll help him every way I can," promised Asher. "If that ole Darran'll let me." He pulled a face. "Are you sure he has to come with us?"

That made Borne chuckle. "I'm sure. You never know, Asher, you might even find yourself learning something of the festival from him."

"From *Darran*? And me a fisherman born and bred?"

"Well, perhaps not," conceded the king. "But you'll humor me and let him think it's possible, won't you?"

Asher rolled his eyes. "Yes, Your Majesty."

The brief amusement in Borne's face died, leaving him tired and sad. "I'm sorry to see you leave us, Asher. I hope some day you'll come back to the City, and bring your father with you."

"Your Majesty . . ." Asher slid off the chair and knelt beside the king's bed. "I don't know what to say except thank you. Reckon if I were leavin' Dorana with less money than I had when I got here, and that'd be bloody near impossible, I'd still be leavin' a wealthy man, 'cause I had the luck to know you. And your son."

"The luck runs both ways, I think." Beckoning Asher close, the king pressed dry and burning lips to his forehead in a kiss. "Barl's blessings go with you, Asher. Your father is a fortunate man."

"Aye, sir. Thank you, sir," said Asher, and made good his escape.

Gar was waiting for him outside the chamber. "Done at last?" he said as they headed for the door. "What did he want to see you about?"

"Makin' sure you don't make a muck of the Sea Harvest Festival," said Asher, after the briefest hesitation. "I'm to hold your hand every step of the way."

Gar snorted. "Not where anybody can see us, you won't be."

"'Course not. Don't want to make that ole Darran jealous, do we?"

Gar choked. "Or Willer." He burst out laughing, all the strain and despair of the last week draining from his face.

Relieved for the moment, dreading the future, Asher laughed with him.

In the aftermath of the announcement that His Majesty had that very morning been pronounced once more fine and dandy by the royal physician Pother Nix, the Green Goose was crammed to the rafters with celebration and a damned fine tune from Humperdy's Band. No sooner had the sun gone down and the last shop shut its doors than the inn began to fill with cheerful Olken ready to raise a mug or many to the king's good health and the Wall's longstanding.

Not that there'd been any fear for the Wall, of course. Everybody knew the king was a powerful strong magician who'd never let that Wall fall down. And anyway, there was always Princess Fane, ready to be WeatherWorker as soon as was needful. And if that wasn't a reason for celebration, then just what bloody well was?

Dathne waited and watched as Matt fought through the heaving, hilarious crowd to the bar for a fresh mug each of ale. Despite the good news about the king she was in no mood for smiling.

After a year without visions, Prophecy was back.

She'd dreamed last night of evil eyes, waiting, and a wind of fury blowing every tree in the Black Woods bare. Of stars bleeding scarlet as they fell from the sky, and the sound of women weeping.

The stubborn silence had continued for so long since her last vision she'd begun to doubt all that had at first felt so clear and certain. If Asher were truly the Innocent Mage, why had Prophecy abandoned her, Jervale's Heir, leaving her ignorant and blind? Where was calamity? What had happened to the Final Days? Had she been wrong after all?

Wait, Veira had counseled her. *After six hundred and forty-four years, what is one more? Prophecy unfolds itself according to its own desires, child. Not ours. You were not wrong. Asher is the one, and his time will come. Wait.*

So she'd waited. Waited and waited and *waited*, filling her days with work and her nights with schooling Asher as best she could, without revealing anything, in whatever arts and knowledge she thought might help him in the hidden days to come. And after a little while had got well used to waiting. To laughing. To his company. So that waiting had stopped feeling like waiting . . . and instead began to feel like happiness.

Now at long last the waiting was over, and all she

could do was long for the silence and nights empty of dreams. For after the dream that had woken her screaming into the dark, there burned in her mind a new knowledge. An understanding that *here* now were the Final Days, counting down to chaos. That the last year had been a kind of gestation, and bloody childbirth waited hungrily, its time almost come. The knowledge sat on her shoulder like a midnight crow, cawing and chittering its fears and foretellings into the dark secret places of her mind where there was no hiding, no kind forgetting, no respite from care.

And to think she'd hoped that maybe, just maybe, the Final Days had somehow passed them by . . .

But she forbade her rediscovered weariness and fear to show in her face as she crunched garlic-roasted nuts and waited for Matt to return with another mug of ale. Still stuck fast in the raucous crowd he turned his head to smile at her, shoulders shrugging an apology. She smiled back, but it was an effort. Then Humperdy's music changed from gleeful laughter to a sweet, slow lament and a bracelet of fingers closed tight about her wrist.

"This be my favorite," Asher announced, his breath tickling her ear, stirring the wayward curls that escaped the confinement of her practical plait. "Dance with me, Dathne."

She hadn't seen him come in. Before she could protest, demur, distract or simply slap him down he'd dragged her into the swaying, close-packed press of bodies on the Goose's tiny excuse for a dance floor. His arms were loosely on her, gathering her close. The smell of him was all around her, clean and male and vaguely redolent of horse, and it was wrong, so wrong, he wasn't for her, couldn't be for her, there was no-one for her. She'd been chosen for other things, and so had he . . .

Wickedly, she let her forehead drop against his broad chest, and for one chorus and half a verse allowed the music to move her as it willed. His arms tightened, and for the first time in a long time . . . ever . . . she felt safe. Secure.

Fool! her inner self screamed and the moment shattered.

She stepped back, easing a proper distance between them. Lightly, brightly, in the bantering tone she'd taken with him from that first day in the bustling marketplace, she said, "So you've come out slumming, have you? Am I to be honored or should I just fall over in surprise?"

He scowled. "Ha ha. I been stuck up in that bloody Tower for a week, haven't I? Taking care of all the bits and bobs that Gar forgot about, seeing as how the ceiling were going to cave in if he didn't finish translating some stupid ole story or other."

"Oh well," she said. "He's been worried about his father." And so had she, and Veira. Remembering anxiety, she asked: "His Majesty's really better?"

Asher nodded, and slyly pulled her closer again. "Oh, aye. At least he seemed well enough when I saw him this morning. Tired but on the mend, just like Nix said."

"You saw the king? This morning?" She stared at him. "In his bedchamber?" And stared a little harder, as some memory chased across his face. "Is something wrong? What did he want?"

He chewed his lip a moment, hesitant, then said, "Gar's going down the coast, to Westwailing. It's nearly Sea Harvest Festival time, and since the king's still too poorly to sing it, Gar's going to. I'm going with him. We leave in three days."

"Oh, I see. Well, it sounds very exciting. I'll look forward to hearing all about it when you get back."

"Thing is . . ." said Asher, after another silent moment. "I ain't coming back."

There were too many people dancing. All the breathable air had been sucked from the smoky room. Bumped and jostled she stood there, and he stood there with her, staring down, anxiety and excitement and a kind of foolhardy bravado lighting him from within.

"I'm sorry?" She almost didn't recognize her own voice, so breathless and uncertain did it sound. "*What* did you say?"

"I'm leaving Dorana. Going back to Restharven. Mayhap I'll stay there, mayhap I'll shift along to one of the other fishing villages. Depends on Da. And my brothers. But—"

"Does the prince know?" she demanded, a little strident, a touch querulous. Be easy, her saner self counseled from a great distance. But easiness was nowhere to be found.

Asher shrugged, uncomfortable. "Not yet."

That made her stare. "You haven't *told* him?"

At least he had the grace to look abashed. "I been meaning to. Now the king's asked me not to. But Gar's always known I were never going stay in the City much above a year."

"I never knew that. You never told me."

He pulled a face. "Figured it were easier all round if I kept that to myself. Nobody but Gar needed to know."

She wanted to slap him. Wanted to scream, *I did*. She said, "And if he says no, you can't leave?"

"He won't. I got his word. I can leave whenever I want to."

"And now you want to." There was a pain in her chest like hot coals, burning. "I can't believe you've never told me. I thought we were friends."

"We are," said Asher unhappily. "You and Matt, you be the best friends I ever had, along with Gar."

She lifted her chin. "And this is how you treat us?"

"Don't be angry, Dathne . . ." Asher brushed her cheek with his fingertips.

She took him by the arm, ungently, and hauled him through the dancers and the drinkers, heedless of the cat-calls and the laughter, outside to the empty street which glowed gently in the golden light from the distant, magic-soaked mountains. Dominating the night sky, Barl's Wall soared effortlessly upwards, losing itself amongst the stars.

"You can't leave," she said fiercely. "Gar needs you."

He pulled his arm free. "My da needs me more."

She took a deep, steadying breath and let it out. Careful handling, always careful, that was the key to Asher. For many more reasons than one. So she calmed her frightened heart and sweetened her voice and said, persuasively, 'You can't be sure of that. But even if it's true, your father has other sons. Gar has only one of you. How will he get on if you leave? You're his strong right hand, Asher. The most important Olken in the kingdom. If you're worried about your father, send for him. You can look after him here as well as there."

Asher shook his head. "He'd hate it here, away from

the ocean. All this dry land, no salt air, no rolling waves. It'd kill him."

"You can't just walk away!"

"Watch me," said Asher, eyebrows knitted, jaw tight.

Stepping close again, she rested her palms flat to his chest. "Please. Don't go."

He stared down at her, his broad and weather-beaten face clouded with unhappiness. His mouth opened and she could see the denial in him, the rejection, the stubborn, ignorant undoing of them all . . . and then he looked at her hands, resting on him, and his expression cleared, vivid as a crack of lightning. Suddenly there was hope in him, and wonder, and a kind of terrified joy.

"Come with me," he countered, and covered her hands with his own.

Noise and light spilled through the alehouse's open door and windows, painting the cobblestones and the cool night air. His hands were warm, the skin callused, working hands, a man's hands. His unexpected touch goosebumped her, shivered the tiny hairs on the back of her neck and stoked the fires banked low and deep within. Harshly, with a piercing reluctance, she pulled her own hands free.

"Asher, be serious."

His face was eager now, smiling. "Just listen, eh? Hear me out. I know you've got the bookshop and all, and they don't be much for reading down Restharven way, but you could change all that. I'm pretty nigh rich now. I could set you up all fine and dandy with another little bookshop and I reckon it'd be only a month or two afore you'd have 'em all eatin' out of your hand, just like you do here."

She stepped back again, shaking her head. "You're drunk."

"Or, or," he continued, heedless, all tangled up in his bright and futile dreams, "you could just come for a visit. For a while. And if you like it, and I know you will, *then* you could stay."

"Oh, *Asher*," she said, torn between tears and temper.

"You work too hard, Dath, and you're always so serious. As if the weight of the Wall rested on your shoulders. It don't. That be King Borne's problem, and Fane's after him. Come with me. I . . . I . . . care for you, Dathne. I don't want to leave you behind."

"You're drunk," she said again, and pressed her fingers to her face. "Or I am. Or I should be. Are you mad? I can't just drop everything and run away to the coast with you, even for only a week or three. What are you doing? Why are you asking me this *now*? What possessed you to say it at all?"

He was blushing. How boyish. How charming. The pillock. "Don't know," he muttered, staring at his expensive shoes. "Been wanting to for a while. Just never could get up the nerve."

She could have hit him. Her fingers clenched to her palms, making fists. Oh, how she wanted to hit him. "I'd say you've got plenty of nerve, Asher of Restharven! I can't come with you. Not next week, or the week after, or the week after that. Not *ever*."

"Why not?" he said roughly. "Ain't I good enough for you?"

Good enough? *Good* enough? Oh, if only he knew. She gentled her voice. "That's not the point. I have work to do that can't be done anywhere else. My place is here in this City, Asher. I'm sorry. I can't do what you want."

"Can't?" he echoed. "Or won't? You're a bookseller, Dathne. You could sell books any ole place. If you wanted to."

She was filling with furious tears. He'd weakened her, damn him. Made her vulnerable in a way she'd never been before. "I'm sorry," she said harshly. "I don't mean to be unkind. I don't want us to part in anger. I don't want us to part at all! But what you want is impossible."

He nodded, slowly. Stared thoughtfully through the Goose's open door. "Is it Matt then? Are you in love with him?"

That surprised her into laughter. "*Matt*? Now you're being ridiculous. Of course I don't love Matt. Asher—"

"Then it's me." His eyes hardened, and he stepped away from her. "Go on. You can say it. I'll not break to tiny pieces and run screaming into the night. Say it."

And now she'd hurt him, truly hurt him. Oh, why hadn't she seen *this*, as well as all the other things? What should she do? Lie and say he meant nothing to her? Or should she defy Prophecy? Break her vow, her solemn oath, and tell him the real reason behind her refusal of him? Tell him the terrible truth of himself, long before it was time for him to know? Risk everything, risk a kingdom and everyone in it, all for the sake of one man's bruised heart? Even if the man was Asher?

Or was she supposed to go with him? Jervale's Heir will guide him, Prophecy said. Did that mean she should abandon her shop and Matt and traipse all the way to Westwailing with him? She would if she had to, but it made no sense. Asher's place was in the Usurper's House.

In the Tower, the palace. He didn't belong on the coast, not any more. Restharven was his past, not his future.

Closing her eyes, she looked into that hidden part of herself that all her life had guided her, ruled her, brought her here, to this place, this time, this terrible moment . . .

Let him go. He will return.

A hesitant voice behind them said, "Eh up. What's going on?"

Matt.

She turned, eyes wide, willing him to go away. "Nothing."

Asher said, "I'm leaving."

"Already? You only just got here. What's the rush? There's a barrel of ale in there with your name on it, you know."

"I mean I'm leaving the City," said Asher, and his expression was cold and distant. "Going home."

Matt was staring, aghast. Joining them in three swift strides he said, "For *good*? No, you can't. Asher, you can't leave. Dathne, *tell* him, tell him he can't—"

She sank her fingertips into his arm, making him wince. "It's his life, Matt. His choice. There's nothing I can say that will make any difference." She looked again at Asher and managed a smile. "I'm sorry. Truly I am."

He didn't smile back. Just turned on his heel and walked away.

"*Dathne!*" said Matt explosively. "What are you doing? Go after him! *Tell* him!"

She stared up the street, at the shrinking shadow that was Asher. Felt the knowledge in her, the certainty, the sorrow yet to come, and slowly shook her head. "It's not time."

With a quick glance over his shoulder to make sure they were alone, Matt pointed one scarred, accusing finger at the shimmering mountains and lowered his voice to a scalding whisper. "I think it is. That damned sorcerer's Wall is all that's standing between us and chaos, Dathne. When it goes, when whatever it is waiting beyond those mountains comes crashing down on all our heads, our only hope will be Asher. He *has* to know."

"And he will," she said steadily. "But not yet."

"Really? Seeing as how he's leaving for good? Dathne, you're wrong. He has to know. And if you won't tell him, I will." Reckless with fright he turned and stamped his way up the rising cobbled street.

Oh, Matt. Dear Matt. Often blind and sometimes foolish Matt. She raised her voice and snapped it at his heels. "*Don't.*"

He stopped, as she knew he would. Waited for her to join him. "He thinks he's leaving for good, Matt, but he's not," she told him. "What he wants isn't there. He'll be back."

Matt's inner turmoil reflected in his face. "Who says? Dathne the bookseller? Or Jervale's Heir?"

"Both of us." She said it quietly, confidently, hiding the hurt. "Matt, just trust me, all right? He will be back."

"*Trust.*" Matt raked his fingers through his close-cropped hair. "It's a little word for a big thing, Dathne. Sooner or later we're going to have to trust *him*, you know. With the truth. With us, and himself." With a jerk of his dark-stubbled chin he looked up the empty street that led to the rarefied air of the palace, and the Tower, and Asher. "With Prophecy."

"Yes," she agreed, knowing it in her bones and in her aching heart. "But not yet."

"Not yet! Not yet!" he shouted in sudden rage, fists clenched. "You keep saying that! You've been saying that for a year now, Dathne! We've been lying to him for a whole damned *year*! When is it going to stop? When will *not yet* become *right now*?"

If she cried nothing would ever be the same again. Her own hands fisted, the blood in her veins on fire, she stared at him. Said coldly: "*Not yet.*"

For long moments he glared back at her. Hated her. Then the angry resistance in him melted, as it always did, and he rubbed his large horseman's hands over his despairing face. "Oh, Dath. I'm sorry. I don't mean to question you, I know you know what's best. I just . . ." He groaned. "Damn. How'd I ever get mixed up in all this anyways?"

She smiled, because he needed to see it, not because she felt like smiling, and stepped close. Eased her arm around him until it lay across his defeated shoulders. "The same way as me and Asher, my friend. You were born for it. And in case you were wondering . . . yes. It's far too late to turn back now."

CHAPTER SEVENTEEN

I can't believe you're really doing this."

With a deft flick of his wrist Asher tipped another forkload of manure onto the muck sack. "Why not? Ain't like I never mucked out horse shit before."

"You know what I mean," said Matt, and kicked the stable door he was leaning over.

Gently pushing Cygnet aside, Asher slid his fork under another pile of manure. In the yard behind him the bustle of afternoon stables half drowned their conversation. Why he'd felt the need to come down here and shovel shit he wasn't sure. Mayhap 'cause this was the last chance he'd ever have to do it. The last chance here, any road. In this stable. In this yard, where it had all begun. It was, he supposed, another goodbye that needed to be said. He glanced up at Matt, then kept working.

"Aye."

"Have you seen Dathne since—"

"No," said Asher, disposing of the manure. He didn't want to, either. Just the thought of what he'd asked her, how she'd answered, could flood him hot with angry embarrassment. Seeing her was impossible. The faster she faded into memory, the happier he'd be.

"Are you going to?"

There were three more piles of manure to collect. Bloody Cygnet; the horse was nowt but a pretty silver shit-maker.

"No."

Another bang as Matt kicked at the stable door again. "Why not? You're leaving tomorrow. She'll be hurt if you don't."

"I doubt it."

"Asher!" Matt's laughter was baffled. "She's your friend. How can you not—"

"Easy!" he shouted, glaring. "Because I don't bloody want to, all right? Because—because—" He couldn't say it. Couldn't make the words leave his mouth. If he didn't say it, maybe that meant it didn't have to be true.

Matt's expression changed. "Oh." In his voice, a sudden understanding. "Oh, Asher. Why didn't you say something?"

Savagely he scooped up another pile of manure and dumped it with the rest. "Because I didn't want to. Anyway, it don't matter."

"Of course it matters. When did you—I mean, how long have you known you . . ."

Asher sighed and let himself collapse against the stable wall. Moodily he poked at the straw with the tips of the fork tines, and watched the lazy swish of Cygnet's tail as the horse nibbled hay. "I don't rightly know. Seems it kind of snuck up on me." He glanced at Matt, then glanced away, not wanting to see the sympathy in his friend's face. "I asked her to come with me."

"Oh," Matt said helplessly. "Asher, I'm sorry. Damn, I wish you'd said something. I could've told you she'd never agree to leave Dorana."

Oh, could he? "It's all right," Asher said curtly. "She told me herself."

"I had no idea you felt that way. No idea at all."

"Why would you?" said Asher, pushing away from the wall and forking up the remaining manure. He needed to get out of here before Matt said something they'd both regret. It looked like he was parting badly from one good friend; he didn't want an argument with Matt to make it two. Not when he had Westwailing looming on his horizon.

"It's what I do," Matt said, almost to himself. "I see things."

Asher snorted. "Around here, maybe, but only 'cause it's your job. And I ain't a part of it, not any more. Not for a long time. Here," he added, and held out the fork for Matt to take. Then he gathered up the corners of the laden muck sack and dragged it towards the stable door. Cygnet huffed through his nostrils and pretended to be terrified. "Let me out."

Matt opened the stable door and stood aside to let him pass. "Still, I wish I'd realized."

"Why?"

"I would've said something," said Matt, bolting the stable door closed again.

Young Fulk scurried past empty-handed. Asher grabbed him by the scruff of the neck and gifted him with the muck sack. "Said what?" he demanded, once the lad was safely on his way to the muck heap. "No offence, Matt, but I don't reckon as it's any of your business.

Unless you got an idea I'd be poaching." Scowling, he watched Bellybone slosh water buckets across the yard. "Is that what this is about?"

"No." Matt spoke absently, as though he'd barely heard the question, or didn't care what it might mean. "Look, I'm sorry you've been hurt but if you had told me I could've spared you some of it. There's no use having feelings for Dathne. She's not that kind of woman."

That snapped his head round. "And what's that s'posed to mean?"

"It means . . ." Matt stared at the ground. "She's not for home and hearth, Asher. Her life is in the bookshop. Business. She belongs here, in the City."

Something else he didn't need Matt to tell him. "I know that now."

"And even if you stayed, it wouldn't make any difference."

He shoved his hands into his pockets. "Well, I ain't staying, am I, so there you are."

"I know, but . . ." Matt shrugged. "Even if you were, Asher. She still wouldn't—well, her answer would be the same. That's all I'm saying."

All this bloody interfering. Friends, eh. Who needed 'em? "Y'know that for a fact, do you?" He sounded waspish. He felt it. Right this moment he could sting, and sting, and sting.

Matt rested a hand on his shoulder. "If you mean has she ever said as much to me, no. She didn't have to. I know her, Asher. We've been friends a long time, and sometimes—not often, but sometimes—she confides in me. Dathne's a . . . a racehorse. Not a broodmare."

Despite the anger and pain, he laughed. "I wouldn't go

round callin' her a horse where she can hear you, Matt. Not less you fancy yourself as a gelding."

"I just wish you'd not told her," said Matt unhappily. "It only makes things harder for her. It's not that she doesn't care, you know. She just doesn't care like that."

"For me?"

"For anybody."

"So, this ain't about you bein' jealous?"

Matt gaped. "No! Me and Dathne, you mean? Barl save me. *No*."

Asher stared, suspicious. "You're sure?"

"Bloody sure. I promise."

Stepping sideways so that Matt's hand was pulled free, he scowled. "Well. Anyways. I did speak to her, didn't I, and I reckon I'm paying dear enough for the mistake without you chewing on my ear for good measure. Now were there anything else? Only I've got to meet with bloody Darran to make sure there's been nowt forgotten for tomorrow."

"Anything else? I don't know. No. Yes. Asher, if going home doesn't work out for you . . ."

Asher began inching towards the gate that led to the Tower. Bloody Darran would start squealing like a hog in the slaughterhouse if he didn't turn up soon. Even worse, if he was late he'd have to apologize, and apologizing to Darran gave him indigestion. "Of course it'll work out. I got it all planned, Matt. Had it planned for years, not just since I came here."

Matt took a step after him. "Yes, but you've been away a long time, Asher. Things change."

He laughed. "Not that much, they don't."

"I know. I know. But if they do. If they have . . ."

The urgency in Matt's voice and face made him stare. Matt as a rule was a placid man. Urgency was saved for important matters like lameness and difficult foalings. He stopped inching towards the gate. "What's going on, Matt? Is there something you ain't tellin' me? D'you know something I don't, and should?"

"No." Matt's expression cleared of everything save a gentle concern. "Of course not. What could I know? I'm just trying to be a good friend."

Damn, he hated saying goodbye. He had to wait a moment before he could trust himself to speak. "You've always been a good friend, Matt. Always, from the first day I got here. I ain't likely to forget it."

Matt smiled. His eyes were melancholy. "I hope not."

He was late. He had to go. "I'll see you in the morning, eh? I need Cygnet saddled by seven, mind."

"He'll be ready."

And there wasn't anything else to say after that. Slipping through the stable-yard gate, he started running for the Tower.

"Ah. Asher," said Darran, poisonously polite. "I'm afraid you've missed most of the discussion."

"Sorry," muttered Asher as he slid into Darran's office. "Got held up."

"Indeed." Darran looked down his bony nose at him. "Well, I'm not inclined to waste time by repeating everything we've already agreed upon. I'll give you your instructions once we're done."

Willer sniggered. He was seated beside the Tower's housekeeper, Mistress Hemshaw, who in turn was wedged into the chair next to Trundal, the palace provisioner.

"Fine," said Asher, burning, and propped himself against the nearest bit of wall.

After confirming with Trundal that everything necessary for the long journey was assembled ready for loading into the wagons, Darran turned to the housekeeper. "Mistress Hemshaw, have you anything else to add?"

She fluffed herself like a broody hen. "No, Darran, save for the matter of His Highness's wardrobe. He's still not made up his mind as to exactly what clothes he wishes to take with him so I can have them properly packed and ready for loading."

Darran's nostrils pinched shut. "I see."

"Don't look at me," said Asher, already bored to sobs and staring out of the office window. "I ain't his nursery maid."

"For the sake of efficiency, shall we pretend otherwise?" said Darran. "Just this once?"

Asher sighed. "Fine. I'll take care of it."

"All that remains, then," Darran continued, "is one final announcement. After due consideration and the proper consultation with His Highness I have decided to allow Willer to accompany us on this historic trip to Westwailing. He shall be our official chronicler of the expedition, charged with the solemn duty of keeping a daily diary and accurately recording every moment of His Highness's triumphant procession."

Willer sat bolt upright and squealed like a girl. "Oh, Darran! Really? Oh, thank you, *thank* you!"

Aye, thought Asher sourly, as Mistress Hemshaw and Trundal dutifully congratulated the little sea slug. Thank you very much, Darran. And Gar. Barl bloody save him. With Darran and now Willer along for the ride, it looked like this was going to be the longest, most tedious trip from Dorana to Westwailing in the history of Lur.

An hour after dawn the next morning Gar's entourage was in the last throes of its preparation to quit the City. Four large covered wagons and a traveling coach crammed nose to tail around the outer edges of the Tower's forecourt. Darran stalked along their length, interrogating the drivers and any menial who couldn't scurry away fast enough. Asher, in counterpoint, crisscrossed the scattering gravel on horseback, barking orders, contradicting Darran, chivvying and bustling and scuttling folk out of his way.

Still put out about Willer being included in the expedition, Gar decided, and swallowed a smile. Oh well. It served him right for being so rude about people who had so many fancy bloody clothes they couldn't make up their mind which three shirts to throw into a suitcase, and did he really think the folk down Westwailing way *cared* whether his britches were blue or crimson? Because, you know, it was damn near certain they didn't.

Every spare inch of the forecourt not occupied with last-minute baggage waiting to be stowed or grooms holding horses or messengers bearing sundry forgotten items was packed shoulder to heel with palace and Tower folk and townspeople, eager to send him on his way with a smile and a wave. Even the surrounding gardens were peppered with grinning faces. Seeing them went some small way to warming the cold hollow space in his chest.

If he wasn't very careful he'd find himself feeling terrified of the job that lay ahead. Terrified of doing something wrong, of looking a fool, of letting his father down when the only thing that mattered, in the end, was making him proud.

Reading his mind as usual his mother said, "It's a shame this expedition doesn't appear on the official calendar. I know the Olken on the coast hold the event close to their hearts. But, for reasons that doubtless seem sanguine to the Privy Council, you must depart without their auspices. When it comes to the Sea Harvest Festival not even your father warrants a goodbye wave from Conroyd, you know." She flickered a smile at him. "Are you so very disappointed?"

They were standing together on the Tower's front steps, pretending to be bored by all the hustle and bustle. With a lifetime of practice behind her, his mother was much better at it than he was. He, lowering though it was to admit, was feeling pretty damned excited.

It was, he supposed, marginally better than feeling terrified.

"Disappointed? Not at all. It was the first thing Darran told me so I've had ample time to recover from my devastation," he replied dryly. "You know as well as I, the minute the Privy Council gets involved in anything the protocol quotient trebles and it takes five times as long to get anything done. On the whole I'm as happy as they are that they're still snoring sweetly in their own little beds."

His mother chuckled. "And of course I needn't mention how sorry your father is that he can't be here to give you his blessing. But Durm and Nix were adamant, and I confess I'm glad of it."

He closed his fingers around hers and squeezed gently.

"I would've been cross beyond measure if I'd seen him here this morning. Joining us for dinner last night pushed him to the limits of his recovery. All that needed to be said between us was said then, and I'm content."

She kissed his cheek. "Good."

"Still," he added, shattering all his excellent intentions, "I thought Fane might come to see us off. And Durm."

His mother hesitated. Smoothed his embroidered linen sleeve with a troubled hand and said, "She's busy with her studies, Gar, and of course needs Durm beside her."

"You mean she's jealous and he's excusing her. As usual."

His mother made a small noise of distress. "Oh, Gar. I thought you'd forgiven her that business with the stick and the rose. I know it was unkind. I've spoken to her most severely on it, she knows—"

"You're mistaken, Mama. I don't care about that," he said impatiently, even though he did. Even though the memory could still freeze his blood. He still didn't know which was worse: that she could have done it or that he could have been so blind, so stupid, as to have let her. She was his only sister. He wanted so much to love her. And even though he knew why she had to make it so difficult, there were times he found it almost impossible.

Now it was his mother's fingers that closed, comforted. "Darling, I—"

Scattering pebbles, Darran appeared before them at the base of the carved sandstone steps, harried, harassed and voluble.

"Your Majesty, Your Highness, please forgive me but I must bring to your attention a catastrophe of—"

"What is it, Darran?" Gar sighed.

"I can't find Willer," said Darran, almost wailing. "He's not in the coach where he's supposed to be, he's not in the office, I can't see him anywhere in the forecourt or its environs and—"

Gar lifted an impatient hand, cutting off the spate of words midflow. Turning to search the crowd in the forecourt he saw his target and raised his voice.

"Asher!"

Asher stopped interrogating a groom and nudged Cygnet sideways with knee and heel. "Yes, Your Highness?" And added, with his first smile of the day, "Morning, Your Majesty."

The queen smiled back. "And to you, Asher."

"Do you know where Willer is?" Gar demanded.

"Were I supposed to?" Asher jerked his head at Darran. "That's his job, ain't it?"

Gar permitted himself a barbed smile. "As of now it's yours. Find him."

Asher scowled, then offered a short, sharp bow. "Yes, sir."

"Thank you, sir," said Darran as Asher rode away.

Gar frowned. "If you kept a better eye on your people, Darran, there'd be no need of thanks. Now hurry up. Call me eccentric but I'd like to leave before noon. Today."

"Yes, Your Highness." Darran bowed. "Your Majesty. Your Highness."

Gar watched him retreat then glanced at his mother and shrugged. "I know I shouldn't show it but he does get on my nerves. If I wasn't afraid it'd bring on a relapse I'd leave him behind with strict instructions to wait hand and foot on Father, just the way he used to."

He expected a short, not wholly undeserved lecture on

the importance of keeping one's temper with the staff, but instead his mother took his arm and drew him four paces back from the forecourt, close to the blue curving brick of the Tower wall. In her eyes was a look he'd never seen before.

"What?" he asked, alarmed. "Mama? Has something—is Father—"

"Hush, Gar, and listen to me." Her voice was low, insistent, her fingers like a vice through his shirt sleeve. "You make jokes, but I'm afraid I can't laugh at them."

He stared. "What do you mean? Are you saying he *is* in danger of relapse? Durm said—Pother Nix said—"

"I know what they said. And they're right, in their own limited fashions. He is recovering well enough from this fever. But, Gar, my dear, the situation is more complicated than that."

"Complicated how?"

She released his arm. "The Weather Magic is a double-edged sword and every time you wield it, you cut yourself a little. Your father has been bleeding to death drop by drop since the day he called his first rainfall."

"*Mama!*" If they'd not been in public he would have pressed his fingers to her mouth. He didn't want to hear this. Not now. Not ever. She'd voiced concerns before, fretted his father's dedication to duty at the expense of his own health many times, but never like this. Never so bleakly or with such cold despair. "Mama, why are you—"

"He's changed, Gar. He's not been the same since that business with the young man from Basingdown. You don't know. You don't live with him. You don't wake to the sound of his weeping in dreams, as I do. You haven't had to watch him shrink from himself, as I have, all because of that one brutally necessary act. He may be your father but he's my husband. And a wife sees things . . ."

He reached for her hand. "I see more than you think, Mama. And I, too, have dreams."

She pulled away from him. "He is weary, Gar! Sick at heart. And the WeatherWorking grows harder and harder with every sunrise. I have asked him to abdicate, *begged* him, but he won't. Fane is still too young, he says, and I know he's right, of course he's right, but even so . . ." With an effort she collected herself. "When the day comes for her to ascend the throne—however that day comes—there *must* be a clean succession. There can be no hint of doubt as to her readiness. Do you understand?"

"Yes, of course, but—"

His mother's eyes were fierce. Pain and brute determination burning there. "No matter what Fane does, Gar. No matter how unkind she may be, it can't matter. Your father isn't blind, he can see when she hurts you, and he mustn't be given any more reason for worry. So you'll have to hide it. However deep the wounds your sister inflicts, he must never see the blood. Now I know you're pained because she's not here this morning to wish you well. I don't care. The more hours she spends in study the sooner she can take the burden of WeatherWorking from your father. And that could mean his life, Gar. His *life*. What are your bruised feelings compared to that?"

He was finding it hard to breathe. "Nothing, Mama, they're nothing, but—"

"Your sister will be the greatest WeatherWorker this kingdom has ever known, but only if she's ready when the time comes. If she's not, if she's forced to it before

Durm has tempered her, she could break. And then what? We look to the likes of Conroyd Jarralt? Pray Barl not, Gar. For then the Wall would surely crumble and the horrors that lie beyond it will overcome us all."

Taking her cold hands in his, holding them tight, he said, coaxingly, "It's been six hundred years since Barl and our ancestors fled Morgan—Morg and his tyranny, Mama. He is long since dead and gone to dust. Nothing but a name used to frighten naughty children. He can't hurt us. In truth, we don't know there are *any* horrors still beyond the Wall."

Again, she pulled her hands free. "We don't know there *aren't*! A man like Morg. A magician of his unspeakable powers and unbridled lust for domination. Who knows what legacy he left behind him? Who can say how far his hand stretched? He may have spawned children. He may have founded a dynasty of tyrants that has stretched from his time to ours. All that stands between us and the fruit of those diseased days, their savagery and their slaughter, is the Wall. Would I stand idly by as your father kills himself by inches to protect it if I didn't believe the sacrifice was necessary? Would I give up a child of my body to the same cruel fate?"

Another word, another syllable, and she would have him in tears. "I know you wouldn't," he said, his voice unsteady. "I wish you'd told me this sooner. I wish I could do more to spare him. I wish—"

She wrapped her arms around him then, and held him close to her breast. "Forgive me!" she breathed, her own voice breaking. "I am all to pieces, dearest. It was wrong of me to speak on it. Especially now. Your father is making a fine recovery and I fear he'd be vexed indeed to learn I'd made you worry!"

She felt as frail as a sparrow. "Don't, Mama. Don't treat me like a child. When I come back we'll speak more on this. We'll find a way to spare him, I promise. You—"

A ripple of laughter, rising to a wave, ran through the crowd that had gathered to see him depart for the coast. His mother loosened her grip and they stepped apart to see what was causing the commotion.

Asher, the thrown stone, jogged his horse down the path from the storehouses at the rear of the Tower. Slung over the front of his saddle was Willer, plump rump quivering like a satin-covered jelly, short legs kicking the innocent air. He was shrieking.

"Put me down! Oaf! Cretin! Barbarian! Put me *down*!"

Ignoring him, Asher jogged on through the crowd's swelling mirth. Reached the foot of the Tower steps and lifted his reins, signaling an indignant Cygnet to stop. He was grinning. "Found 'im," he announced, and slid Willer to the gravel-strewn ground.

Gar sighed. "So I see. Willer? I take it you have an explanation?"

His secretary's assistant, scarlet-faced and puffing like a bellows, staggered in a ragged circle and nearly upended himself in a bow. His blotched face streamed sweat despite the early hour. "Your Hi-Highness! Your Majesty! Your Highness!" Then he turned on Asher. "*You*! You did this on purpose!"

Asher rolled his eyes. Darran, squawking up to join them like an enraged hen, attacked from the rear. "Depend on it, Your Highness, Willer is telling the truth!

From the day he arrived Asher has failed to show me and my staff the veriest *breadcrumb* of respect! He—"

Forgetting his place entirely, Willer interrupted. "He locked me in that storeroom so he could shame me before everyone!"

Asher heaved a vastly put-upon sigh. Ignoring Willer and Darran he looked to his prince. "I didn't."

Abruptly weary of the lot of them, Gar lifted a dismissive hand. "We'll discuss it later."

Willer squeaked. "But, Your *Highness*—"

"Later, I said!" Gar snapped. "It's time to leave."

Willer deflated. Bowed. "Your Majesty. Your Highness."

Ungently maneuvered by Darran, the assistant secretary withdrew. Gar, still watching, smiled a little at the glare with which he scorched an impervious Asher; a degree or two more heat and his irritating friend would be stone dead on the ground and doubtless smoking. Turning his back on them all, he laid a hand against his mother's thin cheek. "Tell the king I shall not fail him. Tell him to rest, and get well. The kingdom needs him."

Her hand came up to cover his and she met his gaze with her restored and customary cool strength. "Barl's blessing on you, my dear. You carry your king and queen's full confidence." She kissed him and stepped back, a determined smile on her lips. Only if he looked deep into her eyes could he see her smothered distress.

"I'll see you in a few weeks," he promised, not daring to say more. Kissed her hand, beckoned for his horse and swung himself into the saddle.

Asher grinned. "No need to fret, Your Majesty. I'll

keep a close eye on him, make sure he don't catch cold or stub his toe."

"I know you will," said Dana. "Goodbye, Asher."

For some reason, Asher started. A flea bite, perhaps, thought Gar. If so then serve him right, with a fulminating Darran still to come.

Asher's grin faded. "Goodbye, Your Majesty." He bowed, a fisted hand pressed close to his heart.

Which was odd, Gar thought, and not the least like Asher, who disdained all public protestations of affection.

As the rumbling cavalcade set forth with himself and Asher in the lead, and the people cheered and the horses tossed their bright heads and jingled their bits, gently excited, he turned to his assistant and said, "So, we're off. Excited?"

Asher was barely paying attention, his frowning gaze scouring the rows of wellwishers left and right. "Not really."

He raised his eyebrows severely. "Not really. The first chance to see your precious ocean again in more than a year, and you're not excited. Asher, I declare, there is no hope for you."

"No," said Asher vaguely, still searching the crowd. "Prob'ly there ain't." Some of the ladies were throwing flowers; absently, out of habit, he caught a dethorned rose and tucked it behind one ear. The black-haired girl who'd tossed it subsided amongst her friends in a flurry of giggles.

Goaded, Gar kicked Asher's ankle. "Looking for somebody special?" he asked in a tone of voice guaranteed to irritate.

Asher snapped his head round. "No," he said shortly,

and after that did not let his gaze stray from the straight road leading out of the City.

Gar grinned. *Yes.* Happy that he'd repaid at least a part of the debt he freshly owed Asher, all too aware of the sibilant dissatisfaction in the coach behind him, he patted Ballodair's warm brown neck and looked forward to the journey ahead.

In her tiny rooms above her bookshop Dathne gathered the tools of her secret business and laid them out on the table by the window. A breeze stirred the curtains and wafted the scent of fresh-picked jasmine through the cramped and book-crammed living room.

A large shallow silver bowl, filled to the brim with un-tainted rainwater.

Three glass vials, unlabeled, and stoppered against leakage.

A sprig of dried tanal leaf, known also by another name, never to be spoken aloud.

The leaf was bitter, flooding her mouth with sharp saliva. She chewed and chewed and chewed again but did not swallow, for that would lead to madness. When the shiny golden foliage was a pulped mass on her tongue, all its properties extracted, she spat the dregs of it into a scrap of rag for later burning. Tipping her head back, closing her eyes, she swilled the acrid saliva around and around her mouth, sieving it through her teeth and over the avid mucous membranes of her gums and palate. Then, giddy with the potency of it, she spat what was left onto the rag with the leaf pulp, and waited.

In time the room grew dim to her sight, even as the sun's bright light flooded through the open window.

When it looked to her as though midnight were upon the world, she reached for the first vial, plucked free its stopper, and dribbled a scant three drops of vervle into the silver basin.

The water bubbled and swirled and turned the color of blood.

Carefully she put the first vial aside and reached for the second. Cloysies' tears. Four drops this time, and this time the water heaved in fury, spitting forth a burned ochre steam. It was pungent, smelling of the grave.

The last vial, its potion the most virulent. Moon-rot. One drop only. The muddy water stirred and seethed, thickened like a porridge and belched a sour, sickly smell. Dathne flared her nostrils to catch it like a horse scenting home, and smiled. The steam thinned, thinned some more, disappeared, and now the water in the basin was black like glass. Reflected on its surface her eyes glowed back at her, gold around the edges, fathomless and wise. She spread her hand above the bowl and spoke aloud the name of he whose image she summoned.

"Asher."

The shiny black water waited motionless in its basin, like a cat before the mouse hole. Breathing in through her nose, and out through her nose, Dathne waited with it, hands loosely resting palm down on the table, head drooping a little as the magic bubbled in her blood.

A small bright light, brighter than a diamond in sunshine, pierced the darkness in the water. Slowly it blossomed, bloomed, opened like a window onto another world. Hazily a picture formed, bleary, the way a woman's sight is bleary upon opening her eyes to the morning after a long hard night.

Dathne eased a sigh from her lungs and leaned a little closer over the basin.

The picture rippled, then coalesced into focus.

Asher. And Gar. And the rest of the prince's troupe, clattering their way over the City's cobblestones, waving to the townsfolk who'd forsaken their beds to wish them good journey. Gar was smiling, laughing, waving left and right. Asher waved too, and smiled after a fashion, but it didn't reach his eyes.

For a long time she sat before the basin, breathing in and breathing out, and watched him. Knowing he rode towards heartbreak and shattered dreams. The exact nature of the pain awaiting him she could not tell, but she felt it as though it were her own. Like a knife in her heart.

Soon after reaching the coast he would return. And she would be waiting for him, whether he wanted her there or not. Because she had to be. Because he needed her, even though he didn't know it.

And Prophecy, her cruel master, would continue.

In sudden anger, sudden fear, her hands plunged into the silver basin of water. Asher's image shattered. The water cleared, became just a jug's worth of rainwater once more. Her heavy head ached. She lowered it into her wet hands and wept.

CHAPTER EIGHTEEN

Without mishap, Gar's mostly cheerful cavalcade made its stately way along the City Road, over the bustling River Gant and away from Dorana and its Home Districts. Leaving the Home farms and orchards in their wake they climbed up the gentle Saffron Hills and down the other side, where the Flatlands spread before them in a tapestry of green and blue and yellow and brown. Tiny birds like bright winged jewels danced among the flowering grasses, flitting from stem to nodding stem. Butterflies floated indolently on the perfumed breeze, and rabbits, startled and scudding, caused the horses to dance on restive hooves.

Just past noon they stopped for luncheon. Two cooks prepared the food while other servants pitched a silk pavilion to protect their prince from the unfettered sun, trapping the wild Flatland grasses beneath carpets of hand-woven splendor. The fresh bloom-laden air turned savory with the spitting smell of venison roasting.

But before food came business. Wedged into a folding chair plumped comfortably with cushions, and appeased with a goblet of wine, Gar reluctantly admitted a poker-backed Darran to his presence. The man was looking even more desiccated than usual. Pique, probably, sucking him dry of life's joy.

"Before you say anything, Darran," he said tersely, "I've spoken to Asher and he assures me that Willer being locked in the storeroom was an accident."

Darran's nostrils pinched tight. "I have no doubt he does, sir."

"Do you imply Asher is lying, Darran? To *me*?"

Darran laced his fingers across his middle and considered the pattern of the carpet beneath his feet for a long moment. "The alternative, sir," he said at last, lifting his gaze, "is to say that Willer is lying to me."

Of course it was. Damn. Gar tossed back the remains of his wine and held out the empty goblet. With only the merest hesitation, his secretary refilled it from the carafe on the sideboard and handed it back.

"I grant you," he said, after another deep swallow of spicy Brosa red, "that Asher mishandled the business. As you very well know, at times he has a . . . dubious sense of humor."

"Dubious, Your Highness?" Darran sniffed. "I submit, sir, that 'dubious' is too mild a word for it."

Barl save him. "That'll do, Darran. I'm not in the mood for semantics."

Stung, Darran dipped his head. "Sir."

Gar glared at his dusty boots. Despite some lingering misgivings, he'd been looking forward to this expedition. Over dinner last night his father had called it "a wonderful adventure. An experience to be savored." And had added, grinning, "So get out there and savor it." Which, all nerves aside, he'd had every intention of doing. But then there'd been his mother's fraught confession, and now *this*.

Damn Asher anyway. And Willer. Idiots, the pair of them. After all this time you'd think they'd have found a way to get along. Or at least squabble in a way that didn't inconvenience *him*. He swallowed another mouthful of wine.

"Frankly, Darran, I see no point in prolonging this unfortunate business. Least said, soonest mended, and so forth."

Clearly Darran didn't agree. His sparse eyebrows lowered and his lips pursed. "Naturally, sir, if you prefer to declare the incident closed—"

"I do."

"I see, sir."

Struck with conscience—after all, Darran did have a point—Gar softened his tone. "Look. Rightly or wrongly, what's done is done. We'll just have to keep them apart as best we can until Willer's bruised pride has mended. And it's not as if he were *hurt* or anything. A trifle bounced, perhaps. But nothing life-threatening."

Darran favored him with a frosty smile. "As you say, sir."

Unaccountably, it made him feel defensive. "For the love of Barl, Darran, we both have better things to do than concern ourselves with such trifling matters. I'm bored with the whole stupid affair. Don't trouble me with it again."

Darran bowed. "Your Highness."

"Just . . . go and relax, Darran. You've been run off your feet the last few days and it's only going to get worse once we reach Westwailing. Take a moment to enjoy the fresh country air. You deserve it."

Another bow. "Your Highness is too kind."

"Not at all," he replied, teeth gritted. "Now don't allow me to detain you any longer. Given our early start and brisk pace, I'm sure you're hungry and thirsty."

As dismissals went, it was mild. Darran offered him a third bow, meticulously calculated to convey respect laced with a deep and grievous disappointment, and withdrew.

A scant moment later Asher entered. "You settle the ole crow then?" he asked, pouring himself a goblet of wine.

"Yes. And for Barl's sake, stop calling him that!"

Asher shrugged. "If you say so."

"I do. And as for Willer—"

"What about him?"

"I want you to apologize."

That snapped Asher's spine straight. "What? Why? How many times do I have to tell you, Gar, I never locked him in that bloody storeroom!"

"I'm not saying you did."

"Fine," said Asher, truculent. "Then I ain't got anything to apologize for, have I?"

Gar's fingers tightened on the stem of his goblet, but he refrained from throwing it: the wine was too good to waste. "It was unkind and unnecessary of you to make him a public laughing stock. I don't care how annoying you find him, you're the Assistant Olken Administrator. People look up to you. You can't go around indulging intemperate whims like that. There are repercussions."

Asher was staring. "Gar . . . it was a *joke*."

"A bad one. Willer is a member of my staff. When you embarrass him, you embarrass me . . . or had you forgotten that?"

"What are you talking about? I was just poking fun at him. It was harmless."

Snapping, Gar put down his goblet. "A year in my service, of dealing with the meisters and mistresses of the guilds and Conroyd Jarralt and *still* you haven't . . . *Nothing* you do is without the potential for harm. Now find Willer and tender him your apology. Or else get back on your precious Cygnet and return to the Tower. I don't care which. The choice is yours."

Asher collapsed into the other chair. "You're serious."

"Congratulations! Light dawns at last!"

"Gar . . ." Asher sat back, his face a mask of baffled concern. "What's got into you? What's going on?"

Damn. After a year of working together Asher knew him too well. The urge to confide, to share the burden of his mother's fears, was almost overwhelming.

What's going on? Not much. My mother's falling to pieces, my sister's a selfish bitch and my father's committing slow suicide for the sake of his kingdom. That's all.

He couldn't do it. Not only was it unfair to Asher, to crush him with such knowledge, it would be in some strange way a betrayal of his father.

Forcing a smile, he shook his head. "There's nothing going on. I've got a headache. From hunger, probably. Please . . . do as I ask. Apologize to that tiresome prat so I'm not forced to spend the next few weeks enduring a pissy Darran and a whinging Willer. I'm not asking you to declare undying devotion! Just say you're sorry. I hardly think it's going to *kill* you."

"Ha," said Asher, standing. "I ain't so sure about that."

"Well, if I'm wrong and you do drop dead at his feet, I promise there'll be a lovely funeral."

"And don't think I won't hold you to it!" retorted Asher, glaring. Then he sat again, abruptly, his expression softening into concern. "Look. I'm sorry, all right? I never meant to raise a ruckus. I thought it were funny. Thought it might give you a laugh. Things've been a mite fraught lately, and . . ." He shrugged. "Guess I were wrong."

The unexpected apology disarmed Gar. Doused his anger and stirred guilt. "I'm sorry too," he replied, frowning at his fingers. "I know I've been short-tempered lately. Unapproachable. This business with the king . . . it frightened me." He managed a faint smile. "And I don't much care for being frightened."

"Who does? But your da's on the mend now. He'll be right as rain in another few days. So you can relax, eh?"

He made himself smile. "I'll relax after you've said your sorries to Willer."

Asher pulled a face and stood again. "Aye. You'll relax and I'll lose my bloody appetite." He shook his head. "Apologize to Willer. Ha! The things I do for you . . ."

With a meaningful grimace he took himself off, wine goblet dangling negligently from his fingers and splashing vintage Brosa red to the carpet like fat drops of blood.

Gar sighed. Reached for his own goblet and drank deep. Asher and Willer and Darran on the same expedition . . . three spiky peas crammed into the same small pod. Barl save him from temperament. And then, suddenly recalling Willer's plump satin buttocks, upended over Asher's saddle and wriggling like two pigs in a blanket, he snorted into his wine. Choked. And laughed till he was breathless.

Asher stamped his way over to where Flavy Bannet was guarding corn cobs boiling in a tub of water and licking his greasy fingers. Five enormous platters of carved meat steamed on the bench beside him, and loaves of bread wrapped in hot cloths sat next to bowls of salad greens.

"Oy," he said, stomach rumbling. "Never you mind shoving food down your own gizzard, Flavy. The prince is nigh to fainting with hunger. How long afore this lot's ready?"

Flavy gave a guilty start and smeared the rest of the grease down the front of his apron. "Five minutes, Asher."

"Aye, well, if it's five and a half, you and me'll be having words, right?" He filched a slice of venison and slouched off to find Willer.

The prissy little sea slug was in the traveling coach, writing in a big leather-bound book. His hysterical account of the historic expedition, most like.

"What do you want?" Willer snapped, pen poised and dripping ink. Noticing, he hissed and fumbled with salt and blotter to undo the worst of the damage.

Asher scowled. "I don't care what you say, it wasn't me who shut you in that bloody storeroom. Like as not you shut yourself in there by accident when you went poking about for biscuits to stuff in your pockets."

Willer sat up. "How dare you! I am no thief! I went into the storeroom to—"

"D'you think I care why you went in there?" said Asher impatiently. "Just shut up and let me apologize, would you?"

"Apologize? *You*?" Willer's voice was curdled with contempt. "You don't know the meaning of the word. And why should I accept? You don't even—"

"One more squeal out of you afore I've finished," threatened Asher, "and you know what you can do with your bloody apology. Right?"

Willer sneered. "I know what *you* can do with it. We both know you're not sorry. The only reason you're groveling to me now is because His Highness is making you do it."

Asher felt his fingers tighten on his goblet almost to breaking point. "And how would you know that, eh? Been spying again, Willer? Been creeping and crawling like a little rat, listening to conversations that ain't none of your business?"

Willer flushed a blotchy red. "I don't know what you're talking about."

Ah ha. Now this was more like it. This was a damned sight better than apologizing. Grinning, Asher propped one foot on the carriage's unfolded bottom step, rested his elbow on his knee and trapped Willer inside the carriage.

"Thought I never noticed you, eh?" he said conversationally. "Must reckon I'm as blind as a bat and deaf as a post to boot. I'll give you this much, Willer. You're a persistent little slug. A year now you've been tryin' to get me in trouble with Gar, haven't you? Or Darran, or the guild meisters, or the Council, or anybody else you reckon'll listen to your lies. Hanging round meeting rooms once everybody else has gone. Chatting up the guild meisters' assistants. Sneaking little looks at messages and letters not addressed to you. Accidentally on purpose eavesdropping over conversations that ain't none of your concern. Looking and looking for something what'll get me fired, or worse. All the time thinking yourself so clever, 'cause nobody ever noticed. Well *I* noticed, Willer. I'd have to be thick as two short planks not to and, trust me, I ain't."

Willer's face had drained from blotchy red to sickly white. "*You're* the liar. You always lie. That's what you are. A rotten born liar."

Still grinning, Asher downed the last half-swallow of wine and dangled the goblet thoughtfully. "You must think I'm as stupid as you are, Willer. Ain't you worked it out yet? You can't hurt me. Not today, not tomorrow, not ever. And not just 'cause Gar's my friend, although he is and that's a part of it. Mainly you can't hurt me 'cause you're a piss-weak little sea slug, and the only reason I ain't squashed you afore now is 'cause I don't care for slug slime on my boots."

Willer leaned close, his writing forgotten. The inkpot tipped, spilling blue all over the plush red velvet carriage cushions. Willer didn't notice. There was spittle in the corner of his down-turned mouth. His eyes gleamed brimful of hate and his soft hands were clenched tight as a tantrum by his sides.

"You'll mind your step if you know what's good for you, Asher. You think I'm the only person who despises you?" he hissed. "A lot of people despise you. They're just not brave enough to come out and say it. And do you know *why* they despise you? Because you think you're untouchable." His voice was shaking, virulent, and his pink skin shone damp with spite. "And you think you're as good as His Highness. Well, you're not. You're still one of us. You'll *never* be one of *them*."

Asher laughed. "I don't want to be one of them. That's your problem, Willer. Not mine."

Willer recoiled as though he'd been slapped. "That's *blasphemy*! You take that back, Asher. *Take it back*!"

Shaking his head, Asher straightened and took his foot from the carriage step. Stared at Willer, who was breathing in such harsh, strangled gasps he looked near to suffocating.

"You're a sorry little man, Willer."

Willer lunged off the carriage cushions. Book, pen and inkpot went flying. Wheezing, trembling, he clutched at the carriage doorway as though his fingers were round Asher's throat.

"Not as sorry as you'll be one day, I promise you!"

Stepping forward again, Asher reached up to Willer's smooth, soft cheek. Patted it gently. "Don't threaten me, Willer. It's a waste of breath, 'cause you ain't got the brains or the balls to see it through." And laughed as Willer jerked away from him. Losing his balance, the slug fell to the carriage floor, where he stuck tight between the seats like a sausage in a bun.

Whistling, tossing his empty goblet from hand to hand, Asher sauntered back to the prince's pavilion, where Gar was wolfing down meat and bread and hot buttered corn. The food was neatly laid out in dishes and platters on a cloth-covered table. At the rich, heady aromas Asher's empty insides contracted and saliva flooded his mouth. He was bloody famished. He nodded to the little pot boy doing double-duty as a serving man and watched greedily as a plate was piled high with food for him.

"So," said Gar around a mouthful of venison, "you saw Willer? He's all sorted out now?"

"Oh, aye," said Asher, taking his plate from the pot boy, hissing as he burned his fingertips on a fat yellow corn cob. "He's well and truly sorted."

Gar, holding out his goblet for another serving of wine, wasn't paying attention. "Good. Now eat quickly, would you? We have to get back on the road."

Asher rolled his eyes. "Yes, Your Highness. Whatever you say, Your Highness."

And laughed as Gar threw a bread crust at him.

Luncheon concluded, they packed up their wagons and continued on their way. The Flatlands unrolled behind them as they chased the sinking sun. As the last of the dusk surrendered to the stars they reached the hamlet of Flat Iron and the Hooting Owl Inn, where it was arranged they'd spend the night. For the first time in his life Gar went to bed without the glow of Barl's Wall gleaming through his bedroom curtains. Strange, it felt, and unsettling, but the long day's riding took its toll and he fell into a weary sleep.

He woke again, hours later, to the sound of rain thrumming the slate roof overhead. For a moment he was confused. How could it be raining? The king was still too weak to WeatherWork. Durm had forbidden it for at least another week; his father had groused about it last night over his invalid's dinner of steamed chicken and mashed carrots.

Then he realized. *Fane*. Of course. This was the perfect opportunity, wasn't it, to get her feet wet, no pun intended. She'd had the Weather Magic for three months now, had undergone the Transference ceremony amid much excitement and celebration and private gloating. Once she'd recovered from the exhaustion that followed the acceptance of such strong magic they'd had a special dinner, just the family and Durm. His father had glowed with pride and his mother had wept. At the time he'd thought that was pride too but now, after their conversation on the Tower's front steps, he wasn't so sure.

"Your father has been bleeding to death, drop by drop, since the day he called his first rainfall."

One day, perhaps sooner than ever he'd imagined, there'd be no blood left for his father to shed. The thought terrified him. Pounded his heart and stiffled the air in his lungs. His mother was wrong. She had to be. She was panicking for no good reason. The king was perfectly fine. Well on the mend. Hadn't Nix said so? And Durm? Surely Durm, his father's trusted friend and adviser, wouldn't lie. Not about that.

But then . . .

If his mother was wrong, why had Durm put Fane through the punishing Transference ceremony a full year earlier than planned? Why would she be up in the Weather Chamber now, bleeding, proving her worth, making it rain, if not to hurry the day when she could be named WeatherWorker in truth? When she could take the crown from their father's head, the burden from his shoulders, and in doing so save his life.

Save his life, and spend her own.

As Fane's gentle rain whispered down the chamber windowpanes, Gar tossed on his pillows, racked with doubt and dark imaginings.

Her first WeatherWorking. He should be pleased.

Proud. She was his only sister, and despite everything he did love her. Sometimes anyway. As often as he could. As often as she'd let him. Already she'd sacrificed so much for the good of their father's kingdom. Slain her childhood, slain whatever dreams she once might have had about her life. He should remember that instead of dwelling on the wounds she inflicted. Should be desperately grateful that her imminent elevation to Weather-Worker meant their mother's dire predictions would never come true.

He was so jealous he could vomit.

Exhausted, he lay in the dark and listened to the rain until it died and the sun broke free of the horizon.

Within half an hour of breakfast the next morning they were on their way once more. Headed for the long road that led, eventually, to the narrow stretch of coastline supporting the fishing towns and villages of Westwailing, Restharven, Dinfingle, Bibford, Chevrock, Rillingcoombe, Tattler's Ear and Struan Caves. All of Lur's fisherfolk were to be found in those eight places. Nowhere else along Lur's three-sided coastline was habitable. For mile upon mile the land stopped abruptly, falling away to the water in sheer cliffs jagged as broken glass. According to Asher, not even a madman would risk a boat and his life in the savage surf that battered itself to foam and ribbons on the rocks that ringed the kingdom.

Gar, not disbelieving exactly, still found it hard to credit. He was the product of an orderly existence. The promise of such excessive disorder was breathtaking. He began to feel truly excited by the prospect of seeing for himself the wild and untamed water that had somehow managed to produce a man like Asher.

The second night of the journey saw them safely bedded down in the town of Chillingbottom, commercial hub of the prosperous horse-farming region known as the Dingles, although nobody, not even Darran, seemed to know exactly why. The third night saw them welcomed with parade, brass band and flatteringly excited locals into the paper-making town of Slumly Corners named, apparently, for the paper-pulping mill around which the township had grown. On the third and fourth nights they camped in the middle of Grayman's Moor. Darran complained that his pallet was lumpy.

After that, Gar found that some of the novelty and excitement wore off, and then some more, and then pretty much all of it, so the journey became little more than a blurred succession of towns and villages and more towns and villages and lots of scenery and waving people and aching buttocks and too much food which he couldn't politely refuse because somebody's wife had always gone to so much trouble to prepare it, sir.

His father had somehow forgotten to mention that aspect of the adventure.

He started running beside Ballodair for part of each day instead of riding him, and not just to give his backside some rest. His leather riding breeches were starting to feel a little tight.

Asher thought it was very funny, and said so. At length.

Nobody else, of course, dared say so much as a word but he could feel them looking. And smiling.

Roll on Westwailing.

One thing did have him puzzled, as they got closer and closer to their destination. He and Asher hadn't discussed it, partly because he'd been drowning in the preparations for the festival, and partly because Asher wasn't the kind of man who waxed lyrical about anything of a personal nature, or welcomed questions—but still, he'd expected *some* comment, some mention, even in passing, of the fact that after more than a year away his friend was returning to what used to be his home.

But no. Asher hadn't said a single word about it. Not back in Dorana while they'd made the preparations for the journey, and not in the last days on the road. Even worse: the closer they got to the coast the more silent and withdrawn he became. Sullen, almost, and annoyingly short-tempered. In fact, here they were scarcely an hour away from Minching Town and their final night's billet, with Westwailing practically close enough to smell, and Asher hadn't said so much as three words since luncheon, nor cracked a smile since sunrise.

It wasn't good enough. At this rate, by the time they did reach Westwailing Asher's mood was likely going to ruin his whole experience of the Sea Harvest Festival.

Well. He wasn't about to put up with *that*. It was time for some answers. Like it or not, Asher was going to be asked some pointed personal questions over dinner that evening. *And* he was going to answer them, whether he wanted to or not.

By the time they straggled to a halt in the cobbled stable yard of The Juggling Crow, Minching Town's best inn, Asher was close to cross-eyed with weariness. For all the riding he'd done since his arrival in the City, after near on two weeks across country his buttocks and thighs were a shrieking anguish and his back felt beaten with red-hot pokers. Mayhap if he slept in a bathtub tonight, and a serving wench got herself assigned to topping him up with boiling water every half-hour or so, he could stomach the thought of one last day in the saddle tomorrow . . .

The Crow's beaming landlord, Meister Grenfall, and his beaming wife and his seven beaming children were waiting for them as they arrived. Beyond any kind of pleasantry save a surly smile, Asher left the social chitchat to Gar, Darran and Willer. Instead he swung himself groaning to the ground and got busy organizing the stabling of the horses and the stowing of the coach and wagons and the securing of the various valuables they were carting all the way to the coast.

The inn's head groom was a bent-backed old gaffer, seen it all, done it at least twice, and not the least bit impressed by princes and their hangers-on or anything about them except, perhaps, the quality of their horseflesh. That had him nodding and smiling, as well it might. Asher, pleased, handed Cygnet and Ballodair to the ole man's underlings without a qualm. There'd be no suggestion of second-best oats and not enough hay here. Not that there had been anywhere else but it never hurt to check. Folks were unchancy at the best of times. The trick was never to let them think they could sell you sardine for shark.

Letting himself into the inn through the back door he heard the now familiar sounds of excitement at Gar's presence under the innkeeper's humble roof. Rightly speaking he ought to follow the laughter and join the prince and Darran and Willer and the rest of them, but he was too damned tired to face it. Instead he asked a pass-

ing maid for directions to the prince's private parlor, declined her offer of an escort and climbed the stairs, hopefully to find brandy and a comfortable chair.

Westwailing tomorrow.

The parlor was blessedly unoccupied, and there was
indeed brandy and armchairs. Also a spinet, a polished
mahogany dining table and a cheerfully crackling fire in
the hearth. He dragged off his boots, poured himself a
generous slosh of comfort, slumped into the nearest chair
and stretched his stockinged feet towards the leaping
warmth.

Westwailing tomorrow.

Imagine. A year and more of dreaming, of planning, of
looking forward to seeing Da again, seeing his pride and
pleasure in a son's job well done—and now that the moment was almost upon him, he was afraid.

Afraid of Da thinking what he'd accomplished this
past year wasn't enough. Of thinking him changed. Of his
brothers ruining everything out of meanness and spite.
Afraid that he hadn't saved enough money after all and
that somehow all his plans of boats would come to nowt.

But that was just him being foolish. He had more than
enough money. It was on the road behind him now, along
with all his other bits and pieces. Had to be, because the
king had promised he'd see to it.

And then there was Gar. He'd long since started to
wish he'd stood up against Borne, fought for his right to
tell the prince he was quitting his position before they left
the City. Then he could have made his own way home in
his own time, with a clean break behind him. He wouldn't
have had to spend the last long days pretending. Keeping
up appearances. Dreading Gar's disappointment and

demands that he stay. Because there would be disappointment. And argument. Shouting, probably, and things thrown in anger.

Not even his brothers could start him throwing things the way Gar could.

The parlor door opened and Gar came in. "There you are." He thanked the maid holding the door open for him and headed for the brandy. The maid curtsied, pink-cheeked, and quietly withdrew. "I was wondering where you were."

Asher sat up a little straighter. "I got a bit of a headache. Couldn't face all the botheration downstairs."

Brandy balloon in hand, Gar turned to consider him. "A headache, eh? I should've thought of that one. Do you know, before this expedition I never would've thought a man could be *welcomed* to death."

Asher grinned, briefly. "They're excited to meet you, is all."

Gar sipped his drink, pulled a little face then took a thoughtful turn about the room. Took a seat at the spinet and tinkled the keys idly. Cheerful chiming music filled the air. Smiling, he swallowed another mouthful of brandy then put down his glass and began to play properly, some highfalutin' fancy tune you'd never hear down at the Goose. "I know," he said, his voice lifted above the intricate music. "I should be flattered, but it's so damned exhausting."

"It ain't just the locals excited, either," said Asher. "Everyone is. Westwailing tomorrow. Reckon those pot boys won't get a wink of sleep tonight. Worse than magpies, they are, chattering."

"Everyone?" said Gar.

"Okay, well, maybe not Darran. But then he ain't the type to be frisking and gambolling like a spring lamb, eh? That ole crow couldn't kick up his heels if his life depended on it, I reckon."

"I wasn't thinking of Darran."

Oh. Guardedly Asher stared at Gar across the top of his brandy. Now what? "Me? I ain't the frisking type either."

Gar changed tunes, started playing a popular tavern ditty instead. "I don't know about that. I've seen you kick up your heels once or twice. That memorable evening at the Vintners' ball leaps immediately to mind . . ."

Asher grinned, remembering. He'd never been so drunk in all his life. It had been a grand fine night, all things considered. Even the next morning's murderous headache had been worth it. Dathne had danced with him, all dressed up in silk and ribbons . . .

"What?" demanded Gar. "Your face just fell a thousand feet. Asher, I wish you'd abandon this mania you have for secrecy and tell me straight out what's bothering you. And don't try to tell me nowt, because we both know lying to me is a waste of time. You've been worried about something for days now. Do you not want to see the coast again? See your family? Is that it? If so, why didn't you say something? There was no need for you to come if you didn't want to. Barl knows I've nursemaid enough in Darran. Did you think I'd be unsympathetic? That I'd force you to come on this trip if you didn't want to?"

As the music flirted in time with the flames in the fireplace, Asher stared at the floor. Damn. For days he'd wanted to break the news. Tender his resignation. Now the chance was handed to him on a silver platter by Gar himself, and he didn't want it. There was going to be such a fuss . . .

"No," he said. "That ain't it."

"Then what?"

Wait till after the festival, the king had said. Don't give him anything else to fret about.

He shrugged. "Nothing."

Gar's warm concern chilled. He stopped playing the spinet and stared. The sudden silence was uncomfortable. "You're lying."

"Nothing important," he amended. "Nothing that can't wait."

"And what if I don't wish it to wait? What if I wish to know right here, right now?"

"Then I'd say it ain't for you to decide. This is my problem, Gar, not yours."

Gar got up from the spinet stool. Paced to the window, then thumped his fist against the wall. Spun around. "Don't you understand, you fool? I'm trying to help!"

"I didn't ask for your help! And anyways, there's nothing you can do."

"You don't know that." Gar pushed away from the wall and threw himself into the nearest armchair. "I spend most of my waking life helping people, one way or another. Why should you be any different?"

Exasperated, Asher glared at him. "Because I am! Because some things can't be helped! Because if you want the truth, Gar, this ain't none of your bloody business!"

Gar looked down his nose. "I'm making it my business."

Stalemate. Asher took a deep breath and unclenched his fists. Losing his temper now would only make things worse. "Don't. You'll only regret it."

Gar laughed, incredulous. "Was that a *threat*?"

Too late, Asher realized his mistake. He should have told a different lie. Instead of denying a problem existed he should've invented a less explosive one. Spun some malarkey about a wobbly wagon wheel, or loose horse shoes. Bleeding piles. Something. Anything. Instead he'd roused Gar's rampant curiosity . . . which nothing but the truth would satisfy.

Well. No point fretting about it now. That boat had well and truly sailed.

"Fine," he said flatly. "You want to know what's bothering me? I'll tell you. But I give you fair warning: you ain't going to like it."

"Anything's preferable to you sitting there telling me bare-faced lies. I deserve more than that, I think."

"Aye," said Asher, sighing. "You do. So here's the thing. Once we're done with the Sea Harvest Festival, I'll not be going back to Dorana with the rest of you. My year's well and truly up, Gar. I'll be going home. To Restharven."

CHAPTER NINETEEN

Silence, as flames crackled in the hearth and some-body's heels thudded along the corridor outside. Then Gar laughed.

"Very funny, Asher. What's the idea? Give me a false shock then ease me into the actual bad news? Don't waste your time, or mine. Dinner will be here shortly. Come. You're not usually so coy. Just tell me the problem and to-gether we'll work it out."

Asher put down his glass. "I ain't being coy, Gar. I'm moving on. Sorry."

Another silence, longer this time. Gar released a shud-dering breath. "You bastard."

He held up his hands. "Gar—"

Gar sat back. His face had lost its color and the look in his eyes was unbearable. "Well, well, well. You know, I pride myself on being something of a judge of character, but you certainly had me fooled. Congratulations. A whole year as my trusted assistant, my indispensable right hand, and you never talked about your brave little plan to go home and buy fishing boats. Not once. Not even in passing. Instead you insinuated your way into the Tower. Into the City. Into my plans. And smiled, saying nothing, as I gave you more and more responsibility. More and more . . . *trust*. As I increased your wages. Twice. Days turned into weeks, weeks into months, and now here we sit a year later. And in all that time, Asher, with all the opportunity in the world, you said not a single, solitary word about leaving."

"I never thought I had to! I told you when you first gave me the sinkin' job, I *told* you I'd not be staying in the City above a year!"

"But you have stayed above a year." Gar's eyes were glittering and he spoke with great care. "Quite some time above a year, as it happens. The anniversary of your arrival in Dorana came and went, Asher, unremarked by you. So what was I to think? That you'd perhaps forgotten? Or changed your mind?"

"Well if that's what you thought, why didn't you say somethin'? Why didn't you ask me?"

"Why should I? It was for you to speak, Asher. Or stay silent. And you did stay silent, even as you continued to accept my money. Naturally I drew my own conclusion. What's more, you continued to stay silent as we looked to the future of Lur. Why, not three days ago we were making plans for the new Thatchers' guildhouse cornerstone ceremony. Remember? The ceremony where you were to make the speech, instead of me?"

"Of course I bloody remember," Asher snapped, slamming his glass onto the table beside his chair. "And if *you* remember, I didn't want to talk about it! It can wait, I said. We got enough to worry on with this bloody festival, I said. But no, you wouldn't leave it alone. You had to talk about the bloody cornerstone ceremony then and there. Just like you had to talk about *this*, even though I made it clear I didn't want to!"

"Were you even going to tell me? Or were you intending to slip away while my back was turned?" Gar was still holding his brandy balloon. If his fingers tightened any more he'd smash it to pieces and slice all his fingers off too, most like. Well, wouldn't that just serve him right? Poking and prying and not taking no for an answer . . .

"Of course I was going to tell you! What kind of a man d'you think I am?"

Gar smiled. "I don't know. But I'm beginning to find out."

Bastard. Asher shoved himself out of his chair and started pacing. It was that or smash his fist into Gar's face. "I meant to tell you weeks ago. But things kept happenin', I kept puttin' it off. And then your da—"

Gar's lips tightened dangerously. "His Majesty, you mean?"

"Aye," said Asher, glaring. "The king."

"What about him?"

"That day he wanted to see us. See me. He asked me straight out, were I stayin' in Dorana or goin' home. And when I told him *goin'*, and soon, he made me promise not to say anythin' to you till after Sea Harvest."

Slowly, precisely, Gar put his brandy balloon down on the floor. "I see."

Cornered, Asher turned on him. "*You* should have bloody asked me, Gar. You should have bothered to find out if my plans had changed. I would've told you. I never been anythin' but straight with you. But no. You just sat back and drew your own conclusion. Assumed my plans had changed, even though I never said so. What did you reckon, eh? That your fancy City and your fancy Tower and all my fancy clothes and gewgaws had somehow seduced me into staying? That I'd forgotten about my da back home in Restharven? Forgotten the promise I made to take care of him now he's gettin' on in years? Is that what you thought of me? Well, shame on you!"

Thinly, with fireshadows dancing over his face, Gar said, "And what about the promise you made me?"

Asher kicked the nearest chair, hard enough to shift it. Hard enough to hurt. "I bloody well kept that too and you know it! A year I'll give you, I said. And so I have. A year and then some. And I never once shirked a day of it. I've worked my arse off for you, Gar. I may have taken your money every week, aye, taken it gladly, but there ain't a single trin of it I didn't earn honest, fair and square!"

Gar's eyebrows lifted in delicate derision. "And yet you seem to have left it all behind. An unfortunate oversight, surely?"

"'Course I haven't bloody left it!" he shouted. "Think I'm stupid, do you? It's on the road behind us. Your da— no, excuse me, His Majesty the king—saw to it for me."

Gar flinched as though he'd been struck. "Did he?" His voice was a whisper. "Did he indeed? How very considerate of him. Well . . . damn him. And damn you too, Asher. Damn you both beyond the—"

A brisk knock sounded on the parlor door and then it opened, admitting a capped and aproned maidservant pushing a trolley laden with an uncorked wine bottle and covered dishes trailing delicious aromas. Seeing the prince, she bobbed a breathless curtsy. "Your Highness, sir, the meister and mistress's compliments, sir, and here's dinner for you and your assistant, just as you requested."

Gar nodded stiffly. "My thanks to your meister and mistress."

With a nervous sideways glance between the two of them the maidservant began unloading the trolley onto the parlor table. First the food, then the wine, and then a place setting of glass, knife, fork and spoon. That done, she began on the second setting.

"Thank you," said Gar. "I'll be dining alone. You may go."

Her startled gaze flickered from him to Asher and back again. Her cheeks flushed deep pink. "Yes, sir, Your Highness. Enjoy your dinner, sir."

Once the door was closed behind her, Gar seated himself at the table. Poured himself a glass of wine then lifted the cover on the first chafing dish, revealing lightly poached salmon in a dill sauce.

"I believe staff meals are served in the kitchen."

Asher dragged his hands over his face. Well, hadn't this turned into a fine mess of fish guts? Bloody Borne and his damned bloody meddling . . . He bit his lip. Took a step closer to the dining table and cleared his throat.

"Gar. I never said this job was for good. I never said that."

Gar savored a bite of the fish. Explored the second chafing dish: roast duck. In the third, garden fresh vegetables swimming in herbed butter. He helped himself to both.

"My meal is getting cold."

Asher scowled. So the prince was going to sulk, was he? Spoiled, stupid pillock that he was. Trying to make

out he was the injured party. Conveniently forgetting—
and oh, wasn't that just like royalty—that other people
had lives and plans and promises that mattered just as
much as theirs.

"You sure the servants' hall ain't too grand for the likes
of me? Maybe I should go out to the kennels, eh? See if
the hounds have left some bones for chewin'? Would you
like that better? Sir?"

Gar speared a mushroom on his fork. Chewed. Swallowed. "It seems to me, Asher, that what I like doesn't interest you in the slightest. I suggest you please yourself.
It appears to be what you're best at, after all."

Asher slammed the parlor door behind him so hard it
was a wonder the hinges didn't spring free of their hous-
ings. Stamped back into his boots and banged his way along
the corridor, down the stairs and back out to the stables
where he knew he'd be welcome. He didn't care about dinner. He'd lost his appetite. For food, for friendship, for
everything else except getting home . . . and leaving all
things Doranen behind him, once and for all.

Once the parlor door closed and he was alone, Gar
pushed his laden plate away. His stomach was churning.
If he ate another mouthful he'd be sick.

That his father could *do* such a thing. Could conspire
behind his back with Asher like that. That Asher would
keep such a secret. It was so demeaning. So patronizing.
So painful.

In his mind's eye he could see them: heads bent close
together as they plotted his unnecessary protection. "Poor
Gar," they must have whispered. "He's the only choice
for the festival, we have to send him, but Barl knows it's

a risk. So let's not tell him you're leaving, shall we? He might get all upset and ruin everything. We'll keep it our little secret." "Certainly, Your Majesty. Anything you say, Your Majesty." "Excellent, Asher, and here's a little something extra for your trouble . . ."

How could they do this to him? How could his father do it? Treat him like—like a *cripple*?

In silence he stared at the dining table and its burden of abruptly unwelcome food. The old inn creaked around him, settling for the night, and the fire slowly crumbled into glowing cinders. But still he sat there, because it occurred to him that Asher might come back to argue some more or state his case or beg for pardon or hurl abuse, or even plates. Barl knew they'd had their disagreements over the past year. Loud, long and heated disagreements, some of them. But in the end they'd always worked things out. In the end they managed to find their way back to common ground and even laugh about whatever it was that had set them fighting.

They'd never walked away without shaking hands, even if it meant agreeing to disagree.

But Asher didn't come back. The food grew cold, then colder, then congealed into pig food. The fire went out and the candles burned down to their sockets.

Eventually, he went to bed.

Standing by the touring coach the next morning, waiting for the signal to leave, Willer glanced left and right, made certain no underling's flapping ears were close enough to hear, and said eagerly to Darran, "Well? What did you find out?"

Darran looked down his long nose. "Really, Willer. You make me sound positively clandestine."

"No!" he protested. "No, not at all, Darran. Discreet. Politic. Tactful."

Instead of answering, Darran snapped his fingers at a passing servant and nodded at the coach door. The servant opened it, pulled down the little steps then stood back so that his superior might enter. Darran acknowledged the courtesy with a nod and took his place inside. Willer, ignoring the servant, climbed in after him.

Seated in safe silence within the coach, Darran arranged himself comfortably against the cushions. Unfolded his working desk from the panel in the coach siding, extracted a sheaf of papers from the cunningly hidden pocket beneath it, perched his glasses on the end of his nose and began reading.

Just barely, Willer stopped himself from screaming. It was a game, Darran's favorite game, Tease the Assistant, and he'd kiss Asher's fingers and call him "sir" before he'd give Darran the satisfaction of another question. Instead he poked around in his own satchel of papers and pulled out the order of events for the festival. He'd already memorized it, of course, but it was just another part of the game. The more eager he appeared, the longer Darran would wait before sharing what he knew. But his eyes, skimming over the notes, scarcely saw them and his mind was filled with things other than the Great Gathering and the Sea Harvest hymn.

Through the carriage's window, he watched as Asher had scowling words with a groom, all the while tugging at his horse's girth straps and waving his hands about.

Temper hung on him like a mantle, thick and black and red.

Movement from the inn's rear entrance caught his attention. The innkeeper, that provincial rustic Greenhill or Grimfulk or some such name. And His Highness. Looking, Willer saw with dawning delight, as mantled in bad humor as Asher. So perhaps the gossip was true. The prince and his ill-chosen personal assistant *were* at odds. At last, at longest, longest last, the first cracks in that Barl-forsaken alliance were beginning to show.

The urgency of preparations escalated sharply as the bustling servants caught sight of their royal master. Willer, all pretense at reading forgotten, leaned forward to better see the look on Asher's face. At first sight of His Highness the upstart froze, mid-complaint. His spine stiffened and his chin came up, all arrogant defiance, no proper humility, no deferential awe. Just pride and consequence and him nothing but an uneducated pedlar of fish carcases when he'd first arrived in Dorana, to fall into luck and attach himself to His Highness like a leech from Boggy Marshes.

Heart pounding, hands clenched, Willer waited for the prince to notice the scullion. When their eyes met it was like the clashing of boulders, the grinding of ice floes in winter River Gant. Asher was the first to look away. Throwing his reins at the chastened groom he busied himself elsewhere as His Highness showed his back to the courtyard, pretending an interest in whatever the innkeeper was squittling about.

Pleasure, warm and liquid, bathed Willer's skin in a languorous, golden glow.

"You're being obvious, Willer," said Darran, chilly with disapproval.

Caught, Willer felt his cheeks burn, and his hands scrambled on the forgotten paperwork. "No, you misunderstand, I—"

Darran raised sparse eyebrows. "I rarely misunderstand anything. Do cultivate a little self-control, dear boy. The man who controls himself controls the world."

"Yes, Darran," he muttered, and smoothed his creased paperwork back into its carry bag.

"Come, come," Darran chided, thin lips curved in a smile, eyes alight with an unfamiliar fire. "This is no time for sulking. Our patience has at last been rewarded, just as I said it would be."

After a long moment's puzzling, Willer shook his head. "I'm sorry, Darran, but I don't know what you mean."

Darran's smile broadened, revealing crooked teeth. "Asher has resigned."

The shock of it stole his breath, so that for several heartbeats all he could do was gape like a country halfwit, mouth slack with disbelief. "No," he managed at last. "*No*! I don't believe it! There must be a mistake!"

Darran looked at him. "I am not in the habit of being mistaken. I had it from His Highness himself who, I suppose you will allow, has some inkling of his own business."

Resigned? Asher had *resigned*? But that wasn't the plan. That wasn't it at all. Asher was to be found out, brought down, revealed to all the world and reviled by it. He wasn't supposed to just . . . just . . . walk away. Not unpunished. Not whole. How could that be?

Darran said, clearly put out, "He will remain behind in Westwailing once the festival has concluded." And when Willer could still do nothing but stare, snapped, "What is the matter with you? Our dearest wish has at last been granted! Asher's ruffian, unseemly influence will soon be gone from court. He will rapidly become nothing more than the memory of a bad taste in the mouth, and I, for one, am highly pleased by this turn of events. If you are wise, Willer, you will be highly pleased too!"

"Yes, Darran," said Willer, discarding with a sharp pain between his ribs his daydreams of Asher's public downfall. "Of course, Darran. As you say. It's for the best. Of course I'm pleased. I'm *very* pleased." And he smiled, a brave smile, as though he weren't sick with disappointment at all.

In the courtyard Asher's voice rose above the general hubbub. "Right-ho! Mount up, climb up and all aboard! We got ourselves a hefty stretch of travelin' yet and the sun ain't standin' still."

Willer settled himself more comfortably against his cushions and pulled out a book. It was, he discovered with faint surprise, some small comfort that from the sound of it Asher was just as unhappy about impending unemployment as *he* was about his lost hope for revenge.

Good, he thought, and snapped over the page with a vindictive thumb. And what's more, after all this riding I hope he gets piles.

The journey continued in silence. Word had spread, as word always does, that there was something seriously amiss between the prince and his assistant. Even if it hadn't, the chilly unaccustomed silence, their haughty, aloof faces, and the way they rode apart and alone would have shouted as much to anyone who knew them even a little. The grooms, the cooks and the pot boys all exchanged swift, eloquent glances, raised their eyebrows, shrugged their shoulders and in the shorthand of discreet employees everywhere said: What's up with them, then, eh? Dunno. Mind yer step, though, for himself's in a temper and no mistake.

The subdued day dragged on. They reached the Coast Road and got their first look at the ocean an hour and a half after leaving Minching Town. At any other time the breathtaking sight would have stopped them all in their tracks, had them gasping and pointing and begging stories from Asher to match the heart-stopping, impossible stretch of ceaseless blue water.

But Asher was hardly even looking at it and neither was the prince, so that was that. The cavalcade trundled on: overheated, overtired and unhappy.

Luncheon was a brief and acrimonious affair on a sparse stretch of salty open heath land. Strange, ugly bushes writhed low to the ground as far as the jaded eye could see; agonized outcroppings of deep purple and red rock clotted the barren landscape. The horses were unhappy, lashing their tails at stinging flies and snapping yellowed teeth at anybody daft enough to stand too close. Gar ate in solitary splendor beneath a parasol. Asher savaged a heel of bread and a hunk of cheese in the shade of the supply wagon and was wisely left alone. From the look on his face, the horses and flies weren't the only creatures in a biting mood.

They didn't rest for long; Darran had them back on the road within the hour, fussing about punctuality and reminding all and sundry that they would have to stop again before reaching Westwailing so that everyone could change into the fresh clothes kept aside for their official arrival and welcome.

After two interminable, buttock-bleeding weeks on the road, the journey was nearly over.

Westwailing welcomed them with open arms, smiling faces and a raucous brass band, whose five burstingly proud members were crowded at the foot of the mayor's beribboned dais, strategically placed at the top end of the High Street. All the gathered fisherfolk of Lur were there, lining the long, downward-winding thoroughfare, perched precariously in trees and on rooftops, dangling daring from open windows, and every one eager for a glimpse of the flaxen-haired prince from that unimaginable place, the City. The air was brisk and laced with salt, flavored with fish. There was a speech from the mayor, mercifully short, and then the brass band played in earnest as His Royal Highness Prince Gar and his royal party minced their recently washed and meticulously reclothed way between the cheering spectators. The mayor and his wife and various other local dignitaries tucked in behind, basking in royalty's reflected glory.

Face schooled firmly into an expression of gratified pleasure, hand raised and waving impartially left, then right, Gar slid his gaze sideways to his scowling companion and said, "Smile. You owe me that much."

Asher manufactured an obedient, empty smile.

Smothering the hurt, Gar looked to the crowd again. Released a sigh, soft as the briny breeze. All these people. All this excitement. They meant nothing. Nothing. They'd cheer a dancing bear just as hard. Cheer harder if it fell on its fat, moth-eaten behind. Would he fall on his tomorrow, during the Sea Harvest Festival? And would they cheer if he did?

Dear Barl, if you can hear me, he said to the vaulting, cloudless sky, lips pressed hard to his holyring, don't let me fall. Please. If you love me . . . don't let me fall.

That night there was a banquet, and the whole town was invited. The Westwailing market square was reserved for the mayor and his important guests but the streets belonged to Lur's fisherfolk. Colored lanterns draped the trees, hung from windows and shop signs, lit the shiny cobbled streets in garish rainbows. Trestle tables and benches marched end to end between the pavements and the air was soaked to the gills with the smoky smells of roasting meat. Hogsheads of wine and ale stood open on every corner, and on this one night alone it was no shame to be merry with grog. Laughter was music, and music was music, with the warring shrill and pipe of a dozen different strumming bands and voices raised in discordant song.

The daily grind of life had been packed away in its battered box, not to be looked at or sighed over for a day, or even two. For now only merriment counted, and ale, and fat roast pork, and the cheerful gossip of those lucky enough to have a caught a glimpse of the Prince from Up Yonder.

In the market square the celebrations were more refined but just as enthusiastic. The same brass band played valiantly in the center of the square, the edges of which had been lined with trestle tables covered in donated best tablecloths and garlanded with scentwax and ruby gloss-glows and pale purple bugles.

The official table stood above the rest, as was only fitting, and was waited on by the self-important few who'd been honored and schooled and reminded and teased and resented on it until they were thinking that mayhap their friends and relations carousin' in the streets had the better bargain after all. For certain, serving the likes of that bossy long streak of cat's piss in black who called hisself "sir" when he caught sight of his face in the mirror, most like, and went by the name of Durgood or some such, well, servin' the likes of him weren't a minute of fun . . . nor the fat, overdressed little creature who followed him around like a bad smell.

But take no never mind of them. There were the prince and the Mayor and Mrs. Mayor and the seven other town and village leaders, and they were gracious enough. Oh, aye, and that other fellow. The Olken. Used to be a local, someone said, vaguely recognizing him, and how had he managed to climb so high above the rest of them? Sitting there in his fancy clothes, with a fancy gewgaw in his ear and silver rings on his fingers flaming blue and red and purple fire in the guttering torchlights. And not hardly speaking a word, neither, black thunderclouds in his face. Who was he? Who were his kin, and what village or town did he once call home?

Busier than seagulls among fish guts, the serving lads and lasses scurried from table to carvery to wine barrel to bread bins and back again, and looked and wondered, and raised their eyebrows at each other as the banquet continued beneath a crystal clear vista of stars.

*   *   *

Asher buried his face in a fresh mug of ale and cursed himself for the greatest fool breathing. They were all staring at him, sink 'em. Even when their heads were turned or they gobbled a plate of food or swallowed an ocean of wine, still they were staring. The minute he opened his mouth he'd branded himself a local, and what a fool he'd been not to have thought on that possibility.

Aye, he had a City accent now, though he'd never noticed it creeping up and would be glad to lose it fast enough, but still he was one of their own and they knew it. And of course Ole Sailor Vem, Restharven's village adjudicator, had took one look at him and nearly fallen over backwards with shock. He was fair worn out with the effort of avoiding the ole codger. Last thing he wanted was to have to tell Vem what he'd been up to. Turned out protocol was good for something after all. Vem would never get up from his table before Gar, and Gar was too busy troughing to be going any place any time soon.

In his ear a familiar voice, laced now with unfamiliar spite. "Stop sulking," Gar advised, a lying smile on his lips. "Did I say you couldn't stay? Stay, if that's what you want. Stay and be damned."

Dumbstruck, he could only stare. What did Gar want him to say? Never mind, it was only a joke, of course I'm coming back to the City with you? Got no life of my own, no plans, no ambitions. The only promise that counts is the one I made to you. So I'll just tag along at your heels until I be old and gray and all my teeth be in a jar. Was *that* what the prince expected?

Then more fool him.

He opened his mouth to say so but was drowned by the

renewed vigor of the band, striking up a lively dance tune.

Gar turned away, offering his arm to the lady mayoress. She blushed and dimpled, the silly cow, as though royalty wouldn't tread on her toes just like her husband, and accepted his invitation. As they ponced their way to the clear space in the middle of the market square other couples joined them, and soon the cobblestones rang beneath jigging feet and stamping heels.

Sailor Vem, safe on the other end of the table, put aside his crumpled napkin and stood.

Asher pushed back his chair, abandoned his barely touched food and slid silently into the night. He thought he heard a disappointed shout behind him, but didn't look back.

Westwailing Harbor was wide of mouth and deep of bottom. Draped over the stone wall separating the general public from the business of catching fish, Asher sucked in a deep double lungful of heady ocean air and marveled at himself for staying away so long.

A wide stone pier jutted from the main wharf, pointing like a finger towards the horizon . . . and the foam and break of the huge, magically protected reef. As a boy, Asher had sat atop a headland at sunrise and watched the morning light glint off the ferocious coral construction and wondered, achingly, what might lie beyond that meeting of sea and sky. Nobody knew. Hardly anybody cared. What did it matter, so long as the fish found their way through the reef and into the harbors, that they might end their days on a dinner plate somewhere?

Their lack of curiosity had enraged him. But that was people for you. They were the same in the City. Day in, day out, that bloody great Wall gleamed and towered and cut them off from whatever lay beyond it, but they didn't care. It was just the Wall, it had always been there and it always would. Anyway, what other kingdom could possibly be better than Lur? Lur was perfection. Let beyond the Wall look after itself.

Not even Dathne cared. Not even Gar. He supposed he didn't even care all that much himself. Just sometimes, looking, he'd be struck with wondering.

Just like he was struck now, gazing out at the serene, silvery waters of Westwailing Harbor, with the sounds of celebration loud still behind him, and the softer slosh and slap of waves before, and a full moon riding high overhead.

The beauty of it seared him. That afternoon, as they traveled the winding road down to the headlands and the salt wind blew off the water and they'd got their first dazzled, dazzling glimpse of the ocean, his eyes had stung with tears. He'd known then that leaving the City, coming home, was the only right thing left for him to do. All the aggravation, now and to come, was worth it, had to be worth it, because there was the ocean. There was his heart, whose muffled beating in a dry city had gone on long enough.

Tomorrow, after the festival, he'd find his father. Kneel at the old man's feet and beg his forgiveness for being away so long. For staying silent. Da would be angry at first, but he'd come round soon enough. They understood each other, he and Da, as his brothers had never understood either of them.

And after that, their new life would start.

Before that, though, he'd try to mend fences with Gar.

It would be a damned shame, after a year of friendship, if they parted so bitterly at odds. Gar wasn't a mean man. He'd just been thoughtless. Was disappointed. Angry that this wasn't a decision he could overturn or overrule. But, just like Da, the prince would come round.

Or if he didn't, it wouldn't be for want of trying.

A giggling couple, courting and fuddled with ale, weaved their arm-in-arm way down the sloping street to the stone wall. They were young and in the full bloom of love. She was short and sweetly plump, he a hand span taller, with the close-cropped hair and muscled arms of a working man. Her eyes were starry for him, her lips red with his kisses. He was peacock proud, walking on a fine cushion of air for all to see.

Asher, caught unprepared and opened to beauty by the night, watched their bodies melt one into the other as they murmured breathlessly into each other's mouths. His heart hitched. *Dathne*.

He must have said something, or made a noise, because the couple broke apart, charming in their confusion. Then, laughing, they drifted away into shadow and the all-consuming fire of private passion.

Asher shook his head, fingers tight on the sharp stones of the harbor-mouth wall. Fool, he cursed himself. There was no point in pining. He'd asked, she'd answered. If he couldn't share his life with Dathne, then mayhap there'd be someone else he could share it with. That could take care of itself too. All that mattered now was he was home, beside the ocean, and he'd never leave it again.

From the direction of the square the sound of footsteps on the pathway, coming closer. He didn't need to look: he knew that slovenly gait. "You followin' me, Willer? Have a care. Folks'll talk."

Willer's snide and snivelling voice said: "So. We're finally rid of you. I must say it took long enough."

He sighed. "Piss off."

"The question everyone's asking, of course, is did he jump or was he pushed?"

"In case you hadn't noticed, we're standin' on the edge of a tidy drop into deep water," said Asher. "So I wouldn't be talkin' so much about jumpin' and pushin' if I were you. The amount of food you shoveled down your gullet tonight, reckon you'd sink faster than a stone."

Laughing softly, Willer drifted forwards until his fat belly met the stone harbor wall. Asher noticed he kept his distance.

Smart man.

"I do hope, Asher," he continued conversationally, "you weren't expecting any public displays of grief over your long-awaited departure. Impassioned pleas for you to stay. A going-away party, or any such thing." He paused, considering. "Although now I come to think of it I could name one or two people who'd happily pay large amounts of money for a 'Praise Barl he's gone' party."

Asher took a deep breath. Let it out, throttling rage and the desire to silence the vomitous sea slug once and for all. He turned his head and looked at Willer, baring his teeth in what wasn't exactly a smile.

"Fancy that. Here's us workin' together all this time and I never knew you for a man who liked livin' dangerous."

Willer laughed again. "You're wasting your breath. You don't frighten me. You never did." He pushed away from the harbor wall. Drifted backwards, and was swallowed by shadows. "Goodnight, Asher. Goodnight and good riddance."

Back in the town square the partying continued. Snatches of music and laughter floated down to the harbor, and drowned in the sighing of the sea. Propped up by the ancient stone wall, Asher listened.

It was a long, long time before he finally turned away from the moonlit water to make his way back to his bed in the mayor's house, where he could sleep away the scant hours before the great event of the morning: the Sea Harvest Festival, and the end of Asher, Assistant Olken Administrator of Lur.

CHAPTER TWENTY

Tell me again," said Gar, reaching for the damp towel Darran held out to him, "whose spectacularly clever idea this was."

"His Majesty's, I believe," Darran replied. His smile was sympathetic. "If it makes you feel any better, sir, His Majesty also became . . . indisposed before his first Sea Harvest Festival."

Sitting on the edge of a chair, his emptied stomach churning, Gar blotted cold sweat from his forehead. He was shivering, even though the Mayor of Westwailing's very best guest room faced full into the morning sun and the chamber's air was warm against his bare chest. Less than an hour before he was due to lead the procession down to the Harbor . . . to lead the Sea Harvest Festival . . . and he was puking his guts into a chamber-pot like a virgin on her wedding night.

Perfect.

He spared Darran a sour glance. "You're just saying that."

"I assure sir, I am not," Darran said blithely. "As it

happens I was in a position to perform for your dear father the same service I perform for you now."

"Really?" Gar considered him. "That's very dedicated of you, Darran. Surely there must be something more edifying you can find to do with your time?"

"Not at all, sir," said Darran as he tidied away the pot and the soiled facecloths. "I consider this opportunity a great honor."

The roiling queasiness was easing. Overcome, possibly, by sheer, fascinated horror. "You think watching me vomit my breakfast into a chamber-pot is an honor? Darran, you really need to get out more."

Darran laughed politely and relieved him of the damp towel. "Your Highness, I have served your father's house since before he was born and I was a small boy, of an age to be trusted with running messages. Serving him once he ascended the throne . . . serving you, now, in whatever capacity I can . . . well, there isn't another Olken in the kingdom who can claim such continuity. Who has been gifted with such trust. How could I be anything but honored?"

Tentatively, Gar straightened. When his stomach didn't revolt, he took a cautiously deep breath. "I suppose."

Darran bowed. "Indeed, sir. Now, as you can see, I've laid your clothes out for you. Of course, if you've changed your mind, then—"

"No," said Gar, glancing at the grass-green silk shirt, the deep blue, gold and crimson brocade weskit embroidered with bullion thread, the sea-blue woollen breeches he'd selected last night. They were as respectable as anything else he'd brought. "Well, not about the clothes anyway. Are you sure I can't change my mind about leading the festival?"

"You are a prince, sir," Darran reminded him with a discreet smile. "You are at liberty to do as you please. But I wouldn't advise it."

"Neither would I. The king would skin me alive." Gar frowned, briefly, the thought of his father still a small, stinging hurt. He banished the pain. There'd be time enough to deal with that upon his return. For now he had to concentrate on the matter at hand. "But even so, I can dream, can't I?"

"Certainly you can, sir," Darran said. "But if I might suggest that you dream and dress at the same time? We are due to leave for the harbor within the half-hour."

Nodding, Gar reached for his shirt. Buttoning it, careful to keep his eyes on the task, he said, "Have you seen Asher this morning?"

Darran stiffened. "Yes, sir. He took breakfast with the rest of the staff in the servants' kitchen."

"And did you convey to him my displeasure at his leaving the banquet so peremptorily last night?"

"I did." Darran's voice was frigid. "He saw fit to inform me that his whereabouts were none of my concern."

Gar glanced at Darran. Noted the burning spots of color in his sallow cheeks. "But not quite as politely as that?"

Darran sniffed. "Not quite, sir. No."

He felt his jaw tighten. Felt the simmering rage surge. "I see."

"If I may be so bold as to suggest it, sir," Darran continued, "you might be best served by dispensing with Asher's services at the festival ceremony this morning. His attendance can achieve no useful purpose and his recent behavior clearly demonstrates a distressing want of conduct and appreciation for his position. Without wishing to cause you further perturbation, I would remind Your Highness that in a short while you shall be the cynosure of all eyes. It would be regrettable indeed should Asher's deplorable conduct in any way reflect poorly upon yourself or His Majesty."

With the last button successfully captured, Gar turned his attention to pulling on his breeches and tucking his shirt tails into their waistband. "No," he said. "He is sworn to me until the end of our stay here and I shall hold him to that oath." Not least because clearly it was the last place Asher wanted to be.

Vindictive? Him? Never.

After a short pause Darran said, "Certainly, sir. If you say so."

Gar shot him a look. "I do. Hand me my weskit."

Darran gave him the brocade vest and adjusted it across his shoulders after he'd shrugged it on. "Your Highness is naturally free to do as you see fit."

"Yes, Darran, I am," he snapped, and eased his feet into his boots. Damn the man; criticizing and judging and never a word out of place . . . "And as I said before, I'll have no gossiping on this, do you hear me? It's between me and Asher and nobody else."

"Sir," said Darran, grossly offended. "I do not stoop to *gossip*."

Gar held out his hand for his circlet of office. The plain one, which had been passed down from father to son since the days of Barl herself. "And there's no point getting huffy with me either."

Lips thin with disapproval, Darran removed the circlet

from its velvet-lined case and with a soft cloth began to buff it to a glowing luster.

"People talk," Gar added as his secretary's careful hands coaxed highlights from the beaten white gold. "It's to be expected. I'd just better not hear about it, that's all I'm saying."

"Sir," said Darran with awful dignity, and handed over the gleaming circlet. "If you will excuse me, Your Highness, I shall ensure that the rest of the party is ready and awaiting your pleasure."

Gar nodded. "As you like. I'll be downstairs shortly." Ignoring Darran's straight-spined departure he laid the circlet on the bed, found a brush and put his hair in order. Then, staring at his immaculate reflection in the chamber's full-length mirror, settled the circlet of office on his head. Behind him, the door opened again. Asher.

The circlet wasn't quite straight; damn thing was always a horror to get right. "Yes?" he asked, fingers cool and steady on the gold.

"Just checking to make sure you be all set." Asher was dressed in dull purple and dark blue, all silk and brocade and leather, thick black hair freshly washed, polished half-boots on his feet. There was nothing of the fisherman about him.

"Of course I'm all set," said Gar. "Do you think I can't get myself dressed for some half-baked country yodeling session without assistance?"

Asher sighed. Came further into the room and kicked the door shut behind him. "Look. Let's not leave it like this, eh? Not when we'll likely never lay eyes on each other again after today. You want me to say I'm sorry? Then I'm sorry. You want me to say it were wrong of me not to drop a hint every now and then? 'When I get back to Restharven,' that kind of thing? Fine. It were wrong. And I know I should've said something the minute I knew my mind was made up to go. But, Gar, I didn't. And you poutin' and stampin' and pullin' faces like a frog on a log over it ain't goin' to change that now. What's done is done. And you did say I had leave to quit you after a year. So can't we just shake on it, eh, and part friends?"

One final nudge and the thin strip of ancient gold was perfectly aligned. It clasped his skull lightly. Only his imagination made it heavy. Gar took a step back from the mirror and eyed himself up and down one last time. He looked fine. Better than fine. He looked every inch a prince. Doranen royalty. Keeper of Barl's Law. Defender of the Realm. Morg's Scourge. Pity about the magic, but there it was. You couldn't have everything, could you?

Letting his gaze slip sideways, he met Asher's uncertain, reflected eyes. "Change your mind."

Across Asher's face, a skittering of emotions: sorrow, anger, an impatient compassion. "I can't."

And there it was. Final as a door slam. Part friends? Not likely. "You're making me late," he said. "Go downstairs and wait with the others."

Correct to a hair's-breadth, Asher bowed. "Yes, Your Highness." The door closed softly behind him.

Gar snatched off his circlet and threw it at the door. Part *friends*? Not likely.

But he wasn't going to think about it. Let Asher toss his life away. Let him wade chin deep in fish guts and end his days scared and shrunken and seasoned with salt, like all the old men of Westwailing. He'd had his chance and turned his back on it. More fool him.

His Royal Highness Prince Gar had more important things to worry about. It was Sea Harvest Festival time, and very soon now he would stand before thousands of the king's subjects and lead them in song and celebration.

Asher? Asher who?

Miles and miles and days away the king disobeys his keepers and calls a fall of rain. The power writhes through his weakened body, finding all the sorry places, and he cannot help but cry. Too soon, too soon, his keepers were right, but the choice was not theirs to make. Was never theirs to make, and the fault was his, to let them make it. Is he not King Borne of Lur, the WeatherWorker? Bound and sworn to solemn duty unto the bitter end? He is. His daughter was not ready for the blade. Had bared her throat to its edge before the proper time . . . and now pays dearly for the privilege.

The ceiling of his Weather Chamber is solid glass. Early autumn sunshine spills across the timber floor, his shaking hands, the map of Lur that guides his heart and mind and tells him where to send the rain, sing the seeds, chill the earth with snow and ice.

But pain shouts more loudly than magic. Drowns it in a scarlet flooding tide. He falls to his knees. To his hands. Stares hotly at the map on the floor, sweating. Stares at Westwailing township, down on the coast. Thinks of his son, serving him, serving Lur, and smiles. Power seethes and surges through him, turning his blood to bubbles. His long silver hair, lank with recent ill health, stirs of its own accord on his shoulders. Crackles with blue sparks that arc and dance and ignite the air.

"Gar," he whispers. "Sing for me, my son. Sing the

harvest. Sing the festival. Sing the health and happiness of the people. Sing well, and make me proud."

Beyond the naked chamber ceiling, the blue sky trembles . . . and across the glowing golden sun a cloud, like gauze.

"Gar!" the king cries, fingers clawed and clutching, his head crowned with a nimbus of unspeakable power. "Barl save me . . . save me . . . save him!"

And then darkness, as the sun goes out.

The festival fishing boat danced on the end of its mooring, sprightly as a lass at her first grown-up party. Mouth dry, heart pounding, Gar imagined himself upon it, upon the ocean, which was vast and blue and very, very deep. He couldn't remember Asher ever saying it was deep.

Yesterday, still seething with anger at the ingrate's intentions; he'd scarcely noticed the immensity of water stretching from the coastline to the horizon. Even though it was the first time he'd ever seen it. Rage had blinded him.

Now, though, *now . . .*

He imagined himself at the mercy of all that wild water, which not even a WeatherWorker's might could tame, and felt a tremble in his bowels.

Fear was unbecoming. Ruthlessly he throttled it. Throttled imagination too. Instead glanced at Asher, who stood at his fisted right hand. Who stared at the ocean and the boat, his unknowable eyes alight with avarice, and who thought both were more important than anything he'd ever achieved . . . had yet to achieve . . . in the City of Dorana.

The Mayor of Westwailing cleared his throat. "Your Highness?"

Gar nodded. Turned his face away from the water. "Of course, sir. We are ready?"

They were standing on a dais that had been erected at the township end of the harbor's pier. Darran and Willer stood behind them in the second row, along with the other dignitaries who represented their local communities. An enormous crush of bodies filled every inch of space along the harbor front, the promenade, the streets winding down to the water. Men, women and children, bright and shining in their once-a-year festival shirts and skirts and hats and trews and painfully polished shoes. And their faces, glowing with anticipation. Eerily silent, like one vast, indrawn breath, they waited for the ceremony to begin.

A flag waved. The mayor bowed to Gar. "We be ready, Your Highness."

And so was he. He thought. He hoped. He'd spent enough time studying for this moment. If he wasn't ready now he had no right to call himself a prince, or the Olken Administrator, or anything but a witless fool. He nodded to the mayor.

"Then let us celebrate the harvest, sir. And Barl's blessings on us all."

The mayor smiled. "Barl's blessings, aye indeed, sir."

Raising his arms Gar took a deep breath. Then, throwing back his head, eyes closed, expression ecstatic, pierced the waiting air with a single, singing word:

"*Rejoice!*"

Like a curlew's cry the sound unwound into the faultless blue sky. And then the cloudless ceiling cracked as thousands of voices, united, replied in heartfelt joy and wonder:

"*We rejoice!*"

The Sea Harvest Festival had begun.

In the king's bedchamber, restrained pandemonium. "You said he was making a fine recovery!" *the queen rages at the royal pothecary.* "You said we were out of the woods!"

"We were, Your Majesty!" *Pother Nix replies.* "But that was before he took it into his mad head to go and make it rain!" *Then he grunts as one flailing royal arm collides with his ribs. Turning on a hapless assistant he snarls,* "Hold him still, I told you! This is not the king, this is a patient! Hold him!"

"Gar!" *the king cries, struggling against the loving hands that crush him to the mattress.* "Sing, my boy! I know you can do it!"

Beyond the chamber's curtained windows, a tempest. Hail rattles the glass like rocks thrown by a rampaging giant. Fane, newly risen from her own sick bed, clutches at her temples. "It hurts!" *she sobs.* "The energies are all wrong, they twist like snakes and cut like knives! Make it stop, Durm, make it stop!"

Durm shakes his head. "I cannot. He has the Weather in his hands and he'll do with it as he wills. As the fever wills." *Looming over Nix, he says,* "Break it, man. Break the magic's hold on him or it shall break us, and all to tiny pieces."

Nix quails. "I shall do my best, Sir."

Durm's lips bare his teeth in a snarling smile. Overhead, a crack of lightning sears pain through every head. "Do better," *he advises.* "Or you'll be midwife to the end of the world."

*   *   *

Drowning in music, Gar clutched the dais railing and marveled at the glorious sound. He'd long since stopped singing, just so he could listen more perfectly. So many voices . . . a harmony he'd never dreamed of. There were tears on his cheeks. The fresh salt air couldn't dry them fast enough, his eyes were over-run with emotion. Why had his father never *said*? "Off to the festival," he'd groan with a smile, and ride away and long days later ride back and never once had he *said*.

There were tears on Asher's cheeks too. He was still singing, his hoarse baritone melding roughly with the mayor's rich tenor, the lady mayoress's true soprano and the motley choir of the other officials. In his face, a fierce exultation. This was his moment, his heritage, his future. He was a sudden stranger.

Beneath the blazing sun the crowd's united, uniting voice made magic of the air. "*Rejoice*," the fisherfolk sang, in descant and harmony, each voice a thread in the marvellous tapestry of sound. "*Prepare*," they sang, and "*Praise the bounteous ocean;*" "*Strength to the fishermen*," they sang. "*Plenty to the harvest. Clear skies and calm seas.*" Even the trees bent to listen, or so it seemed. And in the harbor the fish leapt to hear it. Singly at first, a rainbow flash of fin and scale. Then in pairs. In triplets. Flinging themselves boldly towards the sun.

"*Behold they come!*" the fisherfolk proclaimed, as they raised their hands in welcome and thanks. "*The ocean's bounty, our lives, our living!*"

Slowly, slowly, the harbor began to boil.

*   *   *

As the king thrashes insensible upon his pillows the queen anchors her fingers to Pother Nix's arm. "Do something! He cannot continue like this much longer!"

Princess Fane slumps in a corner, her face blotched with tears, her eyes slitted with pain. Durm sits with her, an arm about her shoulders. In his set face rages a promise of death, or worse. Nix turns away from the mage's terrible eyes, shuddering, and rests trembling fingers on Her Majesty's hand. Another second and her nails will draw his blood.

"I dare not give him more heartsease, Majesty!" he protests. "As it is I have exceeded the proper dosage by some half again . . . one drop more and it may be fatal!"

"Whereas these seizures are a very bromide?" Her Majesty retorts. Her face is frightening. "What good will your caution do us if he dies in delirium?"

Nix presses a hand to his sweaty forehead. They are all looking at him: the queen, the Master Magician, the princess, his apprentices, all desperate for an answer, an ending in smiles and laughter. The stout palace windows rattle and shake as the king's storm lashes without mercy. "Majesty," he implores, "we must wait a little longer before we essay more potions! In conscience I cannot allow otherwise."

The queen draws breath to argue, but before the hot words can scald forth an ominous rumbling fills the air, shaking the weathered stones of the palace walls. Princess Fane leaps to her feet, a startled fawn.

"What is that?" she whispers.

Now the furniture itself is dancing, and the hand-woven rugs beneath their uncertain feet ripple as though afflicted with unnatural life. The small table beneath one *window jumps, pinpricked, and beyond the closed chamber door the sound of screams and unbridled fear. Nix flings out an arm for balance, is steadied by an underling, who must needs clutch a twitching curtain to keep them both upright.*

"Barl save us!" the queen says, and takes her child into her arms. "Is the Wall falling down around our ears then?"

Durm staggers to a window and looks outside. "No," he replies, and even he cannot quite mask his fear. "But the ground moves as though it were alive . . . never before have I seen the like."

Drawn like magnets, every gaze swivels to the epicenter of their lives.

Oblivious and sweat-soaked in his bed the king shakes and shakes, and all around him fair Dorana echoes his wild trembling.

In all his life Gar never imagined he would see a sight like it: the harbor seething with fish, thousands of Olken united in song and hope, the air itself alive with the strength and joy of it. He thought his heart might burst from the beauty.

The Harvest Hymn reached its crescendo. Soaring on wings of worship the massed choir of fisherfolk opened its glorious throat and exalted the final note, the final word, in a multitude of harmonies, the men, the women, the children, hands joined, hearts joined, eyes clear and wide and focused on the future . . . *Rejoice* . . . the music poured forth, unstoppable, inexhaustible, to fill the sun-bright space between sea and sky . . .

Nix cowers as the Master Magician raises clenched fists to his face.

"Fool!" he thunders as the windows crack and splinter to the floor and dislodged roof slates smash to smithereens on the heaving ground outside, so far beneath them. "Must I lay hands upon His Majesty and choke him to stillness before the fabric of the world is torn to pieces and the Wall itself comes tumbling down?"

The queen is bruised and bloody from being thrown against the fireplace. "Do something, Nix!"

Wild rain drives into the chamber, guttering the glimfire and ordinary candles. Nix cries out in pain as razor-edged hail lays open one blanched cheek. "Do what?" he snaps, nerveless fingers fumbling through his box of remedies. "This fit is beyond anything I—"

"Master Nix!" an apprentice shouts. "The king!"

Thrashing in his tangle of blankets and sheets, Borne opens his eyes. His mouth stretches wide, split lips peeling back. He looks demented.

"Rejoice!" he bellows, voice cracked and desperate, rising in a wild despairing scream. "Rejoice rejoice rejoice rejoice rejoice—"

Beyond the jagged gaping windows green and purple clouds writhe in mortal combat. Scarlet lightning spears the ground. Hailstones like hens' eggs pulp the streaming gardens and the felled trees' foliage, gouge great holes in the lovingly tended lawns of the palace grounds. Unleashed rivers pour from the sky.

"Rejoice!" the king commands.

His Majesty's bowed body lifts off the wrecked bed. In concert the palace seems almost to lift off its very foundations in one final upthrusting convulsion. The queen, the Master Magician, the princess, Pother Nix and his three witless apprentices are thrown to the heaving floor.

"Gar!" the king screams. "Gar!"

A mighty crack of thunder explodes directly overhead. A flash of white and scarlet light blinds every uncovered eye. The king collapses unstrung to his waiting blankets. The restless earth is stilled.

Stunned almost to gibbering, Nix raises himself on one throbbing elbow to look outside. He sees the clouds streaming south like a river in springmelt flood, leaving innocent blue sky in their wake. Sunshine glitters on rain-washed grass and shattered glass. A warm and gentle breeze stirs the curtains. His ears ring with silence. Smothering a small sob of pain, Nix gathers his scattered wits and climbs to his feet. He is a man of medicine. There are patients . . .

Chalk-white, stone-still, the king sprawls in a welter of limbs. Bright scarlet flecks his lips, his beard, the rumpled, tangling sheets.

"Your Majesty?" Nix whispers. Around him the stir and mutter of the others as awareness returns. "Your Majesty?"

The king does not reply. Beneath his white skin a delicate tracery of blue. His eyes, heavy-lidded and almost closed, stare without comment at one limply folded hand.

Nix begins to tremble. His fingers flutter, helpless as limed birds. The room is swimming before his eyes.

"Your Majesty . . . !"

Loud enough to crack the sky, the gathered multitude of fisherfolk erupted into raucous cheering. Hats sailed exuberantly into the air, and feet stamped the cobbled ground in excited liberation.

Battered with exhilaration Gar caught Darran's eye, remembered his protocols and gestured for the mayor to lead them off the dais and on to the next stage of the festival. Puffed with pride, the three-man crew for the festival boat was waiting for them at the end of the pier. Introductions were made, hands were shaken and greetings exchanged, and then it was time.

Gar took a deep breath and hoped against all hope that he appeared, if anything, slightly bored. Sailing? Oh yes. Nothing to it. He sailed all the time back home in Dorana.

"After you then, Captain Kremmer," he invited. Kremmer, a grizzled veteran of some forty festivals, touched his salt-stained cap, collected his crew with a nod and boarded the perilously fragile-looking fishing boat.

"All aboard who be comin' aboard, Yer Highness," Kremmer called. "They fish'll be leavin' the harbor directly!"

Tradition mandated that the reigning king or queen—or an appointed representative—joined the festival fishing crew in collecting the harvest's bounty from the ocean. Heart pounding, Gar looked at Westwailing's politely attentive mayor and his colleagues, at Darran and Willer but not at Asher, then finally at the plank of wood linking the pitching boat deck to the solid pier.

It was so *narrow*. Couldn't they have found a fatter tree?

Asher said under his breath, "You'll be fine. A jaunt about the harbor, is all, fetching up a few net loads of fish. You'll be back on dry land afore you know it. And I won't let nowt happen to you on board, I promise."

Diverted, he glanced at Asher. "And what makes you think you're coming?"

Asher blinked, and the edged sympathy in his eyes froze. He leaned close. Whispered. "Only a petty man'd make me stay behind."

He whispered back. "You'll pay for that."

As Asher's eyebrows rose, derisive, Captain Kremmer rang his shiny ship's bell. Darran cleared his throat. "Your Highness . . ."

He got on the damned boat. And so did Asher, along with all the fishing village mayors. Darran and Willer stayed behind. Within moments of boarding, the fishermen had their sleeves rolled up and were doing incomprehensible things with ropes and anchors and tarry, stinking fish nets, their salt-scoured faces alight with vigor and purpose and a pure uncomplicated joy.

"Set yourself here," said Asher, pushing him without ceremony to stand by a stout mast, "and don't touch *nowt*."

As if he needed to be told that. What did Asher think, that his prince harbored secret ambitions to dance about the deck of this tiny wooden bath tub singing jolly sea songs? Ha! It was all he could do not to throw his arms tight about the mast and bellow for his mother like a foal at weaning . . .

. . . but after a few minutes that urge mercifully passed and he stopped thinking about the fathoms of water beneath his unsteady feet and the rapidly retreating harbor behind them and the fact he was on a *boat*, on the *ocean*, Barl save him. Began instead to notice the sharp, clean tang of the snapping breeze and the laughter in the fishermen's faces, in Asher's face, as they shouted in their foreign fishermen's tongue and tossed the nets overboard with practiced ease and an enviable springiness of wrist and arm.

One of the crew squeezed past him to haul on a lever. The middle section of the deck unhinged and dropped inwards, revealing the boat's dark belly and releasing a stomach-rolling whiff of old fish. He felt his face contract in horror and slapped an appalled hand over nose and mouth. The man laughed at him, and he found himself laughing back.

"You be right there, prince?" the fisherman asked, still chuckling. "Fine day for sailin', eh?"

"Oh yes, fine, fine," he replied, answering both questions, and laughed again. "I'm having a wonderful time."

"'Course you be," said the fisherman. "Sailin's a wonderful thing. Mind yerself now, 'cause we be bringin' in the catch."

And so they were. Muscles straining, the crew hauled the nets back on board, bulging with flapping fish. It was like a dance the way they moved together in unison, perfectly poised, perfectly balanced on their toes and heels, no need to ask questions or look to see where the next man was or what he was doing. Seamless, bred and born in their bones and perfected over years and seasons.

Stabbed with jealousy, wrenchingly reminded of the solitary life from which Asher's friendship had rescued him, and to which he must now return unwilling, Gar leaned against the mast, heedless of stains, of splinters, of everything except this extraordinary brotherhood of which he could never be a part.

But Asher could. Asher was. This was his life, his true life, the life he'd been born to and wanted back again.

And who in all honesty could blame him? To be sure he had a fine and fancy life back in Dorana City. He had a good job, one with purpose and value. He had friends. But he didn't have *this*. And this was Asher's blood and breath, as any fool with eyes could see.

The first takings of the festival catch streamed into the boat's hold, four net loads in all. Sweat-streaked and panting, hilarity lighting his face in a way Gar had never seen in twelve months and more of dry City living, Asher wiped tarry fingers on his good breeches and called over, "You be right there, sir?"

He couldn't speak, could only nod and offer a smile, because he knew now he had lost the battle, if it was a battle at all, if one man's life and the way he wanted to live it could actually be fought over.

Jinking in a strong gust of wind, the boat swung suddenly about so he had to grab at the mast to stay upright. "Hang tight," called Asher, grinning wide enough to split his face. "You bloody landlubber!"

He opened his mouth to say something insulting in return, something to show that he understood now, that it was all right, really, and no grudges at all . . . but there was another gust of wind and a sudden convulsion of the deck beneath his feet. On the wind, a terrified crying of voices.

"Barl save us! Look!" Captain Kremmer shouted, and pointed a shaking hand back to port.

Staggering, sea legs nonexistent, Gar shuffled around till he could see Westwailing Harbor, so far behind them. "The Wall protect us," he whispered, and felt his heart seize fast in his chest.

The cloudless blue sky over Westwailing was gone,

consumed by a terrible writhing of purple and black. Scarlet lightning flickered like a snake's tongue. The shrieks and moans of panic-stricken fisherfolk swarming desperately to reach shelter carried over the agitated harbor. As Gar and the crew watched, dumbstruck, thunderbolts tore gaping holes in the tumultuous storm clouds and struck the unprotected ground below. A moment later they heard the booming concussion and the agonized screams of people unable to escape.

Aggressive with fear, Asher navigated the lurching deck to grasp Gar's arm. "This ain't a sea-born storm, it's come from inland. What's goin' on?"

Gar pressed a fist to his lips. "I don't know."

"We got to get back there," said Asher, and let go of Gar's arm to turn on Kremmer. "Captain! Get us about! We got to help those folks!"

"Help them?" Kremmer demanded. The boat plunged through a wave and he was thrown to one knee. "How? Reckon we'll not help ourselves now! Reckon we won't make it off these waters alive! *Look*!"

As one, they turned to look back at the township. Gar felt his mouth suck drier than summer. "Father . . ." he whispered. "Father, what are you doing?"

The lurid clouds were streaking towards them, blown by a howling malevolent wind. The harbor waters churned and rolled, great waves whipping up, dashing foam, blotting out the terrible sky. Thunderbolts rained down, hissing and spitting as they struck the turbulent water.

"Do something, Your Highness!" Westwailing's mayor bellowed. "Or we'll all be drowned for certain sure!"

"I can't!" Gar shouted back. Hating himself. Hating the mayor for asking.

A cold hand closed over his wrist. Asher. "You're sure? You can't even try?"

Gar snatched his arm free. Swallowed bile. "You can ask me that?" he hissed, even as rain sharp as glass began to drive through the murky air to strike flesh without mercy. "After a year in the City, you can ask me *that*?"

Asher stepped back. "Sorry," but the word was whipped out of his mouth and shredded on the rising wind, ominously howling, banshee-voiced and battering. The inadequate fishing smack pitched and tossed, helpless in the face of the climbing waves. Gar and Asher and the rest flailed about the boat, catching hold of whatever could save them from falling, as their vulnerable flesh bruised and split and streamed rain-diluted blood.

"I can't save us!" Gar screamed into the teeth of the wind, into their blank and fear-blanched faces. "I'm *sorry*!"

And then there was no more time for talking, as the storm fell upon them in all its immediate fury.

CHAPTER TWENTY-ONE

Splinters flew as hailstones like rocks battered the deck beneath their feet. Ear-splitting thunder claps exploded in time with the scarlet lightning that rent the sky. Green and purple fingers of cloud stretched down to the white-whipped harbor, sucking up whirlpools of water. Fish plucked from safety spun and spun and spun apart. Flaming thunderbolts sizzled the air and pounded the boat. One struck the Mayor of Chevrock's head clean off his smoking shoulders. Gar felt his stomach heave, tasted acid as he vomited into the howling wind. Then the boat stood on end and he was sliding face down along the deck, collecting splinters and fish scales, tearing his fingernails as he clutched in vain at the weathered timber beneath him. He cried out in pain as his soaked and suffering body collided with some hard wooden surface at the far end of the boat, then again in alarm as the shuddering vessel tipped the other way and he careened back the way he'd come, only just avoiding a plunge into the hold. The other men were shouting too, he could hear them, barely, through the savage noise of the storm.

Something wet and warm ran down his face; he touched his fingers to it, expecting rain, and they came away red. He was bleeding.

"Gar!"

Muzzy, confused, he turned towards Asher's anchoring voice. Pain pulsed in time with his hammering heart.

"Stay down!" Asher bellowed as he kicked himself free of a tangling net, blood dripping down his chin. "You'll be safer that way!"

That made him laugh. Safer? There was no safer, not any more. As though to prove the point, a giant wave punched the fishing boat like a fist, rolled it half over so that he had to throw his arms around the nearest solid something and hold on for his life. Somebody tumbled past him, yelping, to plummet head-first into the fish-laden belly of the boat.

With a snapping crack the sail tore loose, sending the boom swinging wildly out of control. The boat plunged again with a twisting shivering shudder. Tossed into the air like so much soggy kindling, Gar found himself somersaulted to his feet, where he swayed and tottered and tried to get his bearings. Somebody screamed "*Look out!*" and he turned, too late. The swinging boom with its madly flapping canvas caught him across the chest with a dull thud. Drove the gasping air from his lungs and swept him contemptuously into the air. Over the side of the canting fishing boat he tumbled, and into the unruly sea.

An icy coldness closed over his head. Stinging salt surged into his mouth, up his nose, burned out his eyes and swamped his ears. Deaf, dumb and blind he tumbled inside out and upside down, insignificant and unremarked within the vastness of the ocean and the might of the storm. For one heartbeat he struggled, and another, and another. There was a roaring in his head that might have been the storm, or might have been all his trapped cries of protest dying for lack of air. I am drowning, he thought, and could feel only a mild regret. I wonder if Fane will cry at my funeral. I wonder if she'll even bother to come. Then he stopped struggling altogether. Stopped thinking, because it was simply too hard. Instead he surrendered to the water and the dark and waited for death to come on slinking seaweed feet.

A sharp and sudden pain wrenched him out of complacency. He grunted, eyes slitting open. What the—somebody had him by the *hair*, there were fingers in his *hair*, tangling, tugging . . .

Struggling anew he plowed his leaden arms through the oppressive ocean, struck something soft and yielding. No. Some*one*. He wasn't alone. There was somebody in the water with him, there was an arm around his chest, legs kicking behind him, he could see flashes above him through the watery prism of the heaving waves. His head broke the surface and he sucked in great gasps of air, coughing, sneezing.

"I got you!" said Asher, rasping in his ear. "Hang on tight now, I got you!"

Teeth chattering, ice-cold to his marrow, Gar dragged his hair off his face and looked up into the whirling storm clouds overhead. Asher was a fool, he never should have bothered, the waves towered above them like Barl's mountains, waiting to fall, eager to smear them into red stains on the surface of the sea—

The purple and green sky lit up then, with an eye-searing flash brighter than the sun. He cried out and tried to hide from the whiteness of it. With the flash came a crack of sound like the end of the world. For a moment he lost consciousness.

Then he thought he must be dreaming, because he could feel gentle sunlight on his salt-sticky skin and his ears were empty of the howling wind.

Bemused, he opened his eyes.

The storm was gone. Overhead, a limpid blue sky, cloudless. All around them gentle water, flat and calm as a pond. No scarlet lightning. No sizzling thunderbolts. Just out of reach the fishing smack floated like a duck, lightly, on top of the tranquil sea. Someone called, shakily, "Asher! Be that you? D'you got the prince?"

The arm around his chest tightened, relaxed. Asher called back, sounding a little shaky himself, "Aye! We be here! Come get us in, eh?"

"Hang tight, lad, we be comin'!"

Limp as a neck-wrung chicken, Gar stared up into the pristine sky. Sharp pain stung him as his eyes filled with tears. "*Father!*" he cried inside his head, his heart. "*Father . . .*"

Soon after that the sky faded and, with it, all awareness.

He wasn't sorry.

Dorana City was in a screaming uproar. Those streets and alleyways not choked with fallen roof tiles, with shattered glass, broken flowerpots and all other manner of debris, seethed and heaved with bodies, Olken and Doranen alike, as they stumbled about in consternation and full-throated dishevelment. Captain Orrick and his City Guards, as shocked as everybody else, struggled to maintain a semblance of order in the face of flooding due to cracked and gushing water pipes, fires and indiscriminate rushing about in a panic.

Dathne, bruised and battered by shelves of falling books, escaped her upheavaled shop and joined her dazed neighbours in the street. Once sure her friends were for the most part unharmed she made her struggling way to the Tower stable yard to find Matt, and see if together they could make sense of this unexpected calamity.

Prophecy hadn't warned her about *this*. If she weren't so shaken up she'd be furious.

There were no guards on duty at the gate into the palace grounds. Hurrying through unhindered she saw where the earth had lifted and buckled through the garden beds and lawns, tearing the turf to shreds and revealing rich brown dirt like scars. Some trees had fallen; their roots scrabbled at the sky.

Ahead, beyond the gap-toothed circle of oaks, the prince's Tower still stood sentinel. It wasn't till she saw it there, untouched, that she realized the depth of her terror, her fear that it might have come down, pulping everything around it beneath gigantic blocks of blue stone.

The Tower stable yard was buzzing with lads, some bruised and bloody, some whole, all intent on nurturing the nervous, wide-eyed horses who whickered and whinnied and kicked their stable doors in protest.

"Where's Matt? Where's Matt?" she asked them, and they pointed their trembling fingers at the path leading to the pastures beyond the yard. Picking up her skirts, she ran.

And found him sprawled in one of the fields nearest to the stables, his face smeared with blood from a cut along his hairline. In his arms he held the limp body of a young man. There was blood on his hands too, she realized. And down the front of his shirt. Before she could ask if he was all right—

"It's Bellybone," he said numbly, staring up at her with huge, hurt eyes. "He was trying to bring in the colts. One of them kicked him—look . . ."

His stained hand parted the blood-soaked hair on the back of the man's head. Bellybone? Ah yes. She remembered. At eighteen, one of Matt's senior stable hands. A charming rogue, forever pestering her to play a hand of Cock Robin with him down at the Goose. She nearly always refused; her money was too hard-earned to go losing it at cards with a young man who'd made an artform of winning. She leaned a little closer. Frowned.

"He's dead, Matt. His skull's been crushed."

He nodded. "I know."

"I'm sorry."

He turned his head. Following his gaze, she saw a group of gangly young horses huddled in one corner of the field. Another was stretched ominously still on the buckled green grass. There was the faint sound of many flies, buzzing.

"That's Thunder Crow," he said. "He broke both front legs. There was nothing I could do for him, I had to . . . had to cut his throat . . ."

Which explained the blood. Crouching, her eyes hot, she touched her fingertips to his shoulder. "Matt, we have to talk."

Shuddering, he dragged his eyes away from the dead horse. "What happened, Dathne? Is it the end then? Has the Wall begun to crumble? Is the king dead?"

"I don't know. They're not saying anything down in the City. There's been no announcement. It's madness there right now. But I think he must be. The Wall still stands for now, but I think this is the beginning of the end."

"Asher?"

Her fists clenched, echoing her frustration. "I don't know that either. I don't know how far the storm extended or what other districts were struck. The coast is so far away, you'd think he'd be safe . . . but I just don't know. I tried to scry him but the energies are all over the place. I couldn't find a path to him. I couldn't reach Veira either. Perhaps later tonight, when everything's calmed down."

He nodded again, slowly. Looked down at dead Bellybone, then back up at her. "You didn't see this coming, Dathne. Did you?"

She lowered her face to her knees, perilously close to breaking. "No, Matt," she said, her voice muffled in her skirts. "No, I surely didn't."

"What do you think it means?"

"I don't know." She lifted her aching head. "But I expect we'll find out soon enough. Maybe Veira can tell us, once I can reach her."

"Yes," he said. "Maybe she can." Then he frowned. "And what about you? Are you all right?"

She waved a hand. "I'm fine. Which is more than I can say for my poor shop. It's a mess, all the books off the shelves. Windows broken. Half the floorboards have sprung loose. Unless I can find a Doranen willing to lend me a magical hand it'll take days and days to—"

"But you're all right," said Matt, with his dead stable

hand cradled against his chest. "No bones broken. No need for a healer."

He was in shock, she realized. Ridiculously, it was the last thing she'd expected. Matt was her rock, her foundation, the shoulder she leaned on, the hand that she held in moments of quiet desperation. She *needed* him.

And he needed her, at least for the moment.

Kneeling, disregarding his uncoordinated resistance, she gently prised Bellybone from his grasp. Hoisted the limp form over her shoulder and got to her feet. He hadn't been a big man, most stable hands weren't, but still he was heavy enough to make her back and shoulders ache. But that was all right. She could manage.

"Come on, Matt," she said gently, looking down at him. "We need to lay poor Bellybone somewhere cool and quiet and you need to get back to your horses. The other lads will be looking for you. It's Meister Matt they're needing now, more than they've ever needed him before."

Wincing, Matt stood. Without a word took Bellybone from her, turned, and started walking back to the stable yard. After a moment she fell into step behind him. She could just make out the dead youth's eyes, half closed, as his head rested in the hollow between Matt's neck and shoulder.

Damn you, Asher, she thought as a shiver ran through her from head to toe. Damn you, damn you, damn you. You'd better be all right . . .

Hands trembling, Darran added mustard powder to the bowl of freshly boiled water in front of him. The steam spiraling into his face turned abruptly acrid, stinging runny mucus from his nose and tears from his eyes. Well, at least he'd have an excuse now. *Old fool*, he scolded himself, and stirred the browny yellow water with a wooden spoon anxiously provided by the mayor's cook. *He's not dead. You've not failed Their Majesties this time. He's not dead. Think on that, not on what might have been.* He added more mustard to the mix and sloshed it vigorously, blinking and sniffing.

In the deep armchair behind him Gar shifted inside his enveloping blanket. Was that a cough? Had the prince caught a chill, or worse, from his fearful immersion in the ocean? *You should have stopped him, Darran. Who cares what tradition dictates? You should have put your foot down. You knew it was foolhardy for him to risk himself on all that open water with only that Asher for protection. You know what he's like. Any dangerous thing, he'll do, and has done, ever since they told him he was—ever since he realized he would always be . . . different.*

Oh, how he remembered that day. Seared into memory, it was, and even into nightmares sometimes. Five, the prince had been, tall for his age and splendid, just like the early paintings of his mother that hung in the palace's Hall of Memories. Silver-gilt hair and eyes that mirrored every blossoming hope, every dead dream. "No," he'd screamed. "I'm not a cripple, I'm not I'm not I'm not!" Then he'd run away from his parents, from the Master Magician, from his unbearable life, to the stables. "Let him go," the king had said, his deep voice ripe with sorrow and regret. "The sooner he learns he'll not outrun this, the better." And had punished the prince only for galloping his pony into the ground.

He'd been a junior secretary then, and privy to the

calamity only by accident and a handful of urgent letters. For himself he'd have cut the pony's blue-black throat and drunk the steaming blood for breakfast, if it could have changed the terrible truth. If it could have given the prince his magic.

From the armchair, another ominous throat-clearing sound. Barl knew the prince was hardy enough, not in the least prone to distempers and ill humors and the like. But this was different. This was a near drowning and something more terrible besides . . . a bad chest, or even worse, was a distinct possibility.

His innards clutched again, fear yammering at him, twisting him. Old fool! He needs you! Control yourself! He took a deep breath and then began to cough himself, from the mustard fumes. The prince's footbath was thickening nicely. Perhaps a drop more water . . .

When it was just so, and perfect, he blotted his face and hands dry with a towel, picked up the bowl and turned a bright and resolutely calm smile on his employer. "Here we are, sir. A nice hot mustard bath to ward off any chills."

The prince's face still lacked color, the bruises and scrapes he'd suffered standing out like spilt ink on snow. The minute they'd brought him up from the harbor, battered and bloody and stiffening with salt, he'd been put in a hot bath and ruthlessly scrubbed clean. Darran cast yet another prayer of thanks Barlwards, that the prince had been largely insensible throughout the entire unpleasant ordeal.

Inside his nest of blankets Gar lifted heavy-lidded, glowering eyes. "Where's Asher?"

Years of training kept his expression unchanged. "He's

fine. Now if you'll just put your feet in the bowl, sir, you'll feel much better."

"I don't want a damned mustard footbath, Darran!" the prince snarled. "Unless you want to drink it, take it away!" On his marked face a look all too reminiscent of the Master Magician's, when that terrible man was not pleased with the chaff that served him.

Darran put the bowl back on the table. He's upset, he's just upset, of course he's upset. His hands were shaking again. He doesn't mean it, you know he doesn't, he never does. He hasn't thought, he doesn't understand . . .

"I failed them, Darran."

He turned. "Failed who, sir?"

The prince was staring out of the chamber window. His expression was desolate. Disconsolate. "Asher's people. On the boat. In the town. As the storm hit us the mayor begged me to do something. To save them. I couldn't. I failed. Useless, useless *cripple* . . ."

"I'm sure you're no such thing, sir!" Darran's heart-beat stuttered in panic. "I'm sure not even Master Durm himself could have stopped that dreadful storm."

But the prince wasn't listening. "And I lost the heir-loom circlet. It's somewhere at the bottom of Westwailing Harbor."

"Never mind, sir. I'm quite sure that given a choice Their Ma—" He stopped. Breathed deeply for a moment. "The queen would much rather have you back safe and sound than a circlet."

"The king presented it to me on my twelfth birthday." There was grief in the prince's face now, and in his voice, raw as an open wound. "I swore to him I'd look after it. I swore—"

"It doesn't matter, Your Highness," said Darran, trying to soothe. It was hard; he felt jagged with his own distress. "Not compared to—"

"Of course it bloody matters, you stupid old man!" Gar shouted. "That circlet was a treasure, a priceless part of Lur's history. It was a gift from my *father*! How can you stand there and say it doesn't—"

"Because you matter more!" Darran shouted back. "Don't you understand that, you foolish, foolish boy?"

Shocked silence. Horrified, Darran turned away, fists pressed against his chest. Behind him the prince shifted in his blankets. "Darran . . ."

He'd promised himself he wouldn't speak. Had reminded himself over and over that his was the privileged place of servant to the royal family. The creed, unbreakable, was see all and say nothing. He was a man in the autumn of his life, this prince young enough to be a grandson. The onus was on him to behave as was proper, to indulge the hot blood of youth, to wave an indolent hand at intemperate outbursts. To understand and forgive, no matter what the provocation. That was maturity. That was the code.

Without permission his body turned and his mouth opened. His voice emerged, sounding thin, frightened, not his voice at all.

"I remember the day you were born. Your gracious mother placed you in my arms with her own fair hands. You were so tiny. You smiled at me. I know you don't remember, but you did." Memory curved his lips into the answering smile he'd blazed at the little thing.

The prince stared, startled and discomfited. Uncertain,

and in need of a wiser man's guidance though he couldn't see it. "Darran . . ."

It was the vulnerability that shattered the last of his resolve. "I thought you were drowned!" he cried. "I thought I would have to take your broken body back to your mother! Or worse, tell her—tell her you were lost beneath the waves, not even your body to—"

The hot tears behind his eyes burst forth, unstoppable. Flooded with shame he turned away again, hands pressed to his face. Disgraceful, this was *disgraceful* . . . but oh, how dreadful it had been with the storm upon them and the screaming and the howling and the clouds and rain and lightning and thunderbolts, the hail, the blood, the shrieking children, the waves as tall as trees and taller, pounding them to the ground, pounding them to pieces on the cobblestones, and the prince alone out there on the unprotected ocean! Moaning, he pressed his thin fingers to his lips and willed away the raw and recent horror.

"Darran, you musn't," the prince said, his voice strained. "I'm not drowned. I'm not even hurt, not to mention. Just a few bumps and bruises. I know you had a nasty shock, we all did, but we can't go to pieces now. There's too much to do."

He could only nod, couldn't trust his treacherous voice.

The prince said, shifting inside his blanket, "You know what that storm means, Darran. You know what must have happened."

No, no, no. It wasn't true. *Couldn't* be true. Fresh tears brimming he turned, looked at the king's son, whose own eyes were brilliant with unshed grief. "We don't know anything for certain," he whispered.

"*I* know," the prince said starkly. "Barl save me, Darran. I *know*. Such a cataclysm can only be the result of . . . it has happened before, twice—I fear only one conclusion can be drawn! His Majesty is . . . His Majesty has . . ." His expression fractured then, exposing a wasteland of loss. A hand came up to cover his face, fingers white and pressing.

On a choked sob Darran went to him, heedless of protocol, of propriety, of every rule he'd ever followed, every boundary he'd never crossed. He put his arms around the prince's shoulders and held him. "There, there," he said, helpless, washed in his own tears. "There, there."

At length the prince withdrew, pain banished, a new and harder resolve in his eyes. "How bad is it in the township, Darran? The truth."

Oh, how he'd dreaded that question. Prevaricating, he stood and moved away. Smoothed his rumpled vest, his limp collar and sagging sleeves. Took deep, mustard-scented breaths until his heart was racing only a little.

"Bad enough," he replied, and on another breath turned and faced his prince again. "Perhaps half a hundred dead. There seems to be some difficulty in agreeing on a final tally. Some drowned, some struck with debris. Some . . . trampled underfoot in the panic to escape the foreshore." Despite himself he shuddered, seeing again an old woman crushed to a pulp in the first mad stampede. "Injuries, of course. Aid stations have been established in several locations. Doranen healers have been sent for, but Barl alone knows how long they'll take to reach us, even if any are to be found. This is an Olken part of the world, sir. They have their herbalists and their pothecaries, fine people, doing all they can. Of course it's not the same as having a proper Doranen physicker, but they seem to be managing tolerably well."

"What of damage to property?"

"As you can imagine, sir, it is extensive. Trees down, roof tiles blown off, windows shattered. Boats sunk to the bottom of the harbor."

"The Crown will see them right," the prince said, and pulled his blanket closer. "Whoever has lost what is dear in this calamity, he or she shall be recompensed."

Aching, Darran passed a shaking hand across his eyes. *My boy, my boy, and who will recompense you?* His heart broke anew at the thought. "Of course, sir," he said. "I have set Willer to starting the tally in anticipation of such a commitment."

Incredibly, a faint smile. "Your efficiency does you credit, Darran." Then the smile faded. "I must return to the City. Tomorrow, at first light. The rest of today I will inspect as much of the damage as I can. Pay my respects to the bereaved. I'll need you to work with Asher to ensure my speedy leave-taking come the dawn."

"Leave *tomorrow*?" Aghast, he stared at the prince. "But that's impossible! Recall that you nearly drowned, Your Highness! You mustn't exert yourself before a proper medical inspection, by a proper Doranen pothecary! You need rest, sir, and embrocations for your bruises!"

The prince waved an impatient hand. "Don't be ridiculous. The pothers are for those with real injuries. You're making far too much of a few cuts and scrapes. I've had worse falling off my horse out hunting and you know it."

Grimly determined Darran straightened his spine hard and said, lips pinched with disapproval, "I cannot support such behavior, sir."

The prince lurched to his feet, blanket clutched haphazardly about his chest, eyes blazing. "I haven't asked you to support it! I'm telling you what I intend to do! My mother needs me and I will go to her, is that clear?"

Somehow he stood his ground in the face of royal anger. "You are needed *here*, sir."

"I know," the prince replied. "But the queen takes precedence. You will act in my stead, with my voice, my hand. Do whatever needs to be done. I'll support any decision that you make, without reservation. But I am returning to Dorana at dawn."

He was beaten and he knew it, so he bowed, punctiliously. "As you wish, Your Highness."

"No," said the prince, and his face was bleak as winter. "As I must. Now. Where's Asher? I need to talk to him."

"I don't know where he is, sir," he said, scrupulously neutral. "He left the premises against my express request. Something about making sure his family was all right."

The prince paused in midscowl. Let out a deep sigh. "Of course. I should have thought. *Are* they all right?"

Darran lifted an eyebrow. "I'm sure I don't know, sir. All I do know is he had no business leaving without your permission. He has duties, obligations—"

"Oh, for Barl's sake!" the prince snapped. "He has *family*, Darran. For all we know one or all of them could be among the injured. Or the dead. Of course he went to see if they're all right!"

Well, naturally the prince would say that. His judgement was woefully suspect when it came to that ruffian. The prince was a good lad with a kind and lonely heart, ripe pickings for the unscrupulous, the callous and the calculating. "Yes, sir."

The prince sighed and thumped back into his armchair. When he looked up again his expression was wry and cross and irritatedly patient. "You know he saved my life, Darran."

Saved his life. That was how Asher would tell the tale, for certain. Like as not it had been an accident; like as not he'd been flung into the ocean himself and just happened to latch onto His Highness in all the confusion. Circumstance. Serendipity. To suggest that an uncouth savage like Asher could be *heroic*?

With a bow and smile he humored his prince. "Yes, sir."

The prince flicked him a sharp look. "Darran, he did. I was drowning and he saved me."

Prickled by sudden doubt, by the new shadow in the prince's eyes, Darran stared at him. "Drowning?"

"A few more seconds and I would've been dead. Don't let your dislike blind you, Darran. You're a better man than that. I owe Asher my life."

"Yes, sir," he said faintly.

With a dismissive wave of his hand the prince slumped inside his blankets. "Now leave me. Find one of our pigeons and get a message to the queen. Let her know I'm all right and that I'm coming home. And when Asher returns send him to me immediately."

Another bow. He could try arguing some more, but what would be the point? "Certainly, sir. Can I send up something from the kitchens, sir?"

The prince shrugged. "No. Yes. I don't know. Do what you like. Some soup, maybe."

"Yes, sir."

"And Darran?"

Fingers on the door handle, he turned. "Yes, sir?"

The prince was scowling again. "You might as well give me the damned mustard bath. Seeing as it's just sitting there, getting cold."

"Yes, sir," he said, killing the fatuous smile that threatened to spread over his face. "As Your Highness commands. As always."

"Watch out!"

Asher looked up, saw the slithering roof tiles and leapt aside just in time. With a crash and a splintering spray of clay shards the red squares hit the cobblestones beside him. Peering downwards, a pale face mottled with bruises, eyes wide with alarm.

"Be you unhurt?" the man shouted.

"Aye," he called back, but didn't stop, kept on hurrying. If he stopped for every man, woman and child that needed help in these demolished streets he'd not reach the Dancing Dolphin till the middle of next week. That's where he'd find his family. Year in, year out, without alteration, at festival time they stayed at the Dancing Dolphin.

It wasn't a fashionable inn, which was why Da liked it so much. Good food, better ale, soft beds and no gapesters forever goin' on about how they saw the king and what a mighty upstandin' man he be and weren't they lucky to have such a king to help sing in the harvest. *Lucky*. When everybody knew their festival weren't nowt to do with any Doranen. An Olken matter, it was, and the king bein' invited no more than a courtesy when you got right down to it.

Skirting more debris he turned his face away from a woman standing in a doorway with a mute wrapped bundle in her arms and tears pouring down her blanched and sunken cheeks. Ducked up Lickspittle Lane and into

Baitman Alley, which ran along the back of the houses and shops facing onto Seaswell High Street and came out almost opposite the Dolphin at its far end. The damage wasn't so bad along here. The storm seemed to have cut a straight path down through the township and over the water, as though it were alive, as though it knew exactly where it wanted to go and didn't care what it went through to get there.

He didn't want to think about what that might mean. Couldn't be distracted by Gar's problems right now. Right now he had his own.

Heart hammering, uncaring of his cuts and bruises and the pains they caused, he jogged along the alley until he reached its end. Then he stopped, one hand clutching the corner of the building beside him, and stared.

The Dolphin's sign was half torn from its moorings, dangling tipsily groundwards. Two windows on the top floor were broken. Somebody, probably Hiram the innkeeper, had already boarded over the holes.

There were a few tiles missing here and there. By the side door, the old pittypine tree he'd played in as a spratling was half blown over, gnarly roots clotted with dirt and tangled like an old man's fingers. Apart from that, the inn seemed to still be in one piece. Absurdly, his heart lifted. Brothers aside he had good memories of the Dolphin.

Dodging carts and timber-laden packhorses he crossed Harbormaster Street, made his way through the gate and along the path that led to the Dancing Dolphin's front door and banged both fists on it, hard. His heart was beating so violently he thought he could feel his eyes jumping in their sockets.

"Asher!" Hiram exclaimed, his vast belly swathed in a

dark green apron and his wiry hair a little grayer than the last time they'd met. Standing back, the innkeeper swung the door wide open. "Sink me with a rusty anchor! Hepple said he'd seen you ridin' alongside that namby-pamby prince they sent down from the City, and a course I arsked your fambly and they said they knew nowt on it, said you'd took yourself off a year ago and nobody knew where you were, so I reckoned Hepple'd made a head start on the ale this year, but now here you be and by the looks of your fancy togs you ain't a fisherman no more so Hepple were right then, were he?"

"Hiram," said Asher, trying to see round the innkeeper's bulk, "be my family here? Be they all right? Da—"

Hiram shook his head and stood back from the doorway. "Sorry, lad, sorry, here's me gabbin' like a barmaid and you all worrited about your fambly, and speakin' of fambly let me be the first to tell you how bad me and ole Mistress Hiram did feel when we got the news about—"

"Hiram. Stow that gabble afore I slice out your tongue and roast it for dinner."

Silenced midsentence, Hiram turned his head to look at the speaker.

Asher didn't need to look. He knew that voice. Had known it all his life, and the fists that went with it. With a nod and a grim smile at Hiram, he stepped over the Dolphin's threshold and prepared to meet his brothers.

CHAPTER TWENTY-TWO

Warily, Hiram shifted sideways to reveal the inn's modest staircase and a pack of men, descending. Their boots on the uncarpeted treads were loud in the sudden hush. In the lead, of course, as always, lean and mean and warm as midwinter . . .

"Zeth!" Hiram said. "Look who be here!"

Standing still now, scarred fingers taut on the banister, Zeth nodded. "I got eyes, Hiram. I can see."

Hiram cleared his throat. "Aye. Well. I'll just be gettin' on then, eh? You boys have fambly business to take care of, I reckon. Don't need no outsider puttin' in his three cuicks worth, eh? Good to see you again, Asher. Mind you say goodbye, now!"

"Aye," said Asher, his eyes not leaving Zeth's cold face. "That I will, Hiram."

With a last nervous smile, Hiram retreated. Asher closed the inn's front door behind him then stared at his brothers. Coming down the stairs one after the other, oldest to youngest, the way they went everywhere. Zeth. Abel. Josha. Wishus. Niko. Bede. All grimly staring and not a bump or bruise between them. Despite everything, he was relieved. He took a step forward. Shoved his hands in his pockets and shook his head. "That wasn't very polite, Zeth. It's Hiram's inn, you know."

Zeth bared his teeth in a smile. "Come home to lesson us in manners, boy?"

Asher swallowed a stupid reply. At Zeth's back, his other brothers muttered. "There's no need for trouble, Zeth. I just want to see Da."

Zeth's sharp smile widened. He started down the stairs again, the pack of brothers at his heels. He looked . . . older. There was gray in his hair and a new scar on his face, a pink and puckered line slicing through his left eyebrow and down his cheek, making his eyelid droop.

"That be a fancy tongue you got in your head, boy. And fancy clothes on your back too. Where'd you come by them, eh?"

Asher stood his ground. It was an old game this, one they'd played him at all his life. Standover bully-boy tactics. Raised fists and whispered threats. Well, he wasn't in the mood for games and he wasn't afraid of them any more. Realizing that, he nearly laughed out loud. He wasn't afraid of them any more. After a year of Lord Conroyd Jarralt and Master Magician Durm, who was Zeth? Who were any of 'em?

"Don't piss me about, Zeth. Where's Da? I want to see him."

"Curly Thatcher said he saw you ridin' into town alongside the prince," said Zeth, conversational, at the foot of the staircase now and leaning a negligent shoulder against the newel post. Silent and staring, the others spread out behind him. "Sailor Vem said you were troughin' slops with 'im. That where you been this past long while? Hobnobbin' with blondie?"

Asher let the air hiss softly from his lungs. "I don't answer to you, Zeth. Not any more. Now for the last bloody time, I want to see Da. Where is he? Upstairs? Then let me past. You got no right to keep me from him."

Zeth turned his head, swept their brothers with a measuring gaze. Then he looked again at Asher. "No. No, he ain't upstairs."

An icy splinter of fear pierced him. There was something in their faces. A memory in their eyes. "Then where is he, Zeth? I want to know. Now."

Zeth sighed. Inspected his chipped fingernails. Lifted his unfriendly face and said, with all the brutality in him, "Why, he's right where you put 'im, Asher dear. Deep in the cold dark ground."

Boom, boom, boom went Asher's heart. "What d'you mean, in the ground?"

"What d'you reckon I bloody mean!" said Zeth, suddenly savage. "Da's *dead*, boy. Eight months gone. Mast cracked and fell on 'im. Split 'im in half like a rotten apple."

"No," he said. But not because he disbelieved his brother. Not because it wasn't true. The truth of it was raw and bloody in the air between them, in Zeth's voice, his face. In all his brothers' faces. "*No.*"

Zeth heaved another sigh. "'Fraid so. But don't you go feelin' too bad about it. He died screamin' your name." He shrugged. "'Course, his heart were already broke long afore the mast felled 'im. You could say he were a walkin' dead man, really. Ain't that right, boys?"

Shoulder to shoulder his brothers nodded and muttered, thunder on the horizon.

"Over and over the same old questions," said Zeth. "What's happened to my Asher? Where's he gone? Why did he leave me? I'll tell you, boy, it grew a mite wearisome after a while, and that's for sure. Afore long Da weren't altogether right in the head no more. My word, it was the saddest sight I ever saw. That proud ole man, weepin' night after night into his ale pot and sobbin' your name."

"No," whispered Asher. "That's wrong. I left a message. I asked—"

"Message?" said Zeth. "Don't know nowt about any message, boy. Now just you keep your mouth shut, why don't you, and let me finish? As I were sayin'. Day after day, for weeks on end, Da fretted on you. Drove us all mad. Then one night a storm blew in from beyond the reef. Howlin' and wailin' and peltin' us with ice. Da swore he could hear your voice on the wind, callin'. He got to the boats afore we could stop him. Sailed out to find you. Wishus and me, we went after him, but there weren't nowt we could do with him in one boat and us in another. He were sore distracted lookin' for you, Asher, and distraction on a boat be an unchancy thing when there's bad weather about. Prob'ly you might remember that." Zeth's cruel gaze raked him up and down. "Then again, dressed so fancy like a Doranen, might be you don't."

Asher swallowed. There was a roaring in his head, as though the killing storm had returned. "I don't understand. The night I left I gave Jed a message for him. Jed swore blind he'd deliver it so's Da wouldn't worry."

"The night you left, boy, Jed fell down drunk and

cracked his head like a hard-boiled egg." Zeth's eyes were wide with mock sorrow. "There be nowt for Jed these days but sittin' on street corners, droolin'."

No. No, not Jed. Childhood friend. Partner in many a crime. Freckle-faced and easygoing and always game for a lark . . . "You're lying. You'd say anything you could to hurt me, Zeth."

The mock sorrow gone now, Zeth straightened out of his comfortable slouch and took a step closer. His eyes were empty of everything but hate. "I got better ways to hurt you than words, little brother. You should've told us yourself what you had planned."

Asher held his ground, just. "You would've stopped me. Or tried anyways."

"'Course we would've!" Zeth snarled. "You got no business leavin' the family. You owe your life to the family, your breath and your body belong to us. *We* say what's to be done with 'em. *We* say where you go and what you do. Them's the rules."

"Your rules," said Asher. His voice sounded strange, as though it belonged to somebody else. "Not mine. Not any more."

"Da's dead 'cause of you, boy," said Zeth. "You might as well have stuck a guttin' knife in his heart. You should've. Would've been cleaner. Kinder. Quicker. But no. You had to kill him *slow*."

The air in his lungs had turned to ice. He couldn't breathe. "I ain't killed nobody. I'm goin'." Turning his back on them, he reached for the inn's front door.

Zeth growled. "Boys . . ."

Like wolves in the Black Woods they were on him. Clenched fists pummeled him. Vicious kicks felled him.

Fingers snarled in his hair, his clothes, dragged him across the floor and tore the fine vest and shirt off his back. Face down they hauled him up the hard wooden staircase and pinned him to it like a bullock to the slaughter block. There were too many of them and they were too strong, he couldn't escape; nothing had changed, he might as well be a child again and helpless before them as their grieving father drank away all memory of his dead wife, deaf to his youngest son's cries for help as his brothers paid him back for eight years of their mother's love and their father's careless indulgence.

The sound of Zeth's copper-studded belt sliding free of his trousers closed Asher's teeth on his battered lip. Drew blood. Amid his other brothers' eager encouragement, the first blow fell.

When at last their fury was sated and there was nothing left in the world but torn flesh and pain, they dragged him outside and threw him and his stripped-off clothing into the gutter. It was dusk and Harbormaster Street was empty.

"From this day on," said Zeth, standing over him, panting down on him, "you be no kin of ours and Restharven ain't your home. Don't look for shelter anywhere else neither, for we'll be bannin' your name up coast and down. Your fishing dreams are over, little man. Go back to the City and your new blond friends. You be not wanted here."

Asher stared up at his hateful, hating brother. Hot words crowded his throat, clamored for release. *You can't* and *By what right?* and *He were my father too!*

All he could do was moan.

One by one his brothers spat on him to seal the sentence. Then they went back into the Dolphin and slammed the front door behind them.

Floating on a scarlet sea, Asher barely felt the spittle as it trickled through his hair, down his cheeks, between his parted lips.

Da, he cried, though no more sound escaped him. *Da* . . .

Ages later he sat up beneath a starry sky, inch by painful inch, and pulled on his torn shirt. The weskit was beyond saving so he left it in the gutter. Then, wincing at every step, he dragged himself to the nearest ale house. Sat in a dark corner, ignored by the other patrons who'd gathered to share wild stories and lucky escapes, and spent all his money on glorious cider and beer. Once his purse no longer jingled, the barman pushed him into the street and locked the door behind him.

It was late. So late it was early. He laughed aloud at his own clever wit; the harsh sound bounced off the nearest stone wall, echoing. The streets were deserted. All the windows he could see were dark and cold, no friendly lamplight, no warm waiting welcome. Ah, well. Best he got back to the mayor's house. There was a bed there for him at least. For now. And now was all that mattered. He couldn't think past now. Couldn't think at all.

Weaving his way along the uneven pavement he stopped twice to empty his belly onto the cobblestones. Bending over made his head pound like a galloping herd of horses. After the second heaving he had to sit down for a while. Standing up again was . . . interestingly difficult. There was pain in him somewhere but all that lovely cider and beer kept it far, far away. He'd need to drink some more soon, to sternly discourage its approach.

After a wrong turn or three he found the servants' entrance to the mayor's house. The door was locked. Of course. He didn't have the strength to knock, so he kicked instead. Bang, bang, bang. Eventually the door creaked open. Maggoty Darran stood there, nostrils all pinched in, eyes slitted and beady. What a welcome. Maybe he could be sick again, all over the ole crow's shoes. Would that make him go away?

"Where in Barl's name have you been?" Darran hissed. "It's the middle of the night! His Highness has been worried sick!"

"Suck on a blowfish and die," he said, and pushed his way into the house. Tripped over something. A chair. Fell down. Oooh. That hurt. Def'nitely he needed another drink.

After a couple of false starts he found his feet again. Bed. He wanted his bed. There was a staircase in front of him. He didn't like staircases. With a grunt, he started upwards. Behind him came Darran, wittering.

"How *dare* you come back here in this condition! After everything His Highness has been through, how dare you insult him in this fashion!"

At the top of the stairs, turn left. No, right. No, left. Along the corridor, what a nice wall, holding him up. If he fell down now he'd never stand again. He needed a bloody *drink* . . .

"– *disgusting*, that's what you are—"

If he hit Darran, would that shut him up? He'd get into trouble but what did that matter? What did anything matter any more? He swung around, fist clenched. "Shut your trap, you manky ole maggoty man!" he growled. "Shut it afore I shut it for you!"

"How *dare* you!" Darran gasped. "You should be flogged for this!"

He grinned. "Too late."

Darran wasn't listening. "You should—" He swallowed the rest of the sentence. Collected himself, and bowed. "Your Highness."

Asher shuffled round a bit and looked blearily behind him. Gar, tying the belt of his quilted blue dressing-gown as he walked towards them, scrapes and bruises stark on his face, expression grim.

"Hey!" he said, and waved. "Blondie!"

"He's drunk, sir," said Darran.

Gar raised his eyebrows. "No. Really?" Then he sighed. Dragged a hand over his face. "Go to bed, Darran. I'll deal with this." Darran hesitated. Mouth all pruned up. "Go, I said!" Gar snapped, and Darran withdrew.

"Nighty-night!" Asher called after the ole scarecrow.

Gar grabbed him by the shirt front. Shook him. It was a wonder his head didn't fall clean off his shoulders. "Shut up," said Gar. "And come with me."

Stumbling, protesting, he fumbled along the corridor at Gar's heels until they reached the prince's room. Gar opened the door, pushed him inside and closed the door behind them. "You stink of vomit and beer," he said. Curt. Clipped. Eyes and face as hard as a brother's.

Asher shrugged, adrift between the chamber door and the window. "Aye. Well. S'what happens when you spend the night drinkin' ale and pukin'."

"I'm not interested. Get yourself cleaned up and sober. We leave for the City at first light."

"What d'you mean, 'we'? I don't work for you no more, remember?"

"You work for me until I say otherwise."

Asher blinked at him, swaying gently. "Why go back to the City? We only just got here."

There was a muscle leaping along the side of Gar's clenched jaw. "The king is dead."

Asher winced. He really needed another drink. The pain was getting closer and his mouth tasted vile. "How d'you know he's dead? Did Zeth tell you?"

Gar said, "I don't know any Zeth. Now be quiet and listen. We—"

"Cause if Zeth didn't tell you, then—"

Gar shoved him, hard. "I said *be quiet*! What's the matter with you? Didn't you hear me? My father is *dead*!"

That was funny. That was so funny, he had to laugh. "He is? Well, what d'you know? So's mine! You an' me finally got somethin' in common, eh? Aside from the no magic business, I mean. Fancy that."

Gar hit him.

Well. Now he *really* needed another drink. He touched his fingertips to the corner of his mouth. Found blood. Stared at it. Wiped it off on the front of his shirt and headed unsteadily for the door.

"You're not leaving," said Gar.

"Watch me."

As he reached for the door handle Gar pushed him aside, hands flat to his shoulderblades. Pain flared, roared, drove the air from his lungs in an anguished grunt of protest. He fell against the wall, clutching at it to stop himself from falling. Eyes screwed tight shut he pressed his bruised cheek to the pretty wallpaper and waited for the flames to die down.

"What is this?"

Reluctantly he opened his eyes again. Looked at Gar. The prince was staring at his hands. There was blood on them.

"Nowt." He was tired all of a sudden, so terribly tired. "Nothing."

Gar looked at him. "Show me your back."

"No."

"Show me your back or I'll call Darran in here to help me make you!"

And he would, too. Bastard. Wincing, Asher peeled off his once fancy fine silk shirt. Dropped it to the mayor's expensive carpet. Closed his eyes and leaned against the wall for support.

Gar sucked in a quick, sharp breath. "Who did this?"

"Nobody."

"*Asher*." Gar's voice demanded instant obedience. Ha. "An assault on you is an assault on me. I want his name."

He never should have come back. Not to this house. Not to Westwailing. "Leave it be."

"His name, Asher."

Somehow he opened his eyes. "I fell down."

Gar stared, incredulous. "I don't think so."

"I fell down."

"That's a lie!"

"*I fell down*!"

Infuriated, Gar shoved him a second time. He toppled like a stack of bricks, like the roof tiles on the storm-shattered houses of Westwailing. Landed hard, half on his back, and it hurt so much he started laughing because it was that or cry, and he didn't want to cry.

Gar stood over him, fists clenched. "*This isn't funny*!"

"I know," he said, and hid his face against the floor, and kept on laughing.

The sound of bare heels stamping across the carpet. The door, wrenching open. "Darran? What are you doing out here? I told you to go to bed!"

"I know, sir, I'm sorry, sir. Sir, is everything all right?"

"No. I need a pothecary. Find one, wake him up and bring him to me. Now."

"Yes, sir."

The door, closing again. Thump thump of heels. A slithery swish and a bump as Gar slid down the wall to sit on the floor beside him. A quiet voice. "Your father's dead?"

He stopped laughing. "Aye."

"In the storm?"

"An accident. Eight months ago."

"I'm sorry. How did you—"

"My brothers told me."

"Your *brothers* did this?"

"They blame me."

And they weren't the only ones. *He died screamin' your name*. From somewhere beyond the chamber door, the muffled buzz of voices. Gar said, very quietly, "Your brothers did this . . ."

The carpet smelled of dust and salt. "This is nowt, I'm shunned, Gar. Zeth and the rest of 'em, they've banned me. No fishing boats for Asher. Not in Restharven. Not anywhere in Lur." And what was the pain in his flesh compared to that?

A sharp intake of breath. Tense silence. Then: "For how long?"

"Forever."

More slithery sounds as Gar shifted against the wall. "Can they do that?"

Not only could, but had. It was done, and by common fisherfolk law not to be undone. "Aye."

"No. It's not right. Fishing's a dangerous life, how many times have you told me that? Whatever misfortune befell your father, Asher, it wasn't your fault. Don't worry. I'll fix this."

In the cavernous coldness within, a small warm flame. "You can't. It's Olken business. Fishermen's business. You'll make no friends stirrin' that pot. Leave it be."

"Even though they beat you half to death?"

"It ain't that bad," he said, lying. "Reckon I've had worse."

"Really?" Gar scoffed. "When?"

He sighed, even though breathing hurt like fire. "Leave it, Gar."

"How can I? Here you are, beaten to a bloody pulp, denied your heritage, the means by which you choose to make your living, exiled from your home . . . and by your own damned *family*, Asher! *Leave* it? How can I possibly do that?"

"Because I'm asking you to."

Gar muttered something under his breath. He sounded angry. Resentful. "I don't like it."

"You don't have to."

Silence. "Well . . ." Gar's voice was laced with doubt. "If you're sure."

"Damned sure."

"In that case . . . what will you do now?"

Stay curled up on the floor forever and ever. Drag his sorry carcase to another alehouse and drown it in an ocean of alcohol. Find a Doranen magician to turn back time so none of the past year had ever happened. So Jed wasn't a drooling gapwit and Da was still alive.

"I don't know," he said roughly, swallowing tears.

Another silence. Then: "I really do have to leave at first light. Her Majesty will need me."

"Aye."

"I'll take Mishin with me. Or Fitch."

"You'll take me."

"Asher, you can't—"

With a grunt and a groan he rolled over. Sat up, teeth gritted. "You'll take me," he said again with all the force he could muster. He sounded like a half-drowned cat, mewling.

Gar was shaking his head. "You're out of your mind. *Look* at yourself. You *can't* ride all the way back to Dor—"

Despite the pain he reached out and grabbed a handful of Gar's dressing-gown. Bunched it in his fist and shook as hard as the dregs of his strength allowed. "*I have to!*" he said raggedly. "*I can't stay here!*" Perilously close to breaking, to begging, he loosened his fingers and let his hand fall. "I can't stay here."

Gar hesitated. Nodded. "All right. All right, you can come. Provided the pothecary says you're fit."

"Sink the pothecary. I'm fine."

Gar sighed. Shook his head. "Of course you are." Then added, hesitantly, "You don't have to stay in the City afterwards. Not if you don't want to. I gave you my word you could leave my service after a year and of course I'll keep it. I'm sorry I was so angry before. It was unjust." He frowned. "Unprincely."

If he leaned against the wall his back would burst into flames. Pulling up one knee, he rested his aching head. "No. You were right. I should've said something. Anyway. It don't matter now." He sounded bitter. He couldn't help it, and didn't much care.

"You are welcome to stay, of course," Gar said, abruptly formal. "I still need an Assistant Olken Administrator. If you stayed it would save me a lot of work, showing someone else the ropes."

Face hidden, Asher smiled, a sarcastic twist of lip. *If* he stayed? What choice did he have now but to stay? Where else was there for him to go? He couldn't be a fisherman any more. Assistant Olken Administrator was the only work he was fit for now. A dry life the only one that wanted him.

He lifted his head. "I'll stay. You're mad if you think you'll find anybody else to put up with Darran and Willer."

Gar made a small sound of amusement. "Probably that's an exaggeration but . . . good. I'm glad."

With a groan Asher let his head drop again. If he didn't get another drink soon he'd have to start climbing the walls. He glanced at Gar. Saw trenched hollows beneath his eyes, the scouring grief within them.

"You're sure about the king?"

Gar nodded, bleakly. "I'm sure."

When, exactly, did a body fill up with so much pain it couldn't feel any more?

Soon, he hoped.

Gar looked . . . destroyed. He should say something, but the words wouldn't come. And then the door opened and manky ole Darran bustled in with the pothecary. After that the only pain that mattered was the clean, physical kind.

A pity it wasn't likely to stay that way.

Scant hours later, in the cold dawn of the mayor's stable yard, drugged and dour in the saddle, Asher waited as Darran flapped and fuddled over Gar.

"Oh, sir, I do wish you wouldn't do this!"

Gar frowned. "So you've said. And said. Don't say it again."

Darran's lips pressed tight. "No, sir." He looked like he wanted to scream.

Asher knew the feeling.

"You've plenty of coin in your saddlebag, sir," Darran continued. "And as much bread and cheese and sausage as I could pack." He chewed his lip for a moment. Turned abruptly and glared at Asher. "Make sure he sleeps in a decent bed every night, you. Not rough under a hedge by the side of the road or in an open field. You're to look after him, do you hear?"

Asher didn't have the energy to bite. "Aye."

Willer, lurking behind Darran, glared daggers through puffy, bloodshot eyes. Spite and thwarted triumph roiled in him like snakes in a vat of rancid oil. Asher looked away, biting the inside of his cheek. Willer's bitter disappointment was the only good thing about his forced return to Dorana.

Gar hissed through his teeth, impatient. "Thank you, Darran. Asher knows his duty . . . and so do you. Remember, you are my voice here now. Speak softly and with charity to all."

Darran nodded unhappily. "Yes, sir. Safe journey, Your Highness. And my . . ." He flicked a glance at the mayor and his wife, huddled inside their best coats, blinking bleary eyes at the sunrise, ". . . regards, to Her Majesty."

"Yes." Gar turned to his hosts. "My thanks to you and your good lady, Mr. Mayor. I regret that I'm forced to take my leave in such an unseemly fashion."

The mayor bowed. "Aye, Your Highness."

"If there's anything you need, *anything*, don't hesitate to tell Darran. He'll provide it."

"Thank you, Your Highness."

With a final nod at his secretary, Gar nudged Ballodair over to Cygnet. Lowered his voice. "You can do this?"

Asher nodded. Gar's saddlebags may be bulging with food but his own were crammed with little pills and potions from the pothecary. "Aye."

Still Gar stared at him. "I won't spare you."

"I never asked you to."

"I can't," said Gar, anguished. Uncertain. "If the ride is more than you can manage—"

"It won't be."

"But if it *is* . . ."

Asher glanced at the nearby treetops, tipped with light. "Sun's almost up. Are we leavin' or ain't we?"

Side by side they wheeled their horses round and started the long journey back to Dorana.

They followed the wreckage-strewn path of the storm.

If Gar had any opinions regarding the gouged earth

and splintered trees, the flattened crops, the houses peeled like oranges, he didn't share them. Nor did he offer aid or comfort to the grieving Olken they encountered as they rode. He stopped only when necessary: to drink, eat, piss or rest the horses. As far as Asher could tell, nobody recognized them. The prince wore plain brown leathers and a hood. With his bright head covered, from a distance he'd easily be mistaken for Olken, like Asher.

As the sun slid up the sky then down again the miles unrolled behind them. Mindful of all the miles still waiting, Asher hoarded his treasure of pills and potions and accustomed himself to pain.

They were stranded between villages when at last Gar was forced to admit it was time to stop riding. The sun had set and the moon was a remote sliver of light, high and to the west. They halted and considered their choices.

Squinting in the dark, Asher pointed. "There's a barn still standin'."

"That'll do," said Gar. Turning Ballodair's head he kicked the weary horse into a walk. "I won't tell Darran if you don't."

There were rats in the straw and holes in the roof but it was better than nothing. After unsaddling the horses and leaving them to eat a mean double-handful of oats each, they sat in the dark and devoured their own meager dinner of sausage and cheese. They had candles and a flint box but didn't dare use them.

"You all right?" asked Gar for the first time since leaving Westwailing.

Asher started to shrug, then stopped. "I'll manage."

Rustling and dust as Gar shaped straw into a makeshift

mattress and pillow and lay down. "Barring disaster," he said, stifling a sneeze, "I think we might reach Dorana inside a week."

"Aye. Barring disaster. We want to watch the horses, though. Matt'll never speak to us again if we founder 'em."

"I know."

Asher rummaged in his saddlebag, found one of the pother's vials and drank its foul contents, grimacing. After a few moments the raging fire in his flesh faded to a warm glow. Praise Barl. With a sigh of relief he eased himself onto his side and pulled his saddle a little closer for a pillow.

He was so tired he could see purple blotches dancing in the air in front of his face, even without candles. He closed his eyes. One by one, protesting, his muscles relaxed. Sleep beckoned.

In the darkness Gar said softly, "I was five when Durm confirmed what had long been suspected. When I learned I was . . . what I am. Once the first shock wore off I lived in daily fear that my father would no longer love me. I thought I might be farmed out somewhere, perhaps to an Olken family where lack of magic didn't matter. I don't know why I thought that. Children have strange fancies, I suppose. Even at that young age I knew I meant trouble for my parents. Maybe even for the kingdom. Unlike other Doranen families I knew that kings and queens were allowed only one child, one heir . . . and that my father's precious legacy had been squandered on a magickless cripple."

"Sounds daft to me," Asher said drowsily. "Reckon there should be an heir and a spare, at least."

"You're forgetting your history. Trevoyle's Schism. This kingdom was nearly destroyed by brothers and sisters fighting for the right to be named WeatherWorker."

"Didn't anyone think of drawin' straws?"

A breath of brief, wry amusement. "Three months after my true nature was revealed my father took me riding. It was a great treat. He'd been so busy of late, so troubled. I'd heard raised voices. Crying. Somehow I knew it was because of me. We rode for, oh, ages, until we were quite alone, right at the foothills of the mountains. There we stopped and he told me Barl was giving me a sister. I was confused. I thought I wasn't allowed a sister because of who we were. He said I needn't worry about that. All I had to do, he said, was be my new sister's big brother. It was a very important job. I had to love her and take care of her and help her to one day become the greatest WeatherWorker in the history of Lur."

Asher grunted. "Lucky you."

"I remember my father leaned down from his horse, cupped my face in his hands and kissed my forehead. There were tears in his eyes. On his cheeks. He said, 'I will always love you, Gar. I don't know why you were born without magic but I know there must be a reason. Barl has a destiny for you, my son. In my heart I know this is true. All we need is patience, until it's revealed.'"

"Did you believe him?"

"I believe he loved me."

"And what about the destiny thing? Don't s'pose Barl's dropped any hints, has she?"

"He was a father trying to ease his child's pain. What do you think?" Gar said roughly. Then, whispering:

"Blessed Barl, save me. He's gone, he's gone . . . and I don't know how to bear it . . ."

Outside the barn a hunting owl shrieked. The horses lifted their heads and shuffled the straw uneasily. Further away a fox barked. Barked again. Another fox answered it.

I don't know either, thought Asher, but didn't say it. There was no point, Frowning, he felt memory rise like a mist, blotting out the present. Smothering him in the past. "The only time I saw my da cry was the day we buried Ma," he said, almost to himself. "It was a bad day. Not rainin', just a cold, miserable, mizzly drizzle blowin' in from beyond the reef. After they put her in the ground and said what was needed, folks went home. My brothers went home. But Da stayed. Sat in the dirt beside the hole that swallowed her and said her name, over and over. Amaranda. Amaranda. His face was wet. I told myself it was the drizzle but deep down I knew different. I knew it was tears."

"How old were you?"

"Eight, just gone. A spratling. When he wouldn't get up I sat beside 'im. He put his arm around me, which didn't happen often, I said, 'Don't be sad, Da. We'll be right. One day when I be a man growed, and rich, I'll buy us a boat, and we'll call her *Amaranda*. Paint her green and blue, Ma's favorite colors. And nobody but us'll be allowed to sail her. Zeth and the others, we won't let 'em so much as look at her. That boat'll be just for us. I promise. You and me, Da. Together and laughin', eh? You and me.'"

In the soft silence Gar sighed. "I am sorry. About your father. And your friend, too, what was his name—"

Asher felt his fingers close around fistfuls of old straw.

He'd wanted to find him, see him cared for, but there'd been no time. "Jed."

"Yes. Jed. Look . . . Asher . . ." Now the prince sounded hesitant. "You must realize, you *must*, none of what happened is your—"

"I know," he said, hard and fast. To shut Gar up, not because he believed it. "Now I reckon that's enough talkin' for one night. We ought to be savin' our strength for tomorrow, and the day after, and the day after that. We got a long road ahead of us with nowt but heartache at the end of it. So if it's all the same to you I'll go to sleep now. You'd be smart to do the same."

He thought Gar might argue, but he was answered with silence. After a time the prince's breathing slowed and deepened. Hours later he said his father's name but didn't wake.

Eventually Asher escaped into sleep himself . . . and dreamed.

Dawn didn't come soon enough.

CHAPTER TWENTY-THREE

"Well?" Matt leaned over Dathne's shoulder. "Have you got him?"

She pushed him back with a crooked elbow. "Don't crowd me. And be quiet. I need to concentrate."

Beyond her living-room window dusk softened the edges of the City. If only it could soften her too. Flinty, she felt, and rough, like scratched glass. Five days since the storm and still she'd not managed to find Asher in her scrying basin. Twenty times at least she'd tried, tried till her head throbbed to splitting with too much tanal leaf. No luck. First it was the leftover effects of the catastrophic weather, and after that the waves and waves of Doranen magic flowing in and over and round the City as all efforts were made to repair the damage done by wind and water and heaving earth. Even her precious Circle Stone had been affected. She'd finally reached Veira that morning, a quick brush of mind to mind to make sure the old woman was safe. To assure her that she and Matt had escaped calamity unscathed.

Well. Mostly unscathed. Matt still grieved for Bellybone and the dead colt. There was nothing she could do about that, though, so she kept herself focused on what she could do. Find Asher. Confirm that he was safe too, and returning to the City where he belonged. Where Prophecy needed him.

Where she needed him.

"Come on, Dath," said Matt, fretting. "Get on with it. I've got to get back to the yard. There's poultices and dressings to change. Willem's a good lad but he's not quite ready for that on his own just yet."

She swallowed curses. "You were going to stay for dinner. We've not talked decently since the storm, Matt, there's things we must—"

He turned away from her. "I can't. Maybe tomorrow."

"Tomorrow?" she echoed, temper rising. "Are you mad? Look around you, Matt! Think of what's happened! The storm—the king—what do you think is going on? What do you think it all *means*?"

He'd lost weight these last days. His eyes were hollow, his cheeks sunken. The scrapes on his skin had healed but the wounds to his spirit, his soul, still pained him. There was doubt in him now, where once there'd been only blind, stubborn faith.

"I don't know what it means," he said. "All I know is if everything you've seen in your visions is true, Dathne, then this storm was nothing, *nothing*, compared to what's coming. And this storm shook us like a cat with a mouse. Folk *died*, Dath. Children died. And what did we do about it? What could we do? *Nothing*."

"It's not our job to do, Matt! You know that. Our job is to watch. Wait. Follow Prophecy and guide Asher. *He's* the one born for the doing of great things. Not us."

Trembling, he flung himself away from her and paced the room. "Then *find* him, would you? Stop lecturing me and bloody *find* him, Dath! Make sure he ain't dead or broken to pieces in a ditch somewhere! Because if he is— if that's what's happened to him—"

The effort nearly choked her but she held her tongue. Lashing out at Matt would be too easy, not just thanks to the excess of tanal leaf but because he was giving a voice to her own doubts, her own fears, and she didn't want to hear them spoken aloud. In case speaking them made them come true. Lashing out might make her feel better, if only for a moment, but it would hurt him. Hurt them. Their oathsworn bond, and their friendship. The mood she was in, it would be so simple. Undoing the damage would be far more complicated and they didn't have the time.

So instead of shouting back at him, instead of stamping her foot and slapping him, she gentled herself. Went to him and rested her hand on his arm. "Dear Matt. Don't you think I'd know if he were dead? Don't you think Prophecy would've told me?"

His eyes were stark. "Would it? I don't know. Seems to me there's a lot going on that Prophecy's not talkin' about."

Her fingers closed on his shirt sleeve and shook him. "He's not dead," she said fiercely. "Come. Sit down. Hold your tongue. Let me work and I'll prove it to you."

She tugged him towards the table. With a stiffled groan he dropped into a chair. She sat beside him, smiled at him briefly then took another pinch of tanal. Chewed it, spat it out and began again the ritual to open her mind, send it winging through the world in search of her heart's desire.

This time she found it.

Asher rode into the sinking shadows, towards the tow-

*ering might of the Wall. All around him the countryside
was laid to waste. Trees felled. Crops ruined. Grim en-
durance was in his face and the way he sat his stumbling
horse. The set of his slumping shoulders and the bloodless hold he had on the reins.*

Dreamily, held deep within the tanal's insinuating
grasp, she took Matt's hand and pressed his fingers with
her own. "He's coming," she murmured. "I see him."

"Praise Barl," said Matt, his voice unsteady. "He's all
right, then?"

No. There was pain. In the muscle and the mind. The
heartbreak she'd foreseen for him had struck deep. She
could feel it. But it didn't matter. Nothing mattered save
that Prophecy was served once more.

Asher was coming home.

She stirred the basin's water. Broke the link. "Yes.
He's fine."

Sitting back, Matt dragged one hand over his face,
breathing heavily. "Praise Barl." He looked at her. "Praise
Prophecy." His expression altered. "Dath . . ."

"It's all right," she said. "I was nervous too. I think
we'd be fools not to be. These are nervous times, Matt. A
kingdom's at stake."

He nodded slowly. "Nervous. Aye."

She started rolling up her diminished pouch of tanal
leaf. "He's not so far away. They've traveled fast. Tomorrow night, maybe, or early the morning after that, will see
them in the City."

"They?"

She frowned. "The prince is with him." Impatiently
she shook herself free of the melancholy she'd felt from
both men resonating through the scrying spell. "So, you

can rest easy now. Go, if you're going. See to your precious poultices. I'll call if I need you." Reaching across, she tugged at the small calling stone on its leather thong around his neck. "And if I call, come. I worry when you don't answer me. Ignore me again and I'll tell tales on you to Veira, I swear."

He had the good grace to flush. As well he should. Twice since the storm she'd used the crystal to signal she needed him, and twice he'd put his precious damned horses before her.

"I will," he promised. "Dathne . . ." His hand rested on her shoulder. "You look so tired."

And so she was. Tired, and more than tired. Her recent days had been spent fixing the bookshop, helping neighbours, and her nights were twisted with dreams. Not Prophecy, not precisely. Just dark forebodings and uneasy intuitions, riding her hard till morning dragged harsh fingers across her face and she woke, bathed in pale yellow sunshine and sweat.

"I'll stay," said Matt. "You're right. The horses won't die for lack of a poultice. I'll stay and make us soup and we can talk, Dathne. All right?"

Perversely, it wasn't all right. With the last lingering tartness of the tanal on her tongue, her sight just tinged with its golden potency, all she wanted now was to be left alone. To slide between cool sheets in the rose-scented darkness of her bedroom and surrender to sleep.

With luck, she wouldn't dream tonight.

She shook her head. "No. You go. There'll come a time soon when you'll need to leave the horses behind without a second thought. Don't abandon them till you have to. I'll be fine."

His callused hand moved from her shoulder to her cheek. Rested there. "You're sure?"

She stood and moved away from the table. Towards the door. Hinting. "When have you ever known me not sure?"

He laughed, as she'd intended. Collected his coat from the arm of her dilapidated couch then paused in the open doorway. "I'll stay around the stables and call the minute he gets back."

"Good," she said, and closed the door firmly behind him.

Blessedly alone, she stripped off her skirt and blouse and underthings and bathed in a basin of warm water. Then she fell into bed, too weary for even one page of a book. Blew out the candle. Sank into sleep.

And dreamed.

"Look!" said Gar, and lifted an unsteady hand to point. "Dorana."

Anchored to his saddle by habit and exhaustion, Asher blinked groggily and squinted into the distance. Everything looked bleary and his head hurt. Ha! His head? His head, his back, his legs, his toenails . . . "Where?"

"There! See it? That glittering beyond those far trees? It's the sun setting on the palace windows. We're nearly home, praise Barl. Just a few more miles."

"Aye," said Asher, and dragged a filthy sleeve across his dirty, unshaven face. "Good." For him, any road. Gar was nearly home. As for himself . . .

But it was the City, right enough. And about bloody time too. The muddy track they traveled now linked with the great City Road, and that would lead them all the way to the main gates. And through Dorana. And up to the palace, and the Tower, where he'd have to sleep tonight and tomorrow night and the next and—

His blistered fingers tightened on Cygnet's reins; the horse half raised his head, grunting. Poor beast. He was exhausted too. Matt would be furious when he saw how much condition his precious animals had lost. They'd need a week at least of stable rest, and all the grain and mash they could eat, after the punishing ride from Westwailing.

Come to think of it, he could do with a bit of that himself.

"Let's trot a bit," said Gar, his pale voice humming with tension. He looked rough as guts too. Dark gold stubble sandpapered his cheeks and chin. His bloodshot eyes had sunk into their sockets and his dirty hair hung limp and lank. If Darran could see him now he'd most likely faint.

"Trot?" Asher groaned. "Barl bloody save me. Do we have to? My damn spine's near to jolted through the top of my skull."

"And you think mine isn't?" snapped Gar, glaring. "Come on. We can try, at least. If we can I want to—" He stopped, coughing like a man with lungrot. The fit passed eventually, leaving him milk-white and gasping. Waving away Asher's concern he pressed his fingers to his eyes, hard, then let his hand drop. "I'm all right." Glancing at Asher, he frowned. "Which is more than I can say for you. You look worse than I feel, if that's possible. You shouldn't have come. I was mad to let you talk me into it."

"I'm fine," said Asher, then laughed, unamused, because it was such a lie, and he knew it, and Gar knew it, and truly, what was the point? "Don't fret on it. Like you say, this mad ride were my decision, not yours. Besides, what good would not comin' have done me? If I'd stayed behind I'd have killed that ole Darran by now. Or if not him, then def'nitely bloody Willer. And anyway, I've got nowhere else to go, have I?"

The words scalded, bitter as bile. Damn. He'd never meant to say that out loud. Gar's expression was shocked. Hurt. Bewildered.

"What do you mean?"

"Nowt. Nothing. Forget I said it," Asher replied, inwardly cursing. "I'm tired, is all. Not thinkin' straight. And that bloody pother's pills and potions ran out two days ago. You want to trot? We'll trot."

Gar bullied his horse forward, blocking the path. "I thought I made it clear to you, Asher, I wasn't forcing you back here. I *offered* to fix—"

"I know!" said Asher, raising his voice. "It's all right. I didn't mean it. I don't mind comin' back to Dorana. If I can't have the coast, it's as good a place as any to—"

Gar wasn't listening. "You saved my *life*, Asher! Do you think I'd repay that by making you do anything you didn't want to? Is that the kind of man you think I am?"

"Of course it ain't, you bloody fool."

"You saved my life," Gar repeated, and this time it was a whisper. In his scratched and dirty face a memory of wild water, and drowning. "Barl forgive me. Can you believe I *forgot* . . ."

Asher heaved a sigh. "Don't fret on it. Reckon you've had a bit on your mind this last little while."

The uncertainty in Gar's face hardened into resolve. Reaching out he clasped Asher's shoulder, his fingers like a vice. "I can never fully repay you. But if ever you're in need, come to me. Ask, and no matter the favor it will be granted. My word as a prince."

Embarrassed, Asher looked away. "Aye, well . . ."

Gar's fingers tightened to the point of pain. "I mean it."

Asher looked back again. Nodded. "I know. I'll remember. Now if it's all the same to you, can we get on? I'm halfway desperate for a beer and a bath. And Her Majesty must be lookin' out every window for you by now."

Gar released his grip. Backed Ballodair up a pace and dragged the horse's head round till they were facing the City again. "Yes," he said flatly. "You're right. The queen will be waiting."

They stirred the reluctant horses with their spurs and jogged along in silence, too tired to talk further, too full of separate griefs that couldn't be eased with sharing. Rounding a bend in the track they joined the City Road. It crossed open countryside, and the great storm's passage was less evident here. In the distance ahead was the City itself, somnolent in the sinking sunshine.

On they jogged, bringing Dorana closer stride by stride. They traveled the road alone.

After a time they could make out the City walls. They looked intact. So did the enormous City gates, standing wide in welcome. "Reckon the storm left Dorana alone?" asked Asher, shading his eyes and staring. Cygnet dropped into an ambling walk. He didn't have the heart to spur the horse again. Beside him, Gar loosened his reins and let Ballodair follow suit.

"Unlikely. Durm would have organized a Working. Teams of mages to repair the damage. However bad it was in there, I expect it's all back to normal by now."

The City, maybe, but nothing else. With the poor king dead there'd be a new WeatherWorker. Queen Fane. And that was like to make life very, very interesting indeed . . .

Asher scowled at Cygnet's ears. He'd never asked for interesting. He'd never asked for much at all, really. Just some money, and a boat, and a little peace and quiet. And yet it seemed as though he'd asked for more than fate thought right to give him.

It wasn't bloody fair.

Gar said, "Without wishing for another argument, I want to say this. Once we know how things stand in Dorana, once . . . the new order has been established, I think you should take some time to consider your future. I don't want you to feel obliged to continue in my service. You've come a long way from the fisherman turned stable hand I hired a year ago, Asher. I should think you could do anything you wanted now."

Oh, aye. Of course he could. Anything except the only thing that had ever truly mattered. He glanced at Gar sideways. "What did you have in mind?"

Gar's lips quirked in the smallest of smiles. "Oh, I don't know. Perhaps Dathne needs an errand boy in her bookshop."

Asher's stomach clenched. *Dathne*. Damn Gar. He'd been working so hard at not thinking about Dathne.

"I wasn't imagining things, was I?" Gar continued. "You and she—"

"We're friends," he said flatly. "At least we were. Then I left. I ain't sure what we are now."

"You parted badly?"

Asher sighed. "We parted."

"I like Dathne," Gar said thoughtfully. "She's an

uncommon woman. Too good for you really. Take my advice, Asher, and as soon as you can seek her out and ask her—hold on. What's that?"

It was a carriage, flying recklessly towards them. The sound of hooves pounding the hard road carried clearly on the cooling evening air, and the snap of the whip as the driver cracked it over the backs of the galloping horses.

Despite their bone-deep weariness Cygnet and Ballodair broke into a sidling, head-tossing jog. Exchanging looks, Asher and Gar urged them on. The carriage came closer, closer, and they could see it was an open touring model, and that there were two people in the back behind the reinsman. Closer still and the carriage's passengers were on their feet, standing, a dangerous thing to do in a speeding vehicle, holding each other tight and waving. Shouting. Closer again, and they could see that one of the passengers was the queen, was Dana, her long blonde hair streaming behind her, and the other—the other—

"In Barl's blessed name . . ." Gar whispered. He dropped his reins, forgetting entirely to kiss his holyring, and swayed in the saddle. Trained to a hair's-breadth Ballodair skidded to a halt. Asher stopped beside him and stretched out a steadying hand. Heedless, Gar sat and stared as though turned to stone.

The carriage was slowing, Coachman Matcher leaning back and hauling on his lines, shouting at the horses to whoa, whoa. Before it stopped scant feet away the passenger door flew open.

"Papa?" Gar cried, and slithered to the ground. "Papa! *Papa!*"

They ran to each other, father and son. The king was staggering; not strong, but desperate. They collided. Embraced with abandon, laughing, weeping. They pounded each other's shoulders and touched each other's cheeks with trembling fingers. Their joy was incandescent.

Silent as death, Asher watched the ecstatic reunion.

"Where's Da, Zeth? I want to see him."

"Why, he's right where you put 'im, Asher dear. Deep in the cold dark ground."

Stumbling in her haste, the queen joined her husband and their son. Three people tangled into one, and they all cried togther.

Time passed. At length the king, the queen and the prince disentangled themselves and, still exclaiming, walked to the carriage. Climbed inside. Closed the passenger door. Matcher clicked his tongue and picked up his whip. The carriage turned around and the horses, encouraged, broke into a spanking trot. Its passengers continued to hug and hold and never once looked back.

Asher watched them go. Leaned over and picked up Ballodair's abandoned reins. "Come up then, boys," he said, and nudged Cygnet into a reluctant walk. Ears pinned flat to his head, eyes rolling and mouth agape as he leaned against his bridle, rebellious, Ballodair followed.

Together they traveled in the carriage's wake all the way back to the City.

PART THREE

CHAPTER TWENTY-FOUR

By the time Asher finally made it back to the Tower stable yard, it was dark.

The royal carriage had swiftly left him and the horses behind. Suddenly unable to face the City and the welcome he knew he'd receive from its citizens, he decided to ride the long way round to the Tower. Even though he was tired almost beyond bearing and his body hurt so badly the thought of one jolting step more than strictly necessary was a torment. Even though he was freezing cold and dripping sweat at the same time.

Halfway around the City wall's fat circumference he stumbled across Pellen Orrick, who was inspecting the joins between the huge blocks of stone with a lamp strung on the end of a long pole. Dorana's Captain of the City Guard looked immaculate, as usual, but grim and tired around the eyes. There was a smudge of dirt on his cheek and half-healed scrapes on his knuckles.

"Meister Assistant Administrator," Orrick said, and raised his eyebrows. "Welcome back. You look somewhat the worse for wear, if I may say so."

"Only 'cause I am, Captain. What're you doin'?"

"Looking for cracks. The wall's been mended thrice over and passed sound by the Master Magician and Lord Jarralt, but I like to be thorough. So, if you're back, and leading Ballodair, can I take it the prince has also returned?"

Asher nodded. "Aye." He stared at the City's stone wall, because it was better than meeting Pellen Orrick's sharp, considering gaze. "The storm do much damage here, then?"

"Enough."

"Any deaths? Injuries?"

"Too many."

"And are the people behaving 'emselves? Namin' no names, I can think of one or two as might see in all this woe and wail a chance to line their own pockets with somebody else's misfortune. Certain tradesfolk, for instance."

"The same thought had occurred to me," said Orrick, an appreciative glimmer in his dark eyes. "Don't fret. I've my eye on one or two . . . opportunists. Naming no names, of course."

"Good," said Asher. "So there be nowt I need to take care of straightaway?"

Orrick shook his head. "Not straightaway. I've a report on its way to the Tower for you, as it happens. It can wait a day or two, before we meet on it."

"Can it wait a week?" said Asher hopefully.

"Perhaps," said Orrick, smiling. "Now ride on, Meister Assistant. It's an offence to interfere with a guardsman doing his duty, you know."

"Y'don't say," said Asher. "Fancy that." With a gentle

kick and a tug on the reins he urged Cygnet and Ballodair
into a shambling walk and kept on riding. After three
strides he turned his head, just a little, and added over his
shoulder, "Glad to see you're all right, Captain."

Orrick's laughter was soft in the descending dusk.
"And the same to you, Asher. The same to you."

Cheered, Asher continued the long way round and entered Dorana through the private royal gate high up behind the palace. The startled guards waved him through;
he lifted a hand to them, nodding, but didn't dawdle. The
horses picked their way along the bridlepaths and in between the flowerbeds by starlight and the Wall's golden
glow, heads drooping almost to their knees. Ballodair still
dragged sullenly against his bridle, so that Asher thought
his arm must soon pull free from his shoulder.

An energetic chorus of whinnies greeted their plod-
ding entrance into the Tower stable yard. A few of the
lads tumbled downstairs from their dormitory to see what
all the fuss was about. Matt, who was sitting on an upturned bucket mending a head collar by lamplight, leapt
to his feet. Leather, needle and waxed thread fell unheeded to the ground.

"Barl save us," he breathed, coming forward to stare at
the filthy, overwrought horses. "Asher, what have you
done to them?" A wave of his hand brought a gaping lad
over. "Duffy, take Ballodair. Into his stable with him,
quick, and mind you handle him gently. You know what
to do."

As Duffy obeyed, still gaping, Asher wriggled his fingers in greeting. "Hey, Matt."

Matt swore. His hand rested on Cygnet's trembling

shoulder, soothing, stroking. "*Damn* it, Asher. Get off that bloody horse now, before you fall off."

It was an enticing notion. He'd had enough of saddles and horses to last a lifetime. But the ground looked a long way down. He wasn't sure he could reach it safely. The last of his strength had drained away; the stables, the whispering lads, the pools of lamplight and Matt's frowning face all blurred together. The world faded.

"*Asher!*"

He dragged his eyelids open. "I'm right here," he muttered. "Don't shout."

"Where's the prince?"

"Up at the palace, I s'pose." Asher's eyes drifted shut again. "King and queen met us in a carriage, on the road. He went with them."

Matt snapped his fingers at the nearest lad. "Mikel! Off to the Goose with you and bring back a jug of strong cider. On my chit, tell Derrig. Now! Run!" The lad bolted, and Matt came closer. Punched Asher's knee with a light fist. "Reckon the horses aren't the only ones pushed over the line. Can you get down all right?"

The rough, kind voice was almost his undoing. "'Course I can!" he growled. "What d'you take me for, some namby-pamby City Doranen?" Leaning forward, swallowing a groan, he half slithered, half fell out of the saddle. Only Matt's strong arm saved him from humiliation.

"Steady now," his friend said. "I've got you."

On a shuddering, indrawn breath, he managed to straighten. Stared after poor footsore Cygnet as Jim'l led him away. "Sorry about the horses, Matt. We thought the king was dead."

Matt pulled a face. "You weren't the only ones."

"We rode back as fast as we could. Cross-country nearly all the way."

"The storm reached all the way down to the coast?"

"Damn near flattened Westwailing. We were out on the harbor when it hit. Gar almost—" He shook his head. Flaming thunderbolts. Scarlet lightning. Waves towering overhead and the boat standing on end. Gar smashed over the side into the raging ocean. Another memory he wanted no truck with. Not for a good long while, any road.

Matt's fingers tightened on his shoulder. "What is it? What happened?"

"Nothing. It don't matter. Matt . . ." He could feel his knees shake, threatening to buckle. "Reckon I need to sit down."

"Lie down, more like," said Matt, snorting. He slid his arm around Asher's back. "Let's get you—"

No, no, no. That wasn't going to work. Pain streaked his vision blood red. "I can walk," he gasped and managed, just, to pull free.

"There's a cot in the yard office," said Matt, one hand hovering. "We had a horse or two hurt in the worst of it."

He rolled his eyes. "Nursemaid Matt. Horses all right?"

"They will be. Are you walking or talking?"

He took a tentative step forward. "I can do both."

"Maybe, but do you have to?"

The short distance to the office felt almost as long as the ride from Westwailing. Matt shadowed him every inch. Sent the remaining lads back about their business with a barked command. Opened the office door for him and guided him to the cot.

"You had it bad up here too?" he asked as he lowered his abused and shrieking body to the rough bed. Laid his head on a pillow for the first time in days, and closed his eyes. The glory of it stole his breath.

"Bad enough," Matt's voice said above him. He hesitated. "Dathne's fine . . . if you were wondering."

He prised his eyelids open. Was he wondering? No. Maybe. "What about you?"

Matt shrugged. "I'm fine too. Glad you're back."

He wasn't. "And the king's all right then, is he? Not dead, I saw that, but—"

"There was some kind of crisis. That fever. Word is he's well on the mend now. Asher, did you know there's blood on your shirt?"

"I'll survive."

"That's not what I asked." Matt turned away, opened a cupboard and took out a stoppered clay pot of something that smelled potent. "This'll do till we can get Pother Nix to see you."

He groaned. "I don't need that ole bone-botherer fussin' and fartin' all over me."

"Didn't ask you that either," said Matt. "Just hold your tongue for once, if you can, and let somebody help you."

"Nursemaid bloody Matt," Asher muttered, then hissed as Matt pulled his shirt up.

"Well," said Matt eventually, after a humming silence. "Good thing I made up a new batch of ointment, ain't it?"

The first touch of the salve on his wounds had him gasping. Face pressed into the dark anonymity of the pillow, hands fisted by his sides, Asher chewed his lip bloody as Matt's gentle fingers woke fire in his battered flesh. Then, mercifully, the burning faded and instead there was blessed numbness.

Dimly he heard the office door open. Heard Matt say, softly, "Well done, Mikel. Put it on the table there and close the door behind you. Tell Duff and Jim'l I'll be out directly to check on those horses."

The quiet thunk of a stone jug on wood. The door closing again. A sloshing sound as liquid was poured from the jug into something smaller. Then Matt was helping him up. "Drink this." He pressed a mug into his hand. "Derrig's best."

The cold cider slid easily down his dry throat, welcome as a lover's kiss. He emptied the mug in two swallows. Emptied it again. And again. Then he lowered his head to the pillow once more. Was aware, just, of a thin blanket settling over him. Of Matt, staring down at him. Of the yard office receding like a wave from the shore.

He let the waters close over his head and surrendered to sleep.

Two hours later, startled by a sound, Matt looked up from his sleepy vigil in the office to see Gar standing in the open doorway. The prince looked as tired as Asher. Fading bruises marked his face. Some cuts and scratches. Shadows under his eyes.

He stood. "Sorry, Your Highness, I didn't—"

Gar held up his hand and moved to the cot. "It's all right." He was whispering. "How is he?"

Matt shrugged. "I've doctored him as best I can, sir, but it's Pother Nix he's needing."

Gar was frowning down at Asher. "He'll have him. Did he tell you what happened?"

"No, sir."

Gar told him. Briefly. Brutally. "From the day he got here he was planning his triumphant return to Restharven. Imagining his father's pleasure. Daydreaming the boat they'd sail together. And for the last eight months . . ."

Wrung with horrified sympathy, Matt stared at his sleeping friend. "Damn. Sir."

The prince's expression was cool. Guarded. "So long as his brothers live he can never go back to the coast."

Damn. This was what Dathne had foreseen then, when she said so confidently that Asher would return. Not for the first time he felt relief that he was not Jervale's Heir, cursed with foresight and Prophecy.

The prince said, "How are the horses?"

Anger and duty warred. Duty won, just. "They'll do, sir. In time."

Gar wasn't fooled. "I'd have spared them if I could, Matt." He nodded at the cot, where Asher lay on his stomach like a corpse. "I'd have spared him, too."

"Yes, sir."

"He can't stay here."

"I know, sir. I'll see him safe to his own bed once he wakes."

Gar considered him. "You're a good man, Matt. A good friend."

The words twisted his guts like a knife. "I try to be, sir."

"He'll need his friends, I think, in the next little while. He's lost his whole family." The prince shuddered. "I can't imagine . . ."

"No, sir," said Matt. Then added, hesitantly, "Sir, if you don't mind me saying so, you should be in bed too.

You've ridden as far and as hard as Asher. If you want the truth of it, you look fair worn out."

Gar smiled. "Do I?" Stirring, he turned. "I suppose you're right. Show me the horses, quickly, and I'll be on my way."

After the prince had seen his Ballodair, and Cygnet too, fed them carrots and petted them, he left the quiet stable yard. Matt watched him go, then hesitated. He'd thought to wait till morning to tell Dathne of Asher's return. There'd seemed little point in summoning her to the stables at night-time only to show her his sleeping body. But now . . .

His calling stone lay hidden in his pocket, twin to the one Dathne carried. Closing his fingers hard around the small crystal he opened the link between them. Sought her fierce, unquiet mind with his and whispered her name.

Half an hour later she arrived, crackling with excitement. He met her under the stable yard archway. "Where is he?" she demanded. "How long ago did he get back?"

If there was any unease in her, any sense of awkwardness given the manner of her parting with Asher, she didn't show it. But then she wouldn't. "He rode in a short while ago. Dathne . . ."

She was frowning. She knew him so well; it was getting harder to decide if that was a good thing, or a bad. "Tell me."

He repeated what the prince had told him. Watched her closely as she absorbed the news, looking for some small sign of sorrow. Looked in vain. Her eyes glittered. "So. His ties to the past are broken. He belongs to us now."

Sometimes the hardness in her hurt him. "Is that all you can say?"

She met his hot gaze coldly. "It's all that matters."

He tried to turn away from her, tried to hide his eyes. She wouldn't let him. "His father's *dead*, Dathne!" he cried. "Doesn't that mean anything to you?"

"Not what you want it to mean. There'll be a lot more dead fathers in this kingdom if we fail in our duty, Matt." She let go of his arm. "I'll see him now."

"I don't think he wants to see you, Dathne. Not yet, anyway."

She shrugged. "And if he's sleeping, he won't."

He had to wait a moment before he could trust himself to follow her quietly, calmly, into the yard office. She was kneeling beside the cot. Either Asher had rolled himself onto his back, or she'd done it. Her left hand was on his unresponsive wrist and the fingers of her right hand pressed against his forehead.

"What are you doing? He needs to rest."

She looked up. There was the faintest spark of alarm in her eyes. "He has a fever, did you know?"

He realized then that Asher's breathing was loud. Labored. Saw that his face had flushed from pale to hectic. His lips were dry and his head tossed uneasily on the cot's pillow. Taken aback, he clutched at the door. "He was all right when he got here. Exhausted and in pain, but not—"

Her glare scalded him. "Well, he's not all right now!"

No, he wasn't. Matt laid his hand on Asher's burning forehead. Heard the rattle in his chest. Pressed cold fingers to the pulse point in his throat and felt the echoes of his friend's thundering heart. "I'll send for Pother Nix and alert the prince."

She stood, and pulled her shawl tight. "Yes, you do that. I'll tell Veira Asher's back. The Circle can help here. I'll ask her to link with the others in a distant healing."

Matt chewed his lip. "How can that work? They don't even know him."

"They know of him," she snapped. "And it's better than doing nothing."

She'd slap him if he argued, so he nodded and stood aside to let her leave. As the door slammed shut behind her and the sound of her running feet faded, he looked again at Asher.

Then he throttled fear and went outside to rouse the lads.

Dathne was breathless by the time she reached home. Flinging herself up the shop stairs to her apartment, dragging her Circle Stone from its hiding place, dropping to the floor with it in her sweating hands: blind panic consumed her, crowding out all sense and cool collection.

He cannot die, he cannot die, he cannot cannot must not die . . .

She'd never make the connection to Veira like this. Linking the Circle Stones required a peaceful, meditative state. A calm heart. Her hands were shaking.

Setting the crystal aside she lay flat on the floor. Closed her eyes, and made an effort to breathe out the fear.

He cannot die, he cannot die, he cannot cannot must not die . . .

His father was dead. What a cruel thing. What a harsh

way to serve the will of Prophecy. But then Prophecy had no father, no mother, no child, nor even a heart to break. It just was. Implacable. Unknowable. A spear tip lodged deep in the mind. No matter the pain, however the heart-break, Asher would survive his loss. Prophecy needed him. And what Prophecy wanted, Prophecy got, one way or another.

He will not die.

Dathne sat up. Reached for her Circle Stone and called to Veira. "He is returned."

The old woman's relief shuddered through the link between them. *It is soon, then.*

"Yes. The waiting is almost over. The air itself oppresses me, Veira. My skin crawls like an anthill and my nights writhe like a nest of snakes. We are wounded, we are wounded, and soon the blood must flow."

And he is ready?

"He is ill. Prophecy has used him harshly. Body and heart are bruised, and will take time mending. I thought the Circle might—"

A wise suggestion, child. Share him with me now, that I might call for a healing.

So she thought of Asher. Unchained her memory and opened her heart. When it was done:

Oh, child. Child. Dathne . . .

She felt impatience. Stiffled it. "I know. It can't be helped. It doesn't matter. It makes no difference."

No difference? Not to you, mayhap, but –

"Not to him, either. I won't let it. He'll never know."

So far away, Veira sighed. *I pray you're right. Child, the Circle will hold him safe. I have said so. Be at peace now, for as long as peace can last.*

Which wasn't long, thought Dathne, breaking the link, if foresight served her. Which most likely it did.

It always had before now.

Gar was standing in the Tower lobby, sorting through the pile of mail and messages that had been delivered just before breakfast, when his father came through the open doors.

"Demoted to post boy, are we?" Borne asked, grinning.

There was clean, fresh color in the king's face. A vitality to his demeanour Gar hadn't seen for . . . well, come to think of it, not for a very long time. To see it now, to see him whole and happy: it was a joy as sharp as pain.

"Apparently," he replied, grinning back. "It seems I miss Darran more than I anticipated."

"Never mind. He'll be home soon."

Gar pulled a face. "Not soon enough. But please, I implore you, don't ever tell him I said so."

"Your secret is safe with me," his father promised. "Is there anything urgent? Matters that must be tended to immediately?"

He glanced again at the accumulated correspondence. "No. Another report from Darran, as it happens. Things proceed well, he says. I thought to discuss the matter at length at this afternoon's Privy Council meeting."

His father nodded. "I look forward to hearing the details." Then he glanced sideways, up the Tower's spiral staircase. "And how is your assistant this morning?"

Gar followed his father's gaze. Frowned. "There's no change. Nix has been and gone already. He assures me Asher's prolonged stupor is nothing more serious than the protest of an overstrained mind and body. The fever has abated somewhat and his wounds are healing cleanly. He just won't wake up."

"Perhaps he doesn't want to."

"I thought of that," said Gar unhappily. "I can only hope you're wrong. One life is dead to him, it's true, but he's spent the last year making a new life here in Dorana. That life still lives and breathes. Awaits him. He's needed."

Borne nodded. "He knows that. And when he's ready to face that life again, he'll wake. Have faith in good Pother Nix. I'm living proof he's a miracle worker, after all. Without his passion for herb lore, for combining Doranen healing magics with old Olken remedies . . ."

"You'd be dead, like King Drokas and Queen Ninia." Gar shivered. The mere thought made him ill. Calamity had come too close this time. He dropped his voice to a whisper. "WeatherWorking is so cruel. Sometimes I wonder why Barl—"

His father smiled, sadly. "Because she had to. There was no other way. The natural energies her magics control are vast, Gar. Intricate. And the paradise they've bought us must be paid for."

He could no longer hide his pain. Even though he'd sworn never to reveal it. These last days had been too hard. "Paid for with your blood?"

"Yes," his father said simply. "It's our side of the pact, my son. Our way of thanking the Olken people for giving us a home when our own lay in ashes behind us."

"I know, I know, but—"

"Gar, I'm not here to debate history or its consequences," his father said firmly. "I have news. Something's been discovered. Something I think you might find . . . intriguing."

Smothering sorrow, Gar stared at his father. In that ascetic face, excitement. "What?" he said. "What have you found?"

The king crooked his finger. "Come, and I'll show you."

Largely uninhabited since the massive building works undertaken by Queen Antra at the turn of the last century, the Old Palace baked its crumbling stoneworks in the autumn sunshine and dreamed of its glory days, dead and gone.

Looking around the abandoned west wing's deserted central courtyard, Gar recalled the solitary childhood games he'd played here. The empty chambers and echoing corridors had been his private kingdom. Such fantastic dreams he'd woven, fashioned out of rooms piled high with discarded furniture, chests of fabulously outdated clothing, statues and knick-knacks and all manner of mysterious, grown-up things. He'd not been back here in years. The place looked sad now, not alluring. Weeds had long since taken over the flowerbeds he'd once so industriously tended, growing roses and snapdragons for his mother, and creeping wartsease slowly strangled the little row of plumple trees he'd raised for fruit, crisp and juicy and all his own. There were even some gaps in the courtyard walls, where bricks had tumbled as a result of the recent earth tremors.

"It's just through here," said the king. "In the old kitchen courtyard. Mind your step now, the ground is uneven in places."

Gar stared at his father. "What in Barl's name were you doing poking around the Old Palace grounds?"

They squeezed through a half-rotten doorway in the central courtyard wall. "I wasn't. One of the palace cooks made the discovery while searching for her runaway cat. Instead of finding the wretched creature she found this."

This was a huge, gaping hole in the middle of the old kitchen courtyard. The sunshine shafting into it over the roofline of the surrounding buildings revealed, faintly, some kind of chamber far below their feet. It seemed to be lined with shelves. More shelves crammed side by side across the space beneath the ruined ceiling. And on every shelf, books. It was impossible to tell exactly how large the chamber was, but Gar suspected it was a goodly size; the free-standing bookcases stretched beyond the edges of the breach. Aside from that obvious damage, the rest of the old kitchen courtyard appeared intact.

"Barl save us," Gar said as he and his father skirted the hole to join the queen, Durm and Fane, who were standing together a prudent distance from the lip of the rent in the ground.

"Extraordinary, isn't it?" said the king, jubilant. "And to think—"

"At last!" the princess cried. "Durm was just saying you must have found another hole and fallen into it."

Smiling indulgently, the Master Magician rapped her on the head with his knuckles. "I most certainly was not, madam."

She grinned at him. "Well, you were thinking so. Don't try and deny it, I know you too well!"

As the others laughed, Gar sighed. He and his sister had hardly spoken since his return from Westwailing.

Partly it was because he'd been immersed in emergency meetings with his father and both Councils. Also he'd spent a great many hours asleep, recovering from the gruelling cross-country ride. Some of it was because, whenever he could, he'd been sitting with Asher hoping his friend would grow tired of the history book he'd been reading aloud and sit bolt upright, demanding that Gar give over natterin' afore his bloody ears fell off in self-defense.

It hadn't happened yet, but he remained cautiously optimistic.

But he couldn't blame all of the silence between him and Fane on work and worry. More and more, it seemed of late, they simply had less and less to say to one another . . . and they'd never had a great deal in common to start with. The distance between them was troubling. If in truth the king had perished, his sister would now be his queen. And their strained relationship would have made his life a hundred times harder than it already was.

It was time and past time that he found a way to cross the abyss that separated them. One day, Barl pray long hence, she would be the kingdom's WeatherWorker and he would have to bow his knee to her in solemn obedience. Between now and that day he had to find a way to her goodwill. Because if he didn't . . .

She was frowning at him. "What are you staring at?"

"Nothing," he said, with a lightness he was far from feeling. "You look most becoming in that dress. The color suits you."

"Doesn't it?" said the queen, smiling. "I must order a bolt of the fabric for myself."

Fane twitched her skirts of deep primrose silk. She

appeared pleased by the compliment . . . and suspicious too. Typical. "There's something you want?"

Gar stiffled his mother's protest with a glance, and smiled. "Yes, actually," he said, seizing the moment. "Lunch."

"With me?"

"No, with your lap-dog. Of course with you."

Her eyes narrowed. "Why?"

He kept his tone light, though his fingers itched to shake her. "Can't a man ask his sister to lunch without first facing a stern interrogation?"

"Of course he can," said Dana before Fane could answer. "What a lovely idea, Gar. You can make it a picnic. I'll have the kitchen prepare a special basket for you. Would you like chicken, or—"

"My love," said the king, slipping his arm around her shoulders, "I think if we don't turn our attentions to this mysterious chamber at our feet, Durm is going to erupt with impatience."

Dana laughed. "Of course."

Ignoring the calculating looks Fane was shooting him from beneath her carefully lowered lashes, Gar inched a little closer to the edge of the hole and peered downwards. "It looks like a study. Or a library. But what's a library doing here, practically smack bang beneath the Old Palace kitchens? Beneath *anything*?"

"You're the historian of the family," said his father. "You don't recall any mention in palace archives about this study or library or whatever it may be?"

"No," said Gar after a moment's furious thought. "Nothing comes to mind."

"Don't you think it's strange," Fane said suddenly,

"that despite this enormous hole in the ground there's no rubble or dirt down there? Or in the courtyard. At least, nothing that looks fresh."

"I wonder," Dana said slowly. Moving sideways to the nearest stretch of courtyard wall she picked up an ancient, moss-covered lump of rock. Took aim and tossed it at the hole in the ground. There was a vicious crack of sound, a flash of brilliant blue light and a noxious puff of smoke as the stone exploded.

"A shield," said Durm, his eyes glittering. "Barl's eye-teeth, the chamber has a *shield*."

For once, Dana made no complaint about swearing.

Borne stared at his Master Magician. "Why would a library needed shielding?"

"It's obvious," said Fane. "Because it isn't an ordinary library." She was lit up from within, on fire with excitement. "Papa, Durm—do you know what this is? Do you realize what we've found?"

Gar sighed. "Fane . . . no. I'm sorry, but it can't be."

She turned on him. "Why not?"

Helplessly he looked at her. For all her powers she was still a child, and subject to a child's flights of fancy. The last thing he wanted to do was hurt her, but . . . "Because the idea is nothing more than romantic nonsense," he said as kindly as he could. "A fairy tale. At best it's completely unsubstantiated rumor. There's no proof, none at all, that Barl's so-called 'lost library' ever existed."

"It wouldn't matter to you even if there was proof," his sister retorted. "What use would a library filled with arcane magical texts be to you? For all we know you've come across hundreds of references and you've ignored every one of them because either you don't care or you couldn't understand what they meant. Both, probably."

Gar took a deep breath and kept his tone reasonable. Academic. Adult. "Fane, I know what this means to you. I know you want it to be true. You've been fascinated with Barl and Morgan and the doom of the Doranen ever since you were a little girl and I used to read you your bedtime story. But no documents from the time of the Great Flight or the Arrival have survived to the present day. All we've got are oral accounts, recorded years after the fact. A friend of a friend of a friend of a servant who used to clean Barl's boots told me. That kind of thing. We don't know that Barl left behind so much as a note for the kitchen, let alone books of ancient and powerful spells. Certainly not a whole library's worth of them."

Fane pointed at their feet. Her face was flushed with temper. "You don't call that proof?"

"I call it a hole in the ground. Beyond that we don't know anything."

"Nor will we," said Durm sharply, "until we enter the chamber itself and make a thorough examination of its contents."

Borne nodded. "Exactly. My love . . ." He turned to Dana. "You've a knack for finding things. Would you care to nose out the way into this mysterious library for us?"

The queen lowered her unhappy gaze from Gar and Fane to the breached courtyard. Sadness gave way to a sense of purpose. "I can certainly try." She managed a small smile. "No promises, mind." Stretching out her palm, she closed her eyes and whispered under her

breath. The air above her hand quivered. Thickened. Coalesced into a small orange ball of energy.

For a moment the questor hovered there, like a hunting
dog uncertain of the scent. Then it leapt upwards,
swooped over the hole at their feet, circling, buzzing like
a bee—and darted through the main door opening onto
the kitchen courtyard.

"After it!" Borne cried.

Acrimony forgotten, they hurtled in pursuit.

The queen's questor led them through deserted
kitchens, along dusty corridors and down rickety staircases. After a few minutes Durm conjured glimfire to
light their way. On and on they hurried until they reached
an enormous echoing meat larder where once, years and
years before, whole sides of beef and mutton and venison, plucked pheasants, ducks, geese, swans and pea-
cocks had hung from polished hooks dangling from the
ceiling. The hooks remained, tarnished and dulled by age.

"Oh no! It's lost!" Fane cried, almost stamping her
foot with frustration as the orange ball bumped blindly
along the larder's far wall, humming faintly.

"Wait," said Durm, hand lifted.

With a triumphant chime, the questor plunged
through what appeared to be solid whitewashed bricks
and disappeared.

Fane rushed to spread her palms flat to the old, cold
stone. "No! Durm, do something!"

"I have a better idea," the Master Magician suggested.
"You do something. Unlock for us the key to this hidden
door."

"But I . . ." Fane began. Glanced at Gar, then nodded,
her expression hardening. "All right. I will."

Fingertips lightly searching, she explored the section of wall where her mother's seeking spell had disappeared. Lightly frowning, lips pursed and eyes closed, she teased at the stonework.

Gar, watching, felt a familiar stab under his rib cage. When I'm fifty, he thought, despairing, will I still be jealous? Will I never outgrow this useless, unspeakable resentment?

As though reading his son's mind Borne rested a hand on Gar's shoulder and squeezed. Gar smiled at him, a brief, wry quirk of lip, self-mocking. Borne's answering smile was approving, his raised eyebrow a compliment, of sorts.

"I think I have it," Fane murmured indistinctly, with her cheek pressed hard against the stone. "It's a masking incantation all right. So old. So faint. Like a song carried on the breeze over distant water. If it was just a little louder, I could sing it . . ."

Dana was frowning. "Durm, you do this. Please. She's still not fully recovered from her first WeatherWorking, and unravelling another magician's lock-and-key spell is hardly—"

"I'm fine, Mama," said Fane, opening her eyes. "Stop fussing. Anyway, this spell is so old it's practically non-existent. I just need to—ah. There." She stepped back. Struck the wall above her head three sharp blows. "*Impassata*."

The stone rippled. Melted away, to reveal a door-shaped space.

"Well done," Durm said quietly. He turned to the king. "Indulge me, Borne. It may not be safe beyond this portal. Let me take the lead."

"You are far less expendable than I," Borne objected.

Dana took his arm. "Let him."

"My love . . ."

"*Let him.*"

Borne sighed and waved an inviting arm. "Very well then, Master Magician Durm: lead on."

Conjuring fresh glimfire, tossing it into the air, Durm stepped through the unbarred doorway and into the unknown.

CHAPTER TWENTY-FIVE

There was a narrow passageway beyond the meat larder, hung with old cobwebs and starved of clean air. Sneezing, breathing heavily, Gar and his family followed Durm along it. The glimfire illuminating the gloom cast elongated eldritch shadows on the floor and up the walls.

"There," said Durm at last. He pointed. "The questor, do you see it?"

The little ball of orange light hovered further along the passageway, glowing faintly. "What's it found?" said Fane, peering.

With a wave of his finger Durm increased the power of the glimlight. "A door," he said. He nodded at Dana. "My compliments. Your Majesty. We appear to have reached our destination."

Warily, they approached the end of the passageway.

The door barring their progress seemed to be made from solid wood. The dark timber was intricately carved in patterns alien to their eyes. In its center was a seal of faded crimson wax, shot through with green and blue and fashioned into a complicated woven knot. It shimmered in the glimlit air.

"A ward," said Durm, and looked at Dana. "Your Majesty?"

With a snap of her fingers she sent the seeker spell forward, encouraging it to travel through the carved door. The moment it touched the timber the questor exploded in a shower of sparks.

"So," said Borne. He glanced at Durm, eyebrows lifting, and together they stepped up to the door. "The rest of you stay well back," he added over his shoulder. "Any ward that can survive untold centuries and retain any level of potency at all is not to be trifled with."

"Then pray do not trifle," said Dana tartly. "Explaining an exploded king to his kingdom may prove somewhat awkward."

Borne grinned. "Yes, my love."

In cautious unison he and Durm stretched out their hands to the knot of wax centerd on the door. "Can you feel the skill, Borne? Magnificent," the Master Magician murmured. "A work of genius."

"But weakened, yes?" breathed Borne.

Durm nodded. "Yes. Weakened enough to break, I think. Not easily. Not without danger. But it can be broken."

They lowered their hands, stepped back a pace and soberly regarded each other. "The fashioning of that seal," said Borne. "Do you recognize it?"

"I do," said Fane, shrugging aside her mother's restraining hand and crowding forward. "It's Barl's." She spared Gar a look. "That *is* on record. In the *Magia Majestica*. Durm showed it to me." Then, her attention back on the door and her father, she said, "I was right, wasn't I?" She was quivering. "This is Barl's lost library."

"I concede," Borne replied after a pause, "that the door appears to have been sealed by Barl. Beyond that we don't know."

"And we won't until we get in there and look," she replied. "I could do it. I could break the seal. Can I?"

"No!" Borne and Durm spoke together, a single peal of thunder. Borne continued, "Be silent a moment, Fane. I need to think."

"She's right, Borne," Durm said. "We must know what lies beyond this door."

"Must we?" Borne pressed his fingers to his temples as though his head were aching. "Think, Durm. Think what this might mean, if . . . if fantasy were to become fact. If we have indeed found Barl's lost library."

"It could mean the discovery of a lifetime." Durm's eyes were fevered. "After six long centuries we could bridge the gap between ourselves and our ancestors. Once we Doranen were a proud and mighty race of warrior mages. But what are we today? To what ends do we employ our skills? Plumbing. Glimfire. Bookbinding." The contempt in his voice was searing. "We open doors. Close windows. Bloom pretty flowers and keep our clothes clean without soap and water. Domestic comforts and rustic pursuits are our purview now. WeatherWorking aside, that is the length and breadth of our magic. Yet our ancestors had knowledge of spells and incantations that we, pale reflections of their former glory, can only dream of!"

Slowly, Borne nodded. "My friend, that's what frightens me."

"Frightens, Borne?" Durm shook his head. "Why?"

Borne stared. "How can you ask me that? Barl and our ancestors faced a mage war of such cruel violence it was either flee into the bitter unknown or face destruction. That is what might await us beyond this door. After six hundred years of peace, would you loose such evil upon our people again?"

Durm frowned. "You know me better than that."

"I thought I did."

"Majesty . . ." Durm sighed. "Forgive me. In truth, it's most unlikely that this chamber contains books of arcane lore. I fear that great knowledge is long lost to us. But I beg you to consider this. If it is not lost, if we have indeed discovered a buried treasure trove of ancient Doranen magic . . . can you truly contemplate not unburying it?"

"To keep my kingdom safe?" Borne's eyes were stark, haunted. "I'd burn it."

As his father and his father's best friend stared at each other like strangers, Gar cleared his throat. "But, sir . . . what of our history?"

"Our history, Gar, as you damn well know, is blood and terror and exile!" Borne replied. "We came to this land in desperation and in desperation we conquered it. Only Barl's great sacrifice and the willing aid of the Olken people have kept us safe since then. This kingdom's prosperity owes everything to the partnership of mutual trust and obligation between its two peoples. I will not be the one who teaches the meaning of desperation to the descendants of those first Doranen and the Olken who joined with them to make a better world for all."

"But, Papa, nobody's asking you to!" said Fane. "All we're asking for is the chance to see what's behind that door!"

"Borne, dear friend," said Durm. "Your love for this kingdom and its peoples is beyond question. And so, I had thought, is my love for you. Let us cease this profit-less speculation and instead uncover the truth. If we find anything you mislike, anything at all, we can destroy it."

Borne stared at him searchingly. "You could do that?"

Chin lifted, shoulders braced, Durm nodded. "If you told me to, yes. I could. I would. You are my king. I live to serve you, and your kingdom." Stepping close, he rested one hand on the king's shoulder. "Borne. All our long lives have you trusted me. Tell me now, and tell me truly: have I ever failed you?"

Borne shook his head. "Never."

"Then please. I entreat you. Trust me now."

Borne looked at the queen. "My love?"

Dana was pale. "I think we must. Even if you buried this place again and swore us all to silence, who can say how long it would remain secret a second time? And if in the future it was discovered again . . . by someone less scrupulous than you . . . who knows what might happen? For better or worse, we are here now. I think we must act."

Borne took a deep breath and let it escape, harshly. Looked at Durm. "Very well," he said, voice and face grim. "Breach the chamber, Master Magician."

Durm bowed. "Majesty."

Borne glanced at his family. "The rest of you stand well back."

Dana reached for his sleeve and tugged. "And you."

For a moment Gar thought his father might argue. Then the king sighed, and nodded, and urged them all away from Durm and the sealed door.

In the flickering light Durm's expression was grave.

Facing the wooden door he spread his hands wide above the ancient wax seal, tipped his head back, closed his eyes, and sank into a deep meditation.

Gar glanced at his father. Borne looked calm enough, but there was doubt in the droop of his eyelids, and disciplined fear in the tightness of his lips. He reached out a hand and brushed his fingertips against his father's forearm.

"Even if your worst fears are realized and we do find books of magic in there," he said, keeping his voice low, "the danger is remote. Until they're spoken, spells and enchantments are nothing but words on paper."

Borne nodded. "I know. But even so . . ."

"I am ready," Durm announced. "Go further back, all of you. This ward may be breakable but there yet remains enough power to crisp the hair on all your heads, or worse."

"Be careful, Durm," said Borne, shepherding his family to safety.

"And when, old friend, have you ever known me to be otherwise?" Durm raised his right hand and waved it over the seal from left to right, then traced an intricate sigil in the air with his right forefinger. A twisted thread of green glowed briefly in midair, then faded. With his left hand he waved from right to left, and with his left forefinger traced the empty air. A blue thread glowed and died. Three more times to left and right he unwove the seal's bindings, until the faded red wax was untouched by other colors. "There," he said, as the last glow of blue died. "So much for the peripheral wards. Now for the heart ward."

He raised both hands and spread them over the dull red seal of wax. Shoulders hunched with concentration, head tilted forward, he began to breathe heavily, groaning. A thin keening, faint at first, then gaining in strength, reverberated in the musty air.

"Stay here," said Dana as Fane tried to wriggle free of her mother's restraining arm.

"But how can I see what he's doing from way back here?" Fane argued. "If I can just get—"

Borne took her other arm. "Be quiet. Is this a parlor trick for your idle amusement? Hold your tongue and don't distract him. He risks his life for all of us."

Chastened, Fane fell silent.

The keening was loud enough to be painful, drumming against their ears, driving iron nails into their heads. Higher it rose, louder and more shrill. From the seal pulsed a vibrant red light; Durm became a silhouette of fire. He was shuddering.

Then, with a blazing flash of heat, amidst a shriek of surrender from the wax and a cry of agonized triumph from Durm, the ward exploded.

The air in the sealed library smelled peculiar. Faded. Stretched. It tickled Durm's nose and his throat. He stiffled a cough and stared around the chamber as the others spread out, exclaiming. The room was larger than he'd imagined, and every square foot of it was crammed with laden bookshelves. Taller than Borne, they marched in rows, formed little alcoves, lined every available inch of wall. Squashed to the side of the crowded room was a desk with three drawers and a lumpily padded chair. On the face of it, an unremarkable place . . . especially when one considered the remarkable nature of that ward.

Durm fought a shiver. His teeth were still vibrating

from its residual power and his skin felt lightly scorched. On the whole, an unpleasant experience.

But worth it.

I have broken Barl's Seal. The Seal of Blessed Barl herself, greatest magician in the history of Dorana.

And I broke it.

"Are you sure you're all right?" the king asked, turning back to him. "The residual power in that ward was . . . well, I can scarcely believe it, and I saw it with my own eyes. I can't imagine what it felt like."

No, Borne, you couldn't. He waved a deprecating hand. "I'm fine, Your Majesty."

"Are you certain of that?"

"I admit to a moment of discomfort, but only a moment, and it passed swiftly." Unlike the triumph, which would last a lifetime.

"You never cease to impress me," Borne said, shaking his head. Then his smile faded. "Durm—you know it was never a matter of not trusting you."

Dear Borne. A good man, right to the marrow of his thinning bones. Racked always with cares and concerns and a duty that overwhelmed his strength. Haunted by the ghosts of old decisions. Forever doubting. "I know," he replied. Just as he knew, with sorrow, that in this matter, where the king's judgement was concerned, trust was something in short supply. Kings came, and kings went, but magic . . . magic lived forever. And it was up to the kingdom's Master Mage, keeper of the *Magia Majestica*, guardian of the Weather Orb, to ensure it. To give his or her life, if necessary, to its jealous preservation.

So Borne would burn Barl's books of magic, would he?

Over my dead body, old friend. Over my dead and rotting body.

"It's incredible!" the queen exclaimed, running hesitant fingers along the spines of the books before her. "As though the door were closed on them only yesterday. There's been a strong preserving spell cast here. Can you feel it?" She glanced at him. "But I think it's fading, Durm, don't you?"

He shut his eyes and stretched out with that part of his mind concerned with all things magical. Felt the weft and the warp of the incantation. Where it held, and where it was threadbare and unravelling. "Yes," he agreed, as he marveled at the power of an enchantment that could last more than half a millennium. Let there be spells here, oh, let there be spells. We have labored too long in ignorance. "I shall cast another before we leave, to be certain nothing here can be damaged."

"Yes, you must," said Gar, horrified. "This place, these books, are a find of monumental significance. Whatever we need not destroy must be protected."

Borne stared at the gaping hole in the ceiling. The spilling sunlight cast his fever-wasted features into sharp relief. For all his remarkable recovery, still he had meager strength. Durm watched him marvel at the feat of magic used to keep the chamber hidden for so long, and felt a flood of affection. He needs me now more than ever before, to ease his burden. To make the difficult decisions for him. That terrible illness has cost him dearly. He is lost in a wilderness and cannot see the way. But I can. I can.

"We've some six hours before I must go up to the Weather Chamber," Borne said. "Let's see what we can find in that time, hmm?"

Ever headstrong, Fane objected. "I don't see why we should stop exploring just because you're called to the night's WeatherWorking, Papa."

"Because I wish it. Fane . . ." Borne softened his tone. "This library cannot become an obsession. I have duties. You have your studies. Six hours is a long time. Do you really want to waste them in argument?"

"But, Papa, even with four of us we won't be able to check every last book today. There must be hundreds! Why don't we send for help? Lord Jarralt, or—"

"*No!*" Borne took his daughter's chin between his fingers and tilted her face upwards. Blazed his eyes into hers. "There will be no discussion of this place or what we find in it, is that clear? Not until I'm sure it's safe. Not until I know precisely what we've found."

Fane jerked her chin free. "But the Privy Council—"

"Answers to me," Borne said. "Not I to it. I bear the ultimate responsibility here, Fane. The final authority is mine."

"Father's right," Gar told her. "The last thing we need is politics complicating matters."

With an ease perfected by years of practice, Durm hid his contempt. As though a cripple's opinion were relevant, or required. He was here on sufferance, nothing more.

"Come," said the queen, and touched her daughter lightly on the shoulder. "We can work along this shelf together."

"Trust me, Fane," Borne said, and kissed her forehead. "I know I'm only your father, but I do know what I'm doing, truly."

She looked to him, then. To her beloved mentor, Durm. Just the smallest flick of her eyes and the merest twitch of one eyebrow. His precious Fane. The child of his heart, the daughter of his mind and magic. A perfect blending of her parents, yet molded in his image. Trained and tutored and steeped in the ways of enchantment, the lore of *Magia Majestica*. Soon she would be a queen unsurpassed in the history of Lur. In the history of all magical kingdoms, wherever they might be. If any existed beyond the Wall.

He nodded at her, frowning lightly, and she sighed. Pulled a face at her blood-and-bone father. "All right," she answered both of them. "If you say so. But let's get *on* then! Time's wasting!"

Again they separated, each taking a different direction. Gar pulled a book from a shelf above his head and opened it. "It's written in the Old Tongue. Pure as the day Barl came over the mountains."

Fane glanced over her shoulder. "Can you read it?"

He gave her a dark look. "Yes."

"Well, then, what does it say?"

Give the cripple his due, he was an excellent scholar with a talent for language and history. He'd even made a study of the original Olken tongue, though why anyone would bother Durm couldn't fathom. Such endeavours doubtless endeared him to the likes of that repellent Asher, of course, and the native populace in general. Made him feel . . . important. Lacking magic, doubtless he needed something to fill the void. It was a harmless enough pursuit and it made Borne and the queen happy. For himself he didn't much care, really. Once the boy's impediment had been identified, the prince had ceased to be of the least interest to him.

Gar was frowning over the book's first few pages.

"The print is very small," he muttered. "A Doranen type-face I've never seen before . . ."

"You can't read it," said Fane, and turned away.

"I think it's a story," he said, and turned more pages. "I think it's—it's a *romance*." He laughed.

"What?" Fane cried. Took three steps to join him, reached out and plucked the book from his unresisting fingers. "It can't be. You're making it up. Papa, tell him to take this seriously!"

"Let me see," said Dana, and looked for herself. "Well, I'm nowhere near as accomplished as Gar in reading Old Tongue but I think he might be right. Never mind. I was wanting something new to read and I've always been par-tial to romance. This will make a nice change from Vev Gertsik. I find her a trifle florid, I'm afraid."

"Stop fretting, Fane," Borne advised. "And keep searching. If you find anything of a less frivolous nature I suggest you put it on the table there so we can look at it more carefully in due course."

"Huh," said Fane. "*Romance*." Complaining under her breath, she turned back to the bookshelves.

A muttering silence fell as they began to search the shelves in earnest. Gradually the pile of books on the table grew as they each found something to spark interest or excitement.

For himself, Durm was circumspect. Closing his senses to the brief laughter, the exclamations of triumph, the cries of wonder, he quested silent and single-minded for his heart's desire. To maintain appearances he chose volumes at random and added them to the collection on the table. Histories. Fairy tales. Folklore. Of a certain in-terest, to be sure, but of little value compared with the treasure he sought. That he *knew* must be here some-where. *Nobody* sealed a room for six centuries to protect fairy tales. Certainly not a magician like Barl.

Fane balanced her latest find on a crowded corner of the table and pouted. "No magical treatises yet," she said sadly. "And it's been nearly three hours."

"There are still a lot of shelves to investigate," the queen consoled her. "You mustn't be so easily discouraged."

Fane slumped onto the chair with a disconsolate sigh. "But what if we don't find *anything* useful?"

Gar laughed. "Only you could be so short-sighted, Fane. Most of these books in some way or another deal with the original Dorana. The land of our ancestors. Our home, in a way."

"I couldn't care less about what happened six centuries ago in a country that probably doesn't exist any more," she retorted. "The only place that matters now is Lur. And the only thing that matters is finding a book that tells us more about the enchantments our ancestors knew. The ones we've lost. The ones we never knew existed. Durm's right," she added, and glanced at him, bestowing approval. "That's our true heritage. The only heritage that counts. Not that you'd understand." To emphasise her point, she pulled out the desk's top drawer and banged it shut again, hard.

Something inside the drawer rattled. Rolled. Curious, she slid it open again and put her hand inside. When she pulled it out her fingers were clasped tight about some-thing clear and round and the size of an orange.

Gar, tight-lipped and smarting—though she'd only spoken the truth and it was past time he accepted the facts and stopped spitting in the wind—put aside the book he held. "What's that?"

"I don't know," she said, and unfurled her fingers. "A portrait."

Another tedious squabble averted. Borne and the queen exchanged relieved glances and joined their children around the table. Dana caught a proper look at the sphere, and her face contracted in disgust. "Barl's mercy! Get rid of it, Fane. Put it back in the drawer."

Fane ignored her. Instead lifted the sphere until it was level with her eyes and stared intently at the face contained within it. A coldly handsome face, it was, with ice-blue eyes and hair so pale it looked silver. Extravagant cheekbones. Imperious nose. Lips too full and sensuous for a man.

"It's *him,* isn't it?" she breathed. "Morgan. Morg. I always wondered what he looked like."

"Heed your mother," Borne said harshly. "Put it away. Better yet, destroy it. He was a monster."

"No!" said Fane, and curved her hands protectively around the sphere and the face within it. "It's only a portrait, it can't hurt anybody. It must have been Barl's. She must have kept it. Why would she keep it if there was any danger?" She loosened her grip and stared again at the haughty face of evil. "He was so handsome. None of the history books ever mentioned he was handsome."

With a cry of revulsion Borne pulled her round to face him. "What does that signify? Fair of face he may have been but he was even fouler of heart, which is all that matters! Barl *died* to keep this kingdom safe from him, and for six hundred years the kings and queens of Lur have spent their lives ensuring her sacrifice was not in vain. I have spent my life upholding that sacred trust. My *life,* Fane. And next it will be your turn to stand alone in the Weather Chamber with the weight of the Wall crushing your bones to powder. To spend your life in Barl's service in the full knowledge that if you fail you condemn a kingdom to catastrophe. All because of *him*. Because of Morg. You know this. You *know* this. And yet you can sit there and simper and say he was *handsome*?"

As Fane shrank before the king's outrage, pale and brimming with tears, he wrenched the sphere from her loosened clasp and hurled it at the shielded ceiling.

In light and in sound, the sphere vanished.

The queen caught Borne's trembling hands between her own, carried them to her lips and kissed them. "She meant no harm, my love. She doesn't understand yet. How can she?"

"She's not a child any longer!" Borne retorted, and pulled his hands free. "She is the WeatherWorker-in-Waiting, and childhood is yesterday's dream. Durm! What say you to this? I thought you had taught her more than just the right words in the right order at the right time!"

The rebuke, although unjustified, was expected. Pain and fear had made Borne short-tempered of late. Clasping his hands behind his back Durm offered the king a shallow bow. "Majesty. You are right, of course. But while it is true that Morg, in his dedication to dark magics and his unquenchable quest for power, split asunder our ancestral land and drove our forbears into exile and suffering, he was also Morgan, the beloved of our beloved Barl. Perhaps it's not such a bad thing that Her Highness reminds us of that. Certainly it serves to show just how great was her sacrifice, and how even love cannot overcome all."

"We must agree to disagree about love," the queen

said, reaching again for Borne's hand, "but as for the rest
. . . you make your point, Durm."

As always, Borne's anger died as quickly as it ignited.
He put a contrite arm about Fane's shoulders and held her
tightly. "Forgive me, daughter. Illness has left me out of
sorts. I know you meant no harm. But think on what I said
and you'll discover that I am right."

"I know you are," Fane replied, still shaken. "All I
meant was that it's sad. She loved him but she had to run
away to be safe from him. And then she had to die, to
make sure."

"Yes," said Borne. "Yes. It is sad."

"Do you think he ever loved her?" asked Fane. "Really? Truly?"

Borne shook his head. "I don't know."

Gently, the queen said, "It's likely that he did. Once.
Before his soul was warped by the black magics he embraced. You see, my darling Fane, even the purest heart
cannot withstand such evil. Magic isn't always benevolent and kind."

Durm had to bite his lip and turn away at that. Such
sentimental drivel! She and Borne were as bad as each
other. Magic was a tool, nothing more. It served whatever
purpose its wielder decreed and was no more benevolent
or evil than . . . than . . . a chair!

With a strained smile Borne said, "Come. Let's keep
looking. I admit, though I know you're disappointed,
Fane, I find the failure to discover any magical treatises
encouraging. Not all knowledge is a blessing."

And there, sad to say, was the difference between them
laid bare as bones. There could be no meeting of minds
and hearts in this matter. With that simple declaration

Borne showed himself to be unfit, as a mage, to caretake the secrets Barl had hidden somewhere in her lost library.

Fear not, brave lady. I shall find your books of magics and protect them from the well-meaning blunders of my friend. Our heritage will be saved, I swear on my oath as Master Magician.

He returned to the search, and an hour later was rewarded.

It was some strange, unrecognized instinct that drove him into the rib-crushingly small alcove tucked away in one dark corner of the library. A tickle in the mind that enticed, beckoned. Sang with promise and set his heart to racing. Startled, he glanced at Borne, the queen, Fane. Were they suddenly deaf and numbed, then, as crippled as the prince, that they did not feel it? How could that be? It was a mystery . . .

Or was it? Perhaps this was meant. Perhaps this was a simple case of one Master Magician speaking across the centuries to another. Perhaps he was the only one capable of sensing the presence of such spells. Borne was a powerful magician, but his talents had been trained to the weather, shaped and fashioned for a single purpose. Other buds, other shoots, had been ruthlessly pruned years ago. The queen, well, she had talent enough but used it for womanly pursuits only. Hers was a decorous and dainty application of magic. And Fane, for all she burned bright with a raw power unseen for generations, she was still a student. Inexperienced. Her palate had potential, yes, but was yet too broad for subtle flavors.

So Barl's magic sang for him, and him alone.

Unhurried, maintaining his air of scholarly distraction, he eased himself into the small, book-lined space and conjured glimfire to banish the shadows. The light danced along the spines of leather-bound journals pressed cover to cover in the awkward alcove. He trailed his fingers along them and felt the magic sizzle beneath his skin.

Somewhere in here . . . somewhere . . .

Finding the book was like kissing a lightning bolt. He bit his lip to blood to stop from crying out.

It was a slender volume. Cloth-bound, and tucked between the pages of some obscure text on falconry. Trembling, he freed it from captivity and opened the cover. A diary. Handwritten, the ink faded but legible, a collection of notes, a recitation of deeds accomplished, and yes! oh yes! a listing of incantations, pages of them, and they were completely new, had never been heard of before in this kingdom. And all in a handwriting he knew so well, from the WeatherWorking notes and strictures she'd left behind.

This was Barl's diary. These were her secrets. This was what had called to him.

He could have moaned his excitement out loud.

Beyond the alcove, the prince was saying, "—a lifetime's work, Father. I don't know whether to laugh or cry."

I believe I am familiar with the feeling, boy.

"It's certainly a miraculous collection of books, Gar," Borne agreed. "I must say, given the wide range of subject matter and its relative mundanity, I'm at something of a loss to understand why Barl and her followers made such efforts to take this collection with them when they fled."

"Oh, but Father!" the prince said. "Don't you see? They were trying to preserve an entire civilization. To encapsulate untold centuries of lore and learning in a single haphazard collection of books. It's an extraordinary ambition. When I think of them struggling to decide what to take and what must stay behind . . . it breaks my heart."

Borne laughed. "Spoken like a true historian. And you're right, too, about how much work it will take to properly catalog and translate what's here. It must be done with care, and reverence, and most importantly with an eye to the potential dangers such knowledge carries with it. It's not a task to be awarded lightly."

"No," the prince said, his voice sober. "You're right, of course."

"So when can you begin?" his father added.

"Sir?"

"Yes, Royal Curator? That is, if you'd like to be."

As the prince stammered his delight, his surprise, his protestations of faithful duty, and the queen laughed, and the king laughed too, which was good to hear, and Fane muttered sarcasms under her breath, he held Barl's diary in his trembling hands and gave thanks.

"Durm!" the king called, and stood behind him. "The afternoon fades and WeatherWorking time draws near. We should go."

Half turning his head, keeping the diary hidden close against his chest, Durm said, "By all means, Majesty, you go. I am happy to stay working unaccompanied."

"I know," Borne said affectionately. "Given the chance you'd work yourself to a collapse searching for anything remotely magical. I'd rather you didn't. Aside from the deleterious effect on your health, I'd prefer we didn't draw any more attention to this place than is absolutely necessary. Besides, there's always tomorrow."

Argument, however mild, was too dangerous. "That's true," he agreed.

"We'll leave the place warded. It'll be safe enough. And tomorrow we'll finish what we've begun, then decide what next to do." With a glance that encompassed them all, Borne added, "Apart from ourselves, the only person who knows of this place is the servant who discovered the breach in the courtyard. When she told me what she'd found I commanded her to hold her tongue. Tonight I shall fuddle her to make sure she loses all recollection of her little adventure. This library *must* remain a secret. Not a word is to be said to anybody. Is that understood?"

The others nodded and murmured obedience. "As you say, Majesty," Durm agreed again, and slipped Barl's diary inside his robe where it could lie against his ribs, hidden and protected. He loved Borne like a brother but that didn't blind him to the sober truth: the king could not be trusted with this discovery. Not tonight. Perhaps not ever. The thought pained him . . . but never before in his life had pain stood in the way of duty. Nor would it now.

"Durm?" said Fane as she stood back to allow him and her parents to lead the way out of the library. "Is everything all right?"

He smiled at her, Barl's diary a warm and promising weight against his skin. "Foolish girl," he said, and shook his head indulgently. "Of course it is."

CHAPTER TWENTY-SIX

Much later that night, after dinner, having eased Borne down from his WeatherWorking jitters and wrapped him safe in a robe before a roaring fire, with the rest of the palace retired to bed and only a handful of servants scurrying like mice about the corridors, Durm locked himself into his private study and opened Barl's diary.

The book-lined room was hushed. A modest fire crackled in the hearth, scenting the warm air with the spicy freshness of pine. Candles scattered shadows. He'd left one window uncurtained; the glow of Barl's Wall splashed prismed gold light on the carpet as it filtered through Borne's soft rain and the thin glass panes.

Comfortable in robe and slippers, a tankard of mulled wine by his side and his belly groaning pleasurably with food, he crossed his ankles on a hassock, propped his elbows on the arms of his chair and held the book as tenderly as he would a lover, had there ever been one.

"Speak to me, brave lady," he breathed, and began to read.

*   *   *

Hours later, he stirred. The candles were burned down almost to their sockets. The fire had dwindled to ash and cinders. His half-drunk wine sat cold in the tankard, and the remnants of Borne's rain barely trickled down the windowpanes.

"Barl save us," he said aloud; the sound of his voice was a startlement.

The contents of the diary were . . . unspeakable. Borne had been right about one thing: were it to fall into the wrong hands the potential for catastrophe was limitless. Appalling. All their lost powers, in one slim, innocent-seeming volume. Spells of war. Spells of enslavement. Incantations to sear the guarded truth from a captive's mind. Enchantments to suck a soul from its body and trap it for all time in crystal. Summonings to bring forth beasts the like of which he'd never imagined could exist as flesh and blood: dragons, horslirs, trolls, werehags. Incantations of death and destruction that would see Lur laid waste within hours. She had even recorded the most terrible words of all, the words of UnMaking, designed to unknit a man's flesh from bone and undo his place in the world as though he had never been. A desperate spell that would undo the speaker, as well as his victim. Until this moment that incantation had been mere myth. Passed down in secret whispers from Master Magician to Master Magician and never spoken of beneath an open sky. What breed of magician could labor to bring forth such horrors? What man could bend his gifts to birth such monstrosities? Would want to?

Morg.

Praise Barl he was dead then, his like never to be seen again.

The diary wasn't all horror, though. Threaded through the incantations of insanity were more useful applications of magic. Ways of translocating animate matter. Methods of transmuting base metals to gold. Tricks of transcendence. Devices of enhancement.

And a way to see beyond the Wall.

In the Old Tongue, Barl had written:

> So it falls to me, as I knew it would, to keep this place safe for all time. I have made a beginning, with the banishment of all dark and greedy magics from my people's hearts and minds, but that is not enough. There is still Morgan. His shadow has not touched us yet but I fear it will come, sooner rather than later, and only I can prevent it. There is a way. I believe the natural harmonies in this land, combined with our more militant magics, can be fused into a barrier that will never be breached, so long as it is nurtured most diligently and forevermore. Using some new magics that I have devised I will anchor this Wall in the mountains and a reef around the coastline. Sink its strength into the bowels of the world and feed it daily with the weather magic I will create. I will make this place a paradise, so that our children need cry out in fearful dreams no more.

Rereading the hastily scrawled entry Durm felt unexpected tears prick his eyes. The heart of her. The passion, and the courage. The *mastery*. She was the last of the great magicians, the last to create new magic out of old. For six centuries the Master Magicians of Lur had followed the strictest guidelines, first and most sacred of which being *No new magic*. It was too dangerous. New magic, untried and untested, might disturb the precarious balance between the Weather and the Wall. Might bring it down and so unleash chaos. In the early days, according to judicial records, certain magicians had thought the rule did not apply to them.

Their deaths had been slow and spectacular and were recited into memory and repeated in a litany unto this very day by the new generation of Doranen magicians in their schoolrooms.

No new magic.

He agreed with the rule, of course he did. But sometimes he dreamed, he wondered, of what freedom would be like. To experiment. To risk. To create that which had never before existed. To be another Barl. But for that he would need to stand on soil that was not of Lur.

Mouth dry, heart tolling like the Great Bell on Barlsday, he opened the diary again and continued to read what she had written.

But while a locked room is safe, without a key it is also a trap. So I have fashioned one and in time I will use it to open a window in the Wall, that I may see what has become of the world beyond. And if it be safe, then we will go home. I swear it, I swear it on my life. One day we will all go home.

"Poor Lady!" he cried to the glowing barrier beyond his window. "You didn't know the making of your Wall would kill you!"

Home. Somewhere out there, beyond the mountains, lay home, Dorana, the birthplace of their race. Their true cradle. Somewhere beyond the mountains there was a land where magic flourished, where incantation was an artform and not a survival mechanism or a toy, where great men could labor their lives in its mysteries, untrammelled by rules and dire punishments in the breaking of them.

And in his hands, his trembling hands, he held a way to find it.

Six centuries ago Morgan, become Morg, had plunged his people into bloody war. He was dead now, dust and ashes on the wind. A frightful phantom, a legacy well remembered, a lesson never to be unlearned. But he was dead. And the living cried out to be set free.

Hesitantly he turned to the next page of the diary, and looked at the sigils and syllables of the incantation that would allow him the first glimpse beyond the Wall in more than six centuries.

If I tell Borne of this, he will say no. He will burn this book for fear of what might be. The crown has clipped his wings. For him the sky is forever out of reach.

For him. But not for me.

And when it is done and we stand atop the mountains and survey the world made new, he will know I did the right thing, and thank me.

With the spell committed to memory Durm stood in the middle of his study. Prepared to start the incantation—and hesitated.

What he was about to do was extremely dangerous, even for a magician of his talent and experience. There was a chance . . . a small, slim, unlikely chance . . . that something might go wrong. And if it did, and his study's sanctum was invaded by strangers, or even friends, they would discover Barl's diary.

Which would be a disaster, for many reasons.

His study was full of books. He selected one remarkable for its age and loosened, misshapen leather binding, summoned a narrow-bladed dagger from its drawer and carefully unpicked the back cover's stitching. Slid Barl's slender diary between leather and backing, conjured a needle and painstakingly stitched it whole again.

There. Should worse come to worst, nobody would suspect the book had been tampered with. No magical residue would adhere, and there was no sign of fresh stitching. Barl's secret diary would remain a secret.

Misgivings allayed, he put the book back on its shelf and returned to the business of making history.

Raising his left hand, he traced the first sigil in the warm air. Trailing fire, burning with promise, it hung before his face, waiting. And so, turning half a pace to the left, the second sigil. Another half-pace, and then the third. All with the left hand. With the right, he traced three more, with a half-pace turn between each so that at the end he stood within a wheel of burning sigils, each and every one foreign and thrilling to his eye.

Now for the next step.

"Elil'toral!"

In the marrow of his bones and the running of his blood, magic stirred. The sigils bloomed with fresh fire and he felt his skin scorch with the heat.

And the next step.

"*Nen'nonen ra!*"

The sigils quivered. Then, incredibly, began to drift counterclockwise, pirouetting midair like dancers freed from bondage. Slowly at first, then faster, and faster still, until their single shapes were lost and all were a unified burning blur.

And the last.

"*Ma'mun'maht!*"

The spinning wheel of fire snapped in two. Unfurled. Plunged into his chest and transformed him into a living pillar of molten magic. Mouth wide and soundlessly screaming, eyes staring, he glared transfixed at his reflection in the window overlooking the Wall. His bones were melting, his blood boiled, it was pleasure and pain and fear and wonder and power the likes of which he'd never dreamed, never *dreamed* . . .

And then he was streaming out of his body, leaving it behind, an abandoned ramshackle of excess flesh. Riding the arrow of fire he plunged through the windowpane, flew over the City, through the gently dwindling rain, above the fields beyond and the Black Woods at the foot of Barl's Mountains . . . and through the impenetrable Wall as though it were nothing but mist.

It was dark beyond the mountains. A darkness not just of night but of something else as well. Something unseen, yet palpable to his questing mind as it flew over tangled forests and heath-land. In the small distance, lights. Dim. Sallow. But lights, all the same.

With a thought, his arrow of light aimed true towards them and he left Barl's Mountains behind.

A town. Small. Narrow streets, deserted. Iron-barred windows. Doors locked and uninviting. A central marketplace. Wooden gibbets, dangling crow-feasted bodies. Bones gleaming in the sickly moonlight.

What did it mean?

Onwards he flew, his mind seeking, seeking. Somewhere there was fear and a terrible foreboding, but he pushed the feelings aside.

More open countryside. Dispirited trees. Sickly crops. The land looked poisoned. Beaten to its knees. Another town, bigger than the last but shrouded in the same aura of dread.

Something caught his attention. Movement in the empty streets. He swooped closer.

Horror. A patrol of . . . of . . . beasts. Men with the mouths of animals, their eyes black and merciless in their dead white faces. Demons. They carried torches. Set fire to a house. The inhabitants ran screaming, burning. The laughing demons butchered them.

Sickened, he fled the dreadful scene. This could not be all. There was still Dorana, shining bright light in the midst of madness.

More woodland ahead. Thick. Black. Menacing. Out of its creeping darkness a shadow, rising. Man-shaped, with eyes that glowed like the sun and a mouth opened to swallow him alive . . . to swallow the world. It stank of evil incarnate.

Through the whisper-thin link that anchored him to his body he heard himself scream.

The shadow lunged, eyes flaming fire. Words formed in his gibbering mind: *Who are you?*

Terrified to the brink of unreason Durm turned tail and

tled. Away from the woodland. Over the countryside. Over the second township, the first township, flying faster than thought for Barl's Mountains and the Wall and the inviolate safety of home. The magic parted before him and he was through the golden barrier once more, flying over the City rooftops and into his study, back in his body where he belonged.

Housed safely once more in his cage of blood and bone he fell to his knees, retching. Pain windmilled behind his eyes. Shuddering, gasping, he lay on his face, fingers clawed into the carpet, and waited for the world to stop spinning.

At length, when he thought he could trust his legs, he lurched to his feet and stumbled into his little washroom. Splashed water into the basin and sluiced the sweat of fear from, his skin. Slowly, slowly, reason returned. With shaking hands he reached for a towel, blotted the water from his face and looked up to meet his stunned reflection in the mirror.

He wasn't alone.

Behind him stood a man, shadowy and insubstantial, with eyes that glowed like the sun. Coldly handsome, with hair so pale it looked silver. Extravagant cheekbones. Imperious nose. Lips too full and sensuous. The man smiled.

Durm screamed. Turned. Raised a hand in self-defense: to no avail. Morg's shade lunged for him. Was on him. In him. Melted into his flesh like sunlight through snow. Durm's curdling shriek died midbreath. For a single frozen moment he wore two faces: his own, and that of the man stealing his body.

And then time ticked forward . . . and there was but one face in the mirror. Durm's.

But the mind and the soul behind the eyes belonged to Morg.

"Master Durm? Sir? Where would you like the tray put, sir?"

Morg, studying his outstretched hands intently, nodded to the table by the window. "There."

The servant bobbed its head. "Cook said to tell you, sir," it said, uncovering steaming plates and bowls of food and laying them neatly on the blue tablecloth, "we run right out of chinchi eggs so she flipped a couple of bunties instead, seeing as how you like them almost as much, and hope that's right as rain with you."

What was it babbling about? "Yes," he said. "Now get out."

The servant darted him a startled glance. "Yes, sir."

The door clapped shut behind it and he was alone again. Alone with his host . . . and his body.

"I have a body," he marveled to the room at large, and laughed, and laughed, and laughed. And the pleasure of that made him laugh all the more.

Seated at the table, knife and fork held lightly in remembering fingers, he took a deep breath—lungs! I have lungs!—and felt his head swim with the rich aromas. Eggs. Mushrooms. Beef. Gravy. Porridge, with cream and honey. Crusty warm bread soaked in butter. Spiced wine.

Durm ate all this for *breakfast*? No wonder the fool was fat.

Four hundred years had passed since last he'd tasted

food. It was a memory. Less. The memory of a memory, discarded along with all other physical considerations and the inconveniences they entailed. No sacrifice was too great in the service of his higher purpose. So it could not be regret turning down the corners of this borrowed mouth. Could not be longing, remembered. It was the shock of finding himself corporeal once again after so long without flesh or form.

There was no regret. No longing. These emotions were nothing but the taint of the mind that even now gibbered inconsequentially from its cage deep within. Above all else he was an intellect, a necromancer powerful beyond the dreams and imagination of this wittering Durm and the others, the traitorous descendants of treacherous forebears, soon to be returned to the fold.

Soon to be punished.

But until that glorious moment he was also a body. And his body was hungry. Saliva pooled behind his teeth, under his tongue. His belly rumbled. His nostrils flared.

He ate.

The tastes! The textures! Sweet . . . soft . . . runny . . . crunchy . . . it was too much. Too much. After so long, an assault on the senses almost past bearing.

Of course, there were certain drawbacks to being housed within flesh once more. For one he was enslaved to that flesh, was bound by its limitations, would have to tend its needs, dance to its desires—not all of which were as delightful as eating. But no matter. For the short time he'd be lodged here, he could manage.

Of greater concern, but still no serious impediment, the matter of his reach and influence. He knew his own mind. He knew the captive Durm's mind. All others were closed to him. After nearly six centuries of unfettered access to every thought, every whim, every dark dream of the men, women, children and demons in his domain, the stark silence had been, in the first hours of his occupation, distressing. But he was adjusting now to the ringing empty echoes. To the knowledge that in this place his powers were circumscribed. That any attempt to use them, to channel the vast arsenal of magic at his disposal, would melt the meat from Durm's bones and in doing so destroy himself as well.

And that was hardly part of the plan.

It meant he could not afford to be overconfident. He would have to proceed cautiously. Carefully. Housed within this fleshy prison he was, for the first time in centuries, vulnerable. To accident and perhaps more than accident if he raised an unwise suspicion, or misjudged the temperature of a moment.

Not that he rated the danger highly. These feeble halfwit child's-play magicians were so far beneath him he had no need to read their minds to know their hearts. Their capricious faces would tell him everything he required to bring them to their knees before him.

And bring them to their knees he would. Soon he would have the means to chastise these unruly children of Lur. To ripen this sweet plum of a place, that he might pluck it neatly from its nourishing branch and thereafter swallow it whole.

So.

Licking egg-yolk from his fork, he chuckled. Really, this was turning into something of a—now what was the word? Ah yes . . . a holiday.

*   *   *

With his borrowed body bathed and dressed in a fresh robe, he went to the cupboard and withdrew from it an ancient wooden box hasped with silver. Placing it on the table by the window, he sat and considered it. Allowed himself a brief moment of gloating. Deep inside he felt Durm's impotent fingernails, scratching, scratching, desperate to be let out. With a casual swipe of his will he silenced the fat fool and flipped open the box's lid.

Inside, a pearly white globe nestled on a bed of blue velvet. Swirling deep within its heart a flux of colors: gold and green and crimson and purple. One might even call it beautiful, if beauty mattered.

"Barl, Barl, did you truly think you could defeat me? Six years . . . six hundred . . . six thousand . . . you should have known I would never let your treachery go unpunished."

Her fingerprints were all over the thing. Inside it, where the magic dwelled. He could smell them. Taste them. Feel them, like a breeze across his mind, an invisible caress. For six hundred years he had dreamed of confronting her. Vanquishing her. The discovery of the secret to prolonging life and intellect beyond a mere body had been theirs. All these long centuries he'd dreamed of meeting her face to face once more and bringing her to book for her narrow-minded rejection of the greatness he'd planned for both of them.

But even there she had denied him. Spurned their great discovery. Spurned him. Instead of transmuting herself as they'd planned, as they'd promised, she'd squandered her own life in the making of this perfect little kingdom.

In the creation of her damnable Wall, which had held him at bay for longer than any mortal had ever lived.

And in doing so had cheated him, again. Rejected him, again. Defeated him . . .

"Or so you thought, my love. Yet here I am, and here shall I stay, and here will I pull down your Wall and everything behind it you tried so hard to protect."

Ransacking Durm's memories and devising his plan of conquest had been ridiculously simple. The key to the Wall's destruction lay in the magics that held it together, that fed upon themselves and the ordered management of the weather within the kingdom. It was an endless, self-perpetuating cycle: the power of the weather lent power to the magic, just as the strength of the weather helped maintain the invisible bonds that held the Wall inviolate.

Snap one link in the chain and Barl's precious Wall would come tumbling down.

All he had to do was take the Weather Magic into himself, find that one link, the one point that would yield most meekly to his coercion, and then he could just sit back and watch as Barl's defiance unravelled and her defense of this place crumbled. And then he would stretch forth his hand upon the land . . . and his victory would at last be complete.

It had come as something of a surprise to learn that Durm did not possess the Weather Magics. He was their guardian, sworn to the tedious task in an unbroken line from Fuldred, the first Master Mage, appointed by Barl herself. Only the WeatherWorker, and the WeatherWorker-in-Waiting, were permitted to absorb the Weather Magics from the Orb. Not that more people couldn't possess the magic. They just wouldn't. Because Barl told them not to. The idea astounded him. Revolted him. Slaves. These lost Doranen were nothing but slaves who had placed the chains about their minds with their own hands and then had willingly swallowed the key.

Well. Now he would swallow them.

The Weather Magics were absorbed from the Orb intact and self-fulfilling. Whoever had them could immediately use them. Call rain and wind and sunshine and snow, with only a thought. Amazing. Hate her though he might, he conceded that Barl had created a miracle. But even so he would defeat her. After all, he was something of a miracle himself.

With a great surge of satisfaction he removed the Orb from its box. It felt warm, peculiarly alive, all that vibrant, violent magic humming within its fragile shell. Helpless to resist, Durm had given him the words of the Transference spell. He summoned them now. Cupped the Orb in both hands, closed his eyes, spoke them aloud—

—and was thrown across the room in a soundless explosion of heat and light and barrier magic. It seared his mind and scorched his skin and sent his disordered senses reeling. Echoing in his stunned mind, a whispering voice not heard for six hundred years.

No, Morgan. This is not for you. This is never for you. Never . . . never . . . never.

Gasping, retching, he barely made it to Durm's small private privy before he lost his extravagant breakfast down the boghole. From a great distance deep inside he heard the fat fool laughing.

When he was again himself, could stand on steady legs and walk, he returned to the study and stared at the discarded Orb, unsullied, undamaged, unplundered and abandoned on the floor. Barl had anticipated him. Assumed that somehow he would reach this place . . . or at least that he might. And because she knew him as no other body or mind had ever known him, she had devised a way to keep her precious Weather Magics away from him. Safe from him.

A tidal wave of thick red hatred surged within him, robbed him of sight and hearing, clawed his fingers and tore at his throat.

"Bitch! Slut! Treacherous whore! You think this will stop me? You will never stop me! I am Morg! I am invincible and your defeat is a foregone conclusion!"

He picked up the Orb. Put it back in its box. Put the box back in its cupboard, and closed the doors.

So. If he couldn't bring down the Wall this way, he would bring it down in another. In the end the manner of its destruction wasn't important. All that mattered was that he saw it destroyed.

Slumped in a chair, he let his scheming thoughts wander. The key to his victory lay in manipulating the Weather Magics. In using them—their wielder—to bring down the Wall. The king was unassailable. Pointless to try and corrupt the girl, or take her over. Fane's power was extraordinary, perhaps as fine as Barl's had been, and she believed in protecting Barl's Wall as fervently as the rest of them.

Which left only the cripple . . .

Frustrated, he paced Durm's untidy study. There was a way to use the boy, yes, at least in theory, but it would take so *long*. He'd not thought to spend more than days in this place and now he'd be here weeks. The notion was intensely irritating.

But he could sustain a little irritation. Especially when the reward for patience was so great.

And he was in no danger here, provided he remained undiscovered. The greater part of himself that he'd left behind the Wall would wait for his return, their rejoining. Soon enough he would be Morg again. Would slough off this binding vulnerable flesh and once more become immortal, invulnerable spirit.

Soon enough, Barl's Wall would come down.

Some time later, after a second round of bathing and dressing, and fortified with his new plan, he ventured outside to find the king and queen. Thanks to Durm he knew every twist and turn of the palace, every face that passed him. This place was as familiar to him as the contours of his own mind.

Their Majesties—*Majesties*!—were in the palace solar, lingering over breakfast. A pleasant room, with birds and flowers and spilling sunshine. Pink and cream and gold. Pretty colors. Pretty furnishings, too, plump and fringed and tasseled and sparkling in the warm light. How soft they were, in this place, in the delusions of their safety.

"Durm!" the king said. "Come. Sit." There was something vaguely familiar about him. Chances were he was descended directly from Ryal Torvig; the nose was the same, the mouth, and a trick of the eye. Ryal, who'd promised loyalty and delivered betrayal. Ryal, who'd died screaming amidst his own entrails. But it would seem his whore had survived after all, to breed on. A pity.

"Have you eaten?" asked the queen.

"Thank you, yes." He sat. "Forgive the interruption but I needed to speak with you. I have been thinking."

The king plucked a hothouse strawberry from its bowl. Plump and ripely red, it looked delicious. "About?"

"Barl." He felt his emptied stomach spasm. The bitch, the slut, the treacherous whore. "And her library."

"Durm?" the queen asked, teacup paused at her lips. "Are you all right?"

On a deep breath he relaxed. Unclenched his fingers. "Of course. A touch of indigestion."

The king favored him with a wicked grin. "Shall I call for Nix? He has so *many* potions . . ."

Durm would smile at that, so he curved his lips. "That won't be necessary. But I am touched by the thought."

"I thought you might be." The king bit into another succulent strawberry: pink juice dribbled down his chin and the queen, laughing, dabbed him clean with her napkin. "So, you've been thinking about the library. And?"

"And I fear that yesterday I allowed my zeal to override my better judgement," he continued, and assumed a suitably apologetic expression. "Your better judgement."

"How so?"

"Blessed Barl in her infinite wisdom hid that chamber, and those books, for reasons we cannot fathom. I fear we were wrong to ignore that wisdom."

"I don't know what to say," said the king after a lengthy silence. "What's brought about this abrupt change of heart?"

"The thought that we may yet discover treatises of ancient Doranen magic."

Exchanging glances with the queen, the king leaned forward. The hothouse strawberries were forgotten now. "I thought you wanted to find them."

"I did. In truth, part of me still does. But the danger of doing so far outweighs the benefits. If such magics were discovered . . . if they were to fall into the wrong hands . . .

the Wall itself may be destroyed, Borne, and that is unthinkable." For them, at least. For himself, he'd been dreaming, plotting and planning little else for centuries.

The king frowned. "Whose 'wrong hands' concern you the most?"

"My own," said Morg. Seasoning Durm's voice with a rueful, courageous honesty, he continued, "I'm afraid that if I found such magics, if I discovered a book with our arcane heritage writ large upon its pages, I would not resist the temptation to use it. I fear that my zeal and, regrettably, my arrogance—"

"Arrogance?" the king protested. "Durm, what—"

"Please, old friend!" he said, shaking his head. "Can you truly sit there and smile in my eye and say I am not arrogant? I am, and we both know it. And *I* know that my arrogance would indeed overrun my more temperate self, and that in so doing I would bring about calamity and woe."

"This is arrant nonsense!" the king retorted. "You would never, *never*—"

He lifted a hand to halt the passionate spate of words. "It is an unwise man, Majesty, who claims 'never'. I think you told me that once."

The king's pale face was flushed with temper. "I grant you're a passionate man, Durm. Confident in your abilities, as well you should be, because they're prodigious. But you would *never*, and yes I use the word, not unwisely, *never* betray me or my kingdom. And if you think I'm going to sit here and listen to you malign yourself in such a fashion, you—"

"Borne," said the queen, and laid a gentle finger on his wrist. "Let him finish."

Which was interesting. Little ranting Durm knew the queen did not like him overmuch but kept her peace for the sake of her husband. For himself, he found her reservations amusing, springing as they did from her unreasoning love of that mewling monstrosity she called a son and a suspicion that Durm had no real respect for her at all.

And there, little magician, do we find ourselves in agreement, and nobody is more surprised than I to discover we share a toehold of common ground! This queen is no queen at all; your king is blinded by love. And not just for her. For the cripple, too. But let's not be too harsh towards our little princeling, eh? He is, after all, the tool of your destruction and is to be cherished. At least for now.

The king said, subsiding, "He can talk until crows grow on corn stalks, Dana. It still won't make him right."

"Do you say he doesn't know his own heart?" she countered. "Why then have you called for his counsel all these years if you so easily mistrust what he says?"

There was a dangerous glitter in the king's eye. It made him look more than ever like long-dead Ryal. "I think you'd best speak plainly, madam."

"Plainly, then, you should stop bellowing and hear him out," the queen snapped. "Yesterday you were the one saying the library should remain unbreached. Now Durm is agreeing with you, a little late perhaps, but still. Tell me what there is in this to mislike!"

"I mislike," the king said dangerously, "that he would sit there and accuse himself of foul, unspeakable treachery. Even more do I mislike the fact that you don't defend him, even from himself!"

How tedious. As if he had time for wedded spats. "Dear friends," he raised both hands placatingly. "Please do not disagree on my account. Your loyalty moves me almost to tears, Borne, but in this the queen has the right of it. Allow me to know myself and my personal demons a little better than you."

"You are no traitor," said the king. "My life upon it. I cannot believe you would ever put your own desires above the welfare of this kingdom. I *will* not believe it, even if Barl herself should come back from the grave to tell me in person."

"Well, I expect you're right," said Morg, as deep within the darkness trapped Durm wept, inconsolable. "But can you understand I prefer not to put that belief to the test?"

"Yes," the queen said. "Of course we can understand. We understand. The library will be sealed and the secret of its existence will die with us."

Well, that much was certainly true. He turned to the king. "Borne?"

"I confess," the king said slowly, "that I spent an uneasy night. I had bad dreams. *Not* because I mistrust you. Every argument you made yesterday holds true in the light of a new morning. And yet . . ."

"Precisely," he said, smiling. "In the harsh light of day, doubts outweigh daring. Countless thousands of lives depend on us. You were right all along, Borne. The risk is too great."

"So be it." The king grimaced. "Fane will be desolate."

Ah yes. The magical prodigy. He was looking forward to meeting her: Durm considered her quite amazing. "I will deal with Fane," he said. "As WeatherWorker-in-

Waiting, she will understand that we act with the kingdom's best interests at heart."

"And what of Gar?" said the queen. "Borne, he'll be devastated. All those books. You said he could study them, you named him—"

"I know," said the king. "It can't be helped."

"A compromise, perhaps," Morg suggested. "It's clear that what we found yesterday is harmless. His Highness could safely take those books and translate them to his heart's content. If it's made known that those texts comprised the extent of the discovery, all should be well."

"An excellent idea," approved the queen.

The king nodded. "I agree. And it would be a shame to come away from this empty-handed." Sighing, he frowned at the bowl of strawberries.

Finally succumbing to temptation Morg reached for one, though his purged belly was still uneasy. The flavor exploded on his tongue, sweet, so sweet. He almost moaned aloud. When he could speak: "Might I make another suggestion?"

"Of course," said the king.

"Let me be the one to tell the prince of this decision. It will distress him, and since I'm the one responsible for it, it's only fair that I bear the brunt of his displeasure."

"Like Fane, he will understand," the queen said sharply. "Gar is no fool."

A matter for debate, surely. But he smiled at the queen, and spread his hands wide. "That was not my meaning, Majesty. Forgive me if I was unclear."

"Doubtless it's cowardly of me but—very well," said the king. "By all means, break the bad news to Gar."

"Excellent," said Morg, and smiled. "If you'll excuse

me, Majesty, I'll do so directly. When a plan is decided there seems little point in delay. Don't you agree?"

"Certainly," said Borne. And smiled. And flicked his fingers in fond, unsuspecting farewell.

The fool.

CHAPTER TWENTY-SEVEN

He found the cripple in the Tower's foyer, conversing with Nix. No fool, the pother excused himself and withdrew. Since protocol dictated that Durm bow to the prince, Morg lowered his chin, briefly. "Good morning, Your Highness. I hope your health remains robust?"

"Certainly," replied the cripple. He looked wary. "Nix was here to see Asher."

Ah yes. The Olken hero. Morg smothered a sneer; it was important he gained the weakling's trust. "Still not recovered, then? I'm sorry to hear it. The kingdom owes him a great debt."

The cripple's wariness eased. "Indeed. And when he's on his feet again—Barl grant it be soon, now—the debt shall be paid. Durm, what brings you here? Is something wrong?"

He smiled. "Not . . . precisely. Shall we walk?"

To his and Durm's surprise, the cripple took the news well. "I'm sorry, of course," he said as he was circumspectly guided towards the Old Palace. "Sorrier than you'll ever know. But I can't say I wasn't expecting it. A discovery like this—it's too dangerous. His Majesty is absolutely correct in his decision. I consider myself fortunate to be left with any books at all."

"Which is why I have brought you back here now," said Morg, halting before the door that would lead them, eventually, to his bitch lover's long-hidden chamber. "I thought perhaps you and I might take a few moments to look over one or two more shelves. See if there's not something particularly splendid for you to add to your collection."

"Are you sure? Does His Majesty know that—"

"His Majesty trusts me, Your Highness," said Morg. "And so should you. You used to, once upon a time."

"Once upon a time," the cripple replied, "you thought I was my father's son and that together we'd work great magics." Then he shook his head. "I'm sorry. That was uncalled for. Of course I trust you, Durm."

In silence, they continued to the library.

"It's such a pity," the cripple sighed, wandering among the bookshelves, touching their spines with foolish, doting fingers. "Who knows what grand histories of old Dorana are hidden here? What fabulous tales of those glorious long-dead days I'll never get to read. I'm going to spend the rest of my life wondering. Mourning, really."

Morg swung the chamber door shut with a nod. "No, you won't. Eunuch."

The cripple stopped. Stared. "I'm sorry . . . *what* did you just call me?"

"Eunuch," he repeated politely. "It means 'impotent one'. A man bereft of the means by which to perform. Agreed, there is a slight contextual difference, but the spirit of the word still applies. Magically speaking, little princeling, you are *limp*."

The look on the cripple's face was worth quite a lot of the aggravation his treacherous slut was causing him. "I think you must be unwell," the prince said with great care. "I suggest you see Pother Nix immediately, and I'll forget this ever happened."

"Well . . . you're half right." With a casual flick of his fingers he froze the witless natterer where he stood. "Grand histories of old Dorana. You *cretin*," he sneered, and felt contempt twist his borrowed face. "There is nothing grand about those long-dead days! The dynastic squabbling, the interhouse rivalries, the needless shedding of blood. Politics for its own sake. No thought for the purity of our people, no consideration for the future. All they cared about was power for personal aggrandisement. The greatness of our race, the fulfilment of our destiny, meant nothing to them. *Nothing*! They were fools, your ancestors, every last one of them, and Barl the most foolish of all. Did she think I would stand idly by and watch our race tear itself to pieces like a pack of rabid dogs? She said she loved me. How could she love me, yet know me so little?"

The cripple did not answer. Empty of thought, of feeling, a blank sheet of parchment waiting patiently for the pen, it stood tranquilly before him.

"And *you*," he went on, bile and spite scalding. "You think you're safe here? You think it couldn't happen to you? Are you deaf, then, to the growls in the throat of that dog on the Privy Council? You think Jarralt and the rest of his relatives are without ambition? That they don't nurse dreams of crowns and palaces and the crackling fire of

Weather Magic? Hah! Of course they do . . . thanks to you. You blotted the family copybook, boy. You're the crack in your father's armour. The lever by which Conroyd Jarralt would tilt your world on its axis if he could. Tilt and tilt and tilt until it tumbled, and the sky rained fire on all your pretty heads. You think Trevoyle's Schism was bad? Little eunuch, it pales in comparison with the bloodshed I've seen. I stood on top of the tallest tower in all of old Dorana and watched your forebears melt the flesh from each other's bones. Boil brothers' eyes in their cracking sockets. They turned their mansions into charnelhouses and their children into charcoal. *That* is your grand Doranen history. Your glorious past. Your grim future. It's a good thing I'm here, little crippled princeling. I've come to save you from yourselves."

It came as a shock to realize that he was panting. That there was sweat on his brow and his borrowed hands were trembling. He took a deep breath, then spat it out.

"Your precious Wall is offensive to me." He closed in on the cripple to rest Durm's reluctant fingers upon his waiting shoulders. "The time has come for it to fall."

Leaning close, he pressed spittle-flecked lips to the cripple's smooth forehead. Breathed words into the lax body beneath his hands. He felt the muscles leap. Felt the sizzle and swish of the magic as it breached the body's shield, the skin, and raced through blood and sinew.

Brighter than any glimfire ever conjured; colder than any winter ever called: the imprint of Durm's lips burned blue above the bridge of the prince's nose. Burned . . . burned . . . and faded.

Morg turned away. Began sorting through the books

piled on the chamber's old desk. A moment later, the cripple stirred.

"I'm sorry, did you say something, Durm? I'm afraid I
wasn't listening."

"It was nothing, Your Highness," said Morg, and gently smiled. "Nothing at all."

When Asher finally drifted to the surface of his dream-
soaked sleep it was to see Dathne sitting in the chair beside his bed. She looked almost serene. Her hair was
briskly restrained in a plait, laying bare the pure, sharp
lines of her face. She was knitting. Something pink and
fluffy, which was so unlike her he thought for a moment
he must still be lost in fancies.

He felt his heart crack open and all his throttled feelings for her come pouring out.

Glancing up, she saw his open eyes. "Well, well, well,"
she said, tart as fresh lemon. "If it's not Prince Lazybones
himself." Without waiting for an answer she put down her
knitting and picked up a little silver bell from his bedside
table. Then she went to his bedchamber door, opened it
and tinkled the bell into the corridor.

A maid appeared. Cluny. "Yes'm?" she asked.

"Go and tell whoever needs to know it that Asher is
awake."

Cluny squealed. "Oh, yes'm!"

Dathne closed the chamber door on the sound of
Cluny's feet pounding down the spiral staircase and tinkled her way back to the chair by his bed. Replaced the
bell on his bedside table but didn't pick up her knitting.
Instead she sat with her hands folded neatly in her lap and
frowned at him.

"We parted badly, Asher, you and I," she said in that brusque, forthright way he'd come to treasure. "As much my fault as yours. You took me by surprise. More than a year we've known each other, and you never once said anything about . . . feelings."

He found his voice: it felt tentative. "You expecting an apology?"

"No. We all have our secrets. But here's the thing." Still frowning, she smoothed her blue wool skirt over her knees. "I don't love you, Asher. I don't love anyone. But that doesn't mean we can't be friends."

He laughed, though he was anything but amused. How many different pains were there in this world? And was he going to have to feel all of them? "Don't it?"

"Not to me. Of course I can't speak for you, but I'd like to think you felt the same. We've been good friends till now, haven't we? I see no reason to lose that." She hesitated then, and for once looked uncertain. "I don't want to lose that."

His breathing hitched, air catching in his chest. He wanted to reach his hand to her. Touch her. Friendship wasn't nearly enough, but if it was all she had to give him . . . and mayhap in time he could convince her otherwise. Teach her to trust his heart . . . and her own. "My da died."

Her frown softened. "And you're shunned. Forbidden the coast and all eight fishing communities. I know. I'm sorry."

He didn't know what to say to that. Was afraid if he tried to speak, tears would drown the words. "How long since I got back?" he asked when enough time had passed.

"This is the seventh morning since you fell ill." She skimmed his skin with her cool hand and nodded, satisfied. "Do you still hurt?"

For a moment he was confused. Why would he hurt? Then he remembered. His beaten back. His punished body after all that desperate riding. Great waves of furious heat and freezing cold, sweeping him from head to toe as fever claimed him. Closing his eyes he searched himself, and discovered nothing but a lingering lethargy. "No."

She nodded, smiling. "Good."

He looked at her again. Devoured her face with his eyes. She flushed, a small tide of color washing over her cheeks, but she didn't look away. He lifted an eyebrow. "So. Have I missed anythin' exciting?"

She told him. Details of the damaged City. All the repairs, and the official Day of Thanksgiving: wasn't he sorry he'd slept through that? No, not really. The books discovered in the deserted Old Palace. His Highness was like a pig in mud. "Aye, I'll bet," said Asher, rolling his eyes.

"And Westwailing?" he asked when she was finished. "Is everything all right there now?"

"It is according to Darran," she said. "He and Willer got back safely the day before yesterday. The rest of the expedition is following on."

Asher scowled. Bloody Willer. Now if *he'd* gone arse over earholes into the harbor . . .

She smiled. "And your things, and all your money, which the king sent down to the coast for you—they're safely back."

He could only shake his head. "How do you know so much?"

"I make it my business."

"So what caused the storm in the first place?"

Dathne shrugged. "In a nutshell, the king's illness. He was lost in fever. Worried about the prince. The Weather Magics followed the path of his thoughts. And because he was delirious and couldn't control his own power or the way it manifested, we got a storm. It's tragic, but it's nobody's fault." She pulled a face. "The king has been distraught. The minute he was allowed out of bed he went to the City Barlschapel and spent the night on his knees, praying for those who died, and after that he joined in the repairs. I hear Pother Nix was furious, and the queen, but His Majesty refused to yield."

Asher shifted on his pillows. "He's a grand man, is Borne. We're lucky he didn't die."

"You'll get no argument from me," Dathne agreed. Then she grinned. "There's something else as well. Although probably I shouldn't tell you. Probably the prince will want to tell you himself when he gets here."

There were suspicious glints of mischief in her eyes. He mistrusted Dathne's mischief, heartily. "You tell me now."

"No, no," she said, laughing. "He'll be cross as two sticks if I spoil the surprise."

"*Dathne*—" he started, but broke off because the chamber door flew open and Gar strode into the room. Dathne slid off her chair and curtsied.

"Barl save me from all that goes bump in the night!" the prince exclaimed, stopping at the foot of the bed. "It's about damned time you woke up!"

For a moment Asher couldn't speak. Hollow-cheeked and feverish, Gar looked like a man driven to his limit. His crumpled silk shirt was splotched with ink stains and his fine wool breeches had a tear across one knee. "Barl save you, all right! You look bloody dreadful, Gar. What've you been doing?"

"Fretting for you," said Gar, and laughed. There was a shrill edge to the sound and his eyes were wild. "No. Sorry. I've been working my fingers to the bone fulfilling your duties as well as mine and I have to say I'm well sick of it. When are you getting up?"

Asher worked his way upright and rested his shoulderblades against the bedhead. "Dathne said you found some moldy ole books? Bet you've had your nose stuck in 'em day and night without resting and that's what's got you lookin' like death on a toasting fork."

Another grating laugh. "All right, all right. I confess," Gar said. "I have been burning a smidgin of midnight oil translating some moldy ole books, as you so disrespectfully call them." He turned to Dathne and pretended displeasure. "Stealing my thunder, are you, Dathne? I hope you didn't tell him about that other matter!"

Dathne curtsied again. "No, Your Highness."

"I should think not!" Gar rubbed his hands together as though he were trying to start a fire.

"When was the last time you slept?" asked Asher.

"Who needs sleep?" said Gar, derisive. "Besides, you've been snoring enough for the both of us. Now let's stop bleating about me, shall we? Asher, I have a surprise for you. You'll never guess what it is."

Asher pulled a face. "Don't think I want to."

"All right then, I'll tell you. There's to be a parade in your honor."

He stared at Dathne, horrified. She shrugged. He stared at Gar again, still horrified. The silly prat was grinning like a loon. "A *what*?"

"If you don't stop scowling like that your face is going to shatter," said Gar. "And anyway, nothing you can say will make a difference. Their Majesties insist upon a parade so a parade there will be. Darran's been sweating blood over the final details ever since his return. We've just been waiting for you to wake up. It'll start here at the Tower and go all the way through the City, along every main thoroughfare. What do you think about that, eh?"

"I think you be clean out of your pretty yellow head!" said Asher, choking. "A *parade*? I don't want a bloody parade!"

"Well, want it or not, you're getting one," Gar replied. "So I suggest you start practicing your smiling and waving."

Asher slid back down the bed and pulled the blankets over his face. Pulled them away again and said, despairingly, "But *why*?"

Some of the frenetic animation died out of Gar's expression. "Why do you think? Because you saved my life, you fool."

With the dregs of his dwindling strength Asher tugged a pillow from behind his head. "Well, if I'd known it'd mean a bloody parade I'd have damned well let you drown!" And he threw the pillow as hard as he could at Gar's fatuously smiling face.

Shortly afterwards Pother Nix interrupted the ensuing lively discussion by arriving with his basket of pills and potions and demanding privacy for himself and his patient.

"Waving and smiling, Asher, remember?" said Gar, retreating. "Both must be perfect. Darran insists upon it."

Asher glowered. "Ha."

"Come and see me later, if you're able. I'll be working in the library."

"*Ha.*"

"I'm glad you're mended," said Dathne as she stowed her knitting in her string bag. "I'll look for you in the Goose at week's end, same as usual, shall I?"

"Maybe," said Asher.

She smiled, hefting the straps of the bag onto her bony shoulder. "Definitely. Unless I see you in the parade first, of course."

And then she was gone, laughing, and it was just him and the damn bone-botherer. Nix pronounced him sound in wind and limb, which he knew already, then made him drink another damn potion that put him right back to sleep.

When he woke again it was late afternoon and he was alone. For some small time he lay there unmoving. Thinking. About Da. Jed. His brothers. His life. About decisions, and choices, and who controled who.

About how that was all going to change.

Zeth and the rest were due a few unpleasant surprises.

And with that settled he realized he was suddenly sick of pillows and blankets. Cautiously, expecting his legs to fold like a newborn foal's at any moment, he clambered out of bed. His legs held. Amazing. Somebody had left a bowl of fresh fruit on the table. He ate a couple of teshoes and an apple as he wandered around his apartment, just to see if his legs would still take him from here to there and back again without collapsing. They did. He felt fine. Whatever Nix had put in that potion, it had worked a treat. His head was clear, his body free of pain, and he was ready to brave the world beyond his bedchamber. So he found some fresh clothes, pulled them on and left his rooms.

The first person he saw when he reached the Tower lobby was Darran. Looking like a stork on its way to a funeral, same as usual, all black plumage and long spindly legs. He halted abruptly as Asher stepped off the last staircase tread.

"Asher." He moved closer, knobbly fingers clasped in front of him. "You have Pother Nix's leave to be out and about, do you?"

Asher rolled his eyes. "Aye, I be feelin' ever so much better, Darran. Thanks for askin'. I be touched. Honest." He headed for the doors.

"Asher, wait!"

Sighing, Asher waited. "What?"

Darran darted a quick, hunted look about the empty lobby and came closer still. The ole fool's wrinkly throat was working like he'd swallowed an orange whole and couldn't get it down. "I want a word with you."

"About?"

"You saved His Highness's life."

Asher raised his hands palm out. "Darran, if this is about that stupid parade, you're wastin' your breath. I were asleep when Gar and his folks dreamed up that little bit of madness so you can't blame me."

Darran's pinched face was stiff with dislike, and something else. Something Asher couldn't place. "Asher, be quiet. I am perfectly aware that the parade in your honor was requested by Their Majesties. That's not what I wanted to talk to you about."

"Then what?" said Asher impatiently. "I'm tryin' to get out for a breath of fresh air, Darran, in case you haven't noticed. Feels like I ain't seen nowt but the inside of my own eyelids for six months, not six days."

Darran's thin cheeks stained red. "You really are the most impossible man it has ever been my misfortune to know," he snapped. "I merely wanted to say that in saving Prince Gar's life at the risk of your own you demonstrated a courage and sense of honor I heretofore did not suspect you possessed."

Asher thought about that for a moment. "Am I still dreamin' or was that a compliment?"

Darran nodded. "Apparently. Though I'm beginning to wonder why."

"That makes two of us," said Asher, grinning. "Ain't no need for compliments, Darran. I didn't save him for you."

Darran's clasped hands clenched bloodless. "Nevertheless. You saved him."

With a small shock Asher realized then that this wasn't Darran somehow doing him a backhanded bad turn. The ole fool meant every word he was saying. And that was the thing in Darran's expression he'd not been able to place: the bitter taste of swallowed pride. *Bastard*. He sighed. "I had to."

Darran considered him in silence for a long time. "I see," he said at last. "Very well, then." He turned away. Paused, and turned back. "You realize, of course, this in no way implies that I suddenly approve of you, or have changed my opinion that at heart you remain a lawless ruffianly reprobate."

"Of course. Same as it don't imply I reckon you're anything but a dried-up old dog turd."

Darran's lips thinned in a smile. "Precisely."

Honor mutually satisfied, they parted company.

Without making a conscious decision Asher found himself heading for the stables. The autumn air was crisp, the leaves on the trees all around him dying in a riot of crimson and gold. He took a deep, lung-filling breath and was overwhelmingly glad to be alive.

Of course, whether he was glad to be alive here, and not down on the coast, was another matter. Fresh grief stabbed him. *Da*. And Jed. Would there ever be a time when he could think of his father and his friend and not feel pain? It was hard to imagine. Da was dead . . . Jed was addled . . . and he was to blame.

"Barl save us!" Matt cried when Asher entered the stable yard, and dropped the bucket of feed he was carrying. "Look what the cat's dragged in." All around the yard Matt's lads shouted and whistled and catcalled. Matt strode to meet him and, to his extreme surprise, folded him in a ribcracking embrace. "Damn it, Asher, you scared fifty years out of me!"

Warmed, Asher returned the hug. "Sorry."

With a final thump between the shoulderblades, Matt stepped back. "Dath said you were looking fine," he said, eyeing him critically. "And so you are. I heard there were people thinking healing thoughts for you. Barl must have been listening."

Asher stared. There'd been City folk *prayin'* for him?

Damn. That was even worse than a bloody parade. "Cygnet all right?"

Matt laughed. "Cygnet's fine. Ballodair too." Then his smile faded and he stared intently into Asher's face. "I'm sorry about your father. It comes to all of us in time, no escape, but it's still a bad blow."

Especially when you helped it happen. "Aye." He shrugged. "But it's happened. No point fratchin' on it. I'm fine."

Matt looked as though he didn't believe him. One of the drawbacks of friends. "And what about staying in Dorana?"

So. Matt knew the whole of it. Somebody's tongue must be tired of wagging. Gar. Dathne. Fools. Didn't they have nowt better to do than sit around gossiping? Asher felt his expression harden. "I'm thinkin' I might have a quiet word with my brothers on that score."

Matt stared at him, uncertain. "What? You're going back to Restharven? But I thought—"

"You thought right, for now. But only for now. Fishin's in my blood, Matt, same as horses are in yours. I ain't givin' it up. Not on Zeth's say-so. It'll take time, I know, but that's fine. I'll wait."

"For how long?"

He grinned, feeling savage. "A few months. A year. As long as I have to. Sooner or later the tide always turns." He shrugged. Stared around the immaculate stable yard. "And in the meantime, if I can't have the ocean I s'pose Dorana'll do."

Looking relieved, Matt slung an exuberant arm around his shoulders and shook him. "That's the spirit."

"Get off me, y'great lummox!" said Asher, fighting

free. "Stop hangin' round my neck like a girl and show me my poor bloody horse!"

"Heard about your parade," Matt said as they headed for Cygnet's stable. Asher speared him with a look. Matt looked back, innocently smiling. "It's so exciting. Going to wear tinsel in your hair, are you? That should look pretty."

"There'll be tinsel up your arse if you ain't careful," said Asher darkly.

Matt mimed shock. "Asher! Now is that any way for the Hero of Dorana to talk?"

Asher stopped. Stared. "The *what* of *where*?"

Matt's broad, weathered face split into a delighted smile. "That's what they're calling you, down in the City. Haven't you heard?"

Asher hung his head. "I'm goin' to kill Gar for this, I swear. I don't know when, and I don't know where, but I'm goin' to bloody kill him."

Matt just laughed, and laughed, and laughed.

Returning to the Tower after half an hour of feeding Cygnet and Ballodair enough carrots and apples to rupture their guts, Asher could think of nothing but food and putting his feet up. But first he thought he should pay a call on Gar. The prince hadn't looked well, and the last thing anybody needed was him flat on his back with a fever. For one thing it'd mean *he'd* have to take over all the work, and he wasn't in the mood for that at all.

He banged on Gar's library door for five minutes before it opened the width of three thin fingers. "What do you want?" said the prince. "Can't you see I'm busy?"

Asher winced: the words were slurred, spat into his

face on a cloud of bad breath. "Let me in, Gar. I need your ear for a minute or so."

Gar grinned, a ghastly revelation of teeth. "Give me a knife and you can have both of them, provided you go away afterwards and never bother me again."

"*Gar!*"

"Just joking."

"Do I look amused to you? Open the bloody door, would you?"

Gar scowled, resisting. Then he stood aside grumpily. "One minute. Then I'm calling a guard."

Just as grumpily, Asher shoved the door open and marched into the library. "What's goin' on, Gar? I mean, I know you like your books and all, but this is plain ridiculous!"

Gar returned to his desk, which was layered inches deep in paper and parchment and towered with piles of ancient-looking volumes, whose faded titles Asher couldn't read. More books were piled row after row on the floor so there was hardly any space to walk. The library curtains were drawn. Just one lamp was lit. The room looked like a manky bear's cave. Stank like one too, the air thick and overused. Fumbling through the mess, Gar withdrew a single sheet of paper and held it out.

Asher stared suspiciously. "What's that?"

"A list of people you're to see tomorrow. I'm too busy. Find out what they want, give it to them if you can, tell them they'll have to wait to see me if you can't."

Asher ran his eye down the list of names. Mistress Banfrey of the Milliners' Guild. Meister Glospottle of the Dyers' Guild. Captain Orrick—"What's Pellen Orrick want?" he asked, looking up.

"I'm not sure," said Gar, pawing at his damned books again. "Something about crowd control for the parade, I think. It's your parade, you sort it out."

"How many times do I have to say it, Gar? I don't want a damned bloody stupid parade!"

"It's to be held the day after tomorrow by the way," Gar continued, pen raised. "Speak to Darran about the particulars. There's no use asking me, I'm—"

"Too busy," said Asher in disgust. "I'm gettin that. Gar, when were the last time you saw yourself in a mirror? You look like—"

"I'm afraid you'll be taking on quite a lot of extra responsibility for the next good while," said Gar, oblivious. "These books we've found are extraordinary, I can't begin to tell you." He dipped the pen into the inkpot: it came up dry. "Oh." Discarding the pen, he picked up the pot and held it out. "I seem to have run out of ink. Would you mind—"

Asher snatched the pot from him and threw it across the room. "Yes, I'd bloody mind!" he shouted. "Gar, what's the matter with you?"

The prince stood so fast his chair tipped over. "With me? Nothing's the matter with me! I'm busy, that's all! Can't you understand that? Has everyone become very stupid all of a sudden? First Darran, then Nix, now you?" He waved his arm wildly at the room. "Look at all these books, Asher! They are the greatest find in the history of the kingdom! I have to catalog them, I have to translate them, I have to—"

"You have to stop. Afore you fall to pieces entirely." Shoving the list of appointments inside his shirt, he picked up the upended chair and pushed Gar into it.

Stared down into his hollow-eyed, hollow-cheeked face. "You're halfway there already."

For a long time Gar said nothing, just sat bolt upright on his chair wrestling with demons only he could see. Arms folded, expression as mulish as he could make it, Asher waited.

"I do feel . . . a bit strange," Gar confessed at last, slumping a little and rubbing his hands up and down his arms. "Like my skin is crawling with invisible ants. As though there are hundreds and hundreds of tiny firecrackers going off inside my head. If I close my eyes I can see the explosions."

"See? I was right!" said Asher. "Too much readin' *does* rot your brain. Did you tell any of this to that ole bone-botherer?"

"Nix?" Gar shook his head, a kind of convulsive shudder. "No."

"Good. He'd prob'ly just give you something disgustin' to drink." With a silent sigh, Asher hitched his hip onto the corner of the desk. "You're a damn fool, Gar. You said already you ain't been sleeping. When was the last time you ate something?"

Gar waved a vague hand. "Oh. I don't know. I'm pretty sure I had a boiled egg yesterday."

"Look. I don't care how bloody special these moldy ole books are, no book is worth you workin' yourself into a collapse over. You've got to get some rest now, or it'll be your turn to spend a week in bed and then you'll miss the damn parade. And if you think I'm goin' through all that malarkey on my own, then you really have cracked."

"Miss the parade?" Gar managed a small smile. "And

the sight of you smiling and waving and wishing you were anywhere else in the kingdom? Hardly."

"Then you'd best have a bath and a bowl of soup and a good night's sleep, eh?"

Gar turned back to his desk. Brushed his fingers across the nearest open book. "Yes. You're right. I know. I'll just finish this page and—"

Asher slammed the book shut. "*Now.*"

As he closed the library door behind them, one hand on Gar's shoulder to prevent an attempted escape, Asher glanced through the banisters. Darran was standing on the staircase below them, halfway between floors, hands clasped neatly before him. His face was pinched into a worried frown. On seeing Gar the frown eased, just a little. Then he looked at Asher, and raised one eyebrow.

Asher rolled his eyes and kept on walking.

It was late when Dathne was at last able to contact Veira. After the visit with Asher there'd been shop business and errands, and supper with Matt to discuss where they were along Prophecy's mysterious road.

The fact that she still didn't know, and he couldn't help her find out, was something she refused to dwell on.

"Asher is woken, Veira, and taken no harm from his trials. Tell the Circle their healing was a success."

It will lift their hearts to hear it, child.

"Beyond that, I've nothing more to tell."

Nothing? Veira sounded disappointed.

Well, so was she disappointed. Disappointed and guilty and stuck like a cow in the mire. "I'm sorry! If I could force matters, I would. I pray and I pray for Jervale to show me the next step, but there's nothing. Just forebodings and unease."

You knew Asher would return. We must satisfy ourselves with that for now.

"No, Veira, I can't. It's not enough!" The link between them trembled with the violence of her thoughts, her feelings. "Night after night I rack my brains trying to see the way forward, trying to understand how Asher can be the Innocent Mage. What it means that he is in the Usurper's House. How it's possible for the Wall to be brought down when not even the king's cataclysmic fever disturbed it. We are in the Final Days, Veira, I know it in my bones, in my heart. Yet all remains unaltered. Life jogs along, just the same as ever it did. Now that they're safe and the City is healed of damage and things are returning to normal, people have even started making jokes again. *Jokes*. As though any of this was funny!"

Hush, child. You'll make yourself ill with such fretting.

She was already ill. Churned up and quivering. "I feel like I'm somehow suspended between breaths," she said, fists pressed against her chest where her heart was racing. "As though the storm was an inhalation. Any moment now the world will need to exhale again, and when it does . . . when it does . . ." Cross-legged on the floor before her Circle Stone, she began to rock. "I need to be ready. I need to know what to do, how to react, and I don't, Veira. I don't. And I'm so afraid it will mean the ruin of us all. What if I'm wrong about him, Veira, and he's not the Innocent Mage after all? What if I've been wrong about everything?"

Foolish. You are foolish, Dathne. These are but the fancies of an overtired mind. He is who you have named him.

And when the time comes you will know exactly what to do and how to react. Why else would you be Jervale's Heir?

There were tears in her eyes, welling, burning, flowing down her cheeks. "I don't know. I don't know."

I do. Trust me, if for the moment you cannot trust yourself.

Angrily she smeared her cheeks dry. "It's hard. Even with Matt, even with *you* . . . I feel so alone."

You are not alone, child. You are never alone. The Circle stands with you always.

A rolling wave of love flowed through the link between them. Dathne gasped, feeling it fill her, feeling it smother the strident voices of fear and doubt. Her eyes stopped burning. Her racing heart slowed. Her distress eased, so she could sit still once more with her hands quiescent in her lap. "I wish I could meet you, Veira," she whispered. "On the outside, I mean. In the flesh."

Warmth. Pleasure. *When the time comes, child, you will. Now go to bed. Get some sleep. Trust Prophecy.*

Breaking the link, Dathne did as she was told. Went to bed, tried to sleep . . . and found she couldn't.

Instead she lay awake staring at the ceiling. Waiting for the sound of the world exhaling.

CHAPTER TWENTY-EIGHT

Morg reclined in the royal touring carriage in the company of the king, the queen and the princess and considered the excited, flag-waving natives that lined the street on either side of them. A sturdy people, these Olken. Little more than peasants, of course, dirt-grubbers and third-rate merchants, magickless as rocks. But sturdy. And he liked a good sturdy peasant. They made excellent raw material for demons.

The ranks of his demon armies would swell like the belly of a pregnant sow once all these cheering Olken were put to better use.

"Asher! Asher! Barl's blessings on Asher!" cried the crowd.

Riding at the head of the official procession, directly in front of the touring carriage and marching band and the other coaches carrying the rest of the Privy Council, was the prince, all decked out in his best silk and leather, with the sunshine glinting off a silver circlet rammed onto his unworthy head. As they'd gathered before the start of the parade he'd overheard the cripple bemoaning the loss of some other pointless trapping of rank and had been hard put not to hit him. You're a *cripple*, he'd wanted to shout. Don't you understand? This crown or that one, it makes no difference. Dip you head to toe in molten gold and stick rubies big as hen's eggs where your eyes used to be, you'd still be nothing but *dross*.

But he'd held his tongue. There'd be time for harsh truths later.

Beside the cripple rode his brutish peasant friend, object of the crowd's adoration. Reason for this ridiculous procession through the streets of Dorana. Although, to be fair, he couldn't really begrudge the lout his moment of glory. For one thing, without him the cripple would surely be dead and his own plans of conquest severely disarrayed; and for another, this was likely to be the last glorious moment of the peasant's life. Feeling magnanimous, Morg smiled. Let him savor it while he could.

"Enjoying yourself after all, Durm?" said the king, his voice raised to carry over the exuberant blasting of trumpets. "I told you it wouldn't be so bad."

"You did indeed, Your Majesty," Morg replied. "And as usual, you were right. May I say it's a beautiful day for a parade?"

The king offered him a small mocking bow. "I do my humble best."

The crowd continued to shout. "Hail Asher! Hail the Hero of Dorana!" they chanted, and threw flowers and streamers and handfuls of rice.

"Poor Asher," said the queen, stifling an unbecoming giggle and nodding at the lout as he sat his horse ahead of them. "Even the back of his head looks embarrassed. Perhaps we should have thought of another way to thank him, Borne."

"Nonsense, my love," said the king robustly. "This parade is a perfect antidote to the lingering tensions in the City. Look at the people's faces. They're loving it. The very last thing on their minds is the fright I gave them with that unfortunate storm. Besides, what Asher did was heroic and it would be churlish of us not to show our public appreciation."

The princess, barely managing to conceal her lack of enthusiasm for their outing, spoke for the first time since leaving the palace. "Since you mention the storm, Papa, Conroyd Jarralt has done a wonderful job with the restoration effort. Don't you think so?"

The king's lips tightened but he had no choice other than agreement. Thanks to Durm, Morg knew as well as the rest of them that Jarralt had worked ceaselessly for days, alone and in concert with other Doranen magicians, to heal the storm-damaged City and send more teams of magicians into the surrounding districts to effect repairs there as well. Looking at the City now, pristine and sparkling beneath the blue and sunlit sky, a visitor would never believe the wrack and ruin left behind by the lashing force of the king's fever-blasted mind.

"Yes, Fane," the king said curtly. "Jarralt has done his duty, as have all my subjects. I would expect no less."

She wasn't a stupid girl: she knew when to hold her tongue. Pouting, the princess sank once more into silence. The king and queen waved at the gathered masses. So did Fane, after some sharp prompting.

He would have liked to wave himself, simply for the delicious irony of the gesture, but Durm wasn't the hand-waving type, so he kept his fingers folded in his lap and instead took advantage of the opportunity to see Dorana City for the first time since his arrival.

It reminded him of the old Doranen capital, Manitala, where once he'd lived and loved as a mere mortal thing. Lost Manitala, long since destroyed by war and fallen into crumbled decay. That city had looked just like this one, with its brightly colored houses trimmed with flowerboxes and carved frameworks, its bold shopfronts and broad, cobblestoned thoroughfares. With its wide open Central Square, its bubbling fountains, its tree-shaded gardens and its flocks of wheeling songbirds.

Barl had transplanted memories here, as well as magicians.

Wrenching his mind from that unprofitable destination he once more paid attention to the king and queen. She was speaking: "—threatened to take those wretched books away from him if he didn't take better care of himself."

"Oh, Mama," said the princess. "Gar's a grown man. He doesn't need you fussing over him as though he was still three years old."

"A mother never stops fussing no matter what age her children are!" the queen replied. "Rest assured, Fane, I shall be fussing over you and your brother when your hair is gray and your eyesight has grown dim. It's a prerogative of motherhood. You may roll your eyes now, young lady, but you'll be agreeing with me fast enough once you're a mother yourself."

As the princess begged to differ, groaning and laughing, and the king added his own opinions, Morg stopped listening. Drivel, drivel, drivel. Family and its attendant sentimental slop. Yet one more mortal bond he'd left behind without the smallest whimper.

He looked over the heads of the marching band and considered the cripple, still waving to the mawkish crowds. Closing his eyes, he extended his senses and quested for the shape and smell and taste of the spell he'd kissed into the runt's brain. It must be grown and close to bursting by now . . .

With the sun on his face and the sweet scent of autumn roses blowing on the breeze, he smiled. There it was. Squatting in the depths of the cripple's compost mind like a pustuled toad. Black and bloated and ripe with promise.

It was time.

We have been dragged along on this parade today to celebrate one peasant and his transitory moment of glory, he thought, gloating. May I suggest we celebrate this, instead?

With a single, searing thought he triggered the spell— and His Royal Highness Prince Gar fell from his saddle to the cobblestoned road like a poleaxed bullock in the slaughterhouse.

Everybody screamed: the crowd, the queen, the shocked marching trumpeters at whose stumbling feet the cripple landed. The king shouted and even the princess squealed, just a little. The touring carriage stopped in a clatter of hooves. The lout threw himself from the back of his horse, snatched the reins of the cripple's fine beast and shoved them and his own into the hand of a City Guard who'd come running.

Behind them, the remainder of the Privy Council had tumbled from its halted coach and was milling at the door of the touring carriage. Holze, the religious sot, was crying, "Barl save us, Barl save us", as though his life depended on it. Which it did, though he was wasting his breath. Barl was long past helping anybody now. Conroyd Jarralt's expression was harder to read; was that true concern or just a polished mask for public consumption?

Morg considered him carefully. A mask, he decided, crafted to hide an interesting face. In many ways it was a pity he'd been forced to take Magician Durm's body. Conroyd Jarralt was a man much closer to his taste and temperament.

The king got out of the carriage, then the queen close behind and the princess soon after. Morg, mindful of Durm's dignity, followed at a discreet distance. At his heels trailed Holze and Jarralt.

The lout was sprawled in the middle of the road, the cripple dragged across his lap. "I don't understand it!" he panted at the king. "One minute he were makin' a joke, laughin' at me, and the next he just went over! I don't understand it! Someone ought to fetch that bone-botherer Nix, quick!"

Restrained and muttering on three sides was the crowd, flags and flowers forgotten. Ignoring them, the king dropped to his knees and pressed his hand to the cripple's forehead. Morg watched, lending him Durm's apparent, silent support. "He's quite cool," said Borne, fear coated with calm. Leaning close, he patted his son's cheek. "Gar. Gar. Can you hear me?"

"He's been working himself to bits over those moldy ole books," the lout said. "But we had words on it and yesterday he seemed right as rain."

The king spared him a brief smile. "It's all right, Asher. Nobody's blaming you."

"*I'm* blaming me!" retorted the lout. "I'm s'posed to look out for 'im!"

"And you do," said the queen, coming close. She held Fane's hand in hers, tightly. "Why else are we all here?" She glanced at the staring, muttering crowd, then at the king. "We should get him back to the palace, Borne. The carriage will be best, we can—" She stopped, gasping. The cripple's eyes were open, their pupils shrunk to pinpoints, and in their green depths burned an inky flame that flickered and darted like a black toad's tongue. "Durm! Durm, look at this! Have you ever seen anything like it?"

No, Durm hadn't. Neither had Morg, since this was the first time he'd ever artificially induced magic in another person. The effect was certainly impressive. He bent over to get a closer look and cleared his throat. "Your Majesty, we must proceed with care. I have a suspicion as to the root cause of this matter, and if I am proved correct . . ." He paused dramatically, and waited for the unfolding enchantment to finish the sentence for him.

The unfolding enchantment obliged.

With a series of cracks like an exploding string of fireworks the cobblestones beneath the cripple's body and all their feet rippled and split asunder. Pale green shoots erupted from the earth below them, rushing towards the sun. As those in the crowd close enough to witness the miracle shrieked aloud their surprise and consternation, and the lout cursed, and Holze began begging Barl's mercy again, the green shoots darkened their color, increased in size then burst into flower. Within moments the cripple and everyone within ten feet of him were surrounded by a riot of hollyhocks, roses, tulips and snapdragons.

"No!" cried the princess. "No, he can't do this!"

Morg swallowed a smile. Oh dear. Well, he'd never expected her to be happy about it. But then he wasn't doing
this for her, was he?

At his feet, the cripple stirred. His mouth opened. His
arms lifted, slowly, until his fingertips were pointing at
the sky. "*Ni'ala do m'barra. Tu-e. Tu-e.*"

A hush, reverent and waiting. Then sighs, as a golden
rain began to fall.

Gar was dreaming. He knew he was dreaming because he
was doing magic, and that only ever happened in dreams.
These dreams were particularly vivid, though. Visceral,
in a way he'd never before experienced. He was bursting
flowers from the ground and squeezing raw magic from
the sky in fat golden drops. He could feel the crackle of
magic at his fingertips, smell the burned-orange tang of
discharged energy, as real as anything waking could be.
But it wasn't possible. Was it?

He opened his eyes.

"Welcome back," his father greeted him. There were
tears in his eyes.

"Sir?" he said, and was staggered by the sound of his
own voice. Rusty as nails in a bucket, and thin, as though
he'd poured too much of it from his throat and was now
left with only dregs. "What happened?"

"You don't remember?"

He felt so empty. And light. As though he'd float right
off the bed and out of the open window if the blankets
weren't pinning him to the mattress. Remember? Remember what? "What day is it?"

"Still today," his father said, and straightened the edge of his sheet. "You fell off your horse three hours ago."

"Where's Mama?"

"With your sister. She'll be here directly."

The dream lingered, fresh in his memory. The tang of burned orange. Within his mind, a difference. Intangible, but *there*. It was impossible, of course. Grown and magickless men did not spontaneously burst into flower.

Impossible or not, he had to ask. "Sir, when you perform magic . . ."

His father leaned close. "Yes?"

You fool, you fool, it was only a dream . . . "Do you smell anything afterwards? Say, burned orange?"

"No," said his father.

He had to close his eyes, turn his head to the opposite wall. For one brief and burning moment he'd actually believed the dream.

"For me, it's a sharp kind of lemon smell," his father said. "Your mother swears it's fresh baked bread. Fane won't tell us what she smells. It's different, you see, with each of us. Nobody knows why. Something individual in the blood reacting with the energies. Whatever it is, it's personal. Certainly it's not discussed outside the family circle, so I don't recommend you run around asking everybody you meet what they smell when they perform an incantation. It might lead to unpleasantness."

His heart pounded, booming like a drum. "It was a dream. I was only dreaming."

"Were you?" his father whispered.

With fear like an anvil on his chest he lifted one arm from the bed and held out his palm. Recited, silently, the words to conjure glimfire, the first incantation a child is taught. The one Durm had tried to teach him a hundred times, a thousand, and could not. Failure had seared the syllables of the spell into memory.

His flesh crawled. His fingertips tingled. His nose wrinkled: burned orange. He opened his eyes . . . and there was glimfire.

Durm said, "I told you, did I not, that the spell was an easy one?" He'd been shadowed in a corner, unnoticed. Now he came forward to stand by the bed next to the king. He was smiling, one hand on the king's shoulder. It was the face he'd worn all those years ago, before the truth had soured them both. With the snap of his fingers he plucked a dead, dry stick from thin air and held it out. "Make me a rose, Your Highness."

The king stared. "Durm, are you mad? Four hours ago he couldn't even make glimfire! He can't—"

"Can't?" said Durm. "Who are you to say what he can't? We have no idea what his capabilities may be. For all you and I know, Borne, for Gar there *is* no 'can't'."

As his father and Durm locked gazes Gar took the outstretched stick. It was rough and dry to the touch. Truly dead. "I don't know how to—"

"Use your imagination," Durm suggested. "Close your eyes and think of a rose."

Gar shrugged. It couldn't be that simple. Even Fane had found the translation a challenge, and Fane was gifted beyond living memory. But he had nothing to lose by trying; it wasn't as though he were a stranger to failure, after all. He closed his eyes and thought of a rose.

Burned orange. His blood like boiling wine. Searing. Intoxicating. Power, filling him in an unstoppable wave, rolling through him and over him, dragging him under, flinging him high.

"Ow!" he said, and opened his eyes. There was a bead of blood on the tip of his thumb and a rose in his hand. He laughed, a harsh expulsion of air. "I forgot about the thorns."

Durm said, very quietly, "Fane practiced that translation day and night for a month to get it right."

His frowning father reached out and took the rose from him. "There is no precedent for this."

"There is," said Durm. "And then again, there is not. Records show that a late assumption of powers is not unknown."

"Records show that before today the oldest Doranen to finally exhibit his magical heritage was twelve and a half years old!" retorted the king. "Gar is almost twice that!"

Durm shrugged. "Nevertheless . . . it is not unknown."

"So," said Gar. He thought he should be screaming. Dancing. Laughing . . . or crying. He could do none of those things. With the taste of burned oranges still lingering on his tongue and the memory of a power so grand and grim thrumming yet through his bones, all he could do was breathe. "I am a true Doranen after all."

The idea was obliterating. In the blink of an eye his world was filled with possibilities. A wife . . . a family . . . the right to stand equal with the rest of his race . . .

Smiling, weeping, his father leaned forward and kissed him on the cheek. "Yes, my son. Yes. You are a true Doranen."

If one more person tried to squeeze into the Goose, thought Dathne, the walls were going to split asunder and the roof would crash down on all their heads. Matt had to press his lips against her ear and shout to make himself heard above the din.

"But what does it *mean*, Dathne? It don't make any *sense*. One more magician in the Usurper's House makes the Wall safer, doesn't it?"

"I don't know what it means, Matt!" she shouted back. "I told you, I'm stuck. Can't see any further forward than around the next corner, and that's only if I stick my neck out. Looks like we're back to waiting."

"Waiting!" said Matt, disgusted, and drained his tankard dry. "I hate bloody waiting!"

She had to grin. "You sounded just like Asher, then."

"Aye, well, reckon I—" Matt began, imitating, then broke off and pointed at the door. "Speaking of . . ."

A huge clamor from the Goose's patrons rattled the rafters: Asher had arrived. The walls and roof remained intact, just. Aleman Derrig's customers mobbed their man; hands stretched to pluck at his shirt sleeves, to tug at his elbow, to hold him fast and make him answer their quarrelsome questions. He withstood it for a minute then shoved all the shovers aside to climb up onto the bar.

"Shut your damned cakeholes, all of you!" he bellowed. "Shut up and I'll tell you what's the business! Or at least as much as I can!"

A ragged silence fell. Dathne exchanged a raised-eyebrow look with Matt and sat back in her seat, waiting.

"Right," said Asher. He was still dressed in his parade finery, though it was looking a little the worse for wear. He was looking the worse for wear, too, strained about the eyes and tense in the shoulders and back. "His Highness is fine. The king's seen him, the Master Magician's seen him, Royal Pother Nix's seen him. If they thought it'd help they'd get in a vitinery to see him. He ain't dyin'. He ain't even sick. He's just got his magic, is all."

A fresh wave of clamoring questions. Asher let it rage for a moment, looking tired, then lifted both his hands till the racket died down.

"That's all I got to say. There'll be a royal announcement presently, I reckon. In the meantime you could put yourselves to good use and start spreadin' the word."

Laughter, protests and a few jeering catcalls. Asher ignored them. From her booth up the back, Dathne caught his eye. Crooked her finger at him and beckoned. He hesitated, then shook his head and indicated the Goose's door.

"He wants us to meet him outside," said Dathne, and pulled at Matt's arm. "Come on."

The street was almost as packed with people as the inn. Every second one of them recognized Asher and stopped to beg him for news. "This is bloody ridiculous," he muttered, and led them round the back to the Goose's service alley. It stank of stale beer and rotten cabbage.

"The prince is really all right?" said Matt. "You're sure?"

Asher glowered. "No, I just said that 'cause I felt like lyin'."

Dathne shoved Matt with her elbow. "What happens now, do you know?"

"With Gar?" He dragged his fingers through his hair. "Don't have a bloody clue. But I'll tell you what's about to happen with *me*. Come tomorrow I'm goin' to be the only body in that whole bloody Tower workin' as any kind of Olken Administrator. I'm goin' to be up to my bloody eyeballs in Meister Glospottle's piss problems and Mistress Banfrey's lace shortages and Barl bloody knows what else!" His eyes widened in horror. "*Sink me*! I might even have to sit court at Justice Hall!"

Indeed a horrifying thought. Dathne took a deep breath, choked on it, and said, "What about Gar? This magic, it's unprecedented. Do you know how, or—"

"Why no, Dathne, I'm afraid I don't," said Asher with exaggerated care. "My best friend Durm and I ain't had time for today's cozy little chat over afternoon tea."

"All right," she said, recognizing incipient revolt. "Clearly this isn't a good time."

"No, clearly it bloody well ain't!" said Asher.

"Don't shout at her," snapped Matt. "None of this is Dathne's fault."

"Well it ain't my bloody fault either!" shouted Asher. "But who cares? Reckon I'm about to get covered in shit anyway! First Westwailing Harbor, then him and his moldy ole books and now this! Barl bloody knows where we'll end up with this! You should've seen the look on that Fane's face when all those flowers started sproutin'. I'm tellin' you, if looks could kill I reckon we'd've had a head start on a bloody funeral!"

"So . . ." Dathne tried a sympathetic smile, to see if that would calm things down. "You're going to be fairly occupied in the next little while."

The smile worked; Asher deflated, and kicked at the dirty ground. "Looks like."

She patted him on the arm. "Well, you know where I am if there's anything I can do. He must be pleased."

He gave her a blank look. "Who?"

"The prince. He must be pleased that at last he's found his magic."

Asher shrugged. "S'pose. I ain't seen him yet." He sighed. "I'd best get back. That ole Darran's flappin' about like a chicken with its head cut off and bloody Willer's no use at all."

Dathne stared. "Since when have you been so concerned about Darran?"

"I ain't bloody concerned," said Asher. "But if the ole crow does hisself a mischief while he's flappin' you can bet your arse he'll find a way to blame it on me!"

As he stomped off down the alley, Dathne let her head fall against Matt's shoulder. "Jervale protect us."

He nodded. "Dathne, I don't like this."

She stepped away from him. "It's not for you and me to like or dislike. It's Prophecy working itself out. All we can do about it is be patient and see what happens next."

Matt turned away, hands fisted on his hips. "This can't be natural. Magic comin' on a Doranen so late in his life."

"It's unusual, I grant you. But unusual doesn't mean unnatural, Matt. You know as well as I their magic is a spiky thing, abrupt and uncomfortable. We can't ever hope to fully understand it."

He wasn't convinced. "These past days . . . I haven't felt right."

"How do you mean?"

"Don't know, exactly," he said, shaking his head. "Not sure I can put it into words. But I feel the world around us, Dathne, and something's changed."

"Changed how?"

Frustrated, he tugged at his weskit. "I don't *know*, I tell you. Look, I ain't a Seer, like you. I'm not Jervale's Heir.

I don't have visions and I can't scry to save myself. All I'm good at are horses and . . . and . . . feeling the way the world is."

"And you think it feels different?"

"I *know* it does. Different, and worse than different. *Wrong*. I just don't know *how*, exactly."

"Why didn't you say something before now?"

He shrugged. "I thought I was imagining it. I thought it was just jitters, after the storm. Losing Bellybone, and Thunder Crow. Worrying about Asher. It's not like I can prove anything. How can you prove a feeling?"

She sighed. "I'll be honest with you, Matt. I've not felt what you have. But then, as you say, we've all got different talents. You've always been especially tuned to the natural world." She thought hard. "It could be you've sensed Gar's blossoming. Whenever a Doranen child manifests his or her powers it changes the tune magic sings in this place. Being so much older, with his Doranen magic repressed for so long . . . perhaps that's it."

"Perhaps," Matt said after a moment. "But what if it's not?"

Unfairly, she felt a stab of anger at him. As if she didn't have enough to be losing sleep over. Then common sense reasserted itself. No point in having a voice of reason to hand if you stoppered its mouth every time it said something you didn't like. "I'm going to sound like a corncrake, jabbering the same old song over and over again," she sighed. "But—"

"I know," he said glumly. "We just have to wait. Well, like I said before—I hate bloody waiting."

"And so do I hate bloody waiting," she snapped, losing patience. "But we're like a woman with child, Matt.

We've had a long gestation and a false cramp or two and now we're eager for our waters to break. Well, they'll break when they're ready and not before, and sticking a knife between our legs to hasten matters won't do much beyond making us bloody and putting the whole damned business at risk. Is that what you want?"

He was glaring. "Of course it ain't."

"Well, then. It's getting late. Best you go and tend your horses and leave me to decide when we've waited long enough. Seeing as how I am Jervale's Heir."

That earned her an even dirtier look. "Fine." He bowed. "As madam desires."

She let him go unhindered. His ruffled feathers would smooth soon enough. In the meantime, she'd take some time to sink herself in meditation and see if she couldn't sense for herself whatever it was he had felt . . . and been so unnerved by.

In the end Gar sent everyone away. His parents. Durm. Nix. Especially Nix. Yes, it was amazing. Yes, it was a miracle. But dear Barl save him, he needed *solitude*. Time. A chance to breathe and come to terms with this tumultuous reshaping of his life. He couldn't imagine feeling any more shocked and disarrayed than if he'd woken one day and looked in the mirror to find himself female.

Escaping to his private garden, where he could be sure of undisturbed privacy, he sat on a carved wooden bench in the late afternoon sunshine and let the perfumed air caress his skin. Let the birds in the trees around him sing and soothe his overwrought mind.

I am a magician. A true Doranen. My father's son, at last.

He wasn't sure if it was safe to feel so much joy at once. Could mere flesh contain it? Surely not. Surely any moment now his skin must burst and all his joy come pouring out, as golden and as glowing as the magic that burned and bubbled in his blood. In a heartbeat, in the blink of an eye, he was remade. Reborn. And nothing would ever be the same again.

As though to prove it he snapped his fingers and conjured a glowing ball of glimfire. Obedient, opalescent and *there*, right before his eyes, simply because he wished it, the coalesced magic bobbed on the breeze.

Suddenly, one just wasn't enough.

He conjured a second ball. Then a third. Conjured more, until twenty balls of glimfire hovered in the air above him. Enchanted, he conjured them different colors. With a thought, nothing more. The ease of it stole his breath anew. Then he made them dance. Simply, at first, as he sought to find the balance of energy that would keep them under his control. Then more daringly, and more daringly still, until they looped and swirled and flirted like live things, butterflies or birds or some other, magical creatures, celebrating his great good fortune.

Then, without warning, the multicolored balls of glimfire exploded into black smoke. He cried out in shock and protest and sudden fear as through the drifting remnants of his dancing glimfire Fane crossed the close-clipped lawn towards him, her crimson cloak billowing about her like blood. Her face was obdurate, carved in stone. There was no joy in her at all.

He leapt to his feet, furious. "Why did you do that?"

"You think magic's a game? Is that what you think?"

Heart pounding, he watched her halt before him. "No. Of course I don't."

"You think it's all pretty lights and showing off?"

There was pain in her eyes, as well as fury and disgust and something else he couldn't define. He let his own pain show in return. "I don't understand you, Fane. Why can't you be pleased for me?" ·

She laughed. "Are you truly so stupid?"

"I must be. You'll have to explain it to me. Explain why my own sister, my only sister, whom I love, though sometimes she makes it hard, could so resent my miracle."

She didn't answer him straightaway. Pushed past him to the garden bench and sat on it, arms extended along the back, face tipped back to drink the sunshine. He stood there, watching her. Waiting.

"On my fifth birthday," she said at last, eyes closed, "Durm took me to watch Papa work the Weather Magic. The blood and the pain scared me so much he had to take me out of the Weather Chamber and slap me into silence. When I finally stopped screaming, do you know what he said to me?"

Aching, Gar shook his head. "No."

"He said, 'You are this kingdom's only hope. One day it will be your duty to call the rain and the snow, to sing the seeds in springtime and slumber the earth in winter. In doing this you will keep the Wall strong so that no harm can come to us from beyond the mountains. But if you fail, or deny your destiny, the Wall will fall and with it every man, woman and child in the kingdom. Abandon your childish dreams and desires, Fane. You are no ordinary girl, and your life has never been your own.'"

"That was—" He stopped. Cleared his throat. "That was cruel. He shouldn't have done that."

She opened her eyes; they were sharp with derision. "Of course he should. He was right. I was born to be a WeatherWorker. So every day since that one I have sweated and bled and wept, learning how to be one. How to be this kingdom's only hope." She slid off the bench, sinuously, and in her pellucid eyes stirred something dark and dangerous. "I tell you this, brother. I did not sweat and bleed and weep in vain."

He stared at her, helpless. "Fane, you have to believe me, I'm not interested in usurping your place. I don't want to be the next WeatherWorker."

Her tapering fingers became talons and her beautiful face twisted into ugliness, contorted with hate and despair and a lifetime of remembered whispers. "*Liar*! You think I don't know what you're planning? Of course I know. There's only room for one cripple in this family, Gar, we both know that. And now that you've got your precious magic you're going to make sure I'm it! Well, it's not going to happen. Do you hear me? I won't let you cripple me! I'll *kill* you first!"

Gar felt sick, all joy congealed into sorrow. "Fane, this is ridiculous. You don't want to kill me. And even if you did, you couldn't."

"No?" she spat. "I think you'd be surprised at what I can do, *brother*." Clapping her hands hard she conjured glimfire. No pretty colored sphere, but a brute red thing pulsing scarlet with her pain and untamed fury. She aimed it at him, pelted it, and the air sizzled in its wake.

Startled, he raised a hand in self-defense. Thought desperately of shields and barriers and quenching rain. It wasn't enough, or he lacked the skill. Her glimfire scorched him, blistered flesh and singed silk before exploding into a shower of blood-red sparks. "*Hey*! Fane, stop it! You know this is against the law! You know the penalty for dueling with magic! Do you want to cause a scandal? Do you want to bring the king down here?"

Clap clap, went his little sister's hands. Clap, clap, clap. "No," she cried as balls of scarlet glimfire erupted into life around her. "I want everything to be the way it was! You bastard, you *bastard*! Why couldn't you have stayed a bloody cripple! Why didn't he let you drown?"

His heart broke. "Fane! Fane, listen to me—"

"No, I won't listen!" she screamed. "Why should I listen? What can you say that I could *possibly* want to hear?"

He tried again to reach her. Not because he thought he could, but because he had no other choice. "Fane. Please. I'm begging you, stop now before it's too late. Before you go too far. It doesn't have to be like this. I love you. We can work our problems out . . ."

She screamed again, a wordless outpouring of vitriol and hate. Her hands flung wide, her eyes blazed blue in her chalk-white face . . . and suddenly the sky was raining fire.

CHAPTER TWENTY-NINE

Somehow Gar deflected her flaming rage. Managed this time to explode the balls of glimfire she hurled at him before they could touch his exposed and vulnerable flesh. Given no choice he hurled his own fire back at her in wild self-defense. He had no idea where the magic came from, it just welled out of that secret place inside him that nobody, not even Durm, had ever suspected he possessed.

"Fane, for the love of Barl, *stop this*!" he shouted as the air filled with noxious smoke and exploding glimfire, his and hers. The sound of it boomed around his small walled bower, rocketed from brick to brick and sent the songbirds screaming into the sky. "Fane! Are you mad? There are laws!"

But she was beyond reason, beyond hearing. Almost, he realized, staring heartsick into her venomous eyes, beyond sanity.

Her wild attack intensified. It was impossible to destroy all the fireballs she flung at him; those he failed to extinguish engulfed trees, garden benches, flowerbeds. The smoke thickened till she was reduced to a crimson nightmare shadow spewing hate and fire. He defended himself as best he could but she was much more practiced than he. Raw talent was no match for years and years of training.

If this didn't stop soon one of them was going to die.

He thought he heard distant voices, shouting. The madness had to end now, before death and scandal over-took them. The sweat of desperation and fear poured down his face.

She was the most powerful magician born since Barl, or so Durm said. How in the name of their blessed savior was he supposed to stop her?

"Imagine a rose," Durm had told him, and he had, and in his hand he'd held a rose. Now he imagined a whip of glimfire, snapping and curling at his command.

"Bastard!" Fane shrieked as it lashed around her an-kles and tugged her flailing to the grass. She retaliated with a whip of her own and, unburdened by scruples or any kind of reason, aimed for his hands, his throat, his eyes. He couldn't deflect all her strikes.

Soon he began to sting, to burn, to bleed. Began to lose his temper as a lifetime of buried resentments boiled to the surface of his carefully cultivated facade. Spoilt brat. Rotten bitch. Never happy unless she was humiliating him. Taunting him. Hurting him. Whatever had he done to her to deserve such unkind treatment? *Nothing*. All he'd ever done was try to love her. Understand her. For-give her. Defend her to their mother, their father, even though her words and deeds were so often indefensible.

With a supreme effort he evaded another strike and wrapped his lash of glimfire round her body, pinning her *arms* to her sides. She cried out, fingers spasming, and her own whip fell from her fingers to dissolve on the ground in a puff of acrid smoke. She cried out again as he hauled her towards him across the charred and stinking grass. As he seized her by the shoulders and forced her backwards against the rough trunk of the nearest tree. She kicked and cursed him as he framed her face in his hands, palms flat and pressing, holding her so she could look nowhere but into his anguished eyes.

"*Bitch*!" he panted. Sobbed, nearly. "What is *wrong* with you? All I ever wanted was for you to care like I cared! To be my sister as I was your brother. Why is that so hard? Why is that so much to ask? Why in Barl's name do you *hate* me so much?"

She was crying, her contorted face screwed up with rage and hurt. "Why do you think, you stupid bastard? Because they never wanted me! Not for me. Not for myself. Only because you were a failure! The only reason I exist is because you were born *defective*! And now here you are, reborn a magician . . . so what's to become of *me*?"

Her mewling self-pity was his undoing. His fingers tightened on her face, nails digging into her soft flesh. "Who cares?" he hissed. "So you're not the only one with magic, so what? Do you think the world will cease its spinning? Do you expect the Wall to shatter and our lives to end in blood and fire, all because of me? Because at last, *at last*, Barl has delivered me my magic? My *birthright*? Do you think what I now have diminishes you? Little sister, you preen yourself too proudly!"

Her eyes were wide, the pupils cavernous. Flooding tears washed the soot and smoke from her ice-white cheeks. Through distorted lips she choked, "Gar—let go—you're hurting me! You're *hurting* me!"

"Merciful *Barl*!" he shouted, blind and deaf to her pleading. "You are the most selfish creature alive! Have you even given one minute's thought to what *I'm* going through? To what I've gone through my whole life? No, of course you haven't. Because no matter what happens, no matter who is suffering, at the end of the day you're the only one who matters. You! You! You! And you have the temerity to complain that *I'm* hurting *you*?"

Untrammeled at last, his rage would have overpowered him, would have clutched his fingers round her throat and shaken her till she wept her penitence and begged for his mercy, or suffocated.

They were saved from disaster by Asher.

"You damned bloody idiot!" his friend bellowed, hauling him bodily away from Fane, one strong arm anchored round his chest and arm. "Are you out of your mind? What are you doin'? You tryin' to *kill* her?"

Gasping, swearing, he struggled free of Asher's grasp. "Keep out of this! Go away! It's none of your business and you wouldn't understand anyway!"

"*I* wouldn't?" said Asher, glaring. "Me? With my bloody brothers?"

Panting, Gar dragged his charred sleeve across his gritty, sweat-stained face. The rage was still in him, burning, yearning. He throttled the impulse to flatten Asher where he stood. "That's different!"

Asher's expression was profoundly sceptical. "Aye. Right. I forgot. Royalty's got a better class of family strife." He shook his head. "What were you *thinkin'*, Gar? Half the bloody Tower's heard the two of you goin' at each other like alley cats! Darran's pissed his panties twice over! What's got into you? Has all that newfangled magic gone and burned up what little common sense you were born with?" He flung out a hand towards Fane. "She may be sixteen and a pain in the arse, y'fool, but she's still little more than a child! *And* she's your bloody sister!"

As though waking from a nightmare Gar turned and looked at Fane. She'd slid down the tree trunk and was folded at its base, face pressed into the battered ground, weeping fit to break a brother's heart. Fury fled, and sanity abruptly returned. Flooded with sudden shame and self-loathing he went to her. Fell to his knees at her side and gathered her into his arms. For one searing moment she resisted him . . . then crumpled against his chest.

"No, no, don't cry, Fane," he whispered, rocking her. "I'm sorry. I'm sorry. Don't cry. It's all right. Everything will be all right. We'll work this out. I don't know how, but we'll think of something. You're my sister and I'm your brother, and even though you drive me to distraction I love you. Nothing either of us can say or do will ever change that."

She was hidden from him, her voice muffled. "So you say."

"So I promise." He gently shifted her so he could see her tear-stained face. "And I promise something else, too, and Asher will be my witness." He raised his voice. "Won't you, Asher?"

"Aye," said Asher, keeping a discreet distance. "Provided you promise it fast so's we can get out of here."

Ignoring that, Gar took his sister's chin between his fingers and stared unguarded into her face. "The crown is yours, Fane. Only yours. Always yours. You are the WeatherWorker-in-Waiting. On my life, I will never take that from you."

He watched the doubt shift behind her eyes. "On your life?" She shook her head, frowning. Rejecting. "I don't believe you."

She sounded uncertain, though. As though she wanted to believe him but couldn't quite bring herself to make that leap of faith. Despair threatened. He couldn't let this happen. He couldn't allow his miraculous magic to tear their fragile family apart. Not when they should be celebrating.

Inspiration struck. A memory from distant childhood, a time when he and Fane had not yet learned to hate. Holding out his hand he dribbled saliva onto his palm and showed it to her. "You have to believe me. See? I've spit on it. Now. Your turn. Come on."

Her eyes widened. Filled with a brief, incredulous laughter. "No. That's disgusting."

"Spit on it," he insisted.

She shook her head. "It doesn't mean anything."

"Doesn't it?" He bit his lip, thinking. "It meant something when I didn't tell about the gardener's flowerpots. It meant something when you fell off the stable roof that time you thought you could fly. It meant something when—"

"All right!" she cried, torn between laughter and temper. "Shut up. My memory's as good as yours. Better, probably."

"Come on, Fane," he murmured coaxingly. "You know you want to. You know I mean it. Just spit and we can put all this behind us. Start over, on a whole new page. My magic won't change anything for you. I swear it."

She stared at his spittled hand, her dirty face screwed into a frown. Holding his breath he willed her to accept the challenge. Join him halfway. End the destructive, corrosive feud poisoning their family.

She said, still frowning, "Mama doesn't like it when we swear."

His laugh was half a sob. "Mama's not here."

She spat. Pressed her hand on top of his and shook. Then she looked up at him, a little shy, a little defiant. "I'm not really selfish. I'm just focused."

"Focused?" he said, grinning. Light-headed with relief and hope. "So that's what they're calling it these days." Fishing a handkerchief out of his pocket he wiped the tears from her face, then smeared both their hands dry of saliva.

Asher said, agitated, "All done then? All finished swearin' and spittin' and tryin' to kill each other? Good. Then best the pair of you make yourselves scarce. Ain't no tellin' who that ole Darran's gone flappin' to."

Gar nodded. Got to his feet and pulled Fane upright beside him. "You're right. As usual. And then we're going to have to come up with an explanation."

Fane was staring around them, her expression awestruck. "It's going to have to be a pretty good one, Gar."

For the first time he gazed at their erstwhile battleground. His glorious bower was a smoking ruin, splintered and scarred and shredded. Hardly a flower was left untouched. Beneath the smashed branches of one blackened tree, four charred and feathered corpses. The air stank of magic and death, smudged still with drifting smoke.

"Barl save me," he said quietly. Tiredly.

Asher was staring over his shoulder, his face grim.

"Well, somebody bloody better. 'Cause here comes trouble times three."

Gar felt his heart plummet. Wrapping his fingers around his sister's trembling hand, he turned. Took a deep, shuddering breath and prepared to face his father and his father's best friend . . . and his father's bitter enemy.

"*Barl's sacred bones*!" roared Conroyd Jarralt as his fist crashed down upon the Privy Council table. "This is *your* fault, Borne. *You* are to blame for this appalling state of affairs!"

"Now, now, Conroyd—" Barlsman Holze began, his expression pained.

Jarralt turned on him. "Hold your tongue, Holze, you pandering old fool! Don't think I've forgotten *your* part in this!"

Morg had to bite the inside of his cheek to stop himself from laughing aloud; the look on the pandering old fool's face was priceless. But Durm would not have let such an affront to dignity pass unchallenged so he arranged the magician's face into a frown. "Mind yourself, Lord Jarralt. We will swiftly achieve nothing if we cannot control our choler."

Jarralt continued unchastened. "And why should I control my choler, Master Magician? We are facing the gravest crisis this kingdom can know: a divided succession. Not since the days of Trevoyle's Schism have we seen such a barbarous display as provided by Prince Gar and Princess Fane! Control my choler? No, indeed! Rather I should be shouting my outrage from the rooftops of the City. The rooftops, sir!"

Pale and rigidly composed the cripple stirred in his

council seat. "Lord Jarralt, you are gravely mistaken. There is no divided succession. When the time comes I have no intention of challenging my sister for the crown. She has worked for it her whole life. Sacrificed every joy of childhood in service to the goal of serving this kingdom as its queen. As a prince of the ruling house I have my own duties and I am well satisfied with them. Fane will be WeatherWorker hereafter. I do so swear it, in this place at this time before you, my witnesses."

"So you say now," retorted Jarralt. "And it sounds well and good in theory. But a man can change his mind, Your Highness. Especially when lured by the promise of power." Turning his back on the cripple he glared again at the king. "I said this day would come, Borne, didn't I? Do you remember? I said it was a mistake for this Privy Council to side with the General Council and sanction the birth of a second child to your house . . . and a mistake it has proven to be!"

The king lifted burning green eyes to his accuser's face. "Sanction? You imply there was some kind of rule-breaking, Jarralt. We broke no rule."

"You birthed a second child! Trevoyle's Legacy states clearly and unequivocally: *The ruling house shall spawn but one heir, lest discord and strife once more tear the land asunder. One* heir, Your Majesty. And now you have two."

"If you're going to quote law, my lord, do me the courtesy of quoting it accurately," said Borne. "The Legacy goes on to say: *Should the ruling house be robbed of its heir by death untimely, then—*"

Jarralt struck the table again. "But it wasn't, was it? That is precisely my point! Your heir did not die, he—"

"He was magickless!" cried the king. "And what is that if not death, to a Doranen?"

Silence. Morg watched, mildly fascinated, as Jarralt and Holze looked anywhere but at the cripple. The king reached out his hand and laid it on his son's shoulder. "Gar—"

Face white as milk, the cripple shook his head. "It's all right, sir. Your point is valid."

"Hardly!" said Conroyd Jarralt. "Magickless or not you lived. There is no provision in Trevoyle's Legacy for a Doranen heir born without—"

"There wasn't then," interrupted Holze. "There is now. You helped make it so, Conroyd."

Jarralt bowed his head. "Yes. To my everlasting shame, I did. In a moment of weakness I stopped my ears to the counsel of my heart and allowed myself to be swayed against my conscience by you, Holze, and you, Durm, and you, Your Majesty. When we all know you should not have had a voice in the matter at all."

The king smiled thinly. "Because I had a vested interest in the outcome? Whereas you, who would have nominated your house to succeed mine, naturally had nothing but the welfare of the kingdom in mind."

Conroyd Jarralt's handsome face was blotched with venom and spite. "That would have been the proper order of things! The law made no provision for the birth of a cripple. You know it! But you pleaded and you cozened and you convinced us to make an exception. And now look at the result. Your two charming children at each other's throats. Attacking each other with magic. This kingdom poised on the brink of anarchy. And all because of your overweening arrogance and pride. You were ever thus. All your life whatever or whoever you wanted you took, heedless of anybody's best interests but your own."

The king was on his feet. "*Silence*! You go too far, Conroyd!"

"Too far?" Jarralt kicked back his chair and lunged, thrusting his face into the king's. "I think not! I think we've a distance further yet to travel, Borne, you and I. This kingdom's two Councils made a ruinous mistake in letting you and your precious, persuadable queen birth a second child. Blinded by love or seduced by sympathy or simply shouted down, we indulged your intemperate ambition and now the kingdom is asked to pay the price. Well, I say it is too high. The time has come to—"

Holze slapped his palms on the tabletop. His normally mild face was vivid with displeasure. "*Enough*, my lord! Your Majesty! This unseemly brawling will cease immediately! Are we cur dogs in the gutter, to snap and snarl in such a fashion? In Barl's name I tell you to be silent and mindful of your stations!"

Shocked, shamed, the king and his councilor sank back into their seats. Vastly entertained, Morg watched them gather their tattered dignity and studiously examine their fingertips.

Holze glanced at the cripple, sitting in pallid, mortified silence, and said with utmost reason, "No mistake was made. Laws must change to reflect the current reality. When Trevoyle's Legacy was first laid down, centuries ago, there was no record of a magickless heir ever being born. With His Highness incapable, His Majesty was to all intents and purposes childless. He was well within his rights to breed up a new heir to his crown. And since we settled this some seventeen years ago I fail to see why we must revisit the matter now!"

"Why?" said Jarralt, looking up. "Because now it appears we were a trifle premature in our proclamation of Prince Gar's *technical* demise. Now it appears he is a magician of power equal to, if not greater than, his sister. Now we must contemplate a world in which they attempt to burn each other to cinders! And that returns us to my original assessment of the situation: our kingdom faces the dire prospect of a divided succession."

The cripple sighed. "This afternoon's unfortunate incident will not be repeated. You have my solemn word. Besides, it was merely a . . . misunderstanding."

"So you say. But I say we can afford no more 'misunderstandings'. The next one might well do more than char a few trees and rosebushes and kill a handful of birds!"

"Did you not hear my oath, Lord Jarralt?" the cripple snapped. "Do you wish me to open a vein and write it in blood for you? *I will not contest the crown.*"

With a happy, inward sigh Morg cleared his throat. "I'm afraid, Your Highness, the matter is not quite so easily dealt with as that."

Caught unawares, the cripple stared. "Why not?"

"Because this kingdom must be served by the magician best suited to become the WeatherWorker. Family sentiment cannot play any part in the choosing. Once, before your miraculous transformation, Fane was the obvious WeatherWorker-in-Waiting. Now . . ." He shrugged. "The matter is less clear. You must receive the Weather Magic, so that I may properly assess who is most fit to follow in your father's footsteps."

"But—" The cripple turned to his father. "Your Majesty, I can't. The law—"

"Was designed to serve us, Gar," the king said. "And not the other way around. Durm is right. There is only one way to settle the question of who will succeed me."

"No!" the cripple protested. "I won't. I refuse. Not only am I not qualified or prepared or willing, I gave Fane my word I wouldn't usurp her inheritance."

"That promise wasn't yours to give, Gar," the king said heavily. "It's possible that Fane is still the best magician to wear the crown once I am incapable. But it's equally possible that you are the one destined to be Weather Worker after me. We *must* know. Soon, before uncertainty can undermine the kingdom's stability."

The cripple flinched. "She'll think I've betrayed her."

"I shall speak to her. Make her understand."

"You can try," the cripple said. "But I'm afraid—"

With an abruptly raised hand, the king silenced his son. "She will understand."

Jarralt was scowling. "And if His Highness is right and the Princess Fane refuses to accept her displacement? Then I'll be proven right. Your children will come to daggers drawn, and that will lead to civil unrest at the very least. The people have yet to fully recover their faith after your fever-born storm, sir. Once word spreads of today's altercation—"

The king looked grim. "There was no altercation. It was an unwise experiment that got out of hand. His Highness has yet to refine his magical control. Master Magician Durm will be working most closely with him to ensure such an accident does not occur again. That is the explanation to be given, should anybody ask. If I hear of

a different explanation . . . I will know where to look."
His gaze touched Jarralt with frost.

Impervious to cold, Jarralt sneered. "You expect that
sorry tale to hold water?"

"I expect everybody here to make sure it does."

Morg watched, bubbling with private mirth, as the
king and his rebellious privy councilor again locked
gazes. The cripple and the religious sot held their breaths.
Sadly, Jarralt this time gave ground. Lowered his eyes
and nodded. "Yes, Your Majesty."

The king slapped the table. "Then we are adjourned,
save for one last matter. Until further notice, while Gar
devotes himself to arcane study, Asher will be the Acting
Olken Administrator. As such he shall enjoy all powers
and duties previously ascribed to His Highness Prince
Gar in the same capacity. He will attend these Council
meetings and raise his voice with impunity wheresoever
he deems it appropriate. I trust, gentlemen, that when he
makes his first appearance in his new position you will
make him feel right welcome."

Jarralt was displeased. "Are you certain that's wise? I
was told he's been traipsing from tavern to tavern telling
anyone who'll listen that His Highness is now a 'proper'
Doranen. One wonders what kind of Doranen he considered the prince to be before today."

As the cripple and the king exchanged startled glances,
and Holze tut-tutted his disapproval, Morg smothered a
smile. Obedient Asher, following the Master Magician's
suggestion. And in doing so, possibly—hopefully—
weakening his inconvenient friendship with the cripple.

That was important. The sooner Prince Gar relied

solely on the warmth and support of his tutor—kind, patient and understanding Durm—the better.

The cripple said, "There must be some mistake. Asher wouldn't—"

"No mistake," said Jarralt. "I had it from my groom, who was in the tavern at the time. If this is an example of how the Acting Olken Administrator intends to conduct himself, then perhaps—"

"You give unexamined credence to servants' gossip?" replied the cripple. "You surprise me, sir."

"And you surprise me, Your Highness! To place your unquestioning trust in a man who would—"

"If Asher did in fact make this announcement—"

"*If?*" Jarralt stabbed a pointed finger at the cripple's flushed face. "So now you accuse me of lying? To the Privy Council? To *His Majesty*? How dare—"

The king seized his son's wrist with crushing strength. "Let be. Both of you. Conroyd, Gar's unexpected transformation is hardly a secret, seeing as it took place in front of half the City. If Asher did speak on the matter it's hardly a crime. Surely we have more urgent matters to attend to. This Privy Council session is ended. Go about your own business, my lord. Leave Asher to my son."

Jarralt departed, a silent snarl in his eyes. Breaking the uncomfortable silence, Holze turned to the cripple with a gentle smile. "Do you know, in all the unpleasantness I did not think to say how pleased I am for you, Your Highness. I know you'll use this unexpected gift wisely. Barl's blessings upon you, sir."

"Thank you, Holze," the cripple replied, flushing. "You can be sure I'll look for your guidance in the days to come."

As soon as the old dodderer had gone the king released his son's wrist and pulled a face. "Well. That proceeded as I imagined it would."

"I am so sorry, sir," said the cripple. "To have exposed you thus to Conroyd Jarralt and his—"

"He was always going to scream about a divided succession," the king said wearily. "That at least is not your fault. As for the other business . . ." He frowned. "It's over and done with. In the past, and best left there. I need not ask that it never be repeated?"

"No, sir," the cripple agreed, subdued. "You needn't. Sir, might I beg a favor?"

Fingers exploring a flaw in the wooden table, the king sighed. "What?"

"While I accept—reluctantly—that for now at least I must be considered as a potential WeatherWorker-in-Waiting, need Fane be informed immediately? For the first time in years, if ever, she and I are truly talking to one another. I want to give this fledgling bond between us time to strengthen before she learns I am indeed a rival."

Troubled, the king looked to his best friend for advice. Morg seethed. More delay? He was tired of delay, tired of waiting. He wanted this petty kingdom beaten *now*. Crushed *now*. Subordinate to his sublime domination *now*.

But fat Durm would counsel caution. Would side with the cripple, not for any care of it or its feelings but to protect his precious protégé Fane from distress.

He would have to follow suit.

Nodding Durm's head, pursing Durm's lips in a considering smile, he agreed. "Perhaps it would be wise, Your Majesty. Indeed, until I have had time to fully assess

His Highness's breadth and depth of skill, it might be prudent to delay any announcement. If it should prove that Prince Gar is, after all, the moon to your daugher's sun we might well avoid any unnecessary unpleasantness."

"Very true," said the king. "All right. We stay silent for now. But the minute you're sure, Durm, we must proceed. This kingdom cannot afford any more body blows. One way or another the question of the succession must be settled to my satisfaction. Soon."

Morg smiled again, and bowed. Thinking, and so it will be settled, little king. So it will be. But to no-one's satisfaction save my own.

In something of a self-flagellating mood, Gar headed from the Privy Council chamber to his ruined private garden. With most of it comprehensively destroyed perhaps he should take the chance to consider redesigning its layout. This time he could include a small shrine to Barl, for the offering of penance after transgression.

He found his mother there, making repairs.

Not turning at his approach, keeping her attention on the resurrection of a garden seat, she said, "I suppose this was inevitable really. It's not just your world turned topsy-turvy, it's hers too. But we were so elated for you, your father and I, I'm afraid we neglected to consider that." She sighed, and with a snap of her fingers completed the transformation of charred cinders into carved wood. "No doubt that makes us bad parents."

Gar slipped his arms around her waist from behind and kissed her hair. "It makes you nothing of the sort, Mama.

You might as well say this ridiculous eruption between me and Fane makes us bad children."

She covered his hands with hers and squeezed. "Who says I don't?"

Laughing, he slid away from her to sit on the newly restored garden seat. "Ouch, Oh well. I can't say a little scolding is undeserved. I'm sorry, Mama. I should never have let it get so out of hand."

She sat beside him. "No, you shouldn't," she said with mock severity. "Nor should she have used her magic as a weapon. It's strictly forbidden, and nobody knows that better than your sister. But what's done is done, Gar. Best that we all look to the future now." She patted his knee. "Tell me; how are you feeling? Truthfully?"

"Truthfully? Truthfully, Mama, I'm scared spitless. My blood has turned to sparkling wine. My bones are made of molten gold. Every time I open my mouth I'm afraid I'll breathe a cloud of butterflies into the air. The birth of magic is a grim and glorious thing." He hesitated. "Was it like that for you?"

"No." Her expression softened and her tired eyes gazed into the past. "For me, magic crept like the tide upon a beach. Softly. Gradually. Lapping further and further into my life until I looked around and saw only water. I suspect it's much the same for other Doranen. But your magic has crashed upon you violently, like a storm. And like a storm it's left the landscape a little the worse for wear. But we can fix that, Gar. With time. With patience. Most importantly, with love."

Gar considered the wrecked garden. "I hope so." They exchanged a brief smile. "Where's Fane?"

"In bed. Sleeping. I had Nix give her a draft. When she

wakes we'll talk sensibly, mother to daughter. We'll work this out, Gar. We must. The kingdom depends on it. Your father depends on it." Something implacable stole into her voice. "Now, more than ever, we can't let him down."

Gar felt a catch in his throat. Had to blink a few times to clear his blurring vision. "We won't, Mama. *I* won't. I swear by Blessed Barl herself." He kissed his holyring hard enough to hurt. "No matter how this turns out, no matter what I have to do, His Majesty's kingdom will be safe."

She took his hand and pressed her lips to his knuckles. "My darling boy," she whispered, then released him. "Now run away. I want to have this garden tidied up by dinnertime and I'm sure you've got things to do too."

He looked at her, uncertain. "Well . . . that's very generous of you, Mama, but surely I should help you . . ."

She shook her head. "No, Gar. I think you've done more than enough gardening for one day."

Shocked, he stared at her. She stared back. A gurgle of laughter escaped her firmly pressed lips.

"*Mama!*" he protested. "It's not *funny*!"

She struggled for control. "I know, dear. I know. Only . . . look at it!" Her arm swept wide, encompassing every last sorry inch of the ruined bower. "And you were always such a *tidy* boy!"

Stricken, trying to stifle their shrieks, they fell against each other, shoulders shaking. "Oh dear, oh dear," his mother moaned through muffling fingers. "I can't think what's come over me . . ."

Sitting up again, Gar sobered. Dragged his shirt sleeve over his face and heaved a sigh. "Neither can I. I can't imagine what Darran would say if he saw us."

His mother shuddered theatrically. "I can. Thank you, Gar. I'm now perfectly sober." She kissed his cheek. "Off you go. Will you come to dinner?"

"How about breakfast?"

"All right. Till the morning then."

With a smile and a wave he left her to the garden and returned to the Tower, where duty waited.

The first person he saw was Darran.

"Good," he said brusquely, a raised hand silencing the old meddler before he could start asking questions or offering advice. "I wish to address the staff. Have everyone—Tower, grounds and stables—assembled in the foyer ten minutes from now. Where's Asher?"

"Sir?" Darran said faintly. "Yes, sir. Asher's upstairs, as far as I am aware. Sir, if I may just—"

"No," he replied, and turned for the staircase. "You may not."

He found Asher sitting disconsolate at his desk, the week's appointment diary unrolled before him. "That Darran reckons we should cancel *all* your meetings for the week," he said, looking up. "But if we do it means—"

"Never mind that for now." Gar leaned against the nearest chair. "Why did you go from tavern to tavern discussing my condition without first asking?"

Asher sat back. "Well, to start with it were one tavern, the Goose, and to finish, because Durm said to. He wanted me to 'calm the fears of our good City Olken'."

"*Durm* said?" Gar frowned. "Are you sure?"

"Of the two people in this room, Gar, which one's more likely to have a clear recollection of recent events? Me, same as ever and not a whit changed, or you, the man who spent the morning rollin' around on the cobblestones spontaneously sprouting flowers?"

Eyebrows lifted, Gar stared. "'Spontaneously sprouting flowers'?"

"Don't look at me," said Asher, scowling. "You're the one who said I should read more books."

"Feel free to stop at any time," Gar retorted. "So Durm told you to—"

"*Aye*. Why? Is there a problem?"

Puzzled, Gar shook his head. "No. It's nothing. It's just odd he didn't mention it when—" He shrugged. "Never mind." Then he frowned. "Was it only this morning? It feels like a lifetime ago."

"It was," said Asher darkly. "Reckon I've aged fifty bloody years in the last six hours."

Gar smiled. "Well, I wouldn't let that worry you. I promise you don't look a day over sixty. Now come downstairs, would you? I'm about to address the staff."

There was barely enough space for his assembled people to fit in the Tower foyer. Gar stood on the fourth step of the spiral staircase, Asher at his right hand, and looked at all their expectant faces as they crowded knee to hip to shoulder inside the room's circumference.

"My friends," he said, smiling, "as doubtless you all know by now Barl has, in her mysterious and infinite wisdom and despite my advanced years, chosen to bestow upon me the Doranen gift of magic. As I'm sure you can imagine I am both honored and humbled by this momentous event."

"Praise Barl!" said Darran, and started clapping. "Praise Barl most mightily!" The rest of the staff joined in.

After a moment Gar raised his hands. "Thank you. Barl is indeed worthy of our praise and appreciation. Now, I expect you also heard about a little trouble in the garden a while ago."

No applause this time, just shuffling feet and surreptitious glances. He produced a shamefaced smile.

"It galls me to admit, friends, that while Barl may indeed have gifted me with magic she has yet to bestow the wisdom required to use it properly. Both I and the gardening staff would appreciate a mention of this slight omission when next you're in the chapel."

Relieved laughter. A slapped back here and there. Good. Soon the explanation would be running all over the City. As the laughter died down:

"I'm sure you know this will mean some important changes for us all. From tomorrow I shall be consumed with arcane study so that I might learn how best to control and apply my new talents. Therefore Asher shall become our kingdom's Acting Olken Administrator. You know him well now. You trust him, as do I, without reservation. Take your problems to him, no matter how large or small they may be. He will help you, as I have helped you. As one day soon I will help you again, in whatever manner Barl sees fit. Thank you all, for your affection and your service. Barl's blessings be upon you, my friends."

From the rear of the crowd, his stable meister's voice rang out. "Three cheers for the prince, lads and ladies!"

As they cheered and stamped and hooted their approval Gar felt his throat close with tears.

His loyal loving people . . . his newly reconciled sister . . . his magical birthright, burst upon him . . . truly, truly, was ever a prince of Lur so blessed?

He'd never felt so happy in all his life.

CHAPTER THIRTY

N o, no, *no*!" shouted Durm as the wobbling pile of colored wooden blocks tumbled into disarray. "The alignment must be *exact*, that's the entire *point* of this exercise!"

Swallowing rage, choking on humiliation, Gar glared at him. "I'm trying."

Durm bared his teeth. "Not hard enough. Now. Pick up the pieces and we'll start again."

He reached for the nearest block; Durm cuffed the back of his head. "Not with your *fingers*, you fool! With *magic*!"

Gar leapt back from the workbench, shaking. "Hit me again, Durm, and Master Magician or not there *will* be consequences!"

For long moments they seethed silently at each other. Then Durm sighed, deflating, and shook his head. "Forgive me, boy. I know you're doing your best. Magic is hard work. And it must be difficult, trying to reconcile a lifetime's deprivation with a mere month's bounty."

Gar unstiffened his spine. "Durm," he said ruefully, "you have no idea . . ."

A month and still he hadn't quite accepted his new self. It had been a week before he was able to open his eyes in the morning and not call glimfire even before emptying his urgent bladder. And while that panicked need to reassure himself was now past, still the pleasure of his newfound power was so piercing he was sometimes hard put not to embarrass himself by weeping.

Look at me, I made a flower. Look at me, I locked the door. Look at me. Look at me. Look at me.

The wellspring of magic within him was sweeter than wine. It fed his mind, his heart, his soul. If there'd been a way for him to dive headfirst into it and stay there forever he would have.

Sometimes, dragging himself into bed at night so tired after a day of Durm he could hardly raise his arms, he amused himself by conjuring tiny balls of glimfire and dancing them in the darkness like fireflies.

Harmless tricks like that came as easily as breathing now. But *this* . . . the exercises Durm had him working at day after day . . . the struggle to encompass his power, shape it, refine it, control it drop by miserly drop when it thundered through his veins like a waterfall of fire . . .

"You must," his father had said in a moment of privacy. "For the Weather Magic is like a hundred hundred waterfalls and it will crush you to oblivion if you don't learn control."

Remembering, Gar exhaled sharply. Braced his shoulders, lifted his head and met Durm's piercing gaze unflinching.

"Right," he said. "Let's start again."

This time he succeeded. Briefly. The blocks stayed balanced in their tower for a full three seconds before clattering onto the workbench.

"Better," said Durm, and patted him on the shoulder. "Much better. I'm going to leave you to practice now. I have other matters to attend to for the next little while. I'll rejoin you here after lunch, and once you've demonstrated to my satisfaction your mastery of this exercise we shall proceed to the next level."

Dismayed, Gar stared at him, then at the scatter of blocks on the bench. The sweat of effort was still wet on his skin. "The *next* level?"

Durm laughed. "And now you begin to understand, Your Highness. The reward for conquering one challenging task is another *more* challenging task. Welcome to the world of magic, boy."

Sourly, Gar watched him leave. Pretty soon, something would have to be done about all this "boy" business.

Fane appeared at the open doorway. Gar's frown vanished, replaced with a tentative smile. She wandered in, casual in green silk tunic and trousers, and laughed when she saw the tumbled wooden blocks on the bench.

"I remember those," she said, pulling a face. "Bloody things. I used to have nightmares about them."

Cheered, Gar grinned. "Really? That's reassuring. And don't say bloody."

"I will if I want to," she retorted, and poked her tongue out. "Bloody, bloody, bloody. See?"

"Mama doesn't like you swearing," he reminded her, fighting another smile.

"Mama isn't here. Besides, swearing is better than blowing things up."

"What things?"

She shrugged. "Anything I could find, when I couldn't make the magic do what I wanted. Why do you think this work room is so empty?"

He hadn't really noticed. He'd had other, more pressing concerns than a critique of the décor. Looking round the small room, though, seeing it properly for the first time, it did suddenly strike him as a bit on the austere side. Two workbenches, three stools and a cupboard for all of Durm's training knick-knacks. There was a series of shelves on the wall beside the window, but the only thing on them was dust.

"You always did have a temper," he said, reminiscent. Then he hesitated. Dithered for a moment, and decided to plunge in and take his chances. "I don't suppose you've got any useful advice, have you?"

She didn't answer straight away. Instead took a slow turn around the room, one finger upraised and trailing a thin streamer of dark purple smoke. It swirled and scented the room's heavy air. "About?"

He waved his hand in a vague attempt to encompass his new life. "*This*. Magic. Durm. Surviving my arcane education. I'm just beginning the journey, Fane, and you're almost at its end. There must be *something* you can tell me."

She lifted one eyebrow, head turned a little over her shoulder. Her lips curved in a complacent cat's smile. "I'm sure there is. The question is, why should I?"

"It's not a competition!"

"So you say." She draped herself across the other workbench, chin propped winsomely in her hands. "Your promise still stands then, brother dear? My birthright as WeatherWorker remains unchallenged?"

He kept his face blank, just. "My heart remains unchanged. I have no desire to wear His Majesty's crown."

It wasn't a lie. It just wasn't the . . . exact . . . truth.

Eyes narrowed, she stared at him. "I'm not sure I believe you."

"I confess," he said carefully, "to curiosity, and a little envy. WeatherWorking is the most sacred, most revered act of magic in the kingdom. If I said I hadn't wondered what it would be like to work the weather, how it would feel to serve the people in that fashion, then yes, I'd be lying. So I freely admit to you: I have wondered. A part of me does . . . regret. Is that the same as betraying my oath to you? I don't think so. But perhaps you see it differently."

Still she stared, nibbling her lower lip. He held his breath. The newborn bond between them continued tenuous, their common ground still stony. If he lost her now . . .

Sliding off the workbench, Fane twirled a gently curling strand of hair around her finger. "The trick with the wooden blocks," she said severely, "is in balancing the push and the pull of the energies. As I'm sure Durm explained, the blocks have been individually enchanted to repel each other. *Your* job is to subdue the antithetical elements and forge a fluid alliance between the competing vibrations so they can oscillate in harmony, not discordance. Only when you've achieved that will they remain balanced one upon the other."

He rolled his eyes. "Is that all? And here I was thinking it was difficult!"

Her smile was kindly condescending. "Gar, don't be dense. You're a musician, how can you not see the way it should go?"

Frustrated, he glared at the blocks of wood. "What's music got to do with it? I'm not plucking lute strings here, Fane, I'm—"

"*Think*!" she insisted, and clipped him on the back of the head. He winced. Like master, like protege. "How do you play music? One note at a time! How do you balance the blocks, control the energies? One vibration at a time!"

And suddenly it all made sense.

He closed his eyes, sought in the velvet darkness for the sounds, the colors, the tastes of each block's singular identity. Still with his eyes closed, his fingers drifted, his magic unfurled like a seed from its pod. Vibrant with life but at the same time tamed. Only the echo of waterfalls now, waiting for his command. With his mind's eye he saw the tower of blocks whole, cohesive, compliant. Heard the song they should be singing and coaxed them into a choir. The first block—the second block—third, fourth, fifth, sixth . . .

He opened his eyes.

"See?" said Fane. "Simple."

Sturdy as a tree, the wooden tower block sat on the workbench before him. Pleasure like pain suffused him.

"Thank you," he whispered. "Thank you, thank you, thank you."

Unthinking, he hugged her . . . and for the first time since her innocent infancy, she hugged him back.

Asher put down his pen, linked his fingers behind his neck and tugged. All the muscles went *pop-pop-pop* and for a moment the room swam. Groaning, he rolled his head around and around, trying to ease the persistent, nagging ache that had settled at the base of his skull and down into his shoulders.

All day he'd been stuck indoors, working, just as he'd spent nigh on the last six weeks stuck indoors, working. Or stuck indoors taking meetings with guild meisters, with Pellen Orrick, with concerned citizens. For the life of him he couldn't see any hour soon when he *wouldn't* be stuck indoors, working. Reading letters. Writing letters. Reading affidavits. Responding to affidavits. Preparing for meetings. Attending meetings. Reading notices. Drafting notices. Five more minutes of this and he was going to scream. Like a girl.

It hadn't been so bad when he was Gar's assistant. He'd done a lot of going around talking to people, and he'd enjoyed that. Enjoyed poking his nose into other people's businesses, other people's lives. Solving their problems or, if he couldn't, making sure somebody else did. Seeing how the brewers roasted their hops and the cheese makers waxed their wares and the cartwrights made their wheels so round. Especially enjoyed the respect and the welcome and the way they were so proud, because he was one of them elevated near as good as royalty, eh, and sitting in their parlors, taking tea.

But now, with Gar all magically afflicted and everything so up in the air, he'd had to leave all that pleasurable visiting behind. Instead of talking to people he was either listening to them complain in formal meetings or else bloody writing to them and he *hated* writing. It made his fingers ache and his brain buzz and he kept getting ink all over himself. The laundry maids were complaining.

And if all that wasn't bad enough he wasn't getting out to the stables. He wasn't riding or sharing a morning mug of tea with Matt or mucking about with the lads. At this rate Cygnet and the stable meister both were going to forget what he looked like.

Worst of all, his once regular visits down to the Goose had been severely curtailed. With no assistant of his own, and trying to carry his own responsibilities as well as Gar's, his free time had disappeared faster than a jug of ale down a thirsty field-hand's throat.

His nights down at the Goose were *useful*, damn it. All sorts of gossip and titbits he picked up down there. That's how he'd found out about the Guigan brothers and their shifty dealings in stock feed. How he'd put a stop to a right old bust-up between the candle makers and the bee-keepers practically afore it started. How he'd throttled more than a dozen brewing storms. If he couldn't get on down to the Goose nice and regular, who was going to nip all those pesky little problems in the bud, eh?

A nasty, sneaky voice in the back of his mind said: *you could always ask Dathne.*

Scowling, he told the voice to shut its trap. The only good thing to come out of any of this was him not having much time to lay eyes on Dathne. The thought of her was a raw wound, scabbing over. Last thing he needed was to go pickin' and pokin' and scratchin' at that little embarrassment.

I don't love you, Asher. I don't love anyone.

The razor-sharp memory of her cool voice, so controled, so brisk and matter of fact, made him want to throw something. Hit someone. He didn't know whether to be relieved that he didn't have a rival or appalled that he couldn't break down the wall she hid behind and reach the warm and beating heart of her.

He only knew that he missed her, and he never wanted to see her again.

She'd offered her help. If he took her up on that, if he pretended he was happy to be nothing but friends, if he bided his time, like any good angler, and baited his hook with patience and undemanding good company . . .

Codswallop.

Time to face facts. Dathne wasn't interested. The sooner he stopped pining, the better. Starting right now.

Abruptly, savagely sick of his office and his desk and the endless stream of problems he was expected to solve like—ha!—magic, he threw his pen at his inkpot and headed for the stables.

Where he found Matt and Dathne, damn her, sitting in the yard office amusing themselves with cards.

"Thought you had yourself a shop to run?" he demanded from the doorway, not caring overmuch that his sour temper showed.

She exchanged an arched-eyebrow look with Matt, took a moment to consider her hand of cards, put one on the table and slid a replacement from the pile between them, then said, "Poppy's after some extra pocket money so I left her to mind the till for the afternoon. Is that all right with you?"

Her sweetly poisonous tone galled him. "Poppy?" Slouching into the tack room, he pretended to care what was bubbling on the coal-fed burner in the corner. Barley and linseed mash: the fuggy steam of it hit him full in the face, stealing his breath. Out of habit, and because he didn't want to look at bloody Dathne, he grabbed the old wooden stirring spoon and slopped the horse porridge from side to side in its pot.

She was staring at him; he could feel her gaze smoldering his spine. "Aleman Derrig's youngest. Poppeta, commonly known as Poppy. The one who insists on giving you lovelorn glances and free ale when her father's not looking."

He put the spoon aside, the lid back on the porridge pot and turned round. "I know who Poppy is."

Dathne sniffed. "You could've fooled me."

"Aye, well, reckon the village idiot could fool you, Dathne," he sneered, folding his arms across his chest.

There was a half-eaten apple on the table beside her. Flushed with temper she threw it at him, hard, as Matt said protestingly, "Hey now, hey now! What's all this, Asher? There's no call to fratch at Dathne like that!"

He caught the apple, demolished it in three angry bites and lobbed the core into the waste bucket by the sink. "Sorry."

"My, *that* sounded sincere," said Dathne, rolling her eyes. She sounded just like her spicy, spiky self . . . except there was a hint of hurt surprise in her face and the cards in her clutching fingers shook ever so slightly.

He felt like a murderer. "Sorry," he said again, and this time meant it. He crossed to the camp cot against the wall and collapsed onto it. "Don't mind me. I been penned up in that Tower for what feels like three lifetimes, tryin' to come to grips with Meister Glospottle's piss problem."

"Eh?" said Matt. "I thought you had that solved a week ago."

"Aye, well, so did I," said Asher. And added, darkly, "It came back."

"What . . . like a persistent bladder infection?" suggested Dathne delicately.

Matt guffawed. Dathne grinned. And then they were laughing, all three of them, like the good and true friends they were.

"Come on," said Matt, wiping his eyes. "Forget Meister Pissy Glospottle for a bit and play a round of cards with us, eh? We've not laid eyes on you for days now, and we've missed your ugly face. Haven't we, Dath?"

"Speak for yourself," said Dathne, but she was smiling and shoving out the table's third chair with her foot.

He sat down and waited while Matt took back all the cards. As he shuffled them with casual expertise the stable meister said, "How's His Highness getting on then?"

Asher shrugged. "Buggered if I know. Hardly lay eyes on him from sunup to sundown these days. Every time I do catch a glimpse he's rushin' off to practice turning toads into toadstools with that ole Durm. Or his sister, if you can believe that."

Matt started dealing. Dathne, waiting for all her cards to arrive before picking them up, said, "Is he any good?"

Asher laughed. "Don't ask me. Still . . ." He thought for a moment. "Reckon he can't be exactly *bad*, I s'pose. If he were bad he'd be in a worse mood than me, but every time I see him he's smiling."

Dathne and Matt exchanged glances. "Well," she said brightly, and turned her cards over, "isn't that nice for him? I'll start, shall I? Ladies first, and all that horse manure. I wager . . . three cuicks to a demi-trin I'll see full house in seven switches."

Grinning at Matt, who was throwing a theatrical fit at the outrageous wager, Asher sat back in his chair and stared at Dathne while pretending to consider his own cards. For the first time in a long time he felt something approaching happiness.

Friendship was less, far less, than his heart's desire, but if it was all he could get, at least for now, perhaps it wasn't so bad after all.

Morg wrote the note in Durm's cramped and crabby cursive: *Come to my study at dawn.* Sealed it, and gave it to a servant to deliver to the prince.

Duly summoned, the cripple presented himself at sunup the following morning, agog with curiosity. "Durm? Is something wrong?"

Inviting him in with a beckoning finger, Morg closed and warded the suite's double doors and guided him into the library to a seat at the round velvet-covered table by the window. On it was the ancient wooden box housing the Weather Orb.

"What's this?" asked the cripple, examining the box with interest.

Morg sat in the other chair and waved his hand. "Why don't you see for yourself?"

The cripple raised an eyebrow and reached for the box. Went to slide free the pin securing the lid and yelped as the lightly applied ward spell bit him.

Morg laughed. "Did you think I would make it easy? Undo the ward spell."

"I would if I knew how." There was an edge to the cripple's voice.

"You don't need to know how," he countered. "The 'how' is within you, Your Highness. As it was the day your magic revealed itself and I asked you to make a rose. Remember?"

The cripple gave him a look. "I remember that just yesterday you told me I was a cretin and a fool and a disgrace to the memory of my ancestors."

"Academic hyperbole." Morg dismissed the complaint with the wave of one hand. "It was merely enthusiastic encouragement, I assure you."

"Perhaps *over*enthusiastic would be a more accurate description," muttered the cripple. "To be honest, I think I've been doing exceptionally good work of late."

"And so you have, Gar, so you have," Morg soothed. "Why else do you think I've summoned you here this morning?"

"I don't know why you've summoned me. I'm still waiting for you to tell me."

"And I will," Morg promised. "Just as soon as you deactivate the ward spell."

After a single, searching glance at him the cripple reached out to the box and dissolved the lock's guarding enchantment. He laughed. "I did it!"

"Of course you did, Your Highness. I believe there is nothing you can't do, provided you put your mind to it."

"It was so simple!" the cripple exclaimed. "So natural. Just like . . . breathing."

"Of course," agreed Morg. With my help, you deformed monstrosity. "That is how magic should be. The reason you've found it so hard during our lessons is because I've been forcing you to think about it. To analyze it. To apply your powers consciously when in reality they flow most easily from the subconscious part of your mind."

"Then why do it?"

"Because it is necessary. Trust me."

The cripple smiled. "You know I do. Implicitly. Durm . . ."

"Yes, my boy?"

"How is this possible?" the cripple whispered. "How could I have had all this power inside me for so many years and never once *imagined* or suspected or felt so much as a hint of it?"

He smiled and spread his hands wide. "That, I'm afraid, is likely to remain a mystery. Let's just put it down to another of Blessed Barl's miracles, shall we, and continue with our current business. Open the box."

The cripple obeyed, revealing the box's contents. His face stilled. "That's the Weather Orb. Fane described it once. Why are you showing it to me?"

"Why do you think?"

Shoving his chair away from the table, the cripple retreated. "No. It's too soon. Durm, my powers woke from their slumber scant weeks ago! And now you want me to undertake the Transference? Fane studied with you for *years* before—"

Morg shrugged. "You are not your sister. Her powers are great, I don't deny that. But they grew as she did. Matured as she did. I had to wait until she was ready to face the immense tides and tests of the Weather Magic. But your circumstances are very different. Your power has sprung forth fully developed. With you it's not a case of maturation but exploration. And while your power is formidable, Gar, it might yet be that Fane is still the better WeatherWorker. Receiving the incantations is but the first step on the way to determining who ultimately shall be named your father's heir. Even I cannot tell how long it will take you to master their complexities. Or even if you can. Don't you see? The sooner you're given the magics, the sooner can we begin to explore your aptitude for controling and applying them."

"I understand that," the cripple said, still staring at the Orb. Fascinated. Repelled. "But what would a little further delay matter? I need more time, Durm. Time to fully grasp what's happened to me. How I feel about it. What it means, for my future and the future of the kingdom. That's all. Just a little time."

Morg sighed. Lowered his voice and let Durm's face assume a sorrowful, portentous expression. "Your Highness, unwittingly you have put your finger on the very pulse of the matter. Time is the one thing we may not have. To be brutal, and forgive me but there is no other way, we don't know how long your dear father will remain the WeatherWorker. The bulk of his life now lies behind him, spent lavishly in the service of Lur. For the sake of our kingdom we must ensure the succession. If we don't, we give Conroyd Jarralt more grist for his mill. And then he will grind and grind and grind until the flour comes out to bake a bread of *his* liking. Not ours."

The cripple had lost all his color and in his eyes, tears. Stupid, sentimental fool. He'd do better saving his woe for the days to come. Soon he'd have something truly worth weeping for.

"You're certain of this?"

Morg spread his hands. "Alas."

"And once the decision is made, between Fane and myself? What then? Only one can hold the Weather Magic."

Ah. So his little worm was hooked, and wriggling. Morg swallowed a smile. "There is an incantation for Transference reversal. Unpleasant, to be sure, but the effects aren't permanent. Please, Your Highness." He gestured at the empty chair. "I promise, this is how it must be."

The cripple returned to his seat at the table. "You're absolutely certain . . . ?"

"Absolutely, Your Highness. After all, as loyal subjects and men who love our king, we have our duty."

"Duty . . ." The cripple sighed. "Yes. In the end it always comes down to duty, doesn't it?"

Yes indeed. Duty was the magic word. "It does, Your Highness. And like your father you have never shirked your duty, no matter what the personal cost."

The cripple straightened his spine. "Then let's proceed . . . on one condition."

He kept the smile pinned to Durm's lips. "Yes?"

"When it's over I want to be the one to tell Fane. I want to explain to her that I had no choice. That this doesn't mean I'm breaking my word. If I explain, I know she'll understand."

Morg laughed. Did he truly know his sister so little? "Of course, Your Highness. I have no objection. Now. Remove the Orb from its box and hold it lightly in your hands. Clear your mind. Quiet your soul. Look deep into its heart and breathe in . . . out . . . in . . . out . . ."

The incantation of Transference was a complicated one, with five different levels culminating in a single trigger word. As the cripple prepared himself for the assumption of powers, Morg plucked the words of the Transference from Durm's memory and rolled them on his tongue like a gourmand tasting truffles. Yes . . . *yes* . . . it was all so ludicrously simple. All he had to do was change *this* word—and *this* word—and finally *this* one— and all would be well.

For him, at least, if for nobody else in this doomed kingdom.

He looked up. The cripple was ready: centered and silent and waiting, oblivious.

With a smile so wide it felt he could engulf the world in a single bite, as tiny Durm screeched and scrabbled impotent in his cage, Morg triggered the spell.

The cripple screamed. Inside the pulsing Weather Orb the magic writhed like a living thing in torment. The Orb began to glow, brighter and brighter until it burned like a multicolored sun. A shadow touched it: Morg held his breath. Would Barl's magic detect his handiwork in the cripple's mind? Would it reject the prince as it had rejected him?

The shadow faded. Disappeared. Morg released the trapped air from Durm's aching lungs and leaned forward. Watched avidly as the cripple's fingers convulsed around the Orb, blind staring eyes reflecting gold and green and crimson and purple.

It was working.

The radiant light spread from the Orb and over Gar's fingers like butter, melting. Flowed *into* his fingers, his hands, his wrists and through his entire body until he glowed like a lantern made of flesh.

And then the light died, suddenly extinguished. With a moan the cripple collapsed across the table, emptied of incandescence. The Orb rolled from between his lax fingers to rest quiescent against its drab wooden box.

Morg let out a long, shaky breath. Reached for the cripple's lax wrist and felt for a pulse. It was there: scudding, erratic. His chest rose and fell quickly, shallowly.

He'd survived.

As he waited for the cripple to wake from his stupor he stared longingly at the Orb. More than anything he wanted to destroy it, crush it, spill Barl's trapped magic to the floor and smear it into nothingness beneath his victorious, contemptuous heel.

But he couldn't. So he put it back in its box and returned it to the cupboard. Briefly he considered sealing the doors with a killing ward, but discarded the notion. To do so might arouse unwanted curiosity; they were trusting fools, these lost Doranen. The king came here often, and was used to rummaging at will amongst Durm's things. Going to another cupboard he extracted an empty glass globe and its stand and put them on the table. Then he sat back, gloating, and waited.

At length the cripple stirred. Sat up. "Durm." He pressed his fists to his temples. "You should have warned me it would hurt like that. Fane said it was exhausting, but not that there'd be pain. I thought it would tear me apart . . . or turn me to ash."

Morg shrugged. "Such warnings are pointless. One man's pain is another man's pleasure, after all. Each Transfer is different."

The cripple shook his head. "I feel so *strange*. Did the Transfer work? For a moment it felt almost as though the Weather Magic wanted to . . . to reject me. Why would that be?" He laughed, shakily. "Am I still not good enough?"

"You are perfect," Morg said sharply. "But to put your

mind at rest, let us try a small experiment. Here is an
empty vessel. Cast your mind within the void and make it
rain."

"I'm afraid," the cripple whispered.

"You are a prince of royal House Torvig!" thundered
Morg. "Honor your father and make it rain!"

The cripple reached for the clear globe. Held it before
his eyes in silence, gaze unfocused as he searched the
new knowledge within. Then he stirred. Stared into the
globe's vacant heart and spoke. The air within it churned.
Thickened. Turned white. Gray. Black.

Wept.

"Look, Durm," the cripple breathed. There were tears
in his eyes. On his cheeks. There was blood, a tiny trickle,
but he didn't heed it. "I made it rain . . ."

The servants he passed in the corridors on his way to find
Fane spoke to him, but he couldn't hear them. He said
something in return, "Good morning' most probably, but
he couldn't hear himself. Could barely see their faces or
remember their names.

He'd made it rain.

Blessed Barl preserve him, he'd made it rain, and his
life would never be the same again.

He found Fane in the palace solar, eating a solitary
breakfast. The hovering servant bobbed a curtsy. He dismissed her and crossed the marble floor towards his
sister.

Without looking up from her plate she said coldly, "Go
away."

He stopped. Frowned. "Fane . . ."

She reached for her teacup. Sipped. Swallowed. Put it

back in its saucer with a faint *plink*. "Did you think I wouldn't know? Did you think I wouldn't *feel* it?"

He went to her and dropped to one knee beside her chair. "Fane, I'm sorry. It wasn't my idea. I didn't want the weather magic. I *begged* the king to let my promise stand. But the day we fought there was a scene in Privy Council. It was . . . awful. Accusations were made. Conroyd Jarralt—"

"He made you break your word?" Her face was pale, composed. She spoke calmly, with a vague air of disinterest. As she sliced a hothouse teshoe with her sharp little fruit knife her eyes never left his face. "What a bad man."

"I argued. I did. I told them I'd made you a promise. But it was all of them against me. Even Father agreed it had to be done. In the end, it came down to what's best for the kingdom."

She popped a slice of teshoe into her mouth. Chewed. Swallowed. "I'm sure it did."

He put his hand on her arm. "Fane, I wasn't lying. I didn't ask for this. I didn't break my promise willingly. I had no choice."

She reached for a bread roll. The movement broke the contact of his fingers against her sleeve. "So you'd abdicate, would you, if it was decided you'd make the better WeatherWorker? You'd refuse the throne for my sake? Is that what you're saying?"

"Yes!" he cried. Remembered the rain. Cursed. "Perhaps. I don't know." Frustrated, he stood and began to pace around the solar. "It might not be as easy as that. This can't be about what you or I want, Fane. Our personal desires are *nothing* compared to the welfare of the kingdom. It all comes down to duty. You understand that better than anyone."

Fane finished tearing the bread roll into tiny pieces, selected one and smeared it with sweet butter. "Now I'm confused. It's a simple question, Gar: would you abdicate, yes or no?" Still watching him, she ate the bread.

Gar stopped pacing. Returned to her side and again knelt on the chequered tile floor. "I . . . don't think I could. Not if I were truly chosen. But, Fane, I swear, it won't come to that. You are the superior magician, I have no doubt of it, you—"

Fane sat back in her chair. Her eyes were very . . . polite. "So when you swore to me the crown was mine, only mine, always mine, what you really meant was, unless you decided you'd rather it was yours?"

Barl save him. "*No*. I meant what I said, Fane. You have to believe that. I spat on it, remember?"

She smiled. "I remember." Leaning forward, she spat on him. As the hot saliva trickled down his cheek she said, "And now we're even."

He pulled a handkerchief from his pocket and wiped away the spittle. "Please, let's talk about this. I want us to be close, Fane, I want us to be friends, I want—"

"I don't." She picked up her sharp little fruit knife and pointed its tip at him. Sunlight flashed upon the blade. It was a small knife, hardly lethal, but somehow it was worse than a hundred balls of flaming glimfire. "What I want is for you to go away. Now."

He stood. Tucked the soiled handkerchief back in his pocket. The knife was still pointing at him. "I can't leave it like this, Fane."

Her eyes were glittering. With tears, with temper, with implacable hate. "I can."

He reached out his hand to her. "Fane . . . *please* . . ."

With a shriek like a falcon swooping for the kill she lunged across the table. The knife caught him. Cut silk and skin. Spilled blood.

He fled the solar, his wounded arm tucked inside his weskit where no-one could see it. The memory of her face chased him all the way back to the Tower.

CHAPTER THIRTY-ONE

D'you *mind*?" said Asher as his inkpot floated gently past his nose for the third time.

Gar grinned, briefly. "No."

"Well, I do!" Asher snatched the pot to safety. "I got work to finish here. Reports for Pellen Orrick don't write 'emselves and—"

"Would you like them to?"

"What are you hangin' around here like a bad smell for anyways? Ain't you and Durm s'posed to be goin' on a magical field trip or some such shenanigans?"

"He's been delayed. He'll be along in due course."

Asher groaned. "Then why don't you wait for 'im downstairs? No muckin' about, Gar, I'm bloody drownin' here."

Gar looked at the desk crowded with papers and parchment. "So I see."

With a sigh, Asher sat back in his chair. "Truth is, I don't reckon I'll manage much longer without a proper assistant. And *not* that bloody Willer! He's as much use as tits on a bull."

Gar's lips twitched. "All right. Find yourself an assistant

you can work with, if there is such a creature. Offer them thirty trins a week."

"Twenty-five," said Asher, scowling. "No point givin' a body ideas above his station, eh?"

That made him laugh: something of a miracle. "Fine. I don't really care. Just deal with it."

After a considering pause Asher said, "So. Is she talkin' to you yet?"

She. Fane. Gar rubbed the half-healed cut on his forearm and shook his head. "No."

"Aye, well . . . give her time," said Asher. Trying to sound confident. Failing. "She'll come round."

"No, Asher," he replied sadly. Remembering her face. The knife. "Somehow I don't think she will."

Time for a change of subject. "Well," said Asher, "now you've got your floatin' inkpot trick down a treat, when d'you reckon they'll let you out in public to impress the locals?"

Gar shrugged, feigning indifference. "Soon."

"Which means when? Tomorrow? Next week? Next month?"

"I don't know exactly. All Durm will say is *soon*. I think he wants to be certain I'll not disgrace him."

"Bugger what he wants," said Asher, snorting. "Do you feel ready?"

Gar laughed nervously. "Good question. Sometimes I think yes, and other times . . ." He shook his head. "Durm's right. I must be ready. I must have complete control of my power. Revealing my transformation prematurely would be disastrous. This isn't just about me, Asher. You know the political ramifications of this change. For most of my life I've been an object of pity.

Of scorn. An embarrassing aberration. For most of my life I've been more or less invisible, at least to my own race."

"You're forgettin' Lady Scobey."

Gar shuddered. "If only I could. You know, if there's a drawback to my miracle it's knowing she's going to redouble her efforts to match me with her wretched daughter."

Grinning, Asher nodded. "Never mind. She won't be the only one. You'll have your pick of blonde beauties now, I reckon. Lucky bastard."

"Yes," said Gar, his smile sly. "I confess the thought isn't entirely unpalatable. But my search for a bride will have to wait, I'm afraid. First I must leap the hurdle of my past and gain the confidence and trust of my peers. They know me only as a magical failure. As a cripple. I'll have one chance to show them that's no longer true. One chance . . . and if I stumble, I'll not get a second."

"You worried about that?"

Gar hesitated, then flicked his fingers. "Of course not. Not really. I just—"

He was interrupted by a sharp knock on the open office door. Willer. Stiff-necked and stuffy, as usual. "Your Highness," he said, bowing. "Their Majesties are here, and desirous of speaking with you."

"Very well," said Gar. "Show them into the library, then, and—"

"Forgive me, sir. They're outside. In a carriage."

"Oh. All right. Thank you, Willer." Willer bowed and retreated, and Gar raised his eyebrows at Asher. "Coming?"

"You don't listen, do you? All that bloody magic's

bunged up your lugholes worse than earwax. I got *work* to do."

Gar clapped him on the shoulder. "It'll still be here five minutes from now. Come on. You need some fresh air. In case you hadn't noticed you're getting as persnickety as Darran."

The royal carriage was halted at the Tower's front entrance. It wasn't one of the official carriages, enclosed and groaning beneath the weight of gilt and hand-carved curlicues, but the open touring affair used on the day of Asher's parade. Sprawled on its crimson leather seats were his father, his mother and Fane, splendid in brocades, leather and wool. His parents were talking, laughing; Fane was silent, her expression as smooth as glass. Gar tried to smile at her as he came down the sandstone steps but she refused to meet his gaze. He felt a small pain between his ribs, but kept it from his face as he turned the smile towards their parents instead.

"There he is!" said Dana, and beckoned him closer with a gloved hand. "Gar, my love, we're off to Salbert's Eyrie for a family picnic. Just us, nobody else. We had the whole area closed so we could enjoy some privacy. Conjure yourself a warmer coat, because the weather's definitely getting chilly. One for Asher, too. There's more than enough room in the carriage for him and, besides, he's practically family as well."

Gar tried to catch Fane's eye again, and again was unsuccessful. Thwarted, he glanced at the cloudless sky. A family picnic? It was a perfect day for it, certainly. He wished he could go; behind his mother's bright smile and determined gaiety there was strain and a feverish unhappiness.

"Mama, it's a charming idea, truly, but—"

"Come on, Gar," the king said coaxingly. "The snow will be here before long and there'll be no more picnics for months."

"Yes, sir, I realize that, but—"

With a roll of his eyes, Borne turned to Asher. "Well, sir? What about you?"

Asher bowed. "I'd surely come if I could, Your Majesty. Trouble is, Meister Glospottle's still got problems with his piss, y'see, and he's waitin' on me to fix 'em for him."

"And can you?" said the queen. "I'm most anxious for his difficulties to be resolved, Asher."

Another bow. "I be doin' my best, Your Majesty. But it seems there be more to Meister Glospottle's piss problem than meets the eye."

"I see," said the king after a pause. "Well, far be it from me to come between you and Meister Glospottle's . . ." A wicked grin. "Problems. Gar, must I make this a royal command?"

"Even if you did, I'd have to refuse. I'm due to meet with Durm at any moment. My studies—"

"Are swallowing you alive," said Borne. "Barl knows we've hardly seen hide nor hair of you these past long weeks, Gar. There's more to life than magic. Family is important too."

Gar couldn't help himself. For the third time he looked at Fane. This time she let a spasm of emotion cross her face. His heart sank. "Yes, I know that, sir, but—"

"But pleasure," a new voice said urbanely, "needs often take a back seat to duty."

*   *   *

"Durm!" said Borne, startled, and craned his neck. "Where did you spring from? I swear you move more and more like a cat every day."

Standing beside the carriage horses' heads, Morg smiled. Glossy brown beasts, they were, with perfect paces and gentle eyes. Reaching up a casual hand he stroked the nearest soft nose. "Did I hear you aright, Majesty? You're bound on a picnic?"

"To Salbert's Eyrie," said Dana. "Before the snows come. Will you join us?"

"Nothing would give me greater pleasure," said Morg, fingers sliding up and down the horse's nose. Perfect, perfect, so wonderfully perfect. "Salbert's Eyrie is an ideal place for a picnic, but alas, I must decline. His Highness and I still have much work to do. Another day, perhaps. But don't let us detain you any longer on such a superb morning . . . and do think of us slaving away as you quaff your wine and nibble the dainties you've brought in your picnic basket." He sighed. "Life is so cruel, isn't it?"

There was laughter as he pulled a mock-sorrowful face. Lifting his other hand, smiling, he ensured he was touching both horses. Power flowed through his fingers. The horses' liquid brown eyes flared scarlet. He stepped back. "Mind your animals, driver," he admonished the coachman as the horses snorted and pinned their ears back, heads tossing.

Borne looked from the cripple to the lout and shook his head in sorrow. "I can see your minds are quite made up. I confess I'm disappointed, but not surprised. I warn you, though, next time we really won't take no for an answer."

"As His Majesty commands," said Morg, and moved to join the prince at the foot of the Tower steps. "Next time."

"Drive on then, Matcher," said Borne. The coachman picked up his reins and shook his whip and the carriage rolled forward as the horses leaned into their harness.

Morg looked around as Asher came down the rest of the steps. "You should go," the lout said to the prince in an undertone. "When you thought he was dead you'd have given anythin' to spend just one more day with him. Now here's a day bein' handed to you on a silver platter and you're turnin' it down. For what? For *magic*? That's mad. He ain't goin' to live forever, Gar. Go."

Frozen, the cripple stared at the gravel beneath his feet. "You're right," he whispered. "I'm a fool."

"Just remember," the lout added, "you got that meetin' with Matt this afternoon, about this season's two year olds. So don't go gettin' carried away with the scenery and whatnot."

The prince looked up. "It's a picnic, not an expedition. I'll be back in time, don't fret. And tell Darran where I've gone, will you? He'll fuss, otherwise." He turned and pulled an apologetic face. "Sorry, Durm. Studies are canceled for today.' Then he sprang after the carriage, shouting. "Wait! Wait!"

As the carriage stopped and the king turned round in his seat, Morg rested speculative eyes on the lout. "Well, well, well," he murmured. "What a meddlesome young man you are." And could have *killed* him with such pleasure . . .

Defiant, stiff-necked, the lout stared back. "It's only one day. He can put aside his studies for one day. Sir."

"As you say," he said, smiling thinly. "It's only one day."

Seated now in the carriage, the cripple leaned out and waved an arm. "Durm! Come on!" he called. "There's no point in you staying behind now!"

"No," Morg agreed under his breath. "There's no point at all." He waved an acquiescent hand. "I surrender, sir! Your persuasive powers have overcome my better judgement. To Salbert's Eyrie we go!"

Walking slowly, because above all things Durm was a dignified man, Morg closed the distance between himself and the royal carriage, his mind turning over and over as he rearranged his important plans.

Again.

Soon, very soon, he would have to arrange a special reward for the Olken lout Asher.

The carriage bowled along through the lush open countryside, heading for picturesque Salbert's Eyrie lookout. As the horses shied, plunging, Borne spoke over his shoulder to the coachman. "The team seems fresh today, Matcher!"

"That they do, Your Majesty," Matcher replied, forearms rigid as he grasped the reins. "Don't know what's got into them and that's a fact."

"Must be all this crisp autumn air," Borne said. "Mind how you go, won't you?"

"Certainly will, Your Majesty."

Seated opposite him, the queen tipped her face to the sun and sighed. "Oh, it feels so good to be outside. Do you know I've done nothing but chair committee meetings for nearly a week? I declare I don't know how those women can be so staid. That Etienne Jarralt—"

"Ha," said her husband. "I'll gladly swap you the lord for the lady."

Dana sniffed. "No, thank you."

The cripple considered his father. "He's not still complaining, is he?"

"No more than usual," said the king with a dismissive flick of his fingers. "It's all right. Conroyd can't help himself. He's exactly as your mother described him: a dog with a bone. Either he'll bury it and forget where it is, or he'll chew it to pieces and there'll be an end to the discussion."

"With any luck," said the cripple, disdainful, "he'll chew it and choke."

"I think," his sister said distantly, "you should be kinder to him. I don't care what any of you say, he's not a bad man." She was seated with her back to the coachman, beside her mother, curled up in the corner of the wide touring carriage. Her hair was knotted in loops and braids on the top of her head and she was staring with intense concentration at the countryside flashing by. "It's not his fault his ancestor lost Trevoyle's Trials and his house never got to breed up kings. He's a powerful magician. He might have made a very good WeatherWorker."

There was an awkward pause, filled with the pounding of hooves on the roadway and the bouncing creak of the carriage. Morg let his eyelids droop and watched the girl from under his lashes. She was looking very beautiful this morning. A pity the smooth perfection of her forehead was marred by a frown. Tension, arising from resentment of her brother. Foolish child. Life was far too short to

waste in petty squabbling. It was a shame she'd never realized it.

As the carriage picked up a little more speed, Borne
again spoke up. "For the love of Barl, Matcher, must I repeat myself? Slow those damned horses down!"

"Yes, Your Majesty," said Matcher, and once more
hauled on the reins.

Morg let his gaze drift over the greenery by the side of
the road and smiled. Beside him, the cripple shifted on
the red leather seat then leaned forward a little, trying to
catch his sister's attention. "I've not seen you for days,
Fane," he said. "How do your studies progress?"

She sat there like a maiden carved from ice. "Satisfac-
torily."

Her brother nodded. Morg could feel the effort in him
as he tried to chip away her frozen façade. Fool. Didn't
he know by now he was wasting his time? The girl was
just like Barl: a beautiful heartbreaker. "That's good," the
cripple said, trying to sound encouraging. "What incantations are you working on?"

"My own."

The queen tried to smile. Took her daughter's hand in
hers and squeezed. "Come, darling, you can tell us more
than that, can't you? I'd like to hear what you've been
doing, too."

Fane pulled her hand free. "I thought we were leaving
work behind today."

"Don't be rude, Fane," the king said, mildly enough,
but with an undercurrent of warning.

The girl's eyes flashed cold fire. "I'm not rude. I just
don't want to talk about it." Her gaze flickered to the crip-

ple, then elsewhere. "Why don't you ask Gar what he's been doing? I'm sure that's much more exciting."

The king's tired face contracted. "Stop it. I'll have no quarrelling, is that clear? This is a family outing, something to be enjoyed, and I won't have your tiresome jealousy spoiling it."

The cripple lifted one hand. Placating, as always. Pathetic weakling. "Father. Please. She's a right to be hurt. Angry. Willingly or not, I broke my promise to her and—"

Fane sat up. "I don't want you defending me."

"Please," said the queen. "Please can we just—"

"*Enough*!" Borne snapped. "How many times must I say it? I won't tolerate a divided house! I refuse to leave that as my legacy to this kingdom. Not after a lifetime of sacrifice and service. Gar, Fane—one of you will be WeatherWorker after me and the other won't. If you refuse to accept this then anarchy will again stalk this land. In days long hence, once a new generation's blood has soaked into the soil, they'll call it Borne's Schism. Or Gar's. Or Fane's. Is that what you want? Is that how you wish our house to be remembered?"

"Oh, *please*, let's not argue," cried the queen. There was a treacherous break in her voice and her eyes were sheened with tears. "It's such a lovely day. Can't we leave politics behind us for a few hours and enjoy each other's company? I'm so tired of magic and WeatherWorking and worry! Of late I find myself profoundly sorry that Conroyd Jarralt's wretched ancestor *didn't* win Trevoyle's bloody Trials! Then he could be the one with the weight of the kingdom on his shoulders and I could look forward to night after night of sleep unriven by nightmares!"

After a short, stricken silence: "My love . . ." Borne took his wife's hand and pressed it to his lips. "Forgive me. Forgive us all. These past weeks have been hardest on you, I think. You're so busy being strong for everyone around you . . . and we're so used to counting on that strength . . . it's selfish and unfair and we should all know better." He kissed her hand again. "*I* should know better."

"As should I," the cripple said quietly. "I'm sorry, Mama."

"So am I," his sister added, thawing slightly.

Dana put her arm around the girl and hugged her, hard. "I know, darling. It's all right. We've had a lot on our plates lately. That's why today is so important. We must smile. Laugh. Model ourselves on ladies best not mentioned and be frivolous!" She flashed a teasing look at her husband's Master Magician. "Even you, Durm! I am determined that before the day is out I shall see a daisy chain around your neck!"

Morg smiled. "I very much doubt it, madam."

She smiled back, refusing to believe him. Foolish woman. A cautiously companionable silence fell; at length they reached the gated turn-off for the Eyrie. Slowed. Stopped to greet the guards on duty, posted to turn away lesser mortals who might interfere with royalty at play. The horses tossed their heads and fretted, straining in their harness. When the coachman released his hold on their bits they leapt, and the carriage rattled onwards.

"Look," said Fane, pointing. On their left, flashing by as the horses' long strides ate up the road, a painted sign. *Welcome to Salbert's Eyrie.*

"Nearly there," said Dana, and threaded her arm through her daughter's. "Oh, we're going to have a wonderful day. I can feel it in my bones. How long is it since we picnicked together at the Eyrie? It must be nearly a year!" Turning a little, she raised her voice. "Matcher, Matcher, do slow *down*! The countryside is whipping past at such a rate we can scarcely see it, let alone enjoy it!"

"Yes, Your Majesty, sorry, Your Majesty!" said Matcher, and leaned back hard against the horses' iron mouths, grunting with the effort. Morg stared at his straining back, his heaving shoulders. He was wasting his time. The horses' minds were a ferment of madness now. No power under the sun could stop them, save his.

It was nearly time. Shifting a little in his seat, Morg readied himself. Regretted, briefly, Durm's fleshy and ponderous body. Still. He had power enough to overcome the minor impediment. He had power enough for anything . . .

Out of patience entirely, Borne raised his voice. "The Eyrie isn't far from here, Matcher. Stop the carriage and we'll walk the rest of the way. It's a view to be savored, not rushed at. You can take the team back to the stables and return for us this afternoon. Perhaps the extra mileage will cool the heat from their heels."

"Yes, Your Majesty," said Matcher, and signaled his team to drop out of their spanking trot and back to a suitably sedate walk.

Nothing happened.

"Matcher!" Borne said sharply. "I said stop here!"

The coachman fetched a desperate glance over his

shoulder. "I heard you, sire! It's the horses that ain't listening!"

And just as though the words were a signal the spanking trot became a lurching canter, and then a pounding gallop.

"For Barl's sake, Matcher, what are you doing?" Borne shouted. "The Eyrie, man! The *Eyrie*! Stop those bloody horses *now*, before it's too late!"

"I'm trying!" Matcher sobbed. "I can't!"

"Then turn them off the road! Break all their bloody legs if you have to! Barl's sweet love, you fool, do you want to kill us all?"

Matcher gasped. "I can't—they're too strong—"

On a muffled oath, Borne tried to climb up and over the coach railing. Struggled to reach Matcher, to reach the reins, to lend his strength to the coachman's desperate hauling on the demented horses.

The cripple let out a cry and flung himself to the other side of the carriage to join his father and the coachman. Morg shoved him back into his seat.

"What are you doing?" the cripple raged as the king and the coachman wrapped the reins round their forearms and pulled, shouting aloud with the effort. "I have to help!"

"You can't," said Morg. "You might hurt yourself."

Now the king was trying to save them with magic, shouting at the horses at the top of his lungs. Spells of somnolence. Spells of obedience. Even a spell to snap the harness so the carriage could break free. Spell after spell after spell . . . Morg destroyed each and every one with a thought. The carriage swept around the final bend and Dana, staring along the roadway, screamed. Directly ahead was the famous lookout. Spectacular. Untamed. Between disaster and safety, nothing but a stout wooden railing. The roadway curved to the right, intending to guide visitors to the genteel security of picnic grounds and nodding bluebells, of brilliant sunshine and dappled shade.

The carriage hurtled on.

"Durm, *do* something!" screamed Fane, clutching her mother, all beauty consumed by terror. "There *must* be a spell—"

"Oh, there is," Morg said, smiling, and stood.

With a flourish and a single word he froze them all: Matcher, Borne, Fane, Dana and Gar. With another word and the snap of his fingers he sent Gar flying out of the carriage and onto the grassy side of the road. The prince hit the tussocked turf hard, sliding, to fetch up against the trunk of a spindly tree.

With arm upraised Morg opened his mouth to send himself to safety and leave the carriage plunging towards its destruction. But one wheel hit a half-buried rock on the side of the road. Shattered. The carriage leapt into the air and before he could save himself Morg was thrown out. Striking the road hard, splintering fragile bone, tearing vulnerable flesh, he rolled and rolled and rolled until his head struck another rock and his pell-mell progress halted.

By which time the magic-maddened carriage horses had galloped the king, the queen, the princess and their coachman clean through the wooden safety rail and over the edge of Salbert's Eyrie. As though they had wings. As though they could fly. Their screams, falling, echoed the skirling of the eagles that rode the thermals high above the hidden valley floor. Then the screams stopped, abruptly, and a fusillade of echoes rang out as the carriage and its passengers and its horses shattered on the slopes of the unforgiving Eyrie.

And after that: silence.

The story concludes in

THE AWAKENED MAGE

Kingmaker, Kingbreaker
Book Two

ACKNOWLEDGEMENTS

Where to start? This has been an epic journey: thanks are owed to so many people . . .

Stephanie Smith, for believing in me even though the early work was—exceedingly early. And drafty.

The entire HarperCollins Voyager team in Australia, for helping the dream come true.

Australian Literary Management, for taking me on.

Mary, for her keen and critical eye and years of friendship. One serendipitous phone call and a mutual love of "The Sandbaggers". Who'd've thunk it, eh?

Carol, who said it'd happen a long time before I really believed it would.

Jenn, Cindee, Sharon, Gill and Ellen, for being.

My fellow Voyager authors, and the Purple Zoners for the warmth of their welcome.

The Infinitas Writers' Group, and Elaine and Pete and Melissa, for their input and encouragement.

The folk at the original Del Rey Online Writers Workshop, who gave me hope.

Terry Dowling and Kim Wilkins, for the right words at the right time.

The booksellers, for championing Australian writers.

And last, but never least, you . . . the reader . . . for putting your money where my mouth is. Here's hoping your trust hasn't gone unrewarded.

extras

orbit

meet the author

KAREN MILLER was born in Vancouver, Canada, and moved to Australia with her family when she was two. She started writing stories while still in primary school, where she fell in love with speculative fiction after reading *The Lion, the Witch and the Wardrobe*. Over the years she has held down a wide variety of jobs, including horse stud groom in Buckingham, England. She is working on several new novels. Visit the official Karen Miller Web site at www.karenmiller.net.

interview

Have you always wanted to be a writer?

I think so. I recall writing a *Lost in Space* story (complete with illustrations!) when I was still in primary school. From that moment, I was doomed.

What draws you to writing speculative fiction?

When I read *The Lion, the Witch and the Wardrobe*—again in primary school, clearly a formative time—I fell in love with the spec fic genre and read it all through school. I read it today. Spec fic and mystery are my two favorite literary genres. So it seemed natural to write spec fic.

As for selecting fantasy, I think it's because I've always been a history buff, and the two go so well together. In many ways history *is* fantasy—such alien worlds and concepts, yet also such humanity. It provides great inspiration.

How did you come up with the Kingmaker, Kingbreaker story?

The kernel of the idea came to me while I was swimming laps. It was just the fragment of a scene: two friends, one royal, one common, brought to a terrible place of confrontation, where the prince is about to order the commoner's execution. And from that grew the entire saga. Who are these people? How did they get to this pivotal moment? Why is the execution imminent? So I had to go back in time, to find out how it started, then forward to see how it ended . . . and in the process the story was born.

Did the story change much over the course of its writing?

Yes and no. All the basic elements have stayed pretty much the same, although as I wrote various characters assumed more and more importance to how things unfold. For instance, when he first appeared Willer was just a walk-on bit player—but then he took over and became a major villain! That's what makes writing so rewarding. It's a real voyage of discovery, you might think you know what's going on in your story but the characters always have a way of surprising you—and, I hope, the reader!

introducing

If you enjoyed **THE INNOCENT MAGE**,
keep a look out for

THE AWAKENED MAGE

Book 2 of Kingmaker, Kingbreaker
by Karen Miller

With one callused hand shading his eyes, Asher stood on the Tower's sandstone steps and watched the touring carriage with its royal cargo and Master Magician Durm bowl down the driveway, sweep around the bend in the road and disappear from sight. Then he heaved a rib-creaking sigh, turned on his heel and marched back inside. Darran and Willer weren't about, so he left a note saying where Gar had gone and continued on his way.

The trouble with princes he decided, as he thudded up the spiral staircase, was they could go gallivanting off on picnics in the countryside whenever the fancy struck and nobody could stop them. They could say, "Oh look, the sun is shining, the birds are singing, who cares about responsibilities today? I think I'll go romp amongst the bluebells for an hour or three, tra la tra la."

And the trouble with working for princes, he added to himself as he pushed his study door open and stared in heart-sinking dismay at the piles of letters, memorandums and schedules that hadn't magically disappeared from his desk while he was gone, damn it, was that you never got to share in that kind of careless luxury. Some poor fool had to care about those merrily abandoned responsibilities, and just now that poor fool went by the name of Asher.

With a gusty sigh he kicked the door shut, slid reluctantly into his chair and got back to work.

Acridly drowning in Meister Glospottle's pestilent piss problems, he didn't notice time passing as the day's light drained slowly from the sky. He didn't even realize he was no longer alone in his office until a hand pressed his shoulder and a voice said, "Asher? Are you dreamstruck? What's her name?"

Startled, he dropped his pen and spun about in the chair. "Matt! Y'daft blot! You tryin' to give me a heart spasm?"

"No, I'm trying to get your attention," said Matt. He was half grinning, half concerned. "I knocked and knocked till I bruised my knuckles and then I called your name. Twice. What's so important it's turned you deaf?"

"Urine," he said sourly. "You got any?"

Matt blinked. "Well, no. Not on me. Not as such."

"Then you're no bloody use. You might as well push off."

The thing he liked best about Matt was the stable meister's reassuring aura of unflappability. A man could be as persnickety as he liked and all Matt would ever do was smile. The way he was smiling now. "And if I ask why you're in such desperate need of urine, will I be sorry?"

Suddenly aware of stiff muscles and a looming headache, Asher shoved his chair back and stomped around his office. Ha! His cage. "Prob'ly. I know I bloody am. Urine's for gettin' rid of into the nearest chamber pot, not for hoardin' like a miser with gold."

Matt was looking bemused. "Since when did you have the urge to hoard urine?"

"Since never! It's bloody Indigo Glospottle's got the urge, not me."

"I know I'll regret asking this, but how in Barl's name could any man have a shortage of urine?"

"By bein' too clever for his own damned good, that's how!" He propped himself on the windowsill, scowling. "Indigo Glospottle fancies himself something of an artiste, y'see. Good ole-fashioned cloth dyein' like his da did, and his da's da afore him, that ain't good enough for Meister Indigo Glospottle. No. Meister Indigo Glospottle's got to go and think up new ways of dyein' cloth and wool and suchlike, ain't he?"

"Well," said Matt, being fair, "you can't blame the man for trying to improve his business."

"Yes, I can!" he retorted. "When him improvin' his business turns into me losin' precious sleep over another man's urine, you'd better bloody believe I can!" Viciously mimicking, he screwed up his face into Indigo Glospottle's permanently piss-strangled expression and fluted his voice in imitation. " 'Oh, Meister Asher! The blues are so blue and the reds are so red! My customers can't get enough of them! But it's all in the piddle, you see!' Can you believe it? Bloody man can't even bring himself to say piss! He's got to say piddle. Like that'll mean it don't stink as much. 'I need more piddle, Meister Asher! You must find me more piddle!' Because the thing is, y'see, these precious new ways of his use up twice as much piss as the old ways, don't they? And since he's put all the other guild members' noses out of joint with his fancy secret dyein' recipe, they've pulled strings to make sure he can't get all the urine he needs. Now he reckons the only way he's goin' to meet demand is by going door to door with a bucket in one hand and a bottle in the other sayin', 'Excuse me, sir and madam, would you care to make a donation?' And for some strange reason, he ain't too keen on that idea!"

Matt gave a whoop of laughter and collapsed against the nearest bit of empty wall. "Asher!"

Despite his irritation, Asher felt his own lips twitch. "Aye, well, I s'pose I'd be laughin' too if the fool hadn't gone and made his problem my problem. But he has, so I ain't much in the mood for feelin' amused just now."

Matt sobered. "I'm sorry. It all sounds very vexing."

"It's worse than that," he said, shuddering. "If I can't get Glospottle and the guild to reach terms, the whole mess'll end up in Justice Hall. Gar'll skin me alive if that happens. He's got hisself so caught up in his magic the last thing he wants is trouble at Justice Hall. Last thing I want is trouble at Justice Hall, 'cause the way he's been lately he'll bloody tell me to take care of it. Me! Sittin' in that gold chair in front of all those folk, passing judgement like I know what I'm on about! I never signed up for Justice Hall. That's Gar's job. And the sooner he remembers that, and forgets all this magic codswallop, the happier I'll be."

The smile faded from Matt's face. "What if he can't forget—or doesn't want to? He's the king's firstborn son and he's found his magic, Asher. Everything's different now. You know that."

Asher scowled. Aye, he knew it. But that didn't mean he had to like it. Or think about it overmuch, either. Damn it, he wasn't even supposed to be here! He was supposed to be down south on the coast arguing with Da over the best fishing boat to buy and plotting how to outsell his sinkin' brothers three to one. Dorana was meant to be a fast-fading memory by now.

But that dream was dead and so was Da, both smashed to pieces in a storm of ill luck. And he was stuck here, in the City. In the Tower. In his unwanted life as Asher the bloody Acting Olken Administrator. Stuck with Indigo bloody Glospottle and his stinking bloody piss problems.

He met Matt's concerned gaze with a truculent defiance. "Different for him, but not for me. He pays me, Matt. He don't own me."

"No. But in truth, Asher, the way things stand for you now—where else could you go?"

Matt's tentative question stabbed like a knife. "Anywhere I bloody like! My brothers don't own me any more than Gar does! I'm back here for now, not for good. Zeth or no Zeth, I were born a fisherman and I'll die one like my da did afore me."

"I hope you do, Asher," Matt said softly. "There are worse ways to die, I think." Then he shook himself free of melancholy. "Now. Speaking of His Highness, do you know where he is? We've a meeting planned but I can't find him."

"Did you look in his office? His library?"

Matt huffed, exasperated. "I looked everywhere."

"Ask Darran. When it comes to Gar the ole fart's got eyes in the back of his head."

"Darran's out. But Willer's here, the pompous little weasel, and he hasn't seen His Highness either. He said something about a picnic?"

Asher shifted on the windowsill and looked outside. Late afternoon sunshine gilded the trees' autumn-bronzed leaves and glinted off the stables' rooftops. "That was hours ago. They can't still be at the Eyrie. They didn't have that much food with 'em, and it only takes five minutes to admire the view. After that it's just sittin' around makin' small talk and pretendin' Fane don't hate Gar's guts, ain't it? Prob'ly they went straight back to the palace and he's locked hisself up in the magic room with Durm and forgotten all about you."

"No, I'm afraid he hasn't."

Darran. Pale and self-contained, he stood in the open doorway. Nothing untoward showed in his face, but Asher felt a needle of fright prick him between the ribs. He exchanged glances with Matt, and slid off the windowsill. "What?" he said roughly. "What you witterin' on about now?"

"I am not wittering," Darran replied. "I've just come back from business at the palace. The royal family and the Master Magician are not there. Their carriage has yet to return."

Again, Asher glanced out of the window into the rapidly cooling afternoon. "Are you sure?"

Darran's lips thinned. "Perfectly."

Another needle prick, sharper this time. "So what're

you sayin'? You sayin' they got lost between here and Salbert's Eyrie?"

Darran's hands were behind his black velvet back. Something in the set of his shoulders suggested they were clutched tightly together. "I am saying nothing. I am asking if you can think of a reason why the carriage's return might have been so severely delayed. His Majesty was expected for a public park committee meeting an hour ago. There was some . . . surprise . . . at his absence."

Asher bit off a curse. "Don't tell me you ran around bleatin' about the carriage bein' delayed! You know what those ole biddies are like, Darran, they'll—"

"Of course I didn't. I'm old but not yet addled," said Darran. "I informed the committee that His Majesty had been detained with Prince Gar and the Master Magician in matters of a magical nature. They happily accepted the explanation, the meeting continued without further disruption and I returned here immediately."

Grudgingly, Asher gave a nod of approval. "Good."

"And now I'll ask you again," said Darran, unimpressed by the approval. "Can you think of any reason why the carriage hasn't yet returned?"

The needle was stabbing quick and hard now, in time with his pounding heart. "Could be a wheel came off, held 'em up."

Darran snorted. "Any one of them could fix that in a matter of moments with a spell."

"He's right," said Matt.

"Lame horse, then. A stone in the shoe, or a twisted fetlock."

Matt shook his head. "His Highness would've ridden the other one back here to get a replacement."

"You're being ridiculous, Asher," said Darran. "Clutching at exceedingly flimsy straws. So I shall say aloud what we all know we're thinking. There's been an accident."

"Accident my arse!" he snapped. "You're guessin,' and guessin' wrong, I'll bet you anything you like. What kind of an accident could they have trotting to Salbert's Eyrie and back, eh? We're talking about all the most powerful magicians in the kingdom sittin' side by side in the same bloody carriage! There ain't an accident in the world that could touch 'em!"

"Very well," said Darran. "The only other explanation, then, is . . . not an accident."

It took Asher a moment to realize what he meant. "What? Don't be daft! As if anybody would—as if there were even a reason—y'silly ole fool! Flappin' your lips like laundry on a line! They're late, is all. Got 'emselves sidetracked! Decided to go sightseeing further on from the Eyrie and got all carried away! You'll see! Gar'll be bouncing up the staircase any minute now! You'll see!"

There was a moment of held breaths, as all three of them waited for the sound of eager, tapping boot heels and a charming royal apology.

Silence.

"Look, Asher," said Matt, smiling uneasily, "you're most likely right. But to put Darran's mind at rest, why don't you and I ride out to the Eyrie? Chances are we'll meet them on their way back and they'll have a good old laugh at us for worrying."

"An excellent suggestion," said Darran. "I was about to make it myself. Go now. And if—when—you do en-counter them, one of you ride back here immediately so I may send messages to the palace in case tactless tongues are still wagging."

Scowling, Asher nodded. He didn't know which was worse: Darran being right or the needle of fright now lodged so hard and deep in his flesh he could barely breathe.

"Well?" demanded Darran. He sounded almost shrill. "Why are you both still standing there like tree stumps? Go!"

Twenty minutes later they were cantering in circumspect silence along the road that led to Salbert's Eyrie. The day's slow dying cast long shadows before them.

"There's the sign for the Eyrie," shouted Matt, jerking his chin as they pounded by. "It's getting late, Asher. We should've met them by now. This is the only road in or out and the gates at the turn-off were still closed. Surely the king would've left them open if they'd gone on somewhere else from here?"

"Maybe," Asher shouted back. His cold hands tightened on the reins. "Maybe not. Who can tell with royalty? At least there's no sign of an accident."

"So far," said Matt.

They urged their horses onwards with ungentle heels, hearts hammering in time with the dull hollow drumming of hooves. Swept round a gradual, left-handed bend into a stretch of road dotted either side with trees.

Matt pointed. "Barl save me! Is that—"

"Aye!" said Asher, and swallowed sudden nausea.

Gar. Lying half in the road, half on its grassy border. Unconscious . . . or dead.

As one he and Matt hauled against their horses'

mouths and came to a squealing, grunting, head-tossing halt. Asher threw himself from his saddle and stumbled to Gar's side, as Matt grabbed Cygnet's reins to stop the horse from bolting.

"Well?"

Blood and dirt and the green smears of crushed grass marked Gar's skin, his clothes. Shirt and breeches were torn. The flesh beneath them was torn.

"He's alive," Asher said shakily, fingers pressed to the leaping pulse beneath Gar's jaw. Then he ran unsteady hands over the prince's inert body. "Out cold, though. Could be his collarbone's busted. And there's cuts and bruises aplenty, too." His fingers explored Gar's skull. "Got some bumps on his noggin, but I don't think his skull's cracked."

"Flesh and bone heal," said Matt, and dragged a shirt sleeve across his wet face. "Praise Barl he's not dead."

"Aye," said Asher, and took a moment, just a moment, to breathe. When he could, he looked up. Struggled for lightness. "Bloody Darran. He'll be bleating 'I told you so' for a month of Barl's Days now."

Matt didn't laugh. Didn't even smile. "If the prince is here," he said grimly, his horseman's hands white-knuckled, "then where are the others?"

Their eyes met, dreading answers.

"Reckon we'd best find out," said Asher. He shrugged off his jacket, folded it and settled Gar's head gently back to the cushioned ground. Tried to arrange his left arm more comfortably, mindful of the hurt shoulder. "He'll be right, by and by. Let's go."